COLONIAL AND FEDERAL

TO 1800

THE VIKING PORTABLE LIBRARY

AMERICAN
LITERATURE
SURVEY

EDITED BY

Milton R. Stern
The University of Connecticut

AND

Seymour L. Gross
The University of Detroit

COLONIAL AND FEDERAL TO 1800
*General Introduction and Preface by
the Editors*

THE AMERICAN ROMANTICS · 1800–1860
Prefatory Essay by Van Wyck Brooks

NATION AND REGION · 1860–1900
Prefatory Essay by Howard Mumford Jones

THE TWENTIETH CENTURY
Prefatory Essay by Malcolm Cowley

COLONIAL

AND

FEDERAL

TO 1800

REVISED AND EXPANDED

**WITH A GENERAL INTRODUCTION AND
PREFACE BY THE EDITORS**

THE VIKING PRESS · NEW YORK

Revised and expanded edition first published in 1968

Fifth printing July 1971

Published simultaneously in Canada by
The Macmillan Company of Canada Limited

SBN 670-01887-2

Library of Congress catalog card number 62-15079

Printed in U.S.A.

Original edition published 1962, eighth printing 1967

ACKNOWLEDGMENTS

Bradford, William. From *Of Plymouth Plantation* by William Bradford, with an introduction and notes by Samuel Eliot Morison, published by Alfred A. Knopf, Inc., in 1952.

Byrd, William. From *The Secret Diary of William Byrd of Westover, 1709-1712*. Copyright 1941 by Louis B. Wright and Marion Tinling and reprinted by their permission.

Taylor, Edward. "Upon the Sweeping Flood" from "Some Edward Taylor Gleanings" by T. H. Johnson, *The New England Quarterly*, XVI (1943), by permission of The New England Quarterly. All others from *The Poetical Works of Edward Taylor* edited by Thomas H. Johnson, (copyright 1939, Rockland; 1943, Princeton), by permission of Princeton University Press and that of Thomas H. Johnson, and from *The Poems of Edward Taylor* edited by Donald E. Stanford, reprinted by permission of the publisher, Yale University Press.

For Harriet and Elaine

GENERAL

INTRODUCTION

In the spirit of his own time, Emerson insisted that every age must have its original relation to the universe. He reflected an older American belief that no age can hold a mortgage on any future time and that the world is for the living. Our Republic and our national literature share a democratic sense of time in which every age, besides shaping the world that exists, also remakes the past. Given the fact that history is never finally dead, all literary productions of the past can become meaningful in the human mind of the present. What, then, in our living moment, can we see of our identity in the total span of our literature?

One thing stands out clearly: American literature is a rebellious and iconoclastic body of art. The Puritan rebelled against the Anglican, the deist against the Puritan, the romantic against aspects of deism, the naturalist against aspects of romanticism, the symbolist against aspects of naturalism. In each case the rebellion was greeted with cries of outrage and prophecies of doom. It is true that almost any nation's literary history tells the same story: but besides this there is a deeper nay-saying that characterizes American literature and remains constant beneath the shifting faces of rebellion. On the surface it may seem strange that a nation in some ways tending toward a mass identity should produce a literature of which the underlying theme is revolutionary. But when one considers that the artist, with his keener sensibility and articulation, is most aware of tendencies in his society, including those he feels duty-bound to combat, and that the richest heritage of the Republic is its foundation in defense of freedom of the mind, then his rebelliousness becomes natural and inevitable. The American writer's "nay" is but a prelude to his resounding "yea!" uttered in behalf of new experience rather than hoarded conventions.

That constant and subterranean rebellion is a product of many forces which, to this day, make America a puzzle to observers. Our nation was founded in middle-class aspirations that were noble in many ways, but still were capable of creating a business culture in which, as Edwin Arlington Robinson has it, "Your Dollar, Dove and Eagle make a Trinity that even you rate higher than you rate yourselves; it pays, it flatters, and it's new." On the other hand, those same aspirations demanded ideologies in which nothing is held to be greater than the integrity and freedom of the individual. At certain points our nation adopted particular Protestant attitudes that seemed to encourage smug respectability as a substitute for religion. Yet the development of that same Protestantism flowered into the highest insistence that the world has known on the primacy of the poetic imagination.

And still more contradictions. An extreme form of individualism, especially to be noted in the late nineteenth century, was a primitive, often savage, social and economic anarchy: each man for himself, but all with a common goal, which was the sack of a continent blessed with incredible resources that beckoned them ever westward. That same predatory impulse, however, was only one sequel to an image of America as the organic Great New West where the ultimate hungers of men's hearts could be satisfied, where the infinitude of human identity could be realized and personality could be fulfilled. Because the Republic faced away from the Old World, it was founded on a faith in experiment, newness, and youth. So founded, it could threaten to create a society in which age is a sin, human value is measured by personal appearance, and the teenager becomes the arbiter of popular taste. But this same naïve faith and innocence became something more than a mindless subject for the satire of a Sinclair Lewis: it also suggested an image of the American as a man free from stifling precedent who could break through old barriers in science, belief, and social institutions.

Hawthorne, Melville, and Henry James were among

those who saw that a free innocence, though creating a fresh and spontaneous democracy of the heart, was not an unmixed blessing. The American writer had to search for roots and traditions, had to begin all over again the creation of a world with each new piece of writing, had to re-create each time a sense of community and identity. The noble savage had to temper freedom with responsibility and recognize that by virtue of his searching humanity he was inextricably bound up in all human history.

In short, the American writer began to see that there are really two Americas. One is the actual country that shares all the limitations of any human community in the Old World or the New; the other is the ideal America that, as Scott Fitzgerald told us, existed pure only as a wonderful and pathetically adolescent dream. One is a geographic location in the evolution of all human history; the other is a state of being that answers all human hopes. Whenever the ideal was put forward by mistaken patriotism as the real country, American writers protested—sometimes in full and bitter measure, as Mark Twain, for one, has shown. And whenever the actual America threatened to destroy the ideal, American writers have again protested, with profound, poetic vigor, as Thoreau and Whitman have shown. It is because American culture is precariously and magnificently balanced in a bewildering variety of contradictions that the American writer has remained in a state of protest.

This is not to say that the present editors would return to the critical attitude of the 1930's, which regarded literature as a collection of social documents and interpreted every effort of artistic creation as an economic act. Rather, we think that there is a unifying identity in our cultural and intellectual production that is a deliberate dramatization of our total history. It is from this necessary and sensible orientation, as it seems to us, that we see the iconoclasm of the American writer as a major feature in our literature. What he expresses is a whole-voiced rejection of trammeling orthodoxies, conformities, hypocrisies, and delusions, wherever and whenever they are seen on the national landscape. Keeping that spirit in mind, we offer the following selections from American literature as a record of the continuing exploration that develops into and still speaks to our moment of time.

No student of American literature will feel that he has made a reasonably full perusal of the materials unless he has read complete Hawthorne's *The Scarlet Letter,* Thoreau's *Walden,* Melville's *Moby-Dick,* representative poems from Whitman's *Leaves of Grass,* and a novel or two each of James, Hemingway, and Faulkner. Those authors are most profitably read in full-length works; but before the reading revolution brought about by inexpensive paperback reprints, anthologists were forced to present them in more or less fragmented form. That is no longer necessary. The teacher today can include in his course, in addition to anthologized material, such representative works as those mentioned above without feeling that his students are being asked to make an unreasonable expenditure for books.

In view of this change in the practical realities of courses in American literature, we have felt that it was both wise and necessary to omit from our anthology some of the authors who would, in any case, be read under separate cover. By deleting such material, we have been able to provide a wider selection than is usual from other authors, including Edward Taylor, Emily Dickinson, and Stephen Crane, who in many cases would not be read in separate editions. In this revised edition of *American Literature Survey,* we have added some representative works of Melville because it is impossible for students to buy an inexpensive reprint of *Moby-Dick* that also includes some of Melville's shorter fiction. We have added some basic poems by Whitman because in the majority of courses it is not feasible to read the entire *Leaves of Grass* in separate cover. And we have included some works by Henry James for the same reason we included Melville: none of the two or three James novels most commonly assigned is available in a volume that includes his shorter fiction and essays. Given the needs of courses in American literature, we feel that the present volumes maintain a proper balance of materials and meet the widest demands of common practice, flexibility, and usefulness.

As in the first edition of *American Literature Survey,* we have avoided excess editorial apparatus, in the belief that long historical interchapters, copious footnotes, and coercive critical judgments either duplicate or conflict with the teacher's work. The nature of interpretation and emphasis will vary from class to class, from teacher to teacher, and therefore we have been content to provide the student with a basic minimum of biographical, bibliographical, and textual information.

In general the selections are presented chronologically, though not where the logical placement of materials would make strict chronology a meaningless arrangement. In every case we have chosen texts that yield the highest combination of accuracy and readability, a principle which has led us to modernize the spelling and regularize the punctuation of the most reliable texts of some of the early writers. The dates placed after the works indicate publication; a second or third date indicates extensive revisions. In those instances where there has been a significant lapse of time between composition and publication, a "w." stands for date of writing, a "p." for date of publication.

We should like to acknowledge our gratitude to Malcolm Cowley and to Professors Kay House, Richard H. Schramm, A. G. Medlicott, and Edward E. Cassady for their generous advice in the revision of this anthology, and to thank Thomas Timmins and Kenneth Smith for their conscientious efforts in behalf of this work. We owe a special debt of gratitude to Professor Everett H. Emerson for his having quietly pointed out to us several factual errors in the first edition of Volume I.

MILTON R. STERN
SEYMOUR L. GROSS

CONTENTS

PREFACE

☆

"The imagery in these books called the Prophets," asserted Thomas Paine in *The Age of Reason,* "appertains altogether to poetry. It is fictitious and often extravagant, and not admissible in any other kind of writing than poetry." Later on in the same work he adds, "The natural bent of my mind was to science. I had some turn, and I believe some talent, for poetry; but this I rather repressed than encouraged, as leading too much into the field of imagination." The modern reader may smile at the worldly busy-ness of the Enlightenment's republican machine, who is so immersed either in the revolutionary realities of class structure and government or in the Franklinian way to wealth that he can't take time off from the office for such pleasantly superfluous pastimes as merely imaginative literature. Life is real, life is earnest, and the new world in the making demands from the real man a full-time schedule of practical activities.

Paine was speaking out of the American Enlightenment's respect for observed fact, statistics, and reason. He also reflected a national pioneer experience that necessarily demanded a functional pragmatism and utilitarian expediency. The emphasis was on actualities. Yet the prejudices of Paine are not idiosyncratic of the man or even of his age. From the moment the conquistadores saw gold, glory, and God (for many the sequence ran roughly in that order) in the new world until the 1820's, when the "high Germanorum" of European idealism began to make a serious impact upon young American intellectuals—approximately three hundred years!—the literature of and about America was an attempt to find in the historical actuality a realization of that metaphoric new world toward which the European imagination had been sailing, Columbus fashion, since the loss of Eden. The thing to do was to clear these Gardens of the Hesperides, correct whatever blights they might have, pay attention to the immediate problems of building Utopia out of the pristine and uncorrupted wilderness—to concentrate on the immediate actualities of the moment. Thus the Dream and history would be wedded in the continuing discovery of America's unlimited possibilities. It is in this mixture of endless expectation, practical reportage, and expedient usage that our literature begins. A later day found this mixture to be a crazy paradox, an irony, a dialogue between dream and nightmare, between innocence and experience, a discovery of the limitations of "practical" activity. But if it turned out, partly, to be a bitterness and an indictment, in the beginning the word "practical" was a benediction. Alvar Núñez Cabeza de Vaca voiced one of the earliest summations of what people expected from the New West. In his *Relación* he explained that the motivation for his party's travels through the Southwest in the early sixteenth century was the certitude ("We *ever* held it certain," he said) that by directing their footsteps toward the setting sun they would find what their hearts desired.

The Romantics later saw that the Spaniard's expectations were to be charted in a moral continent, by an exploration that did not demand statistics or descriptions of flora and fauna for the uses of commodity, but that demanded the moral imagination. The real world was to be handled not as a photographic sketch (nineteenth-century readers loved the idealized sketch taken for fact, for in it they saw what we have always wanted to see: we *are* God's chosen people in paradise regained, and here is our unretouched snapshot to prove it), but as a metaphor for that unattained America which, somehow, had managed to elude the searchers. So the Romantics changed the instruments of truth for literature—from fact, from polemic, from theological dispute, to the imagination. It was not so much a change, really, as an alternative that had to be created in the face of our continuing insistence upon pragmatic and polemical priorities. So Hawthorne in 1852: "In the old countries, with which fiction has long been conversant, a certain conventional privilege seems to be awarded to the romancer; his work is not put exactly side by side with nature; and he is allowed a license with regard to every-day probability, in view of the improved effects which he is bound to produce thereby. Among ourselves, on the contrary, there is as yet no such Fairy Land, so like the real world, that on a suitable remoteness one can not well tell the difference, but with an atmosphere of strange enchantment, beheld through which the inhabitants have a propriety of their own. This atmosphere is what the American romancer needs. In its absence, the beings of imagination are compelled to show themselves in the same category as actually living mortals; a necessity that generally renders the paint and pasteboard of their composition but too painfully discernible." And speaking of *The Marble Faun* in 1859 he adds, "Italy, as the site of [my] Romance was chiefly valuable to [me] as affording a sort of poetic or fairy precinct, where actualities would not be so terribly insisted upon as they are, and must needs be, in America." By the time a century had gone by, another novelist, Saul Bellow, complained in 1962 that the American writer is presented with many difficulties because of the nation's terrible insistence upon actualities!

Yet, if pre-Romantic American literature insisted upon actualities, as our technological and practical society itself always has, it did so because it believed or tried to make others believe that El Dorado *was* to be found in American actualities, and just around the corner of tomorrow morning in the corridor of history. John Smith (who knew better, as many apologists knew better) wrote description and exhortation which would lure colonists to perform the necessary labor that would make the new plantations profitable. The proper use of one's place in the world would be made by participation in the American experiment. The Puritans also had polemical uses for letters. Literature was good just so far as it kept man's eyes on the laws of ecclesiastical polity and was evil just so far as it distracted him from the hard ways of religion. Justification and sanctification were not merely theological matters, but were translated into voluminous self-defenses and explanations in the building of the visible body of Christ as the pure church of *New* England's New Jerusalem. Cotton Mather suggests the erudition necessary for the task: the lives of the saints and their reading of the Bible gave the "plantation religious" its blueprint. William Bradford and Samuel Sewall are perennial examples of the extent to which the most mundane actuality was invested with divine significance. And, as they indicate, the plainer the language, the simpler the style, the better literature fulfilled the function of justifying the ways of God to man—and, perhaps (particularly after the 1660's), the ways of the saints to the inhabitants. Perhaps nowhere more clearly than in Michael Wigglesworth can the uses of literature as catechism and mnemonic device be seen.

The diction of Nathaniel Ward is a curiosity and an anachronism, but, along with Anne Bradstreet and Edward Taylor, Ward too sees literature as moral, religious, and social instruction. The subterranean passion of Bradstreet, much closer to the surface in her literary superior, Taylor, could become suspect even in a proper literary function, such as meditation (indeed, Taylor distrusted his own poems), "as leading too much into the field of imagination." The Puritans would have disagreed with Thomas Paine about almost everything else, but they would have agreed with him about the uses of writing: to prepare a "how-to" literature of instruction and persuasion, a literature of statement, a literature of actualities.

Such uses remain constant (there are exceptions) for most of the sixteenth, seventeenth, and eighteenth centuries, regardless of the particular ways in which the new world is seen as the New Atlantis. For the conquistador it was a source of wealth and power for his Catholic Majesty; for the Puritan it was a Congregational or Presbyterian clearing in a Papist and Episcopalian landscape; for the adventurer it was a good investment to which people should be beckoned by propaganda of economics, patriotism, social duty, and credits in heaven; for men like Roger Williams and John Woolman it was the establishment of tolerance and good works; for De Crèvecœur it was a place of idyllic rustic cheer seen through the eye of eighteenth-century sentiment, brightly; for Franklin, Paine, Jefferson, the Federalists, it was the establishment of the agrarian society unified by the harmonious laws and logic of Newton's universe. Yet all agree implicitly about the function of literature, with which they tell about their actualities. Even "belles lettres" (whose beginning one usually sees dated with Mather Byles in 1745) such as one

finds in the Connecticut Wits or Royall Tyler are sympto-
matic of the impulse toward the nationalistic essay instructive in manners, morals, native peculiarities and
attitudes.

Yet deep within the rigidly controlled but passionate
Puritanism of the early settlers was the element that prepared for the Romantic liberation of what today we call
"creative writing." That was the burning symbolic imagination of a people who saw every event as being a special
providence, every actuality as having a divine meaning.
The high point of this vision, which prepared for Emerson,
is found in Jonathan Edwards, who took the rational
causal relationships of his eighteenth-century universe and
built them, through his subjective idealism, into the supra-
rational structure of his seventeenth-century heritage. As his
emphasis shifts from mind to heart, the goals of his writing
shift from the actual to the imaginative worlds. Philip
Freneau continues the transition. In many of his nature
poems his deistic rationalism mingles with the imaginative
vision: the mystic sense of nature as organism symbolically
seen is transmitted from the Puritan, through Edwards,
through Freneau (both of whom combine it with the
eighteenth-century emphasis on nature), to Cooper and
Emerson and the birth of American literature proper.

In one sense, then, one can say that the contributions of
the sixteenth, seventeenth, and eighteenth centuries were
negative. That is, they took a concept—the metaphoric
America—which demands treatment by the symbolic imagination precisely because it has proved incapable of .
reduction to a report for the chairman of the board,
precisely because it is the Heavenly City of the western
imagination, and they tried to squeeze it into the language
of history. They can be said to have given the impetus
to the bursting emergence of our national literature by
supplying the negative pressure that led to the explosion.

But that is not enough to say. Within the range of their
rationales for literature, it is difficult to find a better
example of "plain style" than that of Bradford, of devotional lyricism than that of Taylor, of expository prose
and argument than that of Paine or the Federalist papers,
of "pre-Romanticism" than some of Freneau's poems.
Furthermore, their positive contributions beyond the limits
of their uses of literature lie in their themes and attitudes.

They prepared the central *materials* of American literature, rough hewing them out of a new, unknown, and forbiddingly gigantic land. If their instruments were not adequate for creative literature today, they were adequate to themselves. They perpetuated the image of America, that symbolic concept, so enormous an idea, that swelled and strained beneath their various statements of actualities until the surface of their literary purposes could contain it no longer. America, in the fantastic quality of its actualities, has always outgrown those who envision it, just as, equally, it has never been as great as the vision. To the extent that the central subject of American literature is the relation of the American image to American experience, it is silly to dismiss the precolonials and colonials because they lived in their time and not in ours. In their anti-literary pioneer necessities they provided the preconditions of our literature. They nurtured its major themes, for which in gratitude and relief we can look back to them from the advantage of a heightened perspective—which exists because we can stand on their shoulders. Like all people who have participated in American experience, they too, in their own way, seemed to know what the inevitable literature would be all about.

M. R. S.
S. L. G.

COLONIAL AND FEDERAL
TO 1800

JOHN SMITH
(1579–1631)

As though predicting the character of the nation whose way he helped to open, a nation that would relish the frontier tall tale and delight in a sense of newness, Captain John Smith embellished his histories with items that would turn facts into good stories ("if it's not true it should be" might have been his motto), and himself scored two important "firsts." He was the author of the first book written in America in English, *A True Relation of . . . Virginia* (1608), and he founded the first permanent English colony on American soil, at Jamestown in 1607.

Aged twenty-seven by the time he sailed into what is now Hampton Roads, Virginia, he already had behind him a long history of derring-do. He had run away to sea from his home in Lincolnshire when he was fifteen, had soldiered in France and the Low Countries, and had engaged in ten years of warfare and intrigue in Europe, Turkey, and the Near East. Unlike most Elizabethan adventurers, this hard-handed, quick-witted, zestful braggart and soldier of fortune was not an aristocrat. Many of the Jamestown settlers, expecting to find immediate wealth and luxury in the Golden West, were upper-class gentlemen unwilling to soil their hands. But Smith got labor out of them by taking them, as it were, on quick and frequent trips to the woodshed.

He returned to England in October, 1609, only to sail back to the New World for two trips of exploration (1614 and 1615) of the coast of New England (which he named), from Cape Cod to the Penobscot River. In his maps he gave to the features of the coastline many of the English names that they bear to this day. Perhaps the most important aspect of his writings, as the following selection from A Description of New England (1616) indicates, is the reflection of the fervent imperialistic colonialism which motivated his propagandistic presentation of the New World as a rugged place of infinite possibility, thereby helping to set a major facet of the image of America that has stimulated our national literature down to our own time.

His works include A True Relation of Such Occurrences and Accidents of Note as Hath Happened in Virginia since the First Planting of that Colony (1608); A Map of Virginia, with a Description of the Country (1612); A Description of New England (1616); New England's Trials (1620); The General History of Virginia, New England, and the Summer Isles (1624); An Accidence, or The Pathway to Experience Necessary for All Young Seamen (1626); The True Travels, Adventures, and Observations of Captain John Smith (1630); Advertisements for the Unexperienced Planters of New England, or Anywhere (1631).

Accounts of Smith and his works are to be found in M. C. Tyler, A History of American Literature During the Colonial Period, I (1897); E. Arber, Travels and Works of Captain John Smith (revised, with an introduction by A. G. Bradley), 2 vols. (1910); E. K. Chatterton, Captain John Smith (1927); J. G. Fletcher, John Smith—Also Pocahontas (1928); S. E. Morison, Builders of the Bay Colony (1930); C. M. Andrews, The Colonial Period of American History, I (1934); J. S. Morse, "John Smith and His Critics," Journal of Southern History, I (1935); H. M. Jones, "The Literature of Virginia in the Seventeenth Century," Memoirs of the American Academy of Arts and Sciences (1946); B. Smith, Captain John Smith (1953); L. P. Striker, The Life of John Smith, English Soldier (1957); and P. L. Barbour, The Three Worlds of Captain John Smith (1964).

FROM

A Description of New England

Who can desire more content, that hath small means or but only his merit to advance his fortune, than to tread and plant that ground he hath purchased by the hazard of his life? If he have but the taste of virtue and magnanimity, what to such a mind can be more pleasant than planting and building a foundation for his posterity got from the rude earth by God's blessing and his own industry without prejudice to any? If he have any grain of faith or zeal in religion, what can he do less hurtful to any, or more agreeable to God, than to seek to convert those poor savages to know Christ and humanity, whose labors with discretion will triple requite thy charge and pains? What so truly suits with honor and honesty as the discovering things unknown: erecting towns, peopling countries, informing the ignorant, reforming things unjust, teaching virtue; and gain to our native mother country a kingdom to attend her; find employment for those that are idle because they know not what to do—so far from wronging any as to cause posterity to remember thee, and remembering thee, ever honor that remembrance with praise!

Consider: What were the beginnings and endings of the monarchies of the Chaldeans, the Syrians, the Grecians, and Romans, but this one rule? What was it they would not do for the good of the commonwealth or their Mothercity? For example: Rome. What made her such a monarchess, but only the adventures of her youth, not in riots at home, but in dangers abroad and the justice and judgment out of their experience, when they grew aged? What was their ruin and hurt, but this: the excess of idleness, the fondness of parents, the want of experience in magistrates, the admiration of their undeserved honors, the contempt of true merit, their unjust jealousies, their politic incredulities, their hypocritical seeming goodness, and their deeds of secret lewdness? Finally, in fine, growing only formal temporists, all that their predecessors got in many years, they lost in few days. Those by their pain and virtues became lords of the world; they by their ease and vices became slaves to their servants. This is the difference betwixt the use of arms in the field and on the monuments of stones: the golden age and the leaden age, prosperity and misery, justice and corruption, substance and shadows, deeds and words, experience and imagination, making commonwealths and marring commonwealths, the fruits of virtue and the conclusions of vice.

Then, who would live at home idly (or think in himself any worth to live) only to eat, drink, and sleep, and so die? Or by consuming that carelessly, [that] his friends got worthily? Or by using that miserably, that maintained virtue honestly? Or for being descended nobly, pine with the vain vaunt of great kindred in penury? Or (to maintain a silly show of bravery) toil out thy heart, soul, and time basely by shifts, tricks, cards, and dice? Or by relating news of others' actions, shark here or there for a dinner or supper; deceive thy friends by fair promises and dissimulation in borrowing where thou never intendest to pay; offend the laws, surfeit with excess, burden thy country, abuse thy self, despair in want, and then couzen thy kindred, yea even thine own brother, and wish thy parents' death (I will not say damnation) to have their estates though thou seest what honors and rewards the world yet hath for them who will seek them and worthily deserve them?

I would be sorry to offend, or that any should mistake my honest meaning, for I wish good to all, hurt to none. But rich men for the most part are grown to that dotage, through their pride in their wealth, as though there were no accident could end it or their life.

And what hellish care do such take to make it their own misery, and their country's spoil, especially when there is most need of their employment, drawing by all manner of inventions from the Prince and his honest subjects even the vital spirits of their powers and estates as if their bags or brags were so powerful a defense the malicious could not assault them, when they are the only bait to cause us not to be only assaulted, but betrayed and murdered in our own security, ere we well perceive it!

May not the miserable ruin of Constantinople, their impregnable walls, riches, and pleasures [at] last taken by the Turk (which are but a bit, in comparison of their now mightiness) remember us of the effects of private covetousness, at which time the good Emperor held himself rich enough to have such rich subjects, so formal in all excess of vanity, all kind of delicacy and prodigality? His poverty when the Turk besieged, the citizens (whose merchandizing thoughts were only to get wealth, little conceiving the desperate resolution of a valiant expert enemy) left the Emperor so long to his conclusions, having spent all he had to pay his young, raw, discontented soldiers, that suddenly he, they, and their city were all a prey to the devouring Turk. And what they would not spare for the maintenance of them who adventured their lives to defend them, did serve only their enemies to torment them, their friends, and country, and all Christendom to this present day. Let this lamentable example remember you that are rich (see-

ing there are such great thieves in the world to rob you)
not [to] grudge to lend some proportion to breed them that
have little, yet [are] willing to learn how to defend you, for
it is too late when the deed is a-doing.

The Romans' estate hath been worse than this: for the
mere covetousness and extortion of a few of them so
moved the rest, that, not having any employment but contemplation, their great judgments grew to so great malice,
as themselves were sufficient to destroy themselves by faction. Let this move you to embrace employment for those
whose educations, spirits, and judgments want but your
purses; not only to prevent such accustomed dangers, but
also to gain more thereby than you have.

And you fathers, that are either so foolishly fond or so
miserably covetous or so willfully ignorant or so negligently
careless, as that you will rather maintain your children in
idle wantonness till they grow your masters or become so
basely unkind as they wish nothing but your deaths, so that
both sorts grow dissolute; and although you would wish
them anywhere to escape the gallows and ease your cares;
though they spend you here one, two, or three hundred
pound[s] a year, you would grudge to give half so much in
adventure with them to obtain an estate, which in a small
time, but with a little assistance of your providence, might
be better than your own. But if an angel should tell you
that any place yet unknown can afford such fortunes, you
would not believe him, no more than Columbus was believed there was any such land as is now the well known
abounding America, much less such large regions as are
yet unknown, as well in America, as in Africa, and Asia,
and terra incognita, where were courses for gentlemen
(and them that would be so reputed) more suiting their
qualities than begging from their Princes' generous disposition the labors of his subjects and the very marrow of his
maintenance.

I have not been so ill bred, but I have tasted of plenty
and pleasure, as well as want and misery, nor doth necessity yet, or occasion of discontent, force me to these endeavors; nor am I ignorant what small thanks I shall have
for my pains; or that many would have the world imagine
them to be of great judgment, that can but blemish these
my designs by their witty objections and detractions; yet
(I hope) my reasons with my deeds, will so prevail with

some, that I shall not want employment in these affairs to make the most blind see his own senselessness and incredulity; hoping that gain will make them affect that which religion, charity, and the common good cannot. It were but a poor device in me to deceive myself, much more the king, state, my friends and country, with these inducements; which, seeing his Majesty hath given permission, I wish all sorts of worthy, honest, industrious spirits would understand; and if they desire any further satisfaction, I will do my best to give it; not to persuade them to go only, but go with them; not leave them there, but live with them there.

I will not say, but by ill providing and undue managing, such courses may be taken [that] may make us miserable enough. But if I may have the execution of what I have projected, if they want to eat, let them eat or never digest me. If I perform what I say, I desire but that reward out of the gains [which] may suit my pains, quality, and condition. And if I abuse you with my tongue, take my head for satisfaction. If any dislike at the year's end, defraying their charge, by my consent they should freely return. I fear not want of company sufficient, were it but known what I know of those countries; and by the proof of that wealth I hope yearly to return if God please to bless me from such accidents as are beyond my power in reason to prevent. For, I am not so simple to think that ever any other motive than wealth will ever erect there a Commonwealth; or draw company from their ease and humors at home, to stay in New England to effect my purposes.

And lest any should think the toil might be insupportable, though these things may be had by labor and diligence, I assure myself there are [those] who delight extremely in vain pleasure that take much more pains in England to enjoy it than I should do here to gain wealth sufficient. And yet I think they should not have half such sweet content, for our pleasure here is still gains—in England charges and loss. Here nature and liberty affords us that freely which in England we want or it costeth us dearly. What pleasure can be more than—being tired with any occasion ashore in planting vines, fruits, or herbs, in contriving their own grounds to the pleasure of their own minds, their fields, gardens, orchards, buildings, ships, and other works, etc.— to recreate themselves before their own doors in their own boats upon the sea where man, woman, and child, with a small hook and line, by angling, may take diverse sorts of excellent fish at their pleasures! And is it not pretty sport to pull up two pence, six pence, and twelve pence as fast as you can haul and veer a line! He is a very bad fisher [who] cannot kill in one day with his hook and line one, two, or three hundred cods which, dressed and dried, if they be sold there for ten shillings the hundred—though in England they will give more than twenty—may not both the servant, the master, and merchant be well content with this gain? If a man work but three days in seven, he may get more than he can spend unless he will be excessive. Now that carpenter, mason, gardener, tailor, smith, sailor, forgers, or what other, may they not make this a pretty recreation, though they fish but an hour in a day to take more than they eat in a week? Or if they will not eat it because there is so much better choice, yet sell it or change it with the fishermen or merchants for anything they want. And what sport doth yield a more pleasing content and less hurt or charge than angling with a hook, and crossing the sweet air from isle to isle over the silent streams of a calm sea, wherein the most curious may find pleasure, profit, and content?

Thus, though all men be not fishers, yet all men, whatsoever, may in other matters do as well. For necessity doth in these cases so rule a commonwealth and each in their several functions as their labors in their qualities may be as profitable, because there is a necessary mutual use of all.

For gentlemen, what exercise should more delight them than ranging daily those unknown parts, using fowling and fishing for hunting and hawking? And yet you shall see the wild hawks give you some pleasure in seeing them stoop, six or seven after one another, an hour or two together at the schools of fish in the fair harbors, as those ashore at a fowl. And never trouble nor torment yourselves with watching, mewing, feeding, and attending them; nor kill horse and man with running and crying, See you not a hawk? For hunting also, the woods, lakes, and rivers afford not only chase sufficient for any that delights in that kind of toil or pleasure, but such beasts to hunt that, besides the delicacy of their bodies for food, their skins are so rich as may well recompense thy daily labor with a captain's pay.

For laborers, if those that sow hemp, rape, turnips, car-

rots, cabbage, and the like give 20, 30, 40, 50 shillings
yearly for an acre of ground, and meat, drink, and wages
to use it, and yet grow rich; when better—at least as good
—ground may be had and cost nothing but labor, it seems
strange to me any such should there grow poor.

My purpose is not to persuade children from their
parents, men from their wives, nor servants from their
masters: only such as with free consent may be spared; but
that each parish or village in city or country that will but
apparel their fatherless children of thirteen or fourteen
years of age, or young married people that have small
wealth to live on, here by their labor may live exceeding
well, provided always that first there be a sufficient power
to command them, houses to receive them, means to defend them, and meet provisions for them. For any place
may be overlain; and it is most necessary to have a fortress,
ere this grow to practice, and sufficient masters as carpenters, masons, fishers, fowlers, gardeners, husbandmen,
sawyers, smiths, spinsters, tailors, weavers, and such like
to take ten, twelve, or twenty, or as there is occasion, for
apprentices. The masters by this may quickly grow rich;
these may learn their trades themselves to do the like to a
general and an incredible benefit for King and country,
master and servant.

1616

WILLIAM BRADFORD

(1590–1657)

Even among seventeenth-century New Englanders, there are few American writers who disclose such simple integrity and honesty of purpose as William Bradford. A devoted Christian and a benevolent man in an age of high religious fervors, he defected in 1606 from his substantial Yorkshire farm family to join William Brewster, one of the leading Separatists of the village of Scrooby. Scrooby and Bawtry were centers of the Separatists, who felt that they had little hope of purifying the Church of England from within (the Puritan dream). Consequently, they separated—and thus their name—from the Church in the ardor of their agitation for the abolition of episcopacy. In 1609 Bradford left with the Scrooby group for Holland, where he remained for eleven years as a reasonably prosperous weaver. In 1620 he sailed to Plymouth aboard the *Mayflower*.

After John Carver died in 1621, Bradford became the governor of the colony, a post he was to hold, except for intervals totaling five years, for the next thirty-five years. As the foremost citizen of the colony, he spent his life repaying its debts to the London financial backers of the New World enterprise. With great effort and dedication he cleared Plymouth's economic standing by 1650. Certainly the task of establishment was not easy: during the first year alone, fifty of the 102 settlers died, including his wife Dorothy, who drowned after either falling or jumping from shipboard after the first six weeks off the wintry desolation of Cape Cod.

His history, *Of Plymouth Plantation*, begun as a personal

9

journal of his own affairs and those of the colony, recounts the agonies and problems of colonizing, the distinction between the saints (the Separatist elect) and strangers (the non-Separatist settlers), between the congregational independence of Plymouth churches and the pressure for congregational conformity exerted by the rival Massachusetts Bay Colony. Bradford's work, widely used by contemporaries, was the first authoritative source of information about the New England colony, summing up its history through 1646. Written largely before 1647, it was completed in 1650; yet the first full publication of the document had to wait until 1856, after the manuscript was found (in 1855) in the library of the Bishop of London, to which it was carried, probably by Thomas Hutchinson, the loyalist colonial governor. It was returned to Massachusetts in 1897. Its plain style is an expression of the general Puritan concept of literature, which was not to entertain but to instruct. Yet the very unassuming simplicity and directness heighten, by understatement, the struggles, the devotion, and the tough-minded idealism of a man, a people, and an age.

Bradford's works include, besides the history *Of Plymouth Plantation*, a book called *Mourt's Relation*, generally assumed to have been written by Bradford and Edward Winslow. It was first published in 1622 by George Morton under the name of G. Mourt, as editor of the document, whose full title is *A Relation or Journal of the Beginning and Proceedings of the English Plantation Settled at Plymouth*.

Accounts of Bradford and his work, or some editions of the history are to be found in M. C. Tyler, *A History of American Literature During the Colonial Period*, I (1878); J. Shepard, *Governor William Bradford and His Son* (1900); W. Walker, *Ten New England Leaders* (1901); W. T. Davis, ed., *Bradford's History of Plymouth Plantation* (1908); W. C. Ford, ed., *History of Plymouth Plantation*, 2 vols. (1912); A. H. Plumb, *William Bradford of Plymouth* (1920); E. F. Bradford, "Conscious Art in Bradford's *History of Plymouth Plantation*," *New England Quarterly*, I (1928); K. B. Murdock, "Colonial Historians," in Macy, ed., *American Writers on American Literature* (1931); G. F. Willison, *Saints and Strangers* (1945); B. Smith, *Bradford of Plymouth* (1951); S. E. Morison, ed., *Of Plymouth Plantation* (1952); B. Wish, ed., *Of Plymouth Plantation* (1962); and A. J. Wall, Jr., "William Bradford, Colonial Printer," *Proceedings of American Antiquarian Society*, LXXIII (1964).

FROM

Of Plymouth Plantation

FROM BOOK I

[Their voyage to Cape Cod (1620)]

SEPTEMBER 6. These troubles being blown over, and now all being compact together in one ship, they put to sea again with a prosperous wind, which continued divers days together, which was some encouragement unto them; yet, according to the usual manner, many were afflicted with seasickness. And I may not omit here a special work of God's providence. There was a proud and very profane young man, one of the seamen, of a lusty, able body, which made him the more haughty; he would always be contemning the poor people in their sickness and cursing them daily with grievous execrations; and did not let to tell them that he hoped to help to cast half of them overboard before they came to the journey's end, and to make merry with what they had; and if he were by any gently reproved, he would curse and swear most bitterly. But it pleased God before they came half seas over, to smite this young man with a grievous disease, of which he died in a desperate manner, and so was himself the first that was thrown overboard. Thus his curses light on his own head, and it was an astonishment to all his fellows for they noted it to be the just hand of God upon him.

After they had enjoyed fair winds and weather for a season, they were encountered many times with cross winds and met with many fierce storms with which the ship was shroudly [severely] shaken, and her upper works made very leaky; and one of the main beams in the midships was bowed and cracked, which put them in some fear that the ship could not be able to perform the voyage. So some of the chief of the company, perceiving the mariners to fear the sufficiency of the ship as appeared by their mutterings, they entered into serious consultation with the master and other officers of the ship, to consider in time of the danger, and rather to return than to cast themselves into a desperate and inevitable peril. And truly there was great distraction and difference of opinion amongst the mariners themselves; fain would they do what could be done for their wages' sake (being now near half the seas over) and on the other hand they were loath to hazard their lives too desperately. But in examining of all opinions, the master and others affirmed they knew the ship to be strong and firm under water; and for the buckling of the main beam, there was a great iron screw the passengers brought out of Holland, which would raise the beam into his place; the which being done, the carpenter and master affirmed that with a post put under it, set firm in the lower deck and otherways bound, he would make it sufficient. And as for the decks and upper works, they would caulk them as well as they could, and though with the working of the ship they would not long keep staunch, yet there would otherwise be no great danger, if they did not overpress her with sails. So they committed themselves to the will of God and resolved to proceed.

In sundry of these storms the winds were so fierce and the seas so high, as they could not bear a knot of sail, but were forced to hull for divers days together. And in one of them, as they thus lay at hull in a mighty storm, a lusty young man called John Howland, coming upon some occasion above the gratings was, with a seele [lurch] of the ship, thrown into sea; but it pleased God that he caught hold of the topsail halyards which hung overboard and ran out at length. Yet he held his hold (though he was sundry fathoms under water) till he was hauled up by the same rope to the brim of the water, and then with a boat hook and other means got into the ship again and his life saved. And though he was something ill with it, yet he lived many years after and became a profitable member both in church and commonwealth. In all this voyage there died but one of the passengers, which was William Butten, a youth, servant to Samuel Fuller, when they drew near the coast.

But to omit other things (that I may be brief) after long beating at sea they fell with that land which is called Cape Cod, the which being made and certainly known to be it, they were not a little joyful. After some deliberation had amongst themselves and with the master of the ship, they tacked about and resolved to stand for the southward (the wind and weather being fair) to find some place about Hudson's River for their habitation. But after they had sailed that course about half the day, they fell amongst dangerous shoals and roaring breakers, and they were so far entangled therewith as they conceived themselves in great danger; and the wind shrinking upon them withal, they resolved to bear up again for the Cape and thought themselves happy to get out of those dangers before night overtook them, as by God's good providence they did. And the next day they got into the Cape Harbor where they rid in safety.

A word or two by the way of this cape. It was thus first named by Captain Gosnold and his company, Anno 1602, and after by Captain Smith was called Cape James; but it retains the former name amongst seamen. Also, that point which first showed those dangerous shoals unto them they called Point Care, and Tucker's Terror; but the French and Dutch to this day call it Malabar by reason of those perilous shoals and the losses they have suffered there.

Being thus arrived in a good harbor, and brought safe to land, they fell upon their knees and blessed the God of Heaven who had brought them over the vast and furious ocean, and delivered them from all the perils and miseries thereof, again to set their feet on the firm and stable earth, their proper element. And no marvel if they were thus joyful, seeing wise Seneca was so affected with sailing a few miles on the coast of his own Italy, as he affirmed, that he had rather remain twenty years on his way by land than pass by sea to any place in a short time, so tedious and dreadful was the same unto him.

But here I cannot but stay and make a pause, and stand half amazed at this poor people's present condition; and so I think will the reader, too, when he well considers the same. Being thus passed the vast ocean, and a sea of troubles before in their preparation (as may be remembered by that which went before), they had now no friends to welcome them nor inns to entertain or refresh their weather-beaten bodies; no houses or much less towns to repair to, to seek for succor. It is recorded in Scripture as a mercy to the Apostle and his shipwrecked company, that the barbarians showed them no small kindness in refreshing them, but these savage barbarians, when they met with them (as after will appear) were readier to fill their sides full of arrows than otherwise. And for the season it was winter, and they that know the winters of that country know them to be sharp and violent, and subject to cruel and fierce storms, dangerous to travel to known places, much more to search an unknown coast. Besides, what could they see but a hideous and desolate wilderness, full of wild beasts and wild men—and what multitudes there might be of them they knew not. Neither could they, as it were, go up to the top of Pisgah to view from this wilderness a more goodly country to feed their hopes; for which way soever they turned their eyes (save upward to the heavens) they could have little solace or content in respect of any outward objects. For summer being done, all things stand upon them with a weatherbeaten face, and the whole country, full of woods and thickets, represented a wild and savage hue. If they looked behind them, there was the mighty ocean which they had passed and was now as a main bar and gulf to separate them from all the civil parts of the world. If it be said they had a ship to succor them, it is true; but what heard they daily from the master and company? But that with speed they should look out a place (with their shallop) where they would be, at some near distance; for the season was such as he would not stir from thence till a safe harbor was discovered by them, where they would be, and he might go without danger; and that victuals consumed apace but he must and would keep sufficient for themselves and their return. Yea, it was muttered by some that if they got not a place in time, they would turn them and their goods ashore and leave them. Let it also be considered what weak hopes of supply and succor they left behind them, that might bear up their minds in this sad condition and trials they were under; and they could not but be very small. It is true, indeed, the affections and love of their brethren at Leyden was cordial and entire towards them, but they had little power to help them or themselves; and how the case stood between them and the merchants at their coming away hath already been declared.

What could now sustain them but the Spirit of God and His grace? May not and ought not the children of these fathers rightly say: "Our fathers were Englishmen which came over this great ocean, and were ready to perish in this wilderness; but they cried unto the Lord, and He heard their voice and looked on their adversity," etc. "Let them therefore praise the Lord, because He is good: and His mercies endure forever. Yea, let them which have been redeemed of the Lord, show how He hath delivered them from the hand of the oppressor. When they wandered in the desert wilderness out of the way, and found no city to dwell in, both hungry and thirsty, their soul was overwhelmed in them." "Let them confess before the Lord His lovingkindness and His wonderful works before the sons of men."

[How they sought a place of habitation (1620)]

Being thus arrived at Cape Cod the 11th of November, and necessity calling them to look out a place for habitation (as well as the master's and mariners' importunity); they having brought a large shallop with them out of England, stowed in quarters in the ship, they now got her out and set their carpenters to work to trim her up; but being much bruised and shattered in the ship with foul weather, they saw she would be long in mending. Whereupon a few of them tendered themselves to go by land and discover those nearest places, whilst the shallop was in mending; and the rather because as they went into that harbor there seemed to be an opening some two or three leagues off, which the master judged to be a river. It was conceived there might be some danger in the attempt, yet seeing them resolute, they were permitted to go, being sixteen of them well armed under the conduct of Captain Standish, having such instructions given them as was thought meet.

They set forth the 15th of November; and when they had marched about the space of a mile by the seaside, they espied five or six persons with a dog coming towards them, who were savages; but they fled from them and ran up into the woods, and the English followed them, partly to see if they could speak with them, and partly to discover if there might not be more of them lying in ambush. But the Indians seeing themselves thus followed, they again forsook the woods and ran away on the sands as hard as they could, so as they could not come near them but followed them by the track of their feet sundry miles and saw that they had come the same way. So, night coming on, they made their rendezvous and set out their sentinels, and rested in quiet that night; and the next morning followed their track till they had headed a great creek and so left the sands, and turned another way into the woods. But they still followed them by guess, hoping to find their dwellings; but they soon lost both them and themselves, falling into such thickets as were ready to tear their clothes and armor in pieces; but were most distressed for want of drink. But at length they found water and refreshed themselves, being the first New England water they drunk of, and was now in great thirst as pleasant unto them as wine or beer had been in foretimes.

Afterwards they directed their course to come to the other shore, for they knew it was a neck of land they were to cross over, and so at length got to the seaside and marched to this supposed river, and by the way found a pond of clear, fresh water, and shortly after a good quantity of clear ground where the Indians had formerly set corn, and some of their graves. And proceeding further they saw new stubble where corn had been set the same year; also they found where lately a house had been, where some planks and a great kettle was remaining, and heaps of sand newly paddled with their hands. Which, they digging up, found in them divers fair Indian baskets filled with corn, and some in ears, fair and good, of divers colors, which seemed to them a very goodly sight (having never seen any such before). This was near the place of that supposed river they came to seek, unto which they went and found it to open itself into two arms with a high cliff of sand in the entrance but more like to be creeks of salt water than any fresh, for aught they saw; and that there was good harborage for their shallop, leaving it further to be discovered by their shallop, when she was ready. So, their time limited them being expired, they returned to the ship lest they should be in fear of their safety; and took with them part of the corn and buried up the rest. And so, like the men from Eshcol, carried with them of the fruits of the land and showed their brethren; of which, and their return, they were marvelously glad and their hearts encouraged.

After this, the shallop being got ready, they set out again for the better discovery of this place, and the master of the ship desired to go himself. So there went some thirty men but found it to be no harbor for ships but only for boats. There was also found two of their houses covered with mats, and sundry of their implements in them, but the people were run away and could not be seen. Also there was found more of their corn and of their beans of various colors; the corn and beans they brought away, purposing to give them full satisfaction when they should meet with any of them as, about some six months afterward they did, to their good content.

And here is to be noted a special providence of God, and a great mercy to this poor people, that here they got seed to plant them corn the next year, or else they might have starved, for they had none nor any likelihood to get any till the season had been past, as the sequel did manifest. Neither is it likely they had had this, if the first voyage had not been made, for the ground was now all covered with snow and hard frozen; but the Lord is never wanting unto His in their greatest needs; let His holy name have all the praise. . . .

From hence they departed and coasted all along but discerned no place likely for harbor; and therefore hasted to a place that their pilot (one Mr. Coppin who had been in the country before) did assure them was a good harbor, which he had been in, and they might fetch it before night; of which they were glad for it began to be foul weather.

After some hours' sailing it began to snow and rain, and about the middle of the afternoon the wind increased and the sea became very rough, and they broke their rudder, and it was as much as two men could do to steer her with a couple of oars. But their pilot bade them be of good cheer for he saw the harbor; but the storm increasing, and night drawing on, they bore what sail they could to get in, while they could see. But herewith they broke their mast in three pieces and their sail fell overboard in a very grown sea, so as they had like to have been cast away. Yet by God's mercy they recovered themselves, and having the flood with them, struck into the harbor. But when it came to, the pilot was deceived in the place, and said the Lord be merciful unto them for his eyes never saw that place before; and he and the master's mate would have run her ashore in a cove full of breakers before the wind. But a lusty seaman which steered bade those which rowed, if they were men, about with her or else they were all cast away; the which they did with speed. So he bid them be of good cheer and row lustily, for there was a fair sound before them, and he doubted not but they should find one place or other where they might ride in safety. And though it was very dark and rained sore, yet in the end they got under the lee of a small island and remained there all that night in safety. But they knew not this to be an island till morning, but were divided in their minds; some would keep the boat for fear they might be amongst the Indians, others were so wet and cold they could not endure but got ashore, and with much ado got fire (all things being so wet); and the rest were glad to come to them, for after midnight the wind shifted to the northwest and it froze hard.

But though this had been a day and night of much trouble and danger unto them, yet God gave them a morning of comfort and refreshing (as usually He doth to His children) for the next day was a fair, sunshining day, and they found themselves to be on an island secure from the Indians, where they might dry their stuff, fix their pieces and rest themselves; and gave God thanks for His mercies in their manifold deliverances. And this being the last day of the week, they prepared there to keep the Sabbath.

On Monday they sounded the harbor and found it fit for shipping, and marched into the land and found divers cornfields and little running brooks, a place (as they supposed) fit for situation. At least it was the best they could find, and the season and their present necessity made them glad to accept of it. So they returned to their ship again with this news to the rest of their people, which did much comfort their hearts.

On the 15th of December they weighed anchor to go to the place they had discovered, and came within two leagues of it, but were fain to bear up again; but the 16th day, the wind came fair, and they arrived safe in this harbor. And afterwards took better view of the place, and resolved where to pitch their dwelling; and the 25th day began to erect the first house for common use to receive them and their goods.

BOOK II

[The Mayflower Compact (1620)]

I shall a little return back, and begin with a combination made by them before they came ashore; being the first foundation of their government in this place. Occasioned partly by the discontented and mutinous speeches that some of the strangers amongst them had let fall from them in the ship: That when they came ashore they would use their own liberty, for none had power to command them, the patent they had being for Virginia and not for New England, which belonged to another government, with which the Virginia Company had nothing to do. And partly that such an act by them done, this their condition considered, might be as firm as any patent, and in some respects more sure.

The form was as followeth:

IN THE NAME OF GOD, AMEN.

We whose names are underwritten, the loyal subjects of our dread Sovereign Lord King James, by the Grace of God of Great Britain, France, and Ireland King, Defender of the Faith, etc.

Having undertaken, for the Glory of God and advancement of the Christian Faith and Honor of our King and Country, a Voyage to plant the First Colony in the Northern Parts of Virginia, do by these presents solemnly and mutually in the presence of God and one of another, Covenant and Combine ourselves together into a Civil Body Politic, for our better ordering and preservation and furtherance of the ends aforesaid; and by virtue hereof to enact, constitute and frame such just and equal Laws, Ordinances, Acts, Constitutions and Offices, from time to time, as shall be thought most meet and convenient for the general good of the Colony, unto which we promise all due submission and obedience. In witness whereof we have hereunder subscribed our names at Cape Cod, the 11th of November, in the year of the reign of our Sovereign Lord King James, of England, France and Ireland the eighteenth, and of Scotland the fifty-fourth. Anno Domini 1620.

After this they chose, or rather confirmed, Mr. John Carver (a man godly and well approved amongst them) their Governor for that year. And after they had provided a place for their goods, or common store (which were long in unlading for want of boats, foulness of the winter weather and sickness of divers) and begun some small cottages for their habitation; as time would admit, they met and consulted of laws and orders, both for their civil and military government as the necessity of their condition did require, still adding thereunto as urgent occasion in several times, and as cases did require.

In these hard and difficult beginnings they found some discontents and murmurings arise amongst some, and mutinous speeches and carriages in other; but they were soon quelled and overcome by the wisdom, patience, and just and equal carriage of things, by the Governor and better part, which clave faithfully together in the main.

[Sickness and death (1621)]

But that which was most sad and lamentable was, that in two or three months' time half of their company died, especially in January and February, being the depth of winter, and wanting houses and other comforts; being infected with the scurvy and other diseases which this long voyage and their inaccommodate condition had brought upon them. So as there died some times two or three of a day in the foresaid time, that of 100 and odd persons, scarce fifty remained. And of these, in the time of most distress, there was but six or seven sound persons who to their great commendations, be it spoken, spared no pains night nor day, but with abundance of toil and hazard of their own health, fetched them wood, made them fires, dressed them meat, made their beds, washed their loathsome clothes, clothed and unclothed them. In a word, did all the homely and necessary offices for them which dainty and queasy stomachs cannot endure to hear named; and all this willingly and cheerfully, without any grudging in the least, showing herein their true love unto their friends and brethren; a rare example and worthy to be remembered. Two of these seven were Mr. William Brewster, their reverend Elder, and Myles Standish, their Captain and military commander, unto whom myself and many others were much beholden in our low and sick condition. And yet the Lord so upheld these persons as in this general calamity they were not at all infected either with sickness or lameness. And what I have said of these I may say of many others who died in this general visitation, and others yet living; that whilst they had health, yea, or any strength continuing, they were not wanting to any that had need of them. And I doubt not but their recompense is with the Lord.

But I may not here pass by another remarkable passage not to be forgotten. As this calamity fell among the passengers that were to be left here to plant, and were hasted ashore and made to drink water that the seamen might have the more beer, and one [Bradford] in his sickness desiring but a small can of beer, it was answered that if he were their own father he should have none. The disease began to fall amongst them also, so as almost half of their company died before they went away, and many of their officers and lustiest men, as the boatswain, gunner, three quartermasters, the cook and others. At which the Master was something strucken and sent to the sick ashore and told the Governor he should send for beer for them that had need of it, though he drunk water homeward bound.

But now amongst his company there was far another kind of carriage in this misery than amongst the passengers. For they that before had been boon companions in drink and jollity in the time of their health and welfare, began now to desert one another in this calamity, saying they would not hazard their lives for them, they should be infected by coming to help them in their cabins; and so, after they came to lie by it, would do little or nothing for them but, "if they died, let them die." But such of the passengers as were yet aboard showed them what mercy they could, which made some of their hearts relent, as the boatswain (and some others) who was a proud young man and would often curse and scoff at the passengers. But when he grew weak, they had compassion on him and helped him; then he confessed he did not deserve it at their hands, he had abused them in word and deed. "Oh!" (saith he) "you, I now see, show your love like Christians indeed one to another, but we let one another lie and die like dogs." Another lay cursing his wife, saying if it had not been for her he had never come this unlucky voyage, and anon cursing his fellows, saying he had done this and that for some of them; he had spent so much and so much amongst them, and they were now weary of him and did not help him, having need. Another gave his companion all he had, if he died, to help him in his weakness; he went and got a little spice and made him a mess of meat once or twice. And because he died not so soon as he expected, he went amongst his fellows and swore the rogue would cozen him, he would see him choked before he made him any more meat; and yet the poor fellow died before morning.

[Treaty with the Indians (1621)]

All this while the Indians came skulking about them, and would sometimes show themselves aloof off, but when any approached near them, they would run away; and once they stole away their tools where they had been at work and were gone to dinner. But about the 16th of March, a certain Indian came boldly amongst them and spoke to them in broken English, which they could well understand but marveled at it. At length they understood by discourse with him, that he was not of these parts, but belonged to the eastern parts where some English ships came to fish, with whom he was acquainted and could name sundry of them by their names, amongst whom he had got his language. He became profitable to them in acquainting them with many things concerning the state of the country in the east parts where he lived, which was afterwards profitable unto them; as also of the people here, of their names, number and strength, of their situation and distance from this place, and who was chief amongst them. His name was Samoset. He told them also of another Indian whose name was Squanto, a native of this place, who had been in England and could speak better English than himself.

Being, after some time of entertainment and gifts dismissed, a while after he came again, and five more with him, and they brought again all the tools that were stolen away before, and made way for the coming of their great Sachem, called Massasoit. Who, about four or five days after, came with the chief of his friends and other attendance, with the aforesaid Squanto. With whom, after friendly entertainment and some gifts given him, they made a peace with him (which hath now continued this 24 years) in these terms:

1. That neither he nor any of his should injure or do hurt to any of their people.
2. That if any of his did hurt to any of theirs, he should send the offender, that they might punish him.
3. That if anything were taken away from any of theirs, he should cause it to be restored; and they should do the like to his.

4. If any did unjustly war against him, they would aid him; if any did war against them, he should aid them.

5. He should send to his neighbors confederates to certify them of this, that they might not wrong them, but might be likewise comprised in the conditions of peace.

6. That when their men came to them, they should leave their bows and arrows behind them.

After these things he returned to his place called Sowams, some 40 miles from this place, but Squanto continued with them and was their interpreter and was a special instrument sent of God for their good beyond their expectation. He directed them how to set their corn, where to take fish, and to procure other commodities, and was also their pilot to bring them to unknown places for their profit, and never left them till he died. He was a native of this place, and scarce any left alive besides himself. He was carried away with divers others by one Hunt, a master of a ship, who thought to sell them for slaves in Spain. But he got away for England and was entertained by a merchant in London, and employed to Newfoundland and other parts, and lastly brought hither into these parts by one Mr. Dermer, a gentleman employed by Sir Ferdinando Gorges and others for discovery and other designs in these parts.

[The Mayflower departs (1621)]

They now began to dispatch the ship away which brought them over, which lay till about this time, or the beginning of April. The reason on their part why she stayed so long, was the necessity and danger that lay upon them; for it was well towards the end of December before she could land anything here, or they able to receive anything ashore. Afterwards, the 14th of January, the house which they had made for a general rendezvous by casualty fell afire, and some were fain to retire aboard for shelter; then the sickness began to fall sore amongst them, and the weather so bad as they could not make much sooner any dispatch. Again, the Governor and chief of them, seeing so many die and fall down sick daily, thought it no wisdom to send away the ship, their condition considered and the danger they stood in from the Indians, till they could procure some shelter; and therefore thought it better to draw some more charge upon themselves and friends than hazard all. The master and seamen likewise, though before they hasted the passengers ashore to be gone, now many of their men being dead, and of the ablest of them (as is before noted), and of the rest many lay sick and weak; the master durst not put to sea till he saw his men begin to recover, and the heart of winter over.

Afterwards they (as many as were able) began to plant their corn, in which service Squanto stood them in great stead, showing them both the manner how to set it, and after how to dress and tend it. Also he told them, except they got fish and set with it in these old grounds it would come to nothing. And he showed them that in the middle of April they should have store enough come up the brook by which they began to build, and taught them how to take it, and where to get other provisions necessary for them. All which they found true by trial and experience. Some English seed they sowed, as wheat and pease, but it came not to good, either by the badness of the seed or lateness of the season or both, or some other defect.

[New governor, first marriage (1621)]

In this month of April, whilst they were busy about their seed, their Governor (Mr. John Carver) came out of the field very sick, it being a hot day. He complained greatly of his head and lay down, and within a few hours his senses failed, so as he never spake more till he died, which was within a few days after. Whose death was much lamented and caused great heaviness amongst them, as there was cause. He was buried in the best manner they could, with some volleys of shot by all that bore arms. And his wife, being a weak woman, died within five or six weeks after him.

Shortly after, William Bradford was chosen Governor in his stead, and being not recovered of his illness, in which he had been near the point of death, Isaac Allerton was chosen to be an assistant unto him who, by renewed election every year, continued sundry years together. Which I here note once for all.

May 12 was the first marriage in this place which, according to the laudable custom of the Low Countries, in which they had lived, was thought most requisite to be performed by the magistrate, as being a civil thing, upon which many questions about inheritances do depend, with other things most proper to their cognizance and most consonant to the Scriptures (Ruth iv) and nowhere found in the Gospel to be laid on the ministers as a part of their office.

[First harvest (1621)]

They began now to gather in the small harvest they had, and to fit up their houses and dwellings against winter, being all well recovered in health and strength and had all things in good plenty. For as some were thus employed in affairs abroad, others were exercised in fishing, about cod and bass and other fish, of which they took good store, of which every family had their portion. All the summer there was no want; and now began to come in store of fowl, as winter approached, of which this place did abound when they came first (but afterward decreased by degrees). And besides waterfowl there was great store of wild turkeys, of which they took many, besides venison, etc. Besides they had about a peck a meal a week to a person, or now since harvest, Indian corn to that proportion. Which made many afterwards write so largely of their plenty here to their friends in England, which were not feigned but true reports.

[Private and communal farming (1623)]

All this while no supply was heard of, neither knew they when they might expect any. So they began to think how they might raise as much corn as they could, and obtain a better crop than they had done, that they might not still thus languish in misery. At length, after much debate of things, the Governor (with the advice of the chiefest amongst them) gave way that they should set corn every man for his own particular, and in that regard trust to themselves; in all other things to go on in the general way as before. And so assigned to every family a parcel of land, according to the proportion of their number, for that end, only for present use (but made no division for inheritance) and ranged all boys and youth under some family. This had very good success, for it made all hands very industrious, so as much more corn was planted than otherwise would have been by any means the Governor or any other could use, and saved him a great deal of trouble, and gave far better content. The women now went willingly into the field, and took their little ones with them to set corn; which before would allege weakness and inability; whom to have compelled would have been thought great tyranny and oppression.

The experience that was had in this common course and condition, tried sundry years and that amongst godly and sober men, may well evince the vanity of that conceit of Plato's and other ancients applauded by some of later times; that the taking away of property and bringing in community into a commonwealth would make them happy and flourishing; as if they were wiser than God. For this community (so far as it was) was found to breed much confusion and discontent and retard much employment that would have been to their benefit and comfort. For the young men, that were most able and fit for labor and service, did repine that they should spend their time and strength to work for other men's wives and children without any recompense. The strong, or man of parts, had no more in division of victuals and clothes than he that was weak and not able to do a quarter the other could; this was thought injustice. The aged and graver men to be ranked and equalized in labors and victuals, clothes, etc., with the meaner and younger sort, thought it some indignity and disrespect unto them. And for men's wives to be commanded to do service for other men, as dressing their meat, washing their clothes, etc., they deemed it a kind of slavery, neither could many husbands well brook it. Upon the point all being to have alike, and all to do alike, they thought themselves in the like condition, and one as good as another; and so, if it did not cut off those relations that God hath set amongst men, yet it did at least much diminish and take off the mutual respects that should be preserved amongst them. And would have been worse if they had been men of another condition. Let none object this is men's corruption, and nothing to the course itself. I answer, seeing all men have this corruption in them, God in His wisdom saw another course fitter for them.

[Spent victuals (1623)]

But to return. After this course settled, and by that their corn was planted, all their victuals were spent, and they were only to rest on God's providence; at night not many times knowing where to have a bit of anything the next day. And so, as one well observed, had need to pray that God would give them their daily bread, above all people in the world. Yet they bore these wants with great patience and alacrity of spirit; and that for so long a time as for the most part of two years. Which makes me remember what Peter Martyr writes (in magnifying the Spaniards) in his 5th Decade, page 208. "They (saith he) led a miserable life for five days together, with the parched grain of maize only, and that not to saturity"; and then concludes, "that such pains, such labors, and such hunger, he thought none living which is not a Spaniard could have endured."

But alas! these, when they had maize (that is, Indian corn) they thought it as good as a feast, and wanted not only for five days together, but sometime two or three months together, and neither had bread nor any kind of corn. Indeed, in another place, in his 2nd Decade, page 94, he mentions how others of them were worse put to it, where they were fain to eat dogs, toads, and dead men, and so died almost all. From these extremities the Lord in His goodness kept these His people, and in their great wants preserved both their lives and health. Let His name have the praise. Yet let me here make use of his [Peter Martyr's] conclusion, which in some sort may be applied to this people:

"That with their miseries they opened a way to these new lands, and after these storms, with what ease other men came to inhabit in them, in respect of the calamities these men suffered; so as they seem to go to a bride feast where all things are provided for them."

[Morton of Merrymount (1628)]

Hitherto the Indians of these parts had no pieces nor other arms but their bows and arrows, nor of many years after; neither durst they scarce handle a gun, so much were they afraid of them; and the very sight of one, though out of kilter, was a terror unto them. But those Indians to the east parts which had commerce with the French got pieces of them; and they in the end made a common trade of it; and in time our English fishermen, led with the like covetousness, followed their example for their own gain; but upon complaint against them, it pleased the King's Majesty to prohibit the same by a strict proclamation, commanding that no sort of arms or munition should by any of his subjects be traded with them.

About some three or four years before this time, there came over one Captain Wollaston, a man of pretty parts, and with him three or four more of some eminency, who brought with them a great many servants, with provisions and other implements for to begin a plantation; and pitched themselves in a place within the Massachusetts, which they called, after their captain's name, Mount Wollaston—amongst whom was one Mr. Morton, who, it should seem, had some small adventure (of his own or other men's) amongst them, but had little respect amongst them and was slighted by the meanest servants. Having continued there some time and not finding things to answer their expectations, nor profit to arise as they looked for, Captain Wollaston takes a great part of the servants and transports them to Virginia, where he puts them off at good rates, selling their time to other men; and writes back to one Mr. Rasdall, one of his chief partners, and accounted their merchant, to bring another part of them to Virginia likewise, intending to put them off there as he had done the rest. And he, with the consent of the said Rasdall, appointed one Fitcher to be his lieutenant and govern the remains of the plantation till he or Rasdall returned to take further order thereabout. But this Morton above-said, having more craft than honesty (who had been a kind of pettifogger of Furnefell's Inn), in the other's absence watches an opportunity (and commons being but hard amongst them) and got some strong drink and other junkets and made them a feast; and after they were merry, he began to tell them he would give them good counsel.

"You see," saith he, "that many of your fellows are carried to Virginia; and if you stay till this Rasdall return, you will also be carried away and sold for slaves with the rest. Therefore I would advise you to thrust out this Lieutenant

Fitcher; and I, having a part in the plantation, will receive you as my partners and consociates. So may you be free from service; and we will converse, trade, plant, and live together as equals, and support and protect one another," or to like effect. This counsel was easily received; so they took opportunity and thrust Lieutenant Fitcher out of doors and would suffer him to come no more amongst them, but forced him to seek bread to eat and other relief from his neighbors till he could get passages for England.

After this they fell to great licentiousness and led a dissolute life, pouring out themselves into all profaneness. And Morton became lord of misrule and maintained, as it were, a school of atheism. And after they had got some goods into their hands and got much by trading with the Indians, they spent it as vainly, in quaffing and drinking both wine and strong waters in great excess and, as some reported, ten pounds' worth in a morning. They also set up a Maypole, drinking and dancing about it many days together, inviting the Indian women for their consorts, dancing and frisking together like so many fairies (or furies rather), and worse practices, as if they had anew revived and celebrated the feasts of the Roman goddess Flora or the beastly practices of the mad Bacchanalians. Morton likewise (to show his poetry) composed sundry rhymes and verses, some tending to lasciviousness and others to the detraction and scandal of some persons, which he affixed to this idle, or idol, Maypole. They changed also the name of their place; and instead of calling it Mount Wollaston, they call it Merry Mount, as if this jollity would have lasted ever. But this continued not long; for after Morton was sent for England (as follows to be declared), shortly after came over that worthy gentleman, Mr. John Endecott, who brought over a patent under the broad seal for the government of the Massachusetts, who, visiting those parts, caused that Maypole to be cut down and rebuked them for their profaneness and admonished them to look there should be better walking; so they now, or others, changed the name of their place again and called it Mount Dagon.

Now, to maintain this riotous prodigality and profuse excess, Morton, thinking himself lawless and hearing what gain the French and fishermen made by trading of pieces, powder, and shot to the Indians, he, as the head of this consortship, began the practice of the same in these parts. And first he taught them how to use them, to charge and discharge, and what proportion of powder to give the piece, according to the size or bigness of the same, and what shot to use for fowl and what for deer. And having thus instructed them, he employed some of them to hunt and fowl for him so as they became far more active in that employment than any of the English by reason of their swiftness of foot and nimbleness of body, being also quick-sighted, and by continual exercise well knowing the haunts of all sorts of game—so as when they saw the execution that a piece would do and the benefit that might come by the same, they became mad, as it were, after them, and would not stick to give any price they could attain to for them, accounting their bows and arrows but baubles in comparison of them.

And here I may take occasion to bewail the mischief that this wicked man began in these parts, and which since base covetousness prevailing in men that should know better hath now at length got the upper hand and made this thing common, notwithstanding any laws to the contrary, so as the Indians are full of pieces all over, both fowling pieces, muskets, pistols, etc. They have also their moulds to make shot of all sorts, as musket bullets, pistol bullets, swan and goose shot, and of smaller sorts. Yea, some have seen them have their screw-plates to make screw-pins themselves, when they want them, with sundry other implements wherewith they are ordinarily better fitted and furnished than the English themselves. Yea, it is well known that they will have powder and shot when the English want it, nor cannot get it, and that in a time of war or danger, as experience hath manifested, that when lead hath been scarce and men for their own defense would gladly have given a groat a pound, which is dear enough, yet hath it been bought up and sent to other places and sold to such as trade it with the Indians at twelve pence the pound; and it is like they give three or four shillings the pound, for they will have it at any rate. And these things have been done in the same times when some of their neighbors and friends are daily killed by the Indians or are in danger thereof and live but at the Indians' mercy. Yea, some (as they have acquainted them with all other things) have told them how gunpowder is made and all the materials in it, and that they are to be had in their own land; and I am confident could they attain to make saltpeter, they would teach them to make powder. Oh, the horribleness of this villainy! How many both Dutch and English have been lately slain by those Indians, thus furnished, and no remedy provided—nay, the evil more increased and the blood of their brethren sold for gain, as is to be feared! And in what danger all these colonies are in is too well known. Oh, that princes and parliaments would take some timely order to prevent this mischief, and at length to suppress it, by some exemplary punishment upon some of these gain-thirsty murderers (for they deserve no better title) before their colonies in these parts be overthrown by these barbarous savages, thus armed with their own weapons by these evil instruments and traitors to their neighbors and country!

But I have forgotten myself and have been too long in this digression. But now to return, this Morton having thus taught them the use of pieces, he sold them all he could spare. And he and his consorts determined to send for many out of England, and had by some of the ships sent for above a score—the which being known, and his neighbors meeting the Indians in the woods armed with guns in this sort, it was a terror unto them who lived stragglingly and were of no strength in any place. And other places, though more remote, saw this mischief would quickly spread over all, if not prevented. Besides, they saw they should keep no servants, for Morton would entertain any, how vile soever, and all the scum of the country or any discontents would flock to him from all places, if this nest was not broken; and they should stand in more fear of their lives and goods in short time from this wicked and debauched crew than from the savages themselves.

So sundry of the chief of the straggling plantations, meeting together, agreed by mutual consent to solicit those of Plymouth, who were then of more strength than them all, to join with them to prevent the further growth of this mischief, and suppress Morton and his consorts before they grew to further head and strength. Those that joined in this action (and after contributed to the charge of sending him for England) were from Pascataway, Namkeake, Winisimett, Weesagascusett, Natasco, and other places where any English were seated. Those of Plymouth, being thus sought too by their messengers and letters and weighing both their reasons and the common danger, were willing to afford them their help, though themselves had least cause of fear or hurt. So, to be short, they first resolved jointly to write to him, and in a friendly and neighborly way, to admonish him to forbear those courses, and sent a messenger with their letters to bring his answer. But he was so high as he scorned all advice and asked who had to do with him; he had and would trade pieces with the Indians in despite of all, with many other scurrilous terms full of disdain.

They sent to him a second time and bade him be better advised and more temperate in his terms, for the country could not bear the injury he did; it was against their common safety and against the King's proclamation. He answered in high terms as before, and that the King's proclamation was no law, demanding what penalty was upon it. It was answered, more than he could bear, His Majesty's displeasure. But insolently he persisted and said the King was dead and his displeasure with him, and many the like things, and threatened withal that if any came to molest him, let them look to themselves, for he would prepare for them—upon which they saw there was no way but to take him by force; and having so far proceeded, now to give over would make him far more haughty and insolent. So they mutually resolved to proceed and obtained of the Governor of Plymouth to send Captain Standish and some other aid with him to take Morton by force— the which accordingly was done. But they found him to stand stiffly in his defense, having made fast his doors, armed his consorts, set divers dishes of powder and bullets ready on the table; and if they had not been overarmed with drink, more hurt might have been done. They summoned him to yield, but he kept his house, and they could get nothing but scoffs and scorns from him. But at length, fearing they would do some violence to the house, he and some of his crew came out, but not to yield but to shoot. But they were so steeled with drink as their pieces were too heavy for them; himself with a carbine overcharged and almost half filled with powder and shot, as was after found, had thought to have shot Captain Standish; but he stepped to him and put by his piece and took him.

Neither was there any hurt done to any of either side, save that one was so drunk that he ran his own nose upon the point of a sword that one held before him as he entered the house; but he lost but a little of his hot blood. Morton they brought away to Plymouth, where he was kept till a ship went from the Isle of Shoals for England, with which he was sent to the Council of New England; and letters written to give them information of his course and carriage; and also one was sent at their common charge to inform their Honors more particularly, and to prosecute against him. But he fooled off the messenger after he was gone from hence; and though he went for England, yet nothing was done to him, not so much as rebuked, for aught was heard; but returned the next year. Some of the worst of the company were dispersed, and some of the more modest kept the house till he should be heard from. But I have been too long about so unworthy a person, and bad a cause.

w. 1630–1650
p. 1856

THOMAS MORTON
(1575–1646)

To a later, uninvolved age, Thomas Morton, the man who thumbed his nose at the Saints in Plymouth, might very well seem a prototype of American nonconformity and a forerunner of the later revolt against the Puritan ethic. But to William Bradford and the other Pilgrims he was a "wicked and debauched" hedonist whose presence in nearby Merry Mount threatened the holy enterprise in the New World. A lawyer by training and an adventurer by disposition, Morton first came to New England in 1622—the only one of his four visits in which he did not end up in jail. In 1625 he settled with Captain Wollaston on what is now the site of Quincy, Massachusetts; but when Wollaston left for Virginia, Morton remained behind, renamed the community Merry Mount, and became an outrage to his Puritan neighbors. Not only did Morton ridicule the Pilgrims and engage in what they considered licentious Anglican practices, but, worse, he increased the threat to their lives and well-being by selling guns and whisky to the Indians for furs. After setting up a Maypole in Merry Mount, Morton was captured in 1628 by a band of Pilgrims led by Captain Myles Standish and sent back to England under arrest. (It is fascinating to compare Bradford's and Morton's accounts of this incident, and then to see how Nathaniel Hawthorne used these historical materials for his imaginative exploration of the New England character in "The Maypole of Merry Mount.") Morton returned to New England in 1630 for still another round of capture, arrest, and deportation. In England he was released from jail so that he could testify for those High Churchmen who wanted to have the colonial charter revoked. Morton's *New English Canaan*, published in Holland in 1637, deals with Indians, the enchantments of America, and the errors of the Massachusetts Puritans. In 1643 Morton returned to Massachusetts to spend another year in jail before retiring to Maine, where he died in 1646.

Accounts of Morton and his work are to be found in P. Force, *Tracts and Other Papers*, II (1838, 1947); C. F. Adams, Jr., ed., *The New English Canaan* (1883); C. E. Banks, "Thomas Morton of Merry Mount," *Proceedings of the Massachusetts Historical Society*, LVIII (1924), LIX (1925); H. Beston [Sheahan], *A Book of Gallant Vagabonds* (1925); S. E. Morison, *Builders of the Bay Colony* (1930); and D. F. Connors, "Thomas Morton of Merry Mount: His First Arrival in New England," *American Literature*, XI (1939).

FROM

New English Canaan

Of the Revels of New Canaan

The Inhabitants of Pasonagessit, (having translated the name of their habitation from that ancient savage name to Merry Mount, and being resolved to have the new name confirmed for a memorial to after ages,) did devise amongst themselves to have it performed in a solemn manner, with revels and merriment after the old English custom; they prepared to set up a Maypole upon the festival day of Philip and Jacob, and therefore brewed a barrel of excellent beer and provided a case of bottles, to be spent, with other good cheer, for all comers of that day. And because they would have it in a complete form, they had prepared a song fitting to the time and present occasion. And upon Mayday they brought the Maypole to the place appointed, with drums, guns, pistols and other fitting instruments, for that purpose; and there erected it with the help of savages, that came thither of purpose to see the manner of our revels. A goodly pine tree of 80 foot long was reared up, with a pair of buckhorns nailed on somewhat near unto the top of it: where it stood, as a fair sea mark for directions how to find out the way to mine Host of Merry Mount. . . .

The setting up of this Maypole was a lamentable spectacle to the precise Separatists, that lived at New Plymouth. They termed it an Idol; yea, they called it the Calf of Horeb, and stood at defiance with the place, naming it Mount Dagon; threatening to make it a woeful mount and not a merry mount. . . .

There was . . . a merry song made, which, (to make their revels more fashionable,) was sung with a Chorus, every man bearing his part; which they performed in a dance, hand in hand about the Maypole, while one of the Company sung and filled out the good liquor, like Ganymede and Jupiter.

THE SONG

Chor.

  Drink and be merry, merry, merry boys;
  Let all your delight be in the Hymen's joys;
  Io to Hymen, now the day is come,
  About the merry Maypole take a Room.
    Make green garlands, bring bottles out
    And fill sweet Nectar freely about.
    Uncover thy head and fear no harm,
    For here's good liquor to keep it warm.
  Then drink and be merry, &c.
  Io to Hymen, &c.
    Nectar is a thing assigned
    By the Deity's own mind
    To cure the heart oppressed with grief,
    And of good liquors is the chief.
  Then drink, &c.
  Io to Hymen, &c.
    Give to the Melancholy man
    A cup or two of 't now and then;
    This physic will soon revive his blood,
    And make him be of a merrier mood.
  Then drink, &c.
  Io to Hymen, &c.
    Give to the Nymph that's free from scorn
    No Irish stuff nor Scotch over worn.

Lasses in beaver coats come away,
Ye shall be welcome to us night and day.
To drink and be merry, &c.
Io to Hymen, &c.

This harmless mirth made by young men, (that lived in hope to have wives brought over to them, that would save them a labor to make a voyage to fetch any over,) was much distasted of the precise Separatists, that keep much ado about the tithe of meat and cumin, troubling their brains more than reason would require about things that are indifferent: and from that time sought occasion against my honest Host of Merry Mount, to overthrow his undertakings and to destroy his plantation quite and clean. . . .

Of a Great Monster Supposed to Be at Merry Mount; and the Preparation Made to Destroy It

The Separatists, envying the prosperity and hope of the plantation at Merry Mount, (which they perceived began to come forward, and to be in a good way for gain in the beaver trade,) conspired together against mine Host especially, (who was the owner of that plantation,) and made up a party against him; and mustered up what aid they could, accounting of him as of a great monster.

Many threatening speeches were given out both against his person and his habitation, which they divulged should be consumed with fire: And taking advantage of the time when his company, (which seemed little to regard their threats,) were gone up into the Inlands to trade with the savages for beaver, they set upon my honest Host at a place called Wessaguscus, where, by accident, they found him. The inhabitants there were in good hope of the subversion of the plantation at Merry Mount, (which they principally aimed at;) and the rather because mine Host was a man that endeavored to advance the dignity of the Church of England; which they, (on the contrary part,) would labor to vilify with uncivil terms: inveighing against the sacred Book of Common Prayer, and mine Host that used it in a laudable manner amongst his family, as a practice of piety.

There he would be a means to bring sacks to their mill

(such is the thirst after beaver), and helped the conspirators to surprise mine Host (who was there all alone); and they charged him (because they would seem to have some reasonable cause against him, to set a gloss upon their malice) with criminal things which indeed had been done by such a person, but was of their conspiracy; mine Host demanded of the conspirators who it was that was author of that information, that seemed to be their ground for what they now intended. And because they answered they would not tell him, he as peremptorily replied, that he would not stay, whether he had, or he had not done as they had been informed.

The answer made no matter (as it seemed), whether it had been negatively, or affirmatively made; for they had resolved what he should suffer, because (as they boasted) they were now become the greater number: they had shaked off their shackles of servitude, and were become masters, and masterless people.

It appears they were like bears' whelps in former time, when mine Host's plantation was of as much strength as theirs, but now (theirs being stronger), they (like overgrown bears) seemed monstrous. In brief, mine Host must endure to be their prisoner, until they could contrive it so, that they might send him for England (as they said), there to suffer according to the merit of the fact, which they intended to father upon him; supposing (belike) it would prove a heinous crime.

Much rejoicing was made that they had gotten their capital enemy (as they concluded him), whom they purposed to hamper in such sort, that he should not be able to uphold his plantation at Merry Mount.

The conspirators sported themselves at my honest Host, that meant them no hurt, and were so jocund that they feasted their bodies, and fell to tippling as if they had obtained a great prize; like the Trojans when they had the custody of Hippeus' pinetree horse.

Mine Host feigned grief, and could not be persuaded either to eat or drink; because he knew emptiness would be a means to make him as watchful as the geese kept in the Roman Capital: where, on the contrary part, the conspirators would be so drowsy that he might have an opportunity to give them a slip, instead of a tester.

Six persons of the conspiracy were set to watch him at

Wessaguscus: But he kept waking; and in the dead of night, (one lying on the bed for further surety,) up gets mine Host and got to the second door that he was to pass, which, nothwithstanding the lock, he got open, and shut it after him with such violence that it affrighted some of the conspirators. . . .

Their grand leader, Captain Shrimp [i.e. Myles Standish], took on most furiously and tore his clothes for anger, to see the empty nest, and their bird gone.

The rest were eager to have torn their hair from their heads; but it was so short that it would give them no hold. Now Captain Shrimp thought in the loss of this prize, (which he accounted his masterpiece,) all his honor would be lost forever.

In the meantime mine Host was got home to Merry Mount through the woods, eight miles round about the head of the river Monatoquit that parted the two plantations, finding his way by the help of the lightning, (for it thundered as he went terribly;) and there he prepared powder, three pounds dried, for his present employment, and four good guns for him and the two assistants left at his house, with bullets of several sizes, three hundred or thereabouts, to be used if the conspirators should pursue him thither: and these two persons promised their aids in the quarrel, and confirmed that promise with health in good rosa solis.

Now Captain Shrimp, the first captain in the land, (as he supposed,) must do some new act to repair this loss, and, to vindicate his reputation, who had sustained blemish by this oversight, begins now to study, how to repair or survive his honor: in this manner, calling of council, they conclude.

He takes eight persons more to him, and, (like the nine Worthies of New Canaan,) they embark with preparation against Merry Mount, where this monster of a man, as their phrase was, had his den; the whole number, had the rest not been from home, being but seven, would have given Captain Shrimp, (a quondam drummer,) such a welcome as would have made him wish for a drum as big as Diogenes' tub, that he might have crept into it out of sight.

Now the nine Worthies are approached, and mine Host prepared: having intelligence by a savage, that hastened in love from Wessaguscus to give him notice of their intent.

One of mine Host's men proved a craven: the other had proved his wits to purchase a little valor, before mine Host had observed his posture.

The nine Worthies coming before the den of this supposed monster, this seven-headed Hydra, (as they termed him,) and began, like Don Quixote against the windmill, to beat a parley, and to offer quarter, if mine Host would yield; for they resolved to send him to England; and bade him lay by his arms.

But he, (who was the son of a soldier,) having taken up arms in his just defense, replied that he would not lay by those arms, because they were so needful at sea, if he should be sent over. Yet, to save the effusion of so much worthy blood, as would have issued out of the veins of these nine Worthies of New Canaan, if mine Host should have played upon them out at his portholes, (for they came within danger like a flock of wild geese, as if they had been tailed one to another, as colts to be sold at a fair,) mine Host was content to yield upon quarter; and did capitulate with them. In what manner it should be, for more certainty, because he knew what Captain Shrimp was, he expressed that no violence should be offered to his person, none to his goods, nor any of his household: but that he should have his arms, and what else was requisite for the voyage: which their herald returns, it was agreed upon, and should be performed.

But mine Host no sooner had set open the door, and issued out, but instantly Captain Shrimp and the rest of the Worthies stepped to him, laid hold of his arms, and had him down: and so eagerly was every man bent against him, (not regarding any agreement made with such a carnal man,) that they fell upon him as if they would have eaten him: some of them were so violent that they would have a slice with scabbard, and all for haste; until an old soldier, (of the Queen's, as the proverb is,) that was there by accident, clapt his gun under the weapons, and sharply rebuked these Worthies for their unworthy practices. So the matter was taken into more deliberate consideration.

Captain Shrimp, and the rest of the nine Worthies, made themselves, (by this outrageous riot,) masters of mine Host of Merry Mount, and disposed of what he had at his plantation. . . .   1637

EDWARD JOHNSON
(1598–1672)

Arriving in Boston on the same ship with Governor John Winthrop, Edward Johnson represents the average social position of the thousand or so souls who made up the Great Migration to New England in 1630. A ship's carpenter by trade, Johnson, despite the lack of a university education, rose to some prominence in the governments of Massachusetts Bay and in 1640 founded the community at Woburn, Massachusetts. In 1650 he began his epic account of the trials and triumphs of the Puritan experiment in holy living in the western world. It was published in London in 1653 (dated 1654) as *A History of New England*. The book covers the organization of civil, military, and ecclesiastical authority, wars with the Indians, troubles with heretics, commodities, and trade with "Old England." But its running-title, *The Wonder-Working Providence of Sion's Savior in New England*, as the book has come to be known, more nearly reflects the charismatic vision which impelled the work. Sentimental, bombastic, and ornate, Johnson's *History* is not characteristic of Puritan prose in general, which was committed to the decorum of the "plain style." But it is always colorful and vigorous. More important, it enables us who are at such great historical remove from the assumptions and events of the seventeenth-century Puritans to catch something of what it meant emotionally to them to feel that they were God's "chosen" engaged in a holy crusade for Christ against his enemies in the wilderness.

Accounts of the man and his work are to be found in W. F. Poole, ed., *The Wonder-Working Providence* (1867); S. Sewall, *The History of Woburn* (1868); M. C. Tyler, *A History of American Literature,* I (1878); J. F. Jameson, ed., *Johnson's Wonder-Working Providence* (1910); A. Johnson, *A History . . . of One Line of Descent from Captain Edward Johnson* (1914); and M. Kraus, *Writing of American History* (1953).

FROM

The Wonder-Working Providence of Sion's Savior in New England

The Sad Condition of England, When This People Removed

When England began to decline in religion, like lukewarm Laodicea, and instead of purging out Popery, a farther compliance was sought, not only in vain idolatrous ceremonies but also in profaning the Sabbath and, by proclamation throughout their parish churches, exasperating lewd and profane persons to celebrate a Sabbath, like the heathen, to Venus, Bacchus and Ceres, insomuch that the multitude of irreligious lascivious and Popish affected persons spread the whole land like grasshoppers—in this very time, Christ, the glorious king of his churches, raises an army out of our English nation, for freeing his people from their long servitude under usurping prelacy. And because every corner of England was filled with the fury of malignant adversaries, Christ creates a new England to muster up the first of his forces in, whose low condition, little number, and remoteness of place made these adversaries triumph, despising this day of small things. But in this height of their pride, the Lord Christ brought sudden and unexpected destruction upon them. Thus have you a touch of the time when this work began.

Christ Jesus, intending to manifest his kingly office toward his churches more fully than ever yet the sons of men saw, even to the uniting of Jew and Gentile churches in one faith, begins with our English nation (whose former reformation being very imperfect), doth now resolve to cast down their false foundation of prelacy, even in the height of their domineering dignity. And therefore in the year 1628, he stirs up his servants as the heralds of a king to make this proclamation for volunteers, as followeth:

"Oh yes! oh yes! oh yes! All you, the people of Christ that are here oppressed, imprisoned and scurrilously derided, gather yourselves together, your wives and little ones, and answer to your several names as you shall be shipped for his service, in the western world, and more especially for planting the united colonies of New England, where you are to attend the service of the king of kings, upon the divulging of this proclamation by his heralds at arms." . . .

Of the Voluntary Banishment, Chosen by This People of Christ, and Their Last Farewell Taken of Their Country and Friends

And now behold the several regiments of these soldiers of Christ, as they are shipped for his service in the western world, part thereof being come to the town and port of Southampton in England, where they were to be shipped, that they might prosecute this design to the full. One ship called the *Eagle*, they wholly purchase, and many more they hire, filling them with the seed of man and beast to sow this yet untilled wilderness withal, making sale of such land as they possess, to the great admiration of their friends and acquaintance, who thus expostulate with them, "What, will not the large income of your yearly revenue content you, which in all reason cannot choose but be more advantageous both to you and yours, than all that rocky wilderness, whither you are going, to run the hazard of your life? Have you not here your tables filled with great variety of food, your coffers filled with coin, your houses beautifully built and filled with all rich furniture? (Or otherwise) have you not such a gainful trade as none the like in the town where you live? Are you not enriched daily? Are not your children very well provided for as they come to years? (Nay) may you not here as pithily practice the two chief duties of a Christian (if Christ give strength), namely mortification and sanctification, as in any place of the world? What helps can you have there that you must not carry from hence?" With bold resolvedness these stout soldiers of Christ reply: "As Death, the king of terror, with all his dreadful attendance, inhuman and barbarous tortures, doubled and trebled by all the infernal furies, have appeared but light and momentary to the soldiers of Christ Jesus, so also the pleasure, profits, and honors of this world, set forth in their most glorious splendor and magnitude by alluring Lady of Delight, proffering pleasant embraces, cannot entice with her siren songs such soldiers of Christ, whose aims are elevated by him many millions above that brave warrior Ulysses."

Now seeing all can be said will but barely set forth the immovable resolutions that Christ continued in these men, pass on and attend with tears, if thou hast any, the following discourse, while these men, women, and children are taking their last farewell of their native country, kindred, friends, and acquaintance, while the ships attend them. Many make choice of some solitary place to echo out their bowel-breaking affections in bidding their friends farewell. "Dear friends" (says one), "as near as my own soul doth thy love lodge in my breast, with thought of the heart-burning ravishments, that thy heavenly speeches have wrought; my melting soul is poured out at present with these words." Both of them had their farther speech strangled from the depth of their inward dolor, with breast-breaking sobs, till leaning their heads each on other's shoulders, they let fall the salt-dropping dews of vehement affection, striving to exceed one another, much like the departure of David and Jonathan. Having a little eased their hearts with the still streams of tears, they recovered speech again. "Ah! my much honored friend, hath Christ given thee so great a charge as to be leader of his people into that far remote and vast wilderness? Ay, oh, and alas! thou must die there and never shall I see thy face in the flesh again! Wert thou called to so great a task as to pass the precious ocean, and hazard thy person in battle against thousands of malignant enemies there, there were hopes of thy return with triumph; but now after two, three, or four months spent with daily expectation of swallowing waves and cruel pirates, you are to be landed among barbarous

Indians, famous for nothing but cruelty, where you are like to spend your days in a famishing condition for a long space." Scarce had he uttered this, but presently he locks his friend fast in his arms; holding each other thus for some space of time, they weep again. But, as Paul to his beloved flock, the other replies: "What do you, weeping and breaking my heart? I am now prest for the service of our Lord Christ, to rebuild the most glorious edifice of Mount Sion in a wilderness, and as John Baptist, I must cry, 'prepare ye the way of the Lord, make His paths straight,' for behold He is coming again, He is coming to destroy Antichrist, and give the whore double to drink the very dregs of His wrath. Then my dear friend unfold thy hands, for thou and I have much work to do—aye, and all Christian soldiers the world throughout."

Then hand in hand they lead each other to the sandy banks of the brinish ocean, when clenching their hands fast, they unloose not till enforced to wipe their watery eyes, whose constant streams forced a watery path upon their cheeks, which to hide from the eyes of others they shun society for a time, but being called by Occasion, whose bald back part none can lay hold on, they thrust in among the throng now ready to take ship, where they beheld the like affections with their own among divers relations. Husbands and wives with mutual consent are now purposed to part for a time nine hundred leagues asunder, since some providence at present will not suffer them to go together; they resolve their tender affections shall not hinder this work of Christ. The new married and betrothed men, exempt by the law of God from war, now will not claim their privilege, but being constrained by the love of Christ, lock up their natural affections for a time, till the Lord shall be pleased to give them a meeting in this western world, sweetly mixing it with spiritual love in the meantime. Many fathers now take their young Samuels, and give them to this service of Christ all their lives. Brethren, sisters, uncles, nephews, nieces, together with all kindred of blood that binds the bowels of affection in a true lover's knot, can now take their last farewell, each of other, although natural affection will still claim her right, and manifest herself to be in the body by looking out at the windows in a mournful manner. . . .

Of the Wonderful Preparation
the Lord Christ by his Providence,
Wrought for His Peoples' Abode
in This Western World

Now let all men know the admirable acts of Christ for his churches, and chosen, are universally over the whole earth at one and the same time, but sorry man cannot so discourse of them; and therefore let us leave our English nation in way of preparation for this voyage intended, and tell of the marvelous doings of Christ preparing for his peoples' arrival in the western world, whereas the Indians report they beheld to their great wonderment that perspicuous bright blazing comet (which was so famously noted in Europe) anon after sunset it appeared as they say in the southwest, about three hours continuing in their horizon, for the space of thirty sleeps (for so they reckon their days) after which uncouth sight they expected some strange things to follow, and the rather, because not long before the whole nation of the Mattachusets were so affrighted with a ship that arrived in their bay, having never seen any before, thus they report some persons among them discerning a great thing to move toward them upon the waters, wondering what creature it should be, they run with their light canoes, (which are a kind of boats made of birch rinds, and sowed together with the roots of white cedar trees) from place to place, stirring up all their countrymen to come forth, and behold this monstrous thing; at this sudden news the shores for many miles were filled with this naked nation, gazing at this wonder, till some of the stoutest among them manned out these canoes, being armed with bow and arrows, they approached within shot of the ship, being becalmed, they let fly their long shafts at her, which being headed with bone some stuck fast, and others dropped into the water, they wondering it did not cry, but kept quietly on toward them, till all of a sudden the master caused a piece of ordnance to be fired, which stroke such fear into the poor Indians, that they hasted to shore, having their wonders exceedingly increased; but being gotten among their great multitude, they waited to see the sequel with much amazement, till the seamen furling up their sails came to an anchor, manned out their long boat, and went on shore, at whose approach, the Indians fled, although now they saw they were men, who made signs to stay their flight, that they may have trade with them, and to that end they brought certain copper kettles; the Indians by degrees made their approach nearer and nearer till they came to them, when beholding their vessels, which they had set forth before them, the Indians knocking them were much delighted with the sound, and much more astonished to see they would not break, being so thin, for attaining those vessels they brought them much beaver, fraughting them richly away according to their desires, this was the first working providence of Christ to stir up our English nation, to plant these parts in hope of a rich trade for beaverskins, and this made some of our countrymen make their abode in these parts, whom this army of Christ at their coming over found as fit helps to further their design in planting the churches of Christ; who by a more admirable act of his Providence not long after prepared for his peoples' arrival as followeth.

The summer after the blazing star (whose motion in the heavens was from East to West, pointing out to the sons of men the progress of the glorious Gospel of Christ, the glorious King of his churches) even about the year 1618, a little before the removal of that church of Christ from Holland to Plymouth in New England, as the ancient Indians report, there befell a great mortality among them, the greatest that ever the memory of father to son took notice of, chiefly desolating those places, where the English afterward planted the country of Pockanoky, Agissawamg, it was almost wholly deserted, insomuch that the neighbor Indians did abandon those places for fear of death, fleeing more west and by south, observing the east and by northern parts were most smitten with this contagion, the Abarginny men consisting of Mattachusets, Wippanaps and Tarratines were greatly weakened, and more especially the three Kingdoms or Sagamore ships of the Mattachusets, who were before this mortality most populous, having under them seven Dukedoms or petty Sagamores, and the Nianticks and Narrowganssits, who before this came were but of little note, yet were they now not much increased by such as fled thither for fear of death, the Pecods (who retained the name of a warlike people, till afterwards conquered by the English) were also smitten at this time. Their disease being a sore consumption, sweeping away whole families, but chiefly young men and children, the very seeds of increase. Their Powwows, which are their doctors, working partly by charms, and partly by medicine, were much amazed to see their wigwams lie full of dead corpses, and that now neither Squantam nor Abbamocho could help, which are their good and bad god, and also their Powwows themselves were oft smitten with death's stroke, howling and much lamentation was heard among the living, who being possest with great fear, ofttimes left their dead unburied, their manner being such, that they remove their habitations at death of any, this great mortality being an unwonted thing, feared them the more because naturally the country is very healthy. But by this means Christ (whose great and glorious works the earth throughout are altogether for the benefit of his churches and chosen) not only made room for his people to plant; but also tamed the hard and cruel hearts of these barbarous Indians, insomuch that half a handful of his people landing not long after in Plymouth-Plantation, found little resistance. . . .

1654

JOHN WINTHROP

(1588–1649)

John Winthrop embodies the Puritan ideal at its most historically forceful and humanly unlovely. Authoritarian in politics and rigidly orthodox in religion, he was precisely the kind of man the infant colony needed in order "to hew a tabernacle out of the wilderness"; but his emotional coldness, as evidenced in his turning the sufferings and deprivations of the colonists into divine "messages" (which can be seen in some of the following selections) without so much as a human tremor, plus a radical inability to doubt himself, make him difficult to like.

A convert to Congregational Puritanism, Winthrop felt compelled to leave a comfortable situation in England, where he was lord of Groton manor and an important member of the legal profession, when King Charles abrogated the English parliament in 1629. Chosen governor of the colony-to-be before the Great Migration to Massachusetts Bay had even begun, he was one of the dominating influences in its life from its inception in 1630 until his death in 1649. Although his contempt for democracy ("the meanest and worst form of government") motivated him to make autocratic decisions which periodically enraged some of the freemen in the colony, his political philosophy was not so alien to the Puritans' general view of civil polity that they would have been led to repudiate him. Indeed, in 1645 when he was impeached for supposedly exceeding his authority, his speech on liberty (reprinted here) so convinced the people that not only was he acquitted but he was elected governor annually until the year of his death.

Conscious that he was a Moses leading his people into a new Promised Land and that an account of such a great enterprise ought to be recorded, Winthrop began his *Journal* on March 29, 1630, while the fleet was anchored within sight of the New World. He continued the *Journal* intermittently for as long as he lived. Although it lacks the over-arching vision and artistic control of Bradford's *Of Plymouth Plantation*, Winthrop's *Journal* is nevertheless both a valuable record of day-to-day life in New England from 1630 to 1649 and a fascinating glimpse into the Puritan mind as it struggled to accommodate the realities of a hostile environment and an incipient break-up from within to its myth of special destiny.

The *Journal* was first published, incompletely, in 1790; the entire work was edited by James Savage as *The History of New England from 1630–1649* (1825–1826). The standard edition of Winthrop is A. B. Forbes, gen. ed., *Winthrop Papers*, 5 vols. (1929–1947). Accounts of the man and his work are to be found in R. C. Winthrop, *Life and Letters of John Winthrop* (1863–1867); J. H. Twichell, *John Winthrop* (1891); A. Mac-Phail, *Essays in Puritanism* (1905); J. K. Hosmer, ed. *Winthrop's Journals* (1908); S. E. Morison, *Builders of the Bay Colony* (1930); S. Gray, "The Political Thought of John Winthrop," *New England Quarterly*, III (1930); E. A. J. Johnson, "Economic Ideas of John Winthrop," *New England Quarterly*, III (1930); C. E. Banks, *The Winthrop Fleet of 1630* (1930); L. S. Mayo, *The Winthrop Family in America* (1948); M. Savelle, *Seeds of Liberty* (1948); M. Kraus, *Writing of American History* (1953); B. K. Brown, "A Note on the Puritan Concept of Aristocracy," *Mississippi Valley Historical Review*, XLI (1954); E. S. Morgan, *The Puritan Dilemma: The Story of John Winthrop* (1958); R. S. Dunn, *Puritans and Yankees* (1962); and D. B. Rutman, *Winthrop's Boston* (1965).

FROM

Journal

[The Holy Allegory]

[*July 5, 1632*] At Watertown there was (in the view of divers witnesses) a great combat between a mouse and a snake; and, after a long fight, the mouse prevailed and killed the snake. The pastor of Boston, Mr. Wilson, a very sincere, holy man, hearing of it, gave this interpretation:

That the snake was the devil; the mouse was a poor contemptible people, which God had brought hither, which
should overcome Satan here, and dispossess him of his
kingdom. Upon the same occasion, he told the governor,
that, before he was resolved to come into this country, he
dreamed he was here, and that he saw a church arise out
of the earth, which grew up and became a marvelous
goodly church.

[*March 16, 1639*] There was so violent a wind . . . as
the like was not seen since we came into this land. It began in the evening, and increased till midnight. It overturned some new, strong houses; but the Lord miraculously
preserved old, weak cottages. It tore down fences,—people ran out of their houses in the night, etc. There came
such a rain withal, as raised the waters at Connecticut
twenty feet above the meadows, etc. The Indians near
Aquiday being pawwawing in this tempest, the devil came
and fetched away five of them.

[*December 15, 1640*] About this time there fell out a
thing worthy of observation. Mr. Winthrop the younger,
having many books in a chamber where there was corn of
divers sorts, had among them one wherein the Greek testament, the psalms and the common prayer were bound together. He found the common prayer eaten with mice,
every leaf of it, and not any of the two other touched, nor
any other of his books, though there were above a thousand.

[*April 13, 1641*] Upon the Lord's day at Concord two
children were left at home alone, one lying in a cradle,
the other having burned a cloth, and fearing its mother
should see it, thrust it into a hay stack by the door (the
fire not being quite out) whereby the hay and house were
burned and the child in the cradle before they came from
the meeting. About the same time two houses were burned
at Sudbury.

By occasion of these fires I may add another of a different kind, but of much observation. A godly woman of
the church of Boston, dwelling sometimes in London,
brought with her a parcel of very fine linen of great value,
which she set her heart too much upon, and had been at
charge to have it all newly washed, and curiously folded
and pressed, and so left it in press in her parlor over night.

She had a Negro maid went into the room very late, and let fall some snuff of the candle upon the linen, so as by the morning all the linen was burned to tinder, and the boards underneath, and some stools and a part of the wainscot burned, and never perceived by any in the house, though some lodged in the chamber over head, and no ceiling between. But it pleased God that the loss of this linen did her much good, both in taking off her heart from worldly comforts, and in preparing her for a far greater affliction by the untimely death of her husband, who was slain not long after at Isle of Providence.

[*August 15, 1648*] The synod met at Cambridge by adjournment from the (4) (June) last. Mr. Allen of Dedham preached out of Acts 15, a very godly, learned, and particular handling of near all the doctrines and applications concerning that subject with a clear discovery and refutation of such errors, objections, and scruples as had been raised about it by some young heads in the country.

It fell out, about the midst of his sermon, there came a snake into the seat, where many of the elders sate behind the preacher. It came in at the door where people stood thick upon the stairs. Divers of the elders shifted from it, but Mr. Thomson, one of the elders of Braintree, (a man of much faith,) trode upon the head of it, and so held it with his foot and staff with a small pair of grains, until it was killed. This being so remarkable, and nothing falling out but by divine providence, it is out of doubt, the Lord discovered somewhat of his mind in it. The serpent is the devil; the synod, the representative of the churches of Christ in New England. The devil had formerly and lately attempted their disturbance and dissolution; but their faith in the seed of the woman overcame him and crushed his head.

[*July 5, 1643*] There arose a sudden gust at N. W. so violent for half an hour, as it blew down multitudes of trees. It lifted up their meeting house at Newbury, the people being in it. It darkened the air with dust, yet through God's great mercy it did not hurt, but only killed one Indian with the fall of a tree.

[*January 11, 1649*] . . . another child very strangely drowned a little before winter. The parents were also members of the church of Boston. The father had undertaken to maintain the mill-dam, and being at work upon it (with some help he had hired), in the afternoon of the last day of the week, night came upon them before they had finished what they intended, and his conscience began to put him in mind of the Lord's day, and he was troubled, yet went on and wrought an hour within night. The next day, after evening exercise, and after they had supped, the mother put two children to bed in the room where they themselves did lie, and they went out to visit a neighbor. When they returned, they continued about an hour in the room, and missed not the child, but then the mother going to bed, and not finding her youngest child (a daughter about five years of age) after much search she found it drowned in a well in her cellar; which was very observable, as by a special hand of God, that the child should go out of that room into another in the dark, and then fall down at a trap door, or go down the stairs, and so into the well in the farther end of the cellar, the top of the well and the water being even with the ground. But the father, freely in the open congregation, did acknowledge it the righteous hand of God for his profaning his holy day against the checks of his own conscience.

[Several Puritan Ladies]

[MRS. ONION]

[*March 30, 1643*] The wife of one Onion of Roxbury died in great despair: she had been a servant there, and was very stubborn and self-willed. After she was married, she proved very worldly, aiming at great matters. Her first child was still-born, through her unruliness and falling into a fever. She fell withal into great horror and trembling, so as it shook the room, etc., and crying out of her torment, and of her stubbornness and unprofitableness under the means, and her lying to her dame in denying somewhat that in liquorishness she had taken away, and of her worldliness, saying that she neglected her spiritual good for a little worldly trash, and now she must go to everlasting torments, and exhorted others to take heed of such evils, etc., and still crying out O! ten thousand worlds for one drop of Christ, etc. After she had then been silent a few hours, she began to speak again, and being exhorted to consider of God's infinite mercy, etc., she gave still this answer, "I cannot for my life," and so died.

[MARY LATHAM]

[*March 7, 1644*] At this court of assistants one James Britton, a man ill affected both to our church discipline and civil government, and one Mary Latham, a proper young woman about 18 years of age, whose father was a godly man and had brought her up well, were condemned to die for adultery, upon a law formerly made and published in print. It was thus occasioned and discovered. This woman, being rejected by a young man whom she had an affection unto, vowed she would marry the next that came to her, and accordingly, against her friends' minds, she matched with an ancient man who had neither honesty nor ability, and one whom she had no affection unto. Whereupon, soon after she was married, divers young men solicited her chastity, and drawing her into bad company, and giving her wine and other gifts, easily prevailed with her, and among others this Britton. But God smiting him with a deadly palsy and fearful horror of conscience withal, he could not keep secret, but discovered this, and other the like with other women, and was forced to acknowledge the justice of God in that having often called others fools, etc., for confessing against themselves, he was now forced to do the like. The woman dwelt now in Plymouth patent, and one of the magistrates there, hearing she was detected, etc., sent her to us. Upon her examination, she confessed he did attempt the fact, but did not commit it, and witness was produced that testified (which they both confessed) that in the evening of a day of humiliation through the country for England, etc., a company met at Britton's and there continued drinking sack, etc., till late in the night, and then Britton and the woman were seen upon the ground together, a little from the house. It was reported also that she did frequently abuse her husband, setting a knife to his breast and threatening to kill him, calling him old rogue and cuckold, and said she would make him wear horns as big as a bull. And yet some of the magistrates thought the evidence not sufficient against her, because there were not two direct witnesses; but the jury cast her, and then she confessed the fact, and accused twelve others, whereof two were married men. Five of these were apprehended and committed, (the rest were gone,) but denying it, and there being no other witness against them than the testimony of a condemned person, there could be no proceeding against them. The woman proved very penitent, and had deep apprehension of the foulness of her sin, and at length attained to hope of pardon by the blood of Christ, and was willing to die in satisfaction to justice. The man also was very much cast down for his sins, but was loath to die, and petitioned the general court for his life, but they would not grant it, though some of the magistrates spake much for it, and questioned the letter, whether adultery was death by God's law now. This Britton had been a professor in England, but coming hither he opposed our church government, etc., and grew dissolute, losing both power and profession of godliness.

[*March 21, 1644*] They were both executed, they both died very penitently, especially the woman, who had some comfortable hope of pardon of her sin, and gave good exhortation to all young maids to be obedient to their parents, and to take heed of evil company, etc.

[MRS. HOPKINS]

[*April 13, 1645*] Mr. Hopkins, the governor of Hartford upon Connecticut, came to Boston, and brought his wife with him, (a godly young woman, and of special parts,) who was fallen into a sad infirmity, the loss of her understanding and reason, which had been growing upon her divers years, by occasion of her giving herself wholly to reading and writing, and had written many books. Her husband, being very loving and tender of her, was loath to grieve her; but he saw his error, when it was too late. For if she had attended her household affairs, and such things as belong to women, and not gone out of her way and calling to meddle in such things as are proper for men, whose minds are stronger, etc., she had kept her wits, and might have improved them usefully and honorably in the place God had set her. He brought her to Boston, and left her with her brother, one Mr. Yale, a merchant, to

try what means might be had here for her. But no help
could be had.

[ANNE HUTCHINSON]

[*October 21, 1636*] One Mrs. Hutchinson, a member of
the church of Boston, a woman of a ready wit and bold
spirit, brought over with her two dangerous errors: 1. That
the person of the Holy Ghost dwells in a justified person.
2. That no sanctification can help to evidence to us our
justification. From these two grew many branches; as: our
union with the Holy Ghost, so as a Christian remains dead
to every spiritual action, and hath no gifts nor graces, other
than such as are in hypocrites, nor any other sanctification
but the Holy Ghost himself.

[*November 1, 1637*] The Court . . . sent for Mrs.
Hutchinson, and charged her with divers matters, as her
keeping two public lectures every week in her house,
whereto sixty or eighty persons did usually resort, and for
reproaching most of the ministers (*viz.* all except Mr.
Cotton) for not preaching a covenant of free grace, and
that they had not the seal of the spirit, nor were able ministers of the New Testament; which were clearly proved
against her, though she sought to shift it off. And, after
many speeches to and fro, at last she was so full as she
could not contain, but vented her revelations; amongst
which this was one, that she had it revealed to her, that she
should come into New England, and should here be persecuted, and that God would ruin us and our posterity, and
the whole state, for the same. So the Court proceeded and
banished her; but, because it was winter, they committed
her to a private house, where she was well provided, and her
own friends and the elders permitted to go to her, but none
else.

[*March 1, 1638*] While Mrs. Hutchinson continued at
Roxbury, divers of the elders and others resorted to her,
and finding her to persist in maintaining those gross errors
beforementioned . . . she was called. . . . When she appeared, the errors were read to her. . . . These were also
clearly confuted, but yet she held her own; so as the church
(all but two of her sons) agreed she should be admonished,

and because her sons would not agree to it, they were admonished also.

Mr. Cotton pronounced the sentence of admonition with great solemnity, and with much zeal and detestation of her errors and pride of spirit . . . and she was appointed to appear again the next lecture day.

[*March 22, 1638*] Mrs. Hutchinson appeared again (she had been licensed by the Court, in regard she had given hope of her repentance, to be at Mr. Cotton's house, that both he and Mr. Davenport might have the more opportunity to deal with her); and the articles being again read to her, and her answer required, she delivered it in writing, wherein she made a retraction of near all, but with such explanations and circumstances as gave no satisfaction to the church; so as she was required to speak further to them. Then she declared that it was just with God to leave her to herself, as He had done, for her slighting His ordinances, both magistracy and ministry; and confessed that what she had spoken against the magistrates at the Court (by way of revelation) was rash and ungrounded; and desired the church to pray for her. This gave the church good hope of her repentance; but when she was examined about some particulars, as that she had denied inherent righteousness, etc., she affirmed that it was never her judgment; and though it was proved by many testimonies, that she had been of that judgment, and so had persisted, and maintained it by argument against divers, yet she impudently persisted in her affirmation, to the astonishment of all the assembly. So that, after much time and many arguments had been spent to bring her to see her sin, but all in vain, the church, with one consent, cast her out. Some moved to have her admonished once more; but, it being for manifest evil in matter of conversation, it was agreed otherwise; and for that reason also the sentence was denounced by the pastor, matter of manners belonging properly to his place.

After she was excommunicated, her spirits, which seemed before to be somewhat dejected, revived again, and she gloried in her sufferings, saying that it was the greatest happiness, next to Christ, that ever befell her. Indeed, it was a happy day to the churches of Christ here, and to many poor souls who had been seduced by her, who, by what they heard and saw that day, were (through the grace of God) brought off quite from her errors, and settled again in the truth. . . .

After two or three days, the governor sent a warrant to Mrs. Hutchinson to depart this jurisdiction before the last of this month, according to the order of Court, and for that end set her at liberty from her former constraint, so as she was not to go forth of her own house till her departure; and upon the 28th she went by water to her farm at the Mount, where she was to take water, with Mr. Wheelwright's wife and family, to go to Pascataquack; but she changed her mind, and went by land to Providence, and so to the island in the Naragansett Bay, which her husband and the rest of that sect had purchased of the Indians, and prepared with all speed to remove unto. For the Court had ordered that, except they were gone with their families by such a time, they should be summoned to the General Court.

[*September 7, 1638*] Mrs. Hutchinson, being removed to the Isle of Aquiday, in the Naragansett Bay, after her time was fulfilled, . . . was delivered of a monstrous birth, which, being diversely related in the country, [was] declared by Mr. Cotton to signify her error in denying inherent righteousness, but that all was Christ in us, and nothing of ours in our faith, love, etc. . . .

[*March 16, 1639*] At Aquiday . . . Mrs. Hutchinson exercised [sermonized] publicly, and she and her party (some three or four families) would have no magistracy. She sent also an admonition to the church of Boston; but the elders would not read it publicly, because she was excommunicated. By these examples we may see how dangerous it is to slight the censures of the church; for it was apparent that God had given them up to strange delusions.

[*June 21, 1641*] Mrs. Hutchinson and those of Aquiday island broached new heresies every year. Divers of them turned professed Anabaptists, and would not wear any arms, and denied all magistracy among Christians, and maintained that there were no churches since those founded by the apostles and evangelists, nor could any be, nor any pastors ordained, nor seals administered but by such, and that the church was to want all these all the time she continued in the wilderness, as yet she was.

[In August 1643 Mrs. Hutchinson and most of her family

were slaughtered by Indians in what is now New Rochelle, New York; the theocracy in Massachusetts Bay took the news as divine confirmation of their sentence upon her.]

[Liberty and Authority]

[*September 22, 1642*] The sudden fall of land and cattle, and the scarcity of foreign commodities, and money, etc., with the thin access of people from England, put many into an unsettled frame of spirit, so as they concluded there would be no subsisting here, and accordingly they began to hasten away, some to the West Indies, others to the Dutch, at Long Island, etc. (for the governor there invited them by fair offers), and others back for England. . . .

They fled for fear of want, and many of them fell into it, even to extremity, as if they had hastened into the misery which they feared and fled from, besides the depriving themselves of the ordinances and church fellowship, and those civil liberties which they enjoyed here; whereas, such as stayed in their places, kept their peace and ease, and enjoyed still the blessing of the ordinances, and never tasted of those troubles and miseries, which they heard to have befallen those who departed. Much disputation there was about liberty of removing for outward advantages, and all ways were sought for an open door to get out at; but it is to be feared many crept out at a broken wall. For such as come together into a wilderness, where are nothing but wild beasts and beastlike men, and there confederate together in civil and church estate, whereby they do, implicitly at least, bind themselves to support each other, and all of them that society, whether civil or sacred, whereof they are members, how they can break from this without free consent, is hard to find, so as may satisfy a tender or good conscience in time of trial. Ask thy conscience, if thou wouldst have plucked up thy stakes, and brought thy family 3000 miles, if thou hadst expected that all, or most, would have forsaken thee there? Ask again, what liberty thou hast towards others, which thou likest not to allow others towards thyself? For if one may go, another may, and so the greater part, and so church and commonwealth may be left destitute in a wilderness, exposed to misery and reproach, and all for thy ease and pleasure; whereas these all, being now thy brethren, as near to thee as the Israelites were to Moses, it were much safer for thee, after his example, to choose rather to suffer affliction with thy brethren, than to enlarge thy ease and pleasure by furthering the occasion of their ruin.

[*July 3, 1645*] The great questions that have troubled the country, are about the authority of the magistrates and the liberty of the people. It is yourselves who have called us to this office, and being called by you, we have our authority from God, in way of an ordinance, such as hath the image of God eminently stamped upon it, the contempt and violation whereof hath been vindicated with examples of divine vengeance. I entreat you to consider, that when you choose magistrates, you take them from among yourselves, men subject to like passions as you are. Therefore when you see infirmities in us, you should reflect upon your own, and that would make you bear the more with us, and not be severe censurers of the failings of your magistrates, when you have continual experience of the like infirmities in yourselves and others. We account him a good servant, who breaks not his covenant. The covenant between you and us is the oath you have taken of us, which is to this purpose, that we shall govern you and judge your causes by the rules of God's laws and our own, according to our best skill. When you agree with a workman to build you a ship or house, etc., he undertakes as well for his skill as for his faithfulness, for it is his profession, and you pay him for both. But when you call one to be a magistrate, he doth not profess nor undertake to have sufficient skill for that office, nor can you furnish him with gifts, etc., therefore you must run the hazard of his skill and ability. But if he fail in faithfulness, which by his oath he is bound unto, that he must answer for. If it fall out that the case be clear to common apprehension, and the rule clear also, if he transgress here, the error is not in the skill, but in the evil of the will: it must be required of him. But if the case be doubtful, or the rule doubtful, to men of such understanding and parts as your magistrates are, if your magistrates should err here, yourselves must bear it.

For the other point concerning liberty, I observe a great mistake in the country about that. There is a twofold liberty, natural (I mean as our nature is now corrupt) and civil or federal. The first is common to man with beasts and other creatures. By this, man, as he stands in relation to man simply, hath liberty to do what he lists; it is a liberty to evil as well as to good. This liberty is incompatible and inconsistent with authority, and cannot endure the least restraint of the most just authority. The exercise and maintaining of this liberty makes men grow more evil, and in time to be worse than brute beasts: *omnes sumus licentia deteriores.* [We are all worse because of license.] This is that great enemy of truth and peace, that wild beast, which all the ordinances of God are bent against, to restrain and subdue it. The other kind of liberty I call civil or federal, it may also be termed moral, in reference to the covenant between God and man, in the moral law, and the politic covenants and constitutions, amongst men themselves. This liberty is the proper end and object of authority, and cannot subsist without it; and it is a liberty to that only which is good, just, and honest. This liberty you are to stand for, with the hazard (not only of your goods), but of your lives, if need be. Whatsoever crosseth this, is not authority, but a distemper thereof. This liberty is maintained and exercised in a way of subjection to authority; it is of the same kind of liberty wherewith Christ hath made us free. The woman's own choice makes such a man her husband; yet being so chosen, he is her lord, and she is to be subject to him, yet in a way of liberty, not of bondage; and a true wife accounts her subjection her honor and freedom, and would not think her condition safe and free, but in her subjection to her husband's authority. Such is the liberty of the church under the authority of Christ, her king and husband; his yoke is so easy and sweet to her as a bride's ornaments; and if through frowardness or wantonness, etc., she shake it off, at any time, she is at no rest in her spirit, until she take it up again; and whether her lord smiles upon her, and embraceth her in his arms, or whether he frowns, or rebukes, or smites her, she apprehends the sweetness of his love in all, and is refreshed, supported, and instructed by every such dispensation of his authority over her. On the other side, ye know who they are that complain of this yoke and say, let us break their bands, etc., we will not have this man to rule over us. Even so, brethren, it will be between you and your magistrates. If you stand for your natural corrupt liberties, and will do what is good in your own eyes, you will not endure the least weight of authority, but will murmur, and oppose, and be always striving to shake off that yoke; but if you will be satisfied to enjoy such civil and lawful liberties, such as Christ allows you, then will you quietly and cheerfully submit unto that authority which is set over you, in all the administrations of it, for your good. Wherein, if we fail at any time, we hope we shall be willing (by God's assistance) to harken to good advice from any of you, or in any other way of God; so shall your liberties be preserved, in upholding the honor and power of authority amongst you.

w. 1630–1649
p. 1790, 1825–1826

NATHANIEL WARD

(1578–1652)

America has always sharpened the bite and wit of European visitors, and Nathaniel Ward was at least as much a visitor as he was a colonist; yet during his twelve-year stay in New England, he became very much a part of Massachusetts life. The son of a Suffolk Puritan minister, John Ward, Nathaniel was born into a sectarian ecclesiastical atmosphere in which orthodox Puritan doctrine was to be his meat and drink. In his high education he was typical of many influential Puritans, receiving his B. A. in 1599 and his M. A. from Emmanuel College, Cambridge, in 1603. After studying the law at Lincoln's Inn, he went on to become a full-fledged barrister in 1615, but abandoned his legal practice to enter the ministry in 1618. His Puritan leanings became too pronounced for Archbishop Laud, who excommunicated Ward for nonconformity from the Church of England in 1633.

Consequently, Ward migrated to America in 1634 to serve as Pastor at Ipswich, then called Aggawam, which gave "the Simple Cobbler" his "title." After two years, however, ill health forced him to resign his pastorate. Instead of retiring from affairs of church and state, he became a leader of the Massachusetts Bay theocracy until he returned to England in 1646. As a legal authority, in 1638 he drew up a set of Massachusetts laws which were published in 1641 as *The Body of Liberties*, a code that was to become an important feature of the development of American constitutional history.

In American literary history, Ward is remembered for his *The Simple Cobbler*, part of whose original title page indicates its caustic, corrective purposes: *The Simple Cobler of Aggawam in America. Willing to help 'mend his Native Country, lamentably tattered, both in the upper-Leather and sole, with all the honest stitches he can take. And as willing never to bee paid for his work, by Old English wonted pay. It is his Trade to patch all the year long, gratis.* This work, published under the pseudonym of Theodore de la Guard in 1647, following Ward's return to England, is at once typical and exceptional as an example of New England Puritanism. It is exceptional in style (compare it, for instance, with Bradford's writing) in that its rhetoric is fanciful rather than plain, more in keeping with Anglican "metaphysical" style than with the sober restrictions of Puritan literary theory. Often deliberate and subtle artists of "plain style," the Puritans tended to distrust "wit" and conceit almost as much as they did enthusiasm. But although the rhetoric is that of a salty old wit who has seen it all—Ward was sixty-eight when the *Cobbler* was published—the substance is ultra-orthodox. The work advocates persecution for cause of conscience, religious conformity in a sectarian-torn age, and strict conservatism in matters of customs, manners, economics, politics, and church. With its no-nonsense air, *The Simple Cobbler* is an excellent reflection of the strict rigidity of the Massachusetts Bay Puritan.

Ward's works also include *A Religious Retreat Sounded to a Religious Army* (1647) and *A Word to Mr. Peters* (1647).

Accounts of Ward and his work are to be found in J. W. Dean, *A Memoir of the Reverend Nathaniel Ward* [with a bibliography] (1868); M. C. Tyler, *A History of American Literature during the Colonial Period,* I (1897); S. E. Morison, *Builders of the Bay Colony* (1930); and J. Bohi, "Nathaniel Ward, A Sage of Old Ipswich," *Essex Institute Historical Collections,* XCIX (1963).

FROM

The Simple Cobbler of Aggawam

[On Religious Toleration]

Either I am in an apoplexy, or that man is in a lethargy who does not now sensibly feel God shaking the heavens over his head and the earth under his feet: the heavens so as the sun begins to turn into darkness, the moon into blood, the stars to fall down to the ground so that little light of comfort or counsel is left to the sons of men; the earth so as the foundations are failing, the righteous scarce know where to find rest, the inhabitants stagger like drunken men. It is in a manner dissolved both in religions and relations, and no marvel, for they have defiled it by transgressing the laws, changing the ordinances, and breaking the everlasting Covenant. The truths of God are the pillars of the world whereon states and churches may stand quiet if they will; if they will not, He can easily shake them off into delusions and distractions enough.

Satan is now in his passions, he feels his passions approaching, he loves to fish in roiled waters. Though that dragon cannot sting the vitals of the elect mortally, yet that Beelzebub can fly-blow their intellectuals miserably. The finer religion grows, the finer he spins his cobwebs; he will hold pace with Christ so long as his wits will serve him. He sees himself beaten out of gross idolatries, heresies, ceremonies, where the light breaks forth with power. He will, therefore, bestir him to prevaricate evangelical truths and ordinances, that if they will needs be walking yet they shall *laborare varicibus* [labor at cross purposes] and not keep their path. He will put them out of time and place, assassinating for his engineers men of Paracelsian parts, well complexioned for honesty; for such are fittest to mountebank his chemistry into sick churches and weak judgments.

Nor shall he need to stretch his strength over-much in this work. Too many men, having not laid their foundations sure nor ballasted their spirits deep with humility and fear, are pressed enough of themselves to evaporate their own apprehensions. Those that are acquainted with story know it has ever been so in new editions of churches: such as are least able are most busy to putter in the rubbish and to raise dust in the eyes of more steady repairers. Civil commotions make room for uncivil practices; religious mutations, for irreligious opinions. Change of air discovers corrupt bodies; reformation of religion, unsound minds. He that has any well-faced fancy in his crown and does not vent it now, fears the pride of his own heart will dub him dunce forever. Such a one will trouble the whole Israel of God with his most untimely births, though he makes the bones of his vanity stick up to the view and grief of all that are godly wise. The devil desires no better sport than to see light heads handle their heels and fetch their careers in a time when the roof of liberty stands open.

The next perplexed question with pious and ponderous men will be, What should be done for the healing of these comfortless exulcerations? I am the unablest adviser of a thousand, the unworthiest of ten thousand; yet I hope I may presume to assert what follows without just offense.

First, such as have given or taken any unfriendly reports of us New English should do well to recollect themselves. We have been reputed a colluvies of wild opinionists, swarmed into a remote wilderness to find elbow room for our fanatic doctrines and practices. I trust our diligence past and constant sedulity against such persons and courses will plead better things for us. I dare take upon me to be the herald of New England so far as to proclaim to the world, in the name of our colony, that all Familists, Antinomians, Anabaptists, and other enthusiasts shall have free liberty to keep away from us; and such as will come to be gone as fast as they can, the sooner the better.

Secondly, I dare aver that God does nowhere in His word tolerate Christian states to give toleration to such adversaries of His truth, if they have power in their hands to suppress them.

Here is lately brought us an extract of a Magna Carta, so called, compiled between the sub-planters of a West Indian island, whereof the first article of constipulation firmly provides free stableroom and litter for all kind of consciences, be they never so dirty or jadish, making it actionable, yea, treasonable, to disturb any man in his religion or to discommend it, whatever it be. We are very sorry to see such professed profaneness in English professors as industriously to lay their religious foundations on the ruin of true religion, which strictly binds every conscience to contend earnestly for the truth; to preserve unity of spirit, faith, and ordinances; to be all like minded, of one accord, every man to take his brother into his Christian care, to stand fast with one spirit, with one mind, striving together for the faith of the Gospel; and by no means to permit heresies or erroneous opinions. But God, abhorring such loathsome beverages, has in His righteous judgment blasted that enterprise, which might otherwise have prospered well, for aught I know. I presume their case is generally known ere this.

If the devil might have his free option, I believe he would ask nothing else but liberty to enfranchise all false religions and to embondage the true; nor should he need. It is much to be feared that lax tolerations upon state pretences and planting necessities will be the next subtle stratagem he will spread to dis-state the truth of God and supplant the peace of the churches. Tolerations in things tolerable, exquisitely drawn out by the lines of the Scripture and pencil of the spirit, are the sacred favors of truth, the due latitudes of love, the fair compartments of Christian fraternity. But irregular dispensations, dealt forth by the facilities of men, are the frontiers of error, the redoubts of schism, the perilous irritaments of carnal and spiritual enmity.

My heart has naturally detested four things: the standing of the Apocrypha in the Bible; foreigners dwelling in my country to crowd out native subjects into the corners of the earth; alchemized coins; tolerations of divers religions, or of one religion in segregant shapes. He that willingly assents to the last, if he examines his heart by daylight, his conscience will tell him he is either an atheist or a heretic or a hypocrite, or at best a captive to some lust. Poly-piety is the greatest impiety in the world. . . .

Not to tolerate things merely indifferent to weak consciences argues a conscience too strong; pressed uniformity in these causes much disunity. To tolerate more than indifferents is not to deal indifferently with God. He that does it takes His scepter out of His hand and bids Him stand by. Who hath to do to institute religion but God? The power of all religion and ordinances lies in their purity, their purity in their simplicity: then are mixtures pernicious. I lived in a city where a Papist preached in one church, a Lutheran in another, a Calvinist in a third; a Lutheran one part of the day, a Calvinist the other, in the same pulpit. The religion of that place was but motley and meager, their affections leopardlike.

If the whole creature should conspire to do the Creator a mischief or offer Him an insolence, it would be in nothing more than in erecting untruths against His truth, or by sophisticating His truths with human medleys. The removing of some one iota in Scripture may draw out all the life and traverse all the truth of the whole Bible; but to authorize an untruth by a toleration of state is to build a sconce against the walls of heaven, to batter God out of His chair. To tell a practical lie is a great sin, but yet transient; but to set up a theoretical untruth is to warrant every lie that lies from its root to the top of every branch it hath, which are not a few.

I would willingly hope that no member of the Parliament has skilfully ingratiated himself into the hearts of the House that he might watch a time to midwife out some ungracious toleration for his own turn; and for the sake of that, some others. I would also hope that a word of general caution should not be particularly misapplied. I am the freer to suggest it because I know not one man of that mind; my aim is general, and I desire may be so accepted. Yet, good gentlemen, look well about you and remember how Tiberius played the fox with the senate of Rome and how Fabius Maximus cropped his ears for his cunning.

The state is wise, that will improve all pains and patience rather to compose than tolerate differences in religion. There is no divine truth but hath much celestial fire in it from the Spirit of Truth: nor no irreligious untruth without its proportion of antifire from the spirit of error to contradict it. The zeal of the one, the virulency of the other, must necessarily kindle combustions. Fiery diseases seated in the spirit embroil the whole frame of the body; others more external and cool, are less dangerous. They which divide in religion, divide in God; they who divide in him, divide beyond *Genus Generalissimum,* where there is no reconciliation without atonement; that is, without uniting in him, who is One, and in his Truth, which is also one.

Wise are those men who will be persuaded rather to live within the pale of truth where they may be quiet, than in the purlieus where they are sure to be haunted ever and anon, do authority what it can. Every singular opinion has a singular opinion of itself; and he that holds it a singular opinion of himself, and a simple opinion of all contrasentients. He that confutes them, must confute all three at once, or else he does nothing; which will not be done without more stir than the peace of the state or church can endure.

And prudent are those Christians that will rather give

what may be given, than hazard all by yielding nothing. To sell all peace of country to buy some peace of conscience unseasonably is more avarice than thrift, imprudence than patience. They deal not equally, that set any truth of God at such a rate; but they deal wisely that will stay till the market is fallen.

My prognostics deceive me not a little, if once within three seven years, peace prove not such a penny-worth at most marts in Christendom, that he that would not lay down his money, his lust, his opinion, his will, I had almost said the best flower of his crown for it, while he might have had it, will tell his own heart he played the very ill husband.

Concerning tolerations I may further assert: . . .

Frederick, Duke of Saxon, spake not one foot beyond the mark when he said, he had rather the earth should swallow him up quick, than he should give a toleration to any opinion against any truth of God.

He that is willing to tolerate any religion, or discrepant way of religion, besides his own, unless it be in matters merely indifferent, either doubts of his own or is not sincere in it.

He that is willing to tolerate any unsound opinion that his own may also be tolerated, though never so sound, will for a need hang God's Bible at the Devil's girdle.

Every toleration of false religions or opinions has as many errors and sins in it as all the false religions and opinions it tolerates; and one sound, one more.

That state that will give liberty of conscience in matters of religion must give liberty of conscience and conversation in their moral laws, or else the fiddle will be out of tune, and some of the strings crack.

He that will rather make an irreligious quarrel with other religions than try the truth of his own by valuable arguments and peaceable sufferings either his religion or himself is irreligious.

Experience will teach churches and Christians, that it is far better to live in a state united, though a little corrupt, than in a state whereof some part is incorrupt, and all the rest divided.

I am not altogether ignorant of the eight rules given by orthodox divines about giving tolerations, yet with their favor I dare affirm:

That there is no Rule given by God for any state to give an affirmative toleration to any false religion or opinion whatsoever; they must connive in some cases, but may not concede in any.

That the state of England (so far as my intelligence serves) might in time have prevented with ease and may yet without any great difficulty deny both toleration and irregular connivances *salva Republica*.

That if the state of England shall either willingly tolerate, or weakly connive at such courses, the church of that kingdom will sooner become the devil's dancing-school than God's temple; the Civil State a bear-garden than an exchange; the whole realm a Pais base than an England. And what pity it is that that country which has been the staple of truth to all Christiandom, should now become the aviary of errors to the whole world, let every fearing heart judge.

I take liberty of conscience to be nothing but a freedom from sin and error . . . and liberty of error nothing but a prison for conscience. Then small will be the kindness of a state to build such prisons for their subjects.

The Scripture saith, there is nothing makes free but truth, and truth saith, there is no truth but one. If the States of the World would make it their sumoperous care to preserve this one truth in its purity and authority it would ease you of all other political cares. I am sure Satan makes it his grand, if not only task, to adulterate truth; falsehood is his sole scepter, whereby he first ruffled, and ever since ruined the World.

If truth be but one, methinks all the opinionists in England should not be all in that one truth: some of them I doubt are out. He that can extract an unity out of such a disparity, or contract such a disparity into an unity had need be a better artist than ever was Drebell. [Cornelis Drebbel, 1572–1634, a Dutch inventor.]

If two centers (as we may suppose) be in one circle, and lines drawn from both to all the points of the compass, they will certainly cross one another, and probably cut through the centers themselves.

It is said, though a man have light enough himself to see the truth, yet if he hath not enough to enlighten others, he is bound to tolerate them. I will engage myself, that all the devils in *Britanie* shall sell themselves to their shirts to purchase a lease of this position for three of their lives, under the seal of the Parliament.

It is said that men ought to have liberty of their conscience, and that it is persecution to debar them of it: I can rather stand amazed than reply to this. It is an astonishment to think that the brains of men should be parboiled in such impious ignorance. Let all the wits under the heavens lay their heads together and find an assertion worse than this (one excepted) I will petition to be chosen the universal idiot of the world.

It is said that civil magistrates ought not to meddle with ecclesiastical matters.

I would answer to this so well as I could, did I not know that some papers lately brought out of New England are going to the press, wherein the opinions of the Elders there in a late Synod, concerning this point are manifested, which I suppose will give clearer satisfaction than I can.

The true English of all this, their false Latin, is nothing but a general toleration of all opinions: which motion if it be like to take, it were very requisite that the City would repair Paul's with all the speed they can for an English Pantheon, and bestow it upon the sectaries, freely to assemble in. Then there may be some hope that London will be quiet in time.

1647

On Mrs. Bradstreet's Tenth Muse

Mercury showed Apollo Bartas' book,
Minerva this, and wished him well to look
And tell uprightly which did which excel;
He viewed, and viewed, and vowed he could not tell.
They bid him hemisphere his moldy nose
With's cracked leering-glasses, for it would pose
The best brains he had in's old pudding-pan,
Sex weighed, which best, the woman or the man?
He peered, and pored, and glared, and said for wore,
I'm even as wise now as I was before.   10
They both 'gan laugh, and said, it was no mar'l [marvel],
The auth'ress was a right Du Bartas girl.
Good sooth, quoth the old don, tell ye me so,

I muse whither at length these girls will go.
It half revives my chill frost-bitten blood
To see a woman, once, do aught that's good;
And shod by Chaucer's boots and Homer's furs,
Let men look to't—lest women wear the spurs.

1650

SAMUEL SEWALL
(1652–1730)

Samuel Sewall was born in Bishopstoke, England, of dissenting parents who had already visited America. In 1661 they and nine-year-old Samuel escaped the persecutions of the Restoration and became immigrants in the New World. After living in Newbury, Massachusetts, which was founded by the elder Sewall, Samuel moved to Boston, the center of his various activities for the rest of his life. Although he studied theology at Harvard, which was the usual thing for a Puritan son to do, it became clear after his graduation in 1671 that he was not impressive as a preacher. He soon turned to business for a career. In a way, this is the most significant thing about Sewall, for his personality and career offer an outstanding social, economic, and partly temperamental example of how the idealistic Puritans gradually became the shrewdly practical, humorous, bourgeois Yankees. In his own person, Sewall comes to stand as a milestone in the development of American character and values; in him the Puritan magistrate as guardian of all aspects of the public life of the theocracy becomes the philanthropic public benefactor, the ideal man of the later and materialistic age of Benjamin Franklin. Primarily and constantly a pious and affluent merchant, Sewall filled innumerable public positions from 1680 on. At various times he was manager of the colony's printing press in Boston, tax commissioner, deputy to the General Court, and member of the Council. As council member, he journeyed to England with Increase Mather in 1688 in an unsuccessful attempt to have the colonial charter restored. In 1692 he became a judge of the Superior Court and, together

with John Hathorne (so grimly referred to later by his descendant, Nathaniel Hawthorne), one of the seven judges of the
infamous special commission hearing the witchcraft cases of
the Salem hysteria.

When the colony recovered its senses and repented of its
actions, Sewall repudiated his part and that of the courts in
the trials. On January 14, 1697, a day set apart for public
repentance by legislative act, he stood in the Old South
Church to hear his own confession of guilt read to the assembly. He was a Captain of the Honorable Artillery Company, a
probate judge, and the Chief Justice of Massachusetts from
1718 to 1728. Married three times, he had fourteen children
(of whom he survived nine) by his first wife, Hannah, the
daughter of the John Hull to whom Sewall's friend, Edward
Taylor, had come with letters of introduction from England.

Although he was the author of public compositions, including
The Selling of Joseph (1700), America's first anti-slavery tract,
Sewall's fame rests on a document that he never intended for
publication. His *Diary* which, with the exception of eight years
(1677–1685) covered the life and times of the colony from
December 3, 1673, to October 13, 1729, was not published
until 205 years after it was begun. This document presents a
revealing picture of the man: sober, earnestly religious (he
never ceased reading and studying tracts of divinity), decorous,
comically bumbling and righteous at times, obtuse, good-
natured, and well-intentioned—all of which traits are charmingly captured in the sections recounting his courtship of
Madam Winthrop. It is also a most scrupulously kept contemporary record of public activities, reflected through a
representative intelligence that was as aware of the economic
"main chance" and the respectabilities of society as of the
proper roads to Heaven. Yet throughout all of Sewall's writing,
with its official Puritan sternness, its pious platitudes and attitudes, there sounds the optimistic note of expectation and
innocent sincerity which has become so characteristic of the
national mind.

Besides *The Selling of Joseph* and the *Diary* (1878–1882),
Sewall's works include *The Revolution in New England Justified*
(1691); *Phaenomena quaedam Apocalyptica* (1697); and *Proposals Touching the Accomplishment of Prophecies* (1713).

Accounts of Sewall and his works are to be found in J. L.
Sibley, *Biographical Sketches of Graduates of Harvard University*, II (1881); H. C. Lodge, "A Puritan Pepys," *Studies in*

History (1884); N. H. Chamberlain, *Samuel Sewall and the World He Lived In* (1897); M. C. Tyler, *A History of American Literature During the Colonial Period,* II (1897); C. H. C. Howard, "Chief Justice Samuel Sewall," *Essex Institute Historical Collections,* XXXVII (1901); V. L. Parrington, *Main Currents in American Thought,* I (1927); H. W. Lawrence, "Samuel Sewall: Revealer of Puritan New England," *South Atlantic Quarterly,* XXXIII (1934); G. P. Winship, "Samuel Sewall and the New England Company," *Proceedings of the Massachusetts Historical Society,* LXVII (1945); and O. E. Winslow, *Samuel Sewall of Boston* (1964).

FROM

The Diary

Jan. 13 [*1677*]. Giving my chickens meat, it came to my mind that I gave them nothing save Indian corn and water, and yet they eat it and thrived very well, and that that food was necessary for them, how mean soever, which much affected me and convinced what need I stood in of spiritual food, and that I should not nauseate daily duties of prayer, &c.

March 16 [*1677*]. Dr. Alcock dies about midnight. Note, Mrs. Williams told us presently after duties how dangerously ill he was, and to get John to go for his grandmother. I was glad of that information, and resolved to go and pray earnestly for him; but going into the kitchen, fell into discourse with Tim about metals, and so took up the time. The Lord forgive me and help me not to be so slack for time to come, and so easy to disregard and let die so good a resolution. Dr. Alcock was 39 years old.

July 8 [*1677*]. New meeting house *mane* [in the morning]. In sermon time there came in a female Quaker, in a canvas frock, her hair dishevelled and loose like a periwig, her face as black as ink, led by two other Quakers, and two other[s] followed. It occasioned the greatest and most amazing uproar that I ever saw. Isaiah I. 12, 14.

Nov. 12 [*1685*]. . . . the ministers of this town come to the court and complain against a dancing master who seeks to set up here and hath mixed dances, and his time of meeting is Lecture-Day; and 'tis reported he should say that by one play he could teach more divinity than Mr.

Willard or the Old Testament. Mr. Moodey said 'twas not a time for N[ew] E[ngland] to dance. . . .

Sabbath, Jan. 12 [1690]. Richard Dumer, a flourishing youth of 9 years old, dies of the smallpox. I tell Sam. of it and what need he had to prepare for death, and therefore to endeavor really to pray when he said over the Lord's Prayer. He seemed not much to mind, eating an apple; but when he came to say "Our Father," he burst out into a bitter cry, and when I asked what was the matter, and he could speak, he burst out into a bitter cry, and said he was afraid he should die. I prayed with him, and read Scriptures comforting against death, as "O death where is thy sting," &c. All things yours. Life and immortality brought to light by Christ, &c. 'Twas at noon.

March 19 [1691]. Mr. C. Mather preaches the lecture from Mat. 24., and appoint[s] his portion with the hypocrites. In his proem said, *Totus mundus agit histrionem* [the whole world is playing a role]. Said one sign of a hypocrite was for a man to strain at a gnat and swallow a camel. Sign in his throat discovered him. To be zealous against an innocent fashion taken up and used by the best of men, and yet make no conscience of being guilty of great immoralities. 'Tis supposed means wearing of periwigs; said would deny themselves in any thing but parting with an opportunity to do God service; that so might not offend good Christians. Meaning, I suppose, was fain to wear a periwig for his health. I expected not to hear a vindication of periwigs in Boston pulpit by Mr. Mather; however, not from that text. The Lord give me a good heart and help to know, and not only to know but also to do His will, that my heart and head may be His.

Jan. 13 [1696]. . . . When I came in, past 7 at night, my wife met me in the entry and told me Betty had surprised them. I was surprised with the abruptness of the relation. It seems Betty Sewall had given some signs of dejection and sorrow; but a little after dinner she burst out into an amazing cry, which caused all the family to cry too. Her mother asked the reason; she gave none; at last said she was afraid she should go to Hell, her sins were not pardoned. She was first wounded by my reading a Sermon of Mr. Norton's, about the 5th of Jan. . . . Ye shall seek me and shall not find me. . . . Ye shall seek me and shall die in your sins, ran in her mind, and terrified her greatly. And

staying at home Jan. 12, she read out of Mr. Cotton Mather
—"Why hath Satan filled thy heart?" which increased her
fear. Her mother asked her whether she prayed. She answered, "Yes." But feared her prayers were not heard because her sins not pardoned. Mr. Willard . . . sent for.
. . . He came not till after I came home. He discoursed
with Betty, who could not give a distinct account, but was
confused as his phrase was, and as had experienced in himself. Mr. Willard prayed excellently. The Lord bring light
and comfort out of this dark and dreadful cloud, and grant
that Christ's being formed in my dear child may be the
issue of these painful pangs.

Dec. 21 [1696]. A very great snow is on the ground. I
go in the morn to Mr. Willard to entreat him to choose his
own time to come and pray with little Sarah. He comes a
little before night, and prays very fully and well. Mr.
Mather, the President, had prayed with her in the time of
the court's sitting. Dec. 22. being catechising day, I give
Mr. Willard a note to pray for my daughter publicly, which
he did. Note, this morn Madam Elisa Bellingham came to
our house and upbraided me with setting my hand to pass
Mr. Wharton's account to the court where he obtained a
judgment for Eustace's farm. I was wheedled and hec-
tored into that business, and have all along been uneasy in
the remembrance of it; and now there is one come who
will not spare to lay load. The Lord take away my filthy
garments, and give me change of raiment. This day I remove poor little Sarah into my bed-chamber, where, about
break of day Dec. 23, she gives up the ghost in nurse Co-
well's arms. Born, Nov. 21, 1694. Neither I nor my wife
were by, nurse not expecting so sudden a change, and having promised to call us. I thought of Christ's words, could
you not watch with me one hour! and would fain have sat
up with her; but fear of my wife's illness, who is very
valetudinarious, made me to lodge with her in the new hall,
where was called by Jane's cry to take notice of my dead
daughter. Nurse did long and pathetically ask our pardon
that she had not called us, and said she was surprised. Thus
this very fair day is rendered foul to us by reason of the
general sorrow and tears in the family. Master Chiever
was here the evening before; I desired him to pray for my
daughter. The chapter read in course on Dec. 23, m. was
Deut. 22., which made me sadly reflect that I had not been

so thoroughly tender of my daughter, nor so effectually careful of her defense and preservation as I should have been. The good Lord pity and pardon and help for the future as to those God has still left me.

Dec. 25 [1696]. We bury our little daughter. In the chamber Joseph in course reads Ecclesiastes 3rd—a time to be born and a time to die; Elizabeth [reads] Rev. 22. Hannah, the 38th Psalm. I speak to each, as God helped, to our mutual comfort, I hope. I ordered Sam. to read the 102 Psalm. Elisha Cooke, Edw. Hutchinson, John Baily, and Josia Willard bear my little daughter to the tomb.

Note. 'Twas wholly dry, and I went at noon to see in what order things were set, and there I was entertained with a view of, and converse with, the coffins of my dear Father Hull, Mother Hull, cousin Quinsey, and my six children; for the little posthumous was now took up and set in upon that that stands on John's; so are three, one upon another twice, on the bench at the end. My mother lies on a lower bench, at the end, with head to her husband's head. And I ordered little Sarah to be set on her grandmother's feet. 'Twas an awful yet pleasing treat. Having said, "The Lord knows who shall be brought hither next," I came away.

Jan. 14 [1697]. Copy of the bill I put up on Fast day; giving it to Mr. Willard as he passed by; and standing up at the reading of it, and bowing when finished, in the afternoon. [The bill was read as follows:]

Samuel Sewall, sensible of the reiterated strokes of God upon himself and family, and being sensible that as to the guilt contracted upon the opening of the late commission of Oyer and Terminer at Salem (to which the order for this day relates), he is, upon many accounts, more concerned than any that he knows of, desires to take the blame and shame of it, asking pardon of men, and especially desiring prayers that God, who has an unlimited authority, would pardon that sin and all other his sins, personal and relative; and according to His infinite benignity and sovereignty not visit the sin of him, or of any other, upon himself or any of his, nor upon the land; but that He would powerfully defend him against all temptations to sin, for the future, and vouchsafe him the efficacious, saving conduct of His word and spirit.

[For the remainder of his life Sewall set aside an annual penitential day as a penance for the part he played in the witchcraft trials.]

Jan. 14 [*1701*]. Having been certified last night about 10 o'clock of the death of my dear mother at Newbury, Sam. and I set out with John Sewall, the messenger, for that place. Hired horses at Charlestown; set out about 10 o'clock in a great fog. Dined at Lewis's with Mr. Cushing of Salisbury. Sam. and I kept on in Ipswich Road— John went to accompany Bror from Salem. About Mr. Hubbard's in Ipswich farms they overtook us. Sam. and I lodged at Crompton's in Ipswich. Bror and John stood on for Newbury by moonshine. Jan. 15th Sam and I set forward. Brother Northend meets us. Visit Aunt Northend, Mr. Payson. With Bror and sister we set forward for Newbury, where we find that day appointed for the funeral; 'twas a very pleasant, comfortable day. . . .

Nathan Bricket taking in hand to fill the grave, I said, "Forbear a little, and suffer me to say that amidst our bereaving sorrows we have the comfort of beholding this saint put into the rightful possession of that happiness of living desired and dying lamented. She lived commendably four and fifty years with her dear husband, and my dear father. And she could not well brook the being divided from him at her death which is the cause of our taking leave of her in this place. She was a true and constant lover of God's Word, worship, and saints and she always, with a patient cheerfulness, submitted to the divine decree of providing bread for herself and others in the sweat of her brows. And now her infinitely gracious and bountiful Master has promoted her to the honor of higher employments, fully and absolutely discharged from all manner of toil and sweat. My honored and beloved friends and neighbors, my dear mother never thought much of doing the most frequent and homely offices of love for me, and lavished away many thousands of words upon me, before I could return one word in answer. And therefore I ask and hope that none will be offended that I have now ventured to speak one word in her behalf when she herself is become speechless." Made a motion with my hand for the filling of the grave. Note, I could hardly speak for passion and tears.

May 29 [*1720*]. God having in his holy Sovereignty put my wife out of the fore-seat [his wife had died on May 26], I apprehended I had cause to be ashamed of my sin, and to loath myself for it; and retired into my pew. . . . I put up a note to this purpose: Samuel Sewall, deprived of his wife by a very sudden and awful stroke, desires prayers that God would sanctify the same to himself, and children, and family. Writ and sent three; to the South, Old, and Mr. Colman's church.

Sept. 5 [1720]. Going to son Sewall's I there meet with Madam Winthrop, told her I was glad to meet her there, had not seen her a great while; gave her Mr. Home's sermon.

Sept. 30 [1720]. Daughter Sewall acquaints Madam Winthrop that if she pleased to be within at three P.M., I would wait on her. She answered she would be at home.

Oct. 1 [1720]. Saturday. I dine at Mr. Stoddard's; from thence I went to Madam Winthrop's just at three. Spake to her, saying my loving wife died so soon and suddenly, 'twas hardly convenient for me to think of marrying again; however, I came to this resolution, that I would not make my court to any person without first consulting with her. Had a pleasant discourse about seven single persons sitting in the fore-seat September 29th, viz., Madam Rebecca Dudley, Katherine Winthrop, Bridget Usher, Deliverance Legg, Rebecca Lloyd, Lydia Colman, Elizabeth Bellingham. She propounded one and another for me; but none would do; said Mrs. Lloyd was about her age.

Oct. 3 [1720]. Waited on Madam Winthrop again; 'twas a little while before she came in. Her daughter Noyes being there alone with me, I said I hoped my waiting on her mother would not be disagreeable to her. She answered she should not be against that that might be for her comfort. I saluted her, and told her I perceived I must shortly wish her a good time: her mother had told me she was with child and within a month or two of her time. By and by in came Mr. Airs, chaplain of the Castle, and hanged up his hat, which I was a little startled at, it seeming as if he was to lodge there. At last Madam Winthrop came too. After a considerable time I went up to her and said if it might not be inconvenient, I desired to speak with her. She assented, and spake of going into another room; but Mr. Airs and Mrs. Noyes presently rose up and went out, leaving us there alone. Then I ushered in discourse from the names in the fore-seat; at last I prayed that Katherine [Mrs. Winthrop] might be the person assigned for me. She instantly took it up in the way of denial, as if she had catched at an opportunity to do it, saying she could not do it before she was asked. Said that was her mind unless she should change it, which she believed she should not, could not leave her children. I expressed my sorrow that she should do it so speedily, prayed her consideration, and asked her when I should wait on her again. She setting no time, I mentioned that day seven-night. Gave her Mr. Willard's *Fountain*, opened with the little print and verses, saying I hoped if we did well read that book, we should meet together hereafter, if we did not now. She took the book and put it in her pocket. Took leave.

Oct. 6 [1720]. A little after six P.M. I went to Madam Winthrop's. She was not within. I gave Sarah Chickering. the maid, two shillings, Juno, who brought in wood, one shilling. Afterward the nurse came in; I gave her eighteen pence, having no other small bill. After a while Dr. Noyes came in with his mother, and quickly after his wife came in; they sat talking, I think, till eight o'clock. I said I feared I might be some interruption to their business; Dr. Noyes replied pleasantly he feared they might be an interruption to me, and went away. Madam seemed to harp upon the same string. Must take care of her children; could not leave that house and neighborhood where she had dwelt so long. I told her she might do her children as much or more good by bestowing what she laid out in housekeeping, upon them. Said her son would be of age the 7th of August. I said it might be inconvenient for her to dwell with her daughter-in-law, who must be mistress of the house. I gave her a piece of Mr. Belcher's cake and gingerbread wrapped up in a clean sheet of paper; told her of her father's kindness to me when treasurer, and I constable. My daughter Judith was gone from me and I was more lonesome— might help to forward one another in our journey to Canaan. Mr. Eyre came within the door; I saluted him, asked how Mr. Clark did, and he went away. I took leave about 9 o'clock. I told [her] I came now to refresh her memory as to Monday night; said she had not forgot it. In discourse with her, I asked leave to speak with her sister; I meant to gain Madam Mico's favor to persuade her sister. She seemed surprised and displeased, and said she was in the same condition.

Oct. 10 [1720]. . . . In the evening I visited Madam Winthrop, who treated me with a great deal of courtesy;

wine, marmalade. I gave her a *News-Letter* about the Thanksgiving; proposals, for sake of the verses for David Jeffries. She tells me Dr. Increase Mather visited her this day, in Mr. Hutchinson's coach.

It seems Dr. Cotton Mather's chimney fell afire yesterday, so as to interrupt the Assembly A.M. Mr. Cutler ceased preaching ¼ of an hour.

Oct. 11 [*1720*]. I writ a few lines to Madam Winthrop to this purpose: "Madam, These wait on you with Mr. Mayhew's sermon, and account of the state of the Indians on Martha's Vineyard. I thank you for your unmerited favors of yesterday; and hope to have the happiness of waiting on you tomorrow before eight o'clock after noon. I pray God to keep you, and give you a joyful entrance upon the two hundred and twenty-ninth year of Christopher Columbus his discovery; and take leave, who am, Madam, your humble servant.   S.S."

Sent this by Deacon Green, who delivered it to Sarah Chickering, her mistress not being at home.

Oct. 12 [*1720*]. . . . Mrs. Anne Cotton came to door ('twas before eight), said Madam Winthrop was within, directed me into the little room, where she was full of work behind a stand; Mrs. Cotton came in and stood. Madam Winthrop pointed to her to set me a chair. Madam Winthrop's countenance was much changed from what 'twas on Monday, looked dark and lowering. At last the work (black stuff or silk) was taken away; I got my chair in place, had some converse, but very cold and indifferent to what 'twas before. Asked her to acquit me of rudeness if I drew off her glove. Inquiring the reason, I told her 'twas great odds between handling a dead goat and a living lady. Got it off. I told her I had one petition to ask of her— that was that she would take off the negative she laid on me the third of October; she readily answered she could not, and enlarged upon it; she told me of it so soon as she could; could not leave her house, children, neighbors, business. I told her she might do some good to help and support me. Mentioning Mrs. Gookin (Nath.), the Widow Weld was spoken of; said I had visited Mrs. Denison. I told her, "Yes!" Afterward I said if after a first and second vagary she would accept of me returning, her victorious kindness and good will would be very obliging. She thanked me for my book (Mr. Mayhew's sermon), but said not a word of the letter. When she insisted on the negative, I prayed there might be no more thunder and lightning, I should not sleep all night. I gave her Dr. Preston, *The Church's Marriage and the Church's Carriage,* which cost me six shillings at the sale. The door standing open, Mr. Airs came in, hung up his hat, and sat down. After a while, Madam Winthrop moving, he went out. John Eyre looked in; I said, "How do ye?" or, "Your servant, Mr. Eyre," but heard no word from him. Sarah filled a glass of wine; she drank to me, I to her; she sent Juno home with me with a good lantern; I gave her six pence and bid her thank her mistress. In some of our discourse, I told her I had rather go to the stone house adjoining to her than to come to her against her mind. Told her the reason why I came every other night was lest I should drink too deep draughts of pleasure. She had talked of canary; her kisses were to me better than the best canary. Explained the expression concerning Columbus.

Oct. 15 [1720]. I dine on fish and oil at Mr. Stoddard's. Capt. Hill wished me joy of my proceedings, i.e., with M——. Winthrop; Sister Cooper applauded it, spake of visiting her; I said her complaisance of her visit would be obliging to me.

Oct. 16 [1720]. Lord's Day. I upbraided myself that could be so solicitous about earthly things, and so cold and indifferent as to the love of Christ, who is altogether lovely. Mr. Prince administered. Dined at my son's with Mr. Cutler and Mr. Shurtleff. Mr. Cutler preaches in the afternoon from Ezek. 16:30: "How weak is thy heart." Son reads the order for the Thanksgiving.

Oct. 17 [1720]. Monday. Give Mr. Daniel Willard and Mr. Pelatiah Whittemore their oaths to their accounts, and Mr. John Briggs to his, as they are attorneys to Dr. Cotton Mather, administrator to the estate of Nathan Howell, deceased. In the evening I visited Madam Winthrop, who treated me courteously, but not in clean linen as sometimes. She said she did not know whether I would come again or no. I asked her how she could so impute inconstancy to me. (I had not visited here since Wednesday night, being unable to get over the indisposition received by the treatment received that night, and *I must* in it seemed to sound like a made piece of formality.) Gave her this day's *Gazette.* Heard David Jeffries say the Lord's Prayer, and some other portions of the Scriptures. He came to the door and asked me to go into chamber where his grandmother was tending little Katee, to whom she had given physic; but I chose to sit below. Dr. Noyes and his wife came in and sat a considerable time; had been visiting Son and Daughter Cooper. Juno came home with me.

Oct. 18 [1720]. Visited Madam Mico, who came to me in a splendid dress. I said, "It may be you have heard of my visiting Madam Winthrop," her sister. She answered, her sister had told her of it. I asked her good will in the affair. She answered, if her sister were for it, she should not hinder it. I gave her Mr. Homes's sermon. She gave me a glass of canary, entertained me with good discourse and a respectful remembrance of my first wife. I took leave.

Oct. 19 [1720]. Midweek. Visited Madam Winthrop; Sarah told me she was at Mr. Walley's, would not come home till late. I gave her Hannah three oranges with her duty, not knowing whether I should find her or no. Was ready to go home; but said if I knew she was there, I would go thither. Sarah seemed to speak with pretty good courage she would be there. I went and found her there, with Mr. Walley and his wife in the little room below. At seven o'clock I mentioned going home; at eight I put on my coat and quickly waited on her home. She found occasion to speak loud to the servant, as if she had a mind to be known. Was courteous to me, but took occasion to speak pretty earnestly about my keeping a coach. I said 'twould cost £100 per annum; she said 'twould cost but £40. Spake much against John Winthrop, his false-heartedness. Mr. Eyre came in and sat a while; I offered him Dr. Incr. Mather's *Sermons,* whereof Mr. Appleton's ordination sermon was one; said he had them already. I said I would give him another. Exit. Came away somewhat late.

Oct. 20 [1720]. Mr. Colman preaches from Luke 15:10: "Joy among the angels"; made an excellent discourse.

At council, Col. Townsend spake to me of my hood: should get a wig. I said 'twas my chief ornament; I wore it for sake of the day. Brother Odlin, and Sam, Mary, and Jane Hirst dine with us. Promised to wait on the Governor about seven. Madam Winthrop not being at lecture, I went thither first; found her very serene with her daughter Noyes, Mrs. Dering, and the Widow Shipreeve, sitting at a little table, she in her armed chair. She drank to me, and I to Mrs. Noyes. After a while prayed the favor to speak with her. She took one of the candles and went into the best room, closed the shutters, sat down upon the couch. She told me Madam Usher had been there, and said the coach must be set on wheels, and not by rusting. She spake something of my needing a wig. Asked me what her sister said to me. I told her she said if her sister were for it, she would not hinder it. But I told her she did not say she would be glad to have me for her brother. Said, "I shall keep you in the cold"; and asked her if she would be within tomorrow night, for we had had but a running feat. She said she could not tell whether she should or no. I took leave. As were drinking at the Governor's, he said in England the ladies minded little more than that they might have money, and coaches to ride in. I said, "And New England brooks its name." At which Mr. Dudley smiled. Governor said they were not quite so bad here.

Oct. 21 [*1720*]. Friday. My son the minister came to me P.M. by appointment and we pray one for another in the old chamber, more especially respecting my courtship. About six o'clock I go to Madam Winthrop's; Sarah told me her mistress was gone out, but did not tell me whither she went. She presently ordered me a fire; so I went in, having Dr. Sibb's *Bowels* with me to read. I read the two first sermons; still nobody came in. At last about nine o'clock Mr. John Eyre came in; I took the opportunity to say to him as I had done to Mrs. Noyes, that I hoped my visiting his mother would not be disagreeable to him; he answered me with much respect. When 'twas after nine o'clock he of himself said he would go and call her, she was but at one of his brothers'; a while after I heard Madam Winthrop's voice, inquiring something about John. After a good while and clapping the garden door twice or thrice, she came in. I mentioned something of the lateness; she bantered me, and said I was later. She received me courteously. I asked when our proceedings should be made public; she said they were like to be no more public than they were already. Offered me no wine that I remember. I rose up at eleven o'clock to come away, saying I would put on my coat; she offered not to help me. I prayed her that Juno might light me home; she opened the shutter and said 'twas pretty light abroad, Juno was weary and gone to bed. So I came home by star light as well as I could. At my first coming in I gave Sarah five shillings. I writ Mr. Eyre his name in his book with the date October 21, 1720. It cost me eight shillings. *Jehovah jireh!* [God will provide.] Madam told me she had visited M. Mico, Wendell, and William Clark of the South [Church].

Oct. 22 [1720]. Daughter Cooper visited me before my going out of town, stayed till about sunset. I brought her, going near as far as the Orangetree. Coming back, near Leg's Corner, little David Jeffries saw me, and looking upon me very lovingly, asked me if I was going to see his grandmother. I said, "Not tonight." Gave him a penny and bid him present my service to his grandmother.

Oct. 24 [1720]. I went in the hackney coach through the Common, stopped at Madam Winthrop's: had told her I would take my departure from thence. Sarah came to the door with Katee in her arms, but I did not think to take notice of the child. Called her mistress. I told her, being encouraged by David Jeffries' loving eyes and sweet words, I was come to inquire whether she could find in her heart to leave that house and neighborhood, and go and dwell with me at the South End; I think she said softly, "Not yet." I told her it did not lie in my lands to keep a coach. If I should, I should be in danger to be brought to keep company with her neighbor Brooker: he was a little before sent to prison for debt. Told her I had an antipathy against those who would pretend to give themselves, but nothing of their estate. I would a proportion of my estate with myself. And I supposed she would do so. As to a periwig, my best and greatest Friend, I could not possibly have a greater, began to find me with hair before I was born, and had continued to do so ever since; and I could not find in my heart to go to another. She commended the book I gave her, Dr. Preston, *The Church Marriage;* quoted him saying 'twas inconvenient keeping out of a fashion commonly used. I said the time and tide did circumscribe my visit. She gave me a dram of black-cherry brandy, and gave me a lump of the sugar that was in it. She wished me a good journey. I prayed God to keep her, and came away. Had a very pleasant journey to Salem.

Oct. 31 [1720]. She proves her husband's will. At night I visited Madam Winthrop about six P.M. They told me she was gone to Madam Mico's. I went thither and found she was gone; so returned to her house, read the Epistles to the

Galatians, Ephesians in Mr. Eyre's Latin Bible. After the clock struck eight, I began to read the 103 Psalm. Mr. Wendell came in from his warehouse. Asked me if I were alone. Spake very kindly to me, offered me to call Madam Winthrop. I told him she would be angry, had been at Mrs. Mico's; he helped me on with my coat, and I came home; left the *Gazette* in the Bible, which told Sarah of, bid her present my service to Mrs. Winthrop, and tell her I had been to wait on her if she had been at home.

Nov. 1 [*1720*]. I was so taken up that I could not go if I would.

Nov. 2 [*1720*]. Midweek. Went again, and found Mrs. Alden there, who quickly went out. Gave her about ½ pound of sugar almonds, cost three shillings per pound. Carried them on Monday. She seemed pleased with them, asked what they cost. Spake of giving her a hundred pounds per annum if I died before her. Asked her what sum she would give me, if she should die first. Said I would give her time to consider of it. She said she heard as if I had given all to my children by deeds of gift. I told her 'twas a mistake, Point Judith was mine, etc. That in England, I owned, my father's desire was that it should go to my eldest son; 'twas £20 per annum; she thought 'twas forty. I think when I seemed to excuse pressing this, she seemed to think 'twas best to speak of it; a long winter was coming on. Gave me a glass or two of canary.

Nov. 4 [*1720*]. Friday. Went again about seven o'clock; found there Mr. John Walley and his wife; sat discoursing pleasantly. Madam W. served comfits to us. After a while a table was spread, and supper was set. I urged Mr. Walley to crave a blessing; but he put it upon me. About nine they went away. I asked Madam what fashioned necklace I should present her with; she said, "None at all." I asked her whereabout we left off last time, mentioned what I had offered to give her, asked her what she would give me; she said she could not change her condition, she had said so from the beginning, could not be so far from her children, the lecture. Quoted the Apostle Paul affirming that a single life was better than a married. I answered that was for the present distress. Said she had not pleasure in things of that nature as formerly. I said, "You are the fitter to make me a wife." If she held in that mind, I must go home and bewail my rashness in making more haste than good speed.

However, considering the supper, I desired her to be within next Monday night, if we lived so long. Assented. She charged me with saying that she must put away Juno if she came to me; I utterly denied it, it never came in my heart; yet she insisted upon it, saying it came in upon discourse about the Indian woman that obtained her freedom this court. About ten I said I would not disturb the good orders of her house, and came away. She not seeming pleased with my coming away. Spake to her about David Jeffries; had not seen him.

Monday, Nov. 7 [1720]. My son prayed in the old chamber. Our time had been taken up by Son and Daughter Cooper's visit, so that I only read the 130th and 143rd Psalm. 'Twas on the account of my courtship. I went to Mad. Winthrop; found her rocking her little Katee in the cradle. I excused my coming so late: near eight. She set me an armed chair and cushion; and so the cradle was between her armed chair and mine. Gave her the remnant of my almonds; she did not eat of them as before, but laid them away. I said I came to enquire whether she had altered her mind since Friday, or remained of the same mind still. She said, "Thereabouts." I told her I loved her, and was so fond as to think that she loved me. She said [she] had a great respect for me. I told her I had made her an offer without asking any advice; she had so many to advise with that 'twas a hindrance. The fire was come to one short brand besides the block, which brand was set up in end; at last it fell to pieces, and no recruit was made. She gave me a glass of wine. I think I repeated again that I would go home and bewail my rashness in making more haste than good speed. I would endeavor to contain myself, and not go on to solicit her to do that which she could not consent to. Took leave of her. As came down the steps she bid me have a care. Treated me courteously. Told her she had entered the fourth year of her widowhood. I had given her the *News-Letter* before. I did not bid her draw off her glove as sometime I had done. Her dress was not so clean as sometime it had been. *Jehovah jireh!*

Midweek, Nov. 9 [1720]. Dine at Brother Stoddard's; were so kind as to inquire of me if they should invite Madam Winthrop; I answered "No."

w. 1673–1729
p. 1878–1882

FROM
The Selling of Joseph

The numerousness of slaves at this day in the Province, and the uneasiness of them under their slavery, hath put many upon thinking whether the foundation of it be firmly and well laid; so as to sustain the vast weight that is built upon it. It is most certain that all men, as they are sons of Adam, are coheirs; and have equal right unto liberty, and all other outward comforts of life. "God hath given the earth [and all its commodities] unto the sons of Adam," Psal. 115:16. "And hath made of one blood, all nations of men, for to dwell on all the face of the earth, and hath determined the times before appointed, and the bounds of their habitation: That they should seek the Lord. Forasmuch then as we are the offspring of God," etc. Acts 17:26, 27, 29. Now although the title given by the last Adam doth infinitely better men's estates, respecting God and themselves; and grants them a most beneficial and inviolable lease under the broad seal of heaven, who were before only tenants at will: yet through the indulgence of God to our first parents after the fall, the outward estate of all and every of their children, remains the same, as to one another. So that originally, and naturally, there is no such thing as slavery. Joseph was rightfully no more a slave to his brethren, than they were to him: and they had no more authority to sell him, than they had to slay him. And if they had nothing to do to sell him, the Ishmaelites bargaining with them, and paying down twenty pieces of silver, could not make a title. Neither could Potiphar have any better interest in him than the Ismaelites had, Gen. 37:20, 27, 28. For he that shall in this case plead alteration of property, seems to have forfeited a great part of his own claim to humanity. There is no proportion between twenty pieces of silver, and liberty. The commodity itself is the claimer. If Arabian gold be imported in any quantities, most are afraid to meddle with it, though they might have it at easy rates; lest if it should have been wrongfully taken from the owners, it should kindle a fire to the consumption of their whole estate. 'Tis pity there should be more caution used in buying a horse, or a little lifeless dust, than there is in purchasing men and women: whenas they are the off-spring of God, and their liberty is *auro pretiosior omni* [more precious than gold].

And seeing God hath said, "He that stealeth a man and selleth him, or if he be found in his hand, he shall surely be put to death." Exod. 21:16, this law being of everlasting equity, wherein man stealing is ranked among the most atrocious of capital crimes: what louder cry can there be made of that celebrated warning, *caveat emptor* [let the buyer beware]!

And all things considered, it would conduce more to the welfare of the Province, to have white servants for a term of years, than to have slaves for life. Few can endure to hear of a Negro's being made free; and indeed they can seldom use their freedom well; yet their continual aspiring after their forbidden liberty, renders them unwilling servants. And there is such a disparity in their conditions, color and hair, that they can never embody with us, and grow up into orderly families, to the peopling of the land: but still remain in our body politic as a kind of extravasate blood. As many Negro men as there are among us, so many empty places there are in our train bands, and the places taken up of men that might make husbands for our daughters. And the sons of daughters of New England would become more like Jacob, and Rachel, if this slavery were thrust quite out of doors. Moreover, it is too well known what temptations masters are under, to connive at the fornication of their slaves; lest they should be obliged to find them wives, or pay their fines. It seems to be practically pleaded that they might be lawless; 'tis thought much of, that the law should have satisfaction for their thefts, and other immoralities; by which means, holiness to the Lord is more rarely engraven upon this sort of servitude. It is likewise most lamentable to think, how in taking Negroes out of Africa, and selling of them here, that which God has joined together men do boldly rend asunder; men from their country, husbands from their wives, parents from their children. How horrible is the uncleanness, mortality, if not murder, that the ships are guilty of that bring great crowds of these miserable men, and women! Methinks, when we are bemoaning the barbarous usage of our friends and kinsfolk in Africa: it might not be unseasonable to inquire whether we are not culpable in forcing the Africans to become slaves amongst ourselves. And it may be a question whether all the benefit received by Negro slaves, will balance the account of cash laid out upon them; and for the redemption of our own enslaved friends out of Africa; besides all the persons and estates that have perished there.

Objection 1. These blackamoors are of the posterity of Cham, and therefore are under the curse of slavery. Gen. 9:25, 26, 27.

Answer. Of all offices, one would not beg this; viz., uncalled for, to be an executioner of the vindictive wrath of God; the extent and duration of which is to us uncertain. If this ever was a commission, how do we know but that it is long since out of date? Many have found it to their cost, that a prophetical denunciation of judgment against a person or people, would not warrant them to inflict that evil. If it would, Hazael might justify himself in all he did against his master, and the Israelites, from II Kings 8:10, 12.

But it is possible that by cursory reading, this text may have been mistaken. For Canaan is the person cursed three times over, without the mentioning of Cham. Good expositors suppose the curse entailed on him, and that this prophecy was accomplished in the extirpation of the Canaanites, and in the servitude of the Gibeonites. . . . Whereas the blackamoors are not descended of Canaan, but of Cush. Psal. 68:31. "Princes shall come out of Egypt [Mizraim]; Ethiopia [Cush] shall soon stretch out her hands unto God." Under which names, all Africa may be comprehended; and their promised conversion ought to be prayed for. Jer. 13:23. "Can the Ethiopian change his skin?" This shews that black men are the posterity of Cush, who time out of mind have been distinguished by their color. . . .

Objection 2. The *nigers* are brought out of a pagan country, into places where the gospel is preached.

Answer. Evil must not be done, that good may come of it. The extraordinary and comprehensive benefit accruing to the church of God, and to Joseph personally, did not rectify his brethren's sale of him.

Objection 3. The Africans have wars one with another; our ships bring lawful captives taken in those wars.

Answer. For aught is known, their wars are much such

as were between Jacob's sons and their brother Joseph. If they be between town and town, provincial or national, every war is upon one side unjust. An unlawful war can't make lawful captives. And by receiving, we are in danger to promote, and partake in their barbarous cruelties. I am sure, if some gentlemen should go down to the Brewsters to take the air, and fish: and a stronger party from Hull should surprise them, and sell them for slaves to a ship outward bound, they would think themselves unjustly dealt with; both by sellers and buyers. And yet 'tis to be feared, we have no other kind of title to our *nigers*. "Therefore all things whatsoever ye would that men should do to you, do ye even so to them: for this is the law and the prophets." Matt. 7:12.

Objection 4. Abraham had servants bought with his money, and born in his house.

Answer. Until the circumstances of Abraham's purchase be recorded, no argument can be drawn from it. In the meantime, charity obliges us to conclude, that he knew it was lawful and good.

It is observable that the Israelites were strictly forbidden the buying, or selling one another for slaves. Levit. 25:39, 46. Jer. 34:8–22. And God gaged His blessing in lieu of any loss they might conceit they suffered thereby. Deut. 15:18. And since the partition wall is broken down, inordinate self love should likewise be demolished. God expects that Christians should be of a more ingenuous and benign frame of spirit. Christians should carry it to all the world, as the Israelites were to carry it one towards another. And for men obstinately to persist in holding their neighbors and brethren under the rigor of perpetual bondage, seems to be no proper way of gaining assurance that God has given them spiritual freedom. Our blessed Saviour has altered the measures of the ancient love-song, and set it to a most excellent new tune, which all ought to be ambitious of learning. Matt. 5:43, 44. John 13:34. These Ethiopians, as black as they are, seeing they are the sons and daughters of the first Adam, the brethren and sisters of the last Adam, and the offspring of God; they ought to be treated with a respect agreeable.

1700

FROM

Phaenomena quaedam Apocalyptica

As long as Plum Island shall faithfully keep the commanded post, notwithstanding all the hectoring words and hard blows of the proud and boisterous ocean; as long as any salmon or sturgeon shall swim in the streams of Merrimac, or any perch or pickerel in Crane Pond; as long as the sea-fowl shall know the time of their coming, and not neglect seasonably to visit the places of their acquaintance; as long as any cattle shall be fed with the grass growing in the meadows, which do humbly bow down themselves before Turkey-Hill; as long as any sheep shall walk upon Old-Town Hills, and shall from thence pleasantly look down upon the River Parker, and the fruitful marshes lying beneath; as long as any free and harmless doves shall find a white oak or other tree within the township, to perch, or feed, or build a careless nest upon, and shall voluntarily present themselves to perform the office of gleaners after barley harvest; as long as Nature shall not grow old and dote, but shall constantly remember to give the rows of Indian corn their education by pairs; so long shall Christians be born there, and being first made meet, shall from thence be translated to be made partakers of the inheritance of the saints in light.

1697

COTTON MATHER

(1663–1728)

To have been born the descendant of illustrious Puritan ministers was its own lesson in Christian agony; to have been born
thus, complete with an ego aspiring to surpass one's ancestors,
made life an unremittingly tormenting tension of incredible
industry, obsessive piety, hatred, fear, purpose, ambition, and
passion. At least this was true if one was Cotton Mather.

Born in Boston, the son of Increase Mather and a grandson
of both Richard Mather and John Cotton, and blessed with
enormous, though not always a necessarily profound, intellect,
he seems to have needed to justify his existence by keeping one
step ahead of everyone else, intellectually and spiritually. When
he was eight, he was already sermonizing his playmates, as
Jonathan Edwards later was to do; and he could have found
an augury of the uneven public support he achieved as an adult
in the mixed awe and dislike with which the boys reviled him
for his efforts. By the time he entered Harvard College as the
youngest freshman in the school's records (he was aged twelve),
he was experienced in Greek, Latin, Hebrew, and righteous
attitudes. He was graduated at fifteen, earned his M.A. at
nineteen, and abandoning his earlier desire to become a physician, he accepted in 1685 an appointment to become his
father's assistant in the Congregational Second, or Old North,
Church in Boston. Although he did not realize his ambition
to succeed his father as President of Harvard, he remained as
the leader of the congregation.

In every sense the man was a Puritan. Within his own
personality and history he combined the tough-mindedness of
the first generation and the zeal of the disintegrating third
generation. At the time of the Salem madness, he whole-
heartedly endorsed the "war against Satan." His *Memorable
Providences Relating to Witchcraft* (1689) contributed to the

eruption of the general hysteria and his *Wonders of the Invisible World* (1693) condoned its legal findings. Yet in fairness it must be noted that for the fundamentalistic Puritan the world literally was divided into the warring camps of Christ and Satan, spectral occurrences ranked high in the beliefs of even the most educated, and Mather himself, not concurring in the legal admission of black magic "evidences," effectually and publicly repudiated his position and the methods of the courts by 1700.

His fantastic erudition was reflected in his heavily pedantic and allusive style in the 444 items he published during his lifetime, and in his library, which, except for that of William Byrd of Virginia, was the largest private collection in the colonies at the time. His learning and his desire to be in the vanguard led him to liberalisms surprising for a man of his conservative and often reactionary tendencies. As a liberal and a good middle-class antiepiscopacy Protestant, he helped lead the merchants' revolt against Governor Andros. As a liberal and a scientist, in 1721 he championed Zabdiel Boylston's experiments in inoculation against great public opposition. His scientific papers got him elected to the Royal Society in 1713. Actually, there was nothing in Puritan orthodoxy to deny a man's receptiveness to the new science; thus there was no contradiction between Mather's scientific liberalism and his orthodox attempt to restore the third generation to the first-generation days of the colony, when the minister was as magisterially sovereign as the God of Puritan Covenant theology.

Mather's great work, *Magnalia Christi Americana* or *The Ecclesiastical History of New England from Its First Planting* (1702) was an attempt to paint the golden age of American Puritanism in such holy light that his contemporaries would be inspired to lives of emulation; yet he never succeeded in synthesizing his religion and his age, as Jonathan Edwards would do. His *Manuductio ad Ministerium* (1726) was a handbook for new ministers, looking forward to the liberation of the doctrine of works (indeed, Ben Franklin's eighteenth century delighted in Mather's *Bonifacius,* or *Essays to Do Good* [1710]) and backward to a time when the identity of the minister was unquestioned. Fairly typical of colonial life even in being married three times and outliving thirteen of his fifteen children, Mather, in all his learning, dedication, obsessions, and religious devotion, remains one of our best examples of the flowering and fall of the Puritan age.

Besides the works mentioned above, among the most significant of the items in Mather's tremendous bibliography are his *Diary* (1911–1912, ed. W. C. Ford); *A Poem Dedicated to the Memory of . . . Urian Oakes* (1682); *The Present State of New England* (1690); *Some Considerations on the Bills of Credit* (1691); *The Life and Death of the Renowned Mr. John Eliot* (1691); *The Short History of New England* (1694); *A Family Well Ordered* (1699); *Reasonable Religion* (1700); *A Memorial of the Present Deplorable State of New England* (1707); *The Deplorable State of New England* (1708); *Curiosa Americana* (1712–1724); *The Christian Philosopher* (1721); *Some Account of . . . Inoculating . . . the Smallpox* (1721); and *Parentator* (1724).

B. Wendell, *Cotton Mather: the Puritan Priest* (1891, 1963); A. P. Marvin, *The Life and Times of Cotton Mather* (1892); W. C. Ford, ed., *The Diary of Cotton Mather* (1911–1912); R. P. and L. Boas, *Cotton Mather* (1928); T. J. Holmes, *Cotton Mather: A Bibliography of His Works*, 3 vols. (1940); D. DeLevie, "Cotton Mather, Theologian and Scientist," *American Quarterly*, III (1951); K. A. Porter, "A Bright Particular Faith, A. D. 1700: A Portrait of Cotton Mather," *Perspectives U.S.A.*, No. 7 (Spring, 1954); and R. Shryock, *Cotton Mather, First Significant Figure in American Medicine* (1954). O. T. Beall, "Cotton Mather's Early 'Curiosa Americana' and the Boston Philosophical Society of 1683," *William and Mary Quarterly*, XVIII (1961); E. Benz, "Ecumenical Relations Between Boston Puritanism and German Pietism: Cotton Mather and August Hermann Francke," *Harvard Theological Review*, LIV (1961); W. R. Manierre, "Cotton Mather and the Biographical Parallel," *American Quarterly*, XIII (1961); D. Levin, "The Hazing of Cotton Mather," *New England Quarterly*, XXXVI (1963); P. H. Smith, "Politics and Sainthood: Biography by Cotton Mather," *William and Mary Quarterly*, XX (1963); E. E. White, "Cotton Mather's *Manuductio ad Ministerium*," *Quarterly Journal of Speech*, XLIX (1963); W. R. Manierre, ed., *The Diary of Cotton Mather . . . for the Year 1712* (1964); A. Warren, "Grandfather Mather and His Wonder Book," *Sewanee Review*, LXXII (1964); and S. Berkovitch, "New England Epic: Cotton Mather's *Magnalia Christi Americana*," *ELH*, XXXIII (1966).

FROM

The Wonders of the Invisible World

[Martha Carrier]

The New Englanders are a people of God settled in those which were once the devil's territories, and it may easily be supposed that the devil was exceedingly disturbed when he perceived such a people here accomplishing the promise of old made unto our blessed Jesus: that he should have the utmost parts of the earth for his possession. There was not a greater uproar among the Ephesians when the gospel was first brought among them than there was among the powers of the air (after whom those Ephesians walked) when first the silver trumpets of the gospel here made the joyful sound. The devil, thus irritated, immediately tried all sorts of methods to overturn this poor plantation; and so much of the church as was fled into this wilderness immediately found the serpent cast out of his mouth a flood for the carrying of it away. I believe that never were more satanical devices used for the unsettling of any people under the sun than what have been employed for the extirpation of the vine which God has here planted, casting out the heathen and preparing a room before it, and causing it to take deep root and fill the land, so that it sent its boughs unto the Atlantic sea eastward, and its branches unto the Connecticut River westward, and the hills were covered with the shadow thereof. But all those attempts of hell have hitherto been abortive. Many an Ebenezer has been erected unto the praise of God by his poor people here; and having obtained help from God, we continue to this day. Wherefore the devil is now making one attempt more upon us, an attempt more difficult, more surprising, more snarled with unintelligible circumstances than any that we have hitherto encountered, an attempt so critical that if we get well through, we shall soon enjoy halcyon days with all the vultures of hell trodden under our feet. He has wanted his incarnate legions to persecute us as the people of God have in the other hemisphere been persecuted. He has therefore drawn forth his more spiritual ones to make an attack upon us. We have been advised by some credible Christians yet alive that a malefactor, accused of witchcraft as well as murder, and executed in this place more than forty years ago, did then give notice of an horrible plot against the country by witchcraft and a foundation of witchcraft then laid, which if it were not seasonably discovered would probably blow up and pull down all the churches in the country. And we have now with horror seen the discovery of such a witchcraft! An army of devils is horribly broke in upon the place which is the center and, after a sort, the first-born of our English settlements; and the houses of the good people there are filled with the doleful shrieks of their children and servants, tormented by invisible hands with tortures altogether preternatural. After the mischiefs here endeavored and since in part conquered, the terrible plague of evil angels hath made its progress into some other places where other persons have been in like manner, diabolically handled. These, our poor afflicted neighbors, quickly after they become infected and infested with these demons, arrive to a capacity of discerning those which they conceive the shapes of their troublers. And notwithstanding the great and just suspicion that the demons might impose the shapes of innocent persons in their spectral exhibitions upon the sufferers (which may perhaps prove no small part of the witch plot in the issue), yet many of the persons thus represented being examined, several of them have been convicted of a very damnable witchcraft. Yea, more than one twenty have confessed that they have signed unto a book which the devil showed them and engaged in his hellish design of bewitching and ruining our land. We know not, at least I know not, how far the delusions of Satan may be interwoven into some circumstances of the confessions; but one would think all the rules of understanding human affairs are at an end if, after so many most voluntary, harmonious confessions, made by intelligent persons of all ages, in sundry towns, at several times, we must not believe the main strokes wherein those confessions all agree, especially when we have a thousand preternatural things every day before our eyes wherein the confessors do acknowledge their concernment and give demonstration of their being so concerned. If the devils now can strike the minds of men with any poisons of so fine a composition and operation that scores of innocent people shall unite in confessions of a crime which we see actually committed, it is a thing prodigious, beyond the wonders of the former ages, and it threatens no less than a sort of a dissolution upon the world. Now, by these confessions 'tis agreed that the devil has made a dreadful knot of witches in the country, and by the help of witches has dreadfully increased that knot; that these witches have driven a trade of commissioning their confederate spirits to do all sorts of mischiefs to the neighbors, whereupon there have ensued such mischievous consequences upon the bodies and estates of the neighborhood as could not otherwise be accounted for. Yea, that at prodigious witch meetings the wretches have proceeded so far as to concert and consult the methods of rooting out the Christian religion from this country, and setting up instead of it perhaps a more gross diabolism than ever the world saw before. . . .

Martha Carrier was indicted for the bewitching of certain persons, according to the form usual in such cases, pleading not guilty to her indictment. There were first brought in a considerable number of the bewitched persons, who not only made the court sensible of an horrid witchcraft committed upon them, but also deposed that it was Martha Carrier or her shape that grievously tormented them by biting, pricking, pinching, and choking of them. It was further deposed that while this Carrier was on her examination before the magistrates, the poor people were so tortured that everyone expected their death upon the very spot, but that upon the binding of Carrier they were eased. Moreover the look of Carrier then laid the afflicted people for dead, and her touch, if her eye at the same time were off them, raised them again, which things were also now seen upon her trial. And it was testified that upon the mention of some having their necks twisted almost round by the shape of this Carrier, she replied, "It's no matter though their necks had been twisted quite off."

Before the trial of this prisoner several of her own children had frankly and fully confessed not only that they were witches themselves, but that this, their mother, had made them so. This confession they made with great shows of repentance and with much demonstration of truth. They related place, time, occasion; they gave an account of journeys, meetings, and mischiefs by them performed, and were very credible in what they said. Nevertheless, this evidence was not produced against the prisoner at the bar, inasmuch as there was other evidence enough to proceed upon.

Benjamin Abbot gave in his testimony that last March was a twelve-month this Carrier was very angry with him upon laying out some land near her husband's. Her expressions in this anger were that she would stick as close to Abbot as the bark stuck to the tree, and that he should repent of it afore seven years came to an end so as Doctor Prescot should never cure him. These words were heard by others besides Abbot himself, who also heard her say she would hold his nose as close to the grindstone as ever it was held since his name was Abbot. Presently after this he was taken with a swelling in his foot, and then with a pain in his side, and exceedingly tormented. It bred unto a sore, which was lanced by Doctor Prescot, and several gallons of corruption ran out of it. For six weeks it continued very bad, and then another sore bred in his groin, which was also lanced by Doctor Prescot. Another sore then bred in his groin, which was likewise cut and put him to very great misery. He was brought unto death's door and so remained until Carrier was taken and carried away by the constable, from which very day he began to mend and so grew better every day and is well ever since.

Sarah Abbot also, his wife, testified that her husband was not only all this while afflicted in his body, but also that strange, extraordinary, and unaccountable calamities befell his cattle, their death being such as they could guess at no natural reason for.

Allin Toothaker testified that Richard, the son of Martha Carrier, having some difference with him, pulled him down by the hair of the head. When he rose again, he was going to strike at Richard Carrier, but fell down flat on his back to the ground and had not power to stir hand or foot until he told Carrier he yielded, and then he saw the shape of Martha Carrier go off his breast.

This Toothaker had received a wound in the wars, and he now testified that Martha Carrier told him he should never be cured. Just afore the apprehending of Carrier, he could thrust a knitting needle into his wound, four inches deep; but presently after her being seized he was thoroughly healed.

He further testified that when Carrier and he sometimes were at variance she would clap her hands at him and say he should get nothing by it; whereupon he several times lost his cattle by strange deaths, whereof no natural causes could be given.

John Rogger also testified that upon the threatening words of this malicious Carrier his cattle would be strangely bewitched, as was more particularly then described.

Samuel Preston testified that about two years ago, having some difference with Martha Carrier, he lost a cow in a strange, preternatural, unusual manner. And about a month after this, the said Carrier having again some difference with him, she told him he had lately lost a cow and it should not be long before he lost another, which accordingly came to pass; for he had a thriving and well-kept cow which without any known cause quickly fell down and died.

Phebe Chandler testified that about a fortnight before the apprehension of Martha Carrier, on a Lord's day while the psalm was singing in the church, this Carrier then took her by the shoulder and shaking her asked her where she lived. She made no answer, although as Carrier, who lived next door to her father's house, could not in reason but know who she was. Quickly after this, as she was at several times crossing the fields, she heard a voice that she took to be Martha Carrier's; and it seemed as if it was over her head. The voice told her she should within two or three days be poisoned. Accordingly, within such a little time, one half of her right hand became greatly swollen and very painful, as also part of her face, whereof she can give no account how it came. It continued very bad for some days, and several times since she has had a great pain in her breast and been so seized on her legs that she has hardly been able to go. She added that lately, going well to the house of God, Richard, the son of Martha Carrier, looked very earnestly upon her. And immediately her hand, which had formerly been poisoned, as is above said, began to pain her greatly; and she had a strange burning at her stomach, but was then struck deaf so that she could not hear any of the prayer or singing till the two or three last words of the psalm. . . .

One Lacy, who likewise confessed her share in this witchcraft, now testified that she and the prisoner were once bodily present at a witch meeting in Salem village, and that she knew the prisoner to be a witch and to have been at a diabolical sacrament, and that the prisoner was the undoing of her and her children by enticing them into the snare of the devil.

Another Lacy, who also confessed her share in this witchcraft, now testified that the prisoner was at the witch meeting in Salem village, where they had bread and wine administered unto them.

In the time of this prisoner's trial, one Susanna Sheldon in open court had her hands unaccountably tied together with a wheel band so fast that without cutting it could not be loosed. It was done by a specter, and the sufferer affirmed it was the prisoner's.

Memorandum: This rampant hag, Martha Carrier, was the person of whom the confessions of the witches and of her own children among the rest agreed that the devil had promised her she should be queen of hell.

1693

[George Burroughs]

Glad should I have been, if I had never known the name of this man; or never had this occasion to mention so much as the first letters of his name. But the government requiring some account of his trial to be inserted in this book, it becomes me with all obedience to submit unto the order.

I. This G. B. was indicted for witchcrafts, and in the prosecution of the charge against him, he was accused by five or six of the bewitched, as the author of their miseries; he was accused by eight of the confessing witches, as being an head actor at some of their hellish rendezvous, and one who had the promise of being a king in Satan's kingdom, now going to be erected: he was accused by nine persons for extraordinary lifting, and such feats of strength, as could not be done without a diabolical assistance. And for other such things he was accused, until about thirty testimonies were brought in against him; nor were these judged the half of what might have been considered for his conviction: however they were enough to fix the character of a witch upon him, according to the rules of reasoning, by the judicious Gaule, in that case directed.

II. The court being sensible, that the testimonies of the parties bewitched use to have a room among the suspicions or presumptions, brought in against one indicted for witchcraft, there were now heard the testimonies of several persons, who were most notoriously bewitched, and every day tortured by invisible hands, and these now all charged the spectres of G. B. to have a share in their torments. At the examination of this G. B. the bewitched people were grievously harassed with preternatural mischiefs, which could not possibly be dissembled; and they still ascribed it unto the endeavors of G. B. to kill them. And now upon his trial, one of the bewitched persons testified, that in her agonies, a little black-haired man came to her, saying his name was **B.** and bidding her set her hand unto a book which he showed unto her; and bragging that he was a conjurer, above the ordinary rank of witches; that he often persecuted her with the offer of that book, saying, she should be well, and need fear nobody, if she would but sign it; but he inflicted cruel pains and hurts upon her, because of her denying so to do. The testimonies of the other sufferers concurred with these; and it was remarkable, that whereas biting was one of the ways which the witches used for the vexing of the sufferers, when they cried out of G. B. biting them, the print of the teeth would be seen on the flesh of the complainers, and just such a set of teeth as G. B.'s would then appear upon them, which could be distinguished from those of some other men's. Others of them testified, that in their torments, G. B. tempted them to go unto a sacrament, unto which they perceived him with a sound of trumpet summoning of other witches, who quickly after the sound would come from all quarters unto the rendezvous. One of them falling into a kind of trance, afterwards affirmed, that G. B. had carried her into a very high mountain, where he showed her mighty and glorious kingdoms, and said, he would give them all to her, if she would write in his book; but she told him, they were none of his to give; and refused the motions, enduring of much misery for that refusal.

It cost the court a wonderful deal of trouble, to hear the testimonies of the sufferers; for when they were going to give in their depositions, they would for a long time be taken with fits, that made them uncapable of saying anything. The chief judge asked the prisoner, who he thought hindered these witnesses from giving their testimonies? and he answered, he supposed it was the Divel. That honorable person then replied, "How comes the Divel so loath to have any testimony borne against you?" which cast him into very great confusion.

III. It has been a frequent thing for the bewitched people to be entertained with apparitions of ghosts of murdered people, at the same time that the spectres of the witches trouble them. These ghosts do always affright the beholders more than all the other spectral representations; and when they exhibit themselves, they cry out, of being murdered by the witchcrafts or other violences of the persons who are then in spectre present. It is further considerable, that once or twice, these apparitions have been seen by others at the very same time that they have shewn themselves to the bewitched; and seldom have there been these apparitions but when something unusual and suspected had attended the death of the party thus appearing. Some that have been accused by these apparitions, accosting of the bewitched people, who had never heard a word of any such persons ever being in the world, have upon a fair examination freely and fully confessed the murders of those very persons, although these also did not know how the apparitions had complained of them. Accordingly several of the bewitched had given in their testimony, that they had been troubled with the apparitions of two women, who said that they were G. B.'s two wives, and that he had been the death of them; and that the magistrates must be told of it, before whom if B. upon his trial denied it, they did not know but that they should appear again in the court. Now, G. B. had been infamous for the barbarous usage of his two successive wives, all the country over. Moreover, it was testified, the spectre of G. B. threatening of the sufferers told them, he had killed (besides others) Mrs. Lawson and her daughter Ann. And it was noted, that these were the virtuous wife and daughter of one at whom this G. B. might have a prejudice for his being serviceable at Salem Village, from whence himself had in ill terms removed some years before: and that when they died, which was long since, there were some odd circumstances about them, which made some of the attendants there suspect something of witchcraft, though none imagined from what quarter it should come.

Well, G. B. being now upon his trial, one of the bewitched persons was cast into horror at the ghosts of B.'s two deceased wives then appearing before him, and crying for vengeance against him. Hereupon several of the bewitched persons were successively called in, who all not knowing what the former had seen and said, concurred in their horror of the apparition, which they affirmed that he had before him. But he, though much appalled, utterly denied that he discerned anything of it; nor was it any part of his conviction.

IV. Judicious writers have assigned it a great place in the conviction of witches, when persons are impeached by other notorious witches, to be as ill as themselves; especially, if the persons have been much noted for neglecting the worship of God. Now, as there might have been testimonies enough of G. B.'s antipathy to prayer and the other ordinances of God, though by his profession singularly obliged thereunto; so, there now came in against the prisoner the testimonies of several persons, who confessed their own having been horrible witches, and ever since their confessions had been themselves terribly tortured by the divels and other witches, even like the other sufferers; and therein undergone the pains of many deaths for their confessions.

These now testified, that G. B. had been at witch meetings with them, and that he was the person who had seduced and compelled them into the snares of witchcraft: that he promised them fine clothes, for doing it; that he brought puppets to them, and thorns to stick into those puppets, for the afflicting of other people; and that he exhorted them, with the rest of the crew, to bewitch all Salem Village, but be sure to do it gradually, if they would prevail in what they did.

When the Lancashire witches were condemned, I don't remember that there was any considerable further evidence, than that of the bewitched, and than that of some that confessed. We see so much already against G. B. But this being indeed not enough, there were other things to render what had already been produced credible.

V. A famous divine recites this among the convictions of a witch; the testimony of the party bewitched, whether pining or dying; together with the joint oaths of sufficient persons that have seen certain prodigious pranks or feats wrought by the party accused. Now God had been pleased so to leave this G. B. that he had ensnared himself by several instances, which he had formerly given of a preternatural strength, and which were now produced against him. He was a very puny man; yet he had often done things beyond the strength of a giant. A gun of about seven foot barrel, and so heavy that strong men could not steadily hold it out with both hands; there were several testimonies, given in by persons of credit and honor, that he made nothing of taking up such a gun behind the lock, with but one hand, and holding it out like a pistol, at arm's end. G. B. in his vindication was so foolish as to say, that an Indian was there, and held it out at the same time: whereas, none of the spectators ever saw any such Indian; but they supposed the Black Man (as the witches call the Divel; and they generally say he resembles an Indian) might give him that assistance. There was evidence likewise brought in, that he made nothing of taking up whole barrels filled with molasses or cider, in very disadvantageous postures, and carrying of them through the difficultest places out of a canoe to the shore.

Yea, there were two testimonies that G. B. with only putting the forefinger of his right hand into the muzzle of an heavy gun, a fowling-piece of about six or seven foot barrel, did lift up the gun, and hold it out at arm's end; a gun which the deponents though strong men could not with both hands lift up, and hold out at the butt end, as is usual. Indeed, one of these witnesses was over persuaded by some persons to be out of the way upon G. B.'s trial; but he came afterwards with sorrow for his withdraw, and gave in his testimony: nor were either of these witnesses made use of as evidences in the trial.

VI. There came in several testimonies relating to the domestic affairs of G. B. which had a very hard aspect upon him; and not only proved him a very ill man; but also confirmed the belief of the character, which had been already fastened on him.

'Twas testified, that keeping his two successive wives in a strange kind of slavery, he would when he came home from abroad pretend to tell the talk which any had with them; that he has brought them to the point of death, by his harsh dealings with his wives, and then made the people about him to promise that in case death should happen, they would say nothing of it; that he used all means to make his wives write, sign, seal, and swear a covenant, never to reveal any of his secrets; that his wives had privately complained unto the neighbors about frightful apparitions of evil spirits, with which their house was sometimes infested; and that many such things have been whispered among the neighborhood. There were also some other testimonies, relating to the death of people, whereby the consciences of an impartial jury were convinced that G. B. had bewitched the persons mentioned in the complaints. But I am forced to omit several passages, in this, as well as in all the succeeding trials, because the scribes who took notice of them, have not supplied me.

VII. One Mr. Ruck, brother-in-law to this G. B., testified, that G. B. and he himself, and his sister, who was G. B.'s wife, going out for two or three miles to gather strawberries, Ruck with his sister the wife of G. B. rode home very softly, with G. B. on foot in their company. G. B. stepped aside a little into the bushes; whereupon they halted and hallooed for him. He not answering, they went away homewards, with a quickened pace, without any expectation of seeing him in a considerable while; and yet when they were got near home, to their astonishment they found him on foot with them, having a basket of strawberries. G. B. immediately then fell to chiding his wife, on the account of what she had been speaking to her brother, of him, on the road: which when they wondered at, he said, he knew their thoughts. Ruck being startled at that, made some reply, intimating that the Divel himself did not know so far; but G. B. answered, "My God makes known your thoughts unto me." The prisoner now at the bar had nothing to answer unto what was thus witnessed against him, that was worth considering. Only he said, Ruck and his wife left a man with him, when they left him. Which Ruck now affirmed to be false; and when the court asked G. B. what the man's name was? his countenance was much altered; nor could he say, who 'twas. But the court began to think, that he then stepped aside, only that by the assistance of the Black Man, he might put on his invisibility, and in that fascinating mist, gratify his own jealous humour, to hear what they said of him. Which trick of rend'ring themselves invisible, our witches do in their confessions pretend that they sometimes are masters of; and it is the more credible, because there is demonstration that they often render many other things utterly invisible.

VIII. Falt'ring, faulty, unconstant, and contrary answers upon judicial and deliberate examination, are counted some unlucky symptoms of guilt, in all crimes, especially in witchcrafts. Now there never was a prisoner more eminent for them, than G. B. both at his examination and on his trial. His tergiversations, contradictions, and falsehoods were very sensible: he had little to say, but that he had heard some things that he could not prove, reflecting upon the reputation of some of the witnesses. Only he gave in a paper to the jury; wherein, although he had many times before granted, not only that there are witches, but also that the present sufferings of the country are the effect of horrible witchcrafts, yet he now goes to evince it, that there neither are, nor ever were witches, that having made a compact with the Divel, can send a divel to torment other people at a distance. This paper was transcribed out of Ady, which the court presently knew, as soon as they heard it. But he said, he had taken none of it out of any book; for which, his evasion afterwards was, that a gentleman gave him the discourse in a manuscript, from whence he transcribed it.

IX. The jury brought him in guilty. But when he came to die, he utterly denied the fact, whereof he had been thus convicted.

1692

FROM

Magnalia Christi Americana

[The Life of William Bradford]

Omnium somnos illius vigilantia defendit, omnium otium illius labor, omnium delicias illius industria, omnium vacationem illius occupatio. [His vigilance protects everyone's sleep, his labor everyone's rest, his industry everyone's enjoyment, and his effort everyone's leisure.]

It has been a matter of some observation that, although Yorkshire be one of the largest shires in England, yet for all the fires of martyrdom which were kindled in the days of Queen Mary, it afforded no more fuel than one poor leaf; namely, John Leaf, an apprentice, who suffered for the doctrine of the Reformation at the same time and stake with the famous John Bradford. But when the reign of Queen Elizabeth would not admit the reformation of worship to proceed unto those degrees which were proposed and pursued by no small number of the faithful in those days, Yorkshire was not the least of the shires in England that afforded suffering witnesses thereunto. The churches there gathered were quickly molested with such a raging persecution that if the spirit of separation in them did carry them unto a further extreme than it should have done, one blamable cause thereof will be found in the extremity of that persecution. Their troubles made that cold country too hot for them, so that they were under a necessity to seek a retreat in the Low Countries; and yet the watchful malice and fury of their adversaries rendered it almost impossible for them to find what they sought. For them to leave their native soil, their lands, and their friends, and go into a strange place where they must hear foreign language and live meanly and hardly and in other employments than that of husbandry wherein they had been educated, these must needs have been such discouragements as could have been conquered by none save those who sought first the kingdom of God and the righteousness thereof. But that which would have made these discouragements the more unconquerable unto an ordinary faith was the terrible zeal of their enemies to guard all ports and search all ships, that none of them should be carried off. I will not relate the sad things of this kind then seen and felt by this people of God, but only exemplify those trials with one short story. Divers of this people having hired a Dutchman then lying at Hull to carry them over to Holland, he promised faithfully to take them in between Grimsby and Hull; but they coming to the place a day or two too soon, the appearance of such a multitude alarmed the officers of the town adjoining, who came with a great body of soldiers to seize upon them. Now it happened that one boat full of men had been carried aboard, while the women were yet in a bark that lay aground in a creek at low water. The Dutchman, perceiving the storm that was thus beginning ashore, swore by the sacrament that he would stay no longer for any of them; and so taking the advantage of a fair wind then blowing, he put out to sea for Zealand. The women thus left near Grimsby Common, bereaved of their husbands who had been hurried from them, and forsaken of their neighbors, of whom none durst in this fright stay with them, were a very rueful spectacle; some crying for fear, some shaking for cold, all dragged by troops of armed and angry men from one justice to another, till not knowing what to do with them they e'en dismissed them to shift as well as they could for themselves. But by their singular afflictions, and by their Christian behaviors, the cause for which they exposed themselves did gain considerably. In the meantime, the men at sea found reason to be glad that their families were not with them, for they were surprised with an horrible tempest which held them for fourteen days together, in seven whereof they saw not sun, moon, or star, but were driven upon the coast of Norway. The mariners often despaired of life, and once with doleful shrieks gave over all, as thinking the vessel was foundered; but the vessel rose again, and when the mariners with sunk hearts often cried out, "We sink! We sink!" the passengers without such distraction of mind, even while the water was running into their mouths and ears, would cheerfully shout, "Yet, Lord, Thou canst save! Yet, Lord Thou canst save!" And the Lord accordingly brought them at last safe unto their desired haven and not long after helped their distressed relations thither after them, where indeed they found upon almost all accounts a new world, but a world in which they found that they must live like strangers and pilgrims.

Among those devout people was our William Bradford, who was born Anno 1588 in an obscure village called Austerfield, where the people were as unacquainted with the Bible as the Jews do seem to have been with part of it in the days of Josiah; a most ignorant and licentious people, and like unto their priest. Here, and in some other places, he had a comfortable inheritance left him of his honest parents, who died while he was yet a child, and cast him on the education, first of his grandparents, and then of his uncles, who devoted him, like his ancestors, unto the affairs of husbandry. Soon a long sickness kept him as he would afterwards thankfully say, from the vanities of youth, and made him the fitter for what he was afterwards to undergo. When he was about a dozen years old, the reading of the Scriptures began to cause great impressions upon him, and those impressions were much assisted and improved when he came to enjoy Mr. Richard Clifton's illuminating ministry, not far from his abode; he was then also further befriended by being brought into the company and fellowship of such as were then called professors [i.e., of religious faith], though the young man that brought him into it did after become a profane and wicked apostate. Nor could the wrath of his uncles nor the scoff of his neighbors, now curned upon him as one of the Puritans, divert him from his pious inclinations.

At last beholding how fearfully the evangelical and apostolical church form, whereinto the churches of the primitive times were cast by the good spirit of God, had been deformed by the apostasy of the succeeding times, and what little progress the Reformation had yet made in many parts of Christendom towards its recovery, he set himself by reading, by discourse, by prayer, to learn whether it was not his duty to withdraw from the communion of the parish assemblies and engage with some society of the faithful that should keep close unto the written word of God as the rule of their worship. And after many distresses of mind concerning it, he took up a very deliberate and understanding resolution of doing so, which resolution he cheerfully prosecuted, although the provoked rage of his friends tried all the ways imaginable to reclaim him from it; unto all whom his answer was: "Were I like to endanger my life or consume my estate by any ungodly courses, your counsels to me were very seasonable; but you know that I have been diligent and provident in my calling, and not only desirous to augment what I have, but also to enjoy it in your company, to part from which will be as great a cross as can befall me. Nevertheless, to keep a good conscience, and walk in such a way as God has prescribed in His Word, is a thing which I must prefer before you all, and above life itself. Wherefore, since 'tis for a good cause that I am like to suffer the disasters which you lay before me, you have no cause to be either angry with me or sorry for me; yea, I am not only willing to part with every thing that is dear to me in this world for this cause, but I am also thankful that God has given me an heart so to do, and will accept me so to suffer for Him." Some lamented him, some derided him, all dissuaded him; nevertheless the more they did it, the more fixed he was in his purpose to seek the ordinances of the Gospel where they should be dispensed with most of the commanded purity. And the sudden deaths of the chief relations which thus lay at him quickly after convinced him what a folly it had been to have quitted his profession in expectation of any satisfaction from them. So to Holland he attempted a removal.

Having with a great company of Christians hired a ship to transport them for Holland, the master perfidiously betrayed them into the hands of those persecutors who rifled and ransacked their goods and clapped their persons into prison at Boston [England], where they lay for a month together. But Mr. Bradford, being a young man of about eighteen, was dismissed sooner than the rest, so that within a while he had opportunity with some others to get over to Zealand, through perils both by land and sea not inconsiderable; where he was not long ashore ere a viper seized on his hand, that is, an officer, who carried him unto the magistrates, unto whom an envious passenger had accused him as having fled out of England. When the magistrates understood the true cause of his coming thither, they were well satisfied with him; and so he repaired joyfully unto his brethren at Amsterdam, where the difficulties to which he afterwards stooped in learning and serving of a Frenchman at the working of silks were abundantly compensated by the delight wherewith he sat under the shadow of our Lord in His purely dispensed ordinances. At the end of two years, he did, being of age to do it, convert his estate in England into money; but setting up for himself, he found some of his designs by the providence of God frowned upon, which he judged a correction bestowed by God upon him for certain decays of internal piety, whereinto he had fallen. The consumption of his estate he thought came to prevent a consumption in his virtue. But after he had resided in Holland about half a score years, he was one of those who bore a part in that hazardous and generous enterprise of removing into New England, with part of the English church at Leyden, where at their first landing his dearest consort, accidentally falling overboard, was drowned in the harbor; and the rest of his days were spent in the services and the temptations of that American wilderness.

Here was Mr. Bradford in the year 1621, unanimously chosen the governor of the plantation, the difficulties whereof were such that, if he had not been a person of more than ordinary piety, wisdom and courage, he must have sunk under them. He had with a laudable industry been laying up a treasure of experiences, and he had now occasion to use it; indeed, nothing but an experienced man could have been suitable to the necessities of the people.

The potent nations of the Indians, into whose country they were come, would have cut them off if the blessing of God upon his conduct had not quelled them; and if his prudence, justice, and moderation had not overruled them, they had been ruined by their own distempers. One specimen of his demeanor is to this day particularly spoken of. A company of young fellows that were newly arrived were very unwilling to comply with the Governor's order for working abroad on the public account; and therefore on Christmas Day, when he had called upon them, they excused themselves with a pretense that it was against their conscience to work such a day. The Governor gave them no answer, only that he would spare them till they were better informed; but by and by he found them all at play in the street, sporting themselves with various diversions; whereupon, commanding the instruments of their games to be taken from them, he effectually gave them to understand that it was against his conscience that they should play whilst others were at work, and that if they had any devotion to the day, they should show it at home in the exercises of religion, and not in the streets with pastime and frolics; and this gentle reproof put a final stop to all such disorders for the future.

For two years together after the beginning of the colony, whereof he was now governor, the poor people had a great experiment of man's not living by bread alone; for when they were left all together without one morsel of bread for many months one after another, still the good providence of God relieved them and supplied them, and this for the most part out of the sea. In this low condition of affairs, there was no little exercise for the prudence and patience of the Governor, who cheerfully bore his part in all; and, that industry might not flag, he quickly set himself to settle property among the new planters, foreseeing that while the whole country labored upon a common stock, the husbandry and business of the plantation could not flourish, as Plato and others long since dreamed that it would if a community were established. Certainly, if the spirit which dwelt in the old Puritans had not inspired these new planters, they had sunk under the burden of these difficulties; but our Bradford had a double portion of that spirit.

The plantation was quickly thrown into a storm that almost overwhelmed it by the unhappy actions of a minis-

ter sent over from England by the adventurers concerned
for the plantation; but by the blessing of Heaven on the
conduct of the Governor, they weathered out that storm.
Only the adventurers [the English underwriters], hereupon
breaking to pieces, threw up all their concernments with the
infant colony; whereof they gave this as one reason, that the
planters dissembled with his majesty and their friends in
their petition wherein they declared for a church discipline
agreeing with the French and others of the reforming
churches in Europe; whereas 'twas now urged that they
had admitted into their communion a person who at his
admission utterly renounced the churches of England
(which person, by the way, was that very man who had
made the complaints against them); and therefore, though
they denied the names of Brownists, yet they were the thing
[i.e., Congregationalists]. In answer hereunto, the very
words written by the Governor were these: "Whereas you
tax us with dissembling about the French discipline, you
do us wrong, for we both hold and practice the discipline
of the French and other reformed churches (as they have
published the same in the harmony of confessions) according to our means, in effect and substance. But whereas you
would tie us up to the French discipline in every circumstance, you derogate from the liberty we have in Christ
Jesus. The Apostle Paul would have none to follow him
in any thing but wherein he follows Christ; much less ought
any Christian or church in the world to do it. The French
may err, we may err, and other churches may err, and
doubtless do in many circumstances. That honor therefore
belongs only to the infallible Word of God and pure Testament of Christ, to be propounded and followed as the
only rule and pattern for direction herein to all churches
and Christians. And it is too great arrogancy for any men
or church to think that he or they have so sounded the
Word of God unto the bottom as precisely to set down the
churches' discipline without error in substance or circumstance, that no other without blame may digress or differ
in any thing from the same. And it is not difficult to show
that the reformed churches differ in many circumstances
among themselves." By which words it appears how far
he was free from that rigid spirit of separation which broke
to pieces the Separatists themselves in the Low Countries,
unto the great scandal of the reforming churches. He was

indeed a person of a well-tempered spirit; or else it had
been scarce possible for him to have kept the affairs of
Plymouth in so good a temper for thirty-seven years together, in every one of which he was chosen their governor
except the three years wherein Mr. Winslow, and the two
years wherein Mr. Prince, at the choice of the people, took
a turn with him.

The leader of a people in a wilderness had need be a
Moses; and if a Moses had not led the people of Plymouth
colony when this worthy person was their governor, the
people had never with so much unanimity and importunity
still called him to lead them. Among many instances
thereof, let this one piece of self-denial be told for a memorial of him, wheresoever this history shall be considered.
The patent of the colony was taken in his name, running
in these terms: "To William Bradford, his heirs, associates
and assigns"; but when the number of the freemen was
much increased and many new townships erected, the
general court there desired of Mr. Bradford that he would
make a surrender of the same into their hands, which he
willingly and presently assented unto, and confirmed it
according to their desire by his hand and seal, reserving no
more for himself than was his proportion, with others, by
agreement. But as he found the providence of Heaven many
ways recompensing his many acts of self-denial, so he
gave this testimony to the faithfulness of the divine promises: that he had forsaken friends, houses, and lands for
the sake of the gospel, and the Lord gave them him again.
Here he prospered in his estate; and besides a worthy son
which he had by a former wife, he had also two sons and
a daughter by another, whom he married in this land.

He was a person for study as well as action; and hence,
notwithstanding the difficulties through which he passed in
his youth, he attained unto a notable skill in languages; the
Dutch tongue was become almost as vernacular to him as
the English; the French tongue he could also manage; the
Latin and the Greek he had mastered; but the Hebrew he
most of all studied, because, he said, he would see with
his own eyes the ancient oracles of God in their native
beauty. He was also well skilled in history, in antiquity,
and in philosophy; and for theology he became so versed
in it that he was an irrefragable disputant against the errors,
especially those of Anabaptism, which with trouble he saw

rising in his colony; wherefore he wrote some significant things for the confutation of those errors. But the crown of all was his holy, prayerful, watchful and fruitful walk with God, wherein he was very exemplary.

At length he fell into an indisposition of body which rendered him unhealthy for a whole winter; and as the spring advanced, his health declined; yet he felt himself not what he counted sick, till one day; in the night after which, the God of Heaven so filled his mind with ineffable consolations that he seemed little short of Paul, rapt up unto the unutterable entertainments of paradise. The next morning he told his friends that the good spirit of God had given him a pledge of his happiness in another world, and the first fruits of his eternal glory; and on the day following he died, May 9, 1657, in the sixty-ninth year of his age, lamented by all the colonies of New England as a common blessing and father to them all.

1702

FROM

Manuductio ad Ministerium

[Poetic Style]

Poetry, whereof we have now even an antediluvian piece in our hands, has from the beginning been in such request that I must needs recommend unto you some acquaintance with it. Though some have had a soul so unmusical that they have decried all verse as being but a mere playing and fiddling upon words, all versifying as if it were more unnatural than if we should choose dancing instead of walking, and rhyme as if it were but a sort of Morisco dancing with bells, yet I cannot wish you a soul that shall be wholly unpoetical. An old Horace has left us an *Art of Poetry,* which you may do well to bestow a perusal on. And besides your lyric hours, I wish you may so far understand an epic poem that the beauties of an Homer and a Virgil may be discerned with you. As to the moral part of Homer, 'tis true, and let me not be counted a Zoilus for saying so, that by first exhibiting their gods as no better than rogues he set open the floodgates for a prodigious inundation of wickedness to break in upon the nations, and was one of the greatest apostles the devil ever had in the world. Among the rest that felt the ill impressions of this universal corrupter (as men of the best sentiments have called him), one was that overgrown robber of execrable memory whom we celebrate under the name of Alexander the Great, who by his continual admiring and studying of the *Iliad*, and by following that false model of heroic virtue set before him in his Achilles, became one of the worst of men, and at length, inflated with the ridiculous pride of being himself a deity, exposed himself to all the scorn that could belong unto a lunatic. And hence, notwithstanding the veneration which this idol has had, yet Plato banishes him out of a commonwealth, the welfare whereof he was concerned for. Nevertheless, custom or conscience obliges him to bear testimonies unto many points of morality. And it is especially observable that he commonly propounds prayer to Heaven as a most necessary preface unto all important enterprises; and when the action comes on too suddenly for a more extended supplication, he yet will not let it come on without an ejaculation; and he never speaks of any supplication but he brings in a gracious answer to it. I have seen a travesteering high-flyer, not much to our dishonor, scoff at Homer for this, as making his actors to be like those whom the English call Dissenters. But then, we are so much led into the knowledge of antiquities by reading of this poet, and into so many parts of the recondite learning, that notwithstanding some little nods in him, not a few acute pens besides the old bishop of Thessalonica's have got a reputation by regaining us with annotations upon him. Yea, though one can't but smile at the fancy of Croese, who tries with much ostentation of erudition to show that Homer has all along tendered us in a disguise and fable the history of the Old Testament, yet many illustrations of the sacred scriptures I find are to be fetched from him; who indeed had probably read what was extant of them in his days; particularly, our Eighteenth Psalm is what he has evidently imitated. Virgil too, who so much lived upon him, as well as after him, is unaccountably mad upon his fate, which he makes to be he knows not what himself, but superior to gods as well as to men; and through his whole composures he so asserts the doctrine of this nonsensical power as is plainly inconsistent

with all virtue. And what fatal mischief did Fascinator do
to the Roman Empire when, by deifying one great emperor, he taught the successors to claim the adoration of
gods while they were perpetrating the crimes of devils?
I will not be a Carbilius upon him; nor will I say any
thing, how little the married state owes unto one who
writes as if he were a woman-hater; nor what his blunders
are about his poor-spirited and inconsistent hero, for which
many have taxed him. Nevertheless 'tis observed that the
pagans had no rules of manners that were more laudable
and regular than what are to be found in him. And some
have said it is hardly possible seriously to read his works
without being more disposed unto goodness, as well as
being agreeably entertained. Be sure, had Virgil writ before
Plato, his works had not been any of the books prohibited.
But then, this poet also has abundance of rare antiquities
for us, and such things as others besides a Servius have
imagined that they have instructed and obliged mankind
by employing all their days upon. Wherefore if his *Æneid,*
which though it were once near twenty times as big as
he has left it, yet he has left it unfinished, may not appear
so valuable to you that you may think twenty-seven verses
of the part that is the most finished in it worth one-and-
twenty hundred pounds and odd money; yet his *Georgics,*
which he put his last hand unto, will furnish you with
many things far from despicable. But after all, when I said
I was willing that the beauties of these two poets might
become visible to your visive faculty in poetry, I did not
mean that you should judge nothing to be admittable into
an epic poem which is not authorized by their example; but
I perfectly concur with one who is inexpressibly more
capable to be a judge of such a matter than I can be, that
it is a false critic who with a petulant air will insult reason
itself if it presumes to oppose such authority.

I proceed now to say that if (under the guidance of a
Vida) you try your young wings now and then to see what
flights you can make, at least for an epigram, it may a little
sharpen your sense and polish your style for more important performances; for this purpose you are now even
overstocked with patterns, and *poemata passim.* You may,
like Nazianzen, all your days make a little recreation of
poetry in the midst of your more painful studies. Nevertheless, I cannot but advise you, "Withhold thy throat from

thirst." Be not so set upon poetry as to be always poring on the passionate and measured pages. Let not what should be sauce rather than food for you engross all your application. Beware of a boundless and sickly appetite for the reading of the poems, which now the rickety nation swarms withal; and let not the Circean cup intoxicate you. But especially preserve the chastity of your soul from the dangers you may incur by a conversation with muses that are no better than harlots, among which are others besides Ovid's *Epistles,* which for their tendency to excite and foment impure flames and cast coals into your bosom deserve rather to be thrown into the fire than to be laid before the eye which a covenant should be made withal. Indeed, not merely for the impurities which they convey, but also on some other accounts, the powers of darkness have a library among us, whereof the poets have been the most numerous as well as the most venomous authors. Most of the modern plays, as well as the romances and novels and fictions, which are a sort of poems, do belong to the catalogue of this cursed library. The plays, I say, in which there are so many passages that have a tendency to overthrow all piety, that one whose name is Bedford has extracted near seven thousand instances of them from the plays chiefly of but five years preceding, and says awfully upon them, "They are national sins, and therefore call for national plagues; and if God should enter into judgment, all the blood in the nation would not be able to atone for them." How much do I wish that such pestilences, and indeed all those worse than Egyptian toads (the spawns of a Butler, and a Brown, and a Ward, and a company whose name is legion!) might never crawl into your chamber! The unclean spirits that come like frogs out of the mouth of the dragon, and of the beast; which go forth unto the young people of the earth, and expose them to be dealt withal as the enemies of God, in the battle of the Great Day of the Almighty. As for those wretched scribbles of madmen, my son, touch them not, taste them not, handle them not; thou wilt perish in the using of them. They are the dragons whose contagious breath peoples the dark retreats of death. To much better purpose will an excellent but an envied Blackmore feast you than those vile rhapsodies (of that *vinum dæmonium*) [wine of the devil] which you will find always leave a taint upon your mind, and among other ill effects will sensibly indispose you to converse with the holy oracles of God your Saviour.

But there is what I may rather call a parenthesis than a digression, which this may be not altogether an improper place for the introducing of.

There has been a deal of ado about a style, so much that I must offer you my sentiments upon it. There is a way of writing wherein the author endeavors that the reader may have something to the purpose in every paragraph. There is not only a vigor sensible in every sentence, but the paragraph is embellished with profitable references even to something beyond what is directly spoken. Formal and painful quotations are not studied; yet all that could be learnt from them is insinuated. The writer pretends not unto reading, yet he could not have writ as he does if he had not read very much in his time; and his composures are not only a cloth of gold, but also stuck with as many jewels, as the gown of a Russian ambassador. This way of writing has been decried by many, and is at this day more than ever so, for the same reason that in the old story the grapes were decried, that they were not ripe. A lazy, ignorant, conceited set of authors would persuade the whole tribe to lay aside that way of writing, for the same reason that one would have persuaded his brethren to part with the encumbrance of their bushy tails. But however fashion and humor may prevail, they must not think that the club at their coffeehouse is all the world; but there will always be those who will in this case be governed by indisputable reason, and who will think that the real excellency of a book will never lie in saying of little; that the less one has for his money in a book, 'tis really the more valuable for it; and that the less one is instructed in a book, and the more of superfluous margin and superficial harangue, and the less of substantial matter one has in it, the more 'tis to be accounted of. And if a more massy way of writing be never so much disgusted at this day, a better gust will come on, as will some other thing, *quae iam cecidere*. In the meantime, nothing appears to me more impertinent and ridiculous than the modern way (I cannot say rule, for they have none!) of criticizing. The blades that set up for critics, I know not who constituted or commissioned 'em: they appear to me for the most part as contemptible as they are a supercilious generation. For indeed no two of them have the same style; and they are as intolerably cross-grained and severe in their censures upon one another as they are upon the rest of mankind. But while each of them, conceitedly enough, sets up for the standard of perfection, we are entirely at a loss which fire to follow. Nor can you easily find any one thing wherein they agree for their style, except perhaps a perpetual care to give us jejune and empty pages, without such touches of erudition (to speak in the style of an ingenious traveller) as may make the discourses less tedious and more enriching to the mind of him that peruses them. There is much talk of a florid style obtaining among the pens that are most in vogue; but how often would it puzzle one, even with the best glasses, to find the flowers! And if they were to be chastised for it, it would be with as much of justice as Jerome was for being a Ciceronian. After all, every man will have his own style, which will distinguish him as much as his gait; and if you can attain to that which I have newly described, but always writing so as to give an easy conveyance unto your ideas, I would not have you by any scourging be driven out of your gait; but if you must confess a fault in it, make a confession like that of the lad unto his father while he was beating him for his versifying.

However, since every man will have his own style, I would pray that we may learn to treat one another with mutual civilities and condescensions, and handsomely indulge one another in this, as gentlemen do in other matters.

I wonder what ails people, that they can't let Cicero write in the style of Cicero, and Seneca write in the (much other!) style of Seneca, and own that both may please in their several ways.

1726

ROBERT CALEF

(1648–1719)

Robert Calef, a hard-headed cloth merchant who settled in Boston in 1688, was an oasis of sanity during the witchcraft delusions in the 1690's. While the Mathers and other convinced members of the theocracy were pursuing the "witches" during the height of the panic in 1692, Calef was calmly assembling the materials for his attack on the proceedings. These he had published in London in 1700 under the ironic title *More Wonders of the Invisible World*, which accused ministers such as the Mathers of committing murder under the guise of Christianity. In 1694, Calef was a skeptical observer of Cotton Mather's exorcism of the supposedly possessed Margaret Rule. Afraid that Mather would stir up still another public disaster by such carryings-on, he circulated in manuscript an account of the procedure which implied that sexuality rather than morality was at the bottom of the affair. (Margaret found being stroked across the face and naked breast by Mather very soothing.) For this he was arraigned for libel, but the case was dismissed. The following year he attacked Cotton's father, Increase, for suggesting that ministers collect examples of the power of the invisible world. When Calef's book appeared in 1700, Cotton wrote a slashing rejoinder—*Some Few Remarks upon a Scandalous Book* (1701)—and Increase (so the story goes) had it burned in Harvard Yard. Neither response had much effect on its circulation.

Accounts of the man and his work are to be found in George L. Burr, *The Literature of Witchcraft* (1890); George L. Burr, *Narratives of the Witchcraft Cases, 1648–1706* (1914); W. S. Nevins, *Witchcraft in Salem Village in 1692* (1916); Thomas Hutchinson, *History of the Colony and Province of Massachusetts*, L. S. Mayo, ed. (1936); and M. L. Starkey, *The Devil in Massachusetts* (1949).

FROM

More Wonders of the Invisible World

[George Burroughs and Mr. Mather]

The 30th of June, the court according to adjournment again sat; five more were tried, viz., Sarah Good and Rebecca Nurse of Salem Village, Susanna Martin of Amsbury, Elizabeth How of Ipswich, and Sarah Wildes of Topsfield; these were all condemned that sessions, and were all executed on the 19th of July.

At the trial of Sarah Good, one of the afflicted fell in a fit, and after coming out of it, she cried out of the prisoner, for stabbing her in the breast with a knife, and that she had broken the knife in stabbing of her; accordingly a piece of the blade of a knife was found about her. Immediately information being given to the court, a young man was called, who produced a haft and part of the blade, which the court having viewed and compared, saw it to be the same. And upon inquiry the young man affirmed, that yesterday he happened to break that knife, and that he cast away the upper part, this afflicted person being then present. The young man was dismissed, and she was bidden by the court not to tell lies; and was improved (after as she had been before) to give evidence against the prisoners.

At execution, Mr. Noyes urged Sarah Good to confess, and told her she was a witch, and she knew she was a witch, to which she replied, "You are a liar; I am no more a witch than you are a wizard, and if you take away my life, God will give you blood to drink." . . .

August 5. The court again sitting, six more were tried on the same account, viz., Mr. George Burroughs, sometime minister of Wells, John Proctor, and Elizabeth Proctor his wife, with John Willard of Salem Village, George Jacobs, Senior, of Salem, and Martha Carrier of Andover; these were all brought in guilty, and condemned; and were all executed, August 19, except Proctor's wife, who pleaded pregnancy.

Mr. Burroughs was carried in a cart with the others, through the streets of Salem to execution; when he was upon the ladder, he made a speech for the clearing of his innocency, with such solemn and serious expressions, as were to the admiration of all present; his prayer (which he concluded by repeating the Lord's prayer) was so well worded, and uttered with such composedness, and such (at least seeming) fervency of spirit, as was very affecting, and drew tears from many (so that it seemed to some that the spectators would hinder the execution). The accusers said the Black Man stood and dictated to him; as soon as he was turned off, Mr. Cotton Mather, being mounted upon a horse, addressed himself to the people, partly to declare that he was no ordained minister, and partly to possess the people of his guilt; saying, that the Devil has often been transformed into an angel of light; and this did somewhat appease the people, and the executions went on; when he was cut down, he was dragged by the halter to a hole, or grave, between the rocks, about two foot deep, his shirt and breeches being pulled off, and an old pair of trowsers of one executed, put on his lower parts, he was so put in, together with Willard and Carrier, one of his hands and his chin, and a foot of one of them being left uncovered. . . .

And now nineteen persons having been hanged, and one prest to death, and eight more condemned, in all twenty and eight, of which above a third part were members of some of the churches in New England, and more than half of them of a good conversation in general, and not one cleared; about fifty having confessed themselves to be witches, of which not one executed; above an hundred and fifty in prison, and above two hundred more accused; the special commission of oyer and terminer comes to a period, which has no other foundation than the governor's commission; and had proceeded in the manner of swearing witnesses, viz., by holding up the hand (and by receiving evidences in writing), according to the ancient usage of this country; as also having their indictments in English. In the trials, when any were indicted for afflicting, pining, and wasting the bodies of particular persons by witchcraft, it was usual to hear evidence of matter foreign, and of perhaps twenty or thirty years standing, about oversetting carts, the death of cattle, unkindness to relations, or unexpected accidents befalling after some quarrel. Whether this was admitted by the law of England, or by what other law, wants to be determined; the executions seemed mixed, in pressing to death for not pleading, which most agrees with the laws of England, and sentencing women to be hanged for witchcraft, according to the former practice of this country, and not by burning, as is said to have been the law of England. And though the confessing witches were many, yet not one of them that confessed their own guilt, and abode by their confession, were put to death.

.   .   .

[Witchcraft and the Theocracy]

In the times of Sir Edmond Andros's government, Goody Glover, a despised, crazy, ill-conditioned old woman, an Irish Roman Catholic, was tried for afflicting Goodwin's children; by the account of which trial, taken in shorthand for the use of the jury, it may appear that the generality of her answers were nonsense, and her behavior like that of one distracted. Yet the doctors, finding her as she had been for many years, brought her in *compos mentis;* and setting aside her crazy answers to some ensnaring questions, the proof against her was wholly deficient. The jury brought her in guilty.

Mr. Cotton Mather was the most active and forward of any minister in the country in those matters, taking home one of the children, and managing such intrigues with that child, and printing such an account of the whole in his *Memorable Providences,* as conduced much to the kindling of those flames, that in Sir William's time threatened the destruction of this country.

King Saul in destroying the witches out of Israel is thought by many to have exceeded, and in his zeal to have slain the Gibeonites wrongfully under that notion; yet went after this to a witch to know his fortune. For his wrongfully destroying the Gibeonites (besides the judgments of God upon the land) his sons were hanged; and for his going to the witch, himself was cut off. Our Sir William Phips did not do this; but, as appears by this book, had first his fortune told him, (by such as the author counts no better) and though he put it off (to his pastor, who he knew approved not thereof) as if it were brought to him in writing, without his seeking, &c. yet by his bringing it so far, and safe keeping it so many years, it appears he made some account for it; for which he gave the writer, after he had found the wreck, as a reward, more than two hundred pounds. His telling his wife, that he should be a commander, should have a brick house in Greenlane, &c. might be in confidence of some such prediction; and that he could foretell to him that he should be governor of New England, was probably such an one, the scriptures not having revealed it. Such predictions would have been counted, at Salem, pregnant proofs of witchcraft, and much better than what were against several that suffered there. But Sir William, when the witchcrafts at Salem began (in his esteem) to look formidable, that he might act safely in this affair, asked the advice of the ministers in and near Boston. The whole of their advice and answer is printed in *Cases of Conscience,* the last pages. But lest the world should be ignorant who it was that drew the said advice, in this book of the life of Sir William Phips, are these words, *The ministers made to his excellency and the council a return, drawn up at their desire, by Mr. Mather the younger, as I have been informed.* Mr. C. M. therein intending to beguile the world, and make them think that another, and not himself, had taken that notice of his (supposed) good service done therein, which otherwise would have been ascribed to those ministers in general; though indeed the advice then given looks most like a thing of his composing, as carrying both fire to increase, and water to quench, the conflagration; particularly after the devil's testimony, by the supposed afflicted, had so prevailed, as to take away the life of one, and the liberty of an hundred, and the whole country set into a most dreadful consternation, then this advice is given, ushered in with thanks for what was already done, and in conclusion putting the government upon a speedy and vigorous prosecution, according to the laws of God, and the wholesome statutes of the English nation; so adding oil, rather than water, to the flame: for who so little acquainted with the proceedings of England, as not to know that they have taken some methods, with those here used, to discover who were witches? The rest of the advice, consisting of cautions and directions, is inserted in this book of the life of Sir William: so that if Sir William, looking upon the thanks for what was past, and exhortation to proceed, went on to take away the lives of nineteen more, this is according to the advice said to be given him by the ministers; and if the devil, after those executions, be affronted, by disbelieving his testimony, and by clearing and pardoning all the rest of the accused, yet this also is, according to that advice, but to cast the scale. The same that drew this advice saith, in *Wonders of the Invisible World, Enchantments Encountered,* that to have a hand in anything that may stifle or obstruct a regular detection of that witchcraft, is what we may well with a holy fear avoid: their majesties' good subjects must not every day be torn to pieces by horrid witchcraft, and those bloody felons be wholly left unprosecuted; the witchcraft is a business that will not be shammed. The pastor of that church, of which Sir William was a member, being of this principle, and thus declaring it, after the former advice, no wonder though it cast the scale against those cautions. It is rather a wonder that no more blood was shed; for if that advice of his pastor could still have prevailed with the governor, witchcraft had not been so shammed off as it was. Yet now, in this book of the life of Sir William, the pardoning the prisoners when condemned, and clearing the jails, is called a vanquishing the devil; adding this conquest to the rest of the noble achievements of Sir William, though performed not only without, but directly against, his pastor's advice. But this is not all; though this book pretends to raise a statue in honor of Sir William, yet it appears it was the least part of the design of the author to honor him, but it was rather to honor himself, and the ministers; it being so unjust to Sir William, as to give a full account of the cautions given him, but designedly hiding from the reader the encouragements and exhortations to proceed, that were laid before him, (under the name of the ministers' advice;) in effect telling the world that those executions at Salem were without and against the advice of the ministers, exprest in those cautions, purposely hiding their giving thanks for what was already done, and exhorting to proceed; thereby rendering Sir William of so sanguinary a complexion, that the ministers had such cause to fear his going on with the tragedy, though against their advice, that they desired the president to write his *Cases of Conscience,* &c. To plead misinformation will not salve here, however it may seem to palliate other things, but is a manifest, designed travesty, or misrepresentation, of the minister's advice to Sir William, a hiding the truth, and a wronging the dead, whom the author so much pretends to honor; for which the acknowledgments ought to be as universal as the offence. But though the ministers' advice, or rather Mr. Cotton Mather's, was perfectly ambidexter, giving as great or greater encouragement to proceed in those dark methods, than cautions against them; yet many eminent persons being accused, there was a necessity of a stop to be put to it. If it be true, what was said at the council board in answer to the commendations of Sir William for his stopping the proceedings about witchcraft, viz. that it was high time for him to stop it, his own lady being accused; if that assertion were a truth, then New England may seem to be more beholden to the accusers for accusing her, and thereby necessitating a stop, than to Sir William, or to the advice that was given him by his pastor.

Mr. Cotton Mather, having been very forward to write books of witchcraft, has not been so forward either to explain or to defend the doctrinal part thereof; and his belief (which he had a year's time to compose) he durst not venture, so as to be copied. Yet in this book of the life of Sir William he sufficiently testifies his retaining that heterodox belief, seeking by frightful stories of the sufferings of some, and the refined sight of others, &c. to obtrude upon the world, and confirm it in such a belief as hitherto he either cannot or will not defend, as if the blood already shed thereby were not sufficient.

Mr. I. Mather, in his *Cases of Conscience,* tells of a bewitched eye, and that such can see more than others. They were certainly bewitched eyes, that could see as well shut as open, and that could see what never was; that could see the prisoners upon the afflicted, harming them, when those whose eyes were not bewitched could have sworn that they did not stir from the bar. The accusers are said to have suffered much by biting, and the prints of just such a set of teeth, as those they accused had, would be seen on their flesh; but such as had not such bewitched eyes have seen the accusers bite themselves, and then complain of the accused. It has also been seen, when the accused, instead of having just such a set of teeth, has not had one in his head. They were such bewitched eyes, that could see the poisonous powder (brought by spectres) and that could see in the ashes the print of the brand, there invisibly heating to torment the pretended sufferers with, &c.

These, with the rest of such legends, have this direct tendency, viz. to tell the world that the devil is more ready to serve his votaries, by his doing for them things above or against the course of nature, showing himself to them and making explicit contracts with them, &c. than the Divine Being is to his faithful servants; and that as he is willing, so also able, to perform their desires. The way whereby these people are believed to arrive at a power to afflict their neighbors, is by a compact with the devil, and that they have a power to commission him to those evils. However irrational, or unscriptural, such assertions are, yet they seem a necessary part of the faith of such as maintain the belief of such a sort of witches.

As the scriptures know nothing of a covenanting or commissioning witch, so reason cannot conceive how mortals should by their wickedness arrive at a power to commission angels, fallen angels, against their innocent neighbors. But the scriptures are full in it, and the instances numerous, that the Almighty Divine Being has this prerogative, to make use of what instruments he pleaseth, in afflicting any, and consequently to commission devils: and though this word, commissioning, in the author's former books, might be thought to be by inadvertency, yet now, after he hath been cautioned of it, still to persist in it seems highly criminal; and therefore, in the name of God, I here charge such belief as guilty of sacrilege in the highest nature, and so much worse than stealing church plate, &c. as it is a higher offence to steal any of the glorious attributes of the Almighty, to bestow them upon mortals, than it is to steal the utensils appropriated to his service. And whether to ascribe such power of commissioning devils to the worst of men, be not direct blasphemy, I leave to others better able to determine. Where the Pharisees were so wicked as to ascribe to Beelzebub the mighty works of Christ (whereby he did manifestly show forth his power and godhead) then it was that our Savior declared the sin against the Holy Ghost to be unpardonable. . . .

1700

JONATHAN EDWARDS

(1703–1758)

Jonathan Edwards, born in East Windsor, Connecticut, into a long line of clergymen, was the first truly original philosopher and certainly the most brilliant theological mind of the colonies. As a boy he preached to his playmates in a prayer booth built in the meadow behind his house, and he was rigorously educated by his parents in a true discipline of home study. At twelve he entered Yale, where the works of Locke and Newton introduced him to the new currents of eighteenth-century philosophy. Graduated at sixteen, he stayed on to study theology. He became pastor to a Presbyterian congregation in New York, returned to Yale as a tutor, and in 1726 accepted a call to the church in Northampton, Massachusetts, as the associate of his grandfather, Solomon Stoddard, the "Pope" of New England Calvinism. A year later he married Sarah Pierrepont, by whom he had twelve children; she shared with him the fine intensity of mind and feeling that led him to emphasize a renovation of the heart as the ecstatic foundation of true religion.

By the time Edwards became active in the church, even Stoddard had accepted the Half-Way Covenant which allowed partial church membership to all those who considered themselves Christians as the word was defined by the Massachusetts Synod of 1662. Edwards, the leading defender of the Calvinistic orthodoxy of a past age, wished to turn the clock back to the zeal and purity of the first generation, and he argued for full communion only for the elect: those saved by divine grace. But he worked round to a new definition of grace that combined the orthodoxy of the seventeenth century with the psychology of the eighteenth, and did so by means of a subjective

130

idealism that foreshadowed the romantic thought of American Transcendentalism. When Stoddard died in 1729, Edwards began to emphasize the ecstasy that those elected to God's grace would feel in their redemption. Only those, he insisted, who underwent and publicly claimed the emotional experience of purification in spiritual rebirth were entitled to church membership. In 1734, with an increasing flock of "renovated hearts," Edwards began the Great Awakening, wave of religious enthusiasm that was to spread from Maine to Georgia in the 1740's and that was to make evangelical revivalism the folk trend of American Protestantism. His parishioners, however, began to distrust Edwards's fervor as a heretical enthusiasm destructive of the church, and in 1750 they forced him from his pastorate. He went to Stockbridge, Massachusetts, as a minister and a missionary to the Indians. In 1757 he was elected President of Princeton (then the College of New Jersey, and a stronghold of old-line orthodoxy), but three months later he died of smallpox.

Actually Edwards distrusted enthusiasm, always feeling that he could distinguish between the excitement of the moment and the reception of grace. He fought to reattain an earlier Puritan piety in the face of deistic intellectualism and a polite humanitarianism that passed for religion in the increasingly urban and mercantile society of eighteenth-century rationality. "Sarah Pierrepont" indicates the mysticism and holiness with which he fell in love, and the "Personal Narrative" is an example of the delicately calibrated observation with which he chronicled redemption and explored the roots of religious experience. *Sinners in the Hands of an Angry God,* his most famous sermon —too often used erroneously to identify him as a preacher of hellfire and brimstone—and *God Glorified in Man's Dependence* illustrate his insistence upon the orthodox concept of a Sovereign God. His most closely argued and famous defense of Calvinist doctrine is found in *Freedom of the Will,* in which he combined an older orthodoxy with the new empirical psychology of Locke in order to unify man's being and knowing. One of the most important figures in American thought, Edwards illuminates the continuum between the symbolic world view of the Puritans and the idealism of Emerson. Through the continuing influence of Emerson, Edwards is still felt as a force in modern thought.

The titles of some of his most important works are: *God Glorified in the Work of Redemption* (1731); *A Divine and Supernatural Light* (1734); *A Faithful Narrative* (1737); *Sin-*

ners in the Hands of an Angry God (1741); Some Thoughts
Concerning the Present Revival of Religion in New England
(1742); A Treatise Concerning Religious Affections (1746);
A Farewell Sermon Preached at the First Precinct in Northampton (1751); A Careful Enquiry into Freedom of the Will (1754);
The Great Christian Doctrine of Original Sin Defended (1758);
Two Dissertations: Concerning the End for which God Created
the World; The Nature of True Virtue (1765).

Editions and accounts of Edwards and his works are to be
found in S. E. Dwight, ed., The Works of President Edwards,
10 vols. (1829–1830); J. Tracy, The Great Awakening (1841);
A. V. G. Allen, Jonathan Edwards (1889); W. Walker, Ten
New England Leaders (1901); I. W. Riley, American Philosophy: The Early Schools (1907); H. W. Schneider, The Puritan
Mind (1930); F. I. Carpenter, "The Radicalism of Jonathan
Edwards," New England Quarterly, IV (1931); J. Haroutunian,
Piety versus Moralism (1932); A. C. McGiffert, Jonathan Edwards (1932); P. Miller, "The Half Way Covenant," New
England Quarterly, VI (1933); P. Miller, Orthodoxy in Massachusetts (1933); H. M. Jones, "American Prose Style: 1700–
1770," Huntington Library Bulletin, VI (1934); T. Hornberger,
"The Effect of the New Science upon the Thought of Jonathan
Edwards," American Literature, IX (1937); P. Miller, The New
England Mind: The Seventeenth Century (1939); T. H. Johnson, The Printed Writings of Jonathan Edwards, 1703–1758,
A Bibliography (1940); O. E. Winslow, Jonathan Edwards
(1940); E. H. Cady, "The Artistry of Jonathan Edwards," New
England Quarterly, XXII (1949); P. Miller, Jonathan Edwards
(1949); D. Elwood, The Philosophical Theology of Jonathan
Edwards (1960); R. Suter, "The Strange Universe of Jonathan
Edwards," Harvard Theological Review, LIV (1961); E. H.
Davidson, "From Locke to Edwards," Journal of the History of
Ideas, XXIV (1963); L. Howard, ed., "The Mind" of Jonathan
Edwards, A Reconstructed Text (1963); A. O. Aldridge, Jonathan Edwards (1964); D. B. Shea, Jr., "The Art and Instruction of Jonathan Edwards's Personal Narrative," American
Literature, XXXVII (1965); E. Davidson, Jonathan Edwards:
The Narrative of a Puritan Mind (1966); and C. Cherry, The
Theology of Jonathan Edwards: A Reappraisal (1966).

Sarah Pierrepont

They say there is a young lady in [New Haven] who is
beloved of that Great Being, who made and rules the world,
and that there are certain seasons in which this Great
Being, in some way or other invisible, comes to her and
fills her mind with exceeding sweet delight, and that she
hardly cares for anything, except to meditate on Him—
that she expects after a while to be received up where He

is, to be raised up out of the world and caught up into heaven; being assured that He loves her too well to let her remain at a distance from Him always. There she is to dwell with Him, and to be ravished with His love and delight forever. Therefore, if you present all the world before her, with the richest of its treasures, she disregards it and cares not for it, and is unmindful of any pain or affliction. She has a strange sweetness in her mind, and singular purity in her affections; is most just and conscientious in all her conduct; and you could not persuade her to do any thing wrong or sinful, if you would give her all the world, lest she should offend this Great Being. She is of a wonderful sweetness, calmness and universal benevolence of mind; especially after this Great God has manifested Himself to her mind. She will sometimes go about from place to place, singing sweetly; and seems to be always full of joy and pleasure; and no one knows for what. She loves to be alone, walking in the fields and groves, and seems to have some one invisible always conversing with her.

w. 1723
p. 1830

FROM

God Glorified in Man's Dependence

. . . The several ways wherein the dependence of one being may be upon another for its good, and wherein the redeemed of Jesus Christ depend on God for all their good, are these, viz. That they have all their good of Him, and that they have all through Him, and that they have all in Him; that He is the cause and original whence all their good comes, therein it is *of* Him; and that He is the medium by which it is obtained and conveyed, therein they have it *through* Him; and that He is the good itself given and conveyed, therein it is *in* Him. Now those that are redeemed by Jesus Christ do, in all these respects, very directly and entirely depend on God for their all.

First, the redeemed have all their good *of* God. God is the great author of it. He is the first cause of it; and not only so, but He is the only proper cause. It is of God that we have our Redeemer. It is God that has provided a

Savior for us. Jesus Christ is not only of God in His person, as He is the only begotten Son of God, but He is from God, as we are concerned in Him, and in His office of Mediator. He is the gift of God to us: God chose and anointed Him appointed Him His work, and sent Him into the world. And as it is God that gives, so it is God that accepts the Savior. He gives the purchaser, and He affords the thing purchased.

It is of God that Christ becomes ours, that we are brought to Him and are united to Him. It is of God that we receive faith to close with Him, that we may have an interest in him. Eph. ii: 8—"For by grace ye are saved, through faith; and that not of yourselves, it is the gift of God." It is of God that we actually receive all the benefits that Christ has purchased. It is God that pardons and justifies, and delivers from going down to hell; and into His favor the redeemed are received, when they are justified. So it is God that delivers from the dominion of sin, cleanses us from our filthiness, and changes us from our deformity. It is of God that the redeemed receive all their true excellency, wisdom, and holiness: and that two ways, viz. as the Holy Ghost by whom these things are immediately wrought is from God, proceeds from Him, and is sent by Him; and also as the Holy Ghost Himself is God, by whose operation and indwelling the knowledge of God and divine things, a holy disposition and all grace, are conferred and upheld. And though means are made use of in conferring grace on men's souls, yet it is of God that we have these means of grace, and it is He that makes them effectual. It is of God that we have the holy scriptures: they are His word. It is of God that we have ordinances, and their efficacy depends on the immediate influence of His Spirit. The ministers of the gospel are sent of God, and all their sufficiency is of Him. 2 Cor. iv: 7—"We have this treasure in earthen vessels, that the excellency of the power may be of God, and not of us." Their success depends entirely and absolutely on the immediate blessing and influence of God.

1. The redeemed have all from the grace of God. It was of mere grace that God gave us His only begotten Son. The grace is great in proportion to the excellency of what is given. The gift was infinitely precious, because it was of a person infinitely worthy, a person of infinite glory; and also because it was of a person infinitely near and dear to

God. The grace is great in proportion to the benefit we
have given us in Him. The benefit is doubly infinite, in that
in Him we have deliverance from an infinite, because an
eternal misery, and do also receive eternal joy and glory.
The grace in bestowing this gift is great in proportion to
our unworthiness to whom it is given; instead of deserving
such a gift, we merited infinitely ill of God's hands. The
grace is great according to the manner of giving, or in
proportion to the humiliation and expense of the method
and means by which a way is made for our having the gift.
He gave Him to dwell amongst us; He gave Him to us
incarnate, or in our nature; and in the like though sinless
infirmities. He gave Him to us in a low and afflicted state;
and not only so, but as slain, that He might be a feast for
our souls.

The grace of God in bestowing this gift is most free.
It was what God was under no obligation to bestow. He
might have rejected fallen man, as He did the fallen angels.
It was what we never did any thing to merit; it was given
while we were yet enemies, and before we had so much
as repented. It was from the love of God who saw no
excellency in us to attract it; and it was without expectation
of ever being requited for it. And it is from mere grace
that the benefits of Christ are applied to such and such
particular persons. Those that are called and sanctified
are to attribute it alone to the good pleasure of God's
goodness by which they are distinguished. He is sovereign,
and hath mercy on whom He will have mercy.

Man hath now a greater dependence on the grace of
God than he had before the fall. He depends on free
goodness of God for much more than he did then. Then he
depended on God's goodness for conferring the reward of
perfect obedience; for God was not obliged to promise and
bestow that reward. But now we are dependent on the
grace of God for much more; we stand in need of grace,
not only to bestow glory upon us, but to deliver us
from hell and eternal wrath. Under the first covenant we
depended on God's goodness to give us the reward of
righteousness; and so we do now: But we stand in need of
God's free and sovereign grace to give us that righteousness; to pardon our sin, and release us from the guilt and
infinite demerit of it.

And as we are dependent on the goodness of God for

more now than under the first covenant, so we are dependent on a much greater, more free and wonderful goodness.
We are now more dependent on God's arbitrary and sovereign good pleasure. We were in our first estate dependent
on God for holiness. We had our original righteousness
from Him; but then holiness was not bestowed in such a
way of sovereign good pleasure as it is now. Man was
created holy, for it became God to create holy all His
reasonable creatures. It would have been a disparagement
to the holiness of God's nature, if He had made an intelligent creature unholy. But now when fallen man is made
holy, it is from mere and arbitrary grace: God may for
ever deny holiness to the fallen creature if He pleases,
without any disparagement to any of His perfections.

And we are not only indeed more dependent on the
grace of God, but our dependence is much more conspicuous, because our own insufficiency and helplessness
in ourselves is much more apparent in our fallen and
undone state, than it was before we were either sinful or
miserable. We are more apparently dependent on God for
holiness, because we are first sinful, and utterly polluted,
and afterward holy. So the production of the effect is
sensible, and its derivation from God more obvious. If man
was ever holy and always was so, it would not be so apparent, that he had not holiness necessarily, as an inseparable
qualification of human nature. So we are more apparently
dependent on free grace for the favor of God, for we are
first justly the objects of His displeasure, and afterward are
received into favor. We are more apparently dependent on
God for happiness, being first miserable, and afterward
happy. It is more apparently free and without merit in us,
because we are actually without any kind of excellency to
merit, if there could be any such thing as merit in creature-
excellency. And we are not only without any true excellency, but are full of, and wholly defiled with, that which
is infinitely odious. All our good is more apparently from
God, because we are first naked and wholly without any
good, and afterward enriched with all good.

2. We receive all from the power of God. Man's redemption is often spoken of as a work of wonderful power as
well as grace. The great power of God appears in bringing
a sinner from his low state from the depth of sin and
misery, to such an exalted state of holiness and happiness.

Eph. i: 19— "And what is the exceeding greatness of His power to us-ward who believe, according to the working of His mighty power."

We are dependent on God's power through every step of our redemption. We are dependent on the power of God to convert us, and give faith in Jesus Christ, and the new nature. It is a work of creation: "If any man be in Christ, he is a new creature" (2 Cor. v: 17). "We are created in Christ Jesus" (Eph. ii: 10). The fallen creature cannot attain to true holiness, but by being created again, Eph. iv: 24— "And that ye put on the new man, which after God is created in righteousness and true holiness." It is a raising from the dead, Col. ii: 12, 13— "Wherein also ye are risen with him through the faith of the operation of God, who hath raised him from the dead." Yea, it is a more glorious work of power than mere creation, or raising a dead body to life, in that the effect attained is greater and more excellent. That holy and happy being, and spiritual life which is produced in the work of conversion, is a far greater and more glorious effect, than mere being and life. And the state from whence the change is made—a death in sin, a total corruption of nature, and depth of misery—is far more remote from the state attained, than mere death or non-entity.

It is by God's power also that we are preserved in a state of grace. I Pet. i: 5— "Who are kept by the power of God through faith unto salvation." As grace is at first from God, so it is continually from Him, and is maintained by Him, as much as light in the atmosphere is all day long from the sun, as well as at first dawning, or at sun-rising. Men are dependent on the power of God for every exercise of grace, and for carrying on that work in the heart, for subduing sin and corruption, increasing holy principles, and enabling to bring forth fruit in good works. Man is dependent on divine power in bringing grace to its perfection, in making the soul completely amiable in Christ's glorious likeness, and filling of it with a satisfying joy and blessedness; and for the raising of the body to life, and to such a perfect state, that it shall be suitable for a habitation and organ for a soul so perfected and blessed. These are the most glorious effects of the power of God, that are seen in the series of God's acts with respect to the creatures.

Man was dependent on the power of God in his first

estate, but he is more dependent on his power now; he needs God's power to do more things for him, and depends on a more wonderful exercise of His power. It was an effect of the power of God to make man holy at the first; but more remarkably so now, because there is a great deal of opposition and difficulty in the way. It is a more glorious effect of power to make that holy that was so depraved, and under the dominion of sin, than to confer holiness on that which before had nothing of the contrary. It is a more glorious work of power to rescue a soul out of the hands of the devil, and from the powers of darkness, and to bring it into a state of salvation, than to confer holiness where there was no prepossession or opposition. Luke xi: 21, 22— "When a strong man armed keepeth his palace, his goods are in peace; but when a stronger than he shall come upon him, and overcome him, he taketh from him all his armor wherein he trusted, and divideth his spoils." So it is a more glorious work of power to uphold a soul in a state of grace and holiness, and to carry it on till it is brought to glory, when there is so much sin remaining in the heart resisting, and Satan with all his might opposing, than it would have been to have kept man from falling at first, when Satan had nothing in man. Thus we have shown how the redeemed are dependent on God for all their good, as they have all of Him.

Secondly, They are also dependent on God for all, as they have all *through* Him. God is the medium of it, as well as the author and fountain of it. All we have— wisdom, the pardon of sin, deliverance from hell, acceptance into God's favor, grace and holiness, true comfort and happiness, eternal life and glory—is from God by a Mediator; and this Mediator is God; which Mediator we have an absolute dependence upon, as He through whom we receive all. So that here is another way wherein we have our dependence on God for all good. God not only gives us the Mediator, and accepts His mediation, and of His power and grace bestows the things purchased by the Mediator; but He the Mediator is God.

Our blessings are what we have by purchase; and the purchase is made of God, the blessings are purchased of Him, and God gives the purchaser; and only so, but God is the purchaser. Yea, God is both the purchaser and the price; for Christ who is God, purchased these blessings for us, by offering up Himself as the price of our salvation. He purchased eternal life by the sacrifice of Himself. Heb. vii: 27— "He offered up himself." And chap. ix: 26— "He hath appeared to take away sin by the sacrifice of himself." Indeed it was the human nature that was offered; but it was the same person with the divine, and therefore was an infinite price.

As we thus have our good through God, we have a dependence on Him in a respect that man in his first estate had not. Man was to have eternal life then through his own righteousness; so that he had partly a dependence upon what was in himself; for we have a dependence upon that through which we have our good, as well as that from which we have it: and though man's righteousness that he then depended on was indeed from God, yet it was his own, it was inherent in himself; so that his dependence was not so *immediately* on God. But now the righteousness that we are dependent on is not in ourselves, but in God. We are saved through the righteousness of Christ. . . .

1731

Narrative of Surprising Conversions

Dear Sir [Rev. Benjamin Colman]

In answer to your desire, I here send you a particular account of the present extraordinary circumstances of this town, and the neighbouring towns with respect to religion. I have observed that the town for this several years have gradually been reforming; there has appeared less and less of a party spirit, and a contentious disposition, which before had prevailed for many years between two parties in the town. The young people also have been reforming more and more; they by degrees left off their frolicking, and have been observably more decent in their attendance on the public worship. The winter before last there appeared a strange flexibleness in the young people of the town, and an unusual disposition to harken to counsel, on this occasion; it had been their manner of a long time, and for ought I know, always, to make Sabbath day nights and lecture days, to be especially times of diversion, and company keeping: I then preached a sermon on the Sabbath before the lecture, to show them the unsuitableness, and inconvenience of the practice, and to persuade them to reform it; and urged it on heads of families that it should be a thing agreed among them to govern their families, and keep them in at those times. And there happened to be at my house the evening after, men that belonged to the several parts of the town, to whom I moved that they should desire the heads of families, in my name, to meet together in their several neighbourhoods, that they might know each other's minds, and agree every one to restrain his family; which was done, and my motion complied with throughout the town; but the parents found little or no occasion for the exercise of government in the case; for the young people declared themselves convinced by what they had heard, and willing of themselves to comply with the counsel given them; and I suppose it was almost universally complied with thenceforward. After this there began to be a remarkable religious concern among some farm houses, at a place called Pascommuck, and five or six that I hoped were savingly wrought upon there. And in April there was a very sudden and awful death of a young man in town, in the very bloom of his youth, who was violently seized with a pleurisy and taken immediately out of his head, and died in two days; which much affected many young people in the town. This was followed with another death of a young married woman, who was in great distress in the beginning of her illness, but was hopefully converted before her death; so that she died full of comfort, and in a most earnest and moving manner, warning and counselling others, which I believe much contributed to the solemnizing of the spirits of the young people in the town; and there began evidently to appear more of a religious concern upon people's minds. In the fall of the year I moved to the young people that they should set up religious meetings, on evenings after lectures, which they complied with; this was followed with the death of an elderly person in the town, which was attended with very unusual circumstances, which much affected many people. About that time began the great noise that there was in this part of the country about Arminianism, which seemed strangely to be overruled for the promoting of religion; people seemed to be put by it upon enquiring, with concern and engagedness of mind, what was the way of salvation, and what were the terms of our acceptance with God; and what was said publicly on that occasion; however found fault with by many elsewhere, and ridiculed by some, was most evidently attended with a very remarkable blessing of heaven, to the souls of the people in this town, to the giving of them an universal satisfaction and engaging their minds with respect to the thing in question, the more earnestly to seek salvation in the way, that had been made evident to them; and then, a concern about the great things of religion began, about the latter end of December, and the beginning of January, to prevail abundantly in the town, till in a very little time it became universal throughout the town, among old and young, and from the highest to the lowest; all seemed to be seized with a deep concern about their eternal salvation; all the talk in all companies, and upon occasions was upon the things of religion, and no other talk was anywhere relished; and scarcely a single person in the whole town was left unconcerned about the great things of the Eternal World; those that were wont to be the vainest, and loosest persons in town seemed in general to be seized with strong convictions; those that were most disposed to contemn vital and experimental religion, and those that had the greatest conceit of their own reason; the highest families in the town, and the oldest persons in the town, and many little children were affected remarkably; no one family that I know of, and scarcely a person has been exempt and the Spirit of God went on in his saving influences, to the appearance of all human reason and charity, in a truly wonderful and astonishing manner. The news of it filled the neighbouring towns with talk, and there were many in them that scoffed and made a ridicule of the religion that appeared in Northampton; but it was observable that it was very frequent and common that those of other towns that came into this town, and observed how it was here, were greatly affected, and went home with wounded spirits, and were never more able to shake off the impression that it made upon them, till at length there began to appear a general concern in several of the towns in the county; in the month of March the people in New Hadley seemed to be seized with a deep concern about their salvation, all as it were at once, which has continued in a very great degree ever since; about the same time there began to appear the like concern in the west part of Suffield, which has since spread into all parts of the town. It next began to appear at Sunderland, and soon became universal, and to a very great degree. About the same time it began to appear in part of Deerfield, called Green River, and since has filled the town. It began to appear also at a part of Hatfield, and after that the whole town in the second week in April seemed to be seized at once, and there is a great and general concern there. And there gradually got in a considerable degree of the same concern into Hadley old society, and Mr. Hopkins's parish in Springfield, but it is nothing near so great as in many other places. The next place that we heard of was Northfield, where the concern was very great and general. We have heard that there is a considerable degree of it at Longmeadow, and there is something of it in Old Springfield in some parts of the society. About three weeks ago the town of Enfield were struck down as it were at once, the worst persons in the town seemed to be suddenly seized with a great degree of concern about their souls, as I have been informed; and about the same time, Mr. Bull of Westfield [said] that there began to be a great alteration there, and that there had been more done in one week before that time that I spoke with him than had been done in seven year[s] before; the people of Westfield have till now above all other places, made a scoff and derision of this concern at Northampton. There has been a great concern of a like nature at Windsor, on the west side of the river, which began about the same time that it began to be general here at Northampton; and my father has told me that there is an hopeful beginning on the east side in his society. Mr. Noyes writes me word that there is a considerable revival of religion at New-Haven; and I have been credibly informed that there is something of it at Guilford, and Lime, as there also is at Coventry, Bolton, and a society in Lebanon called the Crank; I yesterday saw Mr. White of Bolton, and also last night saw a young man that belongs to Coventry, who gave a very remarkable account of that town, of the manner in which the rude, debauched young people there were suddenly seized with a concern about their souls.

As to the nature of persons' experiences, and the influences of that spirit that there is amongst us, persons when seized with concern are brought to forsake their vices, and ill practices; the looser sort are brought to forsake and to dread their former extravagances; persons are soon brought to have done with their old quarrels; contention and intermeddling with other men's matters seems to be dead amongst us. I believe there never was so much done at confessing of faults to each other, and making up differences, as there has lately been: where this concern comes it immediately puts an end to differences between ministers and people; there was a considerable uneasiness at New Hadley between some of the people and their minister, but when this concern came amongst them it immediately put an end to it, and the people are now universally united to their minister. There was an exceeding alienation at Sunderland, between the minister and many of the people; but when this concern came amongst them it all vanished at once, and the people are universally united, in hearty affection to their minister. There were some men at Deerfield, of turbulent spirits, that kept up an uneasiness there with Mr. Ashley; but one of the chief of them has lately been influenced, fully, and freely to confess his fault to him, and is become his hearty friend.

People are brought off from inordinate engagedness after the world, and have been ready to run into the other extreme of too much neglecting their worldly business and to mind nothing but religion. Those that are under convictions are put upon it earnestly to enquire what they shall do to be saved, and diligently to use appointed means of grace, and apply themselves to all known duty. And those that obtain hope themselves, and the charity of others concerning their good estate, generally seem to be brought to a great sense of their own exceeding misery in a natural condition, and their utter helplessness, and insufficiency for themselves, and their exceeding wickedness and guiltiness in the sight of God; it seldom fails but that each one seems to think himself worse than anybody else, and they are brought to see that they deserve no mercy of God, that all their prayers and pains are exceeding worthless and polluted, and that God, notwithstanding all that they have done, or can do, may justly execute his eternal wrath upon them, and they seem to be brought to a lively sense of the excellency of Jesus Christ and his sufficiency and willingness to save sinners, and to be much weaned in their affections from the world, and to have their hearts filled with love to God and Christ, and a disposition to lie in the dust before him. They seem to have given them a lively conviction of the truth of the Gospel, and the divine authority of the Holy Scriptures; tho they can't have the exercise of this at all times alike, nor indeed of any other grace. They seem to be brought to abhor themselves for the sins of their past life, and to long to be holy, and to live holily, and to God's glory; but at the same time complain that they can do nothing, they are poor impotent creatures, utterly insufficient to glorify their Creator and Redeemer. They commonly seem to be much more sensible of their own wickedness after their conversion than before, so that they are often humbled by it; it seems to them that they are really become more wicked, when at the same time they are evidently full of a gracious spirit: their remaining sin seems to be their very great burthen, and many of them seem to long after heaven, that there they may be rid of sin. They generally seem to be united in dear love, and affection one to another, and to have a love to all mankind: I never saw the Christian spirit in love to enemies so exemplified, in all my life, as I have seen it within this half year. They commonly express a great concern for other's salvation; some say that they think they are far more concerned for other's conversion, after they themselves have been converted, than ever they were for their own; several have thought (though perhaps they might be deceived in it) that they could freely die for the salvation of any soul, of the meanest of mankind, of any Indian in the woods. This town never was so full of love, nor so full of joy, nor so full of distress as it has lately been. Some persons have had those longing desires after Jesus Christ, that have been to that degree as to take away their strength, and very much to weaken them, and make them faint; many have been even overcome with a sense of the dying love of Christ, so that the home of the body has been ready to fail under it; there was once three pious young persons in this town talking together of the dying love of Christ, till they all fainted away; tho tis probable the fainting of the two latter was much promoted by the fainting of the first. Many express a sense of the glory of the divine perfections, and of the excellency and fullness of Jesus Christ, and of their own littleness and unworthiness, in a manner truly wonderful, and almost unparalleled; and so likewise of the excellency and wonderfulness of the way of salvation by Jesus Christ. Their esteem of the Holy Scriptures is exceedingly increased. Many of them say the Bible seems to be a new book to them, as though they never read it before; there have been some instances of persons that by only an accidental sight of the Bible, have been as much moved, it seemed to me, as a lover by the sight of his sweet heart. The preaching of the word is greatly prized by them, they say they never heard preaching before; and so are God's Sabbaths, and ordinances, and opportunities of public worship; the Sabbath is longed for before it comes, some by only hearing the bell ring on some occasion in the week time, have been greatly moved, because it has put them in mind of its ringing to call the people together to worship God. But no part of public worship has commonly put an effect on them as singing God's praises. They have a greater respect to ministers than they used to have, there is scarcely a minister preaches here but gets their esteem and affection. The experiences of some persons lately amongst [us] have been beyond almost all that ever I heard or read of. There is a pious woman in this town that is a very modest bashful person, that was moved by what she heard of the experiences of others earnestly to seek to God to give her more clear manifestations of himself, and evidences of her own good estate, and God answered her request, and gradually gave her more and more of a sense of his glory and love, which she had with intermissions for several days, till one morning the week before last she had it to a more than ordinary degree, and it prevailed more and more till towards the middle of the day, till her nature began to sink under it, as she was alone in the house; but there came somebody into the house, and found her in an unusual, extraordinary frame. She expressed what she saw and felt to him; it came to that at last that they raised the neighbours, they were afraid she would die; I went up to see her and found her perfectly sober and in the exercise of her reason, but having her nature seemingly overborne and sinking, and when she could speak expressing in a manner that can't be described the sense she had of the glory of God, and particularly of such and such perfections, and her own unworthiness, her longing to lie in the dust, sometimes her longing to go to be with Christ, and crying out of the excellency of Christ, and the wonderfulness of his dying love; and so she continued for hours together tho not always in the same degree; at sometimes she was able to discourse to those about her; but it seemed to me if God had manifested a little more of himself to her she would immediately have sunk and her frame dissolved under it. She has since been at my house, and continues as full as she can hold, but looks on herself not as an eminent saint, but as the worst of all, and unworthy to go to speak with a minister; but yet now beyond any great doubt of her good estate. There are two persons that belong to other towns that have had such a sense of God's exceeding greatness and majesty, that they were as it were swallowed up; they both of them told me to that purpose that if they in the time of it had had the least fear that they were not at peace with that great God, they should immediately have died. But there is a very vast variety of degrees of spiritual discoveries, that are made to those that we hope are godly. As there is also in the steps, and method of the spirit's operation in convincing and converting sinners, and the length of time that persons are under conviction before they have comfort. There is an alteration made in the town in a few months that strangers can scarcely [be] conscious of; our church I believe was the largest in New England before, but persons lately have thronged in, so that there are very few adult persons left out. There have been a great multitude hopefully converted, too many, I find, for me to declare abroad with credit to my judgment. The town seems to be full of the presence of God; our young people when they get together instead of frolicking as they used to do are altogether on pious subjects; 'tis so at weddings and on all occasions. The children in this, and the neighbouring towns, have been greatly affected and influenced by the spirit of God, and many of them hopefully changed; the youngest in this town is between 9 and 10 years of age, some of them seem to be full of love to X. [Christ] and have expressed great longings after him and willingness to die, and leave father and mother and all things in the world to go to him, together with a great sense of their unworthiness and admiration at the free grace of God towards them. And there have been many old people, many above fifty and several near seventy that seem to be

wonderfully changed and hopefully new born. The good
people that have been formerly converted in the town
have many of them been wonderfully enlivened and increased. This work seems to be upon every account an
extraordinary dispensation of Providence. 'Tis extraordinary
upon the account of [the] universality of it in affecting
all sorts, high and low, rich and poor, wise and unwise, old
and young, vicious and moral; 'tis very extraordinary as to
the numbers that are hopefully savingly wrought upon, and
particularly the number of aged persons and children and
loose livers; and also on the account of the quickness of
the work of the spirit on them, for many seem to have
been suddenly taken from a loose way of living, and to be
so changed as to become truly holy, spiritual, heavenly
persons; 'tis extraordinary as to the degrees of gracious
communications, and the abundant measures in which the
spirit of God has been poured out on many persons; 'tis
extraordinary as to the extent of it, God's spirit being so
remarkably poured out on so many towns at once, and
its making such swift progress from place to place. The
extraordinariness of the thing has been I believe one
principal cause that people abroad have suspected it. There
have been as I have heard many odd and strange stories
that have been carried about the country of this affair,
which it is a wonder some wisemen should be so ready to
believe. Some indeed under great terrors of conscience have
had impressions on their imaginations; and also under
the power of the spiritual discoveries, they have had
livelily impressed ideas of Christ shedding blood for sinners,
his blood running from his veins, and of Christ in his glory
in Heaven and such like things, but they are always taught,
and have been several times taught in public not to lay the
weight of their hopes on such things and many have nothing of any such imaginations. There have been several
persons that have had their natures overborne under strong
convictions, have trembled, and han't been able to stand,
they have had such a sense of divine wrath; but there are
no new doctrines embraced, but people have been abundantly established in those that we account orthodox; there
is no new way of worship affected. There is no oddity of
behaviour prevails; people are no more superstitious about
their clothes, or any thing else than they used to be; indeed there is a great deal of talk when they are together of

one another's experiences, and indeed no other is to be expected in a town where the concern of the soul, is so universally the concern and that to so great a degree. And doubtless some persons under the strength of impressions that are made on their minds and under the power of strong affections, are guilty of imprudences, their zeal may need to be regulated by more prudence, and they may need a guide to their assistance; as of old when the church of Corinth had the extraordinary gifts of the spirit, they needed to be told by the apostle that the spirit of the Prophets were subject to the Prophets, and that their gifts were to be exercised with prudence, because God was not the author of confusion but of peace. There is no unlovely oddity in people's temper prevailing with this work, but on the contrary the face of things is much changed as to the appearance of a meek, humble, amiable behaviour. Indeed the devil has not been idle, but his hand has evidently appeared in several instances endeavouring to mimic the work of the spirit of God and to cast a slur upon it and no wonder; and there has hereby appeared the need of the watchful eye of skillful guides, and of wisdom from above to direct them. There lately came up hither a couple of ministers from Connecticut, viz. Mr. Lord of Preston, and Mr. Owen of Groton, who had heard of the extraordinary circumstances of this and the neighbouring towns, who had heard the affair well represented by some, and also had heard many reports greatly to its disadvantage, who came on purpose to see and satisfy themselves; and that they might thoroughly acquaint themselves, went about, and spent good part of a day, in hearing the accounts of many of our new converts, and examining of them; which was greatly to their satisfaction and they took particular notice, among other things, of the modesty with which persons gave account of themselves, and said that the one half was not told them, and could not be told them; and that if they renounced these persons' experiences they must renounce Christianity itself. And Mr. Owen said particularly as to their impressions on their imaginations, they were quite different from what had been represented, and that they were no more than might naturally be expected in such cases.

Thus sir I have given you a particular account of this affair which Satan has so much misrepresented in the country. This is a true account of the matter as far as I have opportunity to know, and I suppose I am under greater advantages to know than any person living. Having been thus long in the account, I forbear to make reflections, or to guess what God is about to do; I leave this to you, and shall only say, as I desire always to say from my heart *To God be all the glory whose work alone it is;* and let him have an interest in your prayers, who so much needs divine help at that day, and is your affectionate brother,

and humble servant,

Northampton May 30, 1735.   JTH EDWARDS.

Since I wrote the foregoing letter, there has happened a thing of a very awful nature in the town; my uncle Hawley, the last Sabbath day morning, laid violent hands on himself, and put an end to his life, by cutting his own throat. He had been for a considerable time greatly concerned about the condition of his soul; till, by the ordering of a sovereign Providence he was suffered to fall into deep melancholy, a distemper that the family are very prone to; he was much overpowered by it; the devil took the advantage and drove him into despairing thoughts; he was kept very much awake at nights, so that he had but very little sleep for two months, till he seemed not to have his faculties in his own power; he was in a great measure past a capacity of receiving advice, or being reasoned with. The Coroner's inquest judged him delirious. Satan seems to be in a great rage, at this extraordinary breaking forth of the work of God. I hope it is because he knows that he has but a short time; doubtless he had a great reach, in this violent attack of his against the whole affair. We have appointed a day of fasting in the town this week, by reason of this and other appearances of Satan's rage amongst us against poor souls. I yesterday saw a woman that belongs to Durham, who says there is a considerable revival of religion there.

I AM YOURS &c—

Northampton June 3, 1735.   J.E.

[The foregoing is an earlier and briefer version of the account dated November 6, 1736, and published in 1737 as *A Faithful Narrative of the Surprising Work of God in the Conversion of Many Hundred Souls in Northamp-*

ton and the Neighboring Towns and Villages. In his expansion Edwards omitted his uncle's suicide and included "two particular instances" of the "operations of God's spirit"—Abigail Hutchinson, a young woman, and Phebe Bartlet, a child.]

The Great Awakening in a Four-Year-Old Child

Phebe Bartlet . . . was born in March, 1731. About the latter end of April, or beginning of May, 1735, she was greatly affected by the talk of her brother, who had been hopefully converted a little before at about eleven years of age, and then seriously talked to her about the great things of religion. Her parents did not know of it at that time, and were not wont, in the counsels they gave to their children, particularly to direct themselves to her, being so young, and as they supposed, not capable of understanding. But after her brother had talked to her, they observed her very earnestly listen to the advice they gave to the other children; and she was observed very constantly to retire, several times in a day, as was concluded for secret prayer. She grew more and more engaged in religion, and was more frequent in her closet; till at last she was wont to visit it five or six times a day: and was so engaged in it, that nothing would at any time divert her from her stated closet exercises. Her mother often observed and watched her, when such things occurred, as she thought most likely to divert her, either by putting it out of her thoughts, or otherwise engaging her inclinations; but never could observe her to fail. She mentioned some very remarkable instances.

She once of her own accord spake of her unsuccessfulness, in that she could not find God, or to that purpose. But on Thursday, the last day of July, about the middle of the day, the child being in the closet where it used to retire; its mother heard it speaking aloud; which was unusual, and never had been observed before. And her voice seemed to be as of one exceedingly importunate and engaged; but her mother could distinctly hear only these words, spoken in a childish manner, but with extraordinary earnestness, and out of distress of soul, "Pray, blessed Lord, give me salvation! I pray, beg, pardon all my sins!"

When the child had done prayer, she came out of the closet, sat down by her mother, and cried out aloud. Her mother very earnestly asked her several times, what the matter was, before she would make any answer; but she continued crying and writhing her body to and fro, like one in anguish of spirit. Her mother then asked her, whether she was afraid that God would not give her salvation. She then answered, Yes, I am afraid I shall go to hell! Her mother then endeavoured to quiet her, and told her she would not have her cry, she must be a good girl, and pray every day, and she hoped God would give her salvation. But this did not quiet her at all; she continued thus earnestly crying, and talking on for some time, till at length she suddenly ceased crying, and began to smile, and presently said with a smiling countenance, Mother, the kingdom of heaven is come to me! Her mother was surprised at the sudden alteration, and at the speech; and knew not what to make of it; but at first said nothing to her. The child presently spake again, and said there is another come to me, and there is another, there is three; and being asked what she meant, she answered, one is, Thy will be done, and there is another, Enjoy him for ever; by which it seems, that when the child said, there is three come to me; she meant three passages of her catechism that came to her mind.

After the child had said this, she retired again into her closet; and her mother went over to her brother's, who was next neighbour; and when she came back, the child, being come out of the closet, meets her mother with this cheerful speech: I can find God now! referring to what she had before complained of, that she could not find God. Then the child spoke again, and said, I love God! her mother asked her, how well she loved God, whether she loved God better than her father and mother, she said yes. Then she asked her whether she loved God better than her little sister Rachel.—She answered, Yes, better than any thing! Then her elder sister, referring to her saying, she could find God now, asked her, where she could find God. She answered, in heaven. Why, said she, have you been in heaven? No, said the child. By this it seems not to have been any imagination of any thing seen with bodily eyes, that she called God, when she said, I can find God now. Her mother asked her, whether she was afraid of going to hell, and if that had made her cry? She answered, Yes, I was; but now I shan't. Her mother asked her, whether she thought that God had given her salvation: She answered, Yes. Her mother asked her, When? She answered, To-day. She appeared all that afternoon exceeding cheerful and joyful. One of the neighbours asked her, how she felt herself? She answered, I feel better than I did. The neighbour asked her what made her feel better? She answered, God makes me. That evening as she lay a-bed, she called one of her little cousins to her, who was present in the room, as having something to say to him; and when he came, she told him that heaven was better than earth. The next day, her mother asked her what God made her for? She answered, To serve him; and added, every body should serve God, and get an interest in Christ.

The same day the elder children, when they came home from school, seemed much affected with the extraordinary change that seemed to be made in Phebe. And her sister Abigail standing by, her mother took occasion to counsel her, how to improve her time, to prepare for another world. On which Phebe burst out in tears, and cried out, Poor Nabby! Her mother told her, she would not have her cry, she hoped that God would give Nabby salvation; but that did not quiet her, she continued earnestly crying for some time. When she had in a measure ceased, her sister Eunice being by her, she burst out again, and cried, Poor Eunice! and cried exceedingly; and when she had almost done, she went into another room, and there looked upon her sister Naomi: and burst out again, crying poor Amy! Her mother was greatly affected at such a behaviour in a child, and knew not what to say to her. One of the neighbours coming in a little after, asked her what she had cried for. She seemed at first backward to tell the reason; her mother told her she might tell that person, for he had given her an apple: upon which she said, she cried because she was afraid they would go to hell.

At night, a certain minister, who was occasionally in the town, was at the house, and talked with her of religious things. After he was gone, she sat leaning on the table, with tears running from her eyes; and being asked what made her cry, she said, It was thinking about God. The next day, being Saturday, she seemed great part of the day to be in a very affectionate frame, had four turns of crying, and seemed to endeavour to curb herself, and hide her tears, and was very backward to talk of the occasion. On the Sabbath-day she was asked, whether she believed in God; she answered, Yes. And being told that Christ was the Son of God, she made ready answer, and said, I know it.

From this time there appeared a very remarkable abiding change in the child. She has been very strict upon the Sabbath; and seems to long for the Sabbath-day before it comes, and will often in the week time be enquiring how long it is to the Sabbath-day, and must have the days between particularly counted over, before she will be contented. She seems to love God's house, and is very eager to go thither. Her mother once asked her, why she had such a mind to go? whether it was not to see fine folks? She said, No, it was to hear Mr. Edwards preach. When she is in the place of worship, she is very far from spending her time there as children at her age usually do, but appears with an attention that is very extraordinary for such a child. She also appears very desirous at all opportunities to go to private religious meetings; and is very still and attentive at home, during prayer, and has appeared affected in time of family-prayer. She seems to delight much in hearing religious conversation. When I once was there with some strangers, and talked to her something of religion, she seemed more than ordinarily attentive; and when we were gone, she looked very wistfully after us, and said, I wish they would come again! Her mother asked her, why? Says she, I love to hear 'em talk.

She seems to have very much of the fear of God before her eyes, and an extraordinary dread of sinning against him; of which her mother mentioned the following remarkable instance. Some time in August, the last year, she went with some bigger children, to get some plums in a neighbour's lot, knowing nothing of any harm in what she did; but when she brought some of the plums into the house, her mother mildly reproved her, and told her that she must not get plums without leave, because it was sin: God had commanded her not to steal. The child seemed greatly surprised and burst out in tears, and cried out, I won't have these plums! and turning to her sister Eunice, very earnestly, said to her, Why did you ask me to go to that plum-tree? I should not have gone if you had not asked me. The other children did not seem to be much affected or concerned; but there was no pacifying Phebe. Her mother told her, she might go and ask leave, and then it would not be sin for her to eat them; and sent one of the children to that end; and, when she returned, her mother told her, that the owner had given leave, now she might eat them, and it would not be stealing. This stilled her a little while; but presently she broke out again into an exceeding fit of crying. Her mother asked her, what made her cry again? Why she cried now, since they had asked leave? What it was that troubled her now! And asked her several times very earnestly, before she made any answer; but at last said, it was because, *because it was sin.* She continued a considerable time crying; and said, she would not go again if Eunice asked her an hundred times; and she retained her aversion to that fruit for a considerable time, under the remembrance of her former sin.

She sometimes appears greatly affected, and delighted with texts of scripture that come to her mind. Particularly about the beginning of November, that text came to her mind, Rev. iii. 20: Behold I stand at the door and knock: If any man hear my voice, and open the door, I will come in, and sup with him, and he with me. She spoke of it to those of the family, with great appearance of joy, a smiling countenance, and elevation of voice; and afterwards she went to another room, where her mother overheard her talking very earnestly to the children about it; and particularly heard her say to them, three or four times over, with an air of exceeding joy and admiration, Why it is to sup with God. Some time about the middle of winter, very late in the night, when all were a-bed, her mother perceived she was awake, and heard her, as though she was weeping. She called to her and asked her what was the matter. She answered with a low voice, so that her mother could not hear what she said; but thinking that it might be occasioned by some spiritual affection, said no more to her; but perceived her to lie awake, and to continue in the same frame for a considerable time. The next morning, she asked her whether she did not cry the last night. The child answered, Yes, I did cry a little, for I was thinking about God and Christ, and they loved me. Her mother asked her, whether to think of God and Christ loving her made her cry? she answered, Yes, it does sometimes.

She has often manifested a great concern for the good

of others' souls: and has been wont many times affectionately to counsel the other children. Once, about the latter
end of September, the last year, when she and some others
of the children were in a room by themselves, husking Indian corn, the child, after a while, came out and sat by
the fire. Her mother took notice that she appeared with a
more than ordinary serious and pensive countenance; but
at last she broke silence, and said, I have been talking
to Nabby and Eunice. Her mother asked her what she
had said to them. Why, said she, I told them they must
pray, and prepare to die; that they had but a little while
to live in this world, and they must be always ready.
When Nabby came out, her mother asked her, whether
she had said that to them. Yes, said she, she said that, and
a great deal more. At other times, the child took opportunities to talk to the other children about the great concern of their souls, so as much to affect them. She was
once exceeding importunate with her mother to go with
her sister Naomi to pray: her mother endeavoured to put
her off; but she pulled her by the sleeve, and seemed as
if she would by no means be denied. At last her mother
told her, that Amy must go and pray by herself; but, says
the child, she will not go; and persisted earnestly to beg
of her mother to go with her.

She has discovered an uncommon degree of a spirit of
charity, particularly on the following occasion. A poor
man that lives in the woods, had lately lost a cow that the
family much depended on; and being at the house, he was
relating his misfortune, and telling of the straits and difficulties they were reduced to by it. She took much notice
of it, and it wrought exceedingly on her compassion.
After she had attentively heard him awhile, she went away
to her father, who was in the shop, and entreated him to
give that man a cow: and told him that the poor man had
no cow! that the hunters, or something else, had killed his
cow! and entreated him to give him one of theirs. Her
father told her that they could not spare one. Then she
entreated him to let him and his family come and live at
his house: and had much more talk of the same nature,
whereby she manifested bowels of compassion to the poor.

She has manifested great love to her minister, particularly when I returned from my long journey for my health,
the last fall. When she heard of it, she appeared very joyful at the news, and told the children of it, with an ele-

vated voice, as the most joyful tidings; repeating it over and over, Mr. Edwards is come home! Mr. Edwards is come home! She still continues very constant in secret prayer, so far as can be observed, for she seems to have no desire that others should observe her when she retires, being a child of a reserved temper. Every night before she goes to bed, she will say her catechism, and will by no means miss. She never forgot it but once, and then, after she was a-bed, thought of it, and cried out in tears, I haven't said my catechism! and would not be quieted till her mother asked her the catechism as she lay in bed. She sometimes appears to be in doubt about the condition of her soul; and when asked, whether she thinks that she is prepared for death, speaks something doubtfully about it. At other times she seems to have no doubt; but when asked, replies, Yes, without hesitation. . . .

1736, 1737

Personal Narrative

I had a variety of concerns and exercises about my soul from my childhood; but had two more remarkable seasons of awakening, before I met with that change by which I was brought to those new dispositions, and that new sense of things, that I have since had. The first time was when I was a boy, some years before I went to college, at a time of remarkable awakening in my father's congregation. I was then very much affected for many months, and concerned about the things of religion, and my soul's salvation; and was abundant in duties. I used to pray five times a day in secret, and to spend much time in religious talk with other boys, and used to meet with them to pray together. I experienced I know not what kind of delight in religion. My mind was much engaged in it, and had much self-righteous pleasure; and it was my delight to abound in religious duties. I, with some of my schoolmates, joined together and built a booth in a swamp, in a very retired spot, for a place of prayer. And besides, I had particular secret places of my own in the woods, where I used to retire by myself, and was from time to time much affected. My affections seemed to be lively and easily moved, and I seemed to be in my element when engaged in religious duties. And I am ready to think many are deceived with such affections and such a kind of delight as I then had in religion, and mistake it for grace.

But in process of time, my convictions and affections wore off; and I entirely lost all those affections and delights and left off secret prayer, at least as to any constant performance of it; and returned like a dog to his vomit, and went on in the ways of sin. Indeed I was at times very uneasy, especially towards the latter part of my time at college, when it pleased God to seize me with the pleurisy; in which He brought me nigh to the grave, and shook me over the pit of hell. And yet, it was not long after my recovery, before I fell again into my old ways of sin. But God would not suffer me to go on with my quietness. I had great and violent inward struggles, till, after many conflicts, with wicked inclinations, repeated resolutions, and bonds that I laid myself under by a kind of vows to God, I was brought wholly to break off all former wicked ways and all ways of known outward sin, and to apply myself to seek salvation, and practice many religious duties, but without that kind of affection and delight which I had formerly experienced. My concern now wrought more by inward struggles and conflicts, and self-reflections. I made seeking my salvation the main business of my life. But yet, it seems to me, I sought after a miserable manner; which has made me sometimes since to question whether ever it issued in that which was saving; being ready to doubt, whether such miserable seeking ever succeeded. I was indeed brought to seek salvation in a manner that I never was before. I felt a spirit to part with all things in the world, for an interest in Christ. My concern continued and prevailed with many exercising thoughts and inward struggles, but yet it never seemed to be proper to express that concern by the name of terror.

From my childhood up, my mind had been full of objections against the doctrine of God's sovereignty in choosing whom He would to eternal life, and rejecting whom He pleased, leaving them eternally to perish, and be everlastingly tormented in hell. It used to appear like a horrible doctrine to me. But I remember the time very well when I seemed to be convinced and fully satisfied as to this sovereignty of God and His justice in thus eternally disposing of men according to His sovereign pleasure; but never could give an account, how, or by what means, I was thus convinced, not in the least imagining at the time, nor a long time after, that there was any extraordinary influence of God's Spirit in it. But only that now I saw further, and my reason apprehended the justice and reasonableness of it. However, my mind rested in it; and it put an end to all those cavils and objections. And there has been a wonderful alteration in my mind with respect to the doctrine of God's sovereignty, from that day to this; so that I scarce ever have found so much as the rising of an objection against it, in the most absolute sense, in God's showing mercy to whom He will show mercy, and hardening whom He will. God's absolute sovereignty and justice, with respect to salvation and damnation, is what my mind seems to rest assured of, as much as of any thing that I see with my eyes; at least it is so at times. But I have often, since that first conviction, had quite another kind of sense of God's sovereignty than I had then. I have often since had not only a conviction, but a delightful conviction. The doctrine has very often appeared exceeding pleasant, bright, and sweet.

Absolute sovereignty is what I love to ascribe to God. But my first conviction was not so.

The first instance that I remember of that sort of inward, sweet delight in God and divine things that I have lived much in since, was on reading those words (I Tim. i:17), "Now unto the King eternal, immortal, invisible, the only wise God, be honor and glory forever and ever, Amen." As I read the words, there came into my soul, and was as it were diffused through it, a sense of the glory of the Divine Being; a new sense, quite different from any thing I ever experienced before. Never any words of scripture seemed to me as these words did. I thought within myself, how excellent a being that was, and how happy I should be, if I might enjoy that God and be wrapt up in heaven and be as it were swallowed up in Him forever! I kept saying, and, as it were, singing over these words of scripture to myself; and went to pray to God that I might enjoy Him, and prayed in a manner quite different from what I used to do; with a new sort of affection. But it never came into my thought that there was any thing spiritual or of a saving nature in this.

From about that time, I began to have a new kind of apprehensions and ideas of Christ, and the work of redemption, and the glorious way of salvation by Him. An inward, sweet sense of these things at times came into my hearts; and my soul was led away in pleasant views and contemplations of them. And my mind was greatly engaged to spend my time in reading and meditating on Christ, on the beauty and excellency of His person, and the lovely way of salvation by free grace in Him. I found no books so delightful to me as those that treated of these subjects. Those words (Cant. ii:1) used to be abundantly with me: "I am the Rose of Sharon, and the Lily of the valleys." The words seemed to me sweetly to represent the loveliness and beauty of Jesus Christ. The whole book of Canticles used to be pleasant to me, and I used to be much in reading it about that time; and found from time to time, an inward sweetness that would carry me away in my contemplations. This I know not how to express otherwise, than by a calm, sweet abstraction of soul from all the concerns of this world; and sometimes a kind of vision, or fixed ideas and imaginations, of being alone in the mountains, or some solitary wilderness, far from all mankind, sweetly conversing with Christ, and wrapt and swallowed up in God. The sense I had of divine things would often of a sudden kindle up, as it were, a sweet burning in my heart; an ardor of soul, that I know not how to express.

Not long after I began to experience these things, I gave an account to my father of some things that had passed in my mind. I was pretty much affected by the discourse we had together; and when the discourse was ended, I walked abroad alone, in a solitary place in my father's pasture for contemplation. And as I was walking there and looking up on the sky and clouds, there came into my mind so sweet a sense of the glorious majesty and grace of God, that I know not how to express. I seemed to see them both in a sweet conjunction: majesty and meekness joined together. It was a gentle, and holy majesty; and also a majestic meekness; a high, great, and holy gentleness.

After this my sense of divine things gradually increased, and became more and more lively, and had more of that inward sweetness. The appearance of everything was altered. There seemed to be, as it were, a calm, sweet cast, or appearance of divine glory in almost everything. God's excellency, His wisdom, His purity and love, seemed to appear in everything; in the sun, moon, and stars; in the clouds, and blue sky; in the grass, flowers, trees; in the water, and all nature; which used greatly to fix my mind. I often used to sit and view the moon for continuance; and in the day, spent much time in viewing the clouds and sky, to behold the sweet glory of God in these things; in the meantime, singing forth, with a low voice, my contemplations of the Creator and Redeemer. And scarce anything among all the works of nature was so delightful to me as thunder and lightning; formerly, nothing had been so terrible to me. Before, I used to be uncommonly terrified with thunder, and to be struck with terror when I saw a thunder storm rising; but now, on the contrary, it rejoiced me. I felt God, so to speak, at the first appearance of a thunder storm; and used to take the opportunity at such times to fix myself in order to view the clouds, and see the lightnings play, and hear the majestic and awful voice of God's thunder, which oftentimes was exceedingly entertaining, leading me to sweet contemplations of my great and glorious God. While thus engaged, it always seemed natural to me to sing or chant for my meditations; or to speak my thoughts in soliloquies with a singing voice.

I felt then great satisfaction as to my good state, but that did not content me. I had vehement longings of soul after God and Christ, and after more holiness, wherewith my heart seemed to be full and ready to break; which often brought to my mind the words of the Psalmist, Ps. cxix:28: "My soul breaketh for the longing it hath." I often felt a mourning and lamenting in my heart, that I had not turned to God sooner, that I might have had more time to grow in grace. My mind was greatly fixed on divine things; almost perpetually in the contemplation of them. I spent most of my time in thinking of divine things year after year, often walking alone in the woods, and solitary places for meditation, soliloquy, and prayer, and converse with God; and it was always my manner, at such times, to sing forth my contemplations. I was almost constantly in ejaculatory prayer, wherever I was. Prayer seemed to be natural to me as the breath by which the inward burnings of my heart had vent. The delights which I now felt in the things of religion were of an exceedingly different kind from those before mentioned that I had when a boy; and what I then had no more notion of than one born blind has of pleasant and beautiful colors. They

were of a more inward, pure, soul-animating and refreshing nature. Those former delights never reached the heart,
and did not arise from any sight of the divine excellency of
the things of God or any taste of the soul-satisfying and
life-giving good there is in them.

My sense of divine things seemed gradually to increase,
until I went to preach at New York, which was about a
year and a half after they began; and while I was there,
I felt them, very sensibly, in a higher degree than I had
done before. My longings after God and holiness were
much increased. Pure and humble, holy and heavenly
Christianity, appeared exceedingly amiable to me. I felt a
burning desire to be in every thing a complete Christian
and conform to the blessed image of Christ, and that I
might live, in all things, according to the pure and blessed
rules of the gospel. I had an eager thirsting after progress
in these things, which put me upon pursuing and pressing
after them. It was my continual strife day and night and
constant inquiry how I should *be* more holy, and *live* more
holily, and more becoming a child of God and a disciple
of Christ. I now sought an increase of grace and holiness,
and a holy life, with much more earnestness than ever
I sought grace before I had it. I used to be continually
examining myself, and studying and contriving for likely
ways and means how I should live holily, with far greater
diligence and earnestness, than ever I pursued any thing
in my life; but yet with too great a dependence on my own
strength; which afterwards proved a great damage to me.
My experience had not then taught me, as it has done since,
my extreme feebleness and impotence every manner of
way; and the bottomless depths of secret corruption and
deceit there was in my heart. However, I went on with my
eager pursuit after more holiness and conformity to Christ.

The heaven I desired was a heaven of holiness: to be
with God, and to spend my eternity in divine love and holy
communion with Christ. My mind was very much taken
up with contemplations on heaven, and the enjoyments
there, and living there in perfect holiness, humility and
love. And it used at that time to appear a great part of
the happiness of heaven, that there the saints could express
their love to Christ. It appeared to me a great clog and
burden, that what I felt within I could not express as I
desired. The inward ardor of my soul, seemed to be hin-

dered and pent up, and could not freely flame out as it would. I used often to think, how in heaven this principle should freely and fully vent and express itself. Heaven appeared exceedingly delightful, as a world of love; and that all happiness consisted in living in pure, humble, heavenly, divine love.

I remember the thoughts I used then to have of holiness, and said sometimes to myself, "I do certainly know that I love holiness, such as the gospel prescribes." It appeared to me, that there was nothing in it but what was ravishingly lovely; the highest beauty and amiableness—a divine beauty; far purer than any thing here upon earth; and that every thing else was like mire and defilement in comparison of it.

Holiness, as I then wrote down some of my contemplations on it, appeared to me to be of a sweet, pleasant, charming, serene, calm nature, which brought an inexpressible purity, brightness, peacefulness and ravishment to the soul. In other words, that it made the soul like a field or garden of God, with all manner of pleasant flowers; all pleasant, delightful, and undisturbed; enjoying a sweet calm, and the gently vivifying beams of the sun. The soul of a true Christian, as I then wrote my meditations, appeared like such a little white flower as we see in the spring of the year: low and humble on the ground, opening its bosom to receive the pleasant beams of the sun's glory; rejoicing as it were in a calm rapture; diffusing around a sweet fragrancy; standing peacefully and lovingly, in the midst of other flowers round about; all in like manner opening their bosoms, to drink in the light of the sun. There was no part of creature holiness that I had so great a sense of its loveliness as humility, brokenness of heart and poverty of spirit; and there was nothing that I so earnestly longed for. My heart panted after this, to lie low before God, as in the dust; that I might be nothing, and that God might be ALL, that I might become as a little child.

While at New York, I was sometimes much affected with reflections on my past life, considering how late it was before I began to be truly religious; and how wickedly I had lived till then; and once so as to weep abundantly, and for a considerable time together.

On January 12, 1723, I made a solemn dedication of myself to God, and wrote it down, giving up myself, and all that I had to God: to be for the future in no respect my own, to act as one that had no right to himself, in any respect. And solemnly vowed to take God for my whole portion and felicity; looking on nothing else as any part of my happiness, nor acting as if it were; and His law for the constant rule of my obedience; engaging to fight with all my might, against the world, the flesh and the devil, to the end of my life. But I have reason to be infinitely humbled, when I consider how much I have failed of answering my obligation.

I had then abundance of sweet religious conversation in the family where I lived, with Mr. John Smith and his pious mother. My heart was knit in affection to those in whom were appearances of true piety, and I could bear the thoughts of no other companions but such as were holy and the disciples of the blessed Jesus. I had great longings for the advancement of Christ's kingdom in the world, and my secret prayer used to be in great part taken up in praying for it. If I heard the least hint of any thing that happened in any part of the world, that appeared in some respect or other to have a favorable aspect on the interest of Christ's kingdom, my soul eagerly catched at it, and it would much animate and refresh me. I used to be eager to read public news-letters mainly for that end: to see if I could not find some news favorable to the interest of religion in the world.

I very frequently used to retire into a solitary place on the banks of Hudson's river, at some distance from the city, for contemplation on divine things and secret converse with God; and had many sweet hours there. Sometimes Mr. Smith and I walked there together to converse on the things of God; and our conversation used to turn much on the advancement of Christ's kingdom in the world and the glorious things that God would accomplish for His church in the latter days. I had then, and at other times, the greatest delight in the holy scriptures of any book whatsoever. Oftentimes in reading it, every word seemed to touch my heart. I felt a harmony between something in my heart, and those sweet and powerful words. I seemed often to see so much light exhibited by every sentence, and such a refreshing food communicated, that I could not get along in reading, often dwelling long on one sentence, to see the wonders contained in it. And yet almost every sentence seemed to be full of wonders.

I came away from New York in the month of April, 1723, and had a most bitter parting with Madam Smith and her son. My heart seemed to sink within me at leaving the family and city, where I had enjoyed so many sweet and pleasant days. I went from New York to Weathersfield by water, and as I sailed away, I kept sight of the city as long as I could. However, that night, after this sorrowful parting, I was greatly comforted in God at Westchester, where we went ashore to lodge, and had a pleasant time of it all the voyage to Saybrook. It was sweet to me to think of meeting dear Christians in heaven, where we should never part more. At Saybrook we went ashore to lodge on Saturday, and there kept the Sabbath, where I had a sweet and refreshing season walking alone in the fields.

After I came home to Windsor, I remained much in a like frame of mind as when at New York; only sometimes I felt my heart ready to sink with the thoughts of my friends at New York. My support was in contemplations on the heavenly state, as I find in my diary of May 1, 1723. It was a comfort to think of that state, where there is fulness of joy; where reigns heavenly, calm, and delightful love, without alloy; where there are continually the dearest expressions of this love; where is the enjoyment of the persons loved, without ever parting; where those persons who appear so lovely in this world, will really be inexpressibly more lovely and full of love to us. And how sweetly will the mutual lovers join together to sing the praises of God and the Lamb! How will it fill us with joy to think that this enjoyment, these sweet exercises, will never cease but will last to all eternity! I continued much in the same frame, in the general, as when at New York, till I went to New Haven as tutor to the college; particularly once at Bolton, on a journey from Boston, while walking out alone in the fields. After I went to New Haven I sunk in religion, my mind being diverted from my eager pursuits after holiness by some affairs that greatly perplexed and distracted my thoughts.

In September, 1725, I was taken ill at New Haven, and while endeavoring to go home to Windsor, was so ill at the North Village that I could go no further; where I lay sick for about a quarter of a year. In this sickness God was pleased to visit me again with the sweet influences of His Spirit. My mind was greatly engaged there in divine, pleasant contemplations and longings of soul. I observed that those who watched with me, would often be looking out wishfully for the morning; which brought to my mind those words of the Psalmist, and which my soul with delight made its own language: "My soul waiteth for the Lord, more than they that watch for the morning, I say, more than they that watch for the morning." And when the light of day came in at the windows, it refreshed my soul from one morning to another. It seemed to be some image of the light of God's glory.

I remember about that time I used greatly to long for the conversion of some that I was concerned with. I could gladly honor them and with delight be a servant to them and lie at their feet, if they were but truly holy. But some time after this, I was again greatly diverted in my mind with some temporal concerns that exceedingly took up my thoughts, greatly to the wounding of my soul; and went on through various exercises that it would be tedious to relate, which gave me much more experience of my own heart than ever I had before.

Since I came to this town, I have often had sweet complacency in God, in views of His glorious perfections and the excellency of Jesus Christ. God has appeared to me a glorious and lovely being, chiefly on the account of His holiness. The holiness of God has always appeared to me the most lovely of all His attributes. The doctrines of God's absolute sovereignty and free grace in showing mercy to whom He would show mercy, and man's absolute dependence on the operations of God's Holy Spirit, have very often appeared to me as sweet and glorious doctrines. These doctrines have been much my delight. God's sovereignty has ever appeared to me a great part of His glory. It has often been my delight to approach God and adore Him as a sovereign God and ask sovereign mercy of Him.

I have loved the doctrines of the gospel. They have been to my soul like green pastures. The gospel has seemed to me the richest treasure, the treasure that I have most desired, and longed that it might dwell richly in me. The way of salvation by Christ has appeared, in a general way, glorious and excellent, most pleasant and most beautiful. It has often seemed to me that it would in a great measure spoil heaven to receive it in any other way. That text has often been affecting and delightful to me (Isa. xxxii:2), "A man shall be an hiding place from the wind, and a covert from the tempest, &c."

It has often appeared to me delightful to be united to Christ, to have Him for my head, and to be a member of His body; also to have Christ for my teacher and prophet. I very often think with sweetness and longings and pantings of soul of being a little child, taking hold of Christ to be led by Him through the wilderness of this world. That text (Matt. xviii:3) has often been sweet to me, "except ye be converted and become as little children, &c." I love to think of coming to Christ to receive salvation of Him, poor in spirit, and quite empty of self, humbly exalting Him alone, cut off entirely from my own root in order to grow into and out of Christ, to have God in Christ to be all in all, and to live by faith on the Son of God, a life of humble unfeigned confidence in Him. That scripture has often been sweet to me (Ps. cxv:1), "Not unto us, O Lord, not unto us, but to thy name give glory, for thy mercy and for thy truth's sake." And those words of Christ (Luke x:21), "In that hour Jesus rejoiced in spirit, and said, I thank thee, O Father, Lord of heaven and earth, that thou hast hid these things from the wise and prudent, and hast revealed them unto babes; even so, Father, for so it seemed good in thy sight." That sovereignty of God which Christ rejoiced in seemed to me worthy of such joy, and that rejoicing seemed to show the excellency of Christ, and of what spirit He was.

Sometimes only mentioning a single word caused my heart to burn within me, or only seeing the name of Christ, or the name of some attribute of God. And God has appeared glorious to me on account of the Trinity. It has made me have exalting thoughts of God, that He subsists in three persons: Father, Son and Holy Ghost. The sweetest joys and delights I have experienced have not been those that have arisen from a hope of my own good estate, but in a direct view of the glorious things of the gospel. When I enjoy this sweetness, it seems to carry me above the thoughts of my own estate. It seems at such times a loss that I cannot bear: to take off my eye from the glorious pleasant object I behold without me, to turn my eye in upon myself and my own good estate.

My heart has been much on the advancement of Christ's

kingdom in the world. The histories of the past advancement of Christ's kingdom have been sweet to me. When I have read histories of past ages, the pleasantest thing in all my reading has been to read of the kingdom of Christ being promoted. And when I have expected in my reading to come to any such thing, I have rejoiced in the prospect all the way as I read. And my mind has been much entertained and delighted with the scripture promises and prophecies which relate to the future glorious advancement of Christ's kingdom upon earth.

I have sometimes had a sense of the excellent fulness of Christ and His meetness and suitableness as a Saviour, whereby He has appeared to me, far above all, the chief of ten thousands. His blood and atonement have appeared sweet, and His righteousness sweet; which was always accompanied with ardency of spirit and inward strugglings and breathings, and groanings that cannot be uttered, to be emptied of myself, and swallowed up in Christ.

Once as I rode out into the woods for my health in 1737, having alighted from my horse in a retired place as my manner commonly has been, to walk for divine contemplation and prayer, I had a view (that for me was extraordinary) of the glory of the Son of God as Mediator between God and man, and His wonderful, great, full, pure and sweet grace and love, and meek and gentle condescension. This grace that appeared so calm and sweet appeared also great above the heavens. The person of Christ appeared ineffably excellent with an excellency great enough to swallow up all thought and conception—which continued, as near as I can judge, about an hour; which kept me the greater part of the time in a flood of tears, and weeping aloud. I felt an ardency of soul to be what I know not otherwise how to express: emptied and annihilated; to lie in the dust, and to be full of Christ alone; to love Him with a holy and pure love; to trust in Him; to live upon Him; to serve and follow Him; and to be perfectly sanctified and made pure, with a divine and heavenly purity. I have, several other times, had views very much of the same nature, and which have had the same effects.

I have many times had a sense of the glory of the third person in the Trinity in His office of Sanctifier, in His holy operations, communicating divine light and life to the soul. God, in the communications of His Holy Spirit, has appeared as an infinite fountain of divine glory and sweetness, being full and sufficient to fill and satisfy the soul: pouring forth itself in sweet communications like the sun in its glory, sweetly and pleasantly diffusing light and life. And I have sometimes had an affecting sense of the excellency of the word of God as a word of life: as the light of life, a sweet, excellent, life-giving word, accompanied with a thirsting after that word, that it might dwell richly in my heart.

Often, since I lived in this town, I have had very affecting views of my own sinfulness and vileness, very frequently to such a degree as to hold me in a kind of loud weeping, sometimes for a considerable time together, so that I have often been forced to shut myself up. I have had a vastly greater sense of my own wickedness and the badness of my own heart than ever I had before my conversion. It has often appeared to me that if God should mark iniquity against me, I should appear the very worst of all mankind—of all that have been since the beginning of the world to this time, and that I should have by far the lowest place in hell. When others that have come to talk with me about their soul concerns have expressed the sense they have had of their own wickedness by saying that it seemed to them that they were as bad as the devil himself, I thought their expression seemed exceedingly faint and feeble to represent my wickedness.

My wickedness, as I am in myself, has long appeared to me perfectly ineffable, and swallowing up all thought and imagination, like an infinite deluge, or mountains over my head. I know not how to express better what my sins appear to me to be than by heaping infinite upon infinite, and multiplying infinite by infinite. Very often, for these many years, these expressions are in my mind and in my mouth. "Infinite upon infinite—Infinite upon infinite!" When I look into my heart and take a view of my wickedness, it looks like an abyss infinitely deeper than hell. And it appears to me that were it not for free grace, exalted and raised up to the infinite height of all the fulness and glory of the great Jehovah, and the arm of his power and grace stretched forth in all the majesty of his power, and in all the glory of His sovereignty, I should appear sunk down in my sins below hell itself, far beyond the sight of everything but the eye of sovereign grace, that can pierce even down to such a depth. And yet, it seems to me, that my conviction of sin is exceedingly small and faint. It is enough to amaze me that I have no more sense of my sin. I know certainly, that I have very little sense of my sinfulness. When I have had turns of weeping and crying for my sins, I thought I knew at the time that my repentance was nothing to my sin.

I have greatly longed of late for a broken heart and to lie low before God; and when I ask for humility, I cannot bear the thoughts of being no more humble than other Christians. It seems to me that though their degrees of humility may be suitable for them, yet it would be a vile self-exaltation to me not to be the lowest in humility of all mankind. Others speak of their longing to be "humbled to the dust"; that may be a proper expression for them, but I always think of myself that I ought (and it is an expression that has long been natural for me to use in prayer) "to lie infinitely low before God." And it is affecting to think how ignorant I was, when a young Christian, of the bottomless, infinite depths of wickedness, pride, hypocrisy and deceit, left in my heart.

I have a much greater sense of my universal, exceeding dependence on God's grace and strength, and mere good pleasure, of late, than I used formerly to have, and have experienced more of an abhorrence of my own righteousness. The very thought of any joy arising in me on any consideration of my own amiableness, performances or experiences, or any goodness of heart or life, is nauseous and detestable to me. And yet I am greatly afflicted with a proud and self-righteous spirit, much more sensibly than I used to be formerly. I see that serpent rising and putting forth its head continually, everywhere, all around me.

Though it seems to me that in some respects I was a far better Christian for two or three years after my first conversion than I am now, and lived in a more constant delight and pleasure, yet, of late years, I have had a more full and constant sense of the absolute sovereignty of God and a delight in that sovereignty, and have had more of a sense of the glory of Christ as a Mediator revealed in the gospel. On one Saturday night in particular, I had such a discovery of the excellency of the gospel above all other doctrines, that I could not but say to myself, "This is my chosen light, my chosen doctrine"; and of Christ, "This is my chosen Prophet." It appeared sweet beyond all expression to follow Christ, and to be taught and enlightened and instructed by Him; to learn of Him, and live to Him. Another Saturday night (January, 1739), I had such a sense, how sweet and blessed a thing it was to walk in the way of duty, to do that which was right and meet to be done and agreeable to the holy mind of God, that it caused me to break forth into a kind of loud weeping, which held me some time, so that I was forced to shut myself up, and fasten the doors. I could not but, as it were, cry out, "How happy are they which do that which is right in the sight of God! They are blessed indeed, they are the happy ones!" I had, at the same time, a very affecting sense how meet and suitable it was that God should govern the world and order all things according to His own pleasure; and I rejoiced in it, that God reigned, and that His will was done.

w. c1740

p. 1765

Sinners in the Hands of an Angry God

Deut. 32:35, "Their foot shall slide in due time."

In this verse is threatened the vengeance of God on the wicked unbelieving Israelites, who were God's visible people, and who lived under the means of grace; but who, notwithstanding all God's wonderful works towards them, remained (as ver. 28) void of counsel, having no understanding in them. Under all the cultivations of heaven, they brought forth bitter and poisonous fruit, as in the two verses next preceding the text. The expression I have chosen for my text, *Their foot shall slide in due time,* seems to imply the following things relating to the punishment and destruction to which these wicked Israelites were exposed.

1. That they were always exposed to destruction, as one that stands or walks in slippery places is always exposed to fall. This is implied in the manner of their destruction coming upon them, being represented by their foot sliding. The same is expressed (Ps. 73:18): "Surely thou didst set them in slippery places; thou castedst them down into destruction."

2. It implies that they were always exposed to sudden unexpected destruction, as he that walks in slippery places

is every moment liable to fall; he cannot foresee one moment whether he shall stand or fall the next; and when he does fall, he falls at once without warning, which is also expressed in Ps. 73:18, 19: "Surely thou didst set them in slippery places; thou castedst them down into destruction. How are they brought into desolation as in a moment!"

3. Another thing implied is that they are liable to fall of themselves, without being thrown down by the hand of another, as he that stands or walks on slippery ground needs nothing but his own weight to throw him down.

4. That the reason why they are not fallen already, and do not fall now, is only that God's appointed time is not come. For it is said that when that due time or appointed time comes, "Their foot shall slide." Then they shall be left to fall, as they are inclined by their own weight. God will not hold them up in these slippery places any longer, but will let them go; and then, at that very instant, they shall fall into destruction, as he that stands on such slippery declining ground, on the edge of a pit, he cannot stand alone; when he is let go he immediately falls and is lost.

The observation from the words that I would now insist upon is this: "There is nothing that keeps wicked men at any one moment out of hell but the mere pleasure of God." By the *mere* pleasure of God I mean His *sovereign* pleasure, His arbitrary will, restrained by no obligation, hindered by no manner of difficulty, any more than if nothing else but God's mere will had in the least degree, or in any respect whatsoever, any hand in the preservation of wicked men one moment.

The truth of this observation may appear by the following considerations.

1. There is no want of power in God to cast wicked men into hell at any moment. Men's hands can't be strong when God rises up; the strongest have no power to resist Him, nor can any deliver out of His hands.

He is not only able to cast wicked men into hell, but He can most easily do it. Sometimes an earthly prince meets with a great deal of difficulty to subdue a rebel that has found means to fortify himself, and has made himself strong by the number of his followers. But it is not so with God. There is no fortress that is any defence against the power of God. Though hand join in hand, and vast multitudes of God's enemies combine and associate themselves, they are easily broken in pieces; they are as great heaps of light chaff before the whirlwind, or large quantities of dry stubble before devouring flames. We find it easy to tread on and crush a worm that we see crawling on the earth; so 'tis easy for us to cut or singe a slender thread that any thing hangs by; thus easy is it for God, when He pleases, to cast His enemies down to hell. What are we, that we should think to stand before Him, at whose rebuke the earth trembles, and before whom the rocks are thrown down!

2. They deserve to be cast into hell, so that divine justice never stands in the way; it makes no objection against God's using His power at any moment to destroy them. Yea, on the contrary, justice calls aloud for an infinite punishment of their sins. Divine justice says of the tree that brings forth such grapes of Sodom, "Cut it down, why cumbereth it the ground?" (Luke xiii:7). The sword of divine justice is every moment brandished over their heads, and 'tis nothing but the hand of arbitrary mercy and God's mere will that holds it back.

3. They are already under a sentence of condemnation to hell. They don't only justly deserve to be cast down thither, but the sentence of the law of God, that eternal and immutable rule of righteousness that God has fixed between Him and mankind, is gone out against them· and stands against them, so that they are bound over already to hell (John iii:18): "He that believeth not is condemned already." So that every unconverted man properly belongs to hell; that is his place; from thence he is (John viii:23): "Ye are from beneath," and thither he is bound. 'Tis the place that justice and God's word and the sentence of His unchangeable law assigns to him.

4. They are now the objects of that very same anger and wrath of God that is expressed in the torments of hell; and the reason why they don't go down to hell at each moment is not because God, in whose power they are, is not then very angry with them, as angry as He is with many of those miserable creatures that He is now tormenting in hell and do there feel and bear the fierceness of His wrath. Yea, God is a great deal more angry with great numbers that are now on earth, yea, doubtless, with

many that are now in this congregation, that, it may be, are at ease and quiet, than He is with many of those that are now in the flames of hell.

So that it is not because God is unmindful of their wickedness and don't resent it, that He don't let loose His hand and cut them off. God is not altogether such a one as themselves, though they may imagine Him to be so. The wrath of God burns against them; their damnation don't slumber; the pit is prepared; the fire is made ready; the furnace is now hot, ready to receive them; the flames do now rage and glow. The glittering sword is whet, and held over them, and the pit hath opened her mouth under them.

5. The devil stands ready to fall upon them and seize them as his own, at what moment God shall permit him. They belong to him; he has their souls in his possession and under his dominion. The Scripture represents them as his goods: Luke xi:21. The devils watch them; they are ever by them, at their right hand; they stand waiting for them, like greedy hungry lions that see their prey, and expect to have it, but are for the present kept back. If God should withdraw His hand by which they are restrained, they would in one moment fly upon their poor souls. The old serpent is gaping for them; hell opens its mouth wide to receive them; and if God should permit it, they would be hastily swallowed up and lost.

6. There are in the souls of wicked men those hellish principles reigning that would presently kindle and flame out into hell-fire if it were not for God's restraints. There is laid in the very nature of carnal men a foundation for the torments of hell: there are those corrupt principles in reigning power in them, and in full possession of them, that are seeds of hell-fire. These principles are active and powerful, exceeding violent in their nature, and if it were not for the restraining hand of God upon them, they would soon break out; they would flame out after the same manner as the same corruptions, the same enmity does in the heart of damned souls, and would beget the same torments in 'em as they do in them. The souls of the wicked are in Scripture compared to the troubled sea: Isa. lvii:20. For the present God restrains their wickedness by His mighty power, as He does the raging waves of the troubled sea, saying, "Hitherto shalt thou come, and

no further"; but if God should withdraw that restraining power, it would soon carry all afore it. Sin is the ruin and misery of the soul; it is destructive in its nature, and if God should leave it without restraint, there would need nothing else to make the soul perfectly miserable. The corruption of the heart of man is a thing that is immoderate and boundless in its fury; and while wicked men live here, it is like fire pent up by God's restraints, whenas if it were let loose, it would set on fire the course of nature; and as the heart is now a sink of sin, so, if sin was not restrained, it would immediately turn the soul into a fiery oven, or a furnace of fire and brimstone.

7. It is no security to wicked men for one moment that there are no visible means of death at hand. 'Tis no security to a natural man that he is now in health and that he don't see which way he should now immediately go out of the world by any accident, and that there is no visible danger in any respect in his circumstances. The manifold and continual experience of the world in all ages shows that this is no evidence that a man is not on the very brink of eternity, and that the next step won't be into another world. The unseen, unthought of ways and means of persons' going suddenly out of the world are innumerable and inconceivable. Unconverted men walk over the pit of hell on a rotten covering, and there are innumerable places in this covering so weak that they won't bear their weight, and these places are not seen. The arrows of death fly unseen at noonday; the sharpest sight can't discern them. God has so many different, unsearchable ways of taking wicked men out of the world and sending 'em to hell that there is nothing to make it appear that God had need to be at the expense of a miracle, or go out of the ordinary course of His providence, to destroy any wicked man at any moment. All the means that there are of sinners' going out of the world are so in God's hands and so absolutely subject to His power and determination, that it don't depend at all less on the mere will of God, whether sinners shall at any moment go to hell, than if means were never made use of or at all concerned in the case.

8. Natural men's prudence and care to preserve their own lives, or the care of others to preserve them, don't secure 'em a moment. This, divine providence and universal experience does also bear testimony to. There is this clear

evidence that men's own wisdom is no security to them from death; that if it were otherwise we should see some difference between the wise and politic men of the world and others, with regard to their liableness to early and unexpected death. But how is it in fact? Eccles. ii:16: "How dieth the wise man? As the fool."

9. All wicked men's pains and contrivance they use to escape hell, while they continue to reject Christ and so remain wicked men, don't secure 'em from hell one moment. Almost every natural man that hears of hell flatters himself that he shall escape it; he depends upon himself for his own security; he flatters himself in what he has done, in what he is now doing, or what he intends to do; every one lays out matters in his own mind how he shall avoid damnation, and flatters himself that he contrives well for himself, and that his schemes won't fail. They hear indeed that there are but few saved and that the bigger part of men that have died heretofore are gone to hell, but each one imagines that he lays out matters better for his own escape than others have done; he don't intend to come to that place of torment; he says within himself that he intends to take care that shall be effectual, and to order matters so for himself as not to fail.

But the foolish children of men do miserably delude themselves in their own schemes and in their confidence in their own strength and wisdom; they trust to nothing but a shadow. The bigger part of those that heretofore have lived under the same means of grace, and are now dead, are undoubtedly gone to hell; and it was not because they were not as wise as those that are now alive; it was not because they did not lay out matters as well for themselves to secure their own escape. If it were so that we could come to speak with them and could inquire of them, one by one, whether they expected, when alive, and when they used to hear about hell, ever to be subjects of that misery, we, doubtless, should hear one and another reply, "No, I never intended to come here: I had laid out matters otherwise in my mind; I thought I should contrive well for myself: I thought my scheme good: I intended to take effectual care; but it came upon me unexpected; I did not look for it at that time, and in that manner; it came as a thief: death outwitted me: God's wrath was too quick for me. O my cursed foolishness! I was flattering myself, and pleasing myself with vain dreams of what I would do hereafter; and when I was saying peace and safety, then sudden destruction came upon me."

10. God has laid himself under no obligation, by any promise, to keep any natural man out of hell one moment. God certainly has made no promises either of eternal life or of any deliverance or preservation from eternal death, but what are contained in the covenant of grace, the promises that are given in Christ, in whom all the promises are yea and amen. But surely they have no interest in the promises of the covenant of grace that are not the children of the covenant and that do not believe in any of the promises of the covenant and have no interest in the Mediator of the covenant.

So that, whatever some have imagined and pretended about promises made to natural men's earnest seeking and knocking, 'tis plain and manifest that whatever pains a natural man takes in religion, whatever prayers he makes, till he believes in Christ God is under no manner of obligation to keep him a moment from eternal destruction.

So that thus it is that natural men are held in the hand of God over the pit of hell; they have deserved the fiery pit, and are already sentenced to it; and God is dreadfully provoked, His anger is as great towards them as to those that are actually suffering the executions of the fierceness of His wrath in hell, and they have done nothing in the least to appease or abate that anger; neither is God in the least bound by any promise to hold 'em up one moment; the devil is waiting for them, hell is gaping for them, the flames gather and flash about them, and would fain lay hold on them and swallow them up, the fire pent up in their own hearts is struggling to break out and they have no interest in any Mediator, there are no means within reach that can be any security to them. In short they have no refuge, nothing to take hold of; all that preserves them every moment is the mere arbitrary will and uncovenanted, unobliged forbearance of an incensed God.

APPLICATION. The use may be of awakening to unconverted persons in this congregation. This that you have heard is the case of every one of you that are out of Christ. That world of misery, that lake of burning brimstone, is extended abroad under you. There is the dreadful pit of the glowing flames of the wrath of God; there is hell's wide gaping mouth open; and you have nothing to stand upon, nor any thing to take hold of. There is nothing between you and hell but the air; 'tis only the power and mere pleasure of God that holds you up.

You probably are not sensible of this; you find you are kept out of hell, but don't see the hand of God in it, but look at other things, as the good state of your bodily constitution, your care of your own life, and the means you use for your own preservation. But indeed these things are nothing; if God should withdraw His hand, they would avail no more to keep you from falling than the thin air to hold up a person that is suspended in it.

Your wickedness makes you as it were heavy as lead and to tend downwards with great weight and pressure towards hell; and if God should let you go, you would immediately sink and swiftly descend and plunge into the bottomless gulf, and your healthy constitution, and your own care and prudence, and best contrivance, and all your righteousness, would have no more influence to uphold you and keep you out of hell than a spider's web would have to stop a falling rock. Were it not that so is the sovereign pleasure of God, the earth would not bear you one moment; for you are a burden to it; the creation groans with you; the creature is made subject to the bondage of your corruption, not willingly; the sun don't willingly shine upon you to give you light to serve sin and Satan; the earth don't willingly yield her increase to satisfy your lusts; nor is it willingly a stage for your wickedness to be acted upon; the air don't willingly serve you for breath to maintain the flame of life in your vitals, while you spend your life in the service of God's enemies. God's creatures are good, and were made for men to serve God with, and don't willingly subserve to any other purpose, and groan when they are abused to purposes so directly contrary to their nature and end. And the world would spew you out, were it not for the sovereign hand of Him who hath subjected it in hope. There are the black clouds of God's wrath now hanging directly over your heads, full of the dreadful storm, and big with thunder; and were it not for the restraining hand of God, it would immediately burst forth upon you. The sovereign pleasure of God, for the present, stays His rough wind;

otherwise it would come with fury, and your destruction would come like a whirlwind, and you would be like the chaff of the summer threshing floor.

The wrath of God is like great waters that are dammed for the present; they increase more and more, and rise higher and higher, till an outlet is given; and the longer the stream is stopped, the more rapid and mighty is its course, when once it is let loose. 'Tis true, that judgment against your evil work has not been executed hitherto; the floods of God's vengeance have been withheld; but your guilt in the meantime is constantly increasing, and you are every day treasuring up more wrath; the waters are continually rising, and waxing more and more mighty; and there is nothing but the mere pleasure of God that holds the waters back, that are unwilling to be stopped, and press hard to go forward. If God should only withdraw His hand from the floodgate, it would immediately fly open, and the fiery floods of the fierceness and wrath of God would rush forth with inconceivable fury, and would come upon you with omnipotent power; and if your strength were ten thousand times greater than it is, yea, ten thousands times greater than the strength of the stoutest, sturdiest devil in hell, it would be nothing to withstand or endure it.

The bow of God's wrath is bent, and the arrow made ready on the string, and justice bends the arrow at your heart, and strains the bow, and it is nothing but the mere pleasure of God, and that of an angry God, without any promise or obligation at all, that keeps the arrow one moment from being made drunk with your blood.

Thus are all you that never passed under a great change of heart by the mighty power of the Spirit of God upon your souls; all that were never born again, and made new creatures, and raised from being dead in sin to a state of new and before altogether unexperienced light and life. However you may have reformed your life in many things, and may have had religious affections, and may keep up a form of religion in your families and closets, and in the house of God, and may be strict in it, you are thus in the hands of an angry God. 'Tis nothing but His mere pleasure that keeps you from being this moment swallowed up in everlasting destruction.

However unconvinced you may now be of the truth of what you hear, by and by you will be fully convinced of

it. Those that are gone from being in the like circumstances with you see that it was so with them; for destruction came suddenly upon most of them, when they expected
nothing of it, and while they were saying, "Peace and
safety." Now they see that those things that they depended
on for peace and safety were nothing but thin air and
empty shadows.

The God that holds you over the pit of hell much as one
holds a spider or some loathsome insect over the fire,
abhors you and is dreadfully provoked; His wrath towards
you burns like fire; He looks upon you as worthy of nothing else but to be cast into the fire; He is of purer eyes
than to bear to have you in His sight; you are ten thousand
times so abominable in his eyes, as the most hateful and
venomous serpent is in ours. You have offended Him infinitely more than ever a stubborn rebel did his prince:
and yet it is nothing but His hand that holds you from falling into the fire every moment. 'Tis ascribed to nothing
else that you did not go to hell the last night, that you was
suffered to awake again in this world after you closed your
eyes to sleep; and there is no other reason to be given why
you have not dropped into hell since you arose in the
morning, but that God's hand has held you up. There is
no other reason to be given why you han't gone to hell
since you have sat here in the house of God, provoking
His pure eyes by your sinful wicked manner of attending
His solemn worship. Yea, there is nothing else that is to be
given as a reason why you don't this very moment drop
down into hell.

O sinner! consider the fearful danger you are in. 'Tis a
great furnace of wrath, a wide and bottomless pit, full of
the fire of wrath, that you are held over in the hand of that
God whose wrath is provoked and incensed as much
against you as against many of the damned in hell. You
hang by a slender thread, with the flames of divine wrath
flashing about it and ready every moment to singe it and
burn it asunder; and you have no interest in any Mediator,
and nothing to lay hold of to save yourself, nothing to keep
off the flames of wrath, nothing of your own, nothing that
you ever have done, nothing that you can do, to induce
God to spare you one moment.

And consider here more particularly several things concerning that wrath that you are in such danger of.

1. Whose wrath it is. It is the wrath of the infinite God. If it were only the wrath of man, though it were of the most potent prince, it would be comparatively little to be regarded. The wrath of kings is very much dreaded, especially of absolute monarchs that have the possessions and lives of their subjects wholly in their power, to be disposed of at their mere will. Prov. xx:2: "The fear of a king is as the roaring of a lion: whoso provoketh him to anger sinneth against his own soul." The subject that very much enrages an arbitrary prince is liable to suffer the most extreme torments that human art can invent or human power can inflict. But the greatest earthly potentates, in their greatest majesty and strength, and when clothed in their greatest terrors, are but feeble, despicable worms of the dust in comparison of the great and almighty Creator and King of heaven and earth: it is but little that they can do when most enraged, and when they have exerted the utmost of their fury. All the kings of the earth before God are as grasshoppers; they are nothing and less than nothing: both their love and their hatred is to be despised. The wrath of the great King of kings is as much more terrible than theirs, as his majesty is greater. Luke xii:4, 5: "And I say unto you my friends, Be not afraid of them that kill the body, and after that have no more that they can do. But I will forewarn you whom you shall fear: Fear him, which after he hath killed hath power to cast into hell; yea, I say unto you, Fear him."

2. 'Tis the fierceness of His wrath that you are exposed to. We often read of the fury of God; as in Isa. lix:18: "According to their deeds, accordingly he will repay fury to his adversaries." So Isa. lxvi:15: "For, behold, the Lord will come with fire, and with his chariots like a whirlwind, to render his anger with fury, and his rebuke with flames of fire." And so in many other places. So we read of God's fierceness, Rev. xix:15. There we read of "the winepress of the fierceness and wrath of Almighty God." The words are exceeding terrible: if it had only been said, "the wrath of God," the words would have implied that which is infinitely dreadful: but 'tis not only said so, but "the fjerceness and wrath of God." The fury of God! The fierceness of Jehovah! Oh, how dreadful must that be! Who can utter or conceive what such expressions carry in them! But it is not only said so, but "the fierceness and wrath of

Almighty God." As though there would be a very great manifestation of His almighty power in what the fierceness of His wrath should inflict, as though omnipotence should be as it were enraged, and exerted, as men are wont to exert their strength in the fierceness of their wrath. Oh! then, what will be the consequence! What will become of the poor worm that shall suffer it! Whose hands can be strong! And whose heart endure! To what a dreadful, inexpressible, inconceivable depth of misery must the poor creature be sunk who shall be the subject of this!

Consider this, you that are here present, that yet remain in an unregenerate state. That God will execute the fierceness of His anger implies that He will inflict wrath without any pity. When God beholds the ineffable extremity of your case, and sees your torment so vastly disproportioned to your strength, and sees how your poor soul is crushed, and sinks down, as it were, into an infinite gloom, He will have no compassion upon you, He will not forbear the executions of His wrath, or in the least lighten His hand; there shall be no moderation or mercy, nor will God then at all stay His rough wind; He will have no regard to your welfare, nor be at all careful lest you should suffer too much in any other sense than only that you should not suffer beyond what strict justice requires: nothing shall be withheld because it is so hard for you to bear. Ezek. viii:18: "Therefore will I also deal in fury: mine eye shall not spare, neither will I have pity: and though they cry in mine ears with a loud voice, yet will I not hear them." Now God stands ready to pity you; this is a day of mercy; you may cry now with some encouragement of obtaining mercy: but when once the day of mercy is past, your most lamentable and dolorous cries and shrieks will be in vain; you will be wholly lost and thrown away of God, as to any regard to your welfare; God will have no other use to put you to but only to suffer misery; you shall be continued in being to no other end; for you will be a vessel of wrath fitted to destruction; and there will be no other use of this vessel, but only to be filled full of wrath: God will be so far from pitying you when you cry to Him, that 'tis said He will only "laugh and mock." (Prov. i:25, 26, &c.).

How awful are those words (Isa. lxiii:3) which are the words of the great God: "I will tread them in mine anger, and trample them in my fury; and their blood shall be sprinkled upon my garments, and I will stain all my raiment." 'Tis perhaps impossible to conceive of words that carry in them greater manifestations of these three things, viz., contempt and hatred and fierceness of indignation. If you cry to God to pity you, He will be so far from pitying you in your doleful case or showing you the least regard or favor, that instead of that He'll only tread you under foot; and though He will know that you can't bear the weight of omnipotence treading upon you, yet He won't regard that, but He will crush you under his feet without mercy; He'll crush out your blood, and make it fly, and it shall be sprinkled on His garments, so as to stain all His raiment. He will not only hate you, but He will have you in the utmost contempt; no place shall be thought fit for you but under His feet, to be trodden down as the mire of the streets.

3. The misery you are exposed to is that which God will inflict to that end that He might show what that wrath of Jehovah is. God hath had it in his heart to show to angels and men both how excellent His love is and also how terrible His wrath is. Sometimes earthly kings have a mind to show how terrible their wrath is by the extreme punishments they would execute on those that provoke 'em. Nebuchadnezzar, that mighty and haughty monarch of the Chaldean empire, was willing to show his wrath when enraged with Shadrach, Meshech, and Abednego; and accordingly gave order that the burning fiery furnace should be heated seven times hotter than it was before; doubtless, it was raised to the utmost degree of fierceness that human art could raise it; but the great God is also willing to show His wrath and magnify His awful Majesty and mighty power in the extreme suffering of His enemies. Rom. ix:22: "What if God, willing to show his wrath, and to make his power known, endured with much long-suffering the vessels of wrath fitted to destruction?" And seeing this is His design and what He has determined to show how terrible the unmixed, unrestrained wrath, the fury and fierceness of Jehovah is, He will do it to effect. There will be something accomplished and brought to pass that will be dreadful with a witness. When the great and angry God hath risen up and executed His awful vengeance on the poor sinner, and the wretch is actually suffering the infinite weight and power of His indignation, then will God call upon the whole universe to behold that awful majesty and mighty power that is to

be seen in it (Isa. xxxiii:12, 13, 14): "And the people shall be as the burnings of lime, as thorns cut up shall they be burnt in the fire. Hear, ye that are far off, what I have done; and ye that are near, acknowledge my might. The sinners in Zion are afraid; fearfulness hath surprised the hypocrites," &c.

Thus it will be with you that are in an unconverted state if you continue in it; the infinite might and majesty and terribleness of the Omnipotent God shall be magnified upon you in the ineffable strength of your torments. You shall be tormented in the presence of the holy angels and in the presence of the Lamb; and when you shall be in this state of suffering, the glorious inhabitants of heaven shall go forth and look on the awful spectacle that they may see what the wrath and fierceness of the Almighty is; and when they have seen it, they will fall down and adore that great power and majesty. Isa. lxvi:23, 24: "And it shall come to pass, that from one new moon to another, and from one sabbath to another, shall all flesh come to worship before me, saith the Lord. And they shall go forth, and look upon the carcasses of the men that have transgressed against me: for their worm shall not die, neither shall their fire be quenched; and they shall be an abhorring unto all flesh."

4. It is everlasting wrath. It would be dreadful to suffer this fierceness and wrath of Almighty God one moment; but you must suffer it to all eternity: there will be no end to this exquisite, horrible misery. When you look forward, you shall see a long forever, a boundless duration before you, which will swallow up your thoughts and amaze your soul; and you will absolutely despair of ever having any deliverance, any end, any mitigation, any rest at all; you will know certainly that you must wear out long ages, millions of millions of ages, in wrestling and conflicting with this almighty, merciless vengeance; and then when you have done so, when so many ages have actually been spent by you in this manner, you will know that all is but a point to what remains. So that your punishment will indeed be infinite. Oh, who can express what the state of a soul in such circumstances is! All that we can possibly say about it gives but a very feeble, faint representation of it; it is inexpressible and inconceivable, for "who knows the power of God's anger?"

How dreadful is the state of those that are daily and

hourly in danger of this great wrath and infinite misery! But this is the dismal case of every soul in this congregation that has not been born again, however moral and strict, sober and religious, they may otherwise be. Oh, that you would consider it, whether you be young or old! There is reason to think that there are many in this congregation now hearing this discourse, that will actually be the subjects of this very misery to all eternity. We know not who they are, or in what seats they sit, or what thoughts they now have. It may be they are now at ease, and hear all these things without much disturbance, and are now flattering themselves that they are not the persons, promising themselves that they shall escape. If we knew that there was one person, and but one, in the whole congregation, that was to be the subject of this misery, what an awful thing it would be to think of! If we knew who it was, what an awful sight would it be to see such a person! How might all the rest of the congregation lift up a lamentable and bitter cry over him! But alas! instead of one, how many is it likely will remember this discourse in hell! And it would be a wonder if some that are now present should not be in hell in a very short time, before this year is out. And it would be no wonder if some persons that now sit here in some seats of this meeting-house in health, and quiet and secure, should be there before tomorrow morning. Those of you that finally continue in a natural condition, that shall keep out of hell longest, will be there in a little time! Your damnation don't slumber; it will come swiftly and, in all probability, very suddenly upon many of you. You have reason to wonder that you are not already in hell. 'Tis doubtless the case of some that heretofore you have seen and known, that never deserved hell more than you and that heretofore appeared as likely to have been now alive as you. Their case is past all hope; they are crying in extreme misery and perfect despair. But here you are in the land of the living and in the house of God, and have an opportunity to obtain salvation. What would not those poor, damned, hopeless souls give for one day's such opportunity as you now enjoy!

And now you have an extraordinary opportunity, a day wherein Christ has flung the door of mercy wide open and stands in the door calling and crying with a loud voice to poor sinners; a day wherein many are flocking to Him and pressing into the Kingdom of God. Many are daily coming from the east, west, north and south; many that were very likely in the same miserable condition that you are in are in now a happy state, with their hearts filled with love to Him that has loved them and washed them from their sins in His own blood, and rejoicing in hope of the glory of God. How awful is it to be left behind at such a day! To see so many others feasting, while you are pining and perishing! To see so many rejoicing and singing for joy of heart, while you have cause to mourn for sorrow of heart and howl for vexation of spirit! How can you rest for one moment in such a condition? Are not your souls as precious as the souls of the people at Suffield, where they are flocking from day to day to Christ?

Are there not many here that have lived long in the world that are not to this day born again, and so are aliens from the commonwealth of Israel and have done nothing ever since they have lived but treasure up wrath against the day of wrath? Oh, sirs, your case in an especial manner is extremely dangerous; your guilt and hardness of heart is extremely great. Don't you see how generally persons of your years are passed over and left in the present remarkable and wonderful dispensation of God's mercy? You had need to consider yourselves and wake thoroughly out of sleep; you cannot bear the fierceness and the wrath of the infinite God.

And you that are young men and young women, will you neglect this precious season that you now enjoy, when so many others of your age are renouncing all youthful vanities and flocking to Christ? You especially have now an extraordinary opportunity; but if you neglect it, it will soon be with you as it is with those persons that spent away all the precious days of youth in sin and are now come to such a dreadful pass in blindness and hardness.

And you children that are unconverted, don't you know that you are going down to hell to bear the dreadful wrath of that God that is now angry with you every day and every night? Will you be content to be the children of the devil, when so many other children in the land are converted and are become the holy and happy children of the King of kings?

And let every one that is yet out of Christ and hanging over the pit of hell, whether they be old men and women or middle-aged or young people or little children, now hearken to the loud calls of God's word and providence. This acceptable year of the Lord that is a day of such great favor to some will doubtless be a day of as remarkable vengeance to others. Men's hearts harden and their guilt increases apace at such a day as this, if they neglect their souls. And never was there so great danger of such persons being given up to hardness of heart and blindness of mind. God seems now to be hastily gathering in His elect in all parts of the land, and probably the bigger part of adult persons that ever shall be saved will be brought in now in a little time; and that it will be as it was on that great outpouring of the Spirit upon the Jews in the Apostles' days, the election will obtain and the rest will be blinded. If this should be the case with you, you will eternally curse this day, and will curse the day that ever you was born to see such a season of the pouring out of God's Spirit, and will wish that you had died and gone to hell before you had seen it. Now undoubtedly it is as it was in the days of John the Baptist, the axe is in an extraordinary manner laid at the root of the trees, that every tree that bringeth not forth good fruit may be hewn down and cast into the fire.

Therefore let every one that is out of Christ now awake and fly from the wrath to come. The wrath of Almighty God is now undoubtedly hanging over a great part of this congregation. Let every one fly out of Sodom. "Haste and escape for your lives, look not behind you, escape to the mountain, lest ye be consumed."

1741

FROM

Freedom of the Will

PART I

Sect. I. Concerning the Nature of the Will.

It may possibly be thought that there is no great need of going about to define or describe the Will, this word being generally as well understood as any other words we can use to explain it; and so perhaps it would be, had not philosophers, metaphysicians and polemic divines brought the matter into obscurity by the things they have said of it. But since it is so, I think it may be of some use, and will tend to greater clearness in the following discourse, to say a few things concerning it.

And therefore I observe that the will (without any metaphysical refining) is: That by which the mind chooses any thing. The faculty of the will is that power or principle of mind by which it is capable of choosing: an act of the will is the same as an act of choosing or choice.

If any think it is a more perfect definition of the will to say that it is that by which the soul either chooses or refuses, I am content with it though I think it enough to say it is that by which the soul chooses; for in every act of will whatsoever, the mind chooses one thing rather than another; it chooses something rather than the contrary, or rather than the want or non-existence of that thing. So in every act of refusal, the mind chooses the absence of the thing refused; the positive and the negative are set before the mind for its choice, and it chooses the negative; and the mind's making its choice in that case is properly the act of the will; the will's determining between the two is a voluntary determination; but that is the same thing as making a choice. So that by whatever names we call the act of the will, choosing, refusing, approving, disapproving, liking, disliking, embracing, rejecting, determining, directing, commanding, forbidding, inclining or being averse, being pleased or displeased with—all may be reduced to this act of choosing. . . .

Sect. II. Concerning the Determination of the Will.

By determining the will, if the phrase be used with any meaning, must be intended, causing that the act of the will or choice should be thus, and not otherwise; and the will is said to be determined when, in consequence of some action or influence, its choice is directed to, and fixed upon, a particular object. As when we speak of the determination of motion, we mean causing the motion of the body to be in such a direction, rather than another.

The determination of the will supposes an effect which must have a cause. If the will be determined, there is a determiner. This must be supposed to be intended even by them that say the will determines itself. If it be so, the will is both determiner and determined; it is a cause that acts and produces effects upon itself, and is the object of its own influence and action.

With respect to that grand enquiry, "What determines the will?" it would be very tedious and unnecessary, at present, to examine all the various opinions which have been advanced concerning this matter; nor is it needful that I should enter into a particular discussion of all points debated in disputes on that other question, "Whether the will always follows the last dictate of the understanding?" It is sufficient to my present purpose to say, It is that motive, which, as it stands in the view of the mind, is the strongest, that determines the will. But it may be necessary that I should a little explain my meaning.

By motive, I mean the whole of that which moves, excites, or invites the mind to volition, whether that be one thing singly, or many things conjunctly. Many particular things may concur and unite their strength to induce the mind; and when it is so, all together are as one complex motive. And when I speak of the strongest motive, I have respect to the strength of the whole that operates to induce a particular act of volition, whether that be the strength of one thing alone, or of many together.

Whatever is objectively a motive, in this sense, must be something that is extant in the view of apprehension of the understanding, or perceiving faculty. Nothing can induce or invite the mind to will or act any thing, any further than it is perceived, or is some way or other in the mind's view; for what is wholly unperceived and perfectly out of the mind's view cannot affect the mind at all. It is most evident that nothing is in the mind, or reaches it, or takes any hold of it, any otherwise than as it is perceived or thought of.

And I think it must also be allowed by all that every thing that is properly called a motive, excitement, or inducement to a perceiving, willing agent, has some sort and degree of tendency or advantage to move or excite the will, previous to the effect, or to the act of the will excited. This previous tendency of the motive is what I call the strength of the motive. That motive which has a less degree of previous advantage or tendency to move the will, or which appears less inviting as it stands in the view of the mind, is what I call a weaker motive. On the contrary, that which appears most inviting, and has, by what appears concerning it to the understanding or apprehension, the greatest degree of previous tendency to excite and induce the choice, is what I call the strongest motive. And in this sense, I suppose the will is always determined by the strongest motive.

Things that exist in the view of the mind have their strength, tendency, or advantage to move or excite its will from many things appertaining to the nature and circumstances of the thing viewed, the nature and circumstances of the mind that views, and the degree and manner of its view, of which it would perhaps be hard to make a perfect enumeration. But so much I think may be determined in general, without room for controversy—that whatever is perceived or apprehended by an intelligent and voluntary agent, which has the nature and influence of a motive to volition or choice, is considered or viewed as good; nor has it any tendency to engage the election of the soul in any further degree than it appears such. For to say otherwise, would be to say that things that appear have a tendency, by the appearance they make, to engage the mind to elect them some other way than by their appearing eligible to it—which is absurd. And therefore it must be true, in some sense, that the will always is, as the greatest apparent good is. . . .

Sect. V. Concerning the Notion of Liberty and of Moral Agency.

The plain and obvious meaning of the words freedom and liberty, in common speech, is the power, opportunity, or advantage that any one has to do as he pleases. Or in other words, his being free from hinderance or impediment in the way of doing, or conducting in any respect as he wills. And the contrary to liberty, whatever name we call that by, is a person's being hindered or unable to conduct as he will, or being necessitated to do otherwise.

If this which I have mentioned be the meaning of the word liberty in the ordinary use of language, as I trust that none that has ever learned to talk and is unprejudiced will deny, then it will follow that in propriety of speech neither liberty, nor its contrary can properly be ascribed to any being or thing, but that which has such a faculty, power, or property, as is called will. For that which is possessed of no will cannot have any power or opportunity of doing according to its will, nor be necessitated to act contrary to its will, nor be restrained from acting agreeably to it. And therefore to talk of liberty, or the contrary, as belonging to the very will itself, is not to speak good sense, if we judge of sense and nonsense by the original and proper signification of words. For the will itself is not an agent that has a will, the power of choosing, itself, has not a power of choosing. That which has the power of volition is the man, or the soul, and not the power of volition itself. And he that has the liberty of doing according to his will is the agent who is possessed of the will, and not the will which he is possessed of. We say with propriety that a bird let loose has power and liberty to fly, but not that the bird's power of flying has a power and liberty of flying. To be free is the property of an agent who is possessed of powers and faculties as much as to be cunning, valiant, bountiful, or zealous. But these qualities are the properties of persons and not the properties of properties.

There are two things contrary to what is called liberty in common speech. One is constraint, otherwise called force, compulsion, and coaction, which is a person's being necessitated to do a thing contrary to his will. The other is restraint, which is his being hindered and not having power to do according to his will. But that which has no will cannot be the subject of these things. I need say the less on this head, Mr. Locke having set the same thing forth, with so great clearness, in his *Essay on the Human Understanding*.

But one thing more I would observe concerning what is vulgarly called liberty—namely, that power and opportunity for one to do and conduct as he will, or according to his choice, is all that is meant by it; without taking into the meaning of the word any thing of the cause of that choice or at all considering how the person came to have such a volition; whether it was caused by some external motive or internal habitual bias; whether it was determined by some internal antecedent volition or whether it happened without a cause; whether it was necessarily connected with something foregoing, or not connected. Let the person come by his choice anyhow, yet, if he is able, and there is nothing in the way to hinder his pursuing and executing his will, the man is perfectly free according to the primary and common notion of freedom.

What has been said may be sufficient to show what is meant by liberty, according to the common notions of mankind and in the usual and primary acceptation of the word. But the word, as used by Arminians, Pelagians and others who oppose the Calvinists, has an entirely different signification. These several things belong to their notion of liberty. 1. That it consists in a self-determining power in the will, of a certain sovereignty the will has over itself, and its own acts, whereby it determines its own volitions so as not to be dependent in its determinations on any cause without itself, nor determined by any thing prior to its own acts. 2. Indifference belongs to liberty in their notion of it, or that the mind, previous to the act of volition, be *in equilibrio*. 3. Contingence is another thing that belongs and is essential to it; not in the common acceptation of the word as that has been already explained, but as opposed to all necessity, or any fixed and certain connection with some previous ground or reason of its existence. They suppose the essence of liberty so much to consist in these things, that unless the will of man be free in this sense, he has no real freedom, how much soever he may be at liberty to act according to his will.

A moral agent is a being that is capable of those actions that have a moral quality, and which can properly be denominated good or evil in a moral sense—virtuous or vicious, commendable or faulty. To moral agency belongs a moral faculty, or sense of moral good and evil, or of such a thing as desert or worthiness, of praise or blame, reward or punishment; and a capacity which an agent has of being influenced in his actions by moral inducements or motives, exhibited to the view of understanding and reason, to engage to a conduct agreeable to the moral faculty.

The sun is very excellent and beneficial in its actions and influence on the earth in warming and causing it to bring forth its fruits; but it is not a moral agent: its action, though good, is not virtuous or meritorious. Fire that breaks out in a city and consumes great part of it is very mischievous in its operation; but it is not a moral agent: what it does is not faulty or sinful, or deserving of any punishment. The brute creatures are not moral agents: the actions of some of them are very profitable and pleasant; others are very hurtful; yet seeing they have no moral faculty, or sense of desert, and do not act from choice guided by understanding, or with a capacity of reasoning and reflecting, but only from instinct and are not capable of being influenced by moral inducements, their actions are not properly sinful or virtuous; nor are they properly the subjects of any such moral treatment for what they do as moral agents are for their faults or good deeds.

Here it may be noted that there is a circumstantial difference between the moral agency of a ruler and a subject. I call it circumstantial because it lies only in the difference of moral inducements by which they are capable of being influenced, arising from the difference of circumstances. A ruler acting in that capacity only is not capable of being influenced by a moral law and its sanctions of threatenings and promises, rewards and punishments, as the subject is, though both may be influenced by a knowledge of moral good and evil. And therefore the moral agency of the Supreme Being, who acts only in the capacity of a ruler towards his creatures, and never as a subject, differs in that respect from the moral agency of created intelligent beings. God's actions, and particularly those which He exerts as a moral governor, have moral qualifications and are morally good in the highest degree. They are most perfectly holy and righteous; and we must conceive of Him as influenced in the highest degree by that which, above all others, is properly a moral inducement; viz. the moral good which He sees in such and such things; and therefore He is, in the most proper sense, a moral agent, the source of all moral ability and agency, the fountain and rule of all virtue and moral good, though by reason of His being supreme over all, it is not possible He should be under the influence of law or command, promises or threatenings, rewards or punishments, counsels or warnings. The essential qualities of a moral agent are in God, in the greatest possible perfection—such as understanding, to perceive the difference between moral good and evil; a capacity of discerning that moral worthiness and demerit, by which some things are praiseworthy, others deserving of blame and punishment; and also a capacity of choice, and choice guided by understanding, and a power of acting according to his choice or pleasure, and being capable of doing those things which are in the highest sense praiseworthy. And herein does very much consist that image of God wherein He made man (which we read of Gen. i:26, 27, and chap. ix:6), by which God distinguished man from the beasts, viz. in those faculties and principles of nature, whereby he is capable of moral agency. Herein very much consists the natural image of God; whereas the spiritual and moral image, wherein man was made at first, consisted in that moral excellency with which he was endowed.

1754

FROM

The Nature of True Virtue

Showing Wherein the Essence of True Virtue Consists

Whatever controversies and variety of opinions there are about the nature of virtue, yet all (excepting some skeptics, who deny any real difference between virtue and vice) mean by it something beautiful, or rather some kind of beauty, or excellency. It is not *all* beauty that is called virtue; for instance, not the beauty of a building, of a flower, or of the rainbow: but some beauty belonging to beings that have perception and will. It is not all beauty of mankind that is called virtue; for instance, not the external beauty of the countenance, or shape, gracefulness of motion, or harmony of voice: but it is a beauty that has its original seat in the mind. But yet perhaps not every thing that may be called a beauty of mind is properly called virtue. There is a beauty of understanding and speculation. There is something in the ideas and conceptions of great philosophers and statesmen that may be called beautiful, which is a different thing from what is most commonly meant by virtue. But virtue is the beauty of those qualities and acts of the mind that are of moral nature, i.e., such as are attended with desert or worthiness of praise or blame. Things of this sort, it is generally agreed, so far as I know, are not any thing belonging merely to speculation; but to the disposition and will, or —to use a general word I suppose commonly well understood—the heart. Therefore I suppose I shall not depart from the common opinion when I say that virtue is the beauty of the qualities and exercises of the heart, or those actions which proceed from them. So that when it is inquired, what is the nature of true virtue, this is the same as to inquire, what that is which renders any habit, disposition, or exercise of the heart truly beautiful. I use the phrase *true* virtue, and speak of things *truly* beautiful because I suppose it will generally be allowed that there is a distinction to be made between some things which are truly virtuous, and others which only seem to be virtuous, through a partial and imperfect view of things: that some actions and dispositions appear beautiful if considered partially and superficially, or with regard to some things belonging to them, and in some of their circumstances and tendencies, which would appear otherwise in a more extensive and comprehensive view, wherein they are seen clearly in their whole nature and the extent of their connections in the universality of things. There is a general and a particular beauty. By a particular beauty I mean that by which a thing appears beautiful when considered only with regard to its connection with, and tendency to some particular things within a limited, and, as it were, a private sphere. And a general beauty is that by which a thing appears beautiful when viewed most perfectly, comprehensively and universally, with regard to all its tendencies, and its connections with every thing it stands related to. The former may be without and against the latter. As a few notes in a tune, taken only by themselves and in their relation to one another, may be harmonious; which when considered with respect to all the notes in the tune, or the entire series of sounds they are connected with, may be very discordant and disagreeable—of which more afterwards. That only, therefore, is what I mean by true virtue, which is that, belonging to the heart of an intelligent being, that is beautiful by a general beauty, or beautiful in a comprehensive view as it is in itself and as related to every thing that it stands in connection with. And therefore when we are inquiring concerning the nature of true virtue, viz., wherein this true and general beauty of the heart does most essentially consist, this is my answer to the inquiry:

True virtue most essentially consists in benevolence to being in general. Or perhaps to speak more accurately, it is that consent, propensity and union of heart to being in general, that is immediately exercised in a general good will.

The things which were before observed of the nature of true virtue naturally lead us to such a notion of it. If it has its seat in the heart, and is the general goodness and beauty of the disposition and exercise of that, in the most comprehensive view considered with regard to its universal tendency, and as related to every thing that it stands in connection with; what can it consist in, but a consent and good will to being in general? Beauty does not consist in discord and dissent, but in consent and agreement. And if every intelligent being is some way related to being in general and is a part of the universal system of existence, and so stands in connection with the whole, what can its general and true beauty be but its union and consent with the great whole?

If any such thing can be supposed as a union of heart to some particular being, or number of beings, disposing it to benevolence to a private circle or system of beings which are but a small part of the whole, not implying a tendency to a union with the great system, and not at all inconsistent with enmity towards being in general, this I suppose not to be of the nature of true virtue, although it may in some respects be good, and may appear beautiful in a confined and contracted view of things. But of this more afterwards.

It is abundantly plain by the holy Scriptures, and generally allowed not only by Christian divines but by the more considerable deists, that virtue most essentially consists in love. And I suppose, it is owned by the most considerable writers to consist in general love of benevolence, or kind affection: though it seems to me, the meaning of some in this affair is not sufficiently explained, which perhaps occasions some error or confusion in discourses on this subject.

When I say true virtue consists in love to being in general, I shall not be likely to be understood. [I mean] that no one act of the mind or exercise of love is of the nature of true virtue, but what has being in general, or the great system of universal existence, for its direct and immediate object: so that no exercise of love or kind affection to any one particular being that is but a small part of this whole, has any thing of the nature of true virtue;

but that the nature of true virtue consists in a disposition to benevolence towards being in general—though, from such a disposition may arise exercises of love to particular beings, as objects are presented and occasions arise. No wonder, that he who is of a generally benevolent disposition, should be more disposed than another to have his heart moved with benevolent affection to particular persons whom he is acquainted and conversant with, and from whom arise the greatest and most frequent occasions for exciting his benevolent temper. But my meaning is, that no affections towards particular persons or beings are of the nature of true virtue, but such as arise from a generally benevolent temper, or from that habit or frame of mind wherein consists a disposition to love being in general.

And perhaps it is needless for me to give notice to my readers that when I speak of an intelligent being's having a heart united and benevolently disposed to being in general, I thereby mean *intelligent* being in general. Not inanimate things, or beings that have no perception or will, which are not properly capable objects of benevolence.

Love is commonly distinguished into love of benevolence and love of complacence. Love of benevolence is that affection or propensity of the heart to any being, which causes it to incline to its well being, or disposes it to desire and take pleasure in its happiness. And if I mistake not, it is agreeable to the common opinion that beauty in the object is not always the ground of this propensity, but that there may be such a thing as benevolence, or a disposition to the welfare of those that are not considered as beautiful; unless mere existence be accounted a beauty. And benevolence or goodness in the Divine Being is generally supposed not only to be prior to the beauty of many of its objects, but to their existence: so as to be the ground both of their existence and their beauty, rather than they the foundation of God's benevolence, as it is supposed that it is God's goodness which moved him to give them both being and beauty. So that if all virtue primarily consists in that affection of heart to being, which is exercised in benevolence, or an inclination to its good, then God's virtue is so extended as to include a propensity not only to being actually existing, and actually beautiful, but to possible being, so as to incline him to give being, beauty and happiness. But not now to insist particularly on this. What I would have observed at present is that it must be allowed [that] benevolence doth not necessarily presuppose beauty in its object.

What is commonly called love of complacence presupposes beauty. For it is no other than delight in beauty; or complacence in the person or being beloved for his beauty.

If virtue be the beauty of an intelligent being, and virtue consists in love, then it is a plain inconsistence to suppose that virtue primarily consists in any love to its object for its beauty; either in a love of complacence, which is delight in a being for his beauty, or in a love of benevolence, that has the beauty of its object for its foundation. For that would be to suppose, that the beauty of intelligent beings primarily consists in love to beauty; or, that their virtue first of all consists in their love to virtue, which is an inconsistence, and going in a circle. Because it makes virtue, or beauty of mind, the foundation or first motive of that love wherein virtue originally consists, or wherein the very first virtue consists; or, it supposes the first virtue to be the consequence and effect of virtue. So that virtue is originally the foundation and exciting cause of the very beginning or first being of virtue, which makes the first virtue, both the ground, and the consequence, both cause and effect of itself. Doubtless virtue primarily consists in something else besides any effect or consequence of virtue. If virtue consists primarily in love to virtue, then virtue, the thing loved, is the love of virtue: so that virtue must consist in the love of the love of virtue. And if it be inquired what that virtue is, which virtue consists in the love of the love of, it must be answered, it is the love of virtue. So that there must be the love of the love of the love of virtue, and so on *in infinitum*. For there is no end of going back in a circle. We never come to any beginning, or foundation. For it is without beginning and hangs on nothing.

Therefore if the essence of virtue or beauty of mind lies in love, or a disposition to love, it must primarily consist in something different both from complacence, which is a delight in beauty, and also from any benevolence that has the beauty of its object for its foundation. Because it is absurd to say that virtue is primarily and first of all the consequence of itself. For this makes virtue primarily prior to itself.

Nor can virtue primarily consist in gratitude; or one being's benevolence to another for his benevolence to him. Because this implies the same inconsistence. For it supposes a benevolence prior to gratitude, that is the cause of gratitude. Therefore the first benevolence, or that benevolence which has none prior to it, cannot be gratitude.

Therefore there is room left for no other conclusion than that the primary object of virtuous love is being, simply considered; or, that true virtue primarily consists, not in love to any particular beings, because of their virtue or beauty, nor in gratitude, because they love us; but in a propensity and union of heart to being simply considered; exciting absolute benevolence (if I may so call it) to being in general. I say, true virtue primarily consists in this. For I am far from asserting that there is no true virtue in any other love than this absolute benevolence. But I would express what appears to me to be the truth on this subject, in the following particulars.

The first object of a virtuous benevolence is being, simply considered: and if being, simply considered, be its object, then being in general is its object; and the thing it has an ultimate propensity to is the highest good of being in general. And it will seek the good of every individual being unless it be conceived as not consistent with the highest good of being in general. In which case the good of a particular being, or some beings, may be given up for the sake of the highest good of being in general. And particularly if there be any being that is looked upon as statedly and irreclaimably opposite and an enemy to being in general, then consent and adherence to being in general will induce the truly virtuous heart to forsake that being, and to oppose it.

And further, if being, simply considered, be the first object of a truly virtuous benevolence, then that being who has most of being, or has the greatest share of existence, other things being equal, so far as such a being is exhibited to our faculties or set in our view, will have the greatest share of the propensity and benevolent affection of the heart. I say, other things being equal, especially because there is a secondary object of virtuous benevolence, that I shall take notice of presently. Which is one thing that must be considered as the ground or motive to a purely virtuous benevolence. Pure benevolence in its first exercise is nothing else but being's uniting consent or propensity to being; appearing true and pure by its extending to being in general, and inclining to the general highest good, and to each being, whose welfare is consistent with the highest general good, in proportion to the degree of existence* understood, other things being equal.

The second object of a virtuous propensity of heart is benevolent being. A secondary ground of pure benevolence is virtuous benevolence itself in its object. When any one under the influence of general benevolence sees another being possessed of the like general benevolence, this attaches his heart to him and draws forth greater love to him, than merely his having existence: because so far as the being beloved has love to being in general, so far his own being is, as it were, enlarged, extends to and in some sort comprehends being in general: and therefore he that is governed by love to being in general must of necessity have complacence in him, and the greater degree of benevolence to him, as it were out of gratitude to him for his love to general existence, that his own heart is extended and united to, and so looks on its interest as its own. It is because his heart is thus united to being in general, that he looks on a benevolent propensity to being in general, wherever he sees it, as the beauty of the being in whom it is; an excellency that renders him worthy of esteem, complacence, and the greater good will.

But several things may be noted more particularly concerning this secondary ground of a truly virtuous love.

1. That loving a being on this ground necessarily arises from pure benevolence to being in general, and comes to the same thing. For he that has a simple and pure good will to general entity or existence, must love that temper in others that agrees and conspires with itself. A spirit of consent to being must agree with consent to being. That which truly and sincerely seeks the good of others must approve of, and love, that which joins with him in seeking the good of others.

* I say, in proportion to the degree of existence, because one being may have more existence than another, as he may be greater than another. That which is great, has more existence, and is further from nothing, than that which is little. One being may have every thing positive belonging to it, or every thing which goes to its positive existence (in opposition to defect) in a higher degree than another; or a greater capacity and power, greater understanding, every faculty and every positive quality in a higher degree. An archangel must be supposed to have more existence, and to be every way further removed from nonentity, than a worm, or a flea.

2. This which has been now mentioned as a secondary ground of virtuous love, is the thing wherein true moral or spiritual beauty primarily consists. Yea, spiritual beauty consists wholly in this, and the various qualities and exercises of mind which proceed from it, and the external actions which proceed from these internal qualities and exercises. And in these things consists all true virtue, viz., in this love of being, and the qualities and acts which arise from it.

3. As all spiritual beauty lies in these virtuous principles and acts, so it is primarily on this account they are beautiful, viz., that they imply consent and union with being in general. This is the primary and most essential beauty of every thing that can justly be called by the name of virtue, or is any moral excellency in the eye of one that has a perfect view of things. I say, the primary and most essential beauty because there is a secondary and inferior sort of beauty, which I shall take notice of afterwards.

4. This spiritual beauty that is but a secondary ground of a virtuous benevolence, is the ground not only of benevolence but complacence, and is the primary ground of the latter; that is, when the complacence is truly virtuous. Love to us in particular, and kindness received, may be a secondary ground. But this is the primary objective foundation of it.

5. It must be noted that the degree of the amiableness or valuableness of true virtue, primarily consisting in consent and a benevolent propensity of heart to being in general, in the eyes of one that is influenced by such a spirit, is not in the simple proportion of the degree of benevolent affection seen, but in a proportion compounded of the greatness of the benevolent being or the degree of being and the degree of benevolence. One that loves being in general will necessarily value good will to being in general, wherever he sees it. But if he sees the same benevolence in two beings, he will value it more in two, than in one only, because it is a greater thing, more favorable to being in general, to have two beings to favor it than only one of them. For there is more being that favors being: both together having more being than one alone. So, if one being be as great as two, has as much existence as both together, and has the same degree of general benevolence, it is more favorable to being in general than

if there were general benevolence in a being that had but half that share of existence. As a large quantity of gold, with the same degree of preciousness, i.e., with the same excellent quality of matter, is more valuable than a small quantity of the same metal.

6. It is impossible that any one should truly relish this beauty, consisting in general benevolence, who has not that temper himself. I have observed, that if any being is possessed of such a temper, he will unavoidably be pleased with the same temper in another. And it may in like manner be demonstrated that it is such a spirit, and nothing else, which will relish such a spirit. For if a being, destitute of benevolence, should love benevolence to being in general, it would prize and seek that which it had no value for. Because to love an inclination to the good of being in general would imply a loving and prizing the good of being in general. For how should one love and value a disposition to a thing, or a tendency to promote a thing, and for that very reason, because it tends to promote it, when the thing itself is what he is regardless of, and has no value for, nor desires to have promoted.

w. 1755–1758
p. 1765

THE BAY PSALM BOOK

(1640)

The Whole Book of Psalms Faithfully Translated into English Metre, commonly known as The Bay Psalm Book, has the distinction of being the first book published in the American Colonies. Although there were available to the Puritans several English translations of the Psalms for singing by the entire congregation (a Reformation innovation), most notably the Sternhold-Hopkins version, the American Puritans desired a Psalter which was at once more literal and more Calvinist than those in common use. Accordingly, the project was begun some time in 1636 and published four years later in an edition of seventeen hundred copies. A second edition appeared in 1647.

Although it is almost impossible to ascribe authorship to the individual psalms, such learned divines as John Eliot, Richard Mather, Thomas Welde, John Wilson, Nathaniel Ward, Peter Bulkeley, Thomas Shepard, John Norton, and John Cotton contributed to the enterprise. Cotton, the most powerful member of the theocracy of his time, was the author of the Preface and was probably responsible for the translation of Psalm 23. The translators, as Cotton's Preface emphasizes, were guided by the desire for literal accuracy, not "sweetness" or "elegance." In the late 1640's, however, as Cotton Mather put it a half-century later, it was decided that "a little more of art was to be employed upon the verses" and a "revised and refined" edition was entrusted to Henry Dunster, the president of Harvard, and Richard Lyon. This edition, which added many other biblical songs and hymns, appeared in 1651 and remained standard for about one hundred years. For the sake of comparison, we have included three versions of Psalm 23: the

King James translation (1611), the *Bay Psalm Book* version (1640), and the Dunster-Lyon revision (1651).

Accounts of the work are to be found in M. C. Tyler, *A History of American Literature During the Colonial Period*, I (1878); W. Eames, ed., *The Bay Psalm Book* (1903); H. S. Jantz, "The First Century of New England Verse," *Proceedings of the American Antiquarian Society*, LIII (1944); Z. Haraszti, ed., *The Bay Psalm Book* (1956); and Z. Haraszti, *The Enigma of the Bay Psalm Book* (1956).

FROM

The Preface

The singing of psalms, though it breathe forth nothing but holy harmony, and melody: yet such is the subtlety of the enemy, and the enmity of our nature against the Lord, & his ways, that our hearts can find matter of discord in this harmony, and crotchets of division in this holy melody. For there have been three questions especially stirring concerning singing. First, what psalms are to be sung in churches? whether David's and other scripture psalms, or the psalms invented by the gifts of godly men in every age of the church. Secondly, if scripture psalms, whether in their own words, or in such meter as English poetry is wont to run in? Thirdly, by whom are they to be sung? whether by the whole churches together with their voices? or by one man singing alone and the rest joining in silence, & in the close saying amen.

Touching the first, certainly the singing of David's psalms was an acceptable worship of God, not only in his own, but in succeeding times. . . . So that if the singing David's psalms be a moral duty & therefore perpetual; then we under the New Testament are bound to sing them as well as they under the Old. . . .

As for the scruple that some take at the translation of the book of psalms into meter, because David's psalms were sung in his own words without meter: we answer—First. There are many verses together in several psalms of David which run in rhythms (as those that know the Hebrew and as Buxtorf shows *Thesau.* pa. 029) which shows at least the lawfulness of singing psalms in English rhythms.

Secondly. The psalms are penned in such verses as are suitable to the poetry of the Hebrew language, and not in the common style of such other books of the Old Testament as are not poetical; now no Protestant doubteth but that all the books of the scripture should by God's ordinance be extant in the mother tongue of each nation, that they may be understood of all, hence the psalms are to be translated into our English tongue; and if in our English tongue we are to sing them, then as all our English songs (according to the course of our English poetry) do run in meter, so ought David's psalms to be translated into meter, that so we may sing the Lord's songs, as in our English tongue so in such verses as are familiar to an English ear which are commonly metrical. . . .

Neither let any think, that for the meter's sake we have taken liberty or poetical license to depart from the true and proper sense of David's words in the Hebrew verses, no; but it hath been one part of our religious care and faithful endeavor, to keep close to the original text.

As for other objections taken from the difficulty of Ainsworth's tunes, and the corruptions in our common psalm books, we hope they are answered in this new edition of psalms which we here present to God and his Churches. For although we have cause to bless God in many respects for the religious endeavors of the translators of the psalms into meter usually annexed to our Bibles, yet it is not unknown to the godly learned that they have rather presented a paraphrase than the words of David translated according to the rule 2 *Chron.* 29. 30. and that their addition to the words, detractions from the words are not seldom and rare, but very frequent and many times needless, (which we suppose would not be approved of if the psalms were so translated into prose) and that their variations of the sense, and alterations of the sacred text too frequently, may justly minister matter of offense to them that are able to compare the translation with the text; of which failings, some judicious have oft complained, others have been grieved, whereupon it hath been generally desired, that as we do enjoy other, so (if it were the Lord's will) we might enjoy this ordinance also in its native purity: we have therefore done our endeavor to make a plain and familiar translation of the psalms and words of David into English meter, and have not so much as presumed to paraphrase to give the sense of his meaning in other words; we have therefore attended herein as our chief guide the original, shunning all additions, except such as even the best translators of them in prose supply, avoiding all material detractions from words or sense. . . .

As for our translations, we have with our English Bibles (to which next to the original we have had respect) used the idioms of our own tongue instead of Hebraisms, lest they might seem English barbarisms. Synonymies we use indifferently: as *folk* for *people,* and *Lord* for *Jehovah,* and sometime (though seldom) *God* for *Jehovah;* for which (as for some other interpretations of places cited in the New Testament) we have the scriptures' authority *Ps.* 14. with 53. *Heb.* 1. 6. with *Psalm* 97.7. Where a phrase is doubtful we have followed that which (in our own apprehension) is most genuine & edifying:

Sometime we have contracted, sometime dilated the same Hebrew word, both for the sense and the verse's sake: which dilatation we conceive to be no paraphrastical addition no more than the contraction of a true and full translation to be any unfaithful detraction or diminution: as when we dilate *who healeth* and say *he it is who healeth;* so when we contract, *those that stand in awe of God* and say *God's fearers.* . . . As for all other changes of numbers, tenses, and characters of speech, they are such as either the Hebrew will unforcedly bear, or our English forcibly calls for, or they no way change the sense; and such are printed usually in another character.

If therefore the verses are not always so smooth and elegant as some may desire or expect; let them consider that God's altar needs not our polishings: *Ex. 20.* for we have respected rather a plain translation, than to smooth our verses with the sweetness of any paraphrase, and so have attended conscience rather than elegance, fidelity rather than poetry, in translating the Hebrew words into English language, and David's poetry into English meter; that so we may sing in Sion the Lord's songs of praise according to his own will; until he take us from hence, and wipe away all our tears, & bid us enter into our master's joy to sing eternal Hallelujahs.

1640

Psalm 23

The Lord is my shepherd, I shall not want.

He maketh me to lie down in green pastures: he leadeth me beside the still waters.

He restoreth my soul: he leadeth me in the paths of righteousness, for his name's sake.

Yea though I walk through the valley of the shadow of death, I will fear no evil: for thou art with me, thy rod and thy staff they comfort me.

Thou preparest a table before me, in the presence of mine enemies: thou anointest my head with oil, my cup runneth over.

Surely goodness and mercy shall follow me all the days of my life: and I will dwell in the house of the Lord for ever.

[King James]

The Lord to me a shepherd is,
    want therefore shall not I.
He in the folds of tender grass,
    doth cause me down to lie:
To waters calm me gently leads
    Restore my soul doth he:
he doth in paths of righteousness:
    for his name's sake lead me.
Yea though in valley of death's shade
    I walk, none ill I'll fear: 10
because thou art with me, thy rod,
    and staff my comfort are.
For me a table thou hast spread,
    in presence of my foes:
thou dost anoint my head with oil:
    my cup it overflows.
Goodness & mercy surely shall
    all my days follow me:
and in the Lord's house I shall dwell
    so long as days shall be.   20

[*Bay Psalm* Book]

The Lord to me a shepherd is: want therefore shall not I.
He in the folds of tender grass doth make me down to lie.
He leads me to the waters still. Restore my soul doth he;
In paths of righteousness, he will for his name's sake lead
    me.

In valley of death's shade although I walk I'll fear none ill:
For thou with me thy rod, also thy staff me comfort will.
Thou hast 'fore me a table spread, in presence of my foes:
Thou dost anoint with oil my head, my cup it overflows.

Goodness and mercy my days all shall surely follow me:
And in the Lord's house dwell shall I so long as days shall
    be.

                              [Dunster-Lyon revision]

ANNE BRADSTREET

(c1612–1672)

Anne Bradstreet, born in Northampton, England, was the daughter of Thomas Dudley, steward of the learned Puritan, the Earl of Lincoln. Brought up in aristocratic surroundings, she was given an education unusual for women at the time (at one point she had eight tutors) and enjoyed the resources of the Earl of Lincoln's magnificent library at Sempringham Castle. When she was sixteen she married Simon Bradstreet, a graduate of Emmanuel College, Cambridge, steward of the Countess of Warwick and, in a small way, protégé of Thomas Dudley. When she was eighteen, Anne, Simon, and her parents sailed with John Winthrop aboard the *Arbella* for Massachusetts Bay, where both her husband and her father later became governors. An exemplary wife, mother of eight children, housekeeper, and hostess, she was nevertheless a precursor of the "emancipated woman" of our time because she could not fully reconcile herself to a life completely defined by kitchen, church, and children. Apparently, every moment she could take she devoted to writing verses, letters, and diary notes, in which she showed her learning, her passionate love for her husband and children, her strength of character, and her uneasiness about being unable to submit as dutifully and constantly as a good Puritan matron should to a total acceptance of the orthodox beliefs of her sect.

Her first book was taken in manuscript to London by John Woodbridge, a relative. In 1650 it was published in England under a title not of Mrs. Bradstreet's choosing: *The Tenth Muse Lately Sprung up in America. Or, Severall Poems, Compiled with Great Variety of Wit and Learning, Full of Delight. . . . By a*

Gentlewoman in those Parts. The poems were attempts to versify not only her moral and religious beliefs but also contemporary scientific ideas, and they reflected the faculty psychology, physics, physiology, natural sciences, and "correspondences" of the Renaissance. Published as "Quarternions," the poems included "The Four Elements," "The Four Ages of Man," "The Four Humors in Man's Constitution," "The Four Seasons of the Year," and "The Four Monarchies." As intellectual exercises, they bespeak the influence of Sir Walter Raleigh's *History of the World,* Plutarch, Ussher, Francis Quarles' *Emblems,* the Bible, and most particularly the Sylvester translation of *La Semaine* by Guillaume du Bartas.

Although she wrote in an age of male supremacy, which would not necessarily regard the curiosity of a female poet with unalloyed delight, her works were surprisingly well received by her Puritan contemporaries both at home and in England. The poems were given a second edition in Boston in 1687 under the somewhat chastened title of *Several Poems Compiled with Great Variety of Wit and Learning.* The second edition contained new poems superior to the first, and it is these new poems that have earned Anne Bradstreet a lasting reputation. More personal and universal than the earlier works, they indicate the influence not so much of du Bartas as of Sidney, Spenser, and the English metaphysical poets. Generally acknowledged her best are the "Contemplations," some of which are reprinted here. As literary statements they are indications of the depth of feeling that always ran strongly beneath the decorous and tight control that the Puritan demanded of God's chosen people.

Accounts of Anne Bradstreet and her works are to be found in J. H. Ellis, *The Works of Anne Bradstreet in Prose and Verse* (1867); M. C. Tyler, *A History of American Literature During the Colonial Period,* I (1897); H. Campbell, *Anne Bradstreet and Her Time* (1891); C. E. Norton, *The Poems of Mrs. Anne Bradstreet, Together with Her Prose Remains* (1897); L. Caldwell, *An Account of Anne Bradstreet* (1898); S. E. Morison, *Builders of the Bay Colony* (1930); O. Wegelin, "A List of Editions of the Poems of Anne Bradstreet," *American Book Collector,* IV (1933); "The First Century of New England Verse," *Proceedings of the American Antiquarian Society,* LIII (1944); E. W. White, "The Tenth Muse—A Tercentenary Appraisal of Anne Bradstreet," *William and Mary Quarterly,* VIII (1951); J. K. Piercy, *Anne Bradstreet* (1965); and A. Stanford, "Anne Bradstreet: Dogmatist and Rebel," *New England Quarterly,* XXXIX (1966).

The Prologue

1

To sing of wars, of captains, and of kings,
Of cities founded, commonwealths begun,
For my mean pen are too superior things;
Or how they all, or each, their dates have run;
Let poets and historians set these forth;
My obscure lines shall not so dim their worth.

2

But when my wond'ring eyes and envious heart
Great Bartas' sugared lines do but read o'er,
Fool, I do grudge the muses did not part
'Twixt him and me that overfluent store.   10
A Bartas can do what a Bartas will;
But simple I according to my skill.

3

From schoolboy's tongue no rhet'ric we expect,
Nor yet a sweet consort from broken strings,
Nor perfect beauty where's a main defect.
My foolish, broken, blemished Muse so sings;
And this to mend, alas, no art is able,
'Cause nature made it so irreparable.

4

Nor can I, like that fluent, sweet-tongued Greek
Who lisped at first, in future times speak plain.   20
By art he gladly found what he did seek;
A full requital of his striving pain.
Art can do much, but this maxim's most sure:
A weak or wounded brain admits no cure.

5

I am obnoxious to each carping tongue
Who says my hand a needle better fits;
A poet's pen all scorn I should thus wrong,
For such despite they cast on female wits.
If what I do prove well, it won't advance;
They'll say it's stol'n, or else it was by chance.   30

6

But sure the antique Greeks were far more mild;
Else of our sex why feignèd they those nine,

> [nine: the Muses]

And Poesy made Calliope's own child?
So 'mongst the rest they placed the arts divine,
But this weak knot they will full soon untie:
The Greeks did nought but play the fools and lie.

7

Let Greeks be Greeks, and women what they are;
Men have precedency and still excel.
It is but vain unjustly to wage war;
Men can do best, and women know it well.   40
Pre-eminence in all and each is yours;
Yet grant some small acknowledgement of ours.

8

And O ye high-flown quills that soar the skies,
And ever with your prey still catch your praise,
If e'er you deign these lowly lines your eyes,
Give thyme or parsley wreath; I ask no bays.
This mean and unrefinèd ore of mine
Will make your glistering gold but more to shine.

1650

The Author to Her Book

Thou ill-form'd offspring of my feeble brain,
Who after birth did'st by my side remain,
Till snatcht from thence by friends, less wise than true
Who thee abroad expos'd to public view,
Made thee in rags, halting to th' press to trudge,
Where errors were not lessened (all may judge).
At thy return my blushing was not small,
My rambling brat (in print) should mother call.
I cast thee by as one unfit for light,
Thy visage was so irksome in my sight;   10
Yet being mine own, at length affection would
Thy blemishes amend, if so I could:
I wash'd thy face, but more defects I saw,

And rubbing off a spot, still made a flaw.
I stretcht thy joints to make thee even feet,
Yet still thou run'st more hobbling than is meet;
In better dress to trim thee was my mind,
But nought save home-spun cloth, i' th' house I find.
In this array, 'mongst vulgars mayst thou roam,
In critics' hands beware thou dost not come;   20
And take thy way where yet thou art not known,
If for thy father asked, say, thou hadst none:
And for thy mother, she alas is poor,
Which caus'd her thus to send thee out of door.

                                                          1678

The Flesh and the Spirit

In secret place where once I stood
Close by the banks of lacrim flood, [lacrim: tearful]
I heard two sisters reason on
Things that are past and things to come.
One Flesh was called, who had her eye
On worldly wealth and vanity;
The other Spirit, who did rear
Her thoughts unto a higher sphere.
"Sister," quoth Flesh, "what liv'st thou on—
Nothing but meditation?   10
Doth Contemplation feed thee, so
Regardlessly to let earth go?
Can Speculation satisfy
Notion without Reality? [Notion: knowing]
Dost dream of things beyond the moon,
And dost thou hope to dwell there soon?
Hast treasures there laid up in store,
That all in th' world thou count'st but poor?
Art fancy sick, or turned a sot,
To catch at shadows which are not?   20
Come, come, I'll show unto thy sense
Industry hath its recompense.
What canst desire but thou mayst see
True substance in variety?
Dost honor like? Acquire the same,
As some to their immortal fame;
And trophies to thy name erect

Which wearing time shall ne'er deject.
For riches dost thou long full sore?
Behold enough of precious store.   30
Earth hath more silver, pearls, and gold
Than eyes can see or hands can hold.
Affect'st thou pleasure? Take thy fill,
Earth hath enough of what you will.
Then let not go, what thou mayst find,
For things unknown, only in mind."
Spirit: "Be still, thou unregenerate part;
Disturb no more my settled heart,
For I have vowed (and so will do)
Thee as a foe, still to pursue,   40
And combat with thee will and must
Until I see thee laid in th' dust.
Sisters we are, yea, twins we be,
Yet deadly feud 'twixt thee and me;
For from one father are we not:
Thou by old Adam wast begot,
But my arise is from above,
Whence my dear Father I do love.
Thou speak'st me fair but hat'st me sore;
Thy flattering shows I'll trust no more.   50
How oft thy slave hast thou me made
When I believed what thou hast said,
And never had more cause of woe
Than when I did what thou bad'st do.
I'll stop mine ears at these thy charms
And count them for my deadly harms.
Thy sinful pleasures I do hate,
Thy riches are to me no bait,
Thine honors do nor will I love;
For my ambition lies above.   60
My greatest honor it shall be
When I am victor over thee
And triumph shall, with laurel head,
When thou my captive shalt be led.
How I do live thou need'st not scoff,
For I have meat thou know'st not of,
The hidden manna I do eat,
The word of life it is my meat.
My thoughts do yield me more content
Than can thy hours in pleasure spent.   70

Nor are they shadows which I catch,
Nor fancies vain at which I snatch;
But reach at things that are so high,
Beyond thy dull capacity,
Eternal substance I do see,
With which enriched I would be;
Mine eye doth pierce the heavens, and see
What is invisible to thee.
My garments are not silk nor gold
Nor such like trash which earth doth hold,   80
But royal robes I shall have on
More glorious than the glist'ring sun.
My crown not diamonds, pearls, and gold,
But such as angels' heads infold.
The City where I hope to dwell
There's none on earth can parallel;
The stately walls both high and strong
Are made of precious jasper stone;
The gates of pearl both rich and clear;
And angels are for porters there;   90
The streets thereof transparent gold,
Such as no eye did e'er behold;
A crystal river there doth run,
Which doth proceed from the Lamb's throne;
Of life there are the waters sure,
Which shall remain forever pure;
Nor sun nor moon they have no need,
For glory doth from God proceed;
No candle there, nor yet torchlight,
For there shall be no darksome night.   100
From sickness and infirmity
For evermore they shall be free,
Nor withering age shall e'er come there,
But beauty shall be bright and clear.
This City pure is not for thee,
For things unclean there shall not be.
If I of heaven may have my fill,
Take thou the world, and all that will."

1678

From *Contemplations*

1

Some time now past in the autumnal tide,
When Phoebus wanted but one hour to bed,

[Phoebus: sun god]

The trees all richly clad, yet void of pride,
Were gilded o'er by his rich golden head.
Their leaves and fruits seemed painted, but was true,
Of green, of red, of yellow, mixed hue;
Rapt were my senses at this delectable view.

2

I wist not what to wish, "Yet sure," thought I,
"If so much excellence abide below,
How excellent is He that dwells on high,   10
Whose power and beauty by His works we know?
Sure He is goodness, wisdom, glory, light,
That hath this under world so richly dight:
More heaven than earth was here, no winter and no night."

3

Then on a stately oak I cast mine eye,
Whose ruffling top the clouds seemed to aspire;
How long since thou wast in thine infancy?
Thy strength and stature, more thy years admire.
Hath hundred winters passed since thou wast born,
Or thousand since thou brak'st thy shell of horn?   20
If so, all these as nought eternity doth scorn.

4

Then higher on the glistering sun I gazed,
Whose beams was shaded by the leafy tree;
The more I looked the more I grew amazed,
And softly said, "What glory's like to thee?
Soul of this world, this universe's eye,
No wonder some made thee a deity;
Had I not better known, alas, the same had I.

5

"Thou as a bridegroom from thy chamber rushes
And as a strong man, joys to run a race,   30

The morn doth usher thee with smiles and blushes,
The earth reflects her glances in thy face.
Birds, insects, animals, with vegetive
Thy heart from death and dullness doth revive:
And in the darksome womb of fruitful nature dive.

6

"Thy swift annual and diurnal course,
Thy daily straight and yearly oblique path,
Thy pleasing fervor and thy scorching force,
All mortals here the feeling knowledge hath.
Thy presence makes it day, thy absence night,   40
Quaternal seasons caused by thy might:
Hail, creature full of sweetness, beauty, and delight!

7

"Art thou so full of glory that no eye
Hath strength thy shining rays once to behold?
And is thy splendid throne erect so high
As to approach it can no earthly mould?
How full of glory then must thy Creator be,
Who gave this bright light luster unto thee:
Admired, adored forever, be that majesty!"

8

Silent, alone, where none or saw or heard,   50
In pathless paths I led my wand'ring feet,
My humble eyes to lofty skies I reared,
To sing some song my mazed Muse thought meet.
My great Creator I would magnify,
That nature had thus decked liberally:
But ah, and ah, again, my imbecility!

9

I heard the merry grasshopper then sing,
The black clad cricket bear a second part;
They kept one tune and played on the same string,
Seeming to glory in their little art.   60
Shall creatures abject thus their voices raise,
And in their kind resound their Maker's praise,
Whilst I, as mute, can warble forth no higher lays?

29

Man at the best a creature frail and vain,
In knowledge ignorant, in strength but weak,

Subject to sorrows, losses, sickness, pain,
Each storm his state, his mind, his body break;
From some of these he never finds cessation,
But day or night, within, without, vexation,
Troubles from foes, from friends, from dearest, near'st
    relation.   70

30

And yet this sinful creature, frail and vain,
This lump of wretchedness, of sin and sorrow,
This weather-beaten vessel wracked with pain,
Joys not in hope of an eternal morrow;
Nor all his losses, crosses, and vexation,
In weight, in frequency and long duration,
Can make him deeply groan for that divine translation.

31

The mariner that on smooth waves doth glide
Sings merrily and steers his bark with ease,
As if he had command of wind and tide,   80
And now become great master of the seas;
But suddenly a storm spoils all the sport,
And makes him long for a more quiet port,
Which 'gainst all adverse winds may serve for fort.

32

So he that faileth in this world of pleasure,
Feeding on sweets, that never bit of th' sour,
That's full of friends, of honor, and of treasure,
Fond fool, he takes this earth ev'n for heaven's bower.
But sad affliction comes and makes him see
Here's neither honor, wealth, nor safety;   90
Only above is found all with security.

33

O Time, the fatal wrack of mortal things,
That draws oblivion's curtains over kings,
Their sumptuous monuments, men know them not,
Their names without a record are forgot,
Their parts, their ports, their pomp's all laid in th' dust,
Nor wit nor gold nor buildings 'scape time's rust;
But he whose name is graved in the white stone
Shall last and shine when all of these are gone.

                      1678

An Epitaph on My Dear and Ever Honored Mother

MRS. DOROTHY DUDLEY, WHO DECEASED
DECEMBER 27, 1643,
AND OF HER AGE 61

Here lies

A worthy matron of unspotted life,
A loving mother, and obedient wife,
A friendly neighbor, pitiful to poor,
Whom oft she fed and clothèd with her store;
To servants wisely awful, but yet kind,
And as they did so they reward did find;
A true instructor of her family,
The which she ordered with dexterity;
The public meetings ever did frequent,
And in her closet constant hours she spent;   10
Religious in all her words and ways,
Preparing still for death till end of days;
Of all her children children lived to see,
Then dying, left a blessed memory.

1678

To My Dear and Loving Husband

If ever two were one, then surely we.
If ever man were lov'd by wife, then thee;
If ever wife was happy in a man,
Compare with me ye women if you can.
I prize thy love more than whole mines of gold,
Or all the riches that the East doth hold.
My love is such that rivers cannot quench,
Nor aught but love from thee give recompense.
Thy love is such I can no way repay,
The heavens reward thee manifold I pray.   10
Then while we live, in love let's so persevere,
That when we live no more, we may live ever.

1678

A Letter to Her Husband

Phoebus, make haste: the day's too long; begone;
The silent night's the fittest time for moan.
But stay this once, unto my suit give ear,
And tell my griefs in either hemisphere;
And if the whirling of thy wheels don't drown'd
The woeful accents of my doleful sound,
If in thy swift career thou canst make stay,
I crave this boon, this errand by the way:
Commend me to the man more lov'd than life;
Show him the sorrows of his widowed wife,   10
My dumpish thoughts, my groans, my brackish tears,
My sobs, my longing hopes, my doubting fears;
And if he love, how can he there abide?
My interest's more than all the world beside.
He that can tell the stars or ocean sand,
Or all the grass that in the meads do stand,
The leaves in th' woods, the hail or drops of rain,
Or in a corn-field number every grain,
Or every mote that in the sun-shine hops,
May count my sighs and number all my drops.   20
Tell him the countless steps that thou dost trace
That once a day thy spouse thou mayst embrace;
And when thou canst not treat by loving mouth,
Thy rays afar salute her from the south.
But for one month I see no day, poor soul,
Like those far situate under the pole,
Which day by day long wait for thy arise:
O how they joy when thou dost light the skys.
O Phoebus, hadst thou but thus long from thine
Restrain'd the beams of thy beloved shine,   30
At thy return, if so thou could'st or durst,
Behold a Chaos blacker than the first.
Tell him here's worse than a confused matter—
His little world's a fathom under water;
Nought but the fervor of his ardent beams
Hath power to dry the torrent of these streams.
Tell him I would say more, but cannot well:
Oppressed minds abruptest tales do tell.

Now post with double speed, mark what I say;
By all our loves conjure him not to stay.   40

                                                          1678

Before the Birth of One of Her Children

All things within this fading world have end.
Adversity doth still our joys attend;
No ties so strong, no friends so dear and sweet,
But with death's parting blow are sure to meet.
The sentence passed is most irrevocable,
A common thing, yet, oh, inevitable.
How soon, my dear, death may my steps attend,
How soon it may be thy lot to lose thy friend,
We both are ignorant; yet love bids me
These farewell lines to recommend to thee,   10
That when that knot's untied that made us one
I may seem thine who in effect am none.
And if I see not half my days that are due,
What nature would God grant to yours and you.
The many faults that well you know I have
Let be interred in my oblivion's grave;
If any worth or virtue were in me,
Let that live freshly in thy memory,
And when thou feelest no grief, as I no harms,
Yet love thy dead, who long lay in thine arms;   20
And when thy loss shall be repaid with gains
Look to my little babes, my dear remains,
And if thou love thyself, or lovedst me,
These oh protect from stepdam's injury.
And if chance to thine eyes shall bring this verse,
With some sad sighs honor my absent hearse;
And kiss this paper for thy love's dear sake,
Who with salt tears this last farewell did take.

                                                          1678

Upon the Burning of Our House

July 10th, 1666

In silent night when rest I took,
For sorrow near I did not look,
I waken'd was with thund'ring noise
And piteous shrieks of dreadful voice.
That fearful sound of fire and fire,
Let no man know is my desire.

I, starting up, the light did spy,
And to my God my heart did cry
To strengthen me in my distress
And not to leave me succorless.   10
Then coming out beheld a space,
The flame consume my dwelling place.

And, when I could no longer look,
I blest his Name that gave and took,
That laid my goods now in the dust:
Yea so it was, and so 'twas just.
It was his own: it was not mine;
Far be it that I should repine.

He might of all justly bereft,
But yet sufficient for us left.   20
When by the ruins oft I past,
My sorrowing eyes aside did cast,
And here and there the places spy
Where oft I sat, and long did lie.

Here stood that trunk, and there that chest;
There lay that store I counted best:
My pleasant things in ashes lie,
And them behold no more shall I.
Under thy roof no guest shall sit,
Nor at thy table eat a bit.   30

No pleasant tale shall e'er be told,
Nor things recounted done of old.
No candle e'er shall shine in thee,

Nor bridegroom's voice ere heard shall be.
In silence ever shalt thou lie;
Adieu, adieu; all's vanity.

Then straight I gin my heart to chide,
And did thy wealth on earth abide?
Didst fix thy hope on mould'ring dust,
The arm of flesh didst make thy trust?   40
Raise up thy thoughts above the sky
That dunghill mists away may fly.

Thou hast an house on high erect,
Fram'd by that mighty Architect,
With glory richly furnished,
Stands permanent tho' this be fled.
It's purchased, and paid for too
By him who hath enough to do.

A prize so vast as is unknown,
Yet, by his gift, is made thine own.   50
There's wealth enough, I need no more;
Farewell my pelf, farewell my store.
The world no longer let me love,
My hope and treasure lies above.

1678

In Memory of My Dear Grandchild Elizabeth Bradstreet, Who Deceased August, 1665, Being a Year and a Half Old

Farewell, dear babe, my heart's too much content!
    Farewell, sweet babe, the pleasure of mine eye!
Farewell, fair flower that for a space was lent,
    Then taken away unto eternity!
Blest babe, why should I once bewail thy fate,
Or sigh the days so soon were terminate,
Since thou art settled in an everlasting state?

By nature trees do rot when they are grown,
   And plums and apples throughly ripe do fall,
And corn and grass are in their season mown,   10
   And time brings down what is both strong and tall.
But plants new set to be eradicate,
And buds new blown to have so short a date,
Is by His hand alone that guides nature and fate.

                                    1678

MICHAEL WIGGLESWORTH

(1631–1705)

☆

Michael Wigglesworth was born in England and came to America at the age of seven. He lived in New Haven until he went to Harvard; he was graduated in 1651 and remained as a tutor for three years. He lived out the rest of his essentially uneventful life in Malden, Massachusetts, the place of the ministry to which he was appointed in 1656.

A small man, he was extremely frail and weak until 1686 when, apparently, he attained an Indian summer of health. Because of his physical condition he went to Bermuda for seven months in 1663; there he began to study medicine, which had always interested him. Eventually he became a physician of the body as well as of the soul. Although his household occupied some of his leisure (he was married three times and had eight children), he took to writing in order to spread the doctrine that his frailty frequently kept him from preaching in the pulpit. The most famous result of his efforts was *The Day of Doom*.

Although it is not the best of his verse—and although even the best is something less than true poetry—*The Day of Doom* deservedly remains the most famous of his works. It must be considered in a purely historical light, for it reveals the Puritan notions of poetry much better than do the poems of Anne Bradstreet and Edward Taylor. Cast in familiar, jingling ballad meter, it helped New Englanders to remember the doctrines of righteousness, and children memorized Wigglesworth's doggerel along with the catechism. The ideas seem so harsh today that some commentators have supposed erroneously that Wigglesworth was a morbid fanatic. In reality the poem merely dramatizes the abstractions that all orthodox Puritans agreed upon, and it is interesting for its disclosure of Puritan psychology as well as doctrine. Published in 1662, *The Day of Doom* became America's first best seller, circulating 1800 copies during the first year. It has been estimated that at one time one copy was owned for every thirty-five people in all of New England; every other family must have had *The Day of Doom* on its parlor table. The poem went through ten editions in the next fourteen decades, four in the seventeenth century and six in the eighteenth. In spite of its literary shortcomings, it is still the best "official" statement of the Puritan's attempt to use poetry for a plain exposition of the beliefs by which he tried to live.

Wigglesworth's works include *The Day of Doom: or a Poetical Description of the Great and Last Judgment* (1662); *Meat Out of the Eater* (1670); *Vanity of Vanities* (in the 1673 edition of *Day of Doom*); *Riddles Unriddled* (in the 1689 edition of *Meat Out of the Eater*); and "God's Controversy with New England" (first published, 1873).

Accounts of Wigglesworth and his works are to be found in J. W. Dean, *Sketch of the Life of Rev. Michael Wigglesworth* (1863); "Letters of Michael Wigglesworth to Increase Mather," *Collections of the Massachusetts Historical Society*, Fourth Series, VIII (1868); S. A. Green, "The Day of Doom," *Publications of the Massachusetts Historical Society*, Second Series, IX (1895); M. C. Tyler, *A History of American Literature During the Colonial Period*, II (1897); P. E. More, "The Spirit and Poetry of Early New England," *Shelburne Essays* (1921); F. O. Matthiessen, "Michael Wigglesworth: A Puritan Artist," *New England Quarterly*, I (1928); M. B. Jones, "Notes for a Bibliography of Michael Wigglesworth's *Day of Doom* and *Meat Out of the Eater*," *Proceedings of the American Antiquarian Society*, XXXIX (1930); K. B. Murdock, ed., *The Day of Doom* (1929); E. S. Morgan, ed., "The Diary of Michael Wigglesworth," *Publication of the Colonial Society of Massachusetts*, XXXV (1951); and R. Crowder, *No Featherbed to Heaven: A Biography of Michael Wigglesworth* (1962).

FROM

The Day of Doom

1.

Still was the night, serene and bright,
   when all men sleeping lay;
Calm was the season, and carnal reason
   thought it would last for ay.

The Security of the World before Christ's Coming to Judgment

Luke 12:19

Soul, take thine ease, let sorrow cease,
   much good thou hast in store;
This was their song, their cups among,
   the evening before.

2.

Wallowing in all kind of sin,
   vile wretches lay secure;   10
The best of men had scarcely then
   their lamps kept in good ure;   Mat. 25:5
Virgins unwise, who through disguise
   amongst the best were numbered,
Had closed their eyes; yea, and the wise
   through sloth and frailty slumbered.

3.

Like as of old, when men grow bold,
   God's threatenings to contemn,   Mat. 24:37, 38
Who stopped their ear and would not hear
   when mercy warnèd them,   20
But took their course without remorse
   till God began to pour
Destruction the world upon
   in a tempestuous shower.

4.

They put away the evil day,
   and drowned their cares and fears,
Till drowned were they and swept away
   by vengeance unawares.
So at the last, whilst men slept fast   1 Thes. 5:3
   in their security,   30
Surprised they are in such a snare
   as cometh suddenly.

5.

For at midnight broke forth a light,   The suddenness,
   which turned the night to day,   Majesty, and
                                     Terror of Christ's
And speedily a hideous cry   Appearing
   did all the world dismay.
Sinners awake, their hearts do ache,   Mat. 25:6
   trembling their loins surpriseth,   2 Pet. 3:10
Amazed with fear by what they hear,
   each one of them ariseth.   40

6.

They rush from beds with giddy heads,
   and to their windows run,

Viewing this light which shone more bright
    than doth the noonday sun.   Mat. 24:29, 30
Straightway appears (they see't with tears)
    the Son of God most dread,
Who with his train comes on amain
    to judge both quick and dead.

7.

Before his face the heavens give place,
    and skies are rent asunder,   2 Pet. 3:10   50
With mighty voice and hideous noise,
    more terrible than thunder.
His brightness damps heaven's glorious lamps,
    and makes them hide their heads;
As if afraid and quite dismayed,
    they quit their wonted steads.

8.

Ye sons of men that durst contemn
    the threat'nings of God's word,
How cheer you now? your hearts, I trow,
    are thrilled as with a sword.   60
Now atheist blind, whose brutish mind
    a God could never see,
Dost thou perceive, dost thou believe
    that Christ thy judge shall be?

9.

Stout courages, whose hardiness
    could death and hell outface,
Are you as bold, now you behold
    your judge draw near apace?
They cry, "No, no, alas and woe,
    our courage all is gone;   70
Our hardiness, foolhardiness,
    hath us undone, undone."

10.

No heart so bold but now grows cold   Rev. 6:16
    and almost dead with fear,
No eye so dry but now can cry
    and pour out many a tear.
Earth's potentates and pow'rful states,
    captains and men of might,
Are quite abashed, their courage dashed
    at this most dreadful sight.   80

11.

Mean men lament, great men do rent
   their robes and tear their hair;
They do not spare their flesh to tear   Mat. 24:30
   through horrible despair.
All kindreds wail; their hearts do fail;
   horror the world doth fill
With weeping eyes and loud outcries,
   yet knows not how to kill.

12.

Some hide themselves in caves and delves   Rev. 6:15, 16
   and places under ground,   90
Some rashly leap into the deep
   to 'scape by being drowned,
Some to the rocks (O senseless blocks!)
   and woody mountains run,
That there they might this fearful sight
   and dreaded presence shun.

13.

In vain do they to mountains say,
   "Fall on us and us hide
From Judge's ire, more hot than fire,
   for who may it abide?"   100
No hiding place can from his face
   sinners at all conceal,
Whose flaming eye hid things does spy
   and darkest things reveal.

14.

The Judge draws nigh, exalted high   Mat. 25:31
   upon a lofty throne,
Amidst the throng of angels strong,
   like Israel's holy one.
The excellence of whose presence
   and awful majesty   110
Amazeth Nature and every creature
   doth more than terrify.

15.

The mountains smoke, the hills are shook,   Rev. 6:14
   the earth is rent and torn,
As if she should be clean dissolved
   or from her center borne.
The sea doth roar, forsake the shore,
   and shrinks away for fear.

The wild beasts flee into the sea,
   so soon as he draws near.   120

16.

Whose glory bright, whose wondrous might,
   whose power imperial
So far surpass whatever was
   in realms terrestrial,
That tongues of men (nor angels' pen)
   cannot the same express,
And therefore I must pass it by,
   lest speaking should transgress.

17.

Before his throne a trump is blown,   1 Thes. 4:16
   proclaiming the day of doom,   130
Forthwith he cries, "Ye dead, arise,   Resurrection of the
   and unto judgment come."   Dead
No sooner said but 'tis obeyed;   John 5:28, 29
   sepulchers opened are;
Dead bodies all rise at his call,
   and 's mighty power declare.

18.

Both sea and land, at his command,
   their dead at once surrender;
The fire and air constrained are
   also their dead to tender.   140
The mighty word of this great lord
   links body and soul together,
Both of the just and the unjust,
   to part no more forever.

19.

The same translates from mortal states   The Living
   to immortality   Changed
All that survive and be alive,
   i' th' twinkling of an eye;
That so they may abide for aye   Luke 20:36
   to endless weal or woe,   1 Cor. 15:52   150
Both the renate and reprobate
   are made to die no more.

20.

His wingèd hosts fly through all coasts   All Brought to
   together gathering   Judgment
Both good and bad, both quick and dead,   Mat. 24:31

and all to judgment bring,
Out of their holes these creeping moles
    that hid themselves for fear
By force they take and quickly make
    before the Judge appear.   **160**
            21.

Thus every one before the throne   2 Cor. 5:10
    of Christ the Judge is brought,   The Sheep
Both righteous and impious   Separated from the
    that good or ill had wrought,   Goats
A separation and diff'ring station   Mat. 25
    by Christ appointed is
(To sinners sad) 'twixt good and bad,
    'twixt heirs of woe and bliss.

           .   .   .

           92.

Then were brought nigh a company   Civil Honest Men's
    of civil honest men   Pleas   **170**
That loved true dealing and hated stealing, Luke 18:11
    ne'er wronged their brethren,
Who pleaded thus, "Thou knowest us,
    that we were blameless livers;
No whoremongers, no murderers,
    no quarrelers nor strivers.
           93.
"Idolaters, adulterers,
    church-robbers we were none,
Nor false dealers nor cozeners,
    but paid each man his own.   **180**
Our way was fair, our dealing square,
    we were no wasteful spenders,
No lewd toss-pots, no drunken sots,
    no scandalous offenders.
           94.
"We hated vice and set great price
    by virtuous conversation:
And by the same we got a name
    and no small commendation.
God's laws express that righteousness   1 Sam. 15:22
    is that which He doth prize,   **190**
And to obey, as He doth say,
    is more than sacrifice.

95.

◆Thus to obey hath been our way.
    Let our good deeds, we pray,
Find some regard and some reward
    with Thee, O Lord, this day.
And whereas we transgressors be,   Eccles. 7:20
    of Adam's race were none;
No, not the best but have confessed
    themselves to have misdone."   200

96.

Then answerèd unto their dread   Are Taken Off and
    the Judge: "True piety   Rendered Invalid
God doth desire and eke require   Deut. 10:12
    no less than honesty.   Tit. 2:12
                                          Jam. 2:10
Justice demands at all your hands
    perfect obedience—
If but in part you have come short,
    that is a just offense.

97.

"On earth below, where men did owe
    a thousand pounds and more,   210
Could twenty pence it recompense?
    Could that have closed the score?
Think you to buy felicity
    with part of what's due debt,
Or for desert of one small part
    the whole should be offset?

98.

"And yet that part, whose great desert
    you think to reach so far
For your excuse, doth you accuse   Luke 18:11, 14
    and will your boasting mar.   220
However fair, however square
    your way and work hath been
Before men's eyes, yet God espies
    iniquity therein.

99.

"God looks upon th' affection   1 Sam. 16:7
    and temper of the heart,   2 Chron. 25:2
Not only on the action
    and the external part.
Whatever end vain men pretend,
    God knows the verity: 230

And by the end which they intend,
    their words and deeds doth try.
          100.
"Without true faith, the Scripture saith,   Heb. 11:6
    God cannot take delight
In any deed that doth proceed
    from any sinful wight.
And without love all actions prove   1 Cor. 13:1, 2, 3
    but barren, empty things.
Dead works they be and vanity,
    the which vexation brings.   240
          101.
"Nor from true faith, which quencheth wrath,
    hath your obedience flown,
Nor from true love, which wont to move
    believers, hath it grown.
Your argument shows your intent
    in all that you have done;
You thought to scale heav'n's lofty wall
    by ladders of your own.
          102.
"Your blinded spirit, hoping to merit   Rom. 10:9
    by your own righteousness,   250
Needed no Saviour but your behavior
    and blameless carriages.
You trusted to what you could do,
    and in no need you stood:
Your hearty pride laid Me aside
    and trampled on My blood.
          103.
"All men have gone astray and done
    that which God's laws condemn,
But My purchase and offered grace
    all men did not contemn.   Rom. 9:30, 32   260
The Ninevites and Sodomites   Mat. 11:23, 24
    had no such sin as this—   and 12:41
Yet, as if all your sins were small,
    you say, 'All did amiss.'
          104.
"Again you thought and mainly sought   Mat. 6:5
    a name with men t' acquire;
Pride bare the bell that made you swell
    and your own selves admire.

Mean fruit it is and vile, I wis,
   that springs from such a root: **270**
Virtue divine and genuine
   wonts not from pride to shoot.

      105.
"Such deeds as your are worse than poor.
   They are but sins gilt over
With silver dross, whose glist'ring gloss   Prov. 26:23
   can them no longer cover.   Mat. 23:27
The best of them would you condemn
   and ruin you alone,
Although you were from faults so clear,
   the other you had none.   **280**

      106.
"Your gold is brass, your silver dross,   Prov. 15:8
   your righteousness is sin.   Rom. 3:20
And think you by such honesty
   eternal life to win?
You much mistake if for its sake
   you dream of acceptation,
Whereas the same deserveth shame
   and meriteth damnation."

      . . .

      156.
Then were brought near with trembling fear,
   a number numberless,   **290**
Of blind heathen, and brutish men
   that did God's law transgress;

      157.
Whose wicked ways Christ open lays,   Heathen Men
   and makes their sins appear,   Plead Want of the
                            Written Word
They making pleas their case to ease,
   if not themselves to clear.
"Thy Written Word," say they, "good **Lord**,
   we never did enjoy;
We ne'er refus'd, nor it abus'd;
   Oh, do not us destroy!"   **300**

      158.
"You ne'er abus'd, nor yet refus'd   Mat. 11:22
   my Written Word, you plead;   Luke 12:48
That's true," quoth he, "therefore shall ye
   the less be punishéd.
You shall not smart for any part

of other men's offense,
But for your own transgressi-on
  receive due recompense."
159.

"But we were blind," say they, "in mind;
  too dim was Nature's light,   1 Cor. 1:21   310
Our only guide, as hath been tried, And Insufficiency
  to bring us to the sight   of the Light of
Of our estate degenerate,   Nature
  and curs'd by Adam's Fall;
How we were born and lay forlorn
  in bondage and in thrall.
160.

"We did not know a Christ till now,
  nor how fall'n men be savéd,
Else would we not, right well we wot,
  have so ourselves behavéd.   320
We should have mourn'd, we should have turn'd Mat. 11:21
  from sin at thy Reproof,
And been more wise through thy advice,
  for our own soul's behoof.
161.

"But Nature's light shin'd not so bright,
  to teach us the right way:
We might have lov'd it and well improv'd it,
  and yet have gone astray."
The Judge most High makes this reply: They Are
  "You ignorance pretend,   Answered   330
Dimness of sight, and want of light,
  your course Heav'nward to bend.
162.

"How came your mind to be so blind?   Gen. 1:27
  I once you knowledge gave,   Eccles. 7:29
Clearness of sight and judgment right: Hos. 13:9
  who did the same deprave?
If to your cost you have it lost,
  and quite defac'd the same,
Your own desert hath caus'd the smart;
  you ought not me to blame.   340
163.

"Yourselves into a pit of woe,   Mat. 11:25
  your own transgression led,   compared with 20
                        and 15

If I to none my Grace had shown,
  who had been injured?
If to a few, and not to you,
  I show'd a way of life,
My Grace so free, you clearly see
  gives you no ground of strife.

164.

" 'Tis vain to tell, you wot full well,
  if you in time had known   350
Your misery and remedy,
  your actions had it shown:
You, sinful crew, have not been true   Rom. 1:20, 21, 22
  unto the light of Nature,
Nor done the good you understood,
  nor ownéd your Creator.

165.

"He that the Light, because 'tis slight,
  hath uséd to despise,
Would not the Light shining more bright,   Rom. 2:12, 15 and
  be likely for to prize.   1:32, Mat. 12:41
If you had lov'd, and well improv'd
  your knowledge and dim sight,
Herein your pain had not been vain,
  your plagues had been more light."

166.

Then to the bar all they drew near   Reprobate Infants
  who died in infancy,   Plead for
                                  Themselves
And never had or good or bad   Rev. 20:12, 15
  effected pers'nally;   compared with
                                  Rom. 15:12, 14
But from the womb unto the tomb   and 9:11, 13
  were straightway carriéd,   370
(Or at the least ere they transgress'd)
  who thus began to plead:

167.

"If for our own transgressi-on,   Ezek. 18:2
  or disobedience,
We here did stand at thy left hand,
  just were the recompense;
But Adam's guilt our souls hath spilt,
  his fault is charg'd upon us;
And that alone hath overthrown
  and utterly undone us.   380

168.

"Not we, but he ate of the Tree,
  whose fruit was interdicted;
Yet on us all of his sad Fall
  the punishment's inflicted.
How could we sin that had not been,
  or how is his sin our,
Without consent, which to prevent
  we never had the pow'r?

169.

"O great Creator why was our Nature
  depravéd and forlorn?   390
Why so defil'd, and made so vil'd,
  whilst we were yet unborn?
If it be just, and needs we must
  transgressors reckon'd be,
Thy mercy, Lord, to us afford,   Psa. 51:5
  which sinners hath set free.

170.

"Behold we see Adam set free,
  and sav'd from his trespass,
Whose sinful Fall hath split us all,
  and brought us to this pass.   400
Canst thou deny us once to try,
  or grace to us to tender,
When he finds grace before thy face,
  who was the chief offender?"

171.

Then answeréd the Judge most dread: Their Argument
  "God doth such doom forbid,   Taken Off
                                         Ezek. 18:20
That men should die eternally   Rom. 5:12, 19
  for what they never did.
But what you call old Adam's Fall,
  and only his trespass,   410
You call amiss to call it his,
  both his and yours it was.

172.

"He was design'd of all mankind
  to be a public head;
A common root, whence all should shoot,
  and stood in all their stead.
He stood and fell, did ill or well,   1 Cor. 15:48, 49

not for himself alone,
But for you all, who now his Fall
   and trespass would disown.   420

173.

"If he had stood, then all his brood
   had been establishéd
In God's true love never to move,
   nor once awry to tread;
Then all his race my Father's grace
   should have enjoy'd for ever,
And wicked sprites by subtile sleights
   could them have harméd never.

174.

"Would you have griev'd to have receiv'd
   through Adam so much good,   430
As had been your for evermore,
   if he at first had stood?
Would you have said, 'We ne'er obey'd
   nor did thy laws regard;
It ill befits with benefits,
   us, Lord, to so reward?'

175

"Since then to share in his welfare,
   you could have been content,
You may with reason share in his treason,
   and in the punishment.   440
Hence you were born in state forlorn,   Rom. 5:12
   with natures so depravéd;   Psa. 51:5
Death was your due because that you   Gen. 5:3
   had thus yourselves behavéd.

176.

"You think 'If we had been as he,   Mat. 23:30, 31
   whom God did so betrust,
We to our cost would ne'er have lost
   all for a paltry lust.'
Had you been made in Adam's stead,
   you would like things have wrought,   450
And so into the self-same woe,
   yourselves and yours have brought.

177.

"I may deny you once to try,   Rom. 9:15, 18
   or grace to you to tender,   The Free Gift
                              Rom. 5:15

Though he finds grace before my face
    who was the chief offender;
Else should my grace cease to be grace,
    for it would not be free,
If to release whom I should please
    I have no liberty. 460

178.

"If upon one what's due to none
    I frankly shall bestow,
And on the rest shall not think best
    compassion's skirt to throw,
Whom injure I? will you envy
    and grudge at others' weal?
Or me accuse, who do refuse
    yourselves to help and heal?

179.

"Am I alone of what's my own,   Mat. 20:15
    no Master or no Lord? 470
And if I am, how can you claim
    what I to some afford?
Will you demand grace at my hand,
    and challenge what is mine?
Will you teach me whom to set free,
    and thus my grace confine?

180.

"You sinners are, and such a share   Psa. 58:3
    as sinners, may expect;   Rom. 6.23
                                   Gal. 3:10
Such you shall have, for I do save   Rom. 8:29, 30
    none but mine own Elect.   and 11:7
                                    Rev. 21:27   480
Yet to compare your sin with their   Luke 12:48
    who liv'd a longer time,
I do confess yours is much less,
    though every sin's a crime.

181.

"A crime it is, therefore in bliss   Mat. 11:22
    you may not hope to dwell: The Wicked All
                                    Convinced and
But unto you I shall allow   Put to Silence
    the easiest room in Hell."
The glorious King thus answering,   Rom. 3:19
    they cease, and plead no longer;   Mat. 22:12   490
Their consciences must needs confess
    his reasons are the stronger.

182.

Thus all men's pleas the Judge with ease
   doth answer and confute,
Until that all, both great and small,
   are silencéd and mute.
Vain hopes are cropt, all mouths are stopt,
   sinners have naught to say,
But that 'tis just and equal most
   they should be damn'd for aye.

Behold the
Formidable Estate
of All the
Ungodly, as They
Stand Hopeless
and Helpless
before an
Impartial Judge,
Expecting Their
Final Sentence
Rev. 6:16, 17

500

1662

EDWARD TAYLOR

(c1645–1729)

Although little is known about the early years of America's greatest colonial poet, there are some dependable probabilities. He was born in Leicestershire, England, either in Coventry or Sketchley, probably in 1645, and probably to a dissenting family. In any case, British universities were not hospitable to young Puritans during the persecutions of the 1660's; furthermore, the loyalty oaths required after the Restoration were repugnant to a man of Taylor's persuasions. Thus, armed with letters of introduction to the influential Increase Mather and the moneyed John Hull, Taylor arrived in Boston in July, 1668, a refugee in search of formal education. Subsequently he went to Harvard, where he earned distinctions and became a close friend of Samuel Sewall. He was graduated in 1671 and accepted a call to the ministry at Westfield, Massachusetts. There he spent the remaining fifty-eight years of his life as a physician and a passionate, engaging, and brilliant pastor. He was married twice, had thirteen children, was honored with a Master's degree by Harvard in 1720. With one exception, this sums up what we know of the man's life.

The exception, of course, is the remarkable manuscript book of poetry he produced. Although it is a mistake to think that the ecstasy expressed in his poems was not representative of Puritan piety, Taylor's occasional certitude of bliss and emphasis on joy came close to the heresies of Antinomianism, Pelagianism, and "enthusiasm." At a safe distance in time, his grandson, President Ezra Stiles of Yale, presented the manuscripts to the Yale library in 1883. In 1937, Thomas H. Johnson announced the discovery of this heretofore unknown jewel of colonial literature in an article called "Edward Taylor: Puritan 'Sacred Poet' " (*New England Quarterly*, XXI, 1937). In 1939 Johnson published selections from the manuscripts in *The Poetical Works of Edward Taylor*. The basic groupings of the manuscript book are: "God's Determinations," which in highly unorthodox fashion celebrates the primacy of divine mercy rather than justice for man caught in the continuing war between Christ and Satan; "Five Poems"; and "Sacramental Meditations," which expresses a fervent yearning for and expectation of ecstasy in acceptance by Christ.

Published 210 years after his death, the poems of Edward Taylor mark him as a universal writer whose ardor transcended his Puritanism. He combined the intense and simple sincerity of a William Bradford with the aspiring exaltation of a Jonathan Edwards, merging his fire and humility in the intricate style of the English metaphysicals. Though contemporary with the new poetry of Dryden and Pope, Taylor looked backward to Quarles, Donne, Crashaw, and especially Herbert for a rhetoric that would express his lyrical impulses. The total body of poems, particularly the glowing "Meditations," is of uneven quality, but the best pieces earn Taylor a place in world poetry and easily give him the foremost place in the poetry of Colonial America.

Accounts of Taylor and his works, besides those mentioned above, are to be found in "The Diary of Edward Taylor," *Proceedings of the Massachusetts Historical Society*, XVIII (1881); T. H. Johnson, "Some Edward Taylor Gleanings," *New England Quarterly*, XVI (1943); W. C. Brown, "Edward Taylor: An American Metaphysical," *American Literature*, XVI (1944); N. Wright, "The Morality Tradition in the Poetry of Edward Taylor," *American Literature*, XVIII (1946); S. E. Lind, "Edward Taylor: A Revaluation," *New England Quarterly*, XXI (1948); A. Warren, *Rage for Order* (1948); R. H. **Pearce**, "Edward Taylor: The Poet as Puritan," *New England Quarterly*, XXIII (1950); M. Black, "Edward Taylor: Heaven's Sugar Cake," *New England Quarterly*, XXIX (1956); D. E. Stanford, ed., *The Poems of Edward Taylor* (1960); N. S. Grabo, *Edward Taylor* (1961); D. E. Stanford, "Edward Taylor's Metrical History of Christianity," *American Literature*, XXXIII (1961); N. S. Grabo, ed., *Edward Taylor's Christographia* (1962); J. Clendenning, "Piety and Imagery in Edward Taylor's 'The Reflexion'," *American Quarterly*, XVI (1964); N. S. Grabo, "Edward Taylor's Spiritual Huswifery," PMLA, LXXIX (1964); D. E. Stanford, "Edward Taylor's 'Spiritual Relation,' " *American Literature*, XXXV (1964); J. R. Curtis, "Edward Taylor and

Emily Dickinson: Voices and Visions," *Susquehanna University Studies*, VII (1964); D. Junkins, "Edward Taylor's Revisions," *American Literature*, XXXVII (1965); J. L. Thomas, "Drama and Doctrine in *Gods Determinations*," *American Literature*, XXXVI (1965); D. E. Stanford, *Edward Taylor* (1965); and P. Thorpe, "Edward Taylor as Poet," *New England Quarterly*, XXXIX (1966).

FROM

Preparatory Meditations before My Approach to the Lord's Supper First Series

Prologue

Lord, can a crumb of dust the earth outweigh,
Outmatch all mountains, nay, the crystal sky?
Imbosom in't designs that shall display
And trace into the boundless Deity?
Yea! hand, a pen whose moisture doth gild o'er
Eternal glory with a glorious glor?   [glor: glory]

If it its pen had of an angel's quill,
And sharpened on a precious stone ground tight,
And dipt in liquid gold, and moved by skill,
In crystal leaves should golden letters write,   10
It would but blot and blur, yea, jag and jar
Unless Thou mak'st the pen, and scrivener.

I am this crumb of dust which is designed
To make my pen unto Thy praise alone,
And my dull fancy I would gladly grind
Unto an edge on Zion's precious stone,
And write in liquid gold upon Thy name
My letters till Thy glory forth doth flame.

Let not th' attempts break down my dust, I pray,
Nor laugh Thou them to scorn, but pardon give.   20
Inspire this crumb of dust till it display
Thy glory through't, and then Thy dust shall live.
Its failings then Thou'lt overlook, I trust,
They being slips slipped from Thy crumb of dust.

Thy crumb of dust breathes two words from its breast:
That Thou wilt guide its pen to write aright
To prove Thou art and that Thou art the best,
And show Thy properties to shine most bright.
And then Thy works will shine as flowers on stems
Or as in jewelry shops do gems.   30

w. c1682
p. 1939

Meditation One

What love is this of Thine, that cannot be
    In Thine Infinity, O Lord, confined,
Unless it in Thy very Person see
    Infinity and finity conjoined?
    What? hath Thy Godhead, as not satisfied,
    Married our manhood, making it its bride?

Oh, matchless love! filling Heaven to the brim!
    O'errunning it, all running o'er beside
This World! Nay, overflowing Hell, wherein
    For Thine Elect there rose a mighty tide!   10
    That there our veins might through Thy Person bleed,
    To quench those flames that else would on us feed.

Oh! that my love might overflow my heart,
    To fire the same with love: for love I would.
But oh! my straitened breast! my lifeless spark!
    My fireless flame! What chilly love and cold!
    In measure small, in manner chilly, see!
    Lord, blow the coal! Thy love inflame in me.

w. 1682
p. 1939

The Experience

Oh! that I always breathed in such an air
    As I sucked in, feeding on sweet content,
Dished up unto my soul ev'n in that pray'r
    Poured out to God over last Sacrament.
    What beam of light wrapt up my sight to find
    Me nearer God than e'er came in my mind?

Most strange it was! But yet more strange that shine,
   Which filled my soul then to the brim, to spy
My nature with thy nature all divine
    Together joined in Him that's Thou and I.   10
    Flesh of my flesh, bone of my bone: there's run
    Thy Godhead and my manhood in Thy Son.

Oh! that that flame which Thou didst on me cast
   Might me enflame, and lighten everywhere.
Then Heaven to me would be less at last,
    So much of heaven I should have while here.
    Oh! sweet, though short! I'll not forget the same.
    My nearness, Lord, to Thee did me enflame.

I'll claim my right. Give place, ye angels bright!
   Ye further from the Godhead stand than I.   20
My nature is your Lord, and doth unite
    Better than yours unto the Deity.
    God's throne is first, and mine is next; to you
    Only the place of waiting-men is due.

Oh! that my heart Thy golden harp might be,
   Well tuned by glorious grace, that ev'ry string,
Screwed to the highest pitch, might unto Thee
    All praises wrapt in sweetest music bring.
    I praise Thee, Lord, and better praise Thee would
    If what I had, my heart might ever hold.   30

w. c1683
p. 1939

The Reflection

Lord, art Thou at the table-head above
   Meat, medicine, sweetness, sparkling beauties, to
Enamor souls with flaming flakes of love,
    And not my trencher nor my cup o'erflow?
    Ben't I a bidden guest? Oh! sweat mine eye.
    O'erflow with tears. Oh! draw thy fountains dry.

Shall I not smell Thy sweet, oh! Sharon's rose?
   Shall not mine eye salute Thy beauty? Why?

Shall Thy sweet leaves their beauteous sweets upclose?
  As half ashamed my sight should on them lie?   10
  Woe's me! For this my sigh shall be in grain,
  Offered on sorrow's altar for the same.

Had not my soul's, Thy conduit, pipes stopped been
  With mud, what ravishment would'st Thou convey?
Let grace's golden spade dig till the spring
  Of tears arise, and clear this filth away.
  Lord, let Thy spirit raise, my sighings till
  These pipes my soul do with Thy sweetness fill.

Earth once was paradise of heaven below,
  Till inkfaced sin had it with poison stocked,   20
And chased this paradise away into
  Heaven's upmost loft and it in glory locked.
  But Thou, sweet Lord, hast with Thy golden key
  Unlocked the door and made a golden day.

Once at Thy feast I saw Thee pearl-like stand
  'Tween heaven and earth, where heaven's bright glory all
In streams fell on Thee as a floodgate, and
  Like sun beams through Thee on the world to fall.
  Oh! sugar-sweet then! My dear sweet Lord, I see
  Saints' heaven-lost happiness restored by Thee.   30

Shall heaven and earth's bright glory all up-lie
  Like sun beams bundled in the sun in Thee?
Dost Thou sit, Rose, at table-head, where I
  Do sit, and carv'st no morsel sweet for me?
  So much before, so little now! Sprindge, Lord,
                              [sprindge: spread out]
  Thy rosy leaves, and me their glee afford.

Shall not Thy rose my garden fresh perfume?
  Shall not Thy beauty my dull heart assail?
Shall not Thy golden gleams run through this gloom?
  Shall my black velvet mask Thy fair face veil?   40
  Pass o'er my faults. Shine forth, bright sun: arise!
  Enthrone Thy rosy-self within mine eyes.

                                        w. 1683
                                        p. 1939

Meditation Six

Am I Thy gold? Or purse, Lord, for Thy wealth;
 Whether in mine or mint refined for Thee?
I'm counted so, but count me o'er Thyself,
 Lest gold washed face, and brass in heart I be.
 I fear my touchstone touches when I try
 Me, and my counted gold too overly.

Am I new minted by Thy stamp indeed?
 Mine eyes are dim; I cannot clearly see.
Be Thou my spectacles that I may read
 Thine image and inscription stamped on me.   10
 If Thy bright image do upon me stand,
 I am a golden angel in Thy hand.

         [angel: English gold coin]

Lord, make my soul Thy plate; Thine image bright
 Within the circle of the same enfoil.
And on its brims in golden letters write
 Thy superscription in an holy style.
 Then I shall be Thy money, Thou my hoard:
 Let me Thy angel be, be Thou my Lord.

           w. 1683
           p. 1939

Meditation Eight

John 6.51. I am the living bread

I, kenning through astronomy divine
        [kenning: knowing, seeing]
 The world's bright battlement, wherein I spy
A golden path my pencil cannot line
 From that bright Throne unto my threshold lie,
 And while my puzzled thoughts about it pore,
 I find the bread of life in't at my door.

When that this Bird of Paradise, put in
 This wicker cage (my corpse) to tweedle praise,
Had pecked the fruit forbid, and so did fling
 Away its food, and lost its golden days,   10

It fell into celestial famine sore,
And never could attain a morsel more.

Alas! alas! poor bird! What wilt thou do?
This creature's field no food for souls e'er gave.
And if thou knock at angels' doors, they show
An empty barrel; they no soul-bread have.
Alas! poor bird, the world's white loaf is done
And cannot yield thee here the smallest crumb.

In this sad state, God's tender bowels run
               [bowels: supposed seat of compassion]
Out streams of Grace; and He, to end all strife,   20
The purest wheat in heaven, His dear-dear Son,
Grinds and kneads up into this bread of life,
Which bread of life from heaven down came and stands
Dished on thy table up by angels' hands.

Did God mold up this bread in heaven, and bake,
Which from His table came, and to thine goeth?
Doth He bespeak thee thus? "This soul bread take;
Come, eat thy fill of this, thy God's white loaf.
It's food too fine for angels; yet come, take
And eat thy fill. It's heaven's sugar cake."   30

What grace is this, knead in this loaf? This thing,
Souls are but petty things it to admire.
Ye angels, help! This fill would to the brim
Heav'n's whelmed-down crystal meal-bowl, yea and higher.
This bread of life, dropped in my mouth, doth cry,
"Eat, eat me, soul, and thou shalt never die."

w. 1684
p. 1939

Meditation Twenty
Phil. 2.9. God hath highly exalted him

View, all ye eyes above, this sight which flings
Seraphic fancies in chill raptures high:
A turf of clay, and yet bright glory's King:
From dust to glory angel-like to fly.
A mortal clod immortalized, behold,
Flies through the skies swifter than angels could.

Upon the wings He of the wind rode in
  His bright sedan, through all the silver skies,
And made the azure cloud, His chariot, bring
  Him to the mountain of celestial joys.   10
  The Prince o'th'Air durst not an arrow spend
                           [Prince . . . Air: Satan]
  While through his realm His chariot did ascend.

He did not in a fiery chariot's shine,
  And whirlwind, like Elijah's upward go.
But the golden ladder's jasper rounds did climb
  Unto the heavens high from earth below.
  Each step trod on a gold stepping stone
  Of deity unto His very throne.

Methinks I see Heaven's sparkling courtiers fly,
  In flakes of glory down Him to attend;   20
And hear heart-cramping notes of melody
  Surround His chariot as it did ascend:
  Mixing their music, making every string
  More to enravish, as they this tune sing.

God is gone up with a triumphant shout:
  The Lord with sounding trumpets' melodies:
Sing praise, sing praise, sing praise, sing praises out,
  Unto our King sing praise seraphic-wise!
  Lift up your heads, ye lasting doors, they sing,
  And let the King of Glory enter in.   30

Art Thou ascended up on high, my Lord,
  And must I be without Thee here below?
Art Thou the sweetest joy the Heavens afford?
  Oh! that I with Thee was! What shall I do?
  Should I pluck feathers from an angel's wing,
  They could not waft me up to Thee my King.

Lend me Thy wings, my Lord, I'st fly apace,
  My soul's arms stud with Thy strong quills, true faith;
My quills then feather with Thy saving grace,
  My wings will take the wind Thy Word displayeth.
  Then I shall fly up to Thy glorious throne   40
  With my strong wings whose feathers are Thine own.

                                        w. c1686
                                        p. 1939

Meditation Thirty-Eight
1 John 2.1. An advocate with the Father

Oh! What a thing is man? Lord, who am I?
  That Thou should'st give him law (Oh! golden line)
To regulate his thoughts, words, life thereby?
    And judge him wilt thereby too in Thy time.
    A court of justice Thou in heaven hold'st,
    To try his case while he's here housed on mould.

How do Thy angels lay before Thine eye
  My deeds both white and black I daily do?
How doth Thy court Thou panel'st there them try?
                                        [panel'st: impanel]
    But flesh complains. What right for this? Let's know!   10
    For right or wrong, I can't appear unto't.
    And shall a sentence pass on such a suit?

Soft; blemish not this golden bench or place.
  Here is no bribe, nor colorings to hide,
Nor pettifogger to befog the case;
    But justice hath her glory here well tried;
    Her spotless law all spotted cases tends,
    Without respect or disrespect them ends.

God's judge Himself, and Christ attorney is,
  The Holy Ghost registerer is found.   20
Angels the sergeants are, all creatures kiss
    The book, and do as evidences abound.
    All cases pass according to pure law,
    And in the sentence is no fret nor flaw.

What sayest, my soul? Here all thy deeds are tried.
  Is Christ thy advocate to plead thy cause?
Art thou His client? Such shall never slide.
    He never lost His case: He pleads such laws
    As carry do the same, nor doth refuse
    The vilest sinner's case that doth Him choose.   30

This is His honor, not dishonor. Nay,
  No habeas corpus 'gainst His clients came.
For all their fines His purse doth make down pay.

He non-suits Satan's suit or casts the same.

[casts: defeats]

He'll plead thy case, and not accept a fee.
He'll plead sub forma pauperis for thee.

[sub . . . pauperis: under the form allowed to a person declaring himself a pauper]

My case is bad. Lord, be my advocate.
My sin is red; I'm under God's arrest.
Thou hast the hit of pleading; plead my state.
Although it's bad, Thy plea will make it best.   40
If Thou wilt plead my case before the King,
I'll wagon-loads of love and glory bring.

w. 1690
p. 1939

FROM

Preparatory Meditations
Second Series

Meditation Fifty-six

*John 15.24. Had I not done amongst them the works,
that none other man hath done, etc.*

Should I with silver tools delve through the hill
Of Cordillera for rich thoughts, that I,
My Lord, might weave with an angelic skill
A damask web of velvet verse thereby
To deck Thy works up, all my web would run
To rags and jags so snick-snarled to the thrum.

[thrum: thread by which yarn is tied to the loom]

Thine are so rich, within, without, refined:
No works like Thine. No fruits so sweet that grow
On the trees of righteousness of angel kind
And saints, whose limbs reev'd with them bow down low.

[reev'd: entwined]   10

Should I search o'er the nutmeg garden's shine,
Its fruit in flourish are but skegs to Thine.

[skegs: wild plums]

The clove, when in its white-green'd blossoms shoots,
    Some call the pleasantest scent the world doth show;
None eye e'er saw, nor nose e'er smelled such fruits,
    My Lord, as Thine, Thou tree of life in'ts blow.
    Thou Rose of Sharon, valley's lily true,
    Thy fruits most sweet and glorious ever grew.

Thou art a tree of perfect nature trim,
        Whose golden lining is of perfect grace   20
Perfumed with Deity unto the brim,
    Whose fruits, of the perfection, grow of grace:
    Thy buds, Thy blossoms, and Thy fruits adorn
    Thyself and works, more shining than the morn.

Art, nature's ape, hath many brave things done,
    As the pyramids, the Lake of Meris vast; [Meris: Moeris]
The pensile orchards built in Babylon;
    Psammitich's labyrinth, art's cramping task;
    Archimedes his engines made for war;
    Rome's golden house, Titus his theater.   30

The clock of Strasbourg, Dresden's table sight;
    Regiamont's fly of steel about that flew;
Turrian's wooden sparrows in a flight;
    And th' artificial man Aquinas slew;
    Mark Scaliota's lock and key and chain
    Drawn by a flea in our Queen Betty's reign.

Might but my pen in nature's inventory
    Its progress make, 't might make such things to jump,
All which are but invention's vents or glory,
    Wit's wantonings, and fancy's frolics plump,   40
    Within whose maws lies buried times and treasures,
    Embalmed up in thick-daubed sinful pleasures.

Nature doth better work than art, yet Thine
    Outvie both works of nature and art.
Nature's perfection and the perfect shine
    Of grace attend Thy deed in ev'ry part.
    A thought, a word, and work of Thine will kill
    Sin, Satan, and the curse—and law fulfill.

Thou art the tree of life in paradise,
    Whose lively branches are with clusters hung   50
Of lovely fruits and flowers more sweet than spice;
    Bend down to us and do outshine the sun;
    Delightful unto God, do man rejoice,
    The pleasantest fruits in all God's paradise.

Lord, feed my eyes then with Thy doings rare,
    And fat my heart with these ripe fruits Thou bear'st.
Adorn my life well with Thy works; make fair
    My person with apparel Thou prepar'st.
    My boughs shall loaded be with fruits that spring
    Up from Thy works, while to Thy praise I sing.   60

                                            w. 1703
                                            p. 1939

Meditation Sixty [B]
Cor. 10.4. And all drunk the same spiritual drink

Ye angels bright, pluck from your wings a quill,
    Make me a pen thereof that best will write,
Lend me your fancy and angelic skill
    To treat this theme, more rich than rubies bright.
    My muddy ink and cloudy fancy dark
    Will dull its glory, lacking highest art.

An eye at center righter may describe
    The world's circumferential glory vast,
As in its nutshell bed it snugs fast tied,
    Than any angel's pen can glory cast   10
    Upon this drink drawn from the rock, tapped by
    The rod of God, in Horeb, typically.
            [rock . . . typically: alludes to smiting of rock by
            Moses in Numbers 20:11; rock typified Christ]

Sea water strained through minerals, rocks, and sands,
    Well clarified by sunbeams, dulcified;
Insipid, sordid, swill, dishwater stands.
    But here's a rock of aqua-vitae tried!
    When once God broached it, out a river came
                                    [broached: broke]
    To bathe and bibble in, for Israel's train.

Some rocks have sweat. Some pillars bled out tears,
 But here's a river in a rock up tun'd, [up tun'd: kegged]
Not of sea water nor of swill. It's beer!   21
 No nectar like it! Yet it once unbunged,
 A river down out runs through ages all,
 A fountain oped, to wash off sin and Fall.

Christ is this Horeb's rock; the streams that slide
 A river is of aqua-vitae dear,
Yet costs us nothing, gushing from His side:
 Celestial wine our sin-sunk souls to cheer.
 This rock and water, sacramental cup
 Are made, Lord's Supper wine for us to sup. 30

This rock's the grape that Zion's vineyard bore,
 Which Moses' rod did smiting pound, and press,
Until its blood, the brook of life, run o'er:
 All glorious grace, and gracious righteousness.
 We in this brook must bathe, and with faith's quill
 Suck grace and life out of this rock our fill.

Lord oint me with this petro oil: I'm sick. [petro:rock's]
 Make me drink water of the rock: I'm dry.
Me in this fountain wash: my filth is thick.
 I'm faint: give aqua-vitae or I die.   40
 If in this stream Thou cleanse and cherish me,
 My heart Thy hallelujah's pipe shall be.

          w. 1704
          p. 1939

Meditation One Hundred and Ten
Matt. 26.30. When they had sung an hymn

The angels sang a carol at Thy birth,
 My Lord, and Thou Thyself did'st sweetly sing
An epinicion at Thy death on earth.
       [epinicion: song of triumph]
 An order'st Thine, in memory of this thing,
 Thy Holy Supper, closing it at last
 Up with an hymn, and chok'st the foe thou hast.

This feast Thou mad'st in memory of Thy death,
  Which is dished up most graciously; and towers
Of reeching vapors from Thy Grave (sweet breath)
              [reeching: sweetly smelling]
    Aromatize the skies; that sweetest showers   10
    Richly perfumed by the Holy Ghost,
    Are rained thence upon the church's coast.

Thy grave bears flowers to dress Thy church withal,
  In which Thou dost Thy table dress for Thine
With Gospel carpet, chargers, festival
    And spiritual venison, white bread and wine,
    Being the fruits Thy grave brings forth and hands
    Upon Thy table where Thou waiting stand'st.

Dainties most rich, all spiced o'er with grace,
  That grow out of Thy grave do deck Thy table.   20
To entertain Thy guests, Thou call'st, and place
    Allow'st, with welcome (and this is no fable),
    And with these guests I am invited to't,
    And this rich banquet makes me thus a poet.

Thy cross planted within Thy coffin bears
  Sweet blossoms and rich fruits, whose steams do rise
Out of Thy sepulcher and purge the air
    Of all sins, damps and fogs that choke the skies.
    This fume perfumes saints' hearts as it out peeps
    Ascending up to bury Thee in the reechs.   30

Joy stands on tip-toes all the while Thy guests
  Sit at Thy table, ready forth to sing
Its hallelujahs in sweet music's dress,
    Waiting for organs to employ herein.
    Here matter is allowed to all, rich, high,
    My Lord, to tune Thee hymns melodiously.

Oh! make my heart Thy pipe, the Holy Ghost
  The breath that fills the same and spiritually.
Then play on me, Thy pipe, that is almost
    Worn out with piping tunes of vanity.   40
    Wind music is the best, if Thou delight
    To play the same Thyself, upon my pipe.

Hence make me, Lord, Thy golden trumpet choice,
  And trumpet Thou Thyself upon the same
Thy heart enravishing hymns with sweetest voice.
  When Thou Thy trumpet sound'st, Thy tunes will flame.
  My heart shall then sing forth Thy praises sweet,
  When sounded thus with Thy sepulcher reech.

[reech: breath]

Make too my soul Thy cittern, and its wires
[cittern: cithern, a kind of lute]
  Make my affections; and rub off their rust   **50**
With Thy bright Grace; and screw my strings up higher,
  And tune the same to tune Thy praise most just.
  I'll close Thy Supper then with hymns most sweet,
  Burr'ing Thy grave in Thy sepulcher's reech.

[Burr'ing: sheltering]
w. 1712
p. 1939

FROM

God's Determinations Touching His Elect

The Preface

Infinity, when all things it beheld,
In nothing, and of nothing all did build,
Upon what base was fixed the lathe wherein
He turned this globe and riggaled it so trim?
[riggaled: made a groove for]
Who blew the bellows of His furnace vast?
Or held the mould wherein the world was cast?
Who laid its corner-stone? Or whose command?
Where stand the pillars upon which it stands?
Who laced and filleted the earth so fine [filleted: girded]
With rivers like green ribbons smaragdine?
[smaragdine: emerald] 10
Who made the seas its selvedge, and it locks
Like a quilt ball within a silver box?
Who spread its canopy? Or curtains spun?

Who in this bowling alley bowled the sun?
Who made it always when it rises, set:
To go at once both down and up to get?
Who the curtain rods made for this tapestry?
Who hung the twinkling lanthorns in the sky?
Who? who did this? or who is He? Why, know
It's only Might Almighty this did do.   20
His hand hath made this noble work which stands
His glorious handiwork not made by hands.
Who spake all things from nothing; and with ease
Can speak all things to nothing, if He please.
Whose little finger at His pleasure can
Out mete ten thousand worlds with half a span.
Whose might almighty can by half a look
Root up the rocks and rock the hills by th' roots.
Can take this mighty world up in His hand
And shake it like a squitchen or a wand.
                              [squitchen: switch]   30
Whose single frown will make the heavens shake
Like as an aspen leaf the wind makes quake.
Oh! What a might is this! Whose single frown
Doth shake the world as it would shake it down?
Which all from nothing fet, from nothing all; [fet: fetched]
Hath all on nothing set, lets nothing fall.
Gave all to nothing man indeed, whereby
Through nothing man all might Him glorify.
In nothing then embossed the brightest gem
More precious than all preciousness in them.   40
But nothing man did throw down all by sin,
And darkened that lightsome gem in him,
   That now His brightest diamond is grown
   Darker by far than any coal-pit stone.

                                        w. c1682
                                        p. 1939

The Glory of and Grace in the Church Set Out

   Come now behold
Within this knot what flowers do grow,
   Spangled like gold,
Whence wreaths of all perfumes do flow.

Most curious colors of all sorts you shall
With all sweet spirits scent. Yet that's not all.

    Oh, look and find
These choicest flowers most richly sweet
    Are disciplined
With artificial angels meet.
               [artificial: artificer; meet: appropriate]   10
A heap of pearls is precious, but they shall
When set by art excel. Yet that's not all.

    Christ's spirit showers
Down in his word and sacraments
    Upon these flowers,
The clouds of grace divine contents.
Such things of wealthy blessings on them fall
As make them sweetly thrive. Yet that's not all.

    Yet still behold!
All flourish not at once. We see   20
    While some unfold
Their blushing leaves, some buds there be.
Here's faith, hope, charity in flower, which call
On yonder's in the bud. Yet that's not all.

    But as they stand
Like beauties reeching in perfume,
               [reeching: smelling sweet]
    A divine hand
Does hand them up to glory's room—
Where each in sweetened songs all praises shall
Sing all o'er heaven for aye. And that's but all.   30

w. 1682
p. 1939

The Soul's Admiration Hereupon

What, I such praises sing! How can it be?
    Shall I in heaven sing?
What, I, that scarce durst hope to see,
    Lord, such a thing?
   Though nothing is too hard for Thee,
   One hope hereof seems hard to me.

What, can I ever tune those melodies,
    Who have no tune at all,
Not knowing where to stop nor rise,
    Nor when to fall?   10
  To sing Thy praise I am unfit;
  I have not learned my gamut yet.

But should these praises on stringed instruments
    Be sweetly tuned? I find
I nonplussed am, for no consents   [consents: harmonies]
    I ever mind.
  My tongue is neither quill nor bow,
  Nor can my fingers quavers show. [quavers: eighth notes]

But was it otherwise, I have no kit; [kit: small violin]
    Which though I had, I could   20
Not tune the strings, which soon would slip
    Though others should.
  But should they not, I cannot play,
  But for an F should strike an A.

And should Thy praise upon wind instruments
    Sound all o'er heaven shrill?
My breath will hardly through such vents
    A whistle fill.
  Which though it should, it's past my spell
  By stops and falls to sound it well.   30

How should I then join in such exercise?
    One sight of Thee'll entice
Mine eyes to heft, whose ecstasies [heft: lift]
    Will stob my voice. [stob: stop]
  Hereby mine eyes will bind my tongue
  Unless Thou, Lord, do cut the thong.

What use of useless me then there, poor snake?
    There saints and angels sing
Thy praise in full career, which make
    The heavens to ring.   40
  Yet if Thou wilt, Thou canst me raise
  With angels bright to sing Thy praise.

w. c1683
p. 1939

The Joy of Church Fellowship Rightly Attended

The Joy of Church Fellowship

In heaven soaring up I dropt an ear
  On earth, and, oh! sweet melody!
And listening found it was the saints who were
  Encoached for heaven that sang for joy.
    For in Christ's coach they sweetly sing
    As they to glory ride therein.

Oh, joyous hearts! Enfired with holy flame!
  Is speech thus tasselèd with praise?
Will not your inward fire of joy contain,
  That it in open flames doth blaze?   10
    For in Christ's coach saints sweetly sing
    As they to glory ride therein.

And if a string do slip by chance, they soon
  Do screw it up again, whereby
They set it in a more melodious tune
  And a diviner harmony.
    For in Christ's coach they sweetly sing
    As they to glory ride therein.

In all their acts public and private, nay
  And secret too, they praise impart;   20
But in their acts divine and worship, they
  With hymns do offer up their heart.
    Thus in Christ's coach they sweetly sing
    As they to glory ride therein.

Some few not in; and some, whose time and place
  Block up this coach's way, do go
As travellers afoot, and so do trace
  The road that gives them right thereto.
    While in this coach these sweetly sing
    As they to glory ride therein.   30

                                        w. 1682
                                        p. 1939

FROM

Miscellaneous Poems

Upon a Spider Catching a Fly

Thou sorrow, venom elf.
  Is this thy play,
To spin a web out of thyself
  To catch a fly?
    For why?

I saw a pettish wasp   [pettish: peevish]
  Fall foul therein:
Whom yet thy whorl pins did not clasp
                [whorl pins: arms of spindle's flywheel]
  Lest he should fling
    His sting.   10

But as afraid, remote
  Didst stand hereat,
And with thy little fingers stroke
  And gently tap
    His back.

Thus gently him didst treat
  Lest he should pet,
And in a froppish, waspish heat   [froppish: petulant]
  Should greatly fret
    Thy net.   20

Whereas the silly fly,
  Caught by its leg,
Thou by the throat took'st hastily,
  And 'hind the head
    Bite dead.

This goes to pot, that not
  Nature doth call.   [Nature: common sense]
Strive not above what strength hath got,
  Lest in the brawl
    Thou fall.   30

This fray seems thus to us:
   Hell's Spider gets
His entrails spun to whip cords thus,
   And wove to nets,
     And sets.

To tangle Adam's race
   In's stratagems
To their destructions, spoil'd, made base
   By venom things,
     Damn'd sins.   **40**

But mighty, Gracious Lord,
   Communicate
Thy Grace to break the cord; afford
   Us glory's gate
     And state.

We'll nightingale sing like,
   When perched on high
In glory's cage, Thy glory, bright:
   Yea, thankfully,
     For joy.   **50**

w. c1685
p. 1939

Upon a Wasp Chilled with Cold

The Bear that breathes the northern blast
Did numb, torpedo-like, a wasp   [torpedo: sting-ray fish]
Whose stiffened limbs encramped, lay bathing
In Sol's warm breath and shine as saving,
Which with her hands she chafes and stands
Rubbing her legs, shanks, thighs, and hands.
Her petty toes and fingers' ends
Nipped with this breath, she out extends
Unto the sun, in great desire
To warm her digits at that fire: **10**
Doth hold her temples in this state
Where pulse doth beat, and head doth ache:
Doth turn, and stretch her body small,
Doth comb her velvet capital

As if her little brain-pan were
A volume of choice precepts clear:
As if her satin jacket hot
Contained apothecary's shop
Of Nature's receipts, that prevails
To remedy all her sad ails,   20
As if her velvet helmet high
Did turret rationality.
She fans her wing up to the wind
As if her petticoat were lined
With reason's fleece, and hoises sail   [hoises: hoists]
And humming flies in thankful gale
Unto her dun curled palace hall,
Her warm thanks offering for all.
Lord, clear my misted sight that I
May hence view Thy Divinity,   30
Some sparks whereof Thou up dost hasp   [hasp: shut]
Within this little downy wasp,
In whose small corporation we
A school and a schoolmaster see:
Where we may learn, and easily find
A nimble spirit, bravely mind
Her work in ev'ry limb: and lace
It up neat with a vital grace,
Acting each part though ne'er so small,
Here of this fustian animal,   40
Till I enravished climb into
The Godhead on this ladder do:
Where all my pipes inspired upraise
An Heavenly music, furr'd with praise.   [furr'd: filled]

                                             w. c1683
                                             p. 1943

Housewifery

Make me, O Lord, Thy spinning wheel complete.
    Thy Holy Word my distaff make for me.
                            [distaff: raw wool holder]
Make mine affections Thy swift fliers neat,
                            [fliers: revolving arms]

And make my soul Thy holy spool to be.
My conversation make to be Thy reel,
                              [reel: finished thread holder]
And reel the yarn thereon, spun off Thy wheel.

Make me Thy loom then; knit therein this twine;
    And make Thy Holy Spirit, Lord, wind quills
                                    [quills: spindles]
Then weave the web Thyself. The yarn is fine.
    Thine ordinances make my fulling mills.
                          [fulling: cloth processing]   10
Then dye the same in heavenly colors choice,
All pinked with varnished flowers of Paradise.
                      [pinked: ornamentally perforated]

Then clothe therewith mine understanding, will,
    Affections, judgment, conscience, memory,
My words and actions, that their shine may fill
    My ways with glory and Thee glorify.
    Then mine apparel shall display before Ye
That I am clothed in holy robes for glory.

                                        w. c1685
                                        p. 1939

The Ebb and Flow

When first Thou on me, Lord, wroughtest
        Thy sweet print,
    My heart was made Thy tinder box.
    My affections were Thy tinder in't,
        Where fell Thy sparks by drops.
These holy sparks of heavenly fire that came
Did ever catch and often out would flame.

But now my heart is made Thy censer trim,
    Full of Thy golden altar's fire,
    To offer up sweet incense in   10
        Unto Thyself entire:
I find my tinder scarce Thy sparks can feel
That drop out from Thy holy flint and steel.

Hence doubts out-bud for fear Thy fire in me
  Is a mocking ignis fatuus; [ignis fatuus: false light]
  Or lest Thine altar's fire out be,
    It's hid in ashes thus.
Yet when the bellows of Thy spirit blow
Away mine ashes, then Thy fire doth glow.

w. c1683
p. 1939

Upon the Sweeping Flood

O! that I'd had a tear to've quenched that flame
  Which did dissolve the heavens above
  Into those liquid drops that came
    To drown our carnal love.
Our cheeks were dry and eyes refused to weep.
Tears bursting out ran down the sky's dark cheek.

Were the heavens sick? must we their doctors be
  And physic them with pills, our sin?
  To make them purge and vomit see,
    And excrements out fling?   10
We've grieved them by such physic that they shed
Their excrements upon our lofty heads.

w. 1683
p. 1943

ROGER WILLIAMS
(1603–1683)

The first major voice of freedom in the colonies, Roger Williams was motivated not so much by a desire to democratize the state as by a love for pure religion that could not bear to see any church tainted by civil restrictions. The child of a substantial mercantile family in England, Williams attended Charterhouse School. He became a secretary to the famed Sir Edward Coke, who taught Williams an appreciation of the liberties guarded by the common law and who used his influence to have the young man admitted to Pembroke Hall, Cambridge, where Williams received his B.A. in 1627. Instead of going into the law, he remained at Cambridge to study divinity, became a chaplain in Essex for a short while, and, seeking wider religious horizons, arrived in Massachusetts Bay in 1631.

A Puritan himself, he found, however, that the perspectives allowed by New England orthodoxy were rigorously maintained by force. Instead of accepting the pastorate offered in Boston, he began to oppose Congregational polity with the same vehemence with which he opposed Episcopalian organization, and he rebuked the startled New Englanders for not separating from the episcopacy of the Anglican Church Establishment. Consequently Winthrop and others, assured of knowledge of God's will, blocked him from appointment to a church in Salem, and he worked for two years as a laborer and missionary to the Indians in the Plymouth area before returning to Salem in 1633. Although he was not a defender of all sects (he was displeased, for instance, by Quaker enthusiasm), he began to demand that each sect have the right to worship according to its own lights. The magistrates and ministers squirmed. He further demanded separation of church and state, arguing that Caesar was neither fit nor qualified to impose uniformity on religion, a uniformity that must become false and pernicious because it was imposed. The orthodox howled. When he disputed the validity of the royal charter, arguing that the Bay authorities had no right to expropriate land from the Indians, the Puritans were enraged beyond patience. In October, 1635, the Massachusetts General Court ordered him out, never to stain the colony of the righteous with his dark heresies again. In the early winter of 1636 he fled to Narragansett Bay, where he founded Providence.

Victims of religious, economic, social, and ethnic persecution soon heard of the haven founded by the gentle and tolerant Williams, and began to drift into the Rhode Island settlement. Annoyed by the flourishing existence of Satan in their southern dooryard, Massachusetts Bay attempted to extend its charter to include the Narragansett territories. But in 1644, in England to argue his case, Williams secured the charter himself. In 1663 a new charter granted Rhode Island self-government and full status as a colony; thus some of the basic principles of what was to become the republic were established as operative tenets of government.

Williams himself had become a Baptist, setting up in 1638 the first church of that sect in the New World; later he became a Seeker, feeling that no institutional authority should come between a man and his Bible, a man and his God. He remained a Seeker until he died. His most famous work, *The Bloody Tenent* [Tenet] *of Persecution,* is his side of a debate with that rigid Puritan dynast, John Cotton, concerning persecution for cause of conscience.

A partial list of his works includes *A Key into the Language of America* (1643); *The Bloody Tenent of Persecution, for Cause of Conscience, Discussed* (1644); *The Bloody Tenent Yet More Bloody* (1652); *The Hireling Ministry None of Christs* (1652); and *George Fox Digged Out of His Burrowes* (1676).

Accounts of Williams and his works are to be found in J. D. Knowles, *Memoir of Roger Williams* (1834); H. M. Dexter, *As to Roger Williams* (1876); M. C. Tyler, *A History of American Literature during The Colonial Period,* I (1897); E. J. Carpenter, *Roger Williams* (1909); M. E. Hall, *Roger Williams* (1917); V. L. Parrington, *Main Currents in American Thought,* I (1927); E. Easton, *Roger Williams* (1930); G. A. Stead, "Roger Williams and the Massachusetts Bay," *New England*

Quarterly, VII (1934); F. B. Weiner, "Roger Williams's Contribution to Modern Thought," *Rhode Island Historical Society Collections*, XXVIII (1935); C. M. Andrews, *The Colonial Period of American History*, II (1936); C. S. Longacre, *Roger Williams* (1939); S. H. Brockunier, *The Irrepressible Democrat* (1940); J. Eaton, *Lone Journey* (1944); Perry Miller, *Roger Williams* (1953); O. E. Winslow, *Master Roger Williams* (1957); R. Lowenherz, "Roger Williams and the Great Quaker Debate," *American Studies*, X (1958); and C. Covey, *The Gentle Radical* (1966).

FROM

The Bloody Tenent of Persecution

To Every Courteous Reader:

While I plead the cause of Truth and innocency against the bloody doctrine of persecution for cause of conscience, I judge it not unfit to give alarm to myself and all men to prepare to be persecuted or hunted for cause of conscience.

Whether you stand charged with ten or but two talents, if you hunt any for cause of conscience, how can you say you followest the Lamb of God who so abhorred that practice?

If Paul, if Jesus Christ were present here at London, and the question were proposed what religion would they approve of: the Papists, Prelatists, Presbyterians, Independents, etc. would each say, "Of mine, of mine."

But put the second question: If one of the several sorts should by major vote attain the sword of steel, what weapons doth Christ Jesus authorize them to fight with in His cause? Do not all men hate the persecutor, and every conscience, true or false, complain of cruelty, tyranny, etc.?

Two mountains of crying guilt lie heavy upon the backs of all that name the name of Christ in the eyes of Jews, Turks, and pagans.

First, the blasphemies of their idolatrous inventions, superstitions, and most unchristian conversations.

Secondly, the bloody irreligious and inhumane oppressions and destructions under the mask or veil of the name of Christ, etc.

Oh how like is the jealous Jehovah, the consuming fire, to end these present slaughters in a greater slaughter of the holy witnesses? (Rev. 11.)

Six years preaching so much truth of Christ (as that time afforded in King Edward's days) kindles the flames of Queen Mary's bloody persecutions.

Who can now but expect that after so many scores of years preaching and professing of more truth, and amongst so many great contentions amongst the very best of Protestants, a fiery furnace should be heated; and who does not now see the fires kindling?

I confess I have little hopes till those flames are over, that this discourse against the doctrine of persecution for cause of conscience should pass current—I say not amongst the wolves and lions, but even amongst the sheep of Christ themselves. . . . I have not hid within my breast my soul's belief. And although sleeping on the bed either of the pleasures or profits of sin, you think your conscience bound to smite at him that dares to waken you? Yet in the midst of all these civil and spiritual wars, I hope we shall agree on these particulars:

First, however the proud (upon the advantage of a higher earth or ground) overlook the poor and cry out, "Schismatics! Heretics!, etc.," "Shall blasphemers and seducers escape unpunished? etc.," yet there is a sorer punishment in the Gospel for despising Christ than Moses, even when the despiser of Moses was put to death without mercy (Heb. 10:28,29). He that believeth not shall be damned (Mark 16:16).

Secondly, whatever worship, ministry, ministration, [if] the best and purest are practised without faith and true persuasion that they are the true institutions of God, they are sinful worships, ministries, etc. And however in civil things we may be servants unto men, yet in divine and spiritual things the poorest peasant must disdain the service of the highest prince: Be ye not the servants of men. (I Cor. 14.)

Thirdly, without such search and trial, no man attains this faith and right persuasion. (I Thes. 5.) Try all things.

In vain have English parliaments permitted English Bibles in the poorest English houses and the simplest man or woman to search the scriptures, if yet against their souls' persuasions from the scripture they should be forced (as if they lived in Spain or Rome itself, without the sight of a Bible) to believe as the church believes.

Fourthly, having tried, we must hold fast, . . . we must not let go for all the flea bitings of the present afflictions. Having bought truth dear, we must not sell it cheap; not the least grain of it for the whole world, no not for the saving of souls, though our own most precious; least of all for the bitter sweetening of a little vanishing pleasure; for a little puff of credit and reputation from the changeable breath of uncertain sons of men; for the broken bags of riches on eagles' wings; for a dream of these, any or all of these which on our death-bed vanish and leave tormenting stings behind them.

Oh how much better is it from the love of truth, from the love of the Father of lights, from whence it comes, from the love of the Son of God, who is the way and the truth, to say as He (John 18:37), "For this end was I born, and for this end came I into the world, that I might bear witness to the truth."

Chapter I

TRUTH. In what dark corner of the world, sweet Peace, are we two met? How has this present evil world banished me from all the coasts and quarters of it, and how has the righteous God in judgment taken you from the earth? (Rev. 6:4.)

PEACE. 'Tis lamentably true, blessed Truth, the foundations of the world have long been out of course; the gates of earth and Hell have conspired together to intercept our joyful meeting and our holy kisses. With what a wearied, tired wing have I flown over nations, kingdoms, cities, towns to find out precious truth!

TRUTH. The like inquiries in my flights and travels have I made for peace, and still am told she has left the earth and fled to Heaven.

PEACE. Dear Truth, what is the earth but a dungeon of darkness where truth is not?

TRUTH. And what's the peace thereof but a fleeting dream, thine ape and counterfeit?

PEACE. Oh where's the promise of the God of Heaven that righteousness and peace shall kiss each other?

TRUTH. Patience, sweet Peace; these heavens and earth

are growing old and shall be changed like a garment
(Psalm 102). They shall melt away and be burnt up with
all the works that are therein; and the most high eternal
Creator shall gloriously create new heavens and new earth
wherein dwells righteousness (II Pet. 3). Our kisses then
shall have their endless date of purest and sweetest joys.
Till then both you and I must hope, and wait, and bear the
fury of the Dragon's wrath, whose monstrous lies and
furies shall with himself be cast into the lake of fire—
the second death (Rev. 20).

PEACE. Most precious Truth, you know we are both
pursued and laid for. Mine heart is full of sighs, mine eyes
with tears. Where can I better vent my full oppressed
bosom than into thine, whose faithful lips may for these
few hours revive my drooping, wandering spirits, and here
begin to wipe tears from mine eyes and the eyes of my
dearest children?

TRUTH. Sweet daughter of the God of peace begin. Pour
out your sorrows, vent your complaints! How joyful am I
to improve these precious minutes to revive our hearts,
both yours and mine, and the hearts of all that love the
truth and peace! (Zach. 8.)

PEACE. Dear Truth, I know your birth, your nature,
your delight. They that know you will prize you far above
themselves and [their] lives and sell themselves to buy you.
Well spoke that famous Elizabeth to her famous attorney,
Sir Edward Coke: Mr. Attorney, go on as thou hast begun
and still plead not *pro Domina Regina* but *pro Domina
Veritate* [not for Mistress Queen but for Mistress Truth].

TRUTH. 'Tis true my crown is high, my scepter's strong
to break down strongest holds, to throw down highest
crowns of all that plead (though but in thought) against
me. Some few there are—but oh how few are valiant for
the truth and dare to plead my cause as my witnesses in
sackcloth! (Rev. 11.) While all men's tongues are bent
like bows to shoot out lying words against me!

PEACE. Oh how could I spend eternal days and endless
dates at your holy feet in listening to the precious oracles
of your mouth! All the words of your mouth are truth and
there is no iniquity in them. Your lips drop as the honeycomb. But oh! since we must part anon, let us (as you
said) improve our minutes and (according as you prom-

ised) revive me with your words, which are sweeter than the honey and the honeycomb.

Chapter II

Dear Truth, I have two sad complaints:

First, the most sober of your witnesses that dare to plead your cause, how are they charged to be my enemies —contentious, turbulent, seditious?

Secondly, your enemies, though they speak and rail against you, though they outrageously pursue, imprison, banish, kill your faithful witnesses, yet how is all vermillioned o'er for justice 'gainst the heretics? Yea, if they kindle coals and blow the flames of devouring wars that leave neither spiritual nor civil state, but burns up branch and root, yet how do all pretend an holy war? He that kills, and he that's killed, they both cry out it is for God and for their conscience.

'Tis true, nor one nor other seldom dare to plead the mighty Prince Christ Jesus for their author, yet both (both Protestant and Papist) pretend they have spoke with Moses and the prophets, who all, say they (before Christ came), allowed such holy persecutions, holy wars against the enemies of holy Church.

TRUTH. Dear Peace (to ease your first complaint), 'tis true your dearest sons, most like their mother, peace-keeping, peace-making sons of God, have borne and still must bear the blurs of troublers of Israel and turners of the world upside down. And 'tis true again, what Solomon once spoke: The beginning of strife is as when one lets out water; therefore (says he) leave off contention before it be meddled with. This caveat should keep the banks and sluices firm and strong, that strife, like a breach of waters, break not in upon the sons of men.

Yet strife must be distinguished: it is necessary or unnecessary, godly or ungodly, Christian or unchristian, etc.

It is unnecessary, unlawful, dishonorable, ungodly, unchristian in most cases in the world, for there is a possibility of keeping sweet peace in most cases, and if it be possible, it is the express command of God that peace be kept (Rom. 13).

Again, it is necessary, honorable, godly, etc. with civil

and earthly weapons to defend the innocent and to rescue the oppressed from the violent paws and jaws of oppressing, persecuting Nimrods (Psalm 73, Job 29).

It is as necessary, yea more honorable, godly, and Christian, to fight the fight of faith with religious and spiritual artillery, and to contend earnestly for the faith of Jesus, once delivered to the saints, against all opposers, and the gates of earth and Hell, men or devils, yea against Paul himself or an angel from Heaven, if he bring any other faith or doctrine (Jude 4, Gal. 1:8).

PEACE. With the clashing of such arms am I never wakened. Speak once again (dear Truth) to my second complaint of bloody persecution and devouring wars marching under the colors of upright justice and holy zeal, etc.

TRUTH. My ears have long been filled with a threefold doleful outcry.

First, of one hundred forty-four thousand virgins (Rev. 14) forced and ravished by emperors, kings, and governors to their beds of worship and religion, set up (like Absoloms) on high in their several states and countries.

Secondly, the cry of those precious souls under the altar (Rev. 6), the souls of such as have been persecuted and slain for the testimony and witness of Jesus, whose blood has been spilt like water upon the earth, and that because they have held fast the truth and witness of Jesus, against the worship of the states and times, compelling to an uniformity of state religion.

These cries of murdered virgins—who can sit still and hear? Who can but run with zeal inflamed to prevent the deflowering of chaste souls and spilling of the blood of the innocent? Humanity stirs up and prompts the sons of men to draw material swords for a virgin's chastity and life against a ravishing murderer! And piety and Christianity must needs awaken the sons of God to draw the spiritual sword (the Word of God) to preserve the chastity and life of spiritual virgins, who abhor the spiritual defilements of false worship (Rev. 14).

Thirdly, the cry of the whole earth made drunk with the blood of its inhabitants, slaughtering each other in their blinded zeal, for conscience, for religion, against the Catholics, against the Lutherans, etc.

What fearful cries within these twenty years of hundred thousands men, women, children, fathers, mothers, husbands, wives, brethren, sisters, old and young, high and low—plundered, ravished, slaughtered, murdered, famished! And hence these cries that men fling away the spiritual sword and spiritual artillery (in spiritual and religious causes) and rather trust for the suppression of each other's God, conscience, and religion (as they suppose) to an arm of flesh and a sword of steel.

TRUTH. Sweet Peace, what have you there?

PEACE. Arguments against persecution for cause of conscience.

TRUTH. And what there?

PEACE. An answer to such arguments, contrarily maintaining such persecution for cause of conscience.

TRUTH. These arguments against such persecution, and the answer pleading for it, written (as love hopes) from godly intentions, hearts, and hands, yet in a marvellous different style and manner. The arguments against persecution in milk, the answer for it (as I may say) in blood.

The author of these arguments [against persecution] (as I have been informed) being committed by some then in power, close prisoner to Newgate, for the witness of some truths of Jesus, and having not the use of pen and ink, wrote these arguments in milk, in sheets of paper, brought to him by the woman his keeper, from a friend in London, as the stopples of his milk bottle.

In such paper written with milk nothing will appear, but the way of reading it by fire being known to this friend who received the papers, he transcribed and kept together the papers, although the author himself could not correct, nor view what himself had written.

It was in milk, tending to soul nourishment, even for babes and sucklings in Christ.

It was in milk, spiritually white, pure and innocent, like those white horses of the word of truth and meekness, and the white linen or armor of righteousness, in the army of Jesus (Rev. 6 and 19).

It was in milk, soft, meek, peaceable and gentle, tending both to the peace of souls, and the peace of States and Kingdoms.

PEACE. The answer (though I hope out of milky pure intentions) is returned in blood: bloody and slaughterous conclusions; bloody to the souls of all men, forced to the religion and worship which every civil state or common-weal agrees on, and compels all subjects to in a dissembled uniformity.

Bloody to the bodies, first of the holy witnesses of Christ Jesus, who testify against such invented worships.

Secondly, of the nation and peoples slaughtering each other for their several respective religions and consciences. . . .

PEACE. Pass on, holy Truth, to that similitude whereby they illustrate that negative assertion: "The prince in the ship," they say, "is governor over the bodies of all in the ship; but he has no power to govern the ship or the mariners in the actions of it. If the pilot manifestly err in his action, the prince may reprove him," and so, say they may any passenger; "if he offend against the life or goods of any, the prince may in due time and place punish him, which no private person may."

TRUTH. Although, dear Peace, we both agree that civil powers may not enjoin such devices, no nor enforce on any God's institutions, since Christ Jesus's coming, yet, for further illustration, I shall propose some queries concerning the civil magistrate's passing in the ship of the church, wherein Christ Jesus has appointed his ministers and officers as governors and pilots, etc.

If in a ship at sea, wherein the governor or pilot of a ship undertakes to carry the ship to such a port, the civil magistrate (suppose a king or emperor) shall command the master such and such a course, to steer upon such or such a point, which the master knows is not their course, and which if they steer he shall never bring the ship to that port or harbor: what shall the master do? Surely all men will say, the master of the ship or pilot is to present reasons and arguments from his mariner's art, if the prince be capable of them, or else in humble and submissive manner to persuade the prince not to interrupt them in their course and duty properly belonging to them, to wit, governing of the ship, steering of the course, etc.

If the master of the ship command the mariners thus and thus, in running the ship, managing the helm, trimming the sail, and the prince command the mariners a different or contrary course, who is to be obeyed?

It is confessed that the mariners may lawfully disobey the prince, and obey the governor of the ship in the actions of the ship.

Thirdly, what if the prince have as much skill, which is rare, as the pilot himself? I conceive it will be answered, that the master of the ship and pilot, in what concerns the ship, are chief and above, in respect of their office, the prince himself, and their commands ought to be attended by all the mariners, unless it be in manifest error, wherein it is granted any passenger may reprove the pilot.

Fourthly, I ask, if the prince and his attendants be unskillful in the ship's affairs, whether every sailor and mariner, the youngest and lowest, be not, so far as concerns the ship, to be preferred before the prince's followers, and the prince himself? And their counsel and advice more to be attended to, and their service more to be desired and respected, and the prince to be requested to stand by and let the business alone in their hands?

Fifthly, in case a willful king and his attendants, out of opinion of their skill, or willfulness of passion, would so steer the course, trim sail, etc., as that in the judgment of the master and seamen the ship and lives shall be endangered: whether, in case humble persuasions prevail not, ought not the ship's company to refuse to act in such a course, yea, and, in case power be in their hands, resist and suppress these dangerous practices of the prince and his followers, and so save the ship?

Lastly, suppose the master, out of base fear and cowardice, or covetous desire of reward, shall yield to gratify the mind of the prince, contrary to the rules of art and experience, etc., and the ship come in danger, and perish, and the prince with it: if the master get to shore, whether may he not be justly questioned, yea, and suffer as guilty of the prince's death, and those that perished with him? These cases are clear, wherein, according to this similitude, the prince ought not to govern and rule the actions of the ship, but such whose office, and charge, and skill it is.

The result of all is this: the church of Christ is the ship, wherein the prince—if a member, for otherwise the case is altered—is a passenger. In this ship the officers and governors, such as are appointed by the Lord Jesus, they are the chief, and in those respects above the prince himself, and are to be obeyed and submitted to in their works and administrations, even before the prince himself.

In this respect every Christian in the church, man or woman, if of more knowledge and grace of Christ, ought to be of higher esteem, concerning religion and Christianity, than all the princes in the world who have either none or less grace or knowledge of Christ, although in civil things all civil reverence, honor, and obedience ought to be yielded by all men.

Therefore, if in matters of religion the king command what is contrary to Christ's rule, though according to his persuasion and conscience, who sees not that, according to the similitude, he ought not to be obeyed? Yea, and (in case) boldly, with spiritual force and power, he ought to be resisted. And if any officer of the church of Christ shall out of baseness yield to the command of the prince, to the danger of the church and souls committed to his charge, the souls that perish, notwithstanding the prince's command, shall be laid to his charge.

If so, then I rejoin thus: how agree these truths of this similitude with those former positions, viz., that the civil magistrate is keeper of both tables, that he is to see the church do her duty, that he ought to establish the true religion, suppress and punish the false, and so consequently must discern, judge, and determine what the true gathering and governing of the church is, what the duty of every minister of Christ is, what the true ordinances are, and what the true administrations of them; and where men fail, correct, punish, and reform by the civil sword? I desire it may be answered, in the fear and presence of Him whose eyes are as a flame of fire, if this be not—according to the similitude, though contrary to their scope in proposing of it—to be governor of the ship of the church, to see the master, pilot, and mariners do their duty, in setting the course, steering the ship, trimming the sails, keeping the watch etc., and where they fail, to punish them; and therefore, by undeniable consequence, to judge and determine what their duties are, when they do right, and when they do wrong: and this not only to manifest error, (for then they say every passenger may reprove) but in their ordinary course and practice.

The similitude of a physician obeying the prince in the body politic, but prescribing to the prince concerning the prince's body, wherein the prince, unless the physician manifestly err, is to be obedient to the physician, and not to be judge of the physician in his art, but to be ruled and judged as touching the state of his body by the physician:

I say this similitude and many others suiting with the former of a ship, might be alleged to prove the distinction of the civil and spiritual estate, and that according to the rule of the Lord Jesus in the gospel, the civil magistrate is only to attend the calling of the civil magistracy concerning the bodies and goods of the subjects, and is himself, if a member of the church and within, subject to the power of the Lord Jesus therein, as any member of the church is (I Cor. 5). . . .

1644

Two Poems

1

The courteous Pagan shall condemn
   Uncourteous Englishmen,
Who live like foxes, bears and wolves,
   Or lion in his den.
Let none sing blessings to their souls,
   For that they courteous are:
The wild Barbarians with no more
   Than nature, go so far:
If nature's sons both wild and tame
   Humane and courteous be: 10
How ill becomes it sons of God
   To want Humanity?

2

Boast not, proud English, of thy birth and blood:
   Thy brother Indian is by birth as good.
Of one blood God made him, and thee, and all.
   As wise, as fair, as strong, as personal.
By nature, wrath's his portion, thine, no more
   Till Grace his soul and thine in Christ restore.
Make sure thy second birth, else thou shalt see
   Heaven ope to Indians wild, but shut to thee.

1643

WILLIAM BYRD II

(1674–1744)

William Byrd's was probably the outstanding example (up to the generation of Jefferson) of the brilliant and varied lives led by southern aristocrats. Byrd was born on the family's 26,000-acre James River estate—part of the site now occupied by Richmond, which he founded. The famous estate came to be called "Westover," after the Georgian mansion that Byrd built at enormous expense; and by the time of his death his land holdings totaled 180,000 acres.

Byrd was educated in the law at the Middle Temple in London; in Holland he learned how to conduct business enterprises; and during his five sojourns in England spread over a thirty-five-year period, he spent his time amid the urbane elegance of the *haut monde*. As a frequenter of the courts and coffee houses of Augustan England, he became acquainted with the Earl of Orrery, Wycherley, Congreve, Rowe, Swift, and Pope. At home, he became a member of the House of Burgesses when he was eighteen, founded Petersburg as well as Richmond, was the London agent of the Virginia Assembly, acted as receiver-general of the King's revenues, and in 1709 became a member of the Supreme Council for the remaining thirty-five years of his life. Naturally aligned with the interests of the large planter class and with the insistence on local government that was to produce Jefferson's idea of a republic, Byrd was active in the opposition to Governor Spotswood.

A Virginia gentleman indeed, he combined with his shrewd, wide, and cosmopolitan worldly knowledge an education that allowed him to read three classical and two modern languages.

He built his father's library into a holding of over 3500 volumes, the largest private collection in the colonies. A member of the Royal Society, he wrote various works of history and exploration. Three of them—*The History of the Dividing Line, A Progress to the Mines,* and *A Journey to the Land of Eden* (all published in 1841 in *The Westover Manuscripts,* edited by E. Ruffin)—he had bound for his family library. The first grew out of his membership in the boundary commission that in 1728 set the line between Virginia and North Carolina and was, until the discovery of *The Secret Diary,* his most famous work. The second was a product of his visit to some Virginia iron mines, the third of his visit to North Carolina. Yet he never published anything during his lifetime. He did not consider himself an author so much as a gentleman of letters, reflecting the aristocratic attitude that literature was a closet exercise for the leisure diversion of a small group of intimates.

Although he is remembered as a public figure who was lord of a gracious and representative manor, he is best known for his *Secret Diary.* After its discovery, part of the diary (1709–1712), which was written in code, was decoded and published in 1941 by L. B. Wright and M. Tinling as *The Secret Diary of William Byrd of Westover.* In 1942, the 1739–1742 section was published by M. H. Woodfin and M. Tinling as *Another Secret Diary of William Byrd.* The *Diary* does for southern colonial life what the journals of Bradford and Sewall do for New England. And as in both those examples, the man emerges along with the life and times. Arrogant in his station and authority, Byrd yet remained brightly observant, funny, lusty, and accurate. Like Sewall, he points toward the eighteenth-century ideal of the public steward and man of service, later envisioned by Jefferson as the true American aristocrat of social benevolence and talent.

Besides those mentioned above, the works of Byrd include *The Secret History of the Line* (1929; see W. K. Boyd, below).

Accounts of Byrd and his works are to be found in M. C. Tyler, *A History of American Literature During the Colonial Period,* II (1897); J. S. Basset, ed., *The Writings of Colonel William Byrd* (1901); W. K. Boyd, ed., *William Byrd's Histories of the Dividing Line Betwixt Virginia and North Carolina* (1929), which included the first publication of *The Secret History of the Line;* P. A. Bruce, *The Virginia Plutarch* (1929); R. C. Beatty, *William Byrd of Westover* (1932); J. R. Masterson, "William Byrd in Lubberland," *American Literature,* IX (1937); L. B. Wright, "A Shorthand Diary of William Byrd of Westover," *Huntington Library Quarterly,* II (1939); L. B. Wright,

The First Gentlemen of Virginia (1940); L. B. Wright and M. Tinling, "William Byrd of Westover, an American Pepys," *South Atlantic Quarterly*, XXXIX (1940); L. B. Wright, "William Byrd: Citizen of the Enlightenment," *Anglo-American Cultural Relations in the Seventeenth and Eighteenth Centuries* (1959); U. Troubetzkov, "The Great Dismal Swamp," *Virginia Cavalcade*, X (1961); U. Troubetzkov, "Enough to Keep a Byrd Alive," *Virginia Cavalcade*, XI (1961); R. M. Gummere, "Byrd and Sewall: Two Colonial Classicists," *Transactions of the Colonial Society of Massachusetts*, XLII (1964); and L. B. Wright, ed., *The Prose Works of William Byrd of Westover: Narratives of a Colonial Virginian* (1966).

F R O M

The Secret Diary

October 28 [*1709*]. I rose at 6 o'clock but read nothing because Colonel Randolph came to see me in the morning. I neglected to say my prayers but I ate milk for breakfast. Colonel Harrison's vessel came in from Madeira and brought abundance of letters and among the rest I had ten from Mr. Perry with a sad account of tobacco. We went to court but much time was taken up in reading our letters and not much business was done. About 3 we rose and had a meeting of the College in which it was agreed to turn Mr. Blackamore out from being master of the school for being so great a sot. . . .

October 29 [*1709*]. I rose at 6 o'clock and read nothing because the governors of the College were to meet again. . . . When we met, Mr. Blackamore presented a petition in which he set forth that if the governors of the College would forgive him what was past, he would for the time to come mend his conduct. On which the governors at last agreed to keep him on, on trial, some time longer. Then we went to court where we sat till about 3 o'clock, and then I learned that my sister Custis was at Mr. Bland's. I went to her and there was also Mrs. Chiswell. I went with them to Doctor B-r-t and ate beef for dinner. Here I stayed till 8 o'clock and then walked home. . . .

October 31 [*1709*]. I rose at 6 o'clock and read two chapters in Hebrew and some Greek in Lucian. I said my prayers and ate milk for breakfast. About 10 o'clock we went to court. The committee met to receive proposals for the building [of] the College and Mr. Tullitt undertook it for £2,000 provided he might wood off the College land

and all assistants from England to come at the College's risk. We sat in court till about 4 o'clock and then I rode to Green Springs to meet my wife. I found her there and had the pleasure to learn that all was well at home, thanks be to God. There was likewise Mrs. Chiswell. . . . Then we danced and were merry till about 10 o'clock. I neglected to say my prayers but had good health, and thoughts, and good humor, thanks be to God Almighty. This month I took above 400 of Colonel Quarry in money for bills at an allowance of 10 per cent.

Dec. 25 [*1709*]. I rose at 7 o'clock and ate milk for breakfast. I neglected to say my prayers because of my company. . . . About 11 o'clock the rest of the company ate some broiled turkey for their breakfast. Then we went to church, notwithstanding it rained a little, where Mr. Anderson preached a good sermon for the occasion. I received the Sacrament with great devoutness. After church the same company went to dine with me and I ate roast beef for dinner. In the afternoon Dick Randolph and Mr. Jackson went away and Mr. Jackson rode sidelong like a woman. Then we took a walk about the plantation, but a great fog soon drove us into the house again. In the evening we were merry with nonsense and so were my servants. I said my prayers shortly and had good health, good thoughts, and good humor, thanks be to God Almighty.

Dec. 27 [*1709*]. I rose at 5 o'clock and read a chapter in Hebrew and some Greek in Cassius. I said my prayers and ate milk for breakfast. I danced my dance. When the company came down I ate chocolate likewise with them. Then we played at billiards and tried some of our [tokay]. About 12 o'clock we went to Mr. Harrison's notwithstanding it was extremely cold and I ate some goose. In the afternoon we were very merry by a good fire till 5 o'clock. Then we returned home, where I found all well, thank God. In the evening we played at cards till about 10 o'clock and I lost a crown. I neglected to say my prayers and had good health, good thoughts, and good humor, thanks be to God Almighty.

Dec. 28 [*1709*]. I rose at 6 o'clock and read two chapters in Hebrew and some Greek in Cassius. I said my prayers and ate milk for breakfast. I danced my dance. It continued very cold with a strong wind. About 10 o'clock I ate some chocolate with the rest of the company. Then we played at billiards and I lost. When I was beat out I read something in Dr. Day. About one we went to dinner and I ate boiled pork. In the afternoon we played again at billiards till we lost one of the balls. Then we walked about the plantation and took a slide on the ice. In the evening we played at cards till about 10 o'clock. . . .

Dec. 29 [*1709*]. I rose at 5 o'clock and read two chapters in Hebrew and some Greek in Cassius. . . . Then we took a walk and I slid on skates, notwithstanding there was a thaw. Then we returned and played at billiards till dinner. I ate boiled beef for dinner. In the afternoon we played at billiards again and in the evening took another walk and gave Mr. Isham Randolph two bits to venture on the ice. He ventured and the ice broke with him and took him up to the mid-leg. Then we came home and played a little at whisk but I was so sleepy we soon left off. . . .

March 31 [*1710*]. I rose at 7 o'clock and read some Greek in bed. I said my prayers and ate milk for breakfast. Then about 8 o'clock we got a-horseback and rode to Mr. Harrison's and found him very ill but sensible. Here I met Mr. Bland, who brought me several letters from England and among the rest two from Colonel Blakiston who had endeavored to procure the government of Virginia for me at the price of £1,000 of my Lady Orkney and that my Lord [agreed] but the Duke of Marlborough declared that no one but soldiers should have the government of a plantation, so I was disappointed. God's will be done. From hence I came home where I found all well, thank God. I ate fish for dinner. In the afternoon I went again with my wife to Mr. Harrison's who continued very bad so that I resolved to stay with him all night, which I did with Mr. Anderson and Nat Burwell. He was in the same bad condition till he vomited and then he was more easy. In the morning early I returned home and went to bed. It is remarkable that Mrs. Burwell dreamed this night that she saw a person that with money scales weighed time and declared that there was no more than 18 pennies worth of time to come, which seems to be a dream with some significance either concerning the world or a sick person. In my letters from England I learned that the Bishop of Worcester was of opinion that in the year 1715 the city of Rome would be burnt to the ground, that before the year 1745 the popish religion would be routed out of the world, that before the year 1790 the Jews and Gentiles would be converted to the Christianity, and then would begin the millennium.

April 10 [1710]. I rose at 6 o'clock and wrote several letters to my overseers. I sent early to inquire after Mr. Harrison and received word that he died about 4 o'clock this morning, which completed the 18th day of his sickness, according to Mrs. Burwell's dream exactly. Just before his death he was sensible and desired Mrs. L—— with importunity to open the door because he wanted to go out and could not go till the door was open and as soon as the door was opened he died. The country has lost a very useful man and who was both an advantage and an ornament to it, and I have lost a good neighbor, but God's will be done. . . . My wife rode to Mrs. Harrison's to comfort her and to assure her that I should be always ready to do her all manner of service. My wife returned before dinner. I ate tripe for dinner. In the afternoon we played at piquet. Then I prepared my matters for the General Court. It rained, with the wind at northeast, and it was very cold, and in the night it snowed. I read news. I said my prayers and had good health, good thoughts, and good humor, thank God Almighty.

April 14 [1710]. I rose at 6 o'clock and read some Hebrew and no Greek. I neglected to say my prayers but ate milk for breakfast, but the rest of the company ate meat. About 10 o'clock we walked to Mrs. Harrison's to the funeral, where we found abundance of company of all sorts. Wine and cake were served very plentifully. At one o'clock the corpse began to move and the ship "Harrison" fired a gun every half minute. When we came to church the prayers were first read; then we had a sermon which was an extravagant panegyric or [eulogy]. At every turn he called him "this great man," and not only covered his faults but gave him virtues which he never possessed as well as magnified those which he had. When [the] sermon was done, the funeral service was read and the poor widow trembled extremely. When all was over I put the widow, her daughter, and two sisters into my coach and Colonel Randolph, his wife, Colonel Hill, Mrs. Anderson, and the two B-r-k-s went home with us and I invited several others who would not come. . . .

May 23 [1710]. I rose at 5 o'clock and read two chapters in Hebrew and some Greek in Anacreon. The children were a little better, thank God. . . . My daughter was very ill, but the boy had lost his fever, thank God. I settled some accounts and wrote some commonplace. I ate hashed shoat for dinner. In the afternoon Evie had a sweat that worked pretty well but not long enough, for which I was out of humor with my wife. I read some Italian and some news and then took a walk about the plantation. When I returned I had a great quarrel with my wife, in which she was to blame altogether; however I made the first step to a reconciliation, to [which] she with much difficulty consented. . . .

May 24 [1710]. I rose at 5 o'clock and read a chapter in Hebrew and some Greek in Anacreon. . . . I sent for my cousin Harrison to let Evie blood who was ill. When she came she took away about four ounces. We put on blisters and gave her a glyster which worked very well. Her blood was extremely thick, which is common in distemper of this constitution. About 12 o'clock she began to sweat of herself, which we prompted by tincture of saffron and sage and snakeroot. This made her sweat extremely, in which she continued little or more all night. I ate some fish for dinner. In the afternoon Mr. Anderson whom I had sent for came and approved of what I had done. I persuaded him to stay all night which he agreed to. It rained in the evening. We stayed up till 12 o'clock and Bannister sat up with the child till 12 o'clock and G-r-l till break of day. . . .

May 25 [1710]. . . . Evie was much better, thank God Almighty, and had lost her fever. The boy was better likewise but was restless. It was very hot today. I read some Italian. I ate green peas for dinner. In the afternoon my wife and I cut some [sage] and then I read more Italian. . . . I never was more incommoded with heat in my whole life. . . .

July 15 [1710]. About 7 o'clock the Negro Betty that ran away was brought home. My wife against my will caused little Jenny to be burned with a hot iron, for which I quarreled with her. It was so hot today that I did not intend to go to the launching of Colonel Hill's ship but about 9 o'clock the Colonel was so kind as to come and call us. My wife would not go at first, but with much entreaty she at last consented. About 12 o'clock we went and found abundance of company at the ship and about one she was launched and went off very well, notwithstanding several had believed the contrary. . . .

September 20 [1710]. I rose at 6 o'clock but read nothing because I prepared for the Governor's coming in the evening. I neglected to say my prayers but ate milk for breakfast. I settled several things in my library. All the wood was removed from the place where it used to lay to a better place. I sent John to kill some blue wing and he had good luck. I ate some boiled beef for dinner. In the afternoon all things were put into the best order because Captain Burbydge sent word that the Governor would be here at 4 o'clock but he did not come till 5. Captain Burbydge sent his boat for him and fired as he came up the river. I received at the landing with Mr. C-s and gave him 3 guns. Mr. Clayton and Mr. Robinson came with him. After he had drunk some wine he walked in the garden and in the library till it was dark. Then he went to supper and ate some blue wing. After supper we sat and talked till 9 o'clock. . . .

September 21 [1710]. I rose at 6 o'clock and read nothing but got ready to receive the company. About 8 o'clock the Governor came down. I offered him some of my fine water [?]. Then we had milk, tea, and bread and butter for breakfast. The Governor was pleased with everything and very complaisant. About 10 o'clock Captain Stith came and soon after him Colonel Hill, Mr. Anderson and several others of the militia officers. The Governor was extremely courteous to them. About 12 o'clock Mr. Clayton went to Mrs. Harrison's and then orders were given to bring all the men into the pasture to muster. Just as we got on our horses it began to rain hard; however this did not discourage the Governor but away we rode to the men. It rained half an hour and the Governor mustered them all the while and he presented me to the people to be their Colonel and commander-in-chief. About 3 o'clock we returned to the house and as many of the officers as could sit at the table stayed to dine with the Governor, and the rest went to take part of the hogshead [of punch] in the church yard. We had a good dinner, well served, with which the Governor seemed to be well pleased. I ate venison for dinner. In the evening all the company went away and we took a walk and found a comic freak of a man that was drunk that hung on the pales. Then we went home and played at piquet and I won the pool. About 9 the Governor went to bed. . . .

October 19 [*1710*]. . . . About 11 o'clock I went to court, it being the day appointed for trying the criminals. After we had stayed there about 2 hours we went into Council and then came down to court again, where we stayed till 4 o'clock and then adjourned. Then I went to dine at the Governor's where I ate boiled beef for dinner. In the evening we played at cards and I lost 25 shillings. We played at basset. About 11 o'clock I returned to my lodgings. I recommended to the Governor to get some men from the men-of-war for Colonel Hill's ship. . . .

October 20 [*1710*]. I went to court and gave my judgment in several cases. About 1 o'clock I took some sage and snakeroot. Then I returned into court again and there we sat till 3. Then I wrote a letter to my wife and after that I went to the coffeehouse where I played at hazard and lost 7 pounds and returned home very peaceful. . . .

Dec. 25 [*1710*]. I rose at 5 o'clock and read a chapter in Hebrew and some Greek in Lucian. About 7 o'clock the Negro woman died that was mad yesterday. I said my prayers and ate boiled milk for breakfast. The wind blew very strong and it rained exceedingly. . . . About 11 o'clock we went to church where we had prayers and the Holy Sacrament which I took devoutly. We brought nobody home to dinner. I ate boiled venison. The child was a little better. In the afternoon I took a long walk and I saw several parts of the fence blown down with the wind, which blew very hard last night. In the evening I read a sermon in Mr. Norris but a quarrel which I had with my wife hindered my taking much notice of it. However we were reconciled before we went to bed, but I made the first advance. I neglected to say my prayers but not to eat some milk. I had good health, good thoughts, and indifferent good humor, thank God Almighty.

Feb. 5 [*1711*]. I rose about 8 o'clock and found my cold still worse. I said my prayers and ate milk and potatoes for breakfast. My wife and I quarreled about her pulling her brows. She threatened she would not go to

Williamsburg if she might not pull them; I refused, however, and got the better of her, and maintained my authority. . . .

Nov. 23 [*1711*]. It was very cold this morning. About 11 o'clock I went to the coffeehouse where the Governor also came and from thence we went to the capitol and read the bill concerning ports the first time. We stayed till 3 o'clock and then went to dinner to Marot's but could get none there and therefore Colonel Lewis and I dined with Colonel Duke and I ate broiled chicken for dinner. After dinner we went to Colonel Carter's room where we had a bowl of punch of French brandy and oranges. We talked very lewdly and were almost drunk and in that condition we went to the coffeehouse and played at dice and I lost £12. We stayed at the coffeehouse till almost 4 o'clock in the morning talking with Major Harrison.

Dec. 29 [*1711*]. I rose about 7 o'clock and read two chapters in Hebrew and some Greek in Lucian. I said my prayers and ate boiled milk for breakfast. I had abundance of talk with Mr. G-r-l about the affairs of Falling Creek and he told me some of his wants and so did George Smith, which I endeavored to supply as well as I could. I gave John G-r-l leave to go visit his mother. Poor old Jane died this morning about 9 o'clock and I caused her to be buried as soon as possible because she stank very much. It was not very cold today. I danced my dance. Mr. G-r-l and George Smith went away about 12 o'clock. I ate some broiled goose for dinner. In the afternoon I set my razor, and then went out to shoot with bow and arrow till the evening and then I ran to breathe myself and looked over everything. At night I read some Latin in Terence till about 10 o'clock. I said my prayers and had good health, good thoughts, and good humor, thank God Almighty.

Dec. 30 [*1711*]. I rose about 7 o'clock and read a chapter in Hebrew and three chapters in the Greek Testament. I said my prayers very devoutly and ate boiled milk for breakfast. The weather was very clear and warm so that my wife walked out with Mrs. Dunn and forgot dinner, for which I had a little quarrel with her and another afterwards because I was not willing to let her have a book out of the library. About 12 o'clock came Mr. Bland from

Williamsburg but brought no news. He stayed to dinner and I ate some roast beef. In the afternoon we sat and talked till about 4 o'clock and then I caused my people to set him over the river and then I walked with the women about the plantation till they were very weary. At night we ate some eggs and drank some Virginia beer and talked very gravely without reading anything. However I said my prayers and spoke with all my people. I had good health, good thoughts, and good humor, thank God Almighty. I danced my dance in the morning.

Dec. 31 [*1711*]. I rose about 7 o'clock and read a chapter in Hebrew and six leaves in Lucian. I said my prayers and ate boiled milk for breakfast. The weather continued warm and clear. I settled my accounts and wrote several things till dinner. I danced my dance. I ate some turkey and chine for dinner. In the afternoon I weighed some money and then read some Latin in Terence and then Mr. Mumford came and told me my man Tony had been very sick but he was recovered again, thank God. He told me Robin Bolling had been like to die and that he denied that he was the first to mention the imposition on skins which he certainly did. Then he and I took a walk about the plantation. When I returned I was out of humor to find the Negroes all at work in our chambers. At night I ate some broiled turkey with Mr. Mumford and we talked and were merry all the evening. I said my prayers and had good health, good thoughts, and good humor, thank God Almighty. My wife and I had a terrible quarrel about whipping Eugene while Mr. Mumford was there but she had a mind to show her authority before company but I would not suffer it, which she took very ill; however for peace sake I made the first advance towards a reconciliation which I obtained with some difficulty and after abundance of crying. However it spoiled the mirth of the evening, but I was not conscious that I was to blame in that quarrel.

Jan. 1 [*1712*]. I lay abed till 9 o'clock this morning to bring my wife into temper again and rogered her by way of reconciliation. I read nothing because Mr. Mumford was here, nor did I say my prayers, for the same reason. However I ate boiled milk for breakfast, and after my wife tempted me to eat some pancakes with her. Mr. Mumford and I went to shoot with our bows and arrows but shot nothing, and afterwards we played at billiards till dinner, and when we came we found Ben Harrison there, who dined with us. I ate some partridge for dinner. In the afternoon we played at billiards again and I won two bits. I had a letter from Colonel Duke by H-e the brick-layer who came to offer his services to work for me. Mr. Mumford went away in the evening and John Bannister with him to see his mother. I took a walk about the planta-tion and at night we drank some mead of my wife's making which was very good. I gave the people some cider and a dram to the Negroes. I read some Latin in Terence and had good health, good thoughts, and good humor, thank God Almighty. I said my prayers.

w. 1709–1712
p. 1941

FROM

The History of the Dividing Line

March 10 [*1728*]. The sabbath happened very oppor-tunely to give some ease to our jaded people, who rested religiously from every work, but that of cooking the kettle. We observed very few cornfields in our walks, and those very small, which seemed the stranger to us, because we could see no other tokens of husbandry or improvement. But, upon further inquiry, we were given to understand people only made corn for themselves and not for their stocks, which know very well how to get their own living. Both cattle and hogs ramble into the neighboring marshes and swamps, where they maintain themselves the whole winter long, and are not fetched home till the spring. Thus these indolent wretches, during one half of the year, lose the advantage of the milk of their cattle, as well as their dung, and many of the poor creatures perish in the mire, into the bargain, by this ill management.

Some, who pique themselves more upon industry than their neighbors, will, now and then, in compliment to their cattle, cut down a tree whose limbs are loaded with the moss aforementioned. The trouble would be too great to climb the tree in order to gather this provender, but the shortest way (which in this country is always counted the best) is to fell it, just like the lazy Indians, who do the same by such trees as bear fruit, and so make one harvest for all. By this bad husbandry milk is so scarce, in the winter season, that were a bigbellied woman to long for it, she would lose her longing. And, in truth, I believe this is often the case, and at the same time a very good reason why so many people in this province are marked with a custard complexion.

The only business here is raising of hogs, which is managed with the least trouble, and affords the diet they are most fond of. The truth of it is, the inhabitants of North Carolina devour so much swine's flesh, that it fills them full of gross humors. For want too of a constant supply of salt, they are commonly obliged to eat it fresh, and that begets the highest taint of scurvy. Thus whenever a severe cold happens to constitutions thus vitiated, 'tis apt to improve into the yaws, called there very justly the "country-distemper." This has all the symptoms of the pox, with this aggravation—that no preparation of mercury will touch it. First it seizes the throat, next the palate, and lastly shows its spite to the poor nose, of which 'tis apt in a small time treacherously to undermine the foundation.

This calamity is so common and familiar here, that it ceases to be a scandal, and in the disputes that happen about beauty, the noses have in some companies much ado to carry it. Nay, 'tis said that once, after three good pork years, a motion had like to have been made in the House of Burgesses that a man with a nose should be incapable of holding any place of profit in the province, which extraordinary motion could never have been intended without some hopes of a majority.

Thus, considering the foul and pernicious effects of eating swine's flesh in a hot country, it was wisely forbidden and made an abomination to the Jews, who lived much in the same latitude with Carolina.

March 25 [1728]. The air was chilled this morning with a smart north-west wind, which favored the Dismalites [the party that explored the Dismal Swamp] in their dirty march. They returned by the path they had made in coming out, and with great industry arrived in the evening at the spot where the Line had been discontinued. After so long and laborious a journey, they were glad to repose themselves on their couches of cypress-bark, where their sleep was as sweet as it would have been on a bed of Finland down. In the mean time, we who stayed behind had nothing to do, but to make the best observations we could upon that part of the country. The soil of our landlord's plantation, though none of the best, seemed more fertile than any thereabouts, where the ground is near as sandy as the deserts of Africa, and consequently barren. The road leading from thence to Edenton, being in distance about twenty-seven miles, lies upon a ridge called Sandy Ridge, which is so wretchedly poor that it will not bring potatoes.

The pines in this part of the country are of a different species from those that grow in Virginia: their bearded leaves are much longer and their cones much larger. Each cell contains a seed of the size and figure of a black-eyed pea, which, shedding in November, is very good mast for hogs, and fattens them in a short time. The smallest of these pines are full of cones, which are eight or nine inches long, and each affords commonly 60 or 70 seeds. This kind of mast has the advantage of all other by being more constant, and less liable to be nipped by the frost or eaten by the caterpillars. The trees also abound more with turpentine, and consequently yield more tar than either the yellow or the white pine; and for the same reason make more durable timber for building. The inhabitants hereabouts pick up knots of lightwood in abundance, which they burn into tar, and then carry it to Norfolk or Nansimond for a market. The tar made in this method is the less valuable because it is said to burn the cordage, though it is full as good for all other uses as that made in Sweden and Muscovy.

Surely there is no place in the world where the inhabitants live with less labor than in North Carolina. It approaches nearer to the description of Lubberland than any other, by the great felicity of the climate, the easiness of raising provisions, and the slothfulness of the people. Indian corn is of so great increase that a little pains will subsist a very large family with bread, and then they may have meat without any pains at all, by the help of low grounds, and the great variety of mast that grows on the high land. The men for their parts, just like the Indians, impose all the work upon the poor women. They make their wives rise out of their beds early in the morning, at the same time that they lie and snore till the sun has run one-third of his course and dispersed all the unwholesome damps. Then, after stretching and yawning for half an hour, they light their pipes, and, under the protection of a cloud of smoke, venture out into the open air; though, if it happens to be never so little cold, they quickly return shivering into the chimney corner. When the weather is mild, they stand leaning with both their arms upon the cornfield fence, and gravely consider whether they had best go and take a small heat at the hoe: but generally find reasons to put it off till another time.

Thus they loiter away their lives, like Solomon's sluggard, with their arms across, and at the winding up of the year scarcely have bread to eat. To speak the truth, 'tis a thorough aversion to labor that makes people file off to North Carolina, where plenty and a warm sun confirm them in their disposition to laziness for their whole lives.

March 26 [*1728*]. Since we were like to be confined to this place, till the people returned out of the Dismal, 'twas agreed that our chaplain might safely take a turn to Edenton, to preach the Gospel to the infidels there, and christen their children. He was accompanied thither by Mr. Little, one of the Carolina Commissioners, who, to show his regard for the Church, offered to treat him on the road with a fricassee of rum. They fried half a dozen rashers of very fat bacon in a pint of rum, both which being dished up together, served the company at once for meat and drink. Most of the rum they get in this country comes from New England, and is so bad and unwholesome, that it is not improperly called "kill-devil." It is distilled there from foreign molasses, which, if skilfully managed, yields near gallon for gallon. Their molasses comes from the same country, and has the name of "long sugar" in Carolina, I suppose from the ropiness of it, and serves all the purposes of sugar, both in their eating and drinking.

When they entertain their friends bountifully, they fail not to set before them a capacious bowl of bombo, so called from the Admiral of that name. This is a compound of rum and water in equal parts, made palatable with the said long sugar. As good humor begins to flow, and the bowl to ebb, they take care to replenish it with sheer rum, of which there always is a reserve under the table. But such generous doings happen only when that balsam of life is plenty; for they have often such melancholy times, that neither land-graves nor cassicks can procure one drop for their wives, when they lie in, or are troubled with the colic or vapors. Very few in this country have the industry to plant orchards, which, in a dearth of rum, might supply them with much better liquor. The truth is, there is one inconvenience that easily discourages lazy people from making this improvement: very often, in autumn, when the apples begin to ripen, they are visited with numerous flights of paraqueets, that bite all the fruit to pieces in a moment, for the sake of the kernels. The havoc they make is sometimes so great, that whole orchards are laid waste in spite of all the noises that can be made, or mawkins that can be dressed up to fright 'em away. These ravenous birds visit North Carolina only during the warm season, and so soon as the cold begins to come on, retire back towards the sun. They rarely venture so far north as Virginia, except in a very hot summer, when they visit the most southern parts of it. They are very beautiful; but like some other pretty creatures, are apt to be loud and mischievous.

March 27 [1728]. Betwixt this and Edenton there are many thuckleberry slashes, which afford a convenient harbor for wolves and foxes. The first of these wild beasts is not so large and fierce as they are in other countries more northerly. He will not attack a man in the keenest of his hunger, but run away from him, as from an animal more mischievous than himself. The foxes are much bolder, and will sometimes not only make a stand, but likewise assault any one that would balk them of their prey. The inhabitants hereabouts take the trouble to dig abundance of wolf-pits, so deep and perpendicular, that when a wolf is once tempted into them, he can no more scramble out again, than a husband who has taken the leap can scramble out of matrimony. Most of the houses in this part of the country are log-houses, covered with pine or cypress shingles, 3 feet long, and one broad. They are hung upon laths with pegs, and their doors too turn upon wooden hinges, and have wooden locks to secure them, so that the building is finished without nails or other iron-work. They also set up their pales without any nails at all, and indeed more securely than those that are nailed. There are three rails mortised into the posts, the lowest of which serves as a sill with a groove in the middle, big enough to receive the end of the pales: the middle part of the pale rests against the inside of the next rail, and the top of it is brought forward to the outside of the uppermost. Such wreathing of the pales in and out makes them stand firm, and much harder to unfix than when nailed in the ordinary way.

Within three or four miles of Edenton, the soil appears to be a little more fertile, though it is much cut with slashes, which seem all to have a tendency towards the Dismal. This town is situate on the north side of Albemarle Sound, which is there about five miles over. A dirty slash runs all along the back of it, which in the summer is a foul annoyance, and furnishes abundance of that Carolina plague, mosquitoes. There may be forty or fifty houses, most of them small, and built without expense. A citizen here is counted extravagant, if he has ambition enough to aspire to a brick-chimney. Justice herself is but indifferently lodged, the court-house having much the air of a common tobacco-house. I believe this is the only metropolis in the Christian or Mahomedan world, where there is neither church, chapel, mosque, synagogue, or any other place of public worship of any sect or religion whatsoever. What little devotion there may happen to be is much more private than their vices. The people seem easy without a minister, as long as they are exempted from paying him. Sometimes the society for propagating the Gospel has had the charity to send over missionaries to this country; but unfortunately the priest has been too lewd for the people, or, which oftener happens, they too lewd for the priest. For these reasons these reverend gentlemen have always left their flocks as arrant heathen as they found them. Thus much however may be said for the inhabitants of Edenton, that not a soul has the least taint of hypocrisy, or superstition, acting very frankly and aboveboard in all their excesses.

Provisions here are extremely cheap, and extremely good, so that people may live plentifully at a trifling expense. Nothing is dear but law, physic, and strong drink, which are all bad in their kind, and the last they get with so much difficulty, that they are never guilty of the sin of suffering it to sour upon their hands. Their vanity generally lies not so much in having a handsome dining-room, as a handsome house of office: in this kind of structure they are really extravagant. They are rarely guilty of flattering or making any court to their governors, but treat them with all the excesses of freedom and familiarity. They are of opinion their rulers would be apt to grow insolent, if they grew rich, and for that reason take care to keep them poorer, and more dependent, if possible, than the saints in New England used to do their governors. They have very little coin, so they are forced to carry on their home-traffic with paper-money. This is the only cash that will tarry in the country, and for that reason the discount goes on increasing between that and real money, and will do so to the end of the chapter.

April 7 [*1728*]. The next day being Sunday, we ordered notice to be sent to all the neighborhood that there would be a sermon at this place, and an opportunity of christening their children. But the likelihood of rain got the better of their devotion, and what perhaps, might still be a stronger motive of their curiosity. In the morning we dispatched a runner to the Nottoway Town, to let the Indians know we intended them a visit that evening, and our honest landlord was so kind as to be our pilot thither, being about four miles from his house. Accordingly in the afternoon we marched in good order to the town, where the female scouts, stationed on an eminence for that purpose, had no sooner spied us, but they gave notice of our approach to their fellow-citizens by continual whoops and cries, which could not possibly have been more dismal at the sight of their most implacable enemies. This signal assembled all their great men, who received us in a body, and conducted us into the fort. This fort was a square piece of ground, inclosed with substantial puncheons, or strong palisades, about ten feet high, and leaning a little outwards, to make a scalade more difficult. Each side of the square might be about one hundred yards long, with loop-holes at proper distances, through which they may fire upon the enemy. Within this inclosure we found bark cabins sufficient to lodge all their people, in case they should be obliged to retire thither. These cabins are no other but close arbors made of saplings, arched at the top, and covered so well with bark as to be proof against all weather. The fire is made in the middle, according to the Hibernian fashion, the smoke whereof finds no other vent but at the door, and so keeps the whole family warm, at the expense both of their eyes and complexion. The Indians have no standing furniture in their cabins but hurdles to repose their persons upon, which they cover with mats or deer-skins. We were conducted to the best apartments in the fort, which just before had been made ready for our reception, and adorned with new mats that were sweet and clean. The young men had painted themselves in a hideous manner, not so much for ornament as terror. In that frightful equipage they entertained us with sundry war-dances, wherein they endeavored to look as formidable as possible. The instrument they danced to was an Indian-drum, that is, a large gourd with a skin braced taut over the mouth of it. The dancers all sang to this music, keeping exact time with their feet, while their heads and arms were screwed into a thousand menacing postures. Upon this occasion the ladies had arrayed themselves in all their finery. They were wrapt in their red and blue match-coats, thrown so negligently about them that their mahogany skins appeared in several parts, like the Lacedaemonian damsels of old. Their hair was braided with white and blue peak, and hung gracefully in a large roll upon their shoulders.

This peak consists of small cylinders cut out of a conque-shell, drilled through and strung like beads. It serves them both for money and jewels, the blue being of much greater value than the white, for the same reason that Ethiopian mistresses in France are dearer than French, because they are more scarce. The women wear necklaces and bracelets of these precious materials, when they have a mind to appear lovely. Though their complexions be a little sad-colored, yet their shapes are very straight and well proportioned. Their faces are seldom handsome, yet they have an air of innocence and bashfulness, that with a little less dirt would not fail to make them desirable. Such charms might have had their full effect upon men who had been so long deprived of female conversation, but that the whole winter's soil was so crusted on the skins of those dark angels, that it required a very strong appetite to approach them. The bear's oil, with which they anoint their persons all over, makes their skins soft, and at the same time protects them from every species of vermin that used to be troublesome to other uncleanly people. We were unluckily so many that they could not well make us the complement of bed-fellows, according to the Indian rules of hospitality, though a grave matron whispered one of the Commissioners very civ03ly in the ear, that if her daughter had been but one year older, she should have been at his devotion.

It is by no means a loss of reputation among the Indians for damsels that are single to have intrigues with the men; on the contrary, they count it an argument of superior merit to be liked by a great number of gallants. However, like the ladies that game they are a little mercenary in their amours, and seldom bestow their favors out of stark love and kindness. But after these women have once appropriated their charms by marriage, they are from thenceforth faithful to their vows, and will hardly ever be tempted by an agreeable gallant, or be provoked by a brutal or even by a fumbling husband to go astray. The little work that is done among the Indians is done by the poor women, while the men are quite idle, or at most employed only in the gentlemanly diversions of hunting and fishing.

In this, as well as in their wars, they now use nothing but fire-arms, which they purchase of the English for skins. Bows and arrows are grown into disuse, except only amongst their boys. Nor is it ill policy, but on the contrary very prudent, thus to furnish the Indians with fire-arms, because it makes them depend entirely upon the English, not only for their trade, but even for their subsistence. Besides, they were really able to do more mischief while they made use of arrows, of which they would let silently fly several in a minute with wonderful dexterity, whereas now they hardly ever discharge their fire-locks more than once, which they insidiously do from behind a tree, and then retire as nimbly as the Dutch Horse used to do now and then formerly in Flanders. We put the Indians to no expense, but only of a little corn for our horses, for which in gratitude we cheered their hearts with what rum we had left, which they love better than they do their wives and children. Though these Indians dwell among the English, and see in what plenty a little industry enables them to live, yet they choose to continue in their stupid idleness, and to suffer all the inconveniences of dirt, cold, and want, rather than to disturb their heads with care, or defile their hands with labor.

The whole number of people belonging to the Nottoway Town, if you include women and children, amount to about two hundred. These are the only Indians of any consequence now remaining within the limits of Virginia. The rest are either removed, or dwindled to a very inconsiderable number, either by destroying one another, or else by the small-pox and other diseases. Though nothing has been so fatal to them as their ungovernable passion for rum, with which, I am sorry to say it, they have been but too liberally supplied by the English that live near them.

And here I must lament the bad success Mr. Boyle's charity has hitherto had towards converting any of these poor heathens to Christianity. Many children of our neighboring Indians have been brought up in the College of William and Mary: They have been taught to read and write, and have been carefully instructed in the principles of the Christian religion, till they came to be men. Yet after they returned home, instead of civilizing and converting the rest, they have immediately relapsed into infidelity and barbarism themselves.

And some of them too have made the worst use of the knowledge they acquired among the English, by employing it against their benefactors. Besides, as they unhappily forget all the good they learn, and remember the ill, they are apt to be more vicious and disorderly than the rest of their countrymen. . . .

. . .

I am sorry I can't give a better account of the state of the poor Indians with respect to Christianity, although a great deal of pains has been and still continues to be taken with them. For my part, I must be of opinion, as I hinted before, that there is but one way of converting these poor infidels, and reclaiming them from barbarity, and that is, charitably to intermarry with them, according to the modern policy of the most Christian King in Canada and Louisiana. Had the English done this at the first settlement of the Colony, the infidelity of the Indians had been worn out at this day, with their dark complexions, and the country had swarmed with people more than it does with insects.

It was certainly an unreasonable nicety, that prevented their entering into so good-natured an alliance. All nations of men have the same natural dignity, and we all know that very bright talents may be lodged under a very dark skin. The principal difference between one people and another proceeds only from the different opportunities of improvement.

The Indians by no means want understanding, and are in their figure tall and well-proportioned. Even their copper-colored complexion would admit of blanching, if not in the first, at the farthest in the second generation.

I may safely venture to say, the Indian women would have made altogether as honest wives for the first planters, as the damsels they used to purchase from aboard the ships. It is strange, therefore, that any good Christian should have refused a wholesome, straight bed-fellow, when he might have had so fair a portion with her, as the merit of saving her soul.

w. 1728
p. 1841

JOHN WOOLMAN

(1720–1772)

New Jersey and Pennsylvania offered a sanctuary in which the Quakers could establish families and inaugurate Meetings free of the harsh restrictions and persecutions of the Puritans. John Woolman, the son of a Quaker farm family, was born near Burlington, New Jersey. Growing up in the peace and love of the close Quaker community, the farm lad early became imbued with the sense of gentle and all-embracing love that marks his life and writings. When he was twenty he went to work in a shop where he mastered the skills of tailoring. He kept his own shop in Mount Holly, New Jersey, near the place of his birth, married Sarah Ellis in 1749, and prospered thriftily and unobtrusively. By the time he was twenty-one, he had already begun to visit other Meetings of Friends, and gradually he became a dedicated preacher. When he was thirty-six he gave up keeping shop and devoted himself to traveling among the colonial Meetings and presenting his fellow Friends with the humanitarian ideas which were typical of the man and which he felt should be typical of Quaker practice. He became the focal point of Quaker opposition to slavery. In 1772, to further the work of abolition, he traveled to England, where he died of smallpox.

His *Journal*, essays, and memoirs all present a saint. Motivated by a calm but consuming love for human beings, he opposed economic and social inequities in their every aspect, convinced wealthy Quakers that slaveholding was not consonant with their beliefs, and finally effected an emancipation of all slaves held by Friends. In his own life he increasingly refrained from all acts and products which were in any way connected with the oppression or mistreatment of his fellow beings anywhere, and lived more and more simply until, like Henry Thoreau's, his life was his character, his principles, and his fate. The *Journal* reflects the plain and humble rhetoric of the Friends, but its very purity and casual simplicity disguise the artful care with which Woolman revised much of it. A man of beautiful honesty and largeness of soul, Woolman was deeply concerned that his life and writing should be cast so clearly that all who came to them should be instructed in the ways of Christian equality and love. The *Journal*, published in 1774, two years after Woolman's death, impressed people in many lands, becoming one of the best-loved American books. Among the famous Americans upon whom it left its mark are William Ellery Channing, Whittier, Emerson, and Dreiser.

Besides the *Journal*, Woolman's works include *Some Considerations on the Keeping of Negroes* (1754), the second part being issued in 1762; *Considerations on Pure Wisdom and Human Policy* (1768); *Considerations on the True Harmony of Mankind* (1770); *An Epistle to the Quarterly and Monthly Meeting of Friends* (1772); and *A Plea for the Poor* (1793).

Accounts of Woolman and his works are to be found in J. G. Whittier, ed., *The Journal of John Woolman* (1871); W. T. Shore, *John Woolman, His Life and Our Times* (1913); A. Sharpless, *John Woolman, A Pioneer in Labor Reform* (1920); E. E. Taylor, *John Woolman, Craftsman Prophet* (1920); A. M. Gummere, ed., *The Journal and Essays of John Woolman* (1922); F. V. Morley, *The Taylor of Mount Holly* (1926); J. Whitney, *John Woolman, American Quaker* (1942); C. O. Peare, *John Woolman: Child of Light* (1954); F. B. Tolles, ed., *The Journal of John Woolman and A Plea for the Poor* (1961); E. H. Cady, *John Woolman* (1965); and P. Moulton, "John Woolman: Exemplar of Ethics," *Quaker History*, LIV (1965).

FROM

The Journal

I have often felt a motion of love to leave some hints of my experience of the goodness of God; and pursuant thereto, in the thirty-sixth year of my age, I begin this work.

I was born in Northampton, in Burlington county, in West Jersey, in the year of our Lord 1720; and before I was seven years old I began to be acquainted with the operations of Divine love. Through the care of my parents,

I was taught to read as soon as I was capable of it; and as I went from school one seventh-day, I remember, while my companions went to play by the way, I went forward out of sight, and sitting down, I read the twenty-second chapter of the Revelation: "He showed me a pure river of water of life, clear as crystal, proceeding out of the throne of God and of the lamb," etc.; and in the reading of it, my mind was drawn to seek after that pure habitation, which, I then believed, God had prepared for His servants. The place where I sat, and the sweetness that attended my soul, remain fresh in my memory.

This, and the like gracious visitations, had that effect upon me, that when boys used ill language, it troubled me, and through the continued mercies of God I was preserved from it. The pious instructions of my parents were often fresh in my mind when I happened to be among wicked children, and were of use to me.

My parents, having a large family of children, used frequently, on first days after meeting, to put us to read in the Holy Scriptures, or some religious books, one after another, the rest sitting by without much conversation; which I have since often thought was a good practice. From what I had read, I believed there had been, in past ages, people who walked in uprightness before God, in a degree exceeding any that I knew or heard of now living; and the apprehension of there being less steadiness and firmness amongst people in this age than in past ages, often troubled me while I was still young.

I had a dream about the ninth year of my age as follows. I saw the moon rise near the west, and run a regular course eastward, so swift that in about a quarter of an hour she reached our meridian; when there descended from her a small cloud on a direct line to the earth, which lighted on a pleasant green about twenty yards from the door of my father's house (in which I thought I stood) and was immediately turned into a beautiful green tree. The moon appeared to run on with equal swiftness, and soon set in the east, at which time the sun arose at the place where it commonly doth in the summer, and shining with full radiance in a serene air, it appeared as pleasant a morning as ever I saw.

All this time I stood still in the door, in an awful frame of mind, and observed that as heat increased by the rising

sun, it wrought so powerfully on the little green tree, that
the leaves gradually withered and before noon it appeared
dry and dead. There then appeared a being, small of size,
moving swift from the north southward, called a *"Sun
Worm."*

Though I was a child, this dream was instructive to me.

Another thing remarkable in my childhood was, that
once, as I went to a neighbor's house, I saw, on the way,
a robin sitting on her nest; and as I came near she went off,
but having young ones, flew about, and with many cries
expressed her concern for them. I stood and threw stones
at her, till one striking her, she fell down dead. At first I
was pleased with the exploit; but after a few minutes was
seized with horror, as having, in a sportive way, killed an
innocent creature while she was careful for her young. I
beheld her lying dead, and thought those young ones, for
which she was so careful, must now perish for want of their
dam to nourish them; and after some painful considerations
on the subject, I climbed up the tree, took all the young
birds, and killed them—supposing that better than to leave
them to pine away and die miserably; and believed, in this
case, that Scripture proverb was fulfilled, "The tender
mercies of the wicked are cruel." I then went on my errand,
but, for some hours, could think of little else but the
cruelties I had committed, and was much troubled.

Thus He, whose tender mercies are over all His works,
hath placed that in the human mind, which incites to exercise goodness towards every living creature, and this being
singly attended to, people become tender-hearted and sym-
pathizing; but being frequently and totally rejected, the
mind shuts itself up in a contrary disposition.

About the twelfth year of my age, my father being
abroad, my mother reproved me for some misconduct, to
which I made an undutiful reply; and the next first-day, as
I was with my father returning from meeting, he told me he
understood I had behaved amiss to my mother, and advised
me to be more careful in future. I knew myself blamable,
and in shame and confusion remained silent. Being thus
awakened to a sense of my wickedness, I felt remorse in my
mind, and getting home, I retired and prayed to the Lord to
forgive me; and I do not remember that I ever, after that,
spoke unhandsomely to either of my parents, however
foolish in some other things.

Having attained the age of sixteen, I began to love wanton company; and though I was preserved from profane language or scandalous conduct, still I perceived a plant in me which produced much wild grapes. Yet my merciful Father forsook me not utterly, but at times, through His grace, I was brought seriously to consider my ways; and the sight of my backsliding affected me with sorrow; but for want of rightly attending to the reproofs of instruction, vanity was added to vanity, and repentance. Upon the whole, my mind was more and more alienated from the Truth, and I hastened towards destruction. While I meditate on the gulf towards which I travelled, and reflect on my youthful disobedience, my heart is affected with sorrow.

Advancing in age, the number of my acquaintance increased, and thereby my way grew more difficult. Though I had heretofore found comfort in reading the Holy Scriptures, and thinking on heavenly things, I was now estranged therefrom. I knew I was going from the flock of Christ, and had no resolution to return; hence serious reflections were uneasy to me, and youthful vanities and diversions my greatest pleasure. Running in this road I found many like myself; and we associated in that which is reverse to true friendship. But in this swift race it pleased God to visit me with sickness, so that I doubted of recovering; and then did darkness, horror, and amazement, with full force seize me, even when my pain and distress of body was very great. I thought it would have been better for me never to have had a being, than to see the day which I now saw. I was filled with confusion; and in great affliction, both of mind and body, I lay and bewailed myself. I had not confidence to lift up my cries to God, whom I had thus offended; but in a deep sense of my great folly, I was humbled before Him; and at length, that Word which is as a fire and a hammer, broke and dissolved my rebellious heart, and then my cries were put up in contrition; and in the multitude of His mercies I found inward relief, and felt a close engagement, that if He was pleased to restore my health, I might walk humbly before Him.

After my recovery, this exercise remained with me a considerable time; but by degrees, giving way to youthful vanities, they gained strength, and getting with wanton young people I lost ground. The Lord had been very gracious, and spoke peace to me in the time of my distress;

and I now most ungratefully turned again to folly; on which account, at times I felt sharp reproof, but did not get low enough to cry for help. I was not so hardy as to commit things scandalous; but to exceed in vanity and promote mirth, was my chief study. Still I retained a love and esteem for pious people, and their company brought an awe upon me. My dear parents several times admonished me in the fear of the Lord, and their admonition entered into my heart, and had a good effect for a season; but not getting deep enough to pray rightly, the tempter, when he came, found entrance. I remember once, having spent a part of a day in wantonness, as I went to bed at night, there lay in a window near my bed a Bible, which I opened, and first cast my eye on the text, "we lie down in our shame, and our confusion covers us"; this I knew to be my case; and meeting with so unexpected a reproof, I was somewhat affected with it, and went to bed under remorse of conscience, which I soon cast off again.

Thus time passed on: my heart was replenished with mirth and wantonness, while pleasing scenes of vanity were presented to my imagination, till I attained the age of eighteen years, near which time I felt the judgments of God in my soul like a consuming fire, and looking over my past life, the prospect was moving. I was often sad, and longed to be delivered from those vanities; then, again, my heart was strongly inclined to them, and there was in me a sore conflict. At times I turned to folly; and then again, sorrow and confusion took hold of me. In a while, I resolved totally to leave off some of my vanities; but there was a secret reserve in my heart, of the more refined part of them, and I was not low enough to find true peace. Thus for some months, I had great troubles and disquiet, there remaining in me an unsubjected will, which rendered my labors fruitless, till at length, through the merciful continuance of heavenly visitations, I was made to bow down in spirit before the Most High. I remember one evening I had spent some time in reading a pious author; and walking out alone, I humbly prayed to the Lord for His help, that I might be delivered from those vanities which so ensnared me. Thus, being brought low, He helped me, and as I learned to bear the Cross, I felt refreshment to come from His presence, but not keeping in that strength which gave victory, I lost ground again, the sense of which greatly afflicted me; and

I sought deserts and lonely places, and there with tears did confess my sins to God, and humbly craved help of Him. And I may say with reverence, he was near to me in my troubles, and in those times of humiliation opened my ear to discipline.

I was now led to look seriously at the means by which I was drawn from the pure truth, and learned this—that if I would live in the life which the faithful servants of God lived in, I must not go into company as heretofore, in my own will; but all the cravings of sense must be governed by a Divine principle. In times of sorrow and abasement, these instructions were sealed upon me, and I felt the power of Christ prevail over all selfish desires, so that I was preserved in a good degree of steadiness; and being young, and believing, at that time, that a single life was best for me, I was strengthened to keep from such company as had often been a snare to me.

I kept steady to meetings; spent first-days in the afternoon chiefly in reading the Scriptures, and other good books; and was early convinced in my mind that true religion consisted in an inward life, wherein the heart doth love and reverence God the Creator, and learn to exercise true justice and goodness, not only toward all men, but also toward the brute creatures. That as the mind was moved by an inward principle to love God as an invisible, incomprehensible Being, by the same principle it was moved to love Him in all His manifestations in the visible world. That, as by His breath the flame of life was kindled in all animal and sensible creatures, to say we love God as unseen, and, at the same time, exercise cruelty toward the least creature moving by His life, or by life derived from Him, was a contradiction in itself.

I found no narrowness respecting sects and opinions; but believed that sincere, upright-hearted people, in every society, who truly love God, were accepted of Him.

As I lived under the cross, and simply followed the openings of Truth, my mind, from day to day, was more enlightened; my former acquaintance were left to judge of me as they would, for I found it safest for me to live in private, and to keep these things sealed up in my own breast. While I silently ponder on that change which was wrought in me, I find no language equal to it, nor any means to convey a clear idea of it. I looked upon the works of God in this visible creation, and an awfulness covered me; my heart was tender, and often contrite, and a universal love to my fellow-creatures increased in me. This will be understood by such who have trodden in the same path.

Some glances of real beauty is perceivable in their faces who dwell in true meekness, some tincture of true harmony in the sound of that voice to which divine love gives utterance, and some appearance of right order in their temper and conduct whose passions are fully regulated; yet all these do not fully show forth that inward life to such who have not felt it; but this white stone and new name is known rightly to such only who have it.

Now though I had been thus strengthened to bear the cross, I still found myself in great danger, having many weaknesses attending me, and strong temptations to wrestle with; in the feeling whereof I frequently withdrew into private places, and often with tears besought the Lord to help me, whose gracious ear was open to my cry.

All this time I lived with my parents, and wrought on the plantation; and, having had schooling pretty well for a planter, I used to improve it in winter-evenings and other leisure times; and, being now in the twenty-first year of my age, a man, in much business at shop-keeping and baking, asked me, if I would hire with him to tend shop and keep books. I acquainted my father with the proposal; and, after some deliberation, it was agreed for me to go. I had for a considerable time found my mind less given to husbandry than heretofore, having often in view some other way of living.

At home I had lived retired; and now, having a prospect of being much in the way of company, I felt frequent and fervent cries in my heart to God, the Father of Mercies, that he would preserve me from all taint and corruption; that in this more public employment, I might serve Him, my gracious Redeemer, in that humility and self-denial, with which I had been, in a small degree, exercised in a very private life.

The man, who employed me, furnished a shop in Mount-Holly, about five miles from my father's house, and six from his own; and there I lived alone, and tended his shop. Shortly after my settlement here I was visited by several young people, my former acquaintances, who knew not but vanities would be as agreeable to me now as ever; and, at these times, I cried to the Lord, in secret, for wisdom and strength; for I felt myself encompassed with difficulties, and had fresh occasion to bewail the follies of time past, in contracting a familiarity with libertine people. And, as I had now left my father's house outwardly, I found my heavenly Father to be merciful to me beyond what I can express.

By day I was much amongst people, and had many trials to go through; but, in the evenings I was mostly alone, and may with thankfulness acknowledge, that, in those times, the spirit of supplication was often poured upon me; under which I was frequently exercised, and felt my strength renewed.

In a few months after I came here, my master bought several Scotchmen, servants from on-board a vessel, and brought them to Mount-Holly to sell; and, having sold several, the rest were left to me, one of which was taken sick and died. The latter part of his sickness, he, being delirious, used to curse and swear most sorrowfully; and after he was buried, I was left to sleep alone the next night in the same chamber where he died. I perceived in me a timorousness; I knew however, I had not injured the man, but had assisted in taking care of him according to my capacity; and I was not free to ask any one, on that occasion, to sleep with me: nature was feeble, but every trial was a fresh incitement to give myself up wholly to the service of God, for I found no helper like Him in times of trouble.

After a while, my former acquaintance gave over expecting me as one of their company; and I began to be known to some whose conversation was helpful to me; and now, as I had experienced the love of God, through Jesus Christ, to redeem me from many pollutions, and to be a constant succor to me through a sea of conflicts, with which no person was fully acquainted; and as my heart was often enlarged in this heavenly principle, so I felt a tender compassion for the youth, who remained entangled in the same snares, which had entangled me. From one month to another this love and tenderness increased; and my mind was more strongly engaged for the good of my fellow-creatures. I went to meetings in an awful frame of mind, and endeavoured to be inwardly acquainted with the language of the true Shepherd; and, one day, being under a strong exercise of spirit, I stood up, and said some words in a meeting; but, not keeping close to the divine opening, I said more than was required of me; and being soon sensible of my error, I was afflicted in mind some weeks, without any light or comfort, even to that degree that I could take satisfaction in nothing. I remembered God, and was troubled, and, in the depth of my distress, He had pity upon me, and sent the Comforter; I then felt forgiveness for my offense, and my mind became calm and quiet, being truly thankful to my gracious Redeemer for His mercies; and, after this, feeling the spring of Divine Love opened, and a concern to speak, I said a few words in meeting, in which I found peace; this, I believe, was about six weeks from the first time; and, as I was thus humbled and disciplined under the Cross, my understanding became more strengthened to distinguish the language of pure spirit which inwardly moves upon the heart, and taught me to wait in silence sometimes many weeks together, until I felt that rise which prepares the creature to stand like a trumpet through which the Lord speaks to His flock.

From an inward purifying, and stedfast abiding under it, springs a lively operative desire for the good of others. All faithful people are not called to the public ministry; but whoever are called to it, are called to minister of that which they have tasted and handled spiritually. The outward modes of worship are various; but, wheresoever [any] are true ministers of Jesus Christ, it is from the operation of His spirit upon their hearts, first purifying them, and thus giving them a sense of the conditions of others. The truth was clearly fixed in my mind; and I was taught to watch the pure opening, and to take heed, lest, while I was standing to speak, my own will should get uppermost, and cause me to utter words from worldly wisdom, and depart from the channel of the true gospel-ministry.

In the management of my outward affairs, I may say, with thankfulness, I found truth to be my support; and I was respected in my master's family, who came to live in Mount-Holly within two years after my going there.

About the twenty-third year of my age, I had many fresh and heavenly openings, in respect to the care and providence of the Almighty over his creatures in general, and over man as the most noble amongst those which are visible. And being clearly convinced in my judgment, that to place my whole trust in God was best for me, I felt renewed engagements that in all things I might act on an inward principle of virtue, and pursue worldly business no farther, than as truth opened my way therein.

About the time called Christmas, I observed many people from the country, and dwellers in town, who, resorting to public-houses, spent their time in drinking and vain sports, tending to corrupt one another; on which account I was much troubled. At one house, in particular, there was much disorder; and I believed it was a duty laid on me to go and speak to the master of that house. I considered I was young, and that several elderly friends in town had opportunity to see these things; and though I would gladly have been excused, yet I could not feel my mind clear. The exercise was heavy; and as I was reading what the Almighty said to Ezekiel, respecting his duty as a watchman, the matter was set home more clearly; and then, with prayers and tears, I besought the Lord for His assistance, who in loving-kindness, gave me a resigned heart; then, at a suitable opportunity, I went to the public-house; and, seeing the man amongst a company, I went to him, and told him I wanted to speak with him; so we went aside, and there, in the fear and dread of the Almighty, I expressed to him what rested on my mind; which he took kindly, and afterward showed more regard to me than before. In a few years after he died, middle-aged; and I often thought that, had I neglected my duty in that case, it would have given me great trouble; and I was humbly thankful to my gracious Father, who had supported me therein.

My employer having a Negro woman, sold her, and directed me to write a bill of sale, the man being waiting who had bought her: the thing was sudden; and, though the thoughts of writing an instrument of slavery for one of my fellow-creatures felt uneasy, yet I remembered I was hired by the year, that it was my master who directed me to do it, and that it was an elderly man, a member of our society, who bought her; so, through weakness, I gave way, and wrote it; but, at the executing it, I was so afflicted in my mind, that I said, before my master and the friend, that I believed slave-keeping to be a practice inconsistent with the Christian religion. This in some degree abated my uneasiness; yet, as often as I reflected seriously upon it, I thought I should have been clearer, if I had desired to be excused from it, as a thing against my conscience; for such it was. [And,] some time after this a young man spoke to me to write [an instrument of slavery], he having taken a Negro into his house. I told him I was not easy to write it, for though many kept slaves in our society, as in others, I still believed the practice was not right, and desired to be excused from doing the writing. I spoke to him in good will, and he told me that keeping slaves was not altogether agreeable to his mind, but that the slave being a gift to his wife, he had accepted of her. . . .

Until the year 1756, I continued to retail goods, besides following my trade as a tailor; about which time I grew uneasy on account of my business growing too cumbersome. I began with selling trimmings for garments, and from thence proceeded to sell cloths and linens; and at length, having got a considerable shop of goods, my trade increased every year, and the road to large business appeared open: but I felt a stop in my mind.

Through the mercies of the Almighty, I had, in a good degree, learned to be content with a plain way of living. I had but a small family; my outward affairs had been prosperous and on serious reflection, I believed Truth did not require me to engage in many cumbering affairs. It had generally been my practice to buy and sell things really useful. Things that served chiefly to please the vain mind in people, I was not easy to trade in; seldom did it, and whenever I did, I found it [to] weaken me as a Christian.

The increase of business became my burthen; for though my natural inclination was towards merchandise, yet I believed Truth required me to live more free from outward cumbers. There was now a strife in my mind betwixt the two, and in this exercise my prayers were put up to the Lord, who graciously heard me, and gave me a heart resigned to his holy will; I then lessened my outward business; and as I had opportunity, told my customers of my intention, that they might consider what shop to turn to; and so in a while, wholly laid down merchandise, following my trade as a tailor, myself only, having no prentice. I also had a nursery of apple trees, in which I spent a good deal of time hoeing, grafting, trimming, and inoculating.

In merchandise it is the custom, where I lived, to sell chiefly on credit, and poor people often get in debt; and when payment is expected, having not wherewith to pay, and so their creditors often sue for it at law. Having often observed occurrences of this kind, I found it good for me to advise poor people to take such [goods] as were most useful and not costly.

In the time of trading, I had an opportunity of seeing that a too liberal use of spirituous liquors, and the custom of wearing too costly apparel, led some people into great inconveniences; and these two things appear to be often connected one with the other; for by not attending to that use of things which is consistent with universal righteousness, there is an increase of labor which extends beyond what our heavenly Father intends for us; and by great labor, and often by much sweating in the heat, there is, even among such who are not drunkards, a craving of some liquor to revive the spirits; that, partly by the wanton, luxurious drinking of some, and partly by the drinking of others, led to it through immoderate labor, very great quantities of rum are annually expended in our colonies; of which we should have no need, did we steadily attend to pure wisdom.

Where men take pleasure in feeling their minds elevated with strong drink, and so indulge this appetite as to disorder their understanding, neglect their duty as members in a family or civil society, and cast off all pretence to religion, their case is much to be pitied; and where such whose lives are for the most part regular, and whose examples have a strong influence on the minds of others, adhere to some customs which powerfully draw toward the use of more strong liquor than pure wisdom [directeth the use of;] this also, as it hinders the spreading of the spirit of meekness, and strengthens the hands of the more excessive drinkers, is a case to be lamented.

As [the least] degree of luxury hath some connection with evil, for those who profess to be disciples of Christ, and are looked upon as leaders of the people, to have that mind in them which was also in Him, and so stand separate from every wrong way, is a means of help to the weaker. As I have sometimes been much spent in the heat, and taken spirits to revive me, I have found by experience that the mind is not so calm in such circumstances, nor so fitly disposed for Divine meditation, as when all such extremes are avoided; and I have felt an increasing care to attend to that Holy Spirit which sets right bounds to our desires, and leads those who faithfully follow it to apply all the gifts of Divine Providence to the purposes for which they were intended. Did such who have the care of great estates, attend with singleness of heart to this heavenly Instructor, which so opens and enlarges the mind that men love their neighbors as themselves, they would have wisdom given them to manage, without ever finding occasion to employ some people in the luxuries of life, or to make it necessary for others to labor too hard; but for want of regarding steadily this principle of Divine love, a selfish spirit takes place in the minds of people, which is attended with darkness and manifold confusions in the world.

In the course of my trading, being somewhat affected at the various law suits about collecting money which I saw going forward, on applying to a constable he gave me a list of his proceedings for one year, as follows: to wit, served 267 warrants, 193 summonses, and 17 executions! As to writs served by the sheriff, I got no account of them.

I once had a warrant for an idle man, who I believed was about to run away, which was the only time I applied to the law to recover money.

Though trading in things useful is an honest employ, yet, through the great number of superfluities which are commonly bought and sold, and through the corruptions of the times, they who apply to merchandize for a living have great need to be well experienced in that precept which the prophet Jeremiah laid down for Baruc, his scribe: "Seekest thou great things for thyself? seek them not."

w. 1756–1772
p. 1774

ST. JEAN DE CRÈVECOEUR
(Michel-Guillaume Jean de Crèvecoeur)
(1735–1813)

A French aristocrat of Tory leanings yet a partisan of American life, Crèvecoeur was born in Normandy near Caen. He was given a Jesuit education, went to England to complete his schooling, and in 1754 went to Canada to serve under Montcalm. As a cartographer he became familiar with the Great Lakes region, and after 1759, the wars finished, he toured Pennsylvania, New York, and the Atlantic coast. In 1765 he became a colonial citizen of New York under the name of John Hector St. John (from which his popular name of St. Jean de Crèvecoeur was derived); he married Mehitabel Tippet four years later, settled down to a peaceful and happy farm life in Orange County, and began to record his experiences of American life. When the revolution broke out, all he wanted was pastoral neutrality, an impossibility which made both sides suspicious of him. He had to leave the country, returning to France via England; while in England he found a publisher for the manuscript of impressions of America he had taken with him. The least Tory pieces were published in 1782 as *Letters from an American Farmer*.

The popularity of physiocratic thought as echoed in the *Letters*, the somewhat Rousseauistic idealization of our national life, and the easy epistolary style made the *Letters* an immediate success. Crèvecoeur became fashionable in the salons of Paris, and he was a bright if brief luminary on the European literary horizon. When the war was over, he returned to America immediately, only to find his farm destroyed in an Indian raid, his wife killed, and his three children missing. (He found his children, two of whom had been adopted in Boston.) Through the sympathetic friendship of Franklin and others, he became the French consul in New York City. In 1790, having written agricultural articles for his American neighbors (he introduced alfalfa to this country) and having worked hard for continued good relations between France and America, he returned to Normandy, there to remain for the rest of his life.

In 1925 some American scholars brought to light the unpublished letters. They indicate aristocratic leanings mingled with a humanitarian love of the common man in the American scene. These were published as *Sketches of Eighteenth Century America*. In both books—the second containing an anguish and bitterness absent from the first—Crèvecoeur's Painelike anticlericalism is evident, as is his benevolently optimistic view of the possibilities of human reason. And in both books Crèvecoeur's image of Jeffersonian agrarian society as an actualized fact in the New World is a graceful and optimistic assessment of our culture that illustrates one continuing aspect of our self-view.

More of Crèvecoeur's American travels are recounted in his *Voyage dans la Haute Pennsylvanie et dans l'etat de New-York* (1801) and H. L. Bourdin, R. H. Gabriel, and S. T. Williams, eds., *Sketches of Eighteenth Century America* (1925).

Editions and accounts of Crèvecoeur are to be found in M. C. Tyler, *The Literary History of the American Revolution*, II (1897); J. P. Mitchell, *St. Jean de Crèvecoeur* (1916); V. L. Parrington, *Main Currents in American Thought*, I (1927); G. Chinard, "The American Dream," in R. Spiller *et al.*, eds., *The Literary History of the United States*, I (1948); H. N. Smith, *Virgin Land* (1950); W. B. Blake, ed., *Letters from an American Farmer* (1958); P. G. Adams, tr. and ed., *Crèvecoeur's Eighteenth Century Travels in Pennsylvania and New York* (1961); A. E. Stone, "Crèvecoeur's *Letters* and the Beginnings of an American Literature," *Emory University Quarterly*, XVII (1962); and N. A. Plotkin, "Saint-John de Crèvecoeur Rediscovered: Critic or Panegyrist?" *French Historical Studies*, III (1964).

FROM

Letters from an American Farmer

What Is an American?

I wish I could be acquainted with the feelings and thoughts which must agitate the heart and present themselves to the mind of an enlightened Englishman, when he first lands on this continent. He must greatly rejoice that he lived at a time to see this fair country discovered and settled; he must necessarily feel a share of national pride, when he views the chain of settlement which embellishes these extended shores. When he says to himself, this is the work of my countrymen, who, when convulsed by factions, afflicted by a variety of miseries and wants, restless and impatient, took refuge here. They brought along with them their national genius, to which they prinicipally owe what liberty they enjoy, and what substance they possess. Here he sees the industry of his native country displayed in a new manner, and traces in their works the embryos of all the arts, sciences, and ingenuity which flourish in Europe. Here he beholds fair cities, substantial villages, extensive fields, an immense country filled with decent houses, good roads, orchards, meadows, and bridges, where an hundred years ago all was wild, woody, and uncultivated! What a train of pleasing ideas this fair spectacle must suggest; it is a prospect which must inspire a good citizen with the most heartfelt pleasure. The difficulty consists in the manner of viewing so extensive a scene. He is arrived on a new continent; a modern society offers itself to his contemplation, different from what he had hitherto seen. It is not composed, as in Europe, of great lords who possess everything, and of a herd of people who have nothing. Here are no aristocratical families, no courts, no kings, no bishops, no ecclesiastical dominion, no invisible power giving to a few a very visible one; no great manufacturers employing thousands, no great refinements of luxury. The rich and the poor are not so far removed from each other as they are in Europe. Some few towns excepted, we are all tillers of the earth, from Novia Scotia to West Florida. We are a people of cultivators, scattered over an immense territory, communicating with each other by means of good roads and navigable rivers, united by the silken bands of mild government, all respecting the laws, without dreading their power, because they are equitable. We are all animated with the spirit of an industry which is unfettered and unrestrained, because each person works for himself. If he travels through our rural districts he views not the hostile castle, and the haughty mansion, contrasted with the clay-built hut and miserable cabin, where cattle and men help to keep each other warm, and dwell in meanness, smoke, and indigence. A pleasing uniformity of decent competence appears throughout our habitations. The meanest of our log-houses is a dry and comfortable habitation. Lawyer or merchant are the fairest titles our towns afford; that of a farmer is the only appellation of the rural inhabitants of our country. It must take some time ere he can reconcile himself to our dictionary, which is but short in words of dignity, and names of honor. There, on a Sunday, he sees a congregation of respectable farmers and their wives, all clad in neat homespun, well mounted, or riding in their own humble wagons. There is not among them an esquire, saving the unlettered magistrate. There he sees a parson as simple as his flock, a farmer who does not riot on the labor of others. We have no princes, for whom we toil, starve, and bleed: we are the most perfect society now existing in the world. Here man is free as he ought to be; nor is this pleasing equality so transitory as many others are. Many ages will not see the shores of our great lakes replenished with inland nations, nor the unknown bounds of North America entirely peopled. Who can tell how far it extends? Who can tell the millions of men whom it will feed and contain? for no European foot has as yet travelled half the extent of this mighty continent!

The next wish of this traveller will be to know whence came all these people? They are a mixture of English, Scotch, Irish, French, Dutch, Germans, and Swedes. From this promiscuous breed, that race now called Americans have arisen. The eastern provinces must indeed be excepted, as being the unmixed descendants of Englishmen. I have heard many wish that they had been more intermixed also: for my part, I am no wisher, and think it much better as it has happened. They exhibit a most conspicuous figure in this great and variegated picture; they too enter for a great share in the pleasing perspective displayed in these thirteen provinces. I know it is fashionable to reflect on them, but I respect them for what they have done; for the accuracy and wisdom with which they have settled their territory; for the decency of their manners; for their early love of letters; their ancient college, the first in this hemisphere; for their industry; which to me who am but a farmer, is the criterion of everything. There never was a people, situated as they are, who with so ungrateful a soil have done more in so short a time. Do you think that the monarchial ingredients which are more prevalent in other governments, have purged them from all foul stains? Their histories assert the contrary.

In this great American asylum, the poor of Europe have by some means met together, and in consequence of various causes, to what purpose should they ask one another what countrymen they are? Alas, two thirds of them had no country. Can a wretch who wanders about, who works and starves, whose life is a continual scene of sore affliction or pinching penury; can that man call England or any other kingdom his country? A country that had no bread for him, whose fields procured him no harvest, who met with nothing but the frowns of the rich, the severity of the laws, with jails and punishments; who owned not a single foot of the extensive surface of this planet? No! urged by a variety of motives, here they came. Everything has tended to regenerate them; new laws, a new mode of living, a new social system; here they are become men: in Europe they were as so many useless plants, wanting vegetative mould, and refreshing showers; they withered, and were mowed down by want, hunger, and war; but now by the power of transportation, like all other plants they have taken root and flourished! Formerly they were not numbered in any civil lists of their country, except in those of the poor; here they rank as citizens. By what invisible power has this surprising metamorphosis been performed? By that of the laws and that of their industry. The laws, the indulgent laws, protect them as they arrive, stamping on them the symbol of adoption; they receive ample rewards for their labors; these accumulated rewards procure them lands; those lands confer on them the title of free-men, and to that title every benefit is affixed which men can possibly require. This is the great operation daily performed by our laws. From whence proceed these laws? From our government. Whence the government? It is derived from the original genius and strong desire of the people ratified and confirmed by the crown. This is the great chain which links us all, this is the picture which every province exhibits, Nova Scotia excepted. There the crown has done all; either there were no people who had genius, or it was not much attended to: the consequence is that the province is very thinly inhabited indeed; the power of the crown in conjunction with the musketos has prevented men from settling there. Yet some parts of it flourished once, and it contained a mild harmless set of people. But for the fault of a few leaders, the whole were banished. The greatest political error the crown ever committed in America, was to cut off men from a country which wanted nothing but men!

What attachment can a poor European emigrant have for a country where he had nothing? The knowledge of the language, the love of a few kindred as poor as himself, were the only cords that tied him: his country is now that which gives him land, bread, protection, and consequence. *Ubi panis ibi patria* [The fatherland is where the bread is] is the motto of all emigrants. What then is the American, this new man? He is either an European, or the descendant of an European, hence that strange mixture of blood, which you will find in no other country. I could point out to you a family whose grandfather was an Englishman, whose wife was Dutch, whose son married a French woman, and whose present four sons have now four wives of different nations. *He* is an American, who, leaving behind him all his ancient prejudices and manners, receives new ones from the new mode of life he has embraced, the new government he obeys, and the new rank he holds. He becomes an American by being received in the broad lap of our great *Alma Mater*. Here individuals of all nations are melted into a new race of men, whose labors and posterity will one day cause great changes in the world. Americans are the western pilgrims, who are carrying along with them that great mass of arts, sciences, vigor, and industry which began long since in the east; they will finish the great circle. The Americans were once scattered all over Europe; here they are incorporated into one of the finest systems of population which has ever appeared, and which will hereafter become distinct by the power of the different climates they inhabit. The American ought therefore to love this country much better than that wherein either he or his forefathers were born. Here the rewards of his industry follow with equal steps the progress of his labor; his labor is founded on the basis of nature, *self-interest;* can it want a stronger allurement? Wives and children, who before in vain demanded of him a morsel of bread, now, fat and frolicsome, gladly help their father to clear those fields whence exuberant crops are to arise to feed and to clothe them all; without any part being claimed, either by a despotic prince, a rich abbot, or a mighty lord. Here religion demands but little of him; a small voluntary salary to the minister, and gratitude to God; can he refuse these? The American is a new man, who acts upon new principles; he must therefore entertain new ideas, and form new opinions. From involuntary idleness, servile dependence, penury, and useless labor, he has passed to toils of a very different nature, rewarded by ample subsistence.—This is an American.

British America is divided into many provinces, forming a large association, scattered along a coast 1500 miles extent and about 200 wide. This society I would fain examine, at least such as it appears in the middle provinces; if it does not afford that variety of tinges and gradations which may be observed in Europe, we have colors peculiar to ourselves. For instance, it is natural to conceive that those who live near the sea, must be very different from those who live in the woods; the intermediate space will afford a separate and distinct class.

Men are like plants; the goodness and flavor of the fruit proceeds from the peculiar soil and exposition in which they grow. We are nothing but what we derive from the air we breathe, the climate we inhabit, the government we obey, the system of religion we profess, and the nature of our employment. Here you will find but few crimes; these have acquired as yet no root among us. I wish I was able to trace all my ideas; if my ignorance prevents me from describing them properly, I hope I shall be able to delineate a few of the outlines, which are all I propose.

Those who live near the sea, feed more on fish than on flesh, and often encounter that boisterous element. This renders them more bold and enterprising; this leads them to neglect the confined occupations of the land. They see and converse with a variety of people; their intercourse with mankind becomes extensive. The sea inspires them with a love of traffic, a desire of transporting produce from one place to another; and leads them to a variety of resources which supply the place of labor. Those who inhabit the middle settlements, by far the most numerous, must be very different; the simple cultivation of the earth purifies them, but the indulgences of the government, the soft remonstrances of religion, the rank of independent freeholders, must necessarily inspire them with sentiments

very little known in Europe among people of the same
class. What do I say? Europe has no such class of men;
the early knowledge they acquire, the early bargains they
make, give them a great degree of sagacity. As freemen
they will be litigious; pride and obstinacy are often the
cause of law suits; the nature of our laws and governments
may be another. As citizens it is easy to imagine that they
will carefully read the newspapers, enter into every political
disquisition, freely blame or censure governors and others.
As farmers they will be careful and anxious to get as much
as they can, because what they get is their own. As northern men they will love the cheerful cup. As Christians,
religion curbs them not in their opinions; the general
indulgence leaves every one to think for themselves in
spiritual matters; the laws inspect our actions, our thoughts
are left to God. Industry, good living, selfishness, litigious-
ness, country politics, the pride of freemen, religious indifference, are their characteristics. If you recede still farther
from the sea, you will come into more modern settlements;
they exhibit the same strong lineaments, in a ruder appearance. Religion seems to have still less influence, and their
manners are less improved.

Now we arrive near the great woods, near the last inhabited districts; there men seem to be placed still farther
beyond the reach of government, which in some measure
leaves them to themselves. How can it pervade every
corner; as they were driven there by misfortunes, necessity of beginnings, desire of acquiring large tracts of land,
idleness, frequent want of economy, ancient debt; the re-
union of such people does not afford a very pleasing spectacle. When discord, want of unity and friendship; when
either drunkenness or idleness prevail in such remote
districts; contention, inactivity, and wretchedness must en-
sue. There are not the same remedies to these evils as in a
long established community. The few magistrates they have,
are in general little better than the rest; they are often in a
perfect state of war; that of man against man, sometimes
decided by blows, sometimes by means of the law; that of
man against every wild inhabitant of these venerable woods,
of which they are come to dispossess them. There men appear to be no better than carnivorous animals of a superior
rank, living on the flesh of wild animals when they can
catch them, and when they are not able, they subsist on

grain. He who would wish to see America in its proper light, and have a true idea of its feeble beginnings and barbarous rudiments, must visit our extended line of frontiers where the last settlers dwell, and where he may see the first labors of settlement, the mode of clearing the earth, in all their different appearances; where men are wholly left dependent on their native tempers, and on the spur of uncertain industry, which often fails when not sanctified by the efficacy of a few moral rules. There, remote from the power of example and check of shame, many families exhibit the most hideous parts of our society. They are a kind of forlorn hope, preceding by ten or twelve years the most respectable army of veterans which come after them. In that space, prosperity will polish some, vice and the law will drive off the rest, who uniting again with others like themselves will recede still farther; making room for more industrious people, who will finish their improvements, convert the loghouse into a convenient habitation, and rejoicing that the first heavy labors are finished, will change in a few years that hitherto barbarous country into a fine fertile, well regulated district. Such is our progress, such is the march of the Europeans toward the interior parts of this continent. In all societies there are off-casts; this impure part serves as our precursors or pioneers; my father himself was one of that class, but he came upon honest principles, and was therefore one of the few who held fast; by good conduct and temperance, he transmitted to me his fair inheritance, when not above one in fourteen of his contemporaries had the same good fortune.

Forty years ago this smiling country was thus inhabited; it is now purged, a general decency of manners prevails throughout, and such has been the fate of our best countries.

Exclusive of those general characteristics, each province has its own, founded on the government, climate, mode of husbandry, customs, and peculiarity of circumstances. Europeans submit insensibly to these great powers, and become in the course of a few generations, not only Americans in general, but either Pennsylvanians, Virginians, or provincials under some other name. Whoever traverses the continent must easily observe those strong differences, which will grow more evident in time. The inhabitants of Canada, Massachusetts, the middle provinces, the southern ones will be as different as their climates; their only points of unity will be those of religion and language.

As I have endeavored to show you how Europeans become Americans; it may not be disagreeable to show you likewise how the various Christian sects introduced, wear out, and how religious indifference becomes prevalent. When any considerable number of a particular sect happen to dwell contiguous to each other, they immediately erect a temple, and there worship the Divinity agreeably to their own peculiar ideas. Nobody disturbs them. If any new sect springs up in Europe it may happen that many of its professors will come and settle in America. As they bring their zeal with them, they are at liberty to make proselytes if they can, and to build a meeting and to follow the dictates of their consciences; for neither the government nor any other power interferes. If they are peaceable subjects, and are industrious, what is it to their neighbors how and in what manner they think fit to address their prayers to the Supreme Being? But if the sectaries are not settled close together, if they are mixed with other denominations, their zeal will cool for want of fuel, and will be extinguished in a little time. Then the Americans become as to religion, what they are as to country, allied to all. In them the name of Englishman, Frenchman, and European is lost, and in like manner, the strict modes of Christianity as practised in Europe are lost also. This effect will extend itself still farther hereafter, and though this may appear to you as a strange idea, yet it is a very true one. I shall be able perhaps hereafter to explain myself better; in the meanwhile, let the following example serve as my first justification.

Let us suppose you and I to be travelling; we observe that in this house, to the right, lives a Catholic, who prays to God as he has been taught, and believes in transubstantiation; he works and raises wheat, he has a large family of children, all hale and robust; his belief, his prayers offend nobody. About one mile farther on the same road, his next neighbor may be a good honest plodding German Lutheran, who addresses himself to the same God, the God of all, agreeably to the modes he has been educated in, and believes in consubstantiation; by so doing he scandalizes nobody; he also works in his fields, embellishes the earth, clears swamps, etc. What has the world to do with his Lutheran principles? He persecutes nobody, and nobody persecutes him, he visits his neighbors, and his neighbors visit him. Next to him lives a seceder, the most enthusiastic of all sectaries; his zeal is hot and fiery, but separated as he is from others of the same complexion, he has no congregation of his own to resort to, where he might cabal and mingle religious pride with worldly obstinacy. He likewise raises good crops, his house is handsomely painted, his orchard is one of the fairest in the neighborhood. How does it concern the welfare of the country, or of the province at large, what this man's religious sentiments are, or really whether he has any at all? He is a good farmer, he is a sober, peaceable, good citizen: William Penn himself would not wish for more. This is the visible character, the invisible one is only guessed at, and is nobody's business. Next again lives a Low Dutchman, who implicitly believes the rules laid down by the synod of Dort. He conceives no other idea of a clergyman than that of an hired man; if he does his work well he will pay him the stipulated sum; if not he will dismiss him, and do without his sermons, and let his church be shut up for years. But notwithstanding this coarse idea, you will find his house and farm to be the neatest in all the country; and you will judge by his wagon and fat horses, that he thinks more of the affairs of this world than of those of the next. He is sober and laborious, therefore he is all he ought to be as to the affairs of this life; as for those of the next, he must trust to the great Creator. Each of these people instruct their children as well as they can, but these instructions are feeble compared to those which are given to the youth of the poorest class in Europe. Their children will therefore grow up less zealous and more indifferent in matters of religion than their parents. The foolish vanity, or rather the fury of making proselytes, is unknown here; they have no time, the seasons call for all their attention, and thus in a few years, this mixed neighborhood will exhibit a strange religious medley, that will be neither pure Catholicism nor pure Calvinism. A very perceptible indifference even in the first generation, will become apparent; and it may happen that the daughter of the Catholic will marry the son of the seceder, and settle by themselves at a distance from their parents. What religious education will they give their children? A very imperfect one. If there happens to be in the neighborhood any place of worship, we will suppose a Quaker's meeting; rather than not show their fine clothes, they will go to it, and some of them may perhaps attach themselves to that society. Others will remain in a perfect state of indifference; the children of these zealous parents will not be able to tell what their religious principles are, and their grandchildren still less. The neighborhood of a place of worship generally leads them to it, and the action of going thither is the strongest evidence they can give of their attachment to any sect. The Quakers are the only people who retain a fondness for their own mode of worship; for be they ever so far separated from each other, they hold a sort of communion with the society, and seldom depart from its rules, at least in this country. Thus all sects are mixed as well as all nations; thus religious indifference is imperceptibly disseminated from one end of the continent to the other; which is at present one of the strongest characteristics of the Americans. Where this will reach no one can tell, perhaps it may leave a vacuum fit to receive other systems. Persecution, religious pride, the love of contradiction, are the food of what the world commonly calls religion. These motives have ceased here; zeal in Europe is confined; here it evaporates in the great distance it has to travel; there it is a grain of powder inclosed, here it burns away in the open air, and consumes without effect.

But to return to our back settlers. I must tell you, that there is something in the proximity of the woods, which is very singular. It is with men as it is with the plants and animals that grow and live in the forests; they are entirely different from those that live in the plains. I will candidly tell you all my thoughts but you are not to expect that I shall advance any reasons. By living in or near the woods, their actions are regulated by the wildness of the neighborhood. The deer often come to eat their grain, the wolves to destroy their sheep, the bears to kill their hogs, the foxes to catch their poultry. This surrounding hostility immediately puts the gun into their hands; they watch these animals, they kill some; and thus by defending their property, they soon become professed hunters; this is the progress; once hunters, farewell to the plough. The chase renders them ferocious, gloomy, and unsociable; a hunter wants no neighbor, he rather hates them, because he dreads the competition. In a little time their success in the woods makes them neglect their tillage. They trust to the natural fecundity of the earth, and therefore do little; carelessness in fencing often exposes what little they sow to destruction; they are not at home to watch; in order therefore to make up the deficiency, they go often to the woods. That new mode of life brings along with it a new set of manners, which I cannot easily describe. These new manners being grafted on the old stock, produce a strange sort of lawless profligacy, the impressions of which are indelible. The manners of the Indian natives are respectable, compared with this European medley. Their wives and children live in sloth and inactivity; and having no proper pursuits, you may judge what education the latter receive. Their tender minds have nothing else to contemplate but the example of their parents; like them they grow up a mongrel breed, half civilized, half savage, except nature stamps on them some constitutional propensities. That rich, that voluptuous sentiment is gone that struck them so forcibly; the possession of their freeholds no longer conveys to their minds the same pleasure and pride. To all these reasons you must add their lonely situation, and you cannot imagine what an effect on manners the great distances they live from each other has! Consider one of the last settlements in its first view: of what is it composed? Europeans who have not that sufficient share of knowledge they ought to have in order to prosper; people who have suddenly passed from oppression, dread of government, and fear of laws, into the unlimited freedom of the woods. This sudden change must have a very great effect on most men, and on that class particularly. Eating of wild meat, whatever you may think, tends to alter their temper: though all the proof I can adduce, is that I have seen it: and having no place of worship to resort to, what little society this might afford is denied them. The Sunday meetings, exclusive of religious benefits, were the only social bonds that might have inspired them with some degree of emulation in neatness. Is it then surprising to see men thus situated, immersed in great and heavy labors, degenerate a little? It is rather a wonder the effect is not more diffusive. The Moravians and the Quakers are the only instances in exception to what I have advanced. The first never settle singly, it is a colony of the society which emigrates; they carry with them their forms, worship, rules, and decency: the others never begin so hard, they are always able to buy improvements, in which there is a great advantage, for by that time the country is recovered from its first barbarity. Thus our bad people are those who are half cultivators and half hunters; and the worst of them are those who have degenerated altogether into the hunting state. As old ploughmen and new men of the woods, as Europeans and new made Indians, they contract the vices of both; they adopt the moroseness and ferocity of a native, without his mildness, or even his industry at home. If manners are not refined, at least they are rendered simple and inoffensive by tilling the earth; all our wants are supplied by it, our time is divided between labor and rest, and leaves none for the commission of great misdeeds. As hunters it is divided between the toil of the chase, the idleness of repose, or the indulgence of inebriation. Hunting is but a licentious idle life, and if it does not always pervert good dispositions; yet, when it is united with bad luck, it leads to want: want stimulates that propensity to rapacity and injustice, too natural to needy men, which is the fatal gradation. After this explanation of the effects which follow by living in the woods, shall we yet vainly flatter ourselves with the hope of converting the Indians? We should rather begin with converting our back-settlers; and now if I dare mention the name of religion, its sweet accents would be lost in the immensity of these woods. Men thus placed are not fit either to receive or remember its mild instructions; they want temples and ministers, but as soon as men cease to remain at home, and begin to lead an erratic life, let them be either tawny or white, they cease to be its disciples.

Thus have I faintly and imperfectly endeavored to trace our society from the sea to our woods! yet you must not imagine that every person who moves back, acts upon the same principles, or falls into the same degeneracy. Many families carry with them all their decency of conduct, purity of morals, and respect of religion; but these are scarce, the power of example is sometimes irresistible. Even among these back-settlers, their depravity is greater or less, according to what nation or province they belong. Were I to adduce proofs of this, I might be accused of partiality. If there happen to be some rich intervals, some fertile bottoms, in those remote districts, the people will there prefer tilling the land to hunting, and will attach themselves to it; but even on these fertile spots you may plainly perceive the inhabitants to acquire a great degree of rusticity and selfishness.

It is in consequence of this straggling situation, and the astonishing power it has on manners, that the back-settlers of both the Carolinas, Virginia, and many other parts, have been long a set of lawless people; it has been even dangerous to travel among them. Government can do nothing in so extensive a country, better it should wink at these irregularities, than that it should use means inconsistent with its usual mildness. Time will efface those stains: in proportion as the great body of population approaches them they will reform, and become polished and subordinate. Whatever has been said of the four New England provinces, no such degeneracy of manners has ever tarnished their annals; their back-settlers have been kept within the bounds of decency, and government, by means of wise laws, and by the influence of religion. What a detestable idea such people must have given to the natives of the Europeans! They trade with them, the worst of people are permitted to do that which none but persons of the best characters should be employed in. They get drunk with them, and often defraud the Indians. Their avarice, removed from the eyes of their superiors, knows no bounds; and aided by the little superiority of knowledge, these traders deceive them, and even sometimes shed blood. Hence those shocking violations, those sudden devastations which have so often stained our frontiers, when hundreds of innocent people have been sacrificed for the crimes of a few. It was in consequence of such behavior, that the Indians took the hatchet against the Virginians in 1774. Thus are our first steps trod, thus are our first trees felled, in general, by the most vicious of our people; and thus the path is opened for the arrival of a second and better class, the true American freeholders; the most respectable set of people in this part of the world: respectable for their industry, their happy independence, the great share of freedom they possess, the good regulation of their families and for extending the trade and the dominion of our mother country.

Europe contains hardly any other distinctions but lords and tenants; this fair country alone is settled by freeholders, the possessors of the soil they cultivate, members of the government they obey, and the framers of their own laws, by means of their representatives. This is a thought which you have taught me to cherish; our indifference from Europe, far from diminishing, rather adds to our usefulness and consequence as men and subjects. Had our forefathers remained there, they would only have crowded it, and perhaps prolonged those convulsions which had shook it so long. Every industrious European who transports himself here, may be compared to a sprout growing at the foot of a great tree; it enjoys and draws but a little portion of sap; wrench it from the parent roots, transplant it, and it will become a tree bearing fruit also. Colonists are therefore entitled to the consideration due to the most useful subjects; a hundred families barely existing in some parts of Scotland, will here in six years, cause an annual exportation of 10,000 bushels of wheat: 100 bushels being but a common quantity for an industrious family to sell, if they cultivate good land. It is here then that the idle may be employed, the useless become useful, and the poor become rich; but by riches I do not mean gold and silver, we have but little of those metals; I mean a better sort of wealth, cleared lands, cattle, good houses, good clothes, and an increase of people to enjoy them.

There is no wonder that this country has so many charms, and presents to Europeans so many temptations to remain in it. A traveller in Europe becomes a stranger as soon as he quits his own kingdom; but it is otherwise here. We know, properly speaking, no strangers; this is every person's country; the variety of our soils, situations, climates, governments, and produce, hath something which must please everybody. No sooner does an European arrive, no matter of what condition, than his eyes are opened upon the fair prospect; he hears his language spoke, he retraces many of his own country manners, he perpetually hears the names of families and towns with which he is acquainted; he sees happiness and prosperity in all places disseminated; he meets with hospitality, kindness, and plenty everywhere; he beholds hardly any poor, he seldom hears of punishments and executions; and he wonders at the elegance of our towns, those miracles of industry and freedom. He cannot admire enough our rural districts, our convenient roads, good taverns, and our many accommodations; he involuntarily loves a country where everything is so lovely. When in England, he was a mere Englishman; here he stands on a larger portion of the globe, not less than its fourth part, and may see the productions of the north, in iron and naval stores; the provisions of Ireland, the grain of Egypt, the indigo, the rice of China. He does not find, as in Europe, a crowded society, where every place is over-stocked; he does not feel that perpetual collision of parties, that difficulty of beginning, that contention which oversets so many. There is room for everybody in America; has he any particular talent, or industry? he exerts it in order to procure a livelihood, and it succeeds. Is he a merchant? the avenues of trade are infinite; is he eminent in any respect? he will be employed and respected. Does he love a country life? pleasant farms present themselves; he may purchase what he wants, and thereby become an American farmer. Is he a laborer, sober and industrious? he need not go many miles, nor receive many informations before he will be hired, well fed at the table of his employer, and paid four or five times more than he can get in Europe. Does he want uncultivated lands? thousands of acres present themselves, which he may purchase cheap. Whatever be his talents or inclinations, if they are moderate, he may satisfy them. I do not mean that every one who comes will grow rich in a little time; no, but he may procure an easy, decent maintenance, by his industry. Instead of starving he will be fed, instead of being idle he will have employment; and these are riches enough for such men as come over here. The rich stay in Europe, it is only the middling and the poor that emigrate. Would you wish to travel in independent idleness, from north to south, you will find easy access, and the most cheerful reception at every house; society without ostentation, good cheer without pride, and every decent diversion which the country affords, with little expense. It is no wonder that the European who has lived here a few years, is desirous to remain; Europe with all its pomp, is not to be compared to this continent, for men of middle stations, or laborers.

An European, when he first arrives, seems limited in his intentions, as well as in his views; but he very suddenly alters his scale; two hundred miles formerly appeared a very great distance, it is now but a trifle; he no sooner breathes out air than he forms schemes, and embarks in designs he never would have thought of in his own country. There the plenitude of society confines many useful ideas, and often extinguishes the most laudable schemes which here ripen into maturity. Thus Europeans become Americans.

But how is this accomplished in that crowd of low, indigent people, who flock here every year from all parts of Europe? I will tell you; they no sooner arrive than they immediately feel the good effects of that plenty of provisions we possess: they fare on our best food, and they are kindly entertained: their talents, character, and peculiar industry are immediately inquired into; they find country-men everywhere disseminated, let them come from whatever part of Europe. Let me select one as an epitome of the rest; he is hired, he goes to work, and works moderately; instead of being employed by a haughty person, he finds himself with his equal, placed at the substantial table of the farmer, or else at an inferior one as good; his wages are high, his bed is not like that bed of sorrow on which he used to lie: if he behaves with propriety, and is faithful, he is caressed, and becomes as it were a member of the family. He begins to feel the effects of a sort of resurrection; hitherto he had not lived, but simply vegetated; he now feels himself a man, because he is treated as such; the laws of his own country had overlooked him in his insignificancy; the laws of this cover him with their mantle. Judge what an alteration there must arise in the mind and thoughts of this man; he begins to forget his former servitude and dependence, his heart involuntarily swells and glows; this first swell inspires him with those new thoughts which constitute an American. What love can he entertain for a country where his existence was a burthen to him; if he is a generous good man, the love of this new adoptive parent will sink deep into his heart. He looks around, and sees many a prosperous person, who but a few years before was as poor as himself. This encourages him much, he begins to form some little scheme, the first, alas, he ever formed in his life. If he is wise he thus spends two or three years, in which time he acquires knowledge, the use of tools, the modes of working the lands, felling trees, etc. This prepares the foundation of a good name, the most useful acquisition he can make. He is encouraged, he has gained friends; he is advised and directed, he feels bold, he purchases some land; he gives all the money he has brought over, as well as what he has earned, and trusts to the God of harvests for the discharge of the rest. His good name procures him credit. He is now possessed of the deed, conveying to him and his posterity the fee simple and absolute property of two hundred acres of land, situated on such a river. What an epocha in this man's life! He is become a freeholder, from perhaps a German boor —he is now an American, a Pennsylvanian, an English subject. He is naturalized, his name is enrolled with those of the other citizens of the province. Instead of being a vagrant, he has a place of residence; he is called the inhabitant of such a county, or of such a district, and for the first time in his life counts for something; for hitherto he has been a cypher. I only repeat what I have heard many say, and no wonder their hearts should glow, and be agitated with a multitude of feelings, not easy to describe. From nothing to start into being; from a servant to the rank of a master; from being the slave of some despotic prince, to become a free man, invested with lands, to which every municipal blessing is annexed! What a change indeed! It is in consequence of that change that he becomes an American. This great metamorphosis has a double effect, it extinguishes all his European prejudices, he forgets that mechanism of subordination, that servility of disposition which poverty had taught him; and sometimes he is apt to forget too much, often passing from one extreme to the other. If he is a good man, he forms schemes of future prosperity, he proposes to educate his children better than he has been educated himself; he thinks of future modes of conduct, feels an ardor to labor he never felt before. Pride steps in and leads him to everything that the laws do not forbid: he respects them; with a heartfelt gratitude he looks toward the east, toward that insular government from whose wisdom all his new felicity is derived, and under whose wings and protection he now lives. These reflections constitute him the good man and the good subject. Ye poor Europeans, ye, who sweat, and work for the great— ye, who are obliged to give so many sheaves to the church, so many to your lords, so many to your government, and have hardly any left for yourselves—ye, who are held in less estimation than favorite hunters or useless lap-dogs— ye, who only breathe the air of nature, because it cannot be withheld from you; it is here that ye can conceive the possibility of those feelings I have been describing; it is here the laws of naturalization invite every one to partake of our great labors and felicity, to till unrented, untaxed lands! Many, corrupted beyond the power of amendment, have brought with them all their vices, and disregarding the advantages held to them, have gone on in their former career of iniquity, until they have been overtaken and punished by our laws. It is not every emigrant who succeeds; no, it is only the sober, the honest, and industrious: happy those to whom this transition has served as a powerful spur to labor, to prosperity, and to the good establishment of children, born in the days of their poverty; and who had no other portion to expect but the rags of their parents, had it not been for their happy emigration. Others again, have been led astray by this enchanting scene; their new pride, instead of leading them to the fields, has kept them in idleness; the idea of possessing lands is all that satisfies them—though surrounded with fertility, they have moulded away their time in inactivity, misinformed husbandry, and ineffectual endeavors. How much wiser, in general, the honest Germans than almost all other Europeans; they hire themselves to some of their wealthy landsmen, and in that apprenticeship learn everything that is necessary. They attentively consider the prosperous industry of others, which imprints in their minds a strong desire of possessing the same advantages. This forcible idea never quits them, they launch forth, and by dint of sobriety, rigid parsimony, and the most persevering industry, they commonly succeed. Their astonishment at their first arrival from Germany is very great—it is to them a dream; the contrast must be powerful indeed; they observe their countrymen flourishing in every place; they travel through whole counties where not a word of English is spoken; and in the names and the language of the people, they retrace Germany. They have been an useful acquisition to this continent, and to Pennsylvania in particular; to them it owes some share of its prosperity: to their mechanical knowledge and patience it owes the finest mills in all America, the best teams of horses, and many other advantages. The recollection of their former poverty and slavery never quits them as long as they live.

The Scotch and the Irish might have lived in their own

country perhaps as poor, but enjoying more civil advantages, the effects of their new situation do not strike them so forcibly, nor has it so lasting an effect. From whence the difference arises I know not, but out of twelve families of emigrants of each country, generally seven Scotch will succeed, nine German, and four Irish. The Scotch are frugal and laborious, but their wives cannot work so hard as German women, who on the contrary vie with their husbands, and often share with them the most severe toils of the field, which they understand better. They have therefore nothing to struggle against, but the common casualties of nature. The Irish do not prosper so well; they love to drink and to quarrel; they are litigious, and soon take to the gun, which is the ruin of everything; they seem beside to labor under a greater degree of ignorance in husbandry than the others; perhaps it is that their industry had less scope, and was less exercised at home. I have heard many relate, how the land was parcelled out in that kingdom; their ancient conquest has been a great detriment to them, by over-setting their landed property. The lands possessed by a few, are leased down *ad infinitum,* and the occupiers often pay five guineas an acre. The poor are worse lodged there than anywhere else in Europe; their potatoes, which are easily raised, are perhaps an inducement to laziness; their wages are too low, and their whisky too cheap.

There is no tracing observations of this kind, without making at the same time very great allowances, as there are everywhere to be found, a great many exceptions. The Irish themselves, from different parts of that kingdom, are very different. It is difficult to account for this surprising locality, one would think on so small an island an Irishman must be an Irishman: yet it is not so, they are different in their aptitude to, and in their love of labor.

The Scotch on the contrary are all industrious and saving; they want nothing more than a field to exert themselves in, and they are commonly sure of succeeding. The only difficulty they labor under is, that technical American knowledge which requires some time to obtain; it is not easy for those who seldom saw a tree, to conceive how it is to be felled, cut up, and split into rails and posts.

As I am fond of seeing and talking of prosperous families, I intend to finish this letter by relating to you the history of an honest Scotch Hebridean, who came here in 1774, which will show you in epitome what the Scotch can do, wherever they have room for the exertion of their industry.

Whenever I hear of any new settlement, I pay it a visit once or twice a year, on purpose to observe the different steps each settler takes, the gradual improvements, the different tempers of each family, on which their prosperity in a great nature depends; their different modifications of industry, their ingenuity, and contrivance; for being all poor, their life requires sagacity and prudence. In the evening I love to hear them tell their stories, they furnish me with new ideas; I sit still and listen to their ancient misfortunes, observing in many of them a strong degree of gratitude to God, and the government. Many a well meant sermon have I preached to some of them. When I found laziness and inattention to prevail, who could refrain from wishing well to these new countrymen, after having undergone so many fatigues. Who could withhold good advice? What a happy change it must be, to descend from the high, sterile, bleak lands of Scotland, where everything is barren and cold, to rest on some fertile farms in these middle provinces! Such a transition must have afforded the most pleasing satisfaction.

The following dialogue passed at an outsettlement, where I lately paid a visit:

Well, friend, how do you do now; I am come fifty odd miles on purpose to see you: how do you go on with your new cutting and slashing? Very well, good Sir, we learn the use of the axe bravely, we shall make it out; we have a belly full of victuals every day, our cows run about, and come home full of milk, our hogs get fat of themselves in the woods: Oh, this is a good country! God bless the king, and William Penn; we shall do very well by and by, if we keep our healths. Your log-house looks neat and light, where did you get these shingles? One of our neighbors is a New-England man, and he showed us how to split them out of chestnut-trees. Now for a barn, but all in good time, here are fine trees to build with. Who is to frame it, sure you don't understand that work yet? A countryman of ours who has been in America these ten years, offers to wait for his money until the second crop is lodged in it. What did you give for your land? Thirty-five shillings per acre, payable in seven years. How many acres have you got? An hundred and fifty. That is enough to begin with; is not your land pretty hard to clear? Yes, Sir, hard enough, but it would be harder still if it were ready cleared, for then we should have no timber, and I love the woods much; the land is nothing without them. Have not you found out any bees yet? No, Sir; and if we had we should not know what to do with them. I will tell you by and by. You are very kind. Farewell, honest man, God prosper you; whenever you travel toward ——, inquire for J. S. He will entertain you kindly, provided you bring him good tidings from your family and farm. In this manner I often visit them, and carefully examine their houses, their modes of ingenuity, their different ways; and make them all relate all they know, and describe all they feel. These are scenes which I believe you would willingly share with me. I well remember your philanthropic turn of mind. Is it not better to contemplate under these humble roofs, the rudiments of future wealth and population, than to behold the accumulated bundles of litigious papers in the office of a lawyer? To examine how the world is gradually settled, how the howling swamp is converted into a pleasing meadow, the rough ridge into a fine field; and to hear the cheerful whistling, the rural song, where there was no sound heard before, save the yell of the savage, the screech of the owl, or the hissing of the snake? Here an European, fatigued with luxury, riches, and pleasures, may find a sweet relaxation in a series of interesting scenes, as affecting as they are new. England, which now contains so many domes, so many castles, was once like this; a place woody and marshy; its inhabitants, now the favorite nation for arts and commerce, were once painted like our neighbors. The country will flourish in its turn, and the same observations will be made which I have just delineated. Posterity will look back with avidity and pleasure, to trace, if possible, the era of this or that particular settlement.

Pray, what is the reason that the Scots are in general more religious, more faithful, more honest, and industrious than the Irish? I do not mean to insinuate national reflections, God forbid! It ill becomes any man, and much less an American; but as I know men are nothing of themselves, and that they owe all their different modifications either to government or other local circumstances, there must be some powerful causes which constitute this great national difference.

Agreeable to the account which several Scotchmen have given me of the north of Britain, of the Orkneys, and the Hebride Islands, they seem, on many accounts, to be unfit for the habitation of men; they appear to be calculated only for great sheep pastures. Who then can blame the inhabitants of these countries for transporting themselves hither? This great continent must in time absorb the poorest part of Europe; and this will happen in proportion as it becomes better known; and as war, taxation, oppression, and misery increase there. The Hebrides appear to be fit only for the residence of malefactors, and it would be much better to send felons there than either to Virginia or Maryland. What a strange compliment has our mother country paid to two of the finest provinces in America! England has entertained in that respect very mistaken ideas; what was intended as a punishment, is become the good fortune of several; many of those who have been transported as felons, are now rich, and strangers to the stings of those wants that urged them to violations of the law: they are become industrious, exemplary, and useful citizens. The English government should purchase the most northern and barren of those islands; it should send over to us the honest, primitive Hebrideans, settle them here on good lands, as a reward for their virtue and ancient poverty; and replace them with a colony of her wicked sons. The severity of the climate, the inclemency of the seasons, the sterility of the soil, the tempestuousness of the sea, would afflict and punish enough. Could there be found a spot better adapted to retaliate the injury it had received by their crimes? Some of those islands might be considered as the hell of Great Britain, where all evil spirits should be sent. Two essential ends would be answered by this simple operation. The good people, by emigration, would be rendered happier; the bad ones would be placed where they ought to be. In a few years the dread of being sent to that wintry region would have a much stronger effect than that of transportation.—This is no place of punishment; were I a poor hopeless, breadless Englishman, and not restrained by the power of shame, I should be very thankful for the passage. It is of very little importance how, and in what manner an indigent man arrives; for if he is but sober, honest, and industrious, he has nothing more to ask of heaven. Let him go to work, he will have opportunities enough to earn a comfortable support, and even the means of procuring some land; which ought to be the utmost wish of every person who has health and hands to work. I knew a man who came to this country, in the literal sense of the expression, stark naked; I think he was a Frenchman, and a sailor on board an English man-of-war. Being discontended, he had stripped himself and swam ashore; where, finding clothes and friends, he settled afterwards at Maraneck, in the county of Chester in the province of New York: he married and left a good farm to each of his sons. I knew another person who was but twelve years old when he was taken on the frontiers of Canada, by the Indians; at his arrival at Albany he was purchased by a gentleman, who generously bound him apprentice to a tailor. He lived to the age of ninety, and left behind him a fine estate and a numerous family, all well settled; many of them I am acquainted with.—Where is then the industrious European who ought to despair?

After a foreigner from any part of Europe is arrived, and become a citizen; let him devoutly listen to the voice of our great parent, which says to him, "Welcome to my shores, distressed European; bless the hours in which thou didst see my verdant fields, my fair navigable rivers, and my green mountains!— If thou wilt work, I have bread for thee; if thou wilt be honest, sober, and industrious, I have greater rewards to confer on thee—ease and independence. I will give thee fields to feed and clothe thee; a comfortable fireside to sit by, and tell thy children by what means thou hast prospered; and a decent bed to repose on. I shall endow thee beside with the immunities of a freeman. If thou wilt carefully educate thy children, teach them gratitude to God, and reverence to that government, that philanthropic government, which has collected here so many men and made them happy. I will also provide for thy progeny; and to every good man this ought to be the most holy, the most powerful, the most earnest wish he can possibly form, as well as the most consolatory prospect when he dies. Go thou and work and till; thou shalt prosper, provided thou be just, grateful, and industrious."

w. 1770–1775
p. 1782

BENJAMIN FRANKLIN
(1706–1790)

Benjamin Franklin was born the son of a soapmaker-chandler in Boston during the days of Cotton Mather and Samuel Sewall. He was apprenticed to his half-brother James, founder of the *New England Courant* (1721), for which, at sixteen, Franklin began to write his "Silence Dogood" essays. Considered an atheist in Puritan Boston, he ran off to Philadelphia when he was seventeen. With hard work, thrift, and a sharp eye on "the way to wealth," he had acquired his own printing firm by 1728, intending to make enough money to retire and devote himself to personal and public interests. Twenty years later, aged forty-two, he achieved this goal; and ever since, he has served as the prototypical figure in the Great Success Story of the American middle-class dream. The implications of Franklin's calculating character have since become realized in the "practical" philistinism of one aspect of the national character, the subject of much American writing. This is one truth about Franklin; but it is by no means the whole truth.

Franklin's astonishingly capacious, benevolent, and humorous intellect summed up almost every aspect of developing American values, making him the most many-sided and most representative individual of that germinal age, the Enlightenment. His materialism is not simply the precursor of attitudes later satirized by such writers as Sinclair Lewis; more accurately, it was a reflection of the general deistic belief that free reason and full attention to this world of the present moment would result in a social altruism that would be the best service to God. Indeed, because of Franklin's many services and proposals for human betterment, the age considered him its most pious man. He theorized on the nature of earthquakes, windstorms, air and ocean currents, heat, electricity, and optics. He invented the Franklin stove, bifocals, and the harmonica, and developed street gutters and street lighting. He founded the Library Company of Philadelphia (1731), our first public library; the American Philosophical Society (1743), our first learned society; the University of Pennsylvania (1749), then known as the Academy of Philadelphia; and the Pennsylvania Hospital (1751), our first city hospital. He was clerk of the Colonial Legislature (1736–1751), postmaster of the colonies (1753–1774), a leader in the Albany Congress (1754), the chief colonial voice in London (1757–1775), one of the foremost members of the Second Continental Congress (1775–1776), our representative to France (1777–1785), and the founder of our alliance with that nation. He was one of the sanest voices in the Philadelphia Constitutional Convention (1787), and he designed the treaty terms that closed our revolution. So much is the story of Franklin the story of the founding of the Republic, in its character as well as its history, that we can neither admire nor deprecate him without admiring or deprecating our own culture.

As a writer, he was shrewdly simple and lucid in his prose. His rhetoric and attitudes announce the distrust of mysticism and the hard-headed selflessness so typical of the man and his times. Characteristically, he never considered himself a writer of belles lettres, but rather a didactic author of propaganda and moral and social precepts. Secondarily he was a writer of charmingly witty and benignly satiric bagatelles that displayed the cosmopolitan and urbane sophistication so dear to the Age of Reason. He was also our first folk humorist. Unfortunately, his central work, the *Autobiography*, ends in 1757 with his trip to England as the agent of the colony of Pennsylvania. But the well-known personal history, together with the thirty-three remaining years of his life, furnish us with a picture of an amazing and almost universal genius. A confoundingly representative American and ingenious Yankee, he was so familiar in and with every corner of the Western world and its thought that he was our first international citizen. In his own words, "Where liberty is, there is my country."

Included among the long list of titles by Franklin, in addition to the *Autobiography*, are *The Dogood Papers* (1722); *A Dis-*

sertation on Liberty and Necessity (1725); Articles of Belief and Acts of Religion (1728); Busybody Papers (1728–1729); Essay on Human Vanity (1735); Advice to a Young Man on Choosing a Mistress (1745); Reflections on Courtship and Marriage (1746); Plain Truth (1747); Proposals Relating to the Education of Youth in Pennsylvania (1749); Experiments and Observations on Electricity (1751–1753); Poor Richard's Almanack (1732–1764); Plan for Settling the Western Colonies (1756); The Way to Wealth (1757); Advice to a Young Tradesman (1762); An Edict of the King of Prussia (1773); Rules by which a Great Empire may be Reduced to a Small One (1773); Articles of Confederation (1775); The Ephemera (1778); The Morals of Chess (1779); The Whistle (1779); Dialogue Between Franklin and the Gout (1780); The Handsome and the Deformed Leg (1780); and Information to Those Who Would Remove to America (1784).

Editions and accounts of Franklin and his works are to be found in J. Parton, The Life and Times of Benjamin Franklin, 2 vols. (1864); J. Bigelow, The Life of Benjamin Franklin, 3 vols. (1874); J. B. McMaster, Benjamin Franklin as Man of Letters (1887); P. L. Ford, The Many-Sided Franklin (1899); W. C. Bruce, Benjamin Franklin Self Revealed, 2 vols. (1917); B. Fay, Franklin: The Apostle of Modern Times (1929); V. W. Crane, Benjamin Franklin: Englishman and American (1936); C. Van Doren, Benjamin Franklin (1938); I. B. Cohen, Benjamin Franklin (1953); V. W. Crane, Benjamin Franklin and a Rising People (1954); R. D. Miles, "The American Image of Franklin," American Quarterly, IX (1957); J. Bier, "Franklin's Autobiography: Benchmark of American Literature," Western Humanities Review, XII (1958); R. E. Amacher, Benjamin Franklin (1962); T. Hornberger, Benjamin Franklin (1962); W. Shear, "Franklin's Self-Portrait," Midwest Quarterly, IV (1962); R. F. Sayre, "The Worldly Franklin and the Provincial Critics," Texas Studies in Literature and Language, IV (1963); L. W. Labaree, R. L Ketcham, H. C. Boatfield, and H. H. Fineman, eds., The Autobiography (1964); D. Levin, "The Autobiography of Benjamin Franklin: The Puritan Experimenter in Life and Art," Yale Review, LIII (1964); M. Savelle, "Benjamin Franklin and American Liberalism," Western Humanities Review, XVIII (1964); R. F. Sayre, The Examined Self: Benjamin Franklin, Henry Adams, Henry James (1964); A. O. Aldridge, Benjamin Franklin, Philosopher and Man (1965); P. W. Conner, Poor Richard's Politicks: Benjamin Franklin and His New American Order (1965); R. L. Ketcham, Benjamin Franklin (1965); L. W. Labaree, et al, eds., The Papers of Benjamin Franklin, ten vols. (1959–1966); J. Smith, "Coming of Age in America: Young Ben Franklin and Robin Molineux," American Quarterly, XVII (1965); and C. Lopez, Mon Cher Papa: Franklin and the Ladies of Paris (1966).

A Witch Trial at Mount-Holly

BURLINGTON, Oct. 12. Saturday last at Mount-Holly, about 8 miles from this place, near 300 people were gathered together to see an experiment or two tried on some persons accused of witchcraft. It seems the accused had been charged with making their neighbors' sheep dance in an uncommon manner, and with causing hogs to speak, and sing psalms, &c. to the great terror and amazment of the King's good and peaceful subjects in this province; and the accusers being very positive that if the accused were weighted in scales against a Bible, the Bible would prove too heavy for them; or that, if they were bound and put into the river, they would swim; the said accused desirous to make their innocence appear, voluntarily offered to undergo the said trials, if 2 of the most violent of their accusers would be tried with them. Accordingly the time and place was agreed on, and advertised about the country; the accusers were 1 man and 1 woman; and the accused the same. The parties being met, and the people got together, a grand consultation was held, before they proceeded to trial; in which it was agreed to use the scales first; and a committee of men were appointed to search the men, and a committee of women to search the women, to see if they had any thing of weight about them, particularly pins. After the scrutiny was over, a huge great Bible belonging to the Justice of the place was provided, and a lane through the populace was made from the Justice's house to the scales, which were fixed on a gallows erected for that purpose opposite to the house, that the Justice's wife and the rest of the ladies might see the trial, without coming amongst the mob; and after the manner of Moorfields, a large ring was also made. Then came out of the house a grave tall man carrying the Holy Writ before the supposed wizard, &c. (as solemnly as the sword-bearer of London before the Lord Mayor), the wizard was first put in the scale, and over him was read a chapter out of the Books of Moses, and then the Bible was put in the other scale, (which being kept down before) was immediately let go; but to the great surprise of the spectators, flesh and bones came down plump, and outweighed that great good Book by abundance. After that same manner, the others were served, and their lumps of mortality severally were too heavy for Moses and all the Prophets and Apostles. This being over, the accusers and the rest of the mob, not satisfied with this experiment, would have the trial by water; accordingly a most solemn procession was made to the mill-pond; where both accused and accusers being stripped (saving only to the women their shifts) were bound hand and foot, and severally placed in the water, lengthways, from the side of a barge or flat, having for security only a rope about the middle of each, which was held by some in the flat. The accuser man being thin and spare, with some difficulty began to sink at last; but the rest every one of them swam very light upon the water. A sailor in the flat jumped out upon the back of the man accused, thinking to drive him down to the bottom, but the person bound, without any help came up some time before the other. The woman accuser, being told that she did not sink, would be ducked a second time; when she swam again as light as before. Upon which she declared, that she believed the accused had bewitched her to make her so light, and that she would duck the devil out of her. The accused man, being surprised at his own swimming, was not so confident of his innocence as before, but said, *If I am a witch, it is more than I know.* The more thinking part of the spectators were of opinion, that any person so bound and placed in the water (unless they were mere skin and bones) would swim till their breath was gone, and their lungs filled with water. But it being the general belief of the populace, that the women's shifts, and the garters with which they were bound helped to support them; it is said they are to be tried again the next warm weather, naked.

The Way to Wealth

Courteous Reader

I have heard that nothing gives an author so great pleasure as to find his works respectfully quoted by other learned authors. This pleasure I have seldom enjoyed; for though I have been, if I may say it without vanity, an eminent author of almanacs annually now a full quarter of a century, my brother authors in the same way, for what reason I know not, have ever been very sparing in their applauses; and no other author has taken the least notice of me; so that, did not my writings produce me some solid pudding, the great deficiency of praise would have quite discouraged me.

I concluded at length that the people were the best judges of my merit, for they buy my works; and besides, in my rambles where I am not personally known, I have frequently heard one or other of my adages repeated, with 'as Poor Richard says' at the end on't. This gave me some satisfaction, as it showed not only that my instructions were regarded, but discovered likewise some respect for my authority; and I own that, to encourage the practice of remembering and repeating those wise sentences, I have sometimes *quoted myself* with great gravity.

Judge, then, how much I must have been gratified by an incident I am going to relate to you. I stopped my horse lately where a great number of people were collected at a vendue of merchant goods. The hour of sale not being come, they were conversing on the badness of the times, and one of the company called to a plain, clean old man with white locks: 'Pray, Father Abraham, what think you of the times? Won't these heavy taxes quite ruin the country? How shall we be ever able to pay them? What would you advise us to?' Father Abraham stood up and replied, 'if you'd have my advice, I'll give it you in short, for "A word to the wise is enough," and "Many words won't fill a bushel," as Poor Richard says.' They joined in desiring him to speak his mind, and gathering round him, he proceeded as follows:

'Friends,' says he, 'and neighbors, the taxes are indeed very heavy, and if those laid on by the government were the only ones we had to pay, we might more easily discharge them; but we have many others, and much more grievous to some of us. We are taxed twice as much by our idleness, three times as much by our pride, and four times as much by our folly; and from these taxes the commissioners cannot ease or deliver us by allowing an abatement. However, let us hearken to good advice, and something may be done for us; "God helps them that help themselves," as Poor Richard says in his almanac of 1733.

'It would be thought a hard government that should tax its people one-tenth part of their time, to be employed in its service. But idleness taxes many of us much more, if we reckon all that is spent in absolute sloth, or doing of nothing, with that which is spent in idle employments or amusements that amount to nothing. Sloth, by bringing on diseases, absolutely shortens life. "Sloth, like rust, consumes faster than labor wears; while the used key is always bright," as Poor Richard says. "But dost thou love life? Then do not squander time; for that's the stuff life is made of," as Poor Richard says. How much more than is necessary do we spend in sleep, forgetting that "The sleeping fox catches no poultry," and that "There will be sleeping enough in the grave," as Poor Richard says.

' "If time be of all things the most precious, wasting time must be," as Poor Richard says, "the greatest prodigality"; since, as he elsewhere tells us, "Lost time is never found again"; and "What we call time enough always proves little enough." Let us then up and be doing, and doing to the purpose; so by diligence shall we do more with less perplexity. "Sloth makes all things difficult, but industry all easy," as Poor Richard says; and "He that riseth late must trot all day, and shall scarce overtake his business at night"; while "Laziness travels so slowly that poverty soon overtakes him," as we read in Poor Richard, who adds, "Drive thy business, let not that drive thee"; and "Early to bed, and early to rise, makes a man healthy, wealthy, and wise."

'So what signifies wishing and hoping for better times? We may make these times better if we bestir ourselves. "Industry need not wish," as Poor Richard says, and "He that lives upon hope will die fasting." "There are no gains without pains"; "Then help, hands, for I have no lands," or if I have, they are smartly taxed. And, as Poor Richard likewise observes, "He that hath a trade hath an estate; and he that hath a calling, hath an office of profit and honor"; but then the trade must be worked at, and the calling well followed, or neither the estate nor the office will enable us to pay our taxes. If we are industrious, we shall never starve; for, as Poor Richard says, "At the working man's house hunger looks in but dares not enter." Nor will the bailiff or the constable enter, for "Industry

pays debts, while despair increaseth them," says Poor
Richard. What though you have found no treasure, nor has
any rich relation left you a legacy, "Diligence is the mother
of good luck," as Poor Richard says, and "God gives all
things to industry." "Then plough deep while sluggards
sleep, and you shall have corn to sell and to keep," says
Poor Dick. Work while it is called today, for you know
not how much you may be hindered tomorrow, which
makes Poor Richard say, "One today is worth two tomor-
rows," and farther, "Have you somewhat to do tomorrow,
do it today." If you were a servant, would you not be
ashamed that a good master should catch you idle? Are you
then your own master, "Be ashamed to catch yourself idle,"
as Poor Dick says. When there is so much to be done
for yourself, your family, your country, and your gracious
King, be up by peep of day; "Let not the sun look down
and say, 'Inglorious here he lies.'" Handle your tools
without mittens; remember that "The cat in gloves catches
no mice," as Poor Richard says. 'Tis true there is much to
be done, and perhaps you are weakhanded; but stick to
it steadily, and you will see great effects, for "Constant
dropping wears away stones," and "By diligence and patience the mouse ate in two the cable"; and "Little strokes
fell great oaks," as Poor Richard says in his almanac—
the year I cannot just now remember.

'Methinks I hear some of you say, "Must a man afford
himself no leisure?" I will tell thee, my friend, what Poor
Richard says: "Employ thy time well, if thou meanest to
gain leisure"; and, "Since thou art not sure of a minute,
throw not away an hour." Leisure is time for doing something useful; this leisure the diligent man will obtain, but
the lazy man never; so that, as Poor Richard says, "A
life of leisure and a life of laziness are two things." Do
you imagine that sloth will afford you more comfort than
labor? No, for as Poor Richard says, "Trouble springs from
idleness, and grievous toil from needless ease." "Many,
without labor, would live by their wits only, but they break
for want of stock." Whereas industry gives comfort, and
plenty, and respect: "Fly pleasures, and they'll follow
you." "The diligent spinner has a large shift"; and, "Now
I have a sheep and a cow, everybody bids me good morrow"; all which is well said by Poor Richard.

'But with our industry we must likewise be steady, settled, and careful, and oversee our own affairs with our own eyes, and not trust too much to others; for, as Poor Richard says,

> "I never saw an oft-removèd tree,
>   Nor yet an oft-removèd family,
>   That throve so well as those that settled be."

And again, "Three removes is as bad as a fire"; and again, "Keep thy shop, and thy shop will keep thee"; and again, "If you would have your business done, go; if not, send." And again,

> "He that by the plough would thrive
>   Himself must either hold or drive."

And again, "The eye of a master will do more work than his hands"; and again, "Want of care does us more damage than want of knowledge"; and again, "Not to oversee workmen is to leave them your purse open." Trusting too much to others' care is the ruin of many; for, as the almanac says, "In the affairs of this world men are saved not by faith but by the want of it"; but a man's own care is profitable; for, saith Poor Dick, "Learning is to the studious, and riches to the careful, as well as power to the bold, and heaven to the virtuous"; and farther, "If you would have a faithful servant and one that you like, serve yourself." And again, he adviseth to circumspection and care, even in the smallest matters, because sometimes "A little neglect may breed great mischief"; adding: "For want of a nail the shoe was lost; for want of a shoe the horse was lost; and for want of a horse the rider was lost, being overtaken and slain by the enemy; all for want of care about a horseshoe nail."

'So much for industry, my friends, and attention to one's own business; but to these we must add frugality if we would make our industry more certainly successful. A man may, if he knows not how to save as he gets, keep his nose all his life to the grindstone, and die not worth a groat at last. "A fat kitchen makes a lean will," as Poor Richard says; and

> "Many estates are spent in the getting,
>   Since women for tea forsook spinning and knitting,
>   And men for punch forsook hewing and splitting."

"If you would be wealthy," says he in another almanac, "think of saving as well as of getting: the Indies have not made Spain rich, because her outgoes are greater than her incomes."

'Away then with your expensive follies, and you will not then have so much cause to complain of hard times, heavy taxes, and chargeable families; for, as Poor Dick says,

> "Women and wine, game and deceit
> Make the wealth small and the wants great."

And farther, "What maintains one vice would bring up two children." You may think, perhaps, that a little tea, or a little punch now and then, diet a little more costly, clothes a little finer, and a little entertainment now and then can be no great matter; but remember what Poor Richard says, "Many a little makes a mickle"; and farther, "Beware of little expenses; a small leak will sink a great ship"; and again, "Who dainties love, shall beggars prove"; and moreover, "Fools make feasts, and wise men eat them."

'Here you are all got together at this vendue of fineries and knickknacks. You call them goods; but if you do not take care, they will prove evils to some of you. You expect they will be sold cheap, and perhaps they may for less than they cost; but if you have no occasion for them, they must be dear to you. Remember what Poor Richard says, "Buy what thou hast no need of, and ere long thou shalt sell thy necessaries." And again, "At a great pennyworth pause a while." He means that perhaps the cheapness is apparent only, and not real; or the bargain, by straitening thee in thy business, may do thee more harm than good. For in another place he says, "Many have been ruined by buying good pennyworths." Again, Poor Richard says, " 'Tis foolish to lay out money in a purchase of repentance"; and yet this folly is practiced every day at vendues for want of minding the almanac. "Wise men," as Poor Dick says, "learn by others' harms, fools scarcely by their own"; but *felix quem faciunt aliena pericula cautum* [Fortunate the man whom another's dangers make cautious]. Many a one, for the sake of finery on the back, have gone with a hungry belly and half starved their families. "Silks and satins, scarlet and velvets," as Poor Richard says, "put out the kitchen fire."

'These are not the necessaries of life; they can scarcely be called the conveniences; and yet, only because they look pretty, how many want to have them! The artificial wants of mankind thus become more numerous than the natural; and, as Poor Dick says, "For one poor person, there are an hundred indigent." By these and other extravagancies the genteel are reduced to poverty and forced to borrow of those whom they formerly despised, but who through industry and frugality have maintained their standing; in which case it appears plainly that "A ploughman on his legs is higher than a gentleman on his knees," as Poor Richard says. Perhaps they have had a small estate left them, which they knew not the getting of; they think 'tis day and will never be night, that a little to be spent out of so much is not worth minding. "A child and a fool," as Poor Richard says, "imagine twenty shillings and twenty years can never be spent"; but "Always taking out of the meal-tub, and never putting in, soon comes to the bottom"; then as Poor Dick says, "When the well's dry, they know the worth of water." But this they might have known before if they had taken his advice. "If you would know the value of money, go and try to borrow some"; or "He that goes a-borrowing goes a-sorrowing"; and indeed so does he that lends to such people, when he goes to get it in again. Poor Dick farther advises, and says,

> "Fond pride of dress is sure a very curse;
> E'er fancy you consult, consult your purse."

And again, "Pride is as loud a beggar as want, and a great deal more saucy." When you have bought one fine thing, you must buy ten more, that your appearance may be all of a piece; but Poor Dick says, " 'Tis easier to suppress the first desire than to satisfy all that follow it." And 'tis as truly folly for the poor to ape the rich as for the frog to swell in order to equal the ox.

> "Great estates may venture more,
> But little boats should keep near shore."

'Tis, however, a folly soon punished; for "Pride that dines on vanity sups on contempt," as Poor Richard says. And in another place, "Pride breakfasted with plenty, dined with poverty, and supped with infamy." And after all, of what use is this pride of appearance, for which so much is risked, so much is suffered? It cannot promote health, or ease pain; it makes no increase of merit in the person; it creates envy, it hastens misfortune.

> "What is a butterfly? At best
> He's but a caterpillar drest.
> The gaudy fop's his picture just,"

as Poor Richard says.

'But what madness must it be to run in debt for these superfluities! We are offered by the terms of this vendue six months' credit; and that perhaps has induced some of us to attend it, because we cannot spare the ready money and hope now to be fine without it. But, ah, think what you do when you run in debt; you give to another power over your liberty! If you cannot pay at the time, you will be ashamed to see your creditors; you will be in fear when you speak to him; you will make poor pitiful sneaking excuses, and by degrees come to lose your veracity, and sink into base downright lying; for, as Poor Richard says, "The second vice is lying, the first is running in debt." And again, to the same purpose, "Lying rides upon debt's back." Whereas a free-born Englishman ought not to be ashamed or afraid to see or speak to any man living. But poverty often deprives a man of all spirit and virtue: " 'Tis hard for an empty bag to stand upright," as Poor Richard truly says.

'What would you think of that prince or that government who should issue an edict forbidding you to dress like a gentleman or a gentlewoman on pain of imprisonment or servitude? Would you not say that you were free, have a right to dress as you please, and that such an edict would be a breach of your privileges, and such a government tyrannical? And yet you are about to put yourself under that tyranny, when you run in debt for such dress! Your creditor has authority at his pleasure to deprive you of your liberty by confining you in gaol for life, or to sell you as a servant, if you should not be able to pay him! When you have got your bargain, you may perhaps think little of payments; but "Creditors," Poor Richard tells us, "have better memories than debtors"; and in another place says, "Creditors are a superstitious sect, great observers of set days and times." The day comes round before you are aware, and the demand is made before you are prepared to satisfy it; or, if you bear your debt in mind, the term which at first seemed so long will, as it lessens, appear extremely short. Time will seem to have added wings to his heels as well as shoulders. "Those have a short Lent," saith Poor Richard, "who owe money to be paid at Easter." Then since, as he says, "The borrower is a slave to the lender, and the debtor to the creditor," disdain the chain, preserve your freedom; and maintain your independency. Be industrious and free; be frugal and free. At present, perhaps, you may think yourself in thriving circumstances, and that you can bear a little extravagance without injury; but,

> "For age and want, save while you may;
> No morning sun lasts a whole day,"

as Poor Richard says. Gain may be temporary and uncertain, but ever while you live expense is constant and certain; and " 'Tis easier to build two chimneys than to keep one in fuel," as Poor Richard says. So, "Rather go to bed supperless than rise in debt."

> "Get what you can, and what you get hold;
> 'Tis the stone that will turn all your lead into gold,"

as Poor Richard says. And when you have got the philosopher's stone, sure you will no longer complain of bad times or the difficulty of paying taxes.

'This doctrine, my friends, is reason and wisdom; but after all, do not depend too much upon your own industry, and frugality, and prudence, though excellent things, for they may all be blasted without the blessing of Heaven; and therefore ask that blessing humbly, and be not uncharitable to those that at present seem to want it, but comfort and help them. Remember, Job suffered, and was afterwards prosperous.

'And now to conclude, "Experience keeps a dear school, but fools will learn in no other, and scarce in that"; for it is true, "We may give advice, but we cannot give conduct," as Poor Richard says. However, remember this: "They that won't be counselled can't be helped," as Poor Richard says; and farther, that "If you will not hear reason, she'll surely rap your knuckles." '

Thus the old gentleman ended his harangue. The people

heard it and approved the doctrine, and immediately practiced the contrary, just as if it had been a common sermon;
for the vendue opened, and they began to buy extravagantly, notwithstanding all his cautions and their own fear
of taxes. I found the good man had thoroughly studied my
almanacs and digested all I had dropped on these topics
during the course of five and twenty years. The frequent
mention he made of me must have tired anyone else, but
my vanity was wonderfully delighted with it, though I was
conscious that not a tenth part of the wisdom was my
own which he ascribed to me, but rather the gleanings I
had made of the sense of all ages and nations. However,
I resolved to be the better for the echo of it; and though
I had at first determined to buy stuff for a new coat, I went
away resolved to wear my old one a little longer. Reader,
if thou wilt do the same, thy profit will be as great as mine.
I am, as ever, thine to serve thee.

RICHARD SAUNDERS.
July 7, 1757

FROM

The Autobiography

Twyford, at the Bishop of St. Asaph's, *1771*

DEAR SON:

I have ever had a pleasure in obtaining any little anec-
dotes of my ancestors. You may remember the inquiries
I made among the remains of my relations when you were
with me in England, and the journey I undertook for that
purpose. Now imagining it may be equally agreeable to
you to know the circumstances of *my* life, many of which
you are yet unacquainted with, and expecting a week's
uninterrupted leisure in my present country retirement, I
sit down to write them for you. To which I have besides
some other inducements. Having emerged from the poverty
and obscurity in which I was born and bred to a state of
affluence and some degree of reputation in the world and
having gone so far through life with a considerable share

of felicity, the conducing means I made use of, which with the blessing of God so well succeeded, my posterity may like to know, as they may find some of them suitable to their own situations, and therefore fit to be imitated.

That felicity, when I reflected on it, has induced me sometimes to say that were it offered to my choice I should have no objection to a repetition of the same life from its beginning, only asking the advantages authors have in a second edition to correct some faults of the first. So would I, if I might, besides correcting the faults, change some sinister accidents and events of it for others more favorable. But though this were denied, I should still accept the offer. However, since such a repetition is not to be expected, the next thing most like living one's life over again seems to be a *recollection* of that life, and to make that recollection as durable as possible the putting it down in writing.

Hereby, too, I shall indulge the inclination so natural in old men to be talking of themselves and their own past actions; and I shall indulge it without being troublesome to others, who, through respect to age, might think themselves obliged to give me a hearing, since this may be read or not as any one pleases. And lastly (I may as well confess it, since my denial of it will be believed by nobody), perhaps I shall a good deal gratify my own *vanity*. Indeed, I scarce ever heard or saw the introductory words, "Without vanity I may say," etc., but some vain thing immediately followed. Most people dislike vanity in others, whatever share they have of it themselves; but I give it fair quarter wherever I meet with it, being persuaded that it is often productive of good to the possessor, and to others that are within his sphere of action; and therefore, in many cases, it would not be quite absurd if a man were to thank God for his vanity among the other comforts of life.

And now I speak of thanking God, I desire with all humility to acknowledge that I owe the mentioned happiness of my past life to His kind providence, which led me to the means I used and gave them success. My belief of this induces me to *hope*, though I must not *presume*, that the same goodness will still be exercised towards me, in continuing that happiness or in enabling me to bear a fatal reverse, which I may experience as others have done, the complexion of my future fortune being known to Him only in whose power it is to bless to us even our afflictions.

· · ·

Josiah, my father, married young, and carried his wife with three children into New England about 1682. The conventicles having been forbidden by law and frequently disturbed induced some considerable men of his acquaintance to remove to that country, and he was prevailed with to accompany them thither, where they expected to enjoy their mode of religion with freedom. By the same wife he had four children more born there, and by a second wife ten more, in all seventeen; of which I remember thirteen sitting at one time at his table, who all grew up to be men and women, and married; I was the youngest son, and the youngest child but two, and was born in Boston, New England. My mother, the second wife, was Abiah Folger, a daughter of Peter Folger, one of the first settlers of New England, of whom honorable mention is made by Cotton Mather, in his church history of that country, entitled *Magnalia Christi Americana*, as "a godly, learned Englishman," if I remember the words rightly. I have heard that he wrote sundry small occasional pieces, but only one of them was printed, which I saw now many years since. It was written in 1675, in the homespun verse of that time and people, and addressed to those then concerned in the government there. It was in favor of liberty of conscience, and in behalf of the Baptists, Quakers, and other sectaries that had been under persecution, ascribing the Indian wars and other distresses that had befallen the country to that persecution, as so many judgments of God to punish so heinous an offense, and exhorting a repeal of those uncharitable laws. The whole appeared to me as written with a good deal of decent plainness and manly freedom. The six last concluding lines I remember, though I have forgotten the two first of the stanza; but the purport of them was that his censures proceeded from good-will and, therefore, he would be known as the author,

> "Because to be a Libeller, (says he)
>   I hate it with my Heart.
> From Sherburne Town where now I dwell,
>   My Name I do put here,
> Without Offense, your real Friend,
>   It is Peter Folgier."

My elder brothers were all put apprentices to different trades. I was put to the grammar school at eight years of age, my father intending to devote me, as the tithe of his sons, to the service of the church. My early readiness in learning to read (which must have been very early, as I do not remember when I could not read) and the opinion of all his friends that I should certainly make a good scholar encouraged him in this purpose of his. My uncle Benjamin, too, approved of it, and proposed to give me all his shorthand volumes of sermons, I suppose as a stock to set up with, if I would learn his character. I continued, however, at the grammar school not quite one year, though in that time I had risen gradually from the middle of the class of that year to be the head of it, and farther was removed into the next class above it, in order to go with that into the third at the end of the year. But my father, in the meantime, from a view of the expense of a college education, which having so large a family he could not well afford, and the mean living many so educated were afterwards able to obtain—reasons that he gave to his friends in my hearing—altered his first intention, took me from the grammer school, and sent me to a school for writing and arithmetic, kept by a then famous man, Mr. George Brownell, very successful in his profession generally, and that by mild, encouraging methods. Under him I acquired fair writing pretty soon, but I failed in the arithmetic, and made no progress in it. At ten years old I was taken home to assist my father in his business, which was that of a tallow-chandler and soap-boiler; a business he was not bred to, but had assumed on his arrival in New England, and on finding his dying trade would not maintain his family, being in little request. Accordingly, I was employed in cutting wick for the candles, filling the dipping mold and the molds for cast candles, attending the shop, going of errands, etc.

I disliked the trade, and had a strong inclination for the sea, but my father declared against it; however, living near the water, I was much in and about it, learned early to swim well and to manage boats; and when in a boat or canoe with other boys, I was commonly allowed to govern, especially in any case of difficulty; and upon other occasions I was generally a leader among the boys, and sometimes led them into scrapes, of which I will mention one instance, as it shows an early projecting public spirit, though not then justly conducted.

There was a salt-marsh that bounded part of the mill-pond, on the edge of which, at high water, we used to stand to fish for minnows. By much trampling, we had made it a mere quagmire. My proposal was to build a wharf there fit for us to stand upon, and I showed my comrades a large heap of stones which were intended for a new house near the marsh and which would very well suit our purpose. Accordingly, in the evening, when the workmen were gone, I assembled a number of my playfellows, and, working with them diligently like so many emmets, sometimes two or three to a stone, we brought them all away and built our little wharf. The next morning the workmen were surprised at missing the stones, which were found in our wharf. Inquiry was made after the removers; we were discovered and complained of; several of us were corrected by our fathers; and, though I pleaded the usefulness of the work, mine convinced me that nothing was useful which was not honest.

. . .

From a child I was fond of reading, and all the little money that came into my hands was ever laid out in books. Pleased with the *Pilgrim's Progress,* my first collection was of John Bunyan's works in separate little volumes. I afterwards sold them to enable me to buy R. Burton's *Historical Collections;* they were small chapman's books and cheap, forty or fifty in all. My father's little library consisted chiefly of books in polemic divinity, most of which I read and have since often regretted that at a time when I had such a thirst for knowledge, more proper books had not fallen in my way, since it was now resolved I should not be a clergyman. *Plutarch's Lives* there was, in which I read abundantly, and I still think that time spent to great advantage. There was also a book of Defoe's, called an *Essay on Projects,* and another of Dr. Mather's, called *Essays to Do Good,* which perhaps gave me a turn of thinking that had an influence on some of the principal future events of my life.

This bookish inclination at length determined my father to make me a printer, though he had already one son (James) of that profession. In 1717 my brother James returned from England with a press and letters to set up his business in Boston. I liked it much better than that of my father, but still had a hankering for the sea. To prevent the apprehended effect of such an inclination, my father was impatient to have me bound to my brother. I stood out some time, but at last was persuaded, and signed the indentures when I was yet but twelve years old. I was to serve as an apprentice till I was twenty-one years of age, only I was to be allowed journeyman's wages during the last year. In a little time I made great proficiency in the business and became a useful hand to my brother. I now had access to better books. An acquaintance with the apprentices of booksellers enabled me sometimes to borrow a small one, which I was careful to return soon and clean. Often I sat up in my room reading the greatest part of the night, when the book was borrowed in the evening and to be returned early in the morning, lest it should be missed or wanted.

. . .

There was another bookish lad in the town, John Collins by name, with whom I was intimately acquainted. We sometimes disputed; and very fond we were of argument, and very desirous of confuting one another, which disputatious turn, by the way, is apt to become a very bad habit, making people often extremely disagreeable in company by the contradiction that is necessary to bring it into practice; and thence, besides souring and spoiling the conversation, is productive of disgusts and, perhaps, enmities where you may have occasion for friendship. I had caught it by reading my father's books of dispute about religion. Persons of good sense, I have since observed, seldom fall into it, except lawyers, university men, and men of all sorts that have been bred at Edinburgh.

A question was once, somehow or other, started between Collins and me of the propriety of educating the female sex in learning, and their abilities for study. He was of opinion that it was improper, and that they were naturally unequal to it. I took the contrary side, perhaps a little for dispute's sake. He was naturally more eloquent, had a ready plenty of words, and sometimes, as I thought, bore me down more by his fluency than by the strength of his reasons. As we parted without settling the point, and were not to see one another again for some time, I sat down to put my arguments in writing, which I copied fair and sent to him. He answered, and I replied. Three or four letters of a side had passed, when my father happened to find my papers and read them. Without entering into the discussion, he took occasion to talk to me about the manner of my writing; observed that, though I had the advantage of my antagonist in correct spelling and pointing (which I owed to the printing-house), I fell far short in elegance of expression, in method, and in perspicuity, of which he convinced me by several instances. I saw the justice of his remarks, and thence grew more attentive to the *manner* in writing, and determined to endeavor at improvement.

. . .

When about sixteen years of age I happened to meet with a book, written by one Tryon, recommending a vegetable diet. I determined to go into it. My brother, being yet unmarried, did not keep house, but boarded himself and his apprentices in another family. My refusing to eat flesh occasioned an inconveniency, and I was frequently chid for my singularity. I made myself acquainted with Tryon's manner of preparing some of his dishes, such as boiling potatoes or rice, making hasty pudding, and a few others, and then proposed to my brother, that if he would give me, weekly, half the money he paid for my board, I would board myself. He instantly agreed to it, and I presently found that I could save half what he paid me. This was an additional fund for buying books. But I had another advantage in it. My brother and the rest going from the printing-house to their meals, I remained there alone and dispatching presently my light repast, which often was no more than a biscuit or a slice of bread, a handful of raisins or a tart from the pastry-cook's, and a glass of water, had the rest of the time till their return for study, in which I made the greater progress, from that greater clearness of head and quicker apprehension which usually attend temperance in eating and drinking.

And now it was that, being on some occasion made ashamed of my ignorance in figures, which I had twice failed in learning when at school, I took Cocker's book of arithmetic, and went through the whole by myself with great ease. I also read Seller's and Sturmy's books of navigation, and became acquainted with the little geometry they contain; but never proceeded far in that science. And I read about this time Locke *On Human Understanding,* and the *Art of Thinking,* by Messrs. du Port Royal.

While I was intent on improving my language, I met with an English grammar (I think it was Greenwood's), at the end of which there were two little sketches of the arts of rhetoric and logic, the latter finishing with a specimen of a dispute in the Socratic method; and soon after I procured Xenophon's *Memorable Things of Socrates,* wherein there are many instances of the same method. I was charmed with it, adopted it, dropped my abrupt contradiction and positive argumentation, and put on the humble inquirer and doubter. And being then, from reading Shaftsbury and Collins, become a real doubter in many points of our religious doctrine, I found this method safest for myself and very embarrassing to those against whom I used it; therefore I took a delight in it, practiced it continually, and grew very artful and expert in drawing people, even of superior knowledge, into concessions, the consequences of which they did not foresee, entangling them in difficulties out of which they could not extricate themselves, and so obtaining victories that neither myself nor my cause always deserved. I continued this method some few years, but gradually left it, retaining only the habit of expressing myself in terms of modest diffidence; never using, when I advanced anything that may possibly be disputed, the words *certainly, undoubtedly,* or any others that give the air of positiveness to an opinion; but rather say, I conceive or apprehend a thing to be so or so; it appears to me, or I should think it so or so, for such and such reasons; or I imagine it to be so; or it is so, if I am not mistaken. This habit, I believe, has been of great advantage to me when I have had occasion to inculcate my opinions and persuade men into measures that I have been from time to time engaged in promoting; and, as the chief ends of conversation are to *inform* or to be *informed,* to *please* or to *persuade,* I wish well-meaning, sensible men would not lessen their power of doing good by a positive, assuming manner that seldom fails to disgust, tends to create opposition and to defeat every one of those purposes for which speech was given to us, to wit, giving or receiving information or pleasure. For if you would *inform,* a positive dogmatical manner in advancing your sentiments may provoke contradiction and prevent a candid attention. If you wish information and improvement from the knowledge of others, and yet at the same time express yourself as firmly fixed in your present opinions, modest, sensible men, who do not love disputation, will probably leave you undisturbed in the possession of your error. And by such a manner, you can seldom hope to recommend yourself in *pleasing* your hearers, or to persuade those whose concurrence you desire.

· · ·

My brother had, in 1720 or 21, begun to print a newspaper. It was the second that appeared in America, and was called the *New England Courant*. The only one before it was the *Boston News-Letter*. I remember his being dissuaded by some of his friends from the undertaking, as not likely to succeed, one newspaper being, in their judgment, enough for America. At this time (1771) there are not less than five-and-twenty. He went on, however, with the undertaking, and after having worked in composing the types and printing off the sheets, I was employed to carry the papers through the streets to the customers.

He had some ingenious men among his friends, who amused themselves by writing little pieces for this paper, which gained it credit and made it more in demand, and these gentlemen often visited us. Hearing their conversations, and their accounts of the approbation their papers were received with, I was excited to try my hand among them; but, being still a boy, and suspecting that my brother would object to printing anything of mine in his paper if he knew it to be mine, I contrived to disguise my hand and, writing an anonymous paper, I put it in at night under the door of the printing-house. It was found in the morning and communicated to his writing friends when they called in as usual. They read it, commented on it in my hearing, and I had the exquisite pleasure of finding it met with their approbation, and that, in their different guesses at the author, none were named but men of some character among us for learning and ingenuity. I suppose now that I was rather lucky in my judges, and that perhaps they were not really so very good ones as I then esteemed them.

Encouraged, however, by this, I wrote and conveyed

in the same way to the press several more papers which were equally approved; and I kept my secret till my small fund of sense for such performances was pretty well exhausted, and then I discovered it, when I began to be considered a little more by my brother's acquaintance, and in a manner that did not quite please him, as he thought, probably with reason, that it tended to make me too vain. And perhaps this might be one occasion of the differences that we began to have about this time. Though a brother, he considered himself as my master, and me as his apprentice, and accordingly expected the same services from me as he would from another, while I thought he demeaned me too much in some he required of me, who from a brother expected more indulgence. Our disputes were often brought before our father, and I fancy I was either generally in the right, or else a better pleader, because the judgment was generally in my favor. But my brother was passionate, and had often beaten me, which I took extremely amiss; and, thinking my apprenticeship very tedious, I was continually wishing for some opportunity of shortening it.

· · ·

At length, a fresh difference arising between my brother and me, I took upon me to assert my freedom, presuming that he would not venture to produce the new indentures. It was not fair in me to take this advantage, and this I therefore reckon one of the first errata of my life; but the unfairness of it weighed little with me when under the impressions of resentment for the blows his passion too often urged him to bestow upon me, though he was otherwise not an ill-natured man; perhaps I was too saucy and provoking.

When he found I would leave him, he took care to prevent my getting employment in any other printing-house of the town, by going round and speaking to every master, who accordingly refused to give me work. I then thought of going to New York, as the nearest place where there was a printer. . . . So I sold some of my books to raise a little money, was taken on board privately, and as we had a fair wind, in three days I found myself in New York, near three hundred miles from home, a boy of but seventeen, without the least recommendation to, or knowledge of, any person in the place, and with very little money in my pocket.

My inclinations for the sea were by this time worn out, or I might now have gratified them. But, having a trade, and supposing myself a pretty good workman, I offered my service to the printer in the place, old Mr. William Bradford, who had been the first printer in Pennsylvania, but removed from thence upon the quarrel of George Keith. He could give me no employment, having little to do and help enough already; but, says he, "My son at Philadelphia has lately lost his principal hand, Aquila Rose, by death; if you go thither, I believe he may employ you." Philadelphia was one hundred miles further; I set out, however, in a boat for Amboy, leaving my chest and things to follow me round by sea.

In crossing the bay, we met with a squall that tore our rotten sails to pieces, prevented our getting into the Kill, and drove us upon Long Island. In our way, a drunken Dutchman, who was a passenger too, fell overboard; when he was sinking, I reached through the water to his shock pate, and drew him up, so that we got him in again. His ducking sobered him a little, and he went to sleep, taking first out of his pocket a book, which he desired I would dry for him. It proved to be my old favorite author, Bunyan's *Pilgrim's Progress,* in Dutch, finely printed on good paper, with copper cuts, a dress better than I had ever seen it wear in its own language. I have since found that it has been translated into most of the languages of Europe, and suppose it has been more generally read than any other book, except perhaps the Bible. Honest John was the first that I know of who mixed narration and dialogue, a method of writing very engaging to the reader, who in the most interesting parts finds himself, as it were, brought into the company and present at the discourse. Defoe in his *Crusoe,* his *Moll Flanders, Religious Courtship, Family Instructor,* and other pieces, has imitated it with success; and Richardson has done the same in his *Pamela,* etc.

When we drew near the island, we found it was at a place where there could be no landing, there being a great surf on the stony beach. So we dropped anchor, and swung round towards the shore. Some people came down to the water edge and hallowed to us, as we did to them; but the wind was so high, and the surf so loud, that we could not hear so as to understand each other. There were canoes on the shore, and we made signs, and hallowed that they should fetch us; but they either did not understand us, or thought it impracticable, so they went away, and night coming on, we had no remedy but to wait till the wind should abate; and in the mean time the boatman and I concluded to sleep if we could; and so crowded into the scuttle, with the Dutchman, who was still wet, and the spray, beating over the head of our boat, leaked through to us, so that we were soon almost as wet as he. In this manner we lay all night, with very little rest; but, the wind abating the next day, we made a shift to reach Amboy before night, having been thirty hours on the water, without victuals or any drink but a bottle of filthy rum, the water we sailed on being salt.

. . .

I have been the more particular in this description of my journey, and shall be so of my first entry into that city, that you may in your mind compare such unlikely beginnings with the figure I have since made there. I was in my working dress, my best clothes being to come round by sea. I was dirty from my journey; my pockets were stuffed out with shirts and stockings; I knew no soul nor where to look for lodging. I was fatigued with traveling, rowing, and want of rest; I was very hungry; and my whole stock of cash consisted of a Dutch dollar and about a shilling in copper. The latter I gave the people of the boat for my passage, who at first refused it, on account of my rowing; but I insisted on their taking it, a man being sometimes more generous when he has but a little money than when he has plenty, perhaps through fear of being thought to have but little.

Then I walked up the street, gazing about, till near the market-house I met a boy with bread. I had made many a meal on bread, and, inquiring where he got it, I went immediately to the baker's he directed me to, in Second Street, and asked for biscuit, intending such as we had in Boston; but they, it seems, were not made in Philadelphia. Then I asked for a three-penny loaf, and was told they had none such. So, not considering or knowing the difference of money, and the greater cheapness nor the names of his bread, I bade him give me three-penny-worth of any sort. He gave me, accordingly, three great puffy rolls. I was surprised at the quantity, but took it, and, having no room in my pockets, walked off with a roll under each arm, and eating the other. Thus I went up Market Street as far as Fourth Street, passing by the door of Mr. Read, my future wife's father; when she, standing at the door, saw me, and thought I made, as I certainly did, a most awkward, ridiculous appearance. Then I turned and went down Chestnut Street and part of Walnut Street, eating my roll all the way, and, coming round, found myself again at Market Street wharf, near the boat I came in, to which I went for a draught of the river water; and, being filled with one of my rolls, gave the other two to a woman and her child that came down the river in the boat with us, and were waiting to go farther.

Thus refreshed, I walked again up the street, which by this time had many clean-dressed people in it, who were all walking the same way. I joined them, and thereby was led into the great meeting-house of the Quakers near the market. I sat down among them, and, after looking round awhile and hearing nothing said, being very drowsy through labor and want of rest the preceding night, I fell fast asleep, and continued so till the meeting broke up, when one was kind enough to rouse me. This was, therefore, the first house I was in, or slept in, in Philadelphia.

· · ·

Then I made myself as tidy as I could and went to Andrew Bradford the printer's. I found in the shop the old man his father, whom I had seen at New York, and who, traveling on horseback, had got to Philadelphia before me. He introduced me to his son, who received me civilly, gave me a breakfast, but told me he did not at present want a hand, being lately supplied with one; but there was another printer in town, lately set up, one Keimer, who perhaps might employ me; if not, I should be welcome to lodge at his house, and he would give me a little work to do now and then till fuller business should offer.

· · ·

Keimer's printing-house, I found, consisted of an old shattered press, and one small, worn-out font of English, which he was then using himself, composing an elegy on

Aquila Rose, before mentioned, an ingenious young man, of excellent character, much respected in the town, clerk of the Assembly, and a pretty poet. Keimer made verses too, but very indifferently. He could not be said to write them, for his manner was to compose them in the types directly out of his head. So there being no copy, but one pair of cases, and the elegy likely to require all the letter, no one could help him. I endeavored to put his press (which he had not yet used, and of which he understood nothing) into order fit to be worked with; and, promising to come and print off his elegy as soon as he should have got it ready, I returned to Bradford's, who gave me a little job to do for the present, and there I lodged and dieted. A few days after, Keimer sent for me to print off the elegy. And now he had got another pair of cases, and a pamphlet to reprint, on which he set me to work.

These two printers I found poorly qualified for their business. Bradford had not been bred to it, and was very illiterate; and Keimer, though something of a scholar, was a mere compositor, knowing nothing of presswork. He had been one of the French prophets, and could act their enthusiastic agitations. At this time he did not profess any particular religion, but something of all on occasion; was very ignorant of the world, and had, as I afterward found, a good deal of the knave in his composition. He did not like my lodging at Bradford's while I worked with him. He had a house, indeed, but without furniture, so he could not lodge me; but he got me a lodging at Mr. Read's, before mentioned, who was the owner of his house; and, my chest and clothes being come by this time, I made rather a more respectable appearance in the eyes of Miss Read than I had done when she first happened to see me eating my roll in the street.

. . .

Sir William Keith, governor of the province, was then at Newcastle, and Captain Holmes, happening to be in company with him when my letter came to hand, spoke to him of me, and showed him the letter. The Governor read it, and seemed surprised when he was told my age. He said I appeared a young man of promising parts, and therefore should be encouraged; the printers at Philadelphia were wretched ones; and if I would set up there he made no doubt I should succeed; for his part, he would procure me the public business, and do me every other service in his power. This my brother-in-law afterwards told me in Boston, but I knew as yet nothing of it; when, one day, Keimer and I being at work together near the window, we saw the Governor and another gentleman (which proved to be Colonel French of Newcastle), finely dressed, come directly across the street to our house, and heard them at the door.

Keimer ran down immediately, thinking it a visit to him; but the Governor inquired for me, came up, and with a condescension and politeness I had been quite unused to, made me many compliments, desired to be acquainted with me, blamed me kindly for not having made myself known to him when I first came to the place, and would have me away with him to the tavern, where he was going with Colonel French to taste, as he said, some excellent Madeira. I was not a little surprised, and Keimer stared like a pig poisoned. I went, however, with the Governor and Colonel French to a tavern at the corner of Third Street, and over the Madeira he proposed my setting up my business, laid before me the probabilities of success, and both he and Colonel French assured me I should have their interest and influence in procuring the public business of both governments. On my doubting whether my father would assist me in it, Sir William said he would give me a letter to him, in which he would state the advantages, and he did not doubt of prevailing with him. So it was concluded I should return to Boston in the first vessel, with the Governor's letter recommending me to my father. In the mean time the intention was to be kept secret, and I went on working with Keimer as usual, the Governor sending for me now and then to dine with him—a very great honor I thought it—and conversing with me in the most affable, familiar, and friendly manner imaginable.

· · ·

[Franklin's father declined to set Ben up in business and wrote Keith to this effect.] Sir William, on reading his letter, said he was too prudent. There was great difference in persons; and discretion did not always accompany years, nor was youth always without it. "And since he will not set you up," says he, "I will do it myself. Give me an inventory of the things necessary to be had from England, and

I will send for them. You shall repay me when you are able; I am resolved to have a good printer here, and I am sure you must succeed." This was spoken with such an appearance of cordiality, that I had not the least doubt of his meaning what he said. I had hitherto kept the proposition of my setting up a secret in Philadelphia, and I still kept it. Had it been known that I depended on the Governor, probably some friend that knew him better would have advised me not to rely on him, as I afterwards heard it as his known character to be liberal of promises which he never meant to keep. Yet, unsolicited as he was by me, how could I think his generous offers insincere? I believed him one of the best men in the world.

I presented him an inventory of a little printing-house, amounting by my computation to about one hundred pounds sterling. He liked it, but asked me if my being on the spot in England to choose the types and see that everything was good of the kind might not be of some advantage. "Then," says he, "when there, you may make acquaintances, and establish correspondences in the bookselling and stationery way." I agreed that this might be advantageous. "Then," says he, "get yourself ready to go with *Annis*," which was the annual ship, and the only one at that time usually passing between London and Philadelphia. But it would be some months before *Annis* sailed, so I continued working with Keimer. . . .

I believe I have omitted mentioning that, in my first voyage from Boston, being becalmed off Block Island, our people set about catching cod, and hauled up a great many. Hitherto I had stuck to my resolution of not eating animal food, and on this occasion I considered, with my master Tryon, the taking every fish as a kind of unprovoked murder, since none of them had, or ever could do us any injury that might justify the slaughter. All this seemed very reasonable. But I had formerly been a great lover of fish, and, when this came hot out of the frying-pan, it smelled admirably well. I balanced some time between principle and inclination, till I recollected that, when the fish were opened, I saw smaller fish taken out of their stomachs; then thought I, "if you eat one another, I don't see why we mayn't eat you." So I dined upon cod very heartily, and continued to eat with other people, returning only now and then occasionally to a vegetable diet. So convenient a thing it is to be a *reasonable creature,* since it enables one to find or make a reason for everything one has a mind to do.

· · ·

[In London Franklin discovered that Keith's letters were worthless. But he took this setback philosophically. Undaunted, he got work at a famous printing house, Palmer's.]

At Palmer's I was employed in composing for the second edition of Wollaston's *Religion of Nature.* Some of his reasonings not appearing to me well founded, I wrote a little metaphysical piece in which I made remarks on them. It was entitled *A Dissertation on Liberty and Necessity, Pleasure and Pain.* I inscribed it to my friend Ralph; I printed a small number. It occasioned my being more considered by Mr. Palmer as a young man of some ingenuity, though he seriously expostulated with me upon the principles of my pamphlet, which to him appeared abominable. My printing this pamphlet was another erratum.

· · ·

My pamphlet by some means falling into the hands of one Lyons, a surgeon, author of a book entitled *The Infallibility of Human Judgment,* it occasioned an acquaintance between us. He took great notice of me, called on me often to converse on those subjects, carried me to the Horns, a pale alehouse in —— Lane, Cheapside, and introduced me to Dr. Mandeville, author of the *Fable of the Bees,* who had a club there, of which he was the soul, being a most facetious, entertaining companion. Lyons, too, introduced me to Dr. Pemberton, at Batson's Coffeehouse, who promised to give me an opportunity, some time or other, of seeing Sir Isaac Newton, of which I was extremely desirous; but this never happened.

· · ·

At my first admission into this [Watt's] printing-house I took to working at press, imagining I felt a want of the bodily exercise I had been used to in America, where press-work is mixed with composing. I drank only water; the other workmen, near fifty in number, were great guzzlers of beer. On occasion I carried up and down stairs a large form of types in each hand, when others carried but one in both hands. They wondered to see, from this and several instances, that the "Water-American," as they called me, was *stronger* than themselves, who drank *strong* beer! We had an alehouse boy who attended always in the house to supply the workmen. My companion at the press drank every day a pint before breakast, a pint at breakfast with his bread and cheese, a pint between breakfast and dinner, a pint at dinner, a pint in the afternoon about six o'clock, and another when he had done his day's work. I thought it a detestable custom; but it was necessary, he supposed, to drink *strong* beer, that he might be *strong* to labor. I endeavored to convince him that the bodily strength afforded by beer could only be in proportion to the grain or flour of the barley dissolved in the water of which it was made; that there was more flour in a pennyworth of bread, and therefore, if he would eat that with a pint of water, it would give him more strength than a quart of beer. He drank on, however, and had four or five shillings to pay out of his wages every Saturday night for that muddling liquor; an expense I was free from. And thus these poor devils keep themselves always under.

Watts after some weeks desiring to have me in the composing-room, I left the pressmen; a new *bienvenu* or sum for drink, being five shillings, was demanded of me by the compositors. I thought it an imposition, as I had paid below; the master thought so too, and forbade my paying it. I stood out two or three weeks, was accordingly considered as an excommunicate, and had so many little pieces of private mischief done me, by mixing my sorts, transposing my pages, breaking my matter, etc., etc., and if I were ever so little out of the room, and all ascribed to the chapel ghost, which they said ever haunted those not regularly admitted, that, notwithstanding the master's protection, I found myself obliged to comply and pay the money, convinced of the folly of being on ill terms with those one is to live with continually.

I was now on a fair footing with them, and soon acquired considerable influence. I proposed some reasonable alterations in their chapel laws, and carried them against all opposition. From my example, a great part of them left their muddling breakfast of beer and bread and cheese, finding they could with me be supplied from a neighboring house with a large porringer of hot water-gruel, sprinkled with pepper, crumbed with bread, and a bit of butter in it, for the price of a pint of beer, viz., three halfpence. This was a more comfortable as well as cheaper breakfast, and kept their heads clearer. Those who continued sotting with beer all day, were often, by not paying, out of credit at the alehouse, and used to make interest with me to get beer; their *light,* as they phrased it, *being out.* I watched the paytable on Saturday night, and collected what I stood engaged for them, having to pay sometimes near thirty shillings a week on their accounts. This, and my being esteemed a pretty good Riggite, that is, a jocular verbal satirist, supported my consequence in the society. My constant attendance (I never making a St. Monday) recommended me to the master; and my uncommon quickness at composing occasioned by being put upon all work of dispatch, which was generally better paid. So I went on now very agreeably.

· · ·

[After eighteen months in London, Franklin returned to Philadelphia, where, after working for some time for Keimer, he set up shop for himself "in or about 1729."]

Before I enter upon my public appearance in business, it may be well to let you know the then state of my mind with regard to my principles and morals, that you may see how far those influenced the future events of my life. My parents had early given me religious impressions, and brought me through my childhood piously in the dissenting way. But I was scarce fifteen, when, after doubting by turns of several points, as I found them disputed in the different books I read, I began to doubt of Revelation itself. Some books against deism fell into my hands; they were said to be the substance of sermons preached at Boyle's lectures. It happened that they wrought an effect on me quite contrary to what was intended by them; for the arguments of the deists, which were quoted to be refuted, appeared to me much stronger than the refutations; in short, I soon became a thorough deist. My arguments perverted some others, particularly Collins and Ralph; but each of them having

afterwards wronged me greatly without the least compunc-
tion, and recollecting Keith's conduct towards me (who was
another free-thinker), and my own towards Vernon and
Miss Read, which at times gave me great trouble, I began
to suspect that this doctrine, though it might be true, was
not very useful. My London pamphlet, which had for its
motto these lines of Dryden:

> "Whatever is, is right. Though purblind Man
> Sees but a Part of the Chain, the nearest Link,
> His Eyes not carrying to the equal Beam,
> That poises all, above."

And from the attributes of God, his infinite wisdom, goodness, and power, concluded that nothing could possibly be
wrong in the world, and that vice and virtue were empty
distinctions, no such things existing, appeared now not so
clever a performance as I once thought it; and I doubted
whether some error had not insinuated itself unperceived
into my argument, so as to infect all that followed, as is
common in metaphysical reasonings.

I grew convinced that *truth, sincerity* and *integrity* in
dealings between man and man were of the utmost importance to the felicity of life; and I formed written resolutions (which still remain in my journal book), to practice
them ever while I lived. Revelation had indeed no weight
with me as such; but I entertained an opinion that, though
certain actions might not be bad *because* they were forbidden by it, or good *because* it commanded them, yet probably these actions might be forbidden *because* they were
bad for us, or commanded *because* they were beneficial
to us in their own natures, all the circumstances of things
considered. And this persuasion, with the kind hand of
Providence or some guardian angel, or accidental favorable
circumstances and situations, or all together, preserved me
through this dangerous time of youth, and the hazardous
situations I was sometimes in among strangers, remote
from the eye and advice of my father, without any *willful*
gross immorality or injustice, that might have been expected from my want of religion. I say *willful,* because the
instances I have mentioned had something of *necessity* in
them, from my youth, inexperience, and the knavery of
others. I had therefore a tolerable character to begin the

world with; I valued it properly, and determined to preserve it.

. . .

I had been religiously educated as a Presbyterian; and though some of the dogmas of that persuasion, such as *the eternal decrees of God, election, reprobation, etc.*, appeared to me unintelligible, others doubtful, and I early absented myself from the public assemblies of the sect, Sunday being my studying day, I never was without some religious principles. I never doubted, for instance, the existence of the Deity; that he made the world, and governed it by his Providence; that the most acceptable service of God was the doing good to man; that our souls are immortal; and that all crime will be punished, and virtue rewarded, either here or hereafter. These I esteemed the essentials of every religion; and, being to be found in all the religions we had in our country, I respected them all, though with different degrees of respect, as I found them more or less mixed with other articles, which, without any tendency to inspire, promote, or confirm morality, served principally to divide us, and make us unfriendly to one another. This respect to all, with an opinion that the worst had some good effects, induced me to avoid all discourse that might tend to lessen the good opinion another might have of his own religion; and as our province increased in people, and new places of worship were continually wanted, and generally erected by voluntary contribution, my mite for such purpose, whatever might be the sect, was never refused.

Though I seldom attended any public worship, I had still an opinion of its propriety, and of its utility when rightly conducted, and I regularly paid my annual subscription for the support of the only Presbyterian minister or meeting we had in Philadelphia. He used to visit me sometimes as a friend, and admonish me to attend his administrations, and I was now and then prevailed on to do so, once for five Sundays successively. Had he been in my opinion a good preacher, perhaps I might have continued, notwithstanding the occasion I had for the Sunday's leisure in my course of study; but his discourses were chiefly either polemic arguments, or explications of the peculiar doctrines of our sect, and were all to me very dry, uninteresting, and unedifying, since not a single moral principle was inculcated or enforced, their aim seeming to be rather to make us Presbyterians than good citizens.

. . .

It was about this time I conceived the bold and arduous project of arriving at moral perfection. I wished to live without committing any fault at any time; I would conquer all that either natural inclination, custom, or company might lead me into. As I knew, or thought I knew, what was right and wrong, I did not see why I might not always do the one and avoid the other. But I soon found I had undertaken a task of more difficulty than I had imagined. While my care was employed in guarding against one fault, I was often surprised by another; habit took the advantage of inattention; inclination was sometimes too strong for reason. I concluded, at length, that the mere speculative conviction that it was our interest to be completely virtuous was not sufficient to prevent our slipping; and that the contrary habits must be broken, and good ones acquired and established, before we can have any dependence on a steady, uniform rectitude of conduct. For this purpose I therefore contrived the following method.

In the various enumerations of the moral virtues I had met with in my reading, I found the catalogue more or less numerous, as different writers included more or fewer ideas under the same name. Temperance, for example, was by some confined to eating and drinking, while by others it was extended to mean the moderating every other pleasure, appetite, inclination, or passion, bodily or mental, even to our avarice and ambition. I proposed to myself, for the sake of clearness, to use rather more names, with fewer ideas annexed to each, than a few names with more ideas; and I included under thirteen names of virtues all that at that time occurred to me as necessary or desirable, and annexed to each a short precept, which fully expressed the extent I gave to its meaning.

These names of virtues, with their precepts, were:

1. TEMPERANCE. Eat not to dullness; drink not to elevation.

2. SILENCE. Speak not but what may benefit others or yourself; avoid trifling conversation.

3. ORDER. Let all your things have their places; let each part of your business have its time.

4. RESOLUTION. Resolve to perform what you ought; perform without fail what you resolve.

5. FRUGALITY. Make no expense but to do good to others or yourself; *i.e.,* waste nothing.

6. INDUSTRY. Lose no time; be always employed in something useful; cut off all unnecessary actions.

7. SINCERITY. Use no hurtful deceit; think innocently and justly, and, if you speak, speak accordingly.

8. JUSTICE. Wrong none by doing injuries, or omitting the benefits that are your duty.

9. MODERATION. Avoid extremes; forbear resenting injuries so much as you think they deserve.

10. CLEANLINESS. Tolerate no uncleanliness in body, clothes, or habitation.

11. TRANQUILLITY. Be not disturbed at trifles, or at accidents common or unavoidable.

12. CHASTITY. Rarely use venery but for health or offspring, never to dullness, weakness, or the injury of your own or another's peace or reputation.

13. HUMILITY. Imitate Jesus and Socrates.

My intention being to acquire the *habitude* of all these virtues, I judged it would be well not to distract my attention by attemping the whole at once, but to fix it on one of them at a time; and, when I should be master of that, then to proceed to another, and so on, till I should have gone through the thirteen; and, as the previous acquisition of some might facilitate the acquisition of certain others, I arranged them with that view, as they stand above. *Temperance* first, as it tends to procure that coolness and clearness of head, which is so necessary where constant vigilance was to be kept up, and guard maintained against the unremitting attraction of ancient habits, and the force of perpetual temptations. This being acquired and established, *Silence* would be more easy; and my desire being to gain knowledge at the same time that I improved in virtue, and considering that in conversation it was obtained rather by the use of the ears than of the tongue, and therefore wishing to break a habit I was getting into of prattling, punning, and joking, which only made me acceptable to trifling company, I gave *Silence* the second place. This and the next, *Order,* I expected would allow me more time for attending to my project and my studies. *Resolution,* once become habitual, would keep me firm in my endeavors to obtain all the subsequent virtues; *Frugality* and *Industry* freeing me from my remaining debt, and producing affluence and independence, would make more easy the practice of *Sincerity* and *Justice,* etc., etc. Conceiving then, that, agreeably to the advice of Pythagoras in his Golden Verses, daily examination would be necessary, I contrived the following method for conducting that examination.

I made a little book, in which I allotted a page for each of the virtues. I ruled each page with red ink, so as to have seven columns, one for each day of the week, marking each column with a letter for the day. I crossed these columns with thirteen red lines, marking the beginning of each line with the first letter of one of the virtues, on which line, and in its proper column, I might mark, by a little black spot, every fault I found upon examination to have been committed respecting that virtue upon that day.

I determined to give a week's strict attention to each of the virtues successively. Thus, in the first week, my great guard was to avoid every the least offence against *Temperance,* leaving the other virtues to their ordinary chance, only marking every evening the faults of the day. Thus, if in the first week I could keep my first line, marked T, clear of spots, I supposed the habit of that virtue so much strengthened, and its opposite weakened, that I might venture extending my attention to include the next, and for the following week keep both lines clear of spots. Proceeding thus to the last, I could go through a course complete in thirteen weeks, and four courses in a year. And like him who, having a garden to weed, does not attempt to eradicate all the bad herbs at once, which would exceed his reach and his strength, but works on one of the beds at a time, and, having accomplished the first, proceeds to a second, so I should have, I hoped, the encouraging pleasure

Form of the pages.

TEMPERANCE.						
EAT NOT TO DULLNESS; DRINK NOT TO ELEVATION.						
	S.	M.	T.	W.	T.	F.	S.
T.							
S.	*	*		*		*	
O.	* *	*	*		*	*	*
R.			*			*	
F.		*			*		
I.			*				
S.							
J.							
M.							
C.							
T.							
C.							
H.							

of seeing on my pages the progress I made in virtue, by clearing successively my lines of their spots, till in the end, by a number of courses, I should be happy in viewing a clean book, after a thirteen weeks' daily examination.

• • •

The precept of *Order* requiring that *every part of my business should have its allotted time,* one page in my little book contained the following scheme of employment for the twenty-four hours of a natural day.

I entered upon the execution of this plan for self-examination, and continued it with occasional intermissions for

THE MORNING. *Question.* What good shall I do this day?	5 6 7	Rise, wash and address *Powerful Goodness!* Contrive day's business, and take the resolution of the day; prosecute the present study, and breakfast.
	8 9 10 11	Work.
NOON.	12 1	Read, or overlook my accounts, and dine.
	2 3 4 5	Work.
Question. What good have I done to-day?	6 7 8 9	Put things in their places. Supper. Music or diversion, or conversation. Examination of the day.
NIGHT.	10 11 12 1 2 3 4	Sleep.

some time. I was surprised to find myself so much fuller of faults than I had imagined; but I had the satisfaction of seeing them diminish. To avoid the trouble of renewing now and then my little book, which, by scraping out the marks on the paper of old faults to make room for new ones in a new course, became full of holes, I transferred my tables and precepts to the ivory leaves of a memorandum book, on which the lines were drawn with red ink, that made a durable stain, and on those lines I marked my faults with a black-lead pencil, which marks I could easily wipe out with a wet sponge. After a while I went through one course only in a year, and afterward only one in several years, till at length I omitted them entirely, being employed in voyages and business abroad, with a multiplicity of affairs that interfered; but I always carried my little book with me.

My scheme of ORDER gave me the most trouble; and I found that, though it might be practicable where a man's business was such as to leave him the disposition of his time, that of a journeyman printer, for instance, it was not possible to be exactly observed by a master, who must mix with the world, and often receive people of business at their own hours. *Order,* too, with regard to places for things, papers, etc., I found extremely difficult to acquire. I had not been early accustomed to it, and, having an exceeding good memory, I was not so sensible of the inconvenience attending want of method. This article, therefore, cost me so much painful attention, and my faults in it vexed me so much, and I made so little progress in amendment, and had such frequent relapses, that I was almost ready to give up the attempt and content myself with a faulty character in that respect, like the man who, in buying an ax of a smith, my neighbor, desired to have the whole of its surface as bright as the edge. The smith consented to grind it bright for him if he would turn the wheel; he turned, while the smith pressed the broad face of the ax hard and heavily on the stone, which made the turning of it very fatiguing. The man came every now and then from the wheel to see how the work went on, and at length would take his ax as it was, without farther grinding. "No," said the smith, "turn on, turn on; we shall have it bright by-and-by; as yet, it is only speckled." "Yes," says the man, "but I think I like a speckled ax best." And I believe this may have been the case with many, who having for want of some such means as I employed found the difficulty of obtaining good and breaking bad habits in other points of vice and virtue, have given up the struggle, and concluded that *"a speckled ax was best";* for something that pretended to be reason, was every now and then suggesting to me that such extreme nicety as I exacted of myself might be a kind of foppery in morals, which, if it were known, would make me ridiculous; that a perfect character might be attended with the inconvenience of being envied and hated; and that a benevolent man should allow a few faults in himself, to keep his friends in countenance.

In truth, I found myself incorrigible with respect to Order; and now I am grown old, and my memory bad, I feel very sensibly the want of it. But on the whole, though I never arrived at the perfection I had been so ambitious of obtaining, but fell far short of it, yet I was, by the endeavor, a better and a happier man than I otherwise should have been if I had not attempted it; as those who aim at perfect writing by imitating the engraved copies, though they never reach the wished-for excellence of those copies, their hand is mended by the endeavor, and is tolerable while it continues fair and legible.

It may be well my posterity should be informed that to this little artifice, with the blessing of God, their ancestor owed the constant felicity of his life, down to his 79th year, in which this is written. What reverses may attend the remainder is in the hand of Providence; but if they arrive the reflection on past happiness enjoyed ought to help his bearing them with more resignation. To Temperance he ascribes his long-continued health and what is still left to him of a good constitution; to Industry and Frugality, the early easiness of his circumstances and acquisition of his fortune, with all that knowledge that enabled him to be a useful citizen, and obtained for him some degree of reputation among the learned; to Sincerity and Justice, the confidence of his country, and the honorable employs it conferred upon him; and to the joint influence of the whole mass of the virtues, even in the imperfect state he was able to acquire them, all that evenness of temper, and that cheerfulness in conversation, which makes his company still sought for, and agreeable even to his younger acquaintance. I hope, therefore, that some of my descendants may follow the example and reap the benefit.

. . .

My list of virtues contained at first but twelve; but a Quaker friend having kindly informed me that I was generally thought proud; that my pride showed itself frequently in conversation; that I was not content with being in the right when discussing any point, but was overbearing, and rather insolent, of which he convinced me by mentioning several instances; I determined endeavoring to cure myself, if I could, of this vice or folly among the rest, and I added *Humility* to my list, giving an extensive meaning to the word.

I cannot boast of much success in acquiring the *reality* of this virtue, but I had a good deal with regard to the *appearance* of it. I made it a rule to forbear all direct contradiction to the sentiments of others, and all positive assertion of my own. I even forbid myself, agreeably to the old laws of our Junto, the use of every word or expression in the language that imported a fixed opinion, such as *certainly, undoubtedly,* etc., and I adopted, instead of them, *I conceive, I apprehend,* or *I imagine* a thing to be so or so; or it *so appears to me at present.* When another asserted something that I thought an error, I denied myself the pleasure of contradicting him abruptly, and of showing immediately some absurdity in his proposition; and in answering I began by observing that in certain cases or circumstance his opinion would be right, but in the present case there *appeared* or *seemed* to me some difference, etc. I soon found the advantage of this change in my manner; the conversations I engaged in went on more pleasantly. The modest way in which I proposed my opinions procured them a readier reception and less contradiction; I had less mortification when I was found to be in the wrong, and I more easily prevailed with others to give up their mistakes and join with me when I happened to be in the right.

And this mode, which I at first put on with some violence to natural inclination, became at length so easy, and so habitual to me, that perhaps for these fifty years past no one has ever heard a dogmatical expression escape me. And to this habit (after my character of integrity) I think it principally owing that I had early so much weight with my fellow-citizens when I proposed new institutions, or alterations in the old, and so much influence in public councils when I became a member; for I was but a bad speaker, never eloquent, subject to much hesitation in my choice of words, hardly correct in language, and yet I generally carried my points.

In reality, there is, perhaps, no one of our natural passions so hard to subdue as *pride.* Disguise it, struggle with it, beat it down, stifle it, mortify it as much as one pleases, it is still alive, and will every now and then peep out and and show itself; you will see it, perhaps, often in this history; for, even if I could conceive that I had completely overcome it, I should probably be proud of my humility.

. . .

In 1732 I first published my almanac, under the name of *Richard Saunders*; it was continued by me about twenty-five years, commonly called *Poor Richard's Almanack*. I endeavored to make it both entertaining and useful, and it accordingly came to be in such demand that I reaped considerable profit from it, vending annually near ten thousand. And observing that it was generally read, scarce any neighborhood in the province being without it, I considered it as a proper vehicle for conveying instruction among the common people, who bought scarcely any other books; I therefore filled all the little spaces that occurred between the remarkable days in the calendar with proverbial sentences, chiefly such as inculcated industry and frugality, as the means of procuring wealth, and thereby securing virtue; it being more difficult for a man in want, to act always honestly, as, to use here one of those proverbs, *it is hard for an empty sack to stand upright.*

These proverbs, which contained the wisdom of many ages and nations, I assembled and formed into a connected discourse prefixed to the Almanac of 1757, as the harangue of a wise old man to the people attending an auction. The bringing all these scattered counsels thus into a focus enabled them to make greater impression. The piece, being universally approved, was copied in all the newspapers of the continent; reprinted in Britain on a broadside, to be stuck up in houses; two translations were made of it in French, and great numbers bought by the clergy and gentry, to distribute gratis among their poor parishioners and tenants. In Pennsylvania, as it discouraged useless expense in foreign superfluities, some thought it had its share of influence in producing that growing plenty of money which was observable for several years after its publication.

. . .

In 1739 arrived among us from Ireland the Reverend Mr. Whitefield, who had made himself remarkable there as an itinerant preacher. He was at first permitted to preach in some of our churches; but the clergy taking a dislike to him soon refused him their pulpits, and he was obliged to preach in the fields. The multitudes of all sects and denominations that attended his sermons were enormous, and it was matter of speculation to me, who was one of the number, to observe the extraordinary influence of his oratory on his hearers, and who much they admired and respected him, notwithstanding his common abuse of them, by assuring them they were naturally *half beasts and half devils.* It was wonderful to see the change soon made in the manners of our inhabitants. From being thoughtless or indifferent about religion, it seemed as if all the world were growing religious, so that one could not walk through the town in an evening without hearing psalms sung in different families of every street.

. . .

Mr. Whitefield, in leaving us, went preaching all the way through the colonies to Georgia. The settlement of that province had lately been begun, but, instead of being made with hardy, industrious husbandmen, accustomed to labor, the only people fit for such an enterprise, it was with families of broken shop-keepers and other insolvent debtors, many of indolent and idle habits, taken out of the jails, who, being set down in the woods, unqualified for clearing land, and unable to endure the hardships of a new settlement, perished in numbers, leaving many helpless children unprovided for. The sight of their miserable situation inspired the benevolent heart of Mr. Whitefield with the idea of building an Orphan House there, in which they might be supported and educated. Returning northward, he preached up this charity, and made large collections, for his eloquence had a wonderful power over the hearts and purses of his hearers, of which I myself was an instance.

I did not disapprove of the design, but, as Georgia was then destitute of materials and workmen, and it was proposed to send them from Philadelphia at a great expense, I thought it would have been better to have built the house here, and brought the children to it. This I advised; but he was resolute in his first project, rejected my counsel, and I therefore refused to contribute. I happened soon after to attend one of his sermons, in the course of which I perceived he intended to finish with a collection, and I silently resolved he should get nothing from me. I had in my pocket a handful of copper money, three or four silver dollars, and five pistoles in gold. As he proceeded I began to soften, and concluded to give the coppers. Another stroke of his oratory made me ashamed of that, and determined me to give the silver; and he finished so admirably, that I emptied my pocket wholly into the collector's dish, gold and all.

· · ·

In 1746, being at Boston, I met there with a Dr. Spence, who was lately arrived from Scotland and showed me some electric experiments. They were imperfectly performed, as he was not very expert; but, being on a subject quite new to me, they equally surprised and pleased me. Soon after my return to Philadelphia, our library company received from Mr. P. Collinson, Fellow of the Royal Society of London, a present of a glass tube, with some account of the use of it in making such experiments. I eagerly seized the opportunity of repeating what I had seen at Boston; and by much practice, acquired great readiness in performing those, also, which we had an account of from England, adding a number of new ones. I say much practice, for my house was continually full for some time with people who came to see these new wonders.

· · ·

Obliged as we were to Mr. Collinson for his present of the tube, etc., I thought it right he should be informed of our success in using it, and wrote him several letters containing accounts of our experiments. He got them read in the Royal Society, where they were not at first thought worth so much notice as to be printed in their *Transactions*. One paper, which I wrote for Mr. Kinnersley on the sameness of lightning with electricity, I sent to Dr. Mitchel, an acquaintance of mine, and one of the members also of that society, who wrote me word that it had been read, but was laughed at by the connoisseurs. The papers, however, being shown to Dr. Fothergill, he thought them of too much value to be stifled, and advised the printing of them. Mr. Collinson then gave them to Cave for publication in his *Gentleman's Magazine*; but he chose to print them separately in a pamphlet, and Dr. Fothergill wrote the preface. Cave, it seems, judged rightly for his profit, for by the additions that arrived afterward they swelled to a quarto volume, which has had five editions, and cost him nothing for copy-money.

It was, however, some time before those papers were much taken notice of in England. A copy of them happening to fall into the hands of the Count de Buffon, a philosopher deservedly of great reputation in France, and, indeed, all over Europe, he prevailed with M. Dalibard to translate them into French, and they were printed at Paris. The publication offended the Abbé Nollet, preceptor in natural philosophy to the royal family, and an able experimenter, who had formed and published a theory of electricity, which then had the general vogue. He could not at first believe that such a work came from America, and said it must have been fabricated by his enemies at Paris to decry his system. Afterwards, having been assured that there really existed such a person as Franklin at Philadelphia, which he had doubted, he wrote and published a volume of letters, chiefly addressed to me, defending his theory, and denying the verity of my experiments, and of the positions deduced from them.

I once purposed answering the Abbé, and actually began the answer; but, on consideration that my writings contained a description of experiments which any one might repeat and verify, and if not to be verified, could not be defended; or of observations offered as conjectures, and not delivered dogmatically, therefore not laying me under any obligation to defend them; and reflecting that a dispute between two persons, writing in different languages, might be lengthened greatly by mistranslations, and thence misconceptions of one another's meaning, much of one of the Abbé's letters being founded on an error in the translation, I concluded to let my papers shift for themselves, believing it was better to spend what time I could spare from public business in making new experiments than in disputing about those already made. I therefore never answered M. Nollet, and the event gave me no cause to repent my silence; for my friend M. le Roy, of the Royal Academy of Sciences, took up my cause and refuted him; my book was translated into the Italian, German, and Latin languages; and the doctrine it contained was by degrees universally adopted by the philosophers of Europe, in preference to that of the Abbé; so that he lived to see himself the last of his sect, except Monsieur B——, of Paris, his *élève* and immediate disciple.

What gave my book the more sudden and general celebrity was the success of one of its proposed experiments, made by Messrs. Dalibard and De Lor at Marly, for drawing lightning from the clouds. This engaged the public attention everywhere. M. de Lor, who had an apparatus for experimental philosophy, and lectured in that branch of science, undertook to repeat what he called the Philadelphia Experiments, and after they were performed before the king and court, all the curious of Paris flocked to see them. I will not swell this narrative with an account of that capital experiment, nor of the infinite pleasure I received in the success of a similar one I made soon after with a kite at Philadelphia, as both are to be found in the histories of electricity.

Dr. Wright, an English physician, when at Paris wrote to a friend who was of the Royal Society an account of the high esteem my experiments were in among the learned abroad, and of their wonder that my writings had been so little noticed in England. The society, on this, resumed the consideration of the letters that had been read to them; and the celebrated Dr. Watson drew up a summary account of them, and of all I had afterwards sent to England on the subject, which he accompanied with some praise of the writer. This summary was then printed in their *Transaction*; and some members of the society in London, particularly the very ingenious Mr. Canton, having verified the experiment of procuring lightning from the clouds by a pointed rod, and acquainting them with the success, they soon made me more than amends for the slight with which they had before treated me. Without my having made any application for that honor, they chose me a member, and voted that I should be excused the customary payments, which would have amounted to twenty-five guineas; and ever since have given me their *Transactions* gratis. They also presented me with the gold medal of Sir Godfrey Copley for the year 1753, the delivery of which was accompanied by a very handsome speech of the president, Lord Macclesfield, wherein I was highly honored.

w. 1771–1788
p. 1791–1868

An Edict by the King of Prussia

Dantzick, Sept. 5 [1773]

We have long wondered here at the supineness of the English nation, under the Prussian impositions upon its trade entering our port. We did not, till lately, know the claims, ancient and modern, that hang over that nation, and therefore could not suspect that it might submit to those impositions from a sense of duty, or from principles of equity. The following Edict, just made public, may, if serious, throw some light upon this matter:

"FREDERICK, by the grace of God, King of Prussia, &c. &c. &c. to all present and to come, Health. The peace now enjoyed throughout our dominions, having afforded us leisure to apply ourselves to the regulation of commerce, the improvement of our finances, and at the same time the easing our domestic subjects in their taxes: For these causes and other good considerations us thereunto moving, we hereby make known, that, after having deliberated these affairs in our council, present our dear brothers, and other great officers of the state, members of the same, we, of our certain knowledge, full power, and authority royal, have made and issued this present Edict, viz.

"Whereas it is well known to all the world, that the first German settlements made in the island of Britain were by colonies of people, subjects to our renowned ducal ancestors, and drawn from their dominions, under the conduct of Hengist, Horsa, Hella, Uffa, Cerdicus, Ida, and others; and that the said colonies have flourished under the protection of our august house, for ages past; have never been emancipated therefrom; and yet have hitherto yielded little profit to the same: And whereas we ourself have in the last war fought for and defended the said colonies, against the power of France, and thereby enabled them to make conquests from the said power in America; for which we have not yet received adequate compensation: And whereas it is just and expedient that a revenue should be raised from the said colonies in Britain, towards our indemnification; and that those who are descendants of our ancient subjects, and thence still owe us due obedience, should contribute to the replenishing of our royal coffers, as they must have done, had their ancestors remained in the territories now to us appertaining: We do therefore hereby ordain and command, that, from and after the date of these presents, there shall be levied, and paid to our officers of the customs, on all goods, wares, and merchandizes, and on all grain and other produce of the earth, exported from the said island of Britain, and on all goods of whatever kind imported into the same, a duty of four and a half per cent. ad valorem, for the use of us and our successors. And that the said duty may more effectually be collected, we do hereby ordain, that all ships or vessels bound from Great-Britain to any other part of the world, or from any other part of the world to Great-Britain, shall in their respective voyages touch at our port of Koningsberg, there to be unladen, searched, and charged with the said duties.

"And whereas there hath been from time to time discovered in the said island of Great-Britain, by our colonists there, many mines or beds of iron stone; and sundry subjects of our ancient dominion, skilful in converting the said stone into metal, have in times past transported themselves thither, carrying with them and communicating that art; and the inhabitants of the said island, presuming that they had a natural right to make the best use they could of the natural productions of their country, for their own benefit, have not only built furnaces for smelting the said stone into iron, but have erected plating forges, slitting mills, and steel furnaces, for the more convenient manufacturing of the same, thereby endangering a diminution of the said manufacture in our ancient dominion; we do therefore hereby farther ordain, that, from and after the date hereof, no mill or other engine for slitting or rolling of iron, or any plating forge to work with a tilt-hammer, or any furnace for making steel, shall be erected or continued in the said island of Great-Britain: And the Lord-Lieutenant of every county in the said island is hereby commanded, on information of any such erection within his county, to order and by force to cause the same to be abated and destroyed, as he shall answer the neglect thereof to us at his peril. But we are nevertheless graciously pleased to permit the inhabitants of the said island to transport their iron into Prussia, there to be manufactured, and to them returned, they paying our Prussian subjects for the workmanship, with all the costs of commission, freight, and risk, coming and returning, any thing herein contained to the contrary notwithstanding.

"We do not, however, think fit to extend this our indulgence to the article of wool meaning to encourage not only the manufacturing of woolen cloth, but also the raising of wool, in our ancient dominions; and to prevent both, as much as may be, in our said island, we do hereby absolutely forbid the transportation of wool from thence even to the mother-country, Prussia; And that those islanders may be farther and more effectually restrained in making any advantage of their own wool, in the way of manufacture, we command that none shall be carried out of one county into another, nor shall any worsted, bay, or woolen-yarn, cloth, says, bays, kerseys, serges, frizes, druggets, cloth-serges, shalloons, or any other drapery stuffs, or woolen manufactures whatsoever, made up or mixed with wool in any of the said countries, be carried into any other county, or be water-borne even across the smallest river or creek, on penalty of forfeiture of the same, together with the boats, carriages, horses, &c. that shall be employed in removing them. Nevertheless, our loving subjects there are hereby permitted (if they think proper) to use all their wool as manure, for the improvement of their lands.

"And whereas the art and mystery of making hats hath arrived at great perfection in Prussia; and the making of hats by our remoter subjects ought to be as much as possible restrained: And forasmuch as the islanders before mentioned, being in possession of wool, beaver and other furs, have presumptuously conceived they had a right to make some advantage thereof, by manufacturing the same into hats, to the prejudice of our domestic manufacture: We do therefore hereby strictly command and ordain, that no hats or felts whatsoever, dyed or undyed, finished or unfinished, shall be loaden or put into or upon any vessel, cart, carriage, or horse, to be transported or conveyed out of one county in the said island into another county, or to any other place whatsoever, by any person or persons whatsoever, on pain of forfeiting the same, with a penalty of five hundred pounds sterling for every offence. Nor shall any hat-maker, in any of the said counties, employ more than two apprentices, on penalty of five pounds sterling per month: we intending hereby that such hat-makers, being so restrained, both in the production and sale of their commodity, may find no advantage in continuing their business. But, lest the said islanders should suffer inconveniency by the want of hats, we are farther graciously pleased to permit them to send their beaver furs to Prussia; and we also permit hats made thereof to be exported from Prussia to Britain; the people thus favoured to pay all costs and charges of manufacturing, interest, commission to our merchants, insurance and freight going and returning, as in the case of iron.

"And lastly, being willing farther to favour our said colonies in Britain, we do hereby also ordain and command, that all the thieves, highway and street robbers, house-breakers, forgerers, murderers, s—d—tes, and villains of every denomination, who have forfeited their lives to the law in Prussia, but whom we, in our great clemency, do not think fit here to hang, shall be emptied out of our gaols into the said island of Great-Britain, for the better peopling of that country.

"We flatter ourselves, that these our royal regulations and commands will be thought just and reasonable by our much favoured colonists in England; the said regulations being copied from their own statutes, of 10 and 11 William III. c. 10, 5 Geo. II. c. 22, 23, Geo. II. c. 29, 4 Geo. I. c. 11, and from other equitable laws made by their parliaments; or from instructions given by their Princes; or from resolutions of both House, entered into for the good government of their *own colonies in Ireland and America.*

"And all persons in the said island are hereby cautioned not to oppose in any wise the execution of this our Edict, or any part thereof, such opposition being high treason; of which all who are suspected shall be transported in fetters from Britain to Prussia, there to be tried and executed according to the Prussian law.

"Such is our pleasure.
"Given at Potsdam, this twenty-fifth day of the month of August, one thousand seven hundred and seventy-three, and in the thirty-third year of our reign.

"By the King, in his Council.

"Rechtmaessig [legally], Sec."

Some take this Edict to be merely one of the King's *Jeux d'Esprit*: others suppose it serious, and that he means a quarrel with England; but all here think the assertion it concludes with, "that these regulations are copied from acts of the English parliament respecting their colonies," a very injurious one; it being impossible to believe, that a people distinguished for their love of liberty, a nation so wise, so liberal in its sentiments, so just and equitable towards its neighbours, should, from mean and injudicious views of petty immediate profit, treat its own children in a manner so arbitrary and tyrannical!

1773

The Ephemera

AN EMBLEM OF HUMAN LIFE

You may remember, my dear friend, that when we lately spent that happy day in the delightful garden and sweet society of the Moulin Joly, I stopped a little in one of our walks, and stayed some time behind the company. We had been shown numberless skeletons of a kind of little fly, called an ephemera, whose successive generations, we were told, were bred and expired within the day. I happened to see a living company of them on a leaf, who appeared to be engaged in conversation. You know I understand all the inferior animal tongues: my too great application to the study of them is the best excuse I can give for the little progress I have made in your charming language. I listened through curiosity to the discourse of these little creatures; but as they, in their national vivacity, spoke three or four together, I could make but little of their conversation. I found, however, by some broken expressions that I heard now and then, they were disputing warmly on the merit of two foreign musicians, one a *cousin* [gnat], the other a *moscheto* [mosquito]; in which dispute they spent their time, seemingly as regardless of the shortness of life as if they had been sure of living a month. Happy people! thought I, you live certainly under a wise, just, and mild government, since you have no public grievances to complain of, nor any subject of contention but the perfections and imperfections of foreign music. I turned my head from them to an old grey-headed one, who was single on another leaf, and talking to himself. Being amused with his soliloquy, I put it down in writing, in hopes it will likewise amuse her to whom I am so much indebted for the most pleasing of all amusements, her delicious company and heavenly harmony.

"It was," said he, "the opinion of learned philosophers of our race, who lived and flourished long before my time, that this vast world, the Moulin Joly, could not itself subsist more than eighteen hours; and I think there was some foundation for that opinion, since, by the apparent motion of the great luminary that gives life to all nature, and which in my time has evidently declined considerably towards the ocean at the end of our earth, it must then finish its course, be extinguished in the waters that surround us, and leave the world in cold and darkness, necessarily producing universal death and destruction. I have lived seven of those hours, a great age, being no less than four hundred and twenty minutes of time. How very few of us continue so long! I have seen generations born, flourish, and expire. My present friends are the children and grand-children of the friends of my youth, who are now, alas, no more! And I must soon follow them; for, by the course of nature, though still in health, I cannot expect to live above seven or eight minutes longer. What now avails all my toil and labor, in amassing honey-dew on this leaf, which I cannot live to enjoy! What the political struggles I have been engaged in, for the good of my compatriot inhabitants of this bush, or my philosophical studies for the benefit of our race in general! for, in politics, what can laws do without morals? Our present race of ephemeræ will in a course of minutes become corrupt, like those of other and older bushes, and consequently as wretched. And in philosophy how small our progress! Alas! art is long, and life is short! My friends would comfort me with the idea of a name, they say, I shall leave behind me; and they tell me I have lived long enough to nature and to glory. But what will fame be to an ephemera who no longer exists? And what will become of all history in the eighteenth hour, when the world itself, even the whole Moulin Joly, shall come to its end, and be buried in universal ruin?"

To me, after all my eager pursuits, no solid pleasures now remain, but the reflection of a long life spent in meaning well, the sensible conversation of a few good lady ephemeræ, and now and then a kind smile and a tune from the ever amiable *Brillante*.

B. FRANKLIN
1778

Letters

[*TO PETER COLLINSON*]

[*Philadelphia*] *Oct. 19, 1752*

SIR,

As frequent mention is made in public papers from *Europe* of the success of the *Philadelphia* experiment for drawing the electric fire from clouds by means of pointed rods of iron erected on high buildings, &c., it may be agreeable to the curious to be informed, that the same experiment has succeeded in *Philadelphia*, though made in a different and more easy manner, which is as follows:

Make a small cross of two light strips of cedar, the arms so long as to reach to the four corners of a large thin silk handkerchief when extended; tie the corners of the handkerchief to the extremities of the cross, so you have the body of a kite; which being properly accommodated with a tail, loop, and string, will rise in the air, like those made of paper; but this being of silk, is fitter to bear the wet and wind of a thunder-gust without tearing. To the top of the upright stick of the cross is to be fixed a very sharp-pointed wire, rising a foot or more above the wood. To the end of the twine, next the hand, is to be tied a silk ribbon, and where the silk and twine join, a key may be fastened. This kite is to be raised when a thunder-gust appears to be coming on, and the person who holds the string must stand within a door or window, or under some cover, so that the silk ribbon may not be wet; and care must be taken that the twine does not touch the frame of the door or window. As soon as any of the thunder-clouds come over the kite, the pointed wire will draw the electric fire from them, and the kite, with all the twine, will be electrified, and the loose filaments of the twine will stand out every way, and be attracted by an approaching finger. And when the rain has wet the kite and twine, so that it can conduct the electric fire freely, you will find it stream out plentifully from the key on the approach of your knuckle. At this key the phial may be charged; and from electric fire thus obtained, spirits may be kindled, and all the other electric experiments be performed, which are usually done by the help of a rubbed glass globe or tube, and thereby the sameness of the electric matter with that of lightning completely demonstrated.

B. FRANKLIN

[TO SIR JOSEPH BANKS]

Passy, 27 July, 1783

DEAR SIR,

I received your very kind letter by Dr. Blagden, and esteem myself much honoured by your friendly remembrance. I have been too much and too closely engaged in public affairs, since his being here, to enjoy all the benefit of his conversation you were so good as to intend me. I hope soon to have more leisure, and to spend a part of it in those studies, that are much more agreeable to me than political operations.

I join with you most cordially in rejoicing at the return of peace. I hope it will be lasting, and that mankind will at length, as they call themselves reasonable creatures, have reason and sense enough to settle their differences without cutting throats; for, in my opinion, *there never was a good war, or a bad peace.* What vast additions to the conveniences and comforts of living might mankind have acquired, if the money spent in wars had been employed in works of public utility! What an extension of agriculture, even to the tops of our mountains; what rivers rendered navigable, or joined by canals: what bridges, aqueducts, new roads, and other public works, edifices, and improvements, rendering England a complete paradise, might have been obtained by spending those millions in doing good, which in the last war have been spent in doing mischief; in bringing misery into thousands of families, and destroying the lives of so many thousands of working people, who might have performed the useful labor!

I am pleased with the late astronomical discoveries made by our society. Furnished as all Europe now is with academies of science, with nice instruments and the spirit of experiment, the progress of human knowledge will be rapid, and discoveries made, of which we have at present no conception. I begin to be almost sorry I was born so soon, since I cannot have the happiness of knowing what will be known 100 years hence.

I wish continued success to the labors of the royal society, and that you may long adorn their chair; being, with the highest esteem, dear Sir, &c.,

B. FRANKLIN

P.S. Dr. Blagden will acquaint you with the experiment of a vast globe sent up into the air, much talked of here, and which, if prosecuted, may furnish means of new knowledge.

[*TO EZRA STILES*]

Philadelphia, March 9, 1790

REVEREND AND DEAR SIR,

I received your kind letter of January 28, and am glad you have at length received the portrait of Governor Yale from his family, and deposited it in the College Library. He was a great and good man, and had the merit of doing infinite service to your country by his munificence to that institution. The Honor you propose doing me by placing mine in the same room with his, is much too great for my deserts; but you always had a partiality for me, and to that it must be ascribed. I am however too much obliged to Yale College, the first learned society that took notice of me and adorned me with its honors, to refuse a request that comes from it through so esteemed a friend. But I do not think any one of the portraits you mention, as in my possession, worthy of the place and company you propose to place it in. You have an excellent artist lately arrived. If he will undertake to make one for you, I shall cheerfully pay the expense; but he must not delay setting about it, or I may slip through his fingers, for I am now in my eighty-fifth year, and very infirm.

I send with this a very learned work, as it seems to me, on the ancient Samaritan coins, lately printed in Spain, and at least curious for the beauty of the impression. Please to accept it for your College Library. I have subscribed for the Encyclopædia now printing here, with the intention of presenting it to the College. I shall probably depart before the work is finished, but shall leave directions for its continuance to the end. With this you will receive some of the first numbers.

You desire to know something of my religion. It is the first time I have been questioned upon it. But I cannot take your curiosity amiss, and shall endeavor in a few words to gratify it. Here is my creed. I believe in one God, Creator of the Universe. That he governs it by his Providence. That he ought to be worshipped. That the most acceptable service we render to him is doing good to his other children. That the soul of man is immortal, and will be treated with justice in another life respecting its conduct in this. These I take to be the fundamental principles of all sound religion, and I regard them as you do in whatever sect I meet with them.

As to Jesus of Nazareth, my opinion of whom you particularly desire, I think the system of morals and his religion, as he left them to us, the best the world ever saw or is likely to see; but I apprehend it has received various corrupting changes, and I have, with most of the present dissenters in England, some doubts as to his divinity; though it is a question I do not dogmatize upon, having never studied it, and think it needless to busy myself with it now, when I expect soon an opportunity of knowing the truth with less trouble. I see no harm, however, in its being believed, if that belief has the good consequence, as probably it has, of making his doctrine more respected and better observed; especially as I do not perceive, that the Supreme takes it amiss, by distinguishing the unbelievers in his government of the world with any peculiar marks of his displeasure.

I shall only add, respecting myself, that, having experienced the goodness of that Being in conducting me prosperously through a long life, I have no doubt of its continuance in the next, though without the smallest conceit of meriting such goodness. My sentiments on this head you will see in the copy of an old letter enclosed, which I wrote in answer to one from a zealous religionist, whom I had relieved in a paralytic case by electricity, and who, being afraid I should grow proud upon it, sent me his serious though rather impertinent caution. I send you also the copy of another letter, which will show something of my disposition relating to religion. With great and sincere esteem and affection, I am, Your obliged old friend and most obedient humble servant

B. FRANKLIN

P.S. Had not your College some present of books from the King of France? Please to let me know, if you had an expectation given you of more, and the nature of that expectation? I have a reason for the enquiry.

I confide, that you will not expose me to criticism and censure by publishing any part of this communication to you. I have ever let others enjoy their religious sentiments, without reflecting on them for those that appeared to me unsupportable and even absurd. All sects here, and we have a great variety, have experienced my good will in assisting them with subscriptions for building their new places of worship; and, as I have never opposed any of their doctrines, I hope to go out of the world in peace with them all.

Information for Those Who Would Remove to America

Many persons in Europe, having directly or by letters, expressed to the writer of this, who is well acquainted with North America, their desire of transporting and establishing themselves in that country; but who appear to have formed, thro' ignorance, mistaken ideas and expectations of what is to be obtained there; he thinks it may be useful, and prevent inconvenient, expensive, and fruitless removals and voyages of improper persons, if he gives some clearer and truer notions of that part of the world, than appear to have hitherto prevailed.

He finds it is imagined by numbers, that the inhabitants of North America are rich, capable of rewarding, and disposed to reward, all sorts of ingenuity; that they are at the same time ignorant of all the sciences, and, consequently, that strangers, possessing talents in the belles-lettres, fine arts, &c., must be highly esteemed, and so well paid, as to become easily rich themselves; that there are also abundance of profitable offices to be disposed of, which the natives are not qualified to fill; and that, having few persons of family among them, strangers of birth must be greatly respected, and of course easily obtain the best of those offices, which will make all their fortunes; that the governments too, to encourage emigrations from Europe, not only pay the expense of personal transportation, but give lands gratis to strangers, with Negroes to work for them, utensils of husbandry and stocks of cattle. These are all wild imaginations; and those who go to America with expectations founded upon them will surely find themselves disappointed.

The truth is, that though there are in that country few people so miserable as the poor of Europe, there are also very few that in Europe would be called rich; it is rather a general happy mediocrity that prevails. There are few great proprietors of the soil, and few tenants; most people cultivate their own lands, or follow some handicraft or merchandise; very few rich enough to live idly upon their rents or incomes, or to pay the high prices given in Europe for paintings, statues, architecture, and the other works of art, that are more curious than useful. Hence the natural geniuses, that have arisen in America with such talents, have uniformly quitted that country for Europe, where they can be more suitably rewarded. It is true, that letters and mathematical knowledge are in esteem there, but they are at the same time more common than is apprehended; there being already existing nine colleges or universities, viz. four in New England, and one in each of the provinces of New York, New Jersey, Pennsylvania, Maryland, and Virginia, all furnished with learned professors; besides a number of smaller academies; these educate many of their youth in the languages, and those sciences that qualify men for the professions of Divinity, Law, or Physick. Strangers indeed are by no means excluded from exercising those professions; and the quick increase of inhabitants everywhere gives them a chance of employ, which they have in common with the natives. Of civil offices, or employments, there are few; no superfluous ones, as in Europe; and it is a rule established in some of the states, that no office should be so profitable as to make it desirable. The 36th Article of the Constitution of Pennsylvania, runs expressly in these words; "As every freeman, to preserve his independence, (if he has not a sufficient estate) ought to have some profession, calling, trade, or farm, whereby he may honestly subsist, there can be no necessity for, nor use in, establishing offices of profit; the usual effects of which are dependance and servility, unbecoming freemen, in the possessors and expectants; faction, contention, corruption, and disorder among the people. Wherefore, whenever an office, thro' increase of fees or otherwise, becomes so profitable, as to occasion many to apply for it, the profits ought to be lessened by the Legislature."

These ideas prevailing more or less in all the United States, it cannot be worth any man's while, who has a means of living at home, to expatriate himself, in hopes of obtaining a profitable civil office in America; and, as to military offices, they are at an end with the war, the armies being disbanded. Much less is it advisable for a person to go thither, who has no other quality to recommend him but his birth. In Europe it has indeed its value; but it is a commodity that cannot be carried to a worse market than that of America, where people do not inquire concerning a stranger, *What is he?* but, *What can he do?* If he has any useful art, he is welcome; and if he exercises it, and behaves well, he will be respected by all that know him; but a mere man of quality, who, on that account, wants to live upon the public, by some office or salary, will be despised and disregarded. The husbandman is in honor there, and even the mechanic, because their employments are useful. The people have a saying, that God Almighty is himself a mechanic, the greatest in the Universe; and he is respected and admired more for the variety, ingenuity, and utility of his handyworks, than for the antiquity of his family. They are pleased with the observation of a Negro, and frequently mention it, that *Boccarorra* (meaning the white men) *make de black man workee, make de horse workee, make de ox workee, make ebery ting workee; only de hog. He, de hog, no workee; he eat, he drink, he walk about, he go to sleep when he please, he libb like a gentleman.* According to these opinions of the Americans, one of them would think himself more obliged to a genealogist, who could prove for him that his ancestors and relations for ten generations had been ploughmen, smiths, carpenters, turners, weavers, tanners, or even shoemakers, and consequently that they were useful members of society; than if he could only prove that they were gentlemen, doing nothing of value, but living idly on the labour of others, mere *fruges consumere nati* [born merely to eat up the corn], and otherwise *good for nothing,* till by their death their estates, like the carcass of the Negro's gentleman-hog, come to be *cut up.*

With regard to encouragements for strangers from government, they are really only what are derived from good laws and liberty. Strangers are welcome, because there is room enough for them all, and therefore the old inhabitants are not jealous of them; the laws protect them sufficiently, so that they have no need of the patronage of great men; and every one will enjoy securely the profits of his industry. But, if he does not bring a fortune with him, he must work and be industrious to live. One or two years' residence gives him all the rights of a citizen; but the government does not at present, whatever it may have done in former times, hire people to become settlers, by paying their passages, giving land, Negroes, utensils, stock, or any other kind of emolument whatsoever. In short, America is the land of labour, and by no means what the English call *Lubberland,* and the French *Pays de Cocagne,* where the streets are said to be paved with half-peck loaves, the houses tiled with pancakes, and where the fowls fly about ready roasted, crying, *Come eat me!*

Who then are the kind of persons to whom an emigration to America may be advantageous? And what are the advantages they may reasonably expect?

Land being cheap in that country, from the vast forests still void of inhabitants, and not likely to be occupied in an age to come, insomuch that the propriety of an hundred acres of fertile soil full of wood may be obtained near the frontiers, in many places, for eight or ten guineas, hearty young labouring men, who understand the husbandry of corn and cattle, which is nearly the same in that country as in Europe, may easily establish themselves there. A little money saved of the good wages they receive there, while they work for others, enables them to buy the land and begin their plantation, in which they are assisted by the good-will of their neighbours, and some credit. Multitudes of poor people from England, Ireland, Scotland, and Germany, have by this means in a few years become wealthy farmers, who, in their own countries, where all the lands are fully occupied, and the wages of labour low, could never have emerged from the poor condition wherein they were born.

From the salubrity of the air, the healthiness of the climate, the plenty of good provisions, and the encouragement to early marriages by the certainty of subsistence in cultivating the earth, the increase of inhabitants by natural generation is very rapid in America, and becomes still more so by the accession of strangers; hence there is a continual demand for more artisans of all the necessary and useful kinds, to supply those cultivators of the earth with houses, and with furniture and utensils of the grosser sorts, which cannot so well be brought from Europe. Tolerably good workmen in any of those mechanic arts are sure to find employ, and to be well paid for their work, there being no restraints preventing strangers from exercising any art they understand, nor any permission necessary. If they are poor, they begin first as servants or journeymen; and if they are sober, industrious, and frugal, they soon become masters, establish themselves in business, marry, raise families, and become respectable citizens.

Also, persons of moderate fortunes and capitals, who, having a number of children to provide for, are desirous of bringing them up to industry, and to secure estates for their posterity, have opportunities of doing it in America, which Europe does not afford. There they may be taught and practice profitable mechanic arts, without incurring disgrace on that account, but on the contrary acquiring respect by such abilities. There small capitals laid out in lands, which daily become more valuable by the increase of people, afford a solid prospect of ample fortunes thereafter for those children. The writer of this has known several instances of large tracts of land, bought, on what was then the frontier of Pennsylvania, for ten pounds per hundred acres, which after 20 years, when the settlements had been extended far beyond them, sold readily, without any improvement made upon them, for three pounds per acre. The acre in America is the same with the English acre, or the acre of Normandy.

Those, who desire to understand the state of government

in America, would do well to read the Constitutions of the several States, and the Articles of Confederation that bind the whole together for general purposes, under the direction of one assembly, called the Congress. These Constitutions have been printed, by order of Congress, in America; two editions of them have also been printed in London; and a good translation of them into French has lately been published at Paris.

Several of the princes of Europe having of late years, from an opinion of advantage to arise by producing all commodities and manufactures within their own dominions, so as to diminish or render useless their importations, have endeavoured to entice workmen from other countries by high salaries, privileges, &c. Many persons, pretending to be skilled in various great manufactures, imagining that America must be in want of them, and that the Congress would probably be disposed to imitate the princes above mentioned, have proposed to go over, on condition of having their passages paid, lands given, salaries appointed, exclusive privileges for terms of years, &c. Such persons, on reading the Articles of Confederation, will find, that the Congress have no power committed to them, or money put into their hands, for such purposes; and that if any such encouragement is given, it must be by the government of some separate state. This, however, has rarely been done in America; and, when it has been done, it has rarely succeeded, so as to establish a manufacture, which the country was not yet so ripe for as to encourage private persons to set it up; labour being generally too dear there, and hands difficult to be kept together, every one desiring to be a master, and the cheapness of lands inclining many to leave trades for agriculture. Some indeed have met with success, and are carried on to advantage; but they are generally such as require only a few hands, or wherein great part of the work is performed by machines. Things that are bulky, and of so small value as not well to bear the expense of freight, may often be made cheaper in the country than they can be imported; and the manufacture of such things will be profitable wherever there is a sufficient demand. The farmers in America produce indeed a good deal of wool and flax; and none is exported, it is all worked up; but it is in the way of domestic manufacture, for the use of the family. The buy-

ing up quantities of wool and flax, with the design to employ spinners, weavers, &c., and form great establishments,
producing quantities of linen and woollen goods for sale,
has been several times attempted in different provinces;
but those projects have generally failed, goods of equal
value being imported cheaper. And when the governments have been solicited to support such schemes by encouragements, in money, or by imposing duties on impor-
tation of such goods, it has been generally refused, on
this principle, that, if the country is ripe for the manufacture, it may be carried on by private persons to advantage;
and if not, it is a folly to think of forcing nature. Great
establishments of manufacture require great numbers of
poor to do the work for small wages; these poor are to be
found in Europe, but will not be found in America, till
the lands are all taken up and cultivated, and the excess of
people, who cannot get land, want employment. The manufacture of silk, they say, is natural in France, as that of
cloth in England, because each country produces in plenty
the first material; but if England will have a manufacture
of silk as well as that of cloth, and France one of cloth as
well as that of silk, these unnatural operations must be supported by mutual prohibitions, or high duties on the im-
portation of each other's goods; by which means the workmen are enabled to tax the home consumer by greater
prices, while the higher wages they receive makes them
neither happier nor richer, since they only drink more
and work less. Therefore the governments in America do
nothing to encourage such projects. The people, by this
means, are not imposed on, either by the merchant or
mechanic. If the merchant demands too much profit on
imported shoes, they buy of the shoemaker; and if he
asks too high a price, they take them of the merchant; thus
the two professions are checks on each other. The shoemaker, however, has, on the whole, a considerable profit
upon his labour in America, beyond what he had in Europe, as he can add to his price a sum nearly equal to all
the expenses of freight and commission, risk or insurance,
&c., necessarily charged by the merchant. And the case is
the same with the workmen in every other mechanic art.
Hence it is, that artisans generally live better and more
easily in America than in Europe; and such as are good
economists make a comfortable provision for age, and for

their children. Such may, therefore, remove with advantage to America.

In the long-settled countries of Europe, all arts, trades, professions, farms, &c., are so full, that it is difficult for a poor man, who has children, to place them where they may gain, or learn to gain, a decent livelihood. The artisans, who fear creating future rivals in business, refuse to take apprentices, but upon conditions of money, maintenance, or the like, which the parents are unable to comply with. Hence the youth are dragged up in ignorance of every gainful art, and obliged to become soldiers, or servants, or thieves, for a subsistence. In America, the rapid increase of inhabitants takes away that fear of rivalship, and artisans willingly receive apprentices from the hope of profit by their labour, during the remainder of the time stipulated, after they shall be instructed. Hence it is easy for poor families to get their children instructed; for the artisans are so desirous of apprentices, that many of them will even give money to the parents, to have boys from ten to fifteen years of age bound apprentices to them till the age of twenty-one; and many poor parents have, by that means, on their arrival in the country, raised money enough to buy land sufficient to establish themselves, and to subsist the rest of their family by agriculture. These contracts for apprentices are made before a magistrate, who regulates the agreement according to reason and justice, and, having in view the formation of a future useful citizen, obliges the master to engage by a written indenture, not only that, during the time of service stipulated, the apprentice shall be duly provided with meat, drink, apparel, washing, and lodging, and, at its expiration, with a complete new suit of clothes, but also that he shall be taught to read, write, and cast accounts; and that he shall be well instructed in the art or profession of his master, or some other, by which he may afterwards gain a livelihood, and be able in his turn to raise a family. A copy of this indenture is given to the apprentice or his friends, and the magistrate keeps a record of it, to which recourse may be had, in case of failure by the master in any point of performance. This desire among the masters, to have more hands employed in working for them, induces them to pay the passages of young persons, of both sexes, who, on their arrival, agree to serve them one, two, three, or four years; those, who have already learnt a trade, agreeing for a shorter term, in proportion to their skill, and the consequent immediate value of their service; and those, who have none, agreeing for a longer term, in consideration of being taught an art their poverty would not permit them to acquire in their own country.

The almost general mediocrity of fortune that prevails in America obliging its people to follow some business for subsistence, those vices, that arise usually from idleness, are in a great measure prevented. Industry and constant employment are great preservatives of the morals and virtue of a nation. Hence bad examples to youth are more rare in America, which must be a comfortable consideration to parents. To this may be truly added, that serious religion, under its various denominations, is not only tolerated, but respected and practiced. Atheism is unknown there; infidelity rare and secret; so that persons may live to a great age in that country, without having their piety shocked by meeting with either an atheist or an infidel. And the Divine Being seems to have manifested His approbation of the mutual forbearance and kindness with which the different sects treat each other, by the remarkable prosperity with which He has been pleased to favor the whole country.

1782

THOMAS PAINE

(1737–1809)

Actually Thomas Paine, the boldest freethinker of his time, was born in Norfolk, England, in 1737. Metaphorically he was born in America, aged thirty-seven, in 1774. The son of a Quaker corset maker in Thetford, Paine worked as teacher, corset maker, sailor, tax collector, grocer, tobacconist, propagandist, and rebel without a cause. His first wife died in childbirth and his second left him when he lost his small tobacco shop in Lewes. Driven by the ideas of the Enlightenment, restless, poor, unhappily seeking a meaning and objective for his inner rage, he met Franklin, who gave him a letter of introduction to the colony of Pennsylvania. The canny Ben did not quite know what to make of the soul-hungry and physically starved Tom Paine: his letter is a masterpiece of caution, gingerly handing Paine to the colonies at the end of a pair of tongs. History has justified Franklin's tentativeness: in the course of his life, Paine was considered the most dangerous man alive by England, France, and the United States. To this day reviewers of the man and his life are still compelled by healthy and honest partisanship to make him either a saint or a devil. In any event, Paine was probably the most luminous and heartbreaking figure of the American Revolution.

He found in America's brewing revolution exactly the defense of the underdog and the political exposition of a natural-rights philosophy to which his reading, the age, and his own experiences led him. He made America his true country with a joy and enthusiasm that few patriots have ever felt so deeply. He began to espouse democratic rights, in all their social aspects, in the *Pennsylvania Magazine*, but he really came into his own and into the center of colonial attention with his stirring *Common Sense* (January, 1776), a boldly direct and inspiring call for independence treasonable to the British crown. *Common Sense* sold between 100,000 and 150,000 copies in the first three months of its publication. When fighting broke out, the famous "Crisis" series began to appear, the sixteen papers coming at times when defeat seemed certain and acting as an elixir to the flagging spirits and bodies of the citizen-soldiers. His admirers and detractors both agree that as a writer he was one of the most passionate phrase makers and skillful propagandists the world has ever seen. Washington himself later indicated that Paine's services to the struggle for independence were incalculable.

Paine was an aide in the mission to France in 1781 and went back again to Europe in 1787 in an unsuccessful attempt to find a producer for a single-span iron bridge he had invented. In England he wrote the first part of *The Rights of Man* (1791) in defense of France, revolution, and representative republicanism and in reply to Burke's *Reflections on the French Revolution.* For the second part (1792) he was convicted of libel and treason by the British crown and was banished by England, from which he had already fled to France. One story has it that although there was a price on his head and *The Rights of Man* was banned by the government, smuggled copies of *The Rights* outcirculated the *Reflections* six to one in England. In France he was made a member of the revolutionary Convention, but in 1793 went to prison for ten months for his opposition to the Reign of Terror. On the death of Robespierre, Ambassador James Monroe had him released by claiming him as an American citizen. Paine lived on in Paris until 1802, in dire poverty, until brought back to America by his old friend Thomas Jefferson after the Peace of Amiens. But while Paine had been in prison, he wrote the first part of *The Age of Reason* (1794), which, with the publication of Part Two (1796), became the fullest and most radical statement of deistic rational religion. He had been a public enemy in France and England, and in the reaction to radicalism that seems to be an inevitable consequence of war, *The Age of Reason* made him a public enemy in the United States of America—a name he had been the first to coin. In 1801 there had been a rash of attacks upon his name by orthodox religionists and by those of Federalist political persuasion. The mass of Americans, forgetting his services and for the most part not reading *The Age of Reason* itself, erroneously reviled him as an atheist. Poverty-stricken, proud, broken, and neglected except by his vilifiers, he took increasingly to drink. He died in New Rochelle, New York, disturbed by attacking clergymen even on his deathbed. His bones were removed to England by William Cobbet, and his final grave, if any, is still unknown. Most probably his remains have long since been scattered over the planet by the elements. Yet there is something fitting in that, for Paine not only claimed that all men were his brothers and that to do good was his religion, but he also asserted that the entire world was his village.

In the list of titles by Paine, *Agrarian Justice* (1797) is the most important besides those already mentioned.

Editions or accounts of Paine and his works are to be found in T. C. Rickman, *The Life of Thomas Paine* (1814); M. D. Conway, *The Life of Thomas Paine* (1892); D. E. Wheeler, *The Life and Writings of Thomas Paine*, 10 vols. (1908); W. M. Van der Weyde, *The Life and Works of Thomas Paine*, 10 vols. (1925); H. H. Clark, "Toward a Reinterpretation of Thomas Paine," *American Literature*, V (1933); H. Pearson, *Tom Paine, Friend of Mankind* (1937); F. Smith, *Thomas Paine, Liberator* (1938); P. Davidson, *Propaganda and the American Revolution, 1763–1783* (1941); H. Fast, *Citizen Tom Paine* (1943); P. S. Foner, *The Complete Writings of Thomas Paine*, 2 vols. (1945); W. E. Woodward, *Tom Paine: America's Godfather* (1945); A. O. Aldridge, *Man of Reason: The Life of Thomas Paine* (1959); R. Gimbel, "Thomas Paine Fights for Freedom in Three Worlds: The New, The Old, The Next," *Proceedings American Antiquarian Society*, LXX (1961); J. T. Boulton, "Literature and Politics I. Tom Paine and the Vulgar Style," *Essays in Criticism*, XII (1962); M. O. Kistler, "German-American Liberalism and Thomas Paine," *American Quarterly*, XIV (1962); R. B. Browne, ed., *The Burke-Paine Controversy: Texts and Criticism* (1963); and I. M. Thompson, *The Religious Beliefs of Thomas Paine* (1965).

FROM

The Crisis

Number I

These are the times that try men's souls. The summer soldier and the sunshine patriot will, in this crisis, shrink from the service of his country; but he that stands it *now* deserves the love and thanks of man and woman. Tyranny, like hell, is not easily conquered; yet we have this consolation with us, that the harder the conflict, the more glorious the triumph. What we obtain too cheap, we esteem too lightly: it is dearness only that gives everything its value. Heaven knows how to put a proper price upon its goods; and it would be strange indeed if so celestial an article as FREEDOM should not be highly rated. Britain, with an army to enforce her tyranny, has declared that she has a right not only to tax but "to bind us in all cases whatsoever"; and if being bound in that manner is not slavery, then is there not such a thing as slavery upon earth. Even the expression is impious; for so unlimited a power can belong only to God.

Whether the independence of the continent was declared too soon, or delayed too long, I will not now enter into as an argument; my own simple opinion is, that had it been eight months earlier it would have been much better. We did not make a proper use of last winter; neither could we, while we were in a dependent state. However, the fault, if it were one, was all our own; we have none to blame but ourselves. But no great deal is lost yet. All that Howe has been doing for this month past is rather a ravage than a conquest, which the spirit of the Jerseys a year ago would have quickly repulsed, and which time and a little resolution will soon recover.

I have as little superstition in me as any man living; but my secret opinion has ever been, and still is, that God Almighty will not give up a people to military destruction, or leave them unsupportedly to perish, who have so earnestly and so repeatedly sought to avoid the calamities of war, by every decent method which wisdom could invent. Neither have I so much of the infidel in me as to suppose that he has relinquished the government of the world, and given us up to the care of devils; and as I do not, I cannot see on what grounds the king of Britain can look up to heaven for help against us: a common murderer, a highwayman, or a housebreaker, has as good a pretense as he.

It is surprising to see how rapidly a panic will sometimes run through a country. All nations and ages have been subject to them: Britain has trembled like an ague at the report of a French fleet of flat-bottomed boats; and in the fourteenth century the whole English army, after ravaging the kingdom of France, was driven back like men petrified with fear; and this brave exploit was performed by a few broken forces collected and headed by a woman, Joan of

Arc. Would that heaven might inspire some Jersey maid to spirit up her countrymen, and save her fair fellow sufferers from ravage and ravishment! Yet panics, in some cases, have their uses; they produce as much good as hurt. Their duration is always short; the mind soon grows through them, and acquires a firmer habit than before. But their peculiar advantage is, that they are the touchstones of sincerity and hypocrisy, and bring things and men to light, which might otherwise have lain forever undiscovered. In fact, they have the same effect on secret traitors which an imaginary apparition would have upon a private murderer. They sift out the hidden thoughts of man, and hold them up in public to the world. Many a disguised tory has lately shown his head, that shall penitentially solemnize with curses the day on which Howe arrived upon the Delaware.

As I was with the troops at Fort Lee, and marched with them to the edge of Pennsylvania, I am well acquainted with many circumstances which those who live at a distance know but little or nothing of. Our situation there was exceedingly cramped, the place being a narrow neck of land between the North River and the Hackensack. Our force was inconsiderable, being not one-fourth so great as Howe could bring against us. We had no army at hand to have relieved the garrison, had we shut ourselves up and stood on our defense. Our ammunition, light artillery, and the best part of our stores, had been removed, on the apprehension that Howe would endeavor to penetrate the Jerseys, in which case Fort Lee could be of no use to us; for it must occur to every thinking man, whether in the army or not, that these kind of field forts are only for temporary purposes, and last in use no longer than the enemy directs his force against the particular object which such forts are raised to defend. Such was our situation and condition at Fort Lee on the morning of the 20th of November, when an officer arrived with information that the enemy with 200 boats had landed about seven miles above. Major General Green, who commanded the garrison, immediately ordered them under arms, and sent express to General Washington at the town of Hackensack, distant by the way of the ferry, six miles. Our first object was to secure the bridge over the Hackensack, which laid up the river between the enemy and us, about six miles from us, three from them. General Washington arrived in about three-quarters of an hour, and marched at the head of the troops towards the bridge, which place I expected we should have a brush for; however, they did not choose to dispute it with us, and the greatest part of our troops went over the bridge, the rest over the ferry, except some which passed at a mill on a small creek between the bridge and the ferry, and made their way through some marshy grounds up to the town of Hackensack, and there passed the river. We brought off as much baggage as the wagons could contain, the rest was lost. The simple object was to bring off the garrison and march them on till they could be strengthened by the Jersey or Pennsylvania militia, so as to be enabled to make a stand. We stayed four days at Newark, collected our outposts with some of the Jersey militia, and marched out twice to meet the enemy on being informed that they were advancing, though our numbers were greatly inferior to theirs. Howe, in my little opinion, committed a great error in generalship in not throwing a body of forces off from Staten Island through Amboy, by which means he might have seized all our stores at Brunswick and intercepted our march into Pennsylvania; but if we believe the power of hell to be limited, we must likewise believe that their agents are under some providential control.

I shall not now attempt to give all the particulars of our retreat to the Delaware; suffice it for the present to say that both officers and men, though greatly harassed and fatigued, frequently without rest, covering, or provision— the inevitable consequences of a long retreat—bore it with a manly and martial spirit. All their wishes centered in one; which was, that the country would turn out and help them to drive the enemy back. Voltaire has remarked that King William never appeared to full advantage but in difficulties and in action; the same remark may be made on General Washington, for the character fits him. There is a natural firmness in some minds which cannot be unlocked by trifles, but which, when unlocked, discovers a cabinet of fortitude; and I reckon it among those kinds of public blessings, which we do not immediately see, that God hath blessed him with uninterrupted health, and given him a mind that can even flourish upon care.

I shall conclude this paper with some miscellaneous remarks on the state of our affairs; and shall begin with asking the following question, Why is it that the enemy have left the New England provinces, and made these middle ones the seat of war? The answer is easy: New England is not infested with tories, and we are. I have been tender in raising the cry against these men, and used numberless arguments to show them their danger, but it will not do to sacrifice a world either to their folly or their baseness. The period is now arrived in which either they or we must change our sentiments, or one or both must fall. And what is a tory? Good God! what is he? I should not be afraid to go with a hundred Whigs against a thousand tories, were they to attempt to get into arms. Every tory is a coward; for servile, slavish, self-interested fear is the foundation of toryism; and a man under such influence, though he may be cruel, never can be brave.

But, before the line of irrecoverable separation be drawn between us, let us reason the matter together: Your conduct is an invitation to the enemy, yet not one in a thousand of you has heart enough to join him. Howe is as much deceived by you as the American cause is injured by you. He expects you will all take up arms and flock to his standard with muskets on your shoulders. Your opinions are of no use to him unless you support him personally, for it is soldiers, and not tories, that he wants.

I once felt all that kind of anger, which a man ought to feel, against the mean principles that are held by the tories: A noted one, who kept a tavern at Amboy, was standing at his door, with as pretty a child in his hand, about eight or nine years old, as I ever saw, and after speaking his mind as freely as he thought was prudent, finished with this unfatherly expression, "Well! give me peace in my day." Not a man lives on the continent but fully believes that a separation must some time or other finally take place, and a generous parent should have said, "If there must be trouble, let it be in my day, that my child may have peace"; and this single reflection, well applied, is sufficient to awaken every man to duty. Not a place upon earth might be so happy as America. Her situation is remote from all the wrangling world, and she has nothing to do but to trade with them. A man can distinguish himself between temper and principle; and I am as confident as I am that God governs the world, that America will never be happy till she gets clear of foreign dominion. Wars, without ceasing, will break out till that period arrives, and the continent must in the end be conqueror; for though the flame of liberty may sometimes cease to shine, the coal can never expire.

America did not, nor does not want force; but she wanted a proper application of that force. Wisdom is not the purchase of a day, and it is no wonder that we should err at the first setting off. From an excess of tenderness, we were unwilling to raise an army, and trusted our cause to the temporary defense of a well-meaning militia. A summer's experience has now taught us better; yet with those troops, while they were collected, we were able to set bounds to the progress of the enemy, and thank God! they are again assembling. I always considered militia as the best troops in the world for a sudden exertion, but they will not do for a long campaign. Howe, it is probable, will make an attempt on this city; should he fail on this side the Delaware, he is ruined. If he succeeds, our cause is not ruined. He stakes all on his side against a part on ours; admitting he succeeds, the consequences will be that armies from both ends of the continent will march to assist their suffering friends in the middle states; for he cannot go everywhere—it is impossible. I consider Howe as the greatest enemy the tories have; he is bringing a war into their country, which, had it not been for him and partly for themselves, they had been clear of. Should he now be expelled, I wish with all the devotion of a Christian, that the names of Whig and Tory may never more be mentioned; but should the tories give him encouragement to come, or assistance if he come, I as sincerely wish that our next year's arms may expel them from the continent, and the Congress appropriate their possessions to the relief of those who have suffered in well-doing. A single successful battle next year will settle the whole. America could carry on a two years' war by the confiscation of the property of disaffected persons, and be made happy by their expulsion. Say not that this is revenge; call it rather the soft resentment of a suffering people, who, having no object in view but the good of all, have staked their own all upon a seemingly doubtful event. Yet it is folly to argue against determined hardness; eloquence may strike the ear, and the language of sorrow draw forth the tear of compassion, but nothing can reach the heart that is steeled with prejudice.

Quitting this class of men, I turn with the warm ardor of a friend to those who have nobly stood, and are yet determined to stand the matter out: I call not upon a few, but upon all: not on this State or that State, but on every State: up and help us; lay your shoulders to the wheel; better have too much force than too little, when so great an object is at stake. Let it be told to the future world, that in the depth of winter, when nothing but hope and virtue could survive, that the city and the country alarmed at one common danger, came forth to meet and to repulse it. Say not that thousands are gone—turn out your tens of thousands; throw not the burden of the day upon Providence, but "show your faith by your works," that God may bless you. It matters not where you live, or what rank of life you hold, the evil or the blessing will reach you all. The far and the near, the home counties and the back, the rich and the poor, will suffer or rejoice alike. The heart that feels not now is dead; the blood of his children will curse his cowardice who shrinks back at a time when a little might have saved the whole and made *them* happy. I love the man that can smile in trouble, that can gather strength from distress and grow brave by reflection. It is the business of little minds to shrink; but he whose heart is firm, and whose conscience approves his conduct, will pursue his principles unto death. My own line of reasoning is to myself as straight and clear as a ray of light. Not all the treasures of the world, so far as I believe, could have induced me to support an offensive war, for I think it murder; but if a thief breaks into my house, burns and destroys my property, and kills or threatens to kill me or those that are in it, and to "bind me in all cases whatsoever" to his absolute will, am I to suffer it? What signifies it to me whether he who does it is a king or a common man; my countryman or not my countryman; whether it be done by an individual villain, or an army of them? If we reason to the root of things we shall find no difference; neither can any just cause be assigned why we should punish in the one case and pardon in the other. Let them call me rebel and welcome—I feel no concern from it; but I should suffer the misery of devils, were I to make a whore of my soul by swearing allegiance to one whose character is that of a sottish, stupid, stubborn, worthless, brutish man. I conceive likewise a horrid idea in receiving mercy from a being, who at the last day shall be shrieking to the rocks and mountains to cover him, and fleeing with terror from the orphan, the widow, and the slain of America.

There are cases which cannot be overdone by language, and this is one. There are persons, too, who see not the full extent of the evil which threatens them; they solace themselves with hopes that the enemy, if he succeed, will be merciful. It is the madness of folly, to expect mercy from those who have refused to do justice; and even mercy, where conquest is the object, is only a trick of war. The cunning of the fox is as murderous as the violence of the wolf, and we ought to guard equally against both. Howe's first object is, partly by threats and partly by promises, to terrify or seduce the people to deliver up their arms and receive mercy. The ministry recommended the same plan to Gage, and this is what the tories call making their peace, "a peace which passeth all understanding," indeed! A peace which would be the immediate forerunner of a worse ruin than any we have yet thought of. Ye men of Pennsylvania, do reason upon these things! Were the back counties to give up their arms, they would fall an easy prey to the Indians, who are all armed: this perhaps is what some tories would not be sorry for. Were the home counties to deliver up their arms, they would be exposed to the resentment of the back counties, who would then have it in their power to chastise their defection at pleasure. And were any one State to give up its arms, *that* State must be garrisoned by all Howe's army of Britons and Hessians to preserve it from the anger of the rest. Mutual fear is the principal link in the chain of mutual love; and woe be to that State that breaks the compact. Howe is mercifully inviting you to barbarous destruction, and men must be either rogues or fools that will not see it. I dwell not upon the vapors of imagination; I bring reason to your ears, and, in language as plain as A B C, hold up truth to your eyes.

I thank God that I fear not. I see no real cause for fear. I know our situation well, and can see the way out of it. While our army was collected, Howe dared not risk a battle; and it is no credit to him that he decamped from the White Plains, and waited a mean opportunity to ravage the defenseless Jerseys; but it is great credit to us, that with a handful of men, we sustained an orderly retreat for near a hundred miles, brought off our ammunition, all our field-pieces, the greatest part of our stores, and had four rivers to pass. None can say that our retreat was precipitate; for we were near three weeks in performing it, that the country might have time to come in. Twice we marched back to meet the enemy, and remained out till dark. The sign of fear was not seen in our camp, and had not some of the cowardly and disaffected inhabitants spread false alarms through the country, the Jerseys had never been ravaged. Once more we are again collected and collecting, our new army at both ends of the continent is recruiting fast, and we shall be able to open the next campaign with sixty thousand men, well-armed and clothed. This is our situation, and who will may know it. By perseverance and fortitude we have the prospect of a glorious issue; by cowardice and submission, the sad choice of a variety of evils: a ravaged country—a depopulated city—habitations without safety, and slavery without hope—our homes turned into barracks and bawdy-houses for Hessians—and a future race to provide for, whose fathers we shall doubt of. Look on this picture and weep over it! and if there yet remains one thoughtless wretch who believes it not, let him suffer it unlamented.

COMMON SENSE
December 23, 1776

FROM

The Age of Reason

It has been my intention for several years past to publish my thoughts upon religion. I am well aware of the difficulties that attend the subject, and from that consideration had reserved it to a more advanced period of life. I intended it to be the last offering I should make to my fellow citizens of all nations, and that at a time when the purity of the motive that induced me to it could not admit of a question, even by those who might disapprove the work.

The circumstance that has now taken place in France of the total abolition of the whole national order of priesthood, and of everything appertaining to compulsive systems of religion and compulsive articles of faith, has not only precipitated my intention, but rendered a work of this kind exceedingly necessary, lest in the general wreck of superstition, of false systems of government and false theology, we lose sight of morality, of humanity, and of the theology that is true.

As several of my colleagues, and others of my fellow citizens of France, have given me the example of making their voluntary and individual profession of faith, I also will make mine; and I do this with all that sincerity and frankness with which the mind of man communicates with itself.

I believe in one God, and no more; and I hope for happiness beyond this life.

I believe in the equality of man; and I believe that religious duties consist in doing justice, loving mercy, and endeavoring to make our fellow-creatures happy.

But, lest it should be supposed that I believe in many other things in addition to these, I shall, in the progress of this work, declare the things I do not believe, and my reasons for not believing them.

I do not believe in the creed professed by the Jewish church, by the Roman church, by the Greek church, by the Turkish church, by the Protestant church, nor by any church that I know of. My own mind is my own church.

All national institutions of churches, whether Jewish, Christian or Turkish, appear to me no other than human inventions, set up to terrify and enslave mankind, and monopolize power and profit.

I do not mean by this declaration to condemn those who believe otherwise; they have the same right to their belief as I have to mine. But it is necessary to the happiness of man that he be mentally faithful to himself. Infidelity does not consist in believing or in disbelieving; it consists in professing to believe what he does not believe.

. . .

Soon after I had published the pamphlet *Common Sense* in America, I saw the exceeding probability that a revolution in the system of government would be followed by a revolution in the system of religion. The adulterous connection of church and state, wherever it had taken place, whether Jewish, Christian, or Turkish, had so effectually prohibited, by pains and penalties, every discussion upon established creeds and upon first principles of religion, that until the system of government should be changed, those subjects could not be brought fairly and openly before the world; but that whenever this should be done, a revolution in the system of religion would follow. Human inventions and priestcraft would be detected, and man would return to the pure, unmixed and unadulterated belief of one God, and no more. . . .

Every national church or religion has established itself by pretending some special mission from God, communicated to certain individuals. The Jews have their Moses; the Christians their Jesus Christ, their apostles and saints; and the Turks their Mahomet, as if the way to God was not open to every man alike.

Each of those churches show certain books which they call *revelation,* or the word of God. The Jews say that their word of God was given by God to Moses, face to face; the Christians say their word of God came by divine inspiration; and the Turks say that their word of God (the Koran) was brought by an angel from heaven. Each of those churches accuse the other of unbelief; and for my own part I disbelieve them all.

· · ·

When I am told that the Koran was written in heaven and brought to Mahomet by an angel, the account comes too near the same kind of hearsay evidence and second-hand authority as the former. I did not see the angel myself, and, therefore, I have a right not to believe it.

When also I am told that a woman called the Virgin Mary said, or gave out, that she was with child without any cohabitation with a man, and that her betrothed husband, Joseph, said that an angel told him so, I have a right to believe them or not; such a circumstance required a much stronger evidence than their bare word for it; but we have not even this—for neither Joseph nor Mary wrote any such matter themselves; it is only reported by others that *they said so*—it is hearsay upon hearsay, and I do not choose to rest my belief upon such evidence.

· · ·

It is curious to observe how the theory of what is called the Christian church sprung out of the tail of the heathen mythology. A direct incorporation took place in the first instance, by making the reputed founder to be celestially begotten. The trinity of gods that then followed was no other than a reduction of the former plurality, which was about twenty or thirty thousand; the statue of Mary succeeded the statue of Diana of Ephesus; the deification of heroes changed into the canonization of saints; the mythologists had gods for everything; the Christian mythologists had saints for everything; the church became as crowded with one, as the Pantheon had been with the other, and Rome was the place of both. The Christian theory is little else than the idolatry of the ancient mythologists, accommodated to the purposes of power and revenue; and it yet remains to reason and philosophy to abolish the amphibious fraud.

Nothing that is here said can apply, even with the most distant disrespect, to the real character of Jesus Christ. He was a virtuous and an amiable man. The morality that he preached and practised was of the most benevolent kind; and though similar systems of morality had been preached by Confucius and by some of the Greek philosophers many years before, by the Quakers since, and by many good men in all ages, it has not been exceeded by any.

Jesus Christ wrote no account of himself, of his birth, parentage, or anything else; not a line of what is called the New Testament is of his own writing. The history of him is altogether the work of other people; and as to the account of his resurrection and ascension, it was the necessary counterpart to the story of his birth. His historians, having brought him into the world in a supernatural manner, were obliged to take him out again in the same manner, or the first part of the story must have fallen to the ground.

· · ·

But if objects for gratitude and admiration are our desire, do they not present themselves every hour to our eyes? Do we not see a fair creation prepared to receive us the instant we are born—a world furnished to our hands that cost us nothing? Is it we that light up the sun, that pour down the rain and fill the earth with abundance? Whether we sleep or wake, the vast machinery of the universe still goes on. Are these things, and the blessings they indicate in future, nothing to us? Can our gross feelings be excited by no other subjects than tragedy and suicide? Or is the gloomy pride of man become so intolerable that nothing can flatter it but a sacrifice of the Creator?

I know that this bold investigation will alarm many, but it would be paying too great a compliment to their credulity to forbear it on their account; the times and the subject demand it to be done. The suspicion that the theory of what is called the Christian Church is fabulous is becoming very extensive in all countries; and it will be a consolation to men staggering under that suspicion and doubting what to believe and what to disbelieve, to see the object freely investigated.

. . .

If we permit ourselves to conceive right ideas of things, we must necessarily affix the idea, not only of unchangeableness, but of the utter impossibility of any change taking place, by any means or accident whatever, in that which we would honor with the name of the word of God; and therefore the word of God cannot exist in any written or human language.

The continually progressive change to which the meaning of words is subject, the want of a universal language which renders translation necessary, the errors to which translations are again subject, the mistakes of copyists and printers, together with the possibility of willful alteration, are of themselves evidences that the human language, whether in speech or in print, cannot be the vehicle of the word of God. The word of God exists in something else.

Did the book called the Bible excel in purity of ideas and expression all the books that are now extant in the world, I would not take it for my rule of faith, as being the word of God, because the possibility would nevertheless exist of my being imposed upon. But when I see throughout the greater part of this book scarcely anything but a history of the grossest vices and a collection of the most paltry and contemptible tales, I cannot dishonor my Creator by calling it by his name.

. . .

. . . Man stands in the same relative condition with his Maker as he ever did since man existed, and . . . it is his greatest consolation to think so.

Let him believe this and he will live more consistently and morally than by any other system; it is by his being taught to contemplate himself as an outlaw, as an outcast, as a beggar, as a mumper, as one thrown, as it were, on a dunghill at an immense distance from his Creator, and who must make his approaches by creeping and cringing to intermediate beings, that he conceives either a contemptuous disregard for everything under the name of religion, or becomes indifferent, or turns what he calls devout. In the latter case, he consumes his life in grief, or the affectation of it. His prayers are reproaches. His humility is ingratitude. He calls himself a worm and the fertile earth a dunghill, and all the blessings of life by the thankless name of vanities. He despises the choicest gift of God to man, the gift of reason. And having endeavored to force upon himself the belief of a system against which the reason revolts, he ungratefully calls it *human* reason, as if man could give reason to himself.

Yet, with all this strange appearance of humility and this contempt for human reason, he ventures into the boldest presumptions. He finds fault with everything. His selfishness is never satisfied. His ingratitude is never at an end. He takes on himself to direct the Almighty what to do, even in the government of the universe. He prays dictatorially. When it is sunshine he prays for rain, and when it is rain he prays for sunshine. He follows the same idea in everything that he prays for, for what is the amount of all his prayers but an attempt to make the Almighty change his mind and act otherwise than he does? It is as if he were to say, "Thou knowest not so well as I."

But some, perhaps, will say: Are we to have no word of God—no revelation? I answer, Yes; there is a word of God, there is a revelation.

The word of God is the creation we behold: and it is in this word, which no human invention can counterfeit or alter, that God speaketh universally to man.

Human language is local and changeable, and is therefore incapable of being used as the means of unchangeable and universal information. The idea that God sent Jesus Christ to publish, as they say, the glad tidings to all nations, from one end of the earth to the other, is consistent only with the ignorance of those who knew nothing of the extent of the world, and who believed, as those world-saviours believed, and continued to believe for several centuries (and that in contradiction to the discoveries of philosophers and the experience of navigators), that the earth was flat like a trencher, and that a man might walk to the end of it.

But how was Jesus Christ to make anything known to all nations? He could speak but one language, which was Hebrew, and there are in the world several hundred languages. Scarcely any two nations speak the same language or understand each other; and as to translations, every man who knows anything of languages knows that it is impossible to translate from one language to another, not only without losing a great part of the original, but frequently of mistaking the sense; and besides all this, the art of printing was wholly unknown at the time Christ lived.

It is always necessary that the means that are to accomplish any end be equal to the accomplishment of that end, or the end cannot be accomplished. It is in this that the difference between finite and infinite power and wisdom discovers itself. Man frequently fails in accomplishing his ends, from a natural inability of the power to the purpose and frequently from the want of wisdom to apply power properly. But it is impossible for infinite power and wisdom to fail as man faileth. The means it useth are always equal to the end; but human language, more especially as there is not an universal language, is incapable of being used as an universal means of unchangeable and uniform information, and therefore it is not the means that God uses in manifesting himself universally to man.

It is only in the Creation that all our ideas and conceptions of a word of God can unite. The Creation speaks an universal language, independently of human speech or human language, multiplied and various as they may be. It is an ever-existing original, which every man can read. It cannot be forged; it cannot be counterfeited; it cannot be lost; it cannot be altered; it cannot be suppressed. It does not depend upon the will of man whether it shall be published or not; it publishes itself from one end of the earth to the other. It preaches to all nations and to all worlds; and this word of God reveals to man all that is necessary for man to know of God.

· · ·

It is only by the exercise of reason that man can discover God. Take away that reason, and he would be incapable of understanding anything; and, in this case, it would be just as consistent to read even the book called the Bible to a horse as to a man.

. . .

I recollect not enough of the passages in Job to insert them correctly; but there is one occurs to me that is applicable to the subject I am speaking upon: "Canst thou by searching find out God? Canst thou find out the Almighty to perfection?"

I know not how the printers have pointed this passage, for I keep no Bible; but it contains two distinct questions that admit of distinct answers.

First—Canst thou by searching find out God? Yes; because, in the first place, I know I did not make myself, and yet I have existence; and by searching into the nature of other things, I find out that no other thing could make itself; and yet millions of other things exist; therefore it is that I know, by positive conclusion resulting from this search, that there is a power superior to all those things, and that power is God.

Secondly—Canst thou find out the Almighty to perfection? No; not only because the power and wisdom He has manifested in the structure of the Creation that I behold is to me incomprehensible, but because even this manifestation, great as it is, is probably but a small display of that immensity of power and wisdom by which millions of other worlds, to me invisible by their distance, were created and continue to exist. . . .

As to the Christian system of faith, it appears to me as a species of atheism—a sort of religious denial of God. It professes to believe in a man rather than in God. It is a compound made up chiefly of manism with but little deism, and is as near to atheism as twilight is to darkness. It introduces between man and his Maker an opaque body, which it calls a Redeemer, as the moon introduces her opaque self between the earth and the sun, and it produces by this means a religious or an irreligious, eclipse of light. It has put the whole orbit of reason into shade.

The effect of this obscurity has been that of turning everything upside down and representing it in reverse, and among the revolutions it has thus magically produced, it has made a revolution in theology.

That which is now called natural philosophy, embracing the whole circle of science, of which astronomy occupies the chief place, is the study of the works of God and of the power and wisdom of God in his works, and is the true theology.

As to the theology that is now studied in its place, it is the study of human opinions and of human fancies *concerning* God. It is not the study of God himself in the works that he has made, but in the works or writings that man has made; and it is not among the least of the mischiefs that the Christian system has done to the world that it has abandoned the original and beautiful system of theology, like a beautiful innocent, to distress and reproach, to make room for the hag of superstition.

The Book of Job and the 19th Psalm, which even the Church admits to be more ancient than the chronological order in which they stand in the book called the Bible, are theological orations conformable to the original system of theology. The internal evidence of those orations proves to a demonstration that the study and contemplation of the works of creation and of the power and wisdom of God revealed and manifested in those works, made a great part in the religious devotion of the times in which they were written; and it was this devotional study and contemplation that led to the discovery of the principles upon which what are now called sciences are established; and it is to the discovery of these principles that almost all the arts that contribute to the convenience of human life owe their existence. Every principal art has some science for its parent, though the person who mechanically performs the work does not always, and but very seldom, perceive the connection.

It is a fraud of the Christian system to call the sciences human invention; it is only the application of them that is human. Every science has for its basis a system of principles as fixed and unalterable as those by which the universe is regulated and governed. Man cannot make principles, he can only discover them.

. . .

Since, then, man cannot make principles, from whence did he gain a knowledge of them so as to be able to apply them, not only to things on earth, but to ascertain the motion of bodies so immensely distant from him as all the heavenly bodies are? From whence, I ask, *could* he gain that knowledge but from the study of the true theology?

. . .

It is from the study of the true theology that all our knowledge of science is derived, and it is from that knowledge that all the arts have originated.

The Almighty Lecturer, by displaying the principles of science in the structure of the universe, has invited man to study and to imitation. It is as if He had said to the inhabitants of this globe that we call ours, "I have made an earth for man to dwell upon, and I have rendered the starry heavens visible, to teach him science and the arts. He can now provide for his own comfort *and learn from my munificence to all to be kind to each other.*"

. . .

Our ideas, not only of the almightiness of the Creator, but of His wisdom and His beneficence, become enlarged in proportion as we contemplate the extent and the structure of the universe. The solitary idea of a solitary world, rolling or at rest in the immense ocean of space, gives place to the cheerful idea of a society of worlds, so happily contrived as to administer, even by their motion, instruction to man. We see our own earth filled with abundance, but we forget to consider how much of that abundance is owing to the scientific knowledge the vast machinery of the universe has unfolded.

. . .

But though every created thing is, in [a] sense, a mystery, the word "mystery" cannot be applied to moral truth any more than obscurity can be applied to light. The God in whom we believe is a God of moral truth, and not a God of mystery or obscurity. Mystery is the antagonist of truth. It is a fog of human invention that obscures truth and represents it in distortion. Truth never envelops itself in mystery, and the mystery in which it is at any time enveloped is the work of its antagonist, and never of itself.

Religion, therefore, being the belief of a God and the practice of moral truth, cannot have connection with mystery. The belief of a God, so far from having anything of mystery in it, is of all beliefs the most easy, because it arises to us, as is before observed, out of necessity. And the practice of moral truth, or, in other words, a practical imitation of the moral goodness of God, is no other than our acting toward each other as He acts benignly toward all. We cannot serve God in the manner we serve those who cannot do without such service; and, therefore, the only idea we can have of serving God is that of contributing to the happiness of the living creation that God has made. This cannot be done by retiring ourselves from the society of the world and spending a recluse life in selfish devotion.

.   .   .

Upon the whole, mystery, miracle, and prophecy are appendages that belong to fabulous and not to true religion. They are the means by which so many "Lo, heres!" and "Lo, theres!" have been spread about the world, and religion been made into a trade. The success of one imposter gave encouragement to another, and the quieting salvo of doing some good by keeping up a pious fraud protected them from remorse.

Having now extended the subject to a greater length than I first intended, I shall bring it to a close by abstracting a summary from the whole.

First—That the idea or belief of a word of God existing in print, or in writing, or in speech, is inconsistent in itself for reasons already assigned. These reasons, among many others, are the want of a universal language; the mutability of language; the errors to which translations are subject; the possibility of totally suppressing such a word; the probability of altering it, or of fabricating the whole, and imposing it upon the world.

Do we want to contemplate His power? We see it in the immensity of the Creation. Do we want to contemplate His wisdom? We see it in the unchangeable order by which the incomprehensible whole is governed. Do we want to contemplate His munificence? We see it in the abundance with which He fills the earth. Do we want to contemplate His mercy? We see it in His not withholding that abundance even from the unthankful. In fine, do we want to know what God is? Search not the book called the Scripture, which any human hand might make, but the Scripture called the Creation.

Secondly—That the Creation we behold is the real and everexisting word of God in which we cannot be deceived. It proclaims His power, it demonstrates His wisdom, it manifests His goodness and beneficence.

Thirdly—That the moral duty of man consists in imitating the moral goodness and beneficence of God, manifested in the creation toward all His creatures. That seeing, as we daily do, the goodness of God to all men, it is an example calling upon all men to practise the same toward each other; and, consequently, that everything of persecution and revenge between man and man, and everything of cruelty to animals, is a violation of moral duty.

I trouble not myself about the manner of future existence. I content myself with believing, even to positive conviction, that the Power that gave me existence is able to continue it, in any form and manner He pleases, either with or without this body; and it appears more probable to me that I shall continue to exist hereafter than that I should have had existence, as I now have, before that existence began.

It is certain that in one point all nations of the earth and all religions agree—all believe in a God; the things in which they disagree are the redundancies annexed to that belief; and, therefore, if ever a universal religion should prevail, it will not be by believing anything new, but in getting rid of redundancies and believing as man believed at first. Adam, if ever there were such a man, was created a Deist; but in the meantime, let every man follow, as he has a right to do, the religion and the worship he prefers.

1794

THOMAS JEFFERSON

(1743–1826)

When the inheritance of his wife, Martha Skelton, was combined with his own holdings, Thomas Jefferson controlled over
45,000 acres and more than 200 slaves. He was born to an
aristocratic family, which included the famous Randolphs, on
the western lands of Virginia. He was a graduate of the College of William and Mary (1762) and in 1767 was admitted
to the practice of law in Virginia. As a high-born son of influential people, Jefferson was a member of the House of Burgesses
from 1769 to 1775. Certainly one could expect another William
Byrd from such a background; or at the least, a man acutely
aware of and prepared to defend his privileges and prerogatives.
But in his career Jefferson illustrated his own belief that government can be trusted to the mass of men because leaders come
from the most surprising places.

Instead of producing a man allied to the vested interests, the
Jefferson family produced a brilliant revolutionary and one of
the greatest American voices of democratic principles. An heir
himself, he abolished entail and primogeniture. A slaveholder,
he introduced a bill to prevent the extension of slavery (1784).
A ruler, he said, "I have sworn upon the altar of God eternal
hostility against every form of tyranny over the mind of man."
A brief list of his activities suggests something of this "Renaissance man." He was a member of the Virginia Conventions
(1774–1775), of the Continental Congress (1775–1776), and
of the Virginia Legislature (1776–1779). After serving as Governor of Virginia (1779–1781), delegate to Congress (1783–

1784), and minister to France (1784–1789), he was Secretary of State (1790–1793); Vice President of the United States (1797–1801), and President (1801–1809). His private library of more than 10,000 volumes became the basis of the Library of Congress. Our two-party system and parliamentary rules of government are attributed to Jefferson more than to any other man. He concluded the Louisiana Purchase (1803) and with the Lewis and Clark expedition (1803–1806) opened the westward way that has helped to mold the American imagination. As much as Franklin a genius of "Yankee inventiveness," he was a student of various sciences, poetry, linguistics, education, music, art, and architecture. In his love for republican aims and periods of history, he has left his stamp upon the nation even in such matters as the Greek and Roman tradition of our public architecture.

Again like Franklin, so much is the life of Jefferson the story of the Republic that no list can do more than hint at his significance for American values. A leader in eighteenth-century thought, in which an inestimable portion of the national character was shaped, he insisted that a natural aristocracy of worth must replace an artificial aristocracy of station. He based his arguments on the idea of natural rights and natural law bequeathed him by the political essays of Locke and the physics of Newton. He developed the concept of the independent and individual yeoman, who, because of his close relation to Nature and Nature's God, would be the most purely altruistic and intelligent holder of political power. No form of government, Jefferson maintained, would secure the supremacy of the private and free intelligence so well as a populistic, agrarian, republican democracy. As champion of the untrammeled mind, he effected his belief in the separation of church and state, wide franchise, public education, and assured liberties.

He died, fittingly, on July 4, 1826, the fiftieth anniversary of the Declaration of Independence. The greatness of his life—his insistence on political, religious, and intellectual freedom—is summed up in his instructions for his tombstone. On the page on which he drew a picture of the stone he wrote, ". . . on the faces of the obelisk the following inscription, and not a word more: 'Here was buried Thomas Jefferson, Author of the Declaration of American Independence, of the Statute of Virginia for religious freedom, and Father of the University of Virginia,' because by these, as testimonials that I have lived, I wish most to be remembered."

Besides the "Declaration," the titles of Jefferson's works include *A Summary View of the Rights of British America* (1774); *Notes on the Establishment of a Money Unit* (1784); *Notes on the State of Virginia* (1784–1785); *A Manual of Parliamentary Practise* (1801); *The Address to the Senate on the Fourth of March* (1801); and the *Life of Captain Lewis* (1817).

Editions and accounts of Jefferson and his work are to be found in P. L. Ford, ed., *The Writings of Thomas Jefferson,* 10 vols. (1892–1899); A. A. Lipscomb and A. E. Bergh, eds., *The Writings of Thomas Jefferson,* 20 vols. (1903–1907); C. A. Beard, *Economic Origins of Jeffersonian Democracy* (1915); C. Becker, *The Declaration of Independence* (1922); C. G. Bowers, *Jefferson and Hamilton* (1925); G. Chinard, ed., *The Commonplace Book of Thomas Jefferson* (1926); V. L. Parrington, *Main Currents in American Thought,* I (1927); J. T. Adams, *Jeffersonian Principles* (1928); G. Chinard, *The Literary Bible of Thomas Jefferson* (1928); G. Chinard, *Thomas Jefferson, the Apostle of Americanism* (1929); C. G. Bowers, *Jefferson in Power* (1936); B. Mayo, *Jefferson Himself* (1942); S. K. Padover, *Jefferson* (1942); A. Koch, *The Philosophy of Thomas Jefferson* (1943); C. G. Bowers, *The Young Jefferson* (1945); K. Lehmann-Hartben, *Thomas Jefferson, American Humanist* (1947); D. Malone, *Jefferson the Virginian* (1948); D. Malone, *Jefferson and the Rights of Man* (1951); N. Schachner, *Thomas Jefferson,* 2 vols. (1951); H. M. Jones, *The Pursuit of Happiness* (1953); J. Dos Passos, *The Head and Heart of Thomas Jefferson* (1954); P. Russell, *Jefferson, Champion of the Free Mind* (1956); M. Peterson, *The Jeffersonian Image in the American Mind* (1960); W. S. Howell, "The Declaration of Independence and Eighteenth-Century Logic," *William and Mary Quarterly,* XVIII (1961); D. Malone, *Jefferson and the Ordeal of Liberty* (1962); S. G. Brown, "The Mind of Thomas Jefferson," *Ethics,* LXXIII (1963); E. M. Halliday, "Nature's God and the Founding Fathers'," *American Heritage,* XIV (1963); and J. P. Boyd, ed., *The Papers of Thomas Jefferson,* 17 vols. (1950–1965).

The Unanimous Declaration of the Thirteen United States of America In Congress, July 4, 1776

When in the course of human events it becomes necessary for one people to dissolve the political bands which have connected them with another, and to assume among the powers of the earth the separate and equal station to which the laws of Nature and of Nature's God entitle them, a decent respect to the opinions of mankind requires that they should declare the causes which impel them to the separation.

We hold these truths to be self-evident: that all men are created equal; that they are endowed by their creator with certain unalienable rights; that among these are life, liberty, and the pursuit of happiness; that to secure these rights, governments are instituted among men, deriving their just powers from the consent of the governed; that whenever any form of government becomes destructive of these ends, it is the right of the people to alter or abolish it, and to institute new government, laying its foundations on such principles and organizing its powers in such form as to them shall seem most likely to effect their safety and happiness. Prudence, indeed, will dictate that governments long established should not be changed for light and transient causes; and accordingly all experience hath shown that mankind are more disposed to suffer, while evils are sufferable, than to right themselves by abolishing the forms to which they are accustomed. But when a long train of abuses and usurpations, pursuing invariably the same object, evinces a design to reduce them under absolute despotism, it is their right, it is their duty, to throw off such government, and to provide new guards for their future security.

Such has been the patient suffering of these colonies, and such is now the necessity which constrains them to alter their former systems of government. The history of the present King of Great Britain is a history of repeated injuries and usurpations, all having in direct object the establishment of an absolute tyranny over these States. To prove this, let facts be submitted to a candid world.

He has refused his assent to laws the most wholesome and necessary for the public good.

He has forbidden his governors to pass laws of immediate and pressing importance unless suspended in their operation till his assent should be obtained; and when so suspended, he has utterly neglected to attend to them.

He has refused to pass other laws for the accommodation of large districts of people, unless those people would relinquish the right of representation in the Legislature, a right inestimable to them and formidable to tyrants only.

He has called together legislative bodies at places unusual, uncomfortable, and distant from the depository of their public records for the sole purpose of fatiguing them into compliance with his measures.

He has dissolved representative houses repeatedly for opposing with manly firmness his invasions on the rights of the people.

He has refused for a long time, after such dissolutions, to cause others to be elected; whereby the legislative powers, incapable of annihilation, have returned to the people at large for their exercise; the state remaining in the meantime exposed to all the dangers of invasion from without, and convulsions within.

He has endeavored to prevent the population of these states; for that purpose obstructing the laws for naturalization of foreigners; refusing to pass others to encourage their migrations hither, and raising the conditions of new appropriations of lands.

He has obstructed the administration of justice, by refusing his assent to laws for establishing judiciary powers.

He has made judges dependent on his will alone, for the tenure of their offices, and the amount and payment of their salaries.

He has erected a multitude of new offices, and sent hither swarms of officers to harass our people, and eat out their substance.

He has kept among us, in times of peace, standing armies without the consent of our legislatures.

He has affected to render the military independent of and superior to the civil power.

He has combined with others to subject us to a jurisdiction foreign to our constitution, and unacknowledged by our laws, giving his assent to their acts of pretended legislation; for quartering large bodies of armed troops among them; for protecting them, by a mock trial, from punishment for any murders which they should commit on the inhabitants of these states; for cutting off our trade with all parts of the world; for imposing taxes on us without our consent; for depriving us in many cases of the benefits of trial by jury; for transporting us beyond seas to be tried for pretended offences; for abolishing the free system of English laws in a neighboring province, establishing therein an arbitrary government, and enlarging its boundaries so as to render it at once an example and fit instrument for introducing the same absolute rule into these colonies; for taking away our charters, abolishing our most valuable laws, and altering fundamentally the forms of our government; for suspending our own legislatures, and declaring themselves invested with power to legislate for us in all cases whatsoever.

He has abdicated government here, by declaring us out of his protection and waging war against us.

He has plundered our seas, ravaged our coasts, burnt our towns, and destroyed the lives of our people. He is at this time transporting large armies of foreign mercenaries to complete the works of death, desolation and tyranny, already begun with circumstances of cruelty and perfidy scarcely paralleled in the most barbarous ages, and totally unworthy the head of a civilized nation.

He has constrained our fellow citizens taken captive on the high seas to bear arms against their country, to become the executioners of their friends and brethren, or to fall themselves by their hands.

He has excited domestic insurrections amongst us, and has endeavored to bring on the inhabitants of our frontiers, the merciless Indian savages, whose known rule of warfare, is an undistinguished destruction of all ages, sexes and conditions. In every stage of these oppressions, we have petitioned for redress in the most humble terms: Our repeated petitions have been answered only by repeated injury. A prince whose character is thus marked by every act which may define a tyrant, is unfit to be the ruler of a free people. Nor have we been wanting in attentions to our British brethren. We have warned them from time to time of attempts by their legislature to extend an unwarrantable jurisdiction over us. We have reminded them of the circumstances of our emigration and settlement here. We have appealed to their native justice and magnanimity, and we have conjured them by the ties of our common kindred to disavow these usurpations, which would inevitably interrupt our connections and correspondence. They too have been deaf to the voice of justice and of consanguinity. We must, therefore, acquiesce in the necessity, which denounces our separation, and hold them, as we hold the rest of mankind, enemies in war, in peace friends.—

We, THEREFORE, the representatives of the United States of America, in General Congress assembled, appealing to the Supreme Judge of the world for the rectitude of our intentions, do, in the name and by authority of the good people of these colonies, solemnly publish and declare, That these United Colonies are, and of right ought to be FREE AND INDEPENDENT STATES; that they are absolved from all allegiance to the British crown, and that all political connection between them and the State of Great Britain, is and ought to be totally dissolved; and that as free and independent states, they have full power to levy war, conclude peace, contract alliances, establish commerce, and to do all other acts and things which independent states may of right do.

And for the support of this Declaration, with a firm reliance on the protection of divine Providence, we mutually pledge to each other our lives, our fortunes, and our sacred honor.

1776

FROM

Notes on the State of Virginia

[On religious toleration]

The present state of our laws on the subject of religion is this. The convention of May 1776, in their declaration of rights, declared it to be a truth, and a natural right, that the exercise of religion should be free; but when they proceeded to form on that declaration the ordinance of government, instead of taking up every principle declared in the bill of rights, and guarding it by legislative sanction, they passed over that which asserted our religious rights, leaving them as they found them. The same convention, however, when they met as a member of the general assembly in October 1776, repealed all acts of parliament which had rendered criminal the maintaining any opinions in matters of religion, the forbearing to repair to church, and the exercising any mode of worship; and suspended the laws giving salaries to the clergy, which suspension was made perpetual in October 1779. Statutory oppressions in religion being thus wiped away, we remain at present under those only imposed by the common law, or by our own acts of assembly. At the common law, heresy was a capital offence, punishable by burning. Its definition was left to the ecclesiastical judges, before whom the conviction was, till the statute of the I El. C. I. circumscribed it, by declaring that nothing should be deemed heresy but what had been so determined by authority of the canonical scriptures, or by one of the four first general councils, or by some other council having for the grounds of their declaration the express and plain words of the scriptures. Heresy, thus circumscribed, being an offence at the common law, our act of assembly of October 1777, c. 17 gives cognizance of it to the general court, by declaring that the jurisdiction of that court shall be general in all matters at the common law. The execution is by the writ *De hæretico comburendo*. By our own act of assembly of 1705, c. 30, if a person brought up in the Christian religion denies the being of a God, or the Trinity, or asserts there are more Gods than one, or denies the Christian religion to be true, or the scriptures to be of divine authority, he is punishable on the first offence by incapacity to hold any office or employment ecclesiastical, civil, or military; on the second by disability to sue, to take any gift or legacy, to be guardian, executor or administrator, and by three years imprisonment, without bail. A father's right to the custody of his own children being founded in law on his right of guardianship, this being taken away, they may of course be severed from him and put, by the authority of a court, into more orthodox hands. This is a summary view of that religious slavery under which a people have been willing to remain who have lavished their lives and fortunes for the establishment of their civil freedom. The error seems not sufficiently eradicated, that the operations of the mind, as well as the acts of the body, are subject to the coercion of the laws. But our rulers can have authority over such natural rights, only as we have submitted to them. The rights of conscience we never submitted, we could not submit. We are answerable for them to our God. The legitimate powers of government extend to such acts only as are injurious to others. But it does me no injury for my neighbor to say there are twenty gods, or no god. It neither picks my pocket nor breaks my leg. If it be said his testimony in a court of justice cannot be relied on, reject it then, and be the stigma on him. Constraint may make him worse by making him a hypocrite, but it will never make him a truer man. It may fix him obstinately in his errors, but will not cure them. Reason and free inquiry are the only effectual agents against error. Give a loose to them, they will support the true religion by bringing every false one to their tribunal, to the test of their investigation. They are the natural enemies of error, and of error only. Had not the Roman government permitted free inquiry, Christianity could never have been introduced. Had not free inquiry been indulged, at the era of the reformation, the corruptions of Christianity could not have been purged away. If it be restrained now, the present corruptions will be protected, and new ones encouraged. Was the government to prescribe to us our medicine and diet, our bodies would be in such keeping as our souls are now. Thus in France the emetic was once forbidden as a medicine, and the potato as an article of food. Government is just as infallible, too, when it fixes systems in physics. Galileo was sent to the inquisition for affirming that the earth was a sphere; the government had declared it to be as flat as a trencher, and Galileo was obliged to abjure his error. This error however at length prevailed, the earth became a globe, and Descartes declared it was whirled round its axis by a vortex. The government in which he lived was wise enough to see that this was no question of civil jurisdiction, or we should all have been involved by authority in vortices. In fact the vortices have been exploded, and the Newtonian principle of gravitation is now more firmly established, on the basis of reason, than it would be were the government to step in and to make it an article of necessary faith. Reason and experiment have been indulged, and error has fled before them. It is error alone which needs the support of government. Truth can stand by itself. Subject opinion to coercion: whom will you make your inquisitors? Fallible men; men governed by bad passions, by private as well as public reasons. And why subject it to coercion? To produce uniformity. But is uniformity of opinion desirable? No more than of face and stature. Introduce the bed of Procrustes then, and as there is danger that the large men may beat the small, make us all of a size, by lopping the former and stretching the latter. Difference of opinion is advantageous in religion. The several sects perform the office of a Censor morum over each other. Is uniformity attainable? Millions of innocent men, women and children, since the introduction of Christianity, have been burnt, tortured, fined, imprisoned: yet we have not advanced one inch towards uniformity. What has been the effect of coercion? To make one half the world fools, and the other half hypocrites. To support roguery and error all over the earth. Let us reflect that it is inhabited by a thousand millions of people. That these profess probably a thousand different systems of religion. That ours is but one of that thousand. That if there be but one right, and ours that one, we should wish to see the 999 wandering sects gathered into the fold of truth. But against such a majority we cannot effect this by force. Reason and persuasion are the only practicable instruments. To make way for these, free inquiry must be indulged; and how can we wish others to indulge it while we refuse it ourselves? But every state, says an inquisitor, has established some religion. No two, say I, have established the same. Is this a proof of the infallibility of establishments? Our sister states of Pennsylvania and New York, however, have long subsisted without any establishment at all. The experiment was new and doubtful when they made it. It has answered beyond conception. They flourish infinitely. Religion is well supported; of various kinds indeed, but all good enough; all sufficient to preserve peace and order: or if a sect arises whose tenets would subvert morals, good sense has fair play, and reasons and laughs it out of doors, without suffering the state to be troubled with it. They do not hang more malefactors than we do. They are not more disturbed with religious dissentions. On the contrary, their harmony is unparallelled, and can be ascribed to nothing but their unbounded tolerance, because there is no other circumstance in which they differ from every nation on earth. They have made the happy discovery that the way to silence religious disputes is to take no notice of them. Let us too give this experiment fair play, and get rid, while we may, of those tyrannical laws. It is true we are as yet secured against them by the spirit of the times. I doubt whether the people of this country would suffer an execution for heresy, or a three years imprisonment for not comprehending the mysteries of the trinity. But is the spirit of the people an infallible, a permanent reliance? Is it government? Is this the kind of protection we receive in return for the rights we give up? Besides, the spirit of the times may alter, will alter. Our rulers will become corrupt, our people careless. A single zealot may commence persecutor; and better men be his victims. It can never be too often repeated, that the time for fixing every essential right on a legal basis is while our rulers are honest, and ourselves united. From the conclusion of this war we shall be going down hill. It will not then be necessary to resort every moment to the people for support. They will be forgotten therefore, and their rights disregarded. They will forget themselves, but in the sole faculty of making money, and will never think of uniting to effect a due respect for their rights.

[*On slavery in America*]

There must doubtless be an unhappy influence on the manners of our people produced by the existence of slavery among us. The whole commerce between master and slave is a perpetual exercise of the most boisterous passions, the most unremitting despotism on the one part, and degrading submissions on the other. Our children see this, and learn to imitate it; for man is an imitative animal. This quality is the germ of all education in him. From his cradle to his grave he is learning to do what he sees others do. If a parent could find no motive either in his philanthropy or his self-love, for restraining the intemperance of passion towards his slave, it should always be a sufficient one that his child is present. But generally it is not sufficient. The parent storms, the child looks on, catches the lineaments of wrath, puts on the same airs in the circle of smaller slaves, gives a loose to the worst of passions, and thus nursed, educated, and daily exercised in tyranny, cannot but be stamped by it with odious peculiarities. The man must be a prodigy who can retain his manners and morals undepraved by such circumstances. And with what execration should the statesman be loaded, who, permitting one-half the citizens thus to trample on the rights of the other, transforms those into despots, and these into enemies, destroys the morals of the one part, and the *amor patriae* of the other. For if a slave can have a country in this world, it must be any other in preference to that in which he is born to live and labor for another, in which he must lock up the faculties of his nature, contribute as far as depends on his individual endeavors to the evanishment of the human race, or entails his own miserable condition on the endless generations proceeding from him. With the morals of the people, their industry also is destroyed. For in a warm climate, no man will labor for himself who can make another labor for him. This is so true, that of the proprietors of slaves a very small proportion indeed are ever seen to labor. And can the liberties of a nation be thought secure when we have removed their only firm basis, a conviction in the minds of the people that these liberties are of the gift of God? That they are not to be violated but with His wrath? Indeed I tremble for my country when I reflect that God is just; that his justice cannot sleep forever: that considering numbers, nature and natural means only, a revolution of the wheel of fortune, an exchange of situation is among possible events; that it may become probable by supernatural interference! The Almighty has no attribute which can take side with us in such a contest. But it is impossible to be temperate and to pursue this subject through the various considerations of policy, of morals, of history natural and civil. We must be contented to hope they will force their way into every one's mind. I think a change already perceptible, since the origin of the present revolution. The spirit of the master is abating, that of the slave rising from the dust, his condition mollifying, the way I hope preparing, under the auspices of heaven, for a total emancipation, and that this is disposed, in the order of events, to be with the consent of the masters, rather than by their extirpation.

[On dictatorship]

In December, 1776, our circumstances being much distressed, it was proposed in the house of delegates to create a dictator, invested with every power legislative, executive, and judiciary, civil and military, of life and of death, over our persons and over our properties; and in June 1781, again under calamity, the same proposition was repeated, and wanted a few votes only of being passed.—One who entered into this contest from a pure love of liberty and a sense of injured rights, who determined to make every sacrifice, and to meet every danger for the re-establishment of those rights on a firm basis, who did not mean to expend his blood and substance for the wretched purpose of changing this master for that, but to place the powers of governing him in a plurality of hands of his own choice, so that the corrupt will of no one man might in future oppress him, must stand confounded and dismayed when he is told, that a considerable portion of that plurality had meditated the surrender of them into a single hand, and, in lieu of a limited monarch, to deliver him over to a despotic one! How must he find his efforts and sacrifices abused and baffled, if he may still, by a single vote, be laid prostrate at the feet of one man!

In God's name, from whence have they derived this power? Is it from our ancient laws? None such can be produced. Is it from any principle in our new constitution expressed or implied? Every lineament of that expressed or implied, is in full opposition to it. Its fundamental principle is that the state shall be governed as a commonwealth. It provides a republican organization, proscribes under the name of prerogative the exercise of all powers undefined by the laws, places on this basis the whole system of our laws, and by consolidating them together, chooses that they shall be left to stand or fall together, never providing for any circumstances, nor admitting that such could arise, wherein either should be suspended; no, not for a moment. Our ancient laws expressly declare that those who are but delegates themselves shall not delegate to others powers which require judgment and integrity in their exercise. Or was this proposition moved on a supposed right in the movers, of abandoning their posts in a moment of distress? The same laws forbid the abandonment of that post, even on ordinary occasions; and much more a transfer of their powers into other hands and other forms, without consulting the people. They never admit the idea that these, like sheep or cattle, may be given from hand to hand without an appeal to their own will. Was it from the necessity of the case? Necessities which dissolve a government, do not convey its authority to an oligarchy or a monarchy. They throw back into the hands of the people, the powers they had delegated, and leave them as individuals to shift for themselves. A leader may offer, but not impose himself, nor be imposed on them. Much less can their necks be submitted to his sword, their breath be held at his will or caprice. The necessity which should operate these tremendous effects should at least be palpable and irresistible.

Yet in both instances, where it was feared, or pretended with us, it was belied by the event. It was belied, too, by the preceding experience of our sister states, several of whom had grappled through greater difficulties without abandoning their forms of government. When the proposition was first made, Massachusetts had found even the government of committees sufficient to carry them through an invasion. But we at the time of that proposition, were under no invasion. When the second was made, there had been added to this example those of Rhode Island, New York, New Jersey, and Pennsylvania, in all of which the republican form had been found equal to the task of carrying them through the severest trials. In this state alone did there exist so little virtue, that fear was to be fixed in the hearts of the people, and to become the motive of their exertions, and the principle of their government? The very thought alone was treason against the people; was treason against mankind in general, as riveting forever the chains which bow down their necks by giving to their oppressors a proof, which they would have trumpeted through the universe, of the imbecility of republican government, in times of pressing danger, to shield them from harm. Those who assume the right of giving away the reins of government in any case, must be sure that the herd, whom they hand on to the rods and hatchet of the dictator, will lay their necks on the block when he shall nod to them. But if our assemblies supposed such a resignation in the people, I hope they mistook their character. I am of opinion, that the government, instead of being braced and invigorated for greater exertions under their difficulties, would have been thrown back upon the bungling machinery of county committees for administration, till a convention could have been called, and its wheels again set into regular motion. What a cruel moment was this for creating such an embarrassment, for putting to the proof the attachment of our countrymen to republican government! Those who meant well, of the advocates for this measure—and most of them meant well, for I know them personally, had been their fellow-laborers in the common cause, and had often proved the purity of their principles—had been seduced in their judgment by the example of an ancient republic, whose constitution and circumstances were fundamentally different. They had sought this precedent in the history of Rome, where alone it was to be found, and where at length, too, it had proved fatal. They had taken it from a republic rent by the most bitter factions and tumults, where the government was of a heavy-handed unfeeling aristocracy, over a people ferocious, and rendered desperate by poverty and wretchedness; tumults which could not be allayed under the most trying circumstances, but by the omnipotent hand of a single despot. Their constitution, therefore, allowed a temporary tyrant to be erected, under the name of a Dictator; and that temporary tyrant, after a few examples, became perpetual. They misapplied this precedent to a people mild in their dispositions, patient under their trial, united for the public liberty, and affectionate to their leaders. But if from the constitution of the Roman government there resulted to their Senate a power of submitting all their rights to the will of one man, does it follow that the assembly of Virginia have the same authority? What clause in our constitution has substituted that of Rome, by way of residuary provision, for all cases not otherwise provided for? Or if they may step *ad libitum* [at whim] into any other form of government for precedents to rule us by, for what oppression may not a precedent be found in this world of the *bellum omnium in omnia* [universal strife]? Searching for the foundations of this proposition, I can find none which may pretend a color of right or reason, but the defect before developed, that there being no barrier between the legislative, executive, and judiciary departments, the legislature may seize the whole: that having seized it, and possessing a right to fix their own quorum, they may reduce that quorum to one, whom they may call a chairman, speaker, dictator, or by any other name they please. Our situation is indeed perilous, and I hope my countrymen will be sensible of it and will apply, at a proper season, the proper remedy, which is a convention to fix the constitution, to amend its defects, to bind up the several branches of government by certain laws, which, when they transgress, their acts shall become nullities; to render unnecessary an appeal to the people, or in other words a rebellion, on every infraction of their rights, on the peril that their acquiescence shall be construed into an intention to surrender those rights.

1784–1785

First Inaugural Address

FRIENDS AND FELLOW-CITIZENS:

Called upon to undertake the duties of the first executive office of our country, I avail myself of the presence of that portion of my fellow-citizens which is here assembled to express my grateful thanks for the favor with which they have been pleased to look towards me, to declare a sincere consciousness that the task is above my talents, and that I approach it with those anxious and awful presentiments which the greatness of the charge and the weakness of my powers so justly inspire. A rising nation spread over a wide and fruitful land, traversing all the seas with the rich productions of their industry, engaged in commerce with nations who feel power and forget right, advancing rapidly to destinies beyond the reach of mortal eye—when I contemplate these transcendent objects, and see the honor, the happiness, and the hopes of this beloved country committed to the issue and the auspices of this day, I shrink from the contemplation and humble myself before the magnitude of the undertaking.

Utterly, indeed, should I despair, did not the presence of many whom I here see remind me that in the other high authorities provided by our constitution I shall find resources of wisdom, of virtue, and of zeal on which to rely under all difficulties. To you then, gentlemen, who are charged with the sovereign functions of legislation, and to those associated with you, I look with encouragement for that guidance and support which may enable us to steer with safety the vessel in which we are all embarked, amidst the conflicting elements of a troubled sea.

During the contest of opinion through which we have passed, the animation of discussions and of exertions has sometimes worn an aspect which might impose on strangers unused to think freely and to speak and to write what they think. But this being now decided by the voice of the nation, announced according to the rules of the Constitution, all will of course arrange themselves under the will of the law and unite in common efforts for the common good. All too will bear in mind this sacred principle, that, though the will of the majority is in all cases to prevail, that will, to be rightful, must be reasonable; that the minority possess their equal rights, which equal laws must protect, and to violate would be oppression. Let us then, fellow-citizens, unite with one heart and one mind; let us restore to social intercourse that harmony and affection without which liberty, and even life itself, are but dreary things. And let us reflect that, having banished from our land that religious intolerance under which mankind so long bled and suffered, we have yet gained little if we countenance a political intolerance as despotic, as wicked, and capable of as bitter and bloody persecutions. During the throes and convulsions of the ancient world [the French Revolution], during the agonizing spasms of infuriated man, seeking through blood and slaughter his long-lost liberty, it was not wonderful that the agitation of the billows should reach even this distant and peaceful shore; that this should be more felt and feared by some and less by others; and should divide opinions as to measures of safety. But every difference of opinion is not a difference of principle. We have called by different names brethren of the same principle. We are all Republicans; we are all Federalists. If there be any among us who would wish to dissolve this Union, or to change its republican form, let them stand undisturbed as monuments of the safety with which error of opinion may be tolerated where reason is left free to combat it. I know, indeed, that some honest men have feared that a republican government cannot be strong; that this Government is not strong enough. But would the honest patriot, in the full tide of successful experiment, abandon a government which has so far kept us free and firm, on the theoretic and visionary fear that this Government, the world's best hope, may by possibility want energy to preserve itself? I trust not. I believe this, on the contrary, the strongest government on earth. I believe it the only one where every man, at the call of the law, would fly to the standard of the law; would meet invasions of the public order as his own personal concern. Sometimes it is said that man cannot be trusted with the government of himself. Can he, then, be trusted with the government of others? Or have we found angels in the form of kings to govern him? Let history answer this question.

Let us, then, pursue with courage and confidence our own federal and republican principles, our attachment to union and representative government. Kindly separated by nature and a wide ocean from the exterminating havoc of one quarter of the globe; too high-minded to endure the degradations of the others; possessing a chosen country, with room enough for our descendants to the hundredth and thousandth generation; entertaining a due sense of our equal right to the use of our own faculties, to the acquisitions of our own industry, to honor and confidence from our fellow-citizens, resulting not from birth, but from our actions and their sense of them; enlightened by a benign religion, professed indeed and practiced in various forms yet all of them inculcating honesty, truth, temperance, gratitude, and the love of man, acknowledging and adoring an overruling Providence, which by all its dispensations proves that it delights in the happiness of man here and his greater happiness hereafter—with all these blessings, what more is necessary to make us a happy and a prosperous people? Still one thing more, fellow-citizens—a wise and frugal Government, which shall restrain men from injuring one another, shall leave them otherwise free to regulate their own pursuits of industry and improvement, and shall not take from the mouth of labor the bread it has earned. This is the sum of good government, and this is necessary to close the circle of our felicities.

About to enter, fellow-citizens, on the exercise of duties which comprehend everything dear and valuable to you, it is proper you should understand what I deem the essential principles of our Government, and consequently those which ought to shape its administration I will compress them within the narrowest compass they will bear, stating the general principle, but not all its limitations. Equal and exact justice to all men, of whatever state or persuasion, religious or political; peace, commerce, and honest friendship with all nations, entangling alliances with none; the support of the state governments in all their rights as the most competent administrations for our domestic concerns and the surest bulwarks against antirepublican tendencies; the preservation of the General Government in its whole constitutional vigor, as the sheet anchor of our peace at home and safety abroad; a jealous care of the right of election by the people—a mild and safe corrective of abuses which are lopped by the sword of revolution where peaceable remedies are unprovided; absolute acquiescence in the decisions of the majority, the vital principle of republics, from which is no appeal but to force, the vital principle and immediate parent of despotism; a well-disciplined militia, our best reliance in peace and for the first moments of war, till regulars may relieve them; the supremacy of the civil over the military authority; economy in the public expense, that labor may be lightly burthened; the honest payment of our debts and sacred preservation of the public faith; encouragement of agriculture, and of commerce as its handmaid; the diffusion of information and arraignment of all abuses at the bar of the public reason; freedom of religion; freedom of the press, and freedom of person under the protection of the habeas corpus, and trial by juries impartially selected. These principles form the bright constellation which has gone before us and guided our steps through an age of revolution and reformation. The wisdom of our sages and blood of our heroes have been devoted to their attainment. They should be the creed of our political faith, the text of civic-instruction, the touchstone by which to try the services of those we trust; and should we wander from them in moments of error or of alarm, let us hasten to retrace our steps and to regain the road which alone leads to peace, liberty, and safety.

I repair, then, fellow citizens, to the post you have assigned me. With experience enough in subordinate offices to have seen the difficulties of this the greatest of all, I have learnt to expect that it will rarely fall to the lot of imperfect man to retire from this station with the reputation and the favor which bring him into it. Without pretensions to that high confidence you reposed in our first and greatest revolutionary character, whose preeminent services had entitled him to the first place in his country's love and had destined for him the fairest page in the volume of faithful history, I ask so much confidence only as may give firmness and effect to the legal administration of your affairs. I shall often go wrong through defect of judgment. When right, I shall often be thought wrong by those whose positions will not command a view of the whole ground. I ask your indulgence for my own errors, which will never be intentional, and your support against the errors of others who may condemn what they would not, if seen in all its parts. The

approbation implied by your suffrage is a great consolation
to me for the past; and my future solicitude will be to
retain the good opinion of those who have bestowed it in
advance, to conciliate that of others by doing them all the
good in my power, and to be instrumental to the happiness
and freedom of all.

Relying then on the patronage of your goodwill, I
advance with obedience to the work, ready to retire from
it whenever you become sensible how much better choice
it is in your power to make. And may that Infinite Power
which rules the destinies of the universe lead our councils
to what is best, and give them a favorable issue for your
peace and prosperity.

1801

Letters

[TO JAMES MADISON]

Paris, Dec. 20, 1787

DEAR SIR:

My last to you was of Oct. 8 by the Count de Moustier.
Yours of July 18, Sep. 6, and Oct. 24, have been successively received, yesterday, the day before and three or four
days before that. I have only had time to read the letters,
the printed papers communicated with them, however interesting, being obliged to lie over till I finish my dispatches
for the packet, which dispatches must go from hence the
day after tomorrow. I have much to thank you for. First
and most for the cyphered paragraph respecting myself.
These little informations are very material towards forming
my own decisions. I would be glad even to know when any
individual member thinks I have gone wrong in any instance. If I know myself it would not excite ill blood in
me, while it would assist to guide my conduct, perhaps to
justify it, and to keep me to my duty, alert. I must thank
you too for the information in Thos. Burke's case, tho' you
will have found by a subsequent letter that I have asked of
you a further investigation of that matter. It is to gratify
the lady who is at the head of the Convent wherein my
daughters are, and who, by her attachment and attention

to them, lays me under great obligations. I shall hope therefore still to receive from you the result of the further enquiries my second letter had asked.—The parcel of rice which you informed me had miscarried accompanied my letter to the Delegates of S. Carolina. Mr. Bourgoin was to be the bearer of both and both were delivered together into the hands of his relation here who introduced him to me, and who at a subsequent moment undertook to convey them to Mr. Bourgoin. This person was an engraver particularly recommended to Dr. Franklin and Mr. Hopkinson. Perhaps he may have mislaid the little parcel of rice among his baggage.—I am much pleased that the sale of Western lands is so successful. I hope they will absorb all the certificates of our domestic debt speedily in the first place, and that then offered for cash they will do the same by our foreign one.

The season admitting only of operations in the Cabinet, and these being in a great measure secret, I have little to fill a letter. I will therefore make up the deficiency by adding a few words on the Constitution proposed by our Convention. I like much the general idea of framing a government which should go on of itself peaceably, without needing continual recurrence to the state legislatures. I like the organization of the government into Legislative, Judiciary and Executive. I like the power given the Legislature to levy taxes; and for that reason solely approve of the greater house being chosen by the people directly. For tho' I think a house chosen by them will be very illy qualified to legislate for the Union, for foreign nations &c. yet this evil does not weigh against the good of preserving inviolate the fundamental principle that the people are not to be taxed but by representatives chosen immediately by themselves. I am captivated by the compromise of the opposite claims of the great and little states, of the latter to equal, and the former to proportional influence. I am much pleased too with the substitution of the method of voting by persons, instead of that of voting by states: and I like the negative given to the Executive with a third of either house, though I should have liked it better had the Judiciary been associated for that purpose, or invested with a similar and separate power. There are other good things of less moment. I will now add what I do not like. First the omission of a bill of rights providing clearly and without the aid of sophisms for freedom of religion, freedom of the press, protection against standing armies, restriction against monopolies, the eternal and unremitting force of the habeas corpus laws, and trials by jury in all matters of fact triable by the laws of the land and not by the law of Nations. To say, as Mr. Wilson does that a bill of rights was not necessary because all is reserved in the case of the general government which is not given, while in the particular ones all is given which is not reserved might do for the audience to whom it was addressed, but is surely gratis dictum, opposed by strong inferences from the body of the instrument, as well as from the omission of the clause of our present confederation which had declared that in express terms. It was a hard conclusion to say because there has been no uniformity among the states as to the cases triable by jury, because some have been so incautious as to abandon this mode of trial, therefore the more prudent states shall be reduced to the same level of calamity. It would have been much more just and wise to have concluded the other way that as most of the states had judiciously preserved this palladium, those who had wandered should be brought back to it, and to have established general right instead of general wrong. Let me add that a bill of rights is what the people are entitled to against every government on earth, general or particular, and what no just government should refuse, or rest on inference. The second feature I dislike, and greatly dislike, is the abandonment in every instance of the necessity of rotation in office, and most particularly in the case of the President. Experience concurs with reason in concluding that the first magistrate will always be re-elected if the constitution permits it. He is then an officer for life. This once observed it becomes of so much consequence to certain nations to have a friend or a foe at the head of our affairs that they will interfere with money and with arms. A Galloman or an Angloman will be supported by the nation he befriends. If once elected, and at a second or third election outvoted by one or two votes, he will pretend false votes, foul play, hold possession of the reins of government, be supported by the states voting for him, especially if they are the central ones lying in a compact body themselves and separating their opponents:

and they will be aided by one nation of Europe, while the majority are aided by another. The election of a President of America some years hence will be much more interesting to certain nations of Europe than ever the election of a king of Poland was. Reflect on all the instances in history ancient and modern, of elective monarchies, and say if they do not give foundation for my fears, the Roman emperors, the popes, while they were of any importance, the German emperors till they became hereditary in practice, the kings of Poland, the Deys of the Ottoman dependencies. It may be said that if elections are to be attended with these disorders, the seldomer they are renewed the better. But experience shows that the only way to prevent disorder is to render them uninteresting by frequent changes. An incapacity to be elected a second time would have been the only effectual preventative. The power of removing him every fourth year by the vote of the people is a power which will not be exercised. The king of Poland is removeable every day by the Diet, yet he is never removed.— Smaller objections are the Appeal in fact as well as law, and the binding all persons Legislative, Executive and Judiciary by oath to maintain that constitution. I do not pretend to decide what would be the best method of procuring the establishment of the manifold good things in this constitution, and of getting rid of the bad. Whether by adopting it in hopes of future amendment, or, after it has been duly weighed and canvassed by the people, after seeing the parts they generally dislike, and those they generally approve, to say to them 'We see now what you wish. Send together your deputies again, let them frame a constitution for you omitting what you have condemned, and establishing the powers you approve. Even these will be a great addition to the energy of your government.'—At all events I hope you will not be discouraged from other trials, if the present one should fail of its full effect.—I have thus told you freely what I like and dislike: merely as a matter of curiosity for I know your own judgment has been formed on all these points after having heard every thing which could be urged on them. I own I am not a friend to a very energetic government. It is always oppressive. The late rebellion in Massachusetts has given more alarm than I think it should have done. Calculate that one rebellion in 13 states in the course of 11 years, is but one for each state in a century and a half. No country should be so long without one. Nor will any degree of power in the hands of government prevent insurrections. France with all its despotism, and two or three hundred thousand men always in arms has had three insurrections in the three years I have been here in every one of which greater numbers were engaged than in Massachusetts and a great deal more blood was spilt. In Turkey, which Montesquieu supposes more despotic, insurrections are the events of every day. In England, where the hand of power is lighter than there, but heavier than with us they happen every half dozen years. Compare again the ferocious depredations of their insurgents with the order, the moderation and the almost self extinguishment of ours.—After all, it is my principle that the will of the majority should always prevail. If they approve the proposed Convention in all its parts, I shall concur in it cheerfully, in hopes that they will amend it whenever they shall find it work wrong. I think our governments will remain virtuous for many centuries, as long as they are chiefly agricultural; and this will be as long as there shall be vacant lands in any part of America. When they get piled upon one another in large cities, as in Europe, they will become corrupt as in Europe. Above all things I hope the education of the common people will be attended to; convinced that on their good sense we may rely with the most security for the preservation of a due degree of liberty. I have tired you by this time with my disquisitions and will therefore only add assurances of the sincerity of those sentiments of esteem and attachment with which I am, Dear Sir, your affectionate friend & servant,

TH: JEFFERSON

P.S. The instability of our laws is really an immense evil. I think it would be well to provide in our constitutions that there shall always be a twelvemonth between the ingrossing a bill and passing it: that it should then be offered to its passage without changing a word: and that if circumstances should be thought to require a speedier passage, it should take two thirds of both houses instead of a bare majority.

[*TO BENJAMIN RUSH*]

Washington, April 21, 1803

DEAR SIR:

In some of the delightful conversations with you in the evenings of 1798–99, and which serve as an anodyne to the afflictions of the crisis through which our country was then laboring, the Christian religion was sometimes our topic; and I then promised you, that one day or other, I would give you my views of it. They are the result of a life of inquiry and reflection, and very different from that anti-Christian system imputed to me by those who know nothing of my opinions. To the corruptions of Christianity I am, indeed, opposed; but not to the genuine precepts of Jesus himself. I am a Christian in the only sense he wished any one to be; sincerely attached to his doctrines, in preference to all others, ascribing to himself every *human* excellence; and believing he never claimed any other. At the short interval since these conversations, when I could justifiably abstract my mind from public affairs, the subject has been under my contemplation. But the more I considered it, the more it expanded beyond the measure of either my time or information. In the moment of my late departure from Monticello, I received from Dr. Priestley his little treatise of "Socrates and Jesus Compared." This being a section of the general view I had taken of the field, it became a subject of reflection while on the road, and unoccupied otherwise. The result was to arrange in my mind a syllabus, or outline, of such an estimate of the comparative merits of Christianity, as I wished to see executed by some one of more leisure and information for the task, than myself. This I now send you, as the only discharge of my promise I can probably ever execute. And in confiding it to you, I know it will not be exposed to the malignant perversions of those who make every word from me a text for new misrepresentations and calumnies. I am moreover averse to the communication of my religious tenets to the public because it would countenance the presumption of those who have endeavored to draw them before that tribunal, and to seduce public opinion to erect itself into that inquisition over the rights of conscience, which the laws have so justly proscribed. It behooves every man who values liberty of conscience for himself, to resist invasions of it in the case of others; or their case may, by change of circumstances, become his own. It behooves him, too, in his own case, to give no example of concession, betraying the common right of independent opinion, by answering questions of faith, which the laws have left between God and himself. Accept my affectionate salutations . . .

SYLLABUS OF AN ESTIMATE OF THE MERIT OF THE DOCTRINES OF JESUS, COMPARED WITH THOSE OF OTHERS.

In a comparative view of the ethics of the enlightened nations of antiquity, of the Jews and of Jesus, no notice should be taken of the corruptions of reason among the ancients, to wit, the idolatry and superstitution of the vulgar, nor of the corruptions of Christianity by the learned among its professors.

Let a just view be taken of the moral principles inculcated by the most esteemed of the sects of ancient philosophy, or of their individuals; particularly Pythagoras, Socrates, Epicurus, Cicero, Epictetus, Seneca, Antoninus.

I. PHILOSOPHERS. 1. Their precepts related chiefly to ourselves, and the government of those passions which, unrestrained, would disturb our tranquillity of mind. In this branch of philosophy they were really great.

2. In developing our duties to others, they were short and defective. They embraced, indeed, the circles of kindred and friends, and inculcated patriotism, or the love of our country in the aggregate, as a primary obligation; toward our neighbors and countrymen they taught justice, but scarcely viewed them as within the circle of benevolence. Still less have they inculcated peace, charity, and love to our fellow men, or embraced with benevolence the whole family of mankind.

II. JEWS. 1. Their system was Deism, that is, the belief of one only God. But their ideas of him and of his attributes were degrading and injurious.

2. Their Ethics were not only imperfect, but often irreconcilable with the sound dictates of reason and morality as they respect intercourse with those around us; and repulsive and anti-social, as respecting other nations. They needed reformation, therefore, in an eminent degree.

III. JESUS. In this state of things among the Jews,

Jesus appeared. His parentage was obscure; his condition poor; his education null; his natural endowments great; his life correct and innocent; he was meek, benevolent, patient, firm, disinterested, and of the sublimest eloquence.

The disadvantages under which his doctrines appear are remarkable.

1. Like Socrates and Epictetus, he wrote nothing himself.

2. But he had not, like them, a Xenophon or an Arrian to write for him. I name not Plato, who only used the name of Socrates to cover the whimsies of his own brain. On the contrary, all the learned of his country, entrenched in its power and riches, were opposed to him, lest his labors should undermine their advantages; and the committing to writing his life and doctrines fell on unlettered and ignorant men; who wrote, too, from memory, and not till long after the transactions had passed.

3. According to the ordinary fate of those who attempt to enlighten and reform mankind, he fell an early victim to the jealousy and combination of the altar and the throne at about thirty-three years of age, his reason having not yet attained the maximum of its energy, nor the course of his preaching, which was but of three years at most, presented occasions for developing a complete system of morals.

4. Hence the doctrines which he really delivered were defective as a whole, and fragments only of what he did deliver have come to us mutilated, misstated, and often unintelligible.

5. They have been still more disfigured by the corruptions of schismatizing followers, who have found an interest in sophisticating and perverting the simple doctrines he taught, by engrafting on them the mysticisms of a Grecian sophist, fritting them into subtleties, and obscuring them with jargon, until they have caused good men to reject the whole in disgust, and to view Jesus himself as an impostor.

Notwithstanding these disadvantages, a system of morals is presented to us, which, if filled up in the true style and spirit of the rich fragments he left us, would be the most perfect and sublime that has ever been taught by man.

The question of his being a member of the Godhead, or in direct communication with it, claimed for him, by some of his followers, and denied by others, is foreign to the present view, which is merely an estimate of the intrinsic merit of his doctrines.

1. He corrected the Deism of the Jews, confirming them in their belief of one only God, and giving them juster notions of his attributes and government.

2. His moral doctrines, relating to kindred and friends were more pure and perfect than those of the most correct of the philosophers, and greatly more so than those of the Jews; and they went far beyond both in inculcating universal philanthropy, not only to kindred and friends, to neighbors and countrymen, but to all mankind, gathering all into one family, under the bonds of love, charity, peace, common wants and common aids. A development of this head will evince the peculiar superiority of the system of Jesus over all others.

3. The precepts of philosophy, and of the Hebrew code, laid hold of actions only. He pushed his scrutinies into the heart of man; erected his tribunal in the region of his thoughts, and purified the waters at the fountain head.

4. He taught, emphatically, the doctrines of a future state, which was either doubted or disbelieved by the Jews, and wielded it with efficacy, as an important incentive, supplementary to the other motives to moral conduct.

TH: JEFFERSON

[TO JOHN ADAMS]

Monticello, October 28, 1813

· · · I agree with you that there is a natural aristocracy among men. The grounds of this are virtue and talents. Formerly, bodily powers gave place among the aristoi. But since the invention of gunpowder has armed the weak as well as the strong with missile death, bodily strength, like beauty, good humor, politeness and other accomplishments, has become but an auxiliary ground for distinctions. There is also an artificial aristocracy, founded on wealth and birth, without either virtue or talents; for with these it would belong to the first class. The natural aristocracy I consider as the most precious gift of nature, for the instruction, the trusts, and government of society. And indeed, it would have been inconsistent in creation to have formed man for the social state, and not to have provided virtue and wisdom enough to manage the concerns of the society. May we not even say, that that form of government is the best, which provides the most effectually for a pure selection of these natural aristoi into the offices of government? The artificial aristocracy is a mischievous ingredient in government, and provision should be made to prevent its ascendency. On the question, what is the best provision, you and I differ; but we differ as rational friends, using the free exercise of our own reason, and mutually indulging its errors. You think it best to put the pseudo-aristoi into a separate chamber of legislation, where they may be hindered from doing mischief by their coordinate branches, and where, also, they may be a protection to wealth against the Agrarian and plundering enterprises of the majority of the people. I think that to give them power in order to prevent them from doing mischief, is arming them for it, and increasing instead of remedying the evil. For if the co-ordinate branches can arrest their action, so may they that of the co-ordinates. Mischief may be done negatively as well as positively. Of this, a cabal in the Senate of the United States has furnished many proofs. Nor do I believe them necessary to protect the wealthy because enough of these will find their way into every branch of the legislation, to protect themselves. From fifteen to twenty legislatures of our own, in action for thirty years past, have proved that no fears of an equalization of property are to be apprehended from them. I think the best remedy is exactly that provided by all our constitutions, to leave to the citizens the free election and separation of the aristoi from the pseudo-aristoi, of the wheat from the chaff. In general they will elect the really good and wise. In some instances, wealth may corrupt, and birth blind them; but not in sufficient degree to endanger the society.

It is probable that our difference of opinion may, in some measure, be produced by a difference of character in those among whom we lived. From what I have seen of Massachusetts and Connecticut myself, and still more from what I have heard, and the character given of the former by yourself, who know them so much better, there seems to be in those two States a traditionary reverence for certain families, which has rendered the offices of the government nearly hereditary in those families. I presume that from an early period of your history, members of those families happening to possess virtue and talents, have honestly exercised them for the good of the people, and by their services have endeared their names to them. In coupling Connecticut with you, I mean it politically only; not morally. For having made the Bible the common law of their land, they seemed to have modeled their morality on the story of Jacob and Laban. But although this hereditary succession to office with you, may, in some degree, be founded in real family merit, yet in a much higher degree, it has proceeded from your strict alliance of Church and State. These families are canonised in the eyes of the people on common principles, "you tickle me, and I will tickle you." In Virginia we have nothing of this. Our clergy, before the revolution, having been secured against rivalship by fixed salaries, did not give themselves the trouble of acquiring influence over the people. Of wealth, there were great accumulations in particular families, handed down from generation to generation under the English law of entails. But the only object of ambition for the wealthy was a seat in the King's Council. All their court then was paid to the crown and its creatures; and they Philipised [sided with the King, like Philip of Macedon's bribed supporters] in all collisions between the King and the people. Hence they were unpopular; and that unpopularity continues attached to their names. A Randolph, a Carter, or a Burwell must have great personal superiority over a common competitor to be elected by the people even at this day. At the first session of our legislature after the Declaration of Independence, we passed a law abolishing entails. And this was followed by one abolishing the privilege of primogeniture, and dividing the lands of intestates equally among all their children, or other representatives. These laws, drawn by myself, laid the ax to the foot of pseudo-aristocracy. And had another which I prepared been adopted by the legislature, our work would have been complete. It was a bill for the more general diffusion of learning. This proposed to divide every county into wards of five or six miles square, like your townships; to establish in each ward a free school for reading, writing and common arithmetic; to provide for the annual selection of the best subjects from these schools, who might receive, at the public expense, a higher degree of education at a district school; and from these district schools to select a certain number of the most promising subjects, to be completed at an University, where all the useful sciences should be taught. Worth and genius would thus have been sought out from every condition of life and completely prepared by education for defeating the competition of wealth and birth for public trusts. My proposition had for a further object to impart to these wards those portions of self-government for which they are best qualified, by confiding to them the care of their poor, their roads, police, elections, the nomination of jurors, administration of justice in small cases, elementary exercises of militia; in short, to have made them little republics, with a warden at the head of each, for all those concerns which, being under their eye, they would better manage than the larger republics of the county or State. A general call of ward meetings by their wardens on the same day through the State, would at any time produce the genuine sense of the people on any required point, and would enable the State to act in mass, as your people have so often done, and with so much effect by their town meetings. The law for religious freedom, which made a part of this system, having put down the aristocracy of the clergy, and restored to the citizen freedom of the mind, and those of entails and descents nurturing an equality of condition among them, this on education would have raised the mass of the people to the high ground of moral respectability necessary to their own safety, and to orderly government; and would have completed the great object of qualifying them to select the veritable aristoi, for the trusts of government, to the exclusion of the pseudalists; and the same Theognis who has furnished the epigraphs of your two letters, assures us that Οὐδεμίαν πω Κύρν', ἀγαθοὶ πόλιν ὤλεσαν ἄνδρες [Curnus, good men have never yet destroyed a state].

Although this law has not yet been acted on but in a small and inefficient degree, it is still considered as before the legislature, with other bills of the revised code, not yet taken up, and I have great hope that some patriotic spirit will, at a favorable moment, call it up, and make it the keystone of the arch of our government.

With respect to aristocracy, we should further consider, that before the establishment of the American States, nothing was known to history but the man of the old world, crowded within limits either small or overcharged, and steeped in the vices which that situation generates. A government adapted to such men would be one thing; but a very different one, that for the man of these States. Here every one may have land to labor for himself, if he chooses, or, preferring the exercise of any other industry, may exact for it such compensation as not only to afford a comfortable subsistence, but wherewith to provide for a cessation from labor in old age. Every one, by his property, or by his satisfactory situation, is interested in the support of law and order. And such men may safely and advantageously reserve to themselves a wholesome control over their public affairs, and a degree of freedom, which, in the hands of the *canaille* [rabble] of the cities of Europe, would be instantly perverted to the demolition and destruction of everything public and private. The history of the last twenty-five years of France, and of the last forty years in America, nay of its last two hundred years, proves the truth of both parts of this observation.

But even in Europe a change has sensibly taken place in the mind of man. Science had liberated the ideas of those who read and reflect, and the American example had kindled feelings of right in the people. An insurrection has consequently begun, of science, talents, and courage, against rank and birth, which have fallen into contempt. It has failed in its first effort, because the mobs of the cities, the instrument used for its accomplishment, debased by ignorance, poverty and vice, could not be restrained to rational action. But the world will recover from the panic of this first catastrophe. Science is progressive, and talents and enterprise on the alert. Resort may be had to the people of the country, a more governable power from their principles and subordination; and rank, and birth and tinsel-aristocracy will finally shrink into insignificance, even there. This, however, we have no right to meddle with. It suffices for us, if the moral and physical condition of our own citizens qualifies them to select the able and good for the direction of their government, with a recurrence of elections at such short periods as will enable them to displace an unfaithful servant, before the mischief he meditates may be irremediable.

I have thus stated my opinion on a point on which we differ, not with a view to controversy, for we are both too old to change opinions which are the result of a long life of inquiry and reflection; but on the suggestions of a former letter of yours, that we ought not to die before we have explained ourselves to each other. We acted in perfect harmony, through a long and perilous contest for our liberty and independence. A constitution has been acquired, which, though neither of us thinks perfect, yet both consider as competent to render our fellow citizens the happiest and the securest on whom the sun has ever shone. If we do not think exactly alike as to its imperfections, it matters little to our country, which, after devoting to it long lives of disinterested labor, we have delivered over to our successors in life, who will be able to take care of it and of themselves.

Of the pamphlet on aristocracy which has been sent to you, or who may be its author, I have heard nothing but through your letter. If the person you suspect, it may be known from the quaint, mystical, and hyperbolical ideas, involved in affected, new-fangled and pedantic terms which stamp his writings. Whatever it be, I hope your quiet is not to be affected at this day by the rudeness or intemperance of scribblers; but that you may continue in tranquillity to live and to rejoice in the prosperity of our country, until it shall be your own wish to take your seat among the aristoi who have gone before you. Ever and affectionately yours.

Th: Jefferson

[TO BENJAMIN WATERHOUSE]

Monticello, June 26, 1822

Dear Sir:

I have received and read with thankfulness and pleasure your denunciation of the abuses of tobacco and wine. Yet, however sound in its principles, I expect it will be but a sermon to the wind. You will find it as difficult to inculcate these sanative precepts on the sensualities of the present day as to convince an Athanasian that there is but one God. I wish success to both attempts, and am happy to learn from you that the latter at least is making progress, and the more rapidly in proportion as our Platonizing Christians make more stir and noise about it. The doctrines of Jesus are simple, and tend all to the happiness of man: that there is one only God, and He all perfect; that there is a future state of rewards and punishments; that to love God with all thy heart and thy neighbor as thyself is the sum of religion. These are the great points on which He endeavored to reform the religion of the Jews.

But compare with these the demoralizing dogmas of Calvin: that there are three Gods; that good works, or the love of our neighbor, are nothing; that faith is everything, and the more incomprehensible the proposition, the more merit in its faith; that reason in religion is of unlawful use; that God, from the beginning, elected certain individuals to be saved and certain others to be damned, and that no crimes of the former can damn them, no virtues of the latter save.

Now, which of these is the true and charitable Christian? He who believes and acts on the simple doctrines of Jesus? Or the impious dogmatists, as Athanasians and Calvin? Verily I say these are the false shepherds foretold as to enter not by the door into the sheepfold, but to climb up some other way. They are mere usurpers of the Christian name, teaching a counter-religion made up of the deliria of crazy imaginations as foreign from Christianity as that of Mahomet. Their blasphemies have driven thinking men into infidelity, who have too hastily rejected the supposed author himself with the horrors so falsely imputed to him. Had the doctrines of Jesus been preached always as pure as they came from his lips, the whole civilized world would now have been Christian. I rejoice that in this blessed country of free inquiry and belief, which has surrendered its creed and conscience to neither kings nor priests, the genuine doctrine of only one God is reviving, and I trust that there is not a young man now living in the United States who will not die a Unitarian.

But much I fear that when this great truth shall be re-established, its votaries will fall into the fatal error of fabricating formulas of creed and confessions of faith, the engines which so soon destroyed the religion of Jesus and made of Christendom a mere Aceldama; that they will give up morals for mysteries, and Jesus for Plato. How much wiser are the Quakers, who, agreeing in the fundamental doctrines of the gospel, schismatize about no mysteries, and keeping within the pale of common sense, suffer no speculative differences of opinion, any more than of feature, to impair the love of their brethren. Be this the wisdom of Unitarians, this the holy mantle which shall cover within its charitable circumference all who believe in one God, and who love their neighbor!

. . .

[TO JAMES MONROE]

Monticello, October 24, 1823

DEAR SIR:

The question presented by the letters you have sent me is the most momentous which has ever been offered to my contemplation since that of independence. That made us a nation, this sets our compass and points the course which we are to steer through the ocean of time opening on us. And never could we embark on it under circumstances more auspicious. Our first and fundamental maxim should be, never to entangle ourselves in the broils of Europe. Our second, never to suffer Europe to intermeddle with the cis-Atlantic affairs. America, North and South, has a set of interests distinct from those of Europe, and peculiarly her own. She should therefore have a system of her own, separate and apart from that of Europe. While the last is laboring to become the domicile of despotism, our endeavor should surely be, to make our hemisphere that of freedom. One nation, most of all, could disturb us in this pursuit; she now offers to lead, aid, and accompany us in it. By acceding to her proposition, we detach her from the bands, bring her mighty weight into the scale of free government, and emancipate a continent at one stroke, which might otherwise linger long in doubt and difficulty. Great Britain is the nation which can do us the most harm of any one, or all on earth; and with her on our side we need not fear of the whole world. With her then, we should most sedulously cherish a cordial friendship; and nothing would tend more to knit our affections than to be fighting once more, side by side, in the same cause. Not that I would purchase even her amity at the price of taking part in her wars. But the war in which the present proposition might engage us should that be its consequence, is not her war, but ours. Its object is to introduce and establish the American system, of keeping out of our land all foreign powers, of never permitting those of Europe to intermeddle with the affairs of our nations. It is to maintain our own principle, not to depart from it. And if, to facilitate this, we can effect a division in the body of the European powers, and draw over to our side its most powerful member, surely we should do it. But I am clearly of Mr. Canning's opinion, that it will prevent instead of provoking war. With Great Britain withdrawn from their scale and shifted into that of our two continents, all Europe combined would not undertake such a war. For how would they propose to get at either enemy without superior fleets? Nor is the occasion to be slighted which this proposition offers, of declaring our protest against the atrocious violations of the rights of nations, by the interference of any one in the internal affairs of another, so flagitiously begun by Bonaparte, and now continued by the equally lawless Alliance, calling itself Holy.

But we have first to ask ourselves a question. Do we wish to acquire to our own confederacy any one or more of the Spanish provinces? I candidly confess, that I have ever looked on Cuba as the most interesting addition which could ever be made to our system of States. The control which, with Florida Point, this island would give us over the Gulf of Mexico, and the countries and isthmus bordering on it, as well as all those whose waters flow into it, would fill up the measure of our political well-being. Yet, as I am sensible that this can never be obtained, even with her own consent, but by war; and its independence, which is our second interest, (and especially its independence of England,) can be secured without it, I have no hesitation in abandoning my first wish to future chances, and accepting its independence, with peace and the friendship of England, rather than its association, at the expense of war and her enmity.

I could honestly, therefore, join in the declaration proposed, that we aim not at the acquisition of any of those possessions, that we will not stand in the way of any amicable arrangement between them and the Mother country; but that we will oppose, with all our means, the forcible interposition of any other power, as auxiliary, stipendiary, or under any other form or pretext, and most especially, their transfer to any power by conquest, cession, or acquisition in any other way. I should think it, therefore, advisable, that the Executive should encourage the British government to a continuance in the dispositions expressed in these letters, by an assurance of his concurrence with them as far as his authority goes; and that as it may lead to war, the declaration of which requires an act of Congress, the case shall be laid before them for consideration at their first meeting, and under the reasonable aspect in which it is seen by himself.

I have been so long weaned from political subjects, and have so long ceased to take any interest in them, that I am sensible I am not qualified to offer opinions on them worthy of any attention. But the question now proposed involves consequences so lasting, and effects so decisive of our future destinies, as to rekindle all the interest I have heretofore felt on such occasions, and to induce me to the hazard of opinions, which will prove only my wish to contribute still my mite towards anything which may be useful to our country. And praying you to accept it at only what it is worth, I add the assurance of my constant and affectionate friendship and respect.

TH: JEFFERSON

THE FEDERALIST (1788):

Alexander Hamilton (1757–1804) and James Madison (1751–1836)

☆

The eighty-five *Federalist* papers were written by Hamilton, John Jay (1745–1829), and Madison under the joint pseudonym of "Publius." Generally it is believed that Hamilton, the leading spirit of the enterprise, wrote fifty-one of them, that Madison wrote twenty-six, that Madison and Hamilton wrote three in collaboration, and that Jay wrote five. Seventy-seven of the papers appeared in New York periodicals between October, 1787, and May, 1788. When Hamilton issued the two-volume collection of the essays in 1788, he added the last eight.

Madison grew up in the Virginia-planter class of Jefferson and, like the man under whom he was to serve as Secretary of State, held the liberal views of the Enlightenment; as "The Father of the Constitution," he succeeded Jefferson in the Presidency. Hamilton and Jay represented that aspect of eighteenth-century thought which reflected a profound distrust of the liberal view of man as eminently reasonable, perhaps perfectible, and capable of self-government. An oversimplified yet fair approximation of their attitudes is furnished in their own famous dicta: Hamilton's "The people, Sir, is a great beast" and Jay's "Those who own the country ought to govern it." Although the *Federalist* essays represent a reversal of the philosophy that dictated the rhetoric and the principles of *The Declaration of Independence* and the *Articles of Confederation*, Madison joined in support of the Constitution in an attempt to preserve the ideas of the Revolution (he was the prime mover behind the Bill of Rights) and in the belief that a workable compromise of conflicting beliefs could be effected within the framework of a viable central government. The conflict between what today we would call conservative and liberal was, partly, an issue in which man was seen in Calvinistic light (Hamilton) or in the light of the Age of Reason (Jefferson). For the first, especially considering the economic orientation of Hamilton and Jay and their view of man's depraved tendencies, strong government was needed to establish an unruffled order in which the interests of the nation and of those who controlled the sources of wealth could be protected. For the second (Madison), government was not a desirable end in itself, but a necessary means of protecting the liberties and natural rights of the individual. The brilliance of the men involved, together with the importance of the issues, combined to produce some of the most significant political literature of all time. Ever since the pronouncements of Supreme Court Justices Jay and Marshall, *The Federalist* has been considered a basic source of constitutional law and one of the clearest commentaries on the fundamentals of American government. The following selections represent some of the most important contributions of Hamilton and Madison.

Editions and accounts of the men and their works are to be found in P. L. Ford, ed., *Essays on the Constitution of the United States* (1892); G. Hunt, ed., *The Writings of James Madison*, 9 vols. (1900–1910); G. Hunt, *The Life of James Madison* (1902); H. C. Lodge, ed., *The Works of Alexander Hamilton*, 12 vols. (1904); H. J. Ford, *Alexander Hamilton* (1925); J. T. Adams, ed., *Jeffersonian Principles and Hamiltonian Principles* (1932); F. C. Prescott, ed., *Alexander Hamilton and Thomas Jefferson* (1934); L. K. Caldwell, *The Administrative Theories of Hamilton and Jefferson* (1944); N. Schachner, *Alexander Hamilton* (1946); I. Brant, *James Madison, Father of the Constitution* (1950); A. Koch, *Jefferson and Madison* (1950); L. Hacker, *Alexander Hamilton in the American Tradition* (1957); B. Mitchell, *Alexander Hamilton: The National Adventure, 1788–1804* (1962); and B. Mitchell, "If Hamilton Were Here Today: Some Unanswered Questions," *South Atlantic Quarterly*, LXII (1963).

No. I: *(Hamilton)*

TO THE PEOPLE OF THE STATE OF NEW YORK:

After an unequivocal experience of the inefficiency of the subsisting federal government, you are called upon to deliberate on a new Constitution for the United States of America. The subject speaks its own importance; comprehending in its consequences nothing less than the existence of the UNION, the safety and welfare of the parts of which it is composed, the fate of an empire in many respects the most interesting in the world. It has been frequently remarked that it seems to have been reserved to the people of this country, by their conduct and example, to decide the important question, whether societies of men are really capable or not of establishing good government from reflection and choice, or whether they are forever destined to depend for their political constitutions on accident and force. If there be any truth in the remark, the crisis at which we are arrived may with propriety be regarded as the era in which that decision is to be made; and a wrong election of the part we shall act may, in this view, deserve to be considered as the general misfortune of mankind.

This idea will add the inducements of philanthropy to those of patriotism, to heighten the solicitude which all considerate and good men must feel for the event. Happy will it be if our choice should be directed by a judicious estimate of our true interests, unperplexed and unbiased by considerations not connected with the public good. But this is a thing more ardently to be wished than seriously to be expected. The plan offered to our deliberations affects too many particular interests, innovates upon too many local institutions, not to involve in its discussion a variety of objects foreign to its merits, and of views, passions and prejudices little favorable to the discovery of truth.

Among the most formidable of the obstacles which the new Constitution will have to encounter may readily be distinguished the obvious interest of a certain class of men in every State to resist all changes which may hazard a diminution of the power, emolument, and consequence of the offices they hold under the State establishments; and the perverted ambition of another class of men, who will either hope to aggrandize themselves by the confusions of their country, or will flatter themselves with fairer prospects of elevation from the subdivision of the empire into several partial confederacies than from its union under one government.

It is not, however, my design to dwell upon observations of this nature. I am well aware that it would be disingenuous to resolve indiscriminately the opposition of any set of men (merely because their situations might subject them to suspicion) into interested or ambitious views. Candor will oblige us to admit that even such men may be actuated by upright intentions; and it cannot be doubted that much of the opposition which has made its appearance, or may hereafter make its appearance, will spring from sources, blameless at least, if not respectable—the honest errors of minds led astray by preconceived jealousies and fears. So numerous indeed and so powerful are the causes which serve to give a false bias to the judgment, that we, upon many occasions, see wise and good men on the wrong as well as on the right side of questions of the first magnitude to society. This circumstance, if duly attended to, would furnish a lesson of moderation to those who are ever so much persuaded of their being in the right in any controversy. And a further reason for caution, in this respect, might be drawn from the reflection that we are not always sure that those who advocate the truth are influenced by purer principles than their antagonists. Ambition, avarice, personal animosity, party opposition, and many other motives not more laudable than these, are apt to operate as well upon those who support as those who oppose the right side of a question. Were there not even these inducements to moderation, nothing could be more ill-judged than that intolerant spirit which has, at all times, characterized political parties. For in politics, as in religion, it is equally absurd to aim at making proselytes by fire and sword. Heresies in either can rarely be cured by persecution.

And yet, however just these sentiments will be allowed to be, we have already sufficient indications that it will happen in this as in all former cases of great national discussion. A torrent of angry and malignant passions will be let loose. To judge from the conduct of the opposite parties, we shall be led to conclude that they will mutually hope to evince the justness of their opinions, and to increase the number of their converts by the loudness of their declamations and the bitterness of their invectives. An enlightened zeal for the energy and efficiency of government will be stigmatized as the offspring of a temper fond of despotic power and hostile to the principles of liberty. An over-scrupulous jealousy of danger to the rights of the people, which is more commonly the fault of the head than of the heart, will be represented as mere pretense and artifice, the stale bait for popularity at the expense of the public good. It will be forgotten, on the one hand, that jealousy is the usual concomitant of love, and that the noble enthusiasm of liberty is apt to be infected with a spirit of narrow and illiberal distrust. On the other hand, it will be equally forgotten that the vigor of government is essential to the security of liberty; that, in the contemplation of a sound and well-informed judgment, their interest can never be separated; and that a dangerous ambition more often lurks behind the specious mask of zeal for the rights of the people than under the forbidding appearance of zeal for the firmness and efficiency of government. History will teach us that the former has been found a much more certain road to the introduction of despotism than the latter, and that of those men who have overturned the liberties of republics, the greatest number have begun their career by paying an obsequious court to the people; commencing demagogues, and ending tyrants.

In the course of the preceding observations, I have had an eye, my fellow-citizens, to putting you upon your guard against all attempts, from whatever quarter, to influence your decision, in a matter of the utmost moment to your welfare, by any impressions other than those which may result from the evidence of truth. You will, no doubt, at the same time, have collected from the general scope of them, that they proceed from a source not unfriendly to the new Constitution. Yes, my countrymen, I own to you that, after having given it an attentive consideration, I am clearly of opinion it is your interest to adopt it. I am convinced that this is the safest course for your liberty, your dignity, and your happiness. I affect not reserves which I do not feel. I will not amuse you with an appearance of deliberation when I have decided. I frankly acknowledge to you my convictions, and I will freely lay before you the reasons on which they are founded. The consciousness of good intentions disdains ambiguity. I shall not, however, multiply professions on this head. My motives must remain in the depository of my own breast. My arguments will be open to all, and may be judged of by all. They shall at least be offered in a spirit which will not disgrace the cause of truth.

I propose, in a series of papers, to discuss the following interesting particulars: The utility of the UNION to your political prosperity—The insufficiency of the present Confederation to preserve that Union—The necessity of a government at least equally energetic with the one proposed, to the attainment of this object—The conformity of the proposed Constitution to the true principles of republican government—Its analogy to your own State constitution—and lastly, The additional security which its adoption will afford to the preservation of that species of government, to liberty, and to property.

In the progress of this discussion I shall endeavor to give a satisfactory answer to all the objections which shall have made their appearance, that may seem to have any claim to your attention.

It may perhaps be thought superfluous to offer arguments to prove the utility of the UNION, a point, no doubt, deeply engraved on the hearts of the great body of the people in every State, and one which, it may be imagined, has no adversaries. But the fact is, that we already hear it whispered in the private circles of those who oppose the new Constitution, that the thirteen States are of too great extent for any general system, and that we must of necessity resort to separate confederacies of distinct portions of the whole.[1] This doctrine will, in all probability, be gradually propagated, till it has votaries enough to countenance an open avowal of it. For nothing can be more evident, to those who are able to take an enlarged view of the subject, than the alternative of an adoption of the new Constitution or a dismemberment of the Union. It will therefore be of use to begin by examining the advantages of that Union, the certain evils, and the probable dangers, to which every State will be exposed from its dissolution. This shall accordingly constitute the subject of my next address.

PUBLIUS

No. X: (Madison)

TO THE PEOPLE OF THE STATE OF NEW YORK:

Among the numerous advantages promised by a well-constructed Union, none deserves to be more accurately

---

[1] The same idea, tracing the arguments to their consequences, is held out in several of the late publications against the new Constitution.— PUBLIUS.

developed than its tendency to break and control the violence of faction. The friend of popular governments never finds himself so much alarmed for their character and fate as when he contemplates their propensity to this dangerous vice. He will not fail, therefore, to set a due value on any plan which, without violating the principles to which he is attached, provides a proper cure for it. The instability, injustice, and confusion introduced into the public councils, have, in truth, been the mortal diseases under which popular governments have everywhere perished; as they continue to be the favorite and fruitful topics from which the adversaries to liberty derive their most specious declamations. The valuable improvements made by the American constitutions on the popular models, both ancient and modern, cannot certainly be too much admired; but it would be an unwarrantable partiality to contend that they have as effectually obviated the danger on this side, as was wished and expected. Complaints are everywhere heard from our most considerate and virtuous citizens, equally the friends of public and private faith, and of public and personal liberty, that our governments are too unstable, that the public good is disregarded in the conflicts of rival parties, and that measures are too often decided, not according to the rules of justice and the rights of the minor party, but by the superior force of an interested and overbearing majority. However anxiously we may wish that these complaints had no foundation, the evidence of known facts will not permit us to deny that they are in some degree true. It will be found, indeed, on a candid review of our situation, that some of the distresses under which we labor have been erroneously charged on the operation of our governments; but it will be found, at the same time, that other causes will not alone account for many of our heaviest misfortunes; and, particularly, for that prevailing and increasing distrust of public engagements, and alarm for private rights, which are echoed from one end of the continent to the other. These must be chiefly, if not wholly, effects of the unsteadiness and injustice with which a factious spirit has tainted our public administrations.

By a faction, I understand a number of citizens, whether amounting to a majority or minority of the whole, who are united and actuated by some common impulse of passion, or of interest, adverse to the rights of other citizens, or to the permanent and aggregate interests of the community.

There are two methods of curing the mischiefs of faction: the one, by removing its causes; the other, by controlling its effects.

There are again two methods of removing the causes of faction: the one, by destroying the liberty which is essential to its existence; the other, by giving to every citizen the same opinions, the same passions, and the same interests.

It could never be more truly said than of the first remedy, that it was worse than the disease. Liberty is to faction what air is to fire, an aliment without which it instantly expires. But it could not be less folly to abolish liberty, which is essential to political life, because it nourishes faction, than it would be to wish the annihilation of air, which is essential to animal life, because it imparts to fire its destructive agency.

The second expedient is as impracticable as the first would be unwise. As long as the reason of man continues fallible, and he is at liberty to exercise it, different opinions will be formed. As long as the connection subsists between his reason and his self-love, his opinions and his passions will have a reciprocal influence on each other; and the former will be objects to which the latter will attach themselves. The diversity in the faculties of men, from which the rights of property originate, is not less an insuperable obstacle to a uniformity of interests. The protection of these faculties is the first object of government. From the protection of different and unequal faculties of acquiring property, the possession of different degrees and kinds of property immediately results; and from the influence of these on the sentiments and views of the respective proprietors, ensues a division of the society into different interests and parties.

The latent causes of faction are thus sown in the nature of man; and we see them everywhere brought into different degrees of activity, according to the different circumstances of civil society. A zeal for different opinions concerning religion, concerning government, and many other points, as well of speculation as of practice; an attachment of different leaders ambitiously contending for pre-eminence and power; or to persons of other descriptions whose fortunes have been interesting to the human passions, have, in turn, divided mankind into parties, inflamed them with mutual animosity, and rendered them much more disposed to vex and oppress each other than to co-operate for their common good. So strong is this propensity of mankind to fall into mutual animosities, that where no substantial occasion presents itself, the most frivolous and fanciful distinctions have been sufficient to kindle their unfriendly passions and excite their most violent conflicts. But the most common and durable source of factions has been the various and unequal distribution of property. Those who hold and those who are without property have ever formed distinct interests in society. Those who are creditors, and those who are debtors, fall under a like discrimination. A landed interest, a manufacturing interest, a mercantile interest, a moneyed interest, with many lesser interests, grow up of necessity in civilized nations, and divide them into different classes, actuated by different sentiments and views. The regulation of these various and interfering interests forms the principal task of modern legislation, and involves the spirit of party and faction in the necessary and ordinary operations of the government.

No man is allowed to be a judge in his own cause, because his interest would certainly bias his judgment, and, not improbably, corrupt his integrity. With equal, nay, with greater reason, a body of men are unfit to be both judges and parties at the same time; yet what are many of the most important acts of legislation but so many judicial determinations, not indeed concerning the rights of single persons, but concerning the rights of large bodies of citizens? And what are the different classes of legislators but advocates and parties to the causes which they determine? Is a law proposed concerning private debts? It is a question to which the creditors are parties on one side and the debtors on the other. Justice ought to hold the balance between them. Yet the parties are, and must be, themselves the judges; and the most numerous party, or, in other words, the most powerful faction must be expected to prevail. Shall domestic manufactures be encouraged, and in what degree, by restrictions on foreign manufactures? are questions which would be differently decided by the landed and the manufacturing classes, and probably by neither with a sole regard to justice and the public good. The apportionment of taxes on the various descriptions of property is an act which seems to require the most exact impartiality; yet there is, perhaps, no legislative act in which greater opportunity and temptation are given to a predominant party to trample on the rules of justice. Every shilling with which they overburden the inferior number is a shilling saved to their own pockets.

It is in vain to say that enlightened statesmen will be able to adjust these clashing interests, and render them all subservient to the public good. Enlightened statesmen will not always be at the helm. Nor, in many cases, can such an adjustment be made at all without taking into view indirect and remote considerations, which will rarely prevail over the immediate interest which one party may find in disregarding the rights of another or the good of the whole.

The inference to which we are brought is, that the *causes* of faction cannot be removed, and that relief is only to be sought in the means of controlling its *effects*.

If a faction consists of less than a majority, relief is supplied by the republican principle, which enables the majority to defeat its sinister views by regular vote. It may clog the administration, it may convulse the society; but it will be unable to execute and mask its violence under the forms of the Constitution. When a majority is included in a faction, the form of popular government, on the other hand, enables it to sacrifice to its ruling passion or interest both the public good and the rights of other citizens. To secure the public good and private rights against the danger of such a faction, and at the same time to preserve the spirit and the form of popular government, is then the great object to which our inquiries are directed. Let me add that it is the great desideratum by which this form of government can be rescued from the opprobrium under which it has so long labored, and be recommended to the esteem and adoption of mankind.

By what means is this object obtainable? Evidently by one of two only. Either the existence of the same passion or interest in a majority at the same time must be prevented, or the majority, having such co-existent passion or interest, must be rendered, by their number and local situation, unable to concert and carry into effect schemes of oppression. If the impulse and the opportunity be suffered to coincide, we well know that neither moral nor religious motives can be relied on as an adequate control. They are not found to be such on the injustice and violence of individuals, and lose their efficacy in proportion to the number combined together, that is, in proportion as their efficacy becomes needful.

From this view of the subject it may be concluded that a pure democracy, by which I mean a society consisting of a small number of citizens, who assemble and administer the government in person, can admit of no cure for the mischiefs of faction. A common passion or interest will, in almost every case, be felt by a majority of the whole; a communication and concert result from the form of government itself; and there is nothing to check the inducements to sacrifice the weaker party or an obnoxious individual. Hence it is that such democracies have ever been spectacles of turbulence and contention; have ever been found incompatible with personal security or the rights of property; and have in general been as short in their lives as they have been violent in their deaths. Theoretic politicians, who have patronized this species of government, have erroneously supposed that by reducing mankind to a perfect equality in their political rights, they would, at the same time, be perfectly equalized and assimilated in their possessions, their opinions, and their passions.

A republic, by which I mean a government in which the scheme of representation takes place, opens a different prospect, and promises the cure for which we are seeking. Let us examine the points in which it varies from pure democracy, and we shall comprehend both the nature of the cure and the efficacy which it must derive from the Union.

The two great points of difference between a democracy and a republic are: first, the delegation of the government, in the latter, to a small number of citizens elected by the rest; secondly, the greater number of citizens, and greater sphere of country, over which the latter may be extended.

The effect of the first difference is, on the one hand, to refine and enlarge the public views, by passing them through the medium of a chosen body of citizens, whose wisdom may best discern the true interest of their country, and whose patriotism and love of justice will be least likely to sacrifice it to temporary or partial considerations. Under such a regulation, it may well happen that the public voice, pronounced by the representatives of the people, will be more consonant to the public good than if pronounced by the people themselves, convened for the purpose. On the other hand, the effect may be inverted. Men of factious tempers, of local prejudices, or of sinister designs, may, by intrigue, by corruption, or by other means, first obtain the suffrages, and then betray the interests, of the people. The question resulting is, whether small or extensive republics are more favourable to the election of proper guardians of the public weal; and it is clearly decided in favor of the latter by two obvious considerations:

In the first place, it is to be remarked that, however small the republic may be, the representatives must be raised to a certain number, in order to guard against the cabals of a few; and that, however large it may be, they must be limited to a certain number, in order to guard against the confusion of a multitude. Hence the number of representatives in the two cases not being in proportion to that of the two constituents, and being proportionally greater in the small republic, it follows that, if the proportion of fit characters be not less in the large than in the small republic, the former will present a greater option, and consequently a greater probability of a fit choice.

In the next place, as each representative will be chosen by a greater number of citizens in the large than in the small republic, it will be more difficult for unworthy candidates to practise with success the vicious arts by which elections are too often carried; and the suffrages of the people being more free, will be more likely to center in men who possess the most attractive merit and the most diffusive and established character.

It must be confessed that in this, as in most other cases, there is a mean, on both sides of which inconveniences will be found to lie. By enlarging too much the number of electors, you render the representative too little acquainted with all their local circumstances and lesser interests; as by reducing it too much, you render him unduly attached to these, and too little fit to comprehend and pursue great and national objects. The federal Constitution forms a happy combination in this respect; the great and aggregate interests being referred to the national, the local and particular to the State legislatures.

The other point of difference is, the greater number of

citizens and extent of territory which may be brought within the compass of republican than of democratic government; and it is this circumstance principally which renders factious combinations less to be dreaded in the former than in the latter. The smaller the society, the fewer probably will be the distinct parties and interests composing it; the fewer the distinct parties and interests, the more frequently will a majority be found of the same party; and the smaller the number of individuals composing a majority, and the smaller the compass within which they are placed, the more easily will they concert and execute their plans of oppression. Extend the sphere, and you take in a greater variety of parties and interests; you make it less probable that a majority of the whole will have a common motive to invade the rights of other citizens; or if such a common motive exists, it will be more difficult for all who feel it to discover their own strength, and to act in unison with each other. Besides other impediments, it may be remarked that, where there is a consciousness of unjust or dishonorable purposes, communication is always checked by distrust in proportion to the number whose concurrence is necessary.

Hence, it clearly appears, that the same advantage which a republic has over a democracy, in controlling the effects of faction, is enjoyed by a large over a small republic—is enjoyed by the Union over the States composing it. Does the advantage consist in the substitution of representatives whose enlightened views and virtuous sentiments render them superior to local prejudices and to schemes of injustice? It will not be denied that the representation of the Union will be most likely to possess these requisite endowments. Does it consist in the greater security afforded by a greater variety of parties, against the event of any one party being able to outnumber and oppress the rest? In an equal degree does the increased variety of parties comprised within the Union increase this security? Does it, in fine, consist in the greater obstacles opposed to the concert and accomplishment of the secret wishes of an unjust and interested majority? Here, again, the extent of the Union gives it the most palpable advantage.

The influence of factious leaders may kindle a flame within their particular States, but will be unable to spread a general conflagration through the other States. A religious sect may degenerate into a political faction in a part of the Confederacy; but the variety of sects dispersed over the entire face of it must secure the national councils against any danger from that source. A rage for paper money, for an abolition of debts, for an equal division of property, or for any other improper or wicked project, will be less apt to pervade the whole body of the Union than a particular member of it; in the same proportion as such a malady is more likely to taint a particular county or district, than an entire State.

In the extent and proper structure of the Union, therefore, we behold a republican remedy for the diseases most incident to republican government. And according to the degree of pleasure and pride we feel in being republicans, ought to be our zeal in cherishing the spirit and supporting the character of Federalists.

PUBLIUS

No. XXIII: (Hamilton)

TO THE PEOPLE OF THE STATE OF NEW YORK:

The necessity of a Constitution, at least equally energetic with the one proposed, to the preservation of the Union, is the point at the examination of which we are now arrived.

This inquiry will naturally divide itself into three branches—the objects to be provided for by the federal government, the quantity of power necessary to the accomplishment of those objects, the persons upon whom that power ought to operate. Its distribution and organization will properly claim our attention under the succeeding head.

The principal purposes to be answered by union are these—the common defense of the members; the preservation of the public peace, as well against internal convulsions as external attacks; the regulation of commerce with other nations and between the States; the superintendence of our intercourse, political and commercial, with foreign countries.

The authorities essential to the common defense are these: to raise armies; to build and equip fleets; to prescribe rules for the government of both; to direct their operations; to provide for their support. These powers ought to exist without limitation, because it is impossible to foresee or define the extent and variety of national exigencies, or the correspondent extent and variety of the means which may be necessary to satisfy them. The circumstances that endanger the safety of nations are infinite, and for this reason no constitutional shackles can wisely be imposed on the power to which the care of it is committed. This power ought to be co-extensive with all the possible combinations of such circumstances; and ought to be under the direction of the same councils which are appointed to preside over the common defense.

This is one of those truths which, to a correct and unprejudiced mind, carries its own evidence along with it; and may be obscured, but cannot be made plainer by argument or reasoning. It rests upon axioms as simple as they are universal; the *means* ought to be proportioned to the *end;* the persons, from whose agency the attainment of any *end* is expected, ought to possess the *means* by which it is to be attained.

Whether there ought to be a federal government entrusted with the care of the common defense, is a question in the first instance open for discussion; but the moment it is decided in the affirmative, it will follow, that that government ought to be clothed with all the powers requisite to complete execution of its trust. And unless it can be shown that the circumstances which may affect the public safety are reducible within certain determinate limits; unless the contrary of this position can be fairly and rationally disputed, it must be admitted, as a necessary consequence, that there can be no limitation of that authority which is to provide for the defense and protection of the community, in any matter essential to its efficacy—that is, in any matter essential to the formation, direction, or support of the national forces.

Defective as the present Confederation has been proved to be, this principle appears to have been fully recognized by the framers of it; though they have not made proper or adequate provision for its exercise. Congress have an unlimited discretion to make requisitions of men and money; to govern the army and navy; to direct their operations. As their requisitions are made constitutionally binding upon the States, who are in fact under the most solemn obligation to furnish the supplies required of them, the intention evidently was, that the United States should command whatever resources were by them judged requisite to the "common defense and general welfare." It was presumed that a sense of their true interests, and a regard to the dictates of good faith, would be found sufficient pledges for the punctual performance of the duty of the members to the federal head.

The experiment has, however, demonstrated that this expectation was ill-founded and illusory; and the observations, made under the last head, will, I imagine, have sufficed to convince the impartial and discerning, that there is an absolute necessity for an entire change in the first principles of the system; that if we are in earnest about giving the Union energy and duration, we must abandon the vain project of legislating upon the States in their collective capacities; we must extend the laws of the federal government to the individual citizens of America; we must discard the fallacious scheme of quotas and requisitions, as equally impracticable and unjust. The result from all this is that the Union ought to be invested with full power to levy troops; to build and equip fleets; and to raise the revenues which will be required for the formation and support of an army and navy, in the customary and ordinary modes practiced in other governments.

If the circumstances of our country are such as to demand a compound instead of a simple, a confederate instead of a sole, government, the essential point which will remain to be adjusted will be to discriminate the objects, as far as it can be done, which shall appertain to the different provinces or departments of power; allowing to each the most ample authority for fulfilling the objects committed to its charge. Shall the Union be constituted the guardian of the common safety? Are fleets and armies and revenues necessary to this purpose? The government of the Union must be empowered to pass all laws, and to make all regulations which have relation to them. The same must be the case in respect to commerce, and to every other matter to which its jurisdiction is permitted to extend. Is the administration of justice between the citizens of the same State the proper department of the local governments? These must possess all the authorities which are connected with this object, and with every other that may be allotted to their particular cognizance and direction. Not to confer in each case a degree of power commensurate to the end, would be to violate the most obvious rules of prudence and propriety, and improvidently to trust the great interests of the nation to hands which are disabled from managing them with vigor and success.

Who so likely to make suitable provisions for the public defense as that body to which the guardianship of the public safety is confided; which, as the center of information, will best understand the extent and urgency of the dangers that threaten; as the representative of the whole, will feel itself most deeply interested in the preservation of every part; which, from the responsibility implied in the duty assigned to it, will be most sensibly impressed with the necessity of proper exertions; and which, by the extension of its authority throughout the States, can alone establish uniformity and concert in the plans and measures by which the common safety is to be secured? Is there not a manifest inconsistency in devolving upon the federal government the care of the general defense, and leaving in the State governments the *effective* powers by which it is to be provided for? Is not a want of cooperation the infallible consequence of such a system? And will not weakness, disorder, an undue distribution of the burdens and calamities of war, an unnecessary and intolerable increase of expense, be its natural and inevitable concomitants? Have we not had unequivocal experience of its effects in the course of the revolution which we have just accomplished?

Every view we may take of the subject, as candid inquirers after truth, will serve to convince us, that it is both unwise and dangerous to deny the federal government an unconfined authority, as to all those objects which are intrusted to its management. It will indeed deserve the most vigilant and careful attention of the people, to see that it be modeled in such a manner as to admit of its being safely vested with the requisite powers. If any plan which has been, or may be, offered to our consideration, should not, upon a dispassionate inspection, be found to answer this description, it ought to be rejected. A government, the constitution of which renders it unfit to be trusted with all the powers which a free people ought to delegate to any government, would be an unsafe and improper depository of the national interests. Wherever those can with propriety be confided, the coincident powers may safely accompany them. This is the true result of all just reasoning upon the subject. And the adversaries of the plan promulgated by the convention ought to have confined themselves to showing that the internal structure of the proposed government was such as to render it unworthy of the confidence of the people. They ought not to have wandered into inflammatory declamations and unmeaning cavils about the extent of the powers. The powers are not too extensive for the objects of federal administration, or, in other words, for the management of our national interests; nor can any satisfactory argument be framed to show that they are chargeable with such an excess. If it be true, as has been insinuated by some of the writers on the other side, that the difficulty arises from the nature of the thing, and that the extent of the country will not permit us to form a government in which such ample powers can safely be reposed, it would prove that we ought to contract our views, and resort to the expedient of separate confederacies, which will move within more practicable spheres. For the absurdity must continually stare us in the face of confiding to a government the direction of the most essential national interests, without daring to trust it to the authorities which are indispensable to their proper and efficient management. Let us not attempt to reconcile contradictions, but firmly embrace a rational alternative.

I trust, however, that the impracticability of one general system cannot be shown. I am greatly mistaken, if anything of weight has yet been advanced of this tendency; and I flatter myself that the observations which have been made in the course of these papers have served to place the reverse of that position in as clear a light as any matter still in the womb of time and experience can be susceptible of. This, at all events, must be evident, that the very difficulty itself, drawn from the extent of the country, is the strongest argument in favor of an energetic government; for any other can certainly never preserve the Union of so large an empire. If we embrace the tenets of those who oppose the adoption of the proposed Constitution, as the standard of our political creed, we cannot fail to verify the gloomy doctrines which predict the impracticability of a national system pervading entire limits of the present Confederacy.

PUBLIUS

THE CONNECTICUT WITS:

John Trumbull (1750–1831), Timothy Dwight (1752–1817), Joel Barlow (1754–1812)

The Connecticut Wits—also called the Yale Poets, the Hartford Wits, or the Wicked Wits—were not a school, a movement, or an association. They were an accident of similar beliefs and literary interests grouped in a single time and place: Hartford, Connecticut, in the middle and late 1780's. The group included, among others, Barlow, Dwight, Hopkins, Humphreys, and Trumbull. Of these only Barlow, Dwight, and Trumbull retain any repute, frail as it is; yet they were considered eminent men of letters in their own day. They occupy a transitional and peripheral place in American literary history, and are remembered not so much for the virtues of their own works as for their joint value as representatives of the early stirrings of national literary consciousness. In addition to their separate publications they collaborated in efforts such as *The Anarchiad* and *The Echo*.

Federalistic and orthodox in what remained of Calvinistic religious leanings, they devoted themselves to satires of the contemporary scene, of democratic politics, of deism, of physiocratic economics, of almost all the liberal manifestations of the day. To them as much as to anyone is owed the lingering conservatism that for so long characterized Connecticut and Yale as strongholds of New England orthodoxy and aristocratic manners. Their works in prose and verse, generally polished and graceful, are a token of America's deliberate and self-conscious entrance into the world of belles lettres; they handle American materials derivatively in the various manners of Pope, Butler, Addison, Swift, and Goldsmith. Their popularity was a result of nationalism, patriotism, and fashion rather than excellence; even at the height of their own times, the work they produced fell short—by the distance of a culture and an age—of establishing a true native literature.

If the Wits had a literary leader, it was probably John Trumbull. He entered Yale at thirteen, was graduated in 1767, received his M.A. in 1770, and stayed on as a tutor. His interest in literature as an enjoyable humanizing force led him to agitate for the ventilation of Yale's stuffy curriculum by introducing the study of English letters, modern languages, and rhetoric. His *Progress of Dulness* is our first satire on the groves of academe, a subject now much in fashion. He studied law under John Adams, attended the Continental Congress in Philadelphia, went to Hartford in 1781, practiced law, entered politics, and became a Justice in Connecticut's Supreme Court.

Among his works are *An Essay on the Use and Advantages of the Fine Arts* (1770); *An Elegy on the Death of Mr. Buckingham St. John* (1771); *The Progress of Dulness* (1773); and *M'Fingal* (1782).

Editions and accounts of the man and his work are to be found in Trumbulls' own edition of *The Poetical Works of John Trumbull*, 2 vols. (1820); J. H. Trumbull, *The Origin of M'Fingal* (1868); M. C. Tyler, *The Literary History of the American Revolution*, I (1897); H. A. Beers, *The Connecticut Wits and Other Essays* (1920); A. Cowie, *John Trumbull, Connecticut Wit* (1936); A. Cowie, "John Trumbull," *Dictionary of American Biography* (1936); A. Cowie, "John Trumbull as a Critic of Poetry," *New England Quarterly*, XI (1938); B. Granger, "John Trumbull and Religion," *American Literature*, XXIII (1951); and E. T. Bowden, ed. *The Satiric Poems of John Trumbull* (1962).

If the Wits had a dean, it was probably Timothy Dwight. Born in Northampton, grandson of Jonathan Edwards, he had the mind of a Mather—well-stocked, legalistic, not profoundly creative—and like a Mather he was the archspokesman of conservatism and orthodoxy in his day. He too entered Yale at thirteen, was graduated in 1769, and went back to Yale as a tutor. In 1777 he became an army chaplain for two years, and in 1783 he accepted a call to the pastorate in Greenfield Hill, Connecticut. As a teacher at Yale he had been immensely popular, stimulating his students by championing creative literature. In 1795 he became president of his alma mater, where he exercised a far-reaching and dogmatic influence in his curiously mixed role of man of letters and educator on the one hand and enemy of the new on the other. Temperamentally he must have been the kind of man Emerson later had in mind when he chastised the retrogressive tendencies in another New England university.

His work includes *A Dissertation on . . . the Bible* (1772); *The Conquest of Canaan* (1785); *The Triumph of Infidelity* (1788); *Greenfield Hill* (1794); *The Nature and Danger of Infidel Philosophy* (1798); *Theology Explained and Defended* (1818–1819); and *Travels in New England and New York* (1821–1822).

Accounts of Dwight and his works are to be found in B. Silliman, *A Sketch of the Life and Character of President Timothy Dwight* (1817); M. C. Tyler, *Three Men of Letters* (1895); V. L. Parrington, *Main Currents in American Thought*, I (1927); C. E. Cunningham, *Timothy Dwight* (1942); L. Howard, *The Connecticut Wits* (1943); R. E. Lee, "Timothy Dwight and the Boston Palladium," *New England Quarterly*, XXV (1962); and E. S. Morgan, "Ezra Stiles and Timothy Dwight," *Proceedings of the Massachusetts Historical Society*, LXXII (1963).

If the Wits had a renegade, it was certainly Joel Barlow. He was born in Redding, Connecticut, put in his stint at Yale, was graduated in 1778, and tutored there until he became an army chaplain in 1780. He settled in Hartford, sharing the ideas of his fellow Wits. But in 1788 he went to France as a land-company agent (his business enterprises in Europe earned him a large fortune) and was caught up by the philosophy of Condorcet and Holbach, whom he came to know. Not only did he become a radical and a deist, but he also became a friend of Thomas Paine and was made an honorary citizen of the French Republic. His *Advice to the Privileged Orders* is a direct statement of his new and deep opposition to aristocracy and Toryism. When he returned to America in 1805 he passed by provincial and reactionary Hartford to make his home (in no little splendor) in cosmopolitan Washington. In 1811 he returned to Europe as ambassador to Napoleon, and he died in Poland during the retreat from Moscow.

His bibliography includes, besides the *Advice*, *The Hasty Pudding* (1796), his most famous work, a mock-heroic inspired by a meal of the native American dish served him in France; *The Political Writings of Joel Barlow* (1796); *Prospectus for a National Institution* (1806); and *The Columbiad* (1807).

In addition to the listings under the bibliographies for Trumbull and Dwight, accounts of Barlow and his work are to be found in C. B. Todd, *The Life and Letters of Joel Barlow* (1886);

T. Zunder, *The Early Days of Joel Barlow* (1934); J. Dos Passos, *The Ground We Stand On* (1941); J. Blau, "Joel Barlow, Enlightened Religionist," *Journal of the History of Ideas*, X (1949); James Woodress, *A Yankee's Odyssey: The Life of Joel Barlow* (1958); and M. McGuire, "Barlow, Man of Freedom," *Personalist*, XLII (1961).

JOHN TRUMBULL

FROM

The Progress of Dulness

[*Tom Brainless*]

"Our Tom has grown a sturdy boy;
His progress fills my heart with joy;
A steady soul, that yields to rule,
And quite ingenious too, at school.
Our master says, (I'm sure he's right,)
There's not a lad in town so bright.
He'll cypher bravely, write and read,
And say his catechism and creed,
And scorns to hesitate or falter
In Primer, Spelling-book or Psalter.   10
Hard work indeed, he does not love it;
His genius is too much above it.
Give him a good substantial teacher,
I'll lay he'd make a special preacher.
I've loved good learning all my life;
We'll send the lad to college, wife."
    Thus swayed by fond and sightless passion,
His parents hold a consultation;
If on their couch, or round their fire,
I need not tell, nor you enquire.   20
    The point's agreed; the boy well pleased,
From country cares and labor eased;
No more to risk by break of day
To drive home cows, or deal out hay;
To work no more in snow or hail,
And blow his fingers o'er the flail,
Or mid the toils of harvest sweat
Beneath the summer's sultry heat,
Serene, he bids the farm, good-bye,

And quits the plough without a sigh.   30
Propitious to their constant friend,
The powers of idleness attend.
   So to the priest in form he goes,
Prepared to study and to doze.
The parson, in his youth before,
Had run the same dull progress o'er;
His sole concern to see with care
His church and farm in good repair.
His skill in tongues, that once he knew,
Had bid him long, a last adieu;   40

                    . . .

   Two years thus spent in gathering knowledge,
The lad sets forth t'unlade at college,
While down his sire and priest attend him,
To introduce and recommend him;
Or if detained, a letter's sent
Of much apocryphal content,
To set him forth, how dull soever,
As very learn'd and very clever;
A genius of the first emission,
With burning love for erudition;   50
So studious he'll outwatch the moon
And think the planets set too soon.
He had but little time to fit in;
Examination too must frighten.
Depend upon't he must do well,
He knows much more than he can tell;
Admit him, and in little space
He'll beat his rivals in the race;
His father's incomes are but small,
He comes now, if he come at all.   60
   So said, so done, at college now
He enters well, no matter how;
New scenes awhile his fancy please,
But all must yield to love of ease.
In the same round condemned each day,
To study, read, recite and pray;
To make his hours of business double—
He can't endure th' increasing trouble;
And finds at length, as times grow pressing,
All plagues are easier than his lesson.   70

With sleepy eyes and count'nance heavy,
With much excuse of *non paravi,*
Much absence, *tardes* and *egresses,*
The college-evil on him seizes.
Then ev'ry book, which ought to please,
Stirs up the seeds of dire disease;
Greek spoils his eyes, the print's so fine,
Grown dim with study, or with wine;
Of Tully's latin much afraid,
Each page, he calls the doctor's aid;   80
While geometry, with lines so crooked,
Sprains all his wits to overlook it.
His sickness puts on every name,
Its cause and uses still the same;
'Tis tooth-ache, cholic, gout or stone,
With phases various as the moon;
But though through all the body spread,
Still makes its cap'tal seat, the head.
In all diseases, 'tis expected,
The weakest parts be most infected.   90

· · ·

Kind head-ache hail! thou blest disease,
The friend of idleness and ease;
Who mid the still and dreary bound
Where college walls her sons surround,
In spite of fears, in justice' spite,
Assumest o'er laws dispensing right,
Sett'st from his task the blunderer free,
Excused by dulness and by thee.
The vot'ries bid a bold defiance
To all the calls and threats of science,   100
Slight learning human and divine,
And hear no prayers, and fear no fine.
And yet how oft the studious gain,
The dulness of a lettered brain;
Despising such low things the while
As English grammar, phrase and style;
Despising ev'ry nicer art,
That aids the tongue, or mends the heart;
Read ancient authors o'er in vain,
Nor taste one beauty they contain;   110
Humbly on trust accept the sense,

But deal for words at vast expense;
Search well how every term must vary
From Lexicon to Dictionary;
And plodding on in one dull tone,
Gain ancient tongues and lose their own,
Bid every graceful charm defiance,
And woo the skeleton of science.

. . .

Oh! might I live to see that day,
When sense shall point to youths their way;   120
Through every maze of science guide;
O'er education's laws preside;
The good retain, with just discerning
Explode the quackeries of learning;
Give ancient arts their real due,
Explain their faults, and beauties too;
Teach where to imitate, and mend,
And point their uses and their end.
Then bright philosophy would shine,
And ethics teach the laws divine;   130
Our youths might learn each nobler art,
That shows a passage to the heart;
From ancient languages well known
Transfuse new beauties to our own;
With taste and fancy well refined,
Where moral rapture warms the mind,
From schools dismissed, with lib'ral hand,
Spread useful learning o'er the land;
And bid the eastern world admire
Our rising worth, and bright'ning fire.   140
    But while through fancy's realms we roam,
The main concern is left at home;
Returned, our hero still we find
The same, as blundering, and as blind.
    Four years at college dozed away
In sleep, and slothfulness and play,
Too dull for vice, with clearest conscience,
Charged with no fault but that of nonsense,
And nonsense long, with serious air,
Has wandered unmolested there,   150
He passes trial, fair and free,
And takes in form his first degree.

A scholar see him now commence
Without the aid of books or sense;
For passing college cures the brain,
Like mills to grind men young again.
The scholar-dress, that once array'd him,
The charm, *Admitto te ad gradum,*
With touch of parchment can refine,
And make the veriest coxcomb shine,   160
Confer the gift of tongues at once,
And fill with sense the vacant dunce.
So kingly crowns contain quintessence
Of worship, dignity and presence;
Give learning, genius, virtue, worth,
Wit, valor, wisdom, and so forth;
Hide the bald pate, and cover o'er
The cap of folly worn before.

   Our hero's wit and learning now may
Be proved by token of diploma,   170
Of that diploma, which with speed
He learns to construe and to read;
And stalks abroad with conscious stride,
In all the airs of pedant pride,
With passport signed for wit and knowledge,
And current under seal of college.

   Few months now past, he sees with pain
His purse as empty as his brain;
His father leaves him then to fate,
And throws him off, as useless weight;   180
But gives him good advice, to teach
A school at first, and then to preach.

   Thou reason'st well; it must be so;
For nothing else thy son can do.
As thieves of old, t'avoid the halter,
Took refuge in the holy altar;
Oft dulness flying from disgrace
Finds safety in that sacred place;
There boldly rears his head, or rests
Secure from ridicule or jests;   190
Where dreaded satire may not dare
Offend his wig's extremest hair;
Where scripture sanctifies his strains,
And reverence hides the want of brains.

   Next see our youth at school appear,

Procured for forty pounds a year;
His ragged regiment round assemble,
Taught, not to read, but fear and tremble.
Before him, rods prepare his way,
Those dreaded antidotes to play.   200
Then throned aloft in elbow chair,
With solemn face and awful air,
He tries, with ease and unconcern,
To teach what ne'er himself could learn;
Gives law and punishment alone,
Judge, jury, bailiff, all in one;
Holds all good learning must depend
Upon his rod's extremest end,
Whose great electric virtue's such,
Each genius brightens at the touch;   210
With threats and blows, incitements pressing,
Drives on his lads to learn each lesson;
Thinks flogging cures all moral ills,
And breaks their heads to break their wills. . . .
    Now to some priest, that's famed for teaching,
He goes to learn the art of preaching;
And settles down with earnest zeal
Sermons to study, and to steal.
Six months from all the world retires
To kindle up his covered fires. . . .   220
    At length, matured the grand design,
He stalks abroad, a grave divine.
    Mean while, from every distant seat,
At stated time the clergy meet,
Our hero comes, his sermons reads,
Explains the doctrine of his creeds,
A license gains to preach and pray,
And makes his bow, and goes his way.
    What though his wits could ne'er dispense
One page of grammar, or of sense;   230
What though his learning be so slight,
He scarcely knows to spell or write;
What though his skull be cudgel-proof!
He's orthodox, and that's enough.

[Harriet Simper]

A judge of modes in silks and satins,
From tassels down to clogs and pattens;

A genius, that can calculate
When modes of dress are out of date,
Cast the nativity with ease
Of gowns, and sacks and negligees,   240
And tell, exact to half a minute,
What's out of fashion and what's in it;
And scanning all with curious eye,
Minutest faults in dresses spy;
(So in nice points of sight, a flea
Sees atoms better far than we;)
A patriot too, she greatly labors,
To spread her arts among her neighbors,
Holds correspondences to learn
What facts the female world concern,   250
To gain authentic state-reports
Of varied modes in distant courts,
The present state and swift decays
Of tuckers, handkerchiefs, and stays,
The colored silk that beauty wraps,
And all the rise and fall of caps.
Then shines, a pattern to the fair,
Of mien, address and modish air,
Of every new, affected grace,
That plays the eye, or decks the face,   260
The artful smile, that beauty warms,
And all the hypocrisy of charms.
    On Sunday, see the haughty maid
In all the glare of dress arrayed,
Decked in her most fantastic gown,
Because a stranger's come to town.
Heedless at church she spends the day,
For homelier folks may serve to pray,
And for devotion those may go,
Who can have nothing else to do.   270
Beauties at church must spend their care in
Far other work, than pious hearing;
They've beaux to conquer, belles to rival;
To make them serious were uncivil.
For, like the preacher, they each Sunday
Must do their whole week's work in one day.
    As though they meant to take by blows
Th' opposing galleries of beaux,
To church the female squadron move,

All armed with weapons used in love.   280
Like colored ensigns gay and fair,
High caps rise floating in the air;
Bright silk its varied radiance flings,
And streamers wave in kissing-strings;
Each bears th' artill'ry of her charms,
Like training bands at viewing arms.

So once, in fear of Indian beating,
Our grandsires bore their guns to meeting,
Each man equipped on Sunday morn,
With psalm-book, shot and powder-horn;   290
And looked in form, as all must grant,
Like th' ancient, true church militant;
Or fierce, like modern deep divines,
Who fight with quills, like porcupines.

Or let us turn the style and see
Our belles assembled o'er their tea;
Where folly sweetens ev'ry theme,
And scandal serves for sugared cream.

"And did you hear the news? (they cry)
The court wear caps full three feet high,   300
Built gay with wire, and at the end on't,
Red tassels streaming like a pendant.
Well sure, it must be vastly pretty;
'Tis all the fashion in the city.
And were you at the ball last night?
Well, Chloe looked like any fright;
Her day is over for a toast;
She'd now do best to act a ghost.
You saw our Fanny; envy must own
She figures, since she came from Boston.   310
Good company improves one's air—
I think the troops were stationed there.
Poor Cœlia ventured to the place;
The small-pox quite has spoiled her face,
A sad affair, we all confest:
But providence knows what is best.
Poor Dolly, too, that writ the letter
Of love to Dick; but Dick knew better;
A secret that; you'll not disclose it;
There's not a person living knows it.   320
Sylvia shone out, no peacock finer;
I wonder what the fops see in her.

Perhaps 'tis true what Harry maintains,
She mends on intimate acquaintance."
    Yet that we fairly may proceed,
We own that ladies sometimes read,
And grieve, that reading is confined
To books that poison all the mind;
Novels and plays (where shines displayed
A world that nature never made),   330
Which swell their hopes with airy fancies,
And amorous follies of romances;
Inspire with dreams the witless maiden
On flowery vales and fields Arcadian,
And constant hearts no chance can sever,
And mortal loves, that last for ever.
    For while she reads romance, the fair one
Fails not to think herself the heroine;
For every glance, or smile, or grace,
She finds resemblance in her face,   340
Expects the world to fall before her,
And every fop she meets adore her.
Thus HARRIET reads, and reading really
Believes herself a young Pamela,
The high-wrought whim, the tender strain
Elate her mind and turn her brain:
Before her glass, with smiling grace,
She views the wonders of her face;
There stands in admiration moveless,
And hopes a Grandison, or Lovelace.   350
    Then shines she forth, and round her hovers,
The powdered swarm of bowing lovers;
By flames of love attracted thither,
Fops, scholars, dunces, cits, together.
No lamp exposed in nightly skies,
E'er gathered such a swarm of flies;
Or flame in tube electric draws
Such thronging multitudes of straws.
(For I shall still take similes
From fire electric when I please.)   360
    With vast confusion swells the sound,
When all the coxcombs flutter round.
What undulation wide of bows!
What gentle oaths and am'rous vows!
What double entendres all so smart!

What sighs hot-piping from the heart!
What jealous leers! what angry brawls
To gain the lady's hand at balls!
What billet-doux, brimful of flame!
Acrostics lined with HARRIET's name!   370
What compliments, o'er-strained with telling
Sad lies of Venus and of Helen!
What wits half-cracked with commonplaces
On angels, goddesses and graces!
On fires of love what witty puns!
What similes of stars and suns!
What cringing, dancing, ogling, sighing,
What languishing for love, and dying!

. . .

Poor Harriet now hath had her day;
No more the beaux confess her sway;   380
New beauties push her from the stage;
She trembles at th' approach of age,
And starts to view the altered face,
That wrinkles at her in her glass:
So Satan, in the monk's tradition,
Feared, when he met his apparition.
At length her name each coxcomb cancels
From standing lists of toasts and angels;
And slighted where she shone before,
A grace and goddess now no more,   390
Despised by all, and doomed to meet
Her lovers at her rival's feet,
She flies assemblies, shuns the ball,
And cries out, vanity, on all;
Affects to scorn the tinsel-shows
Of glittering belles and gaudy beaux;
Nor longer hopes to hide by dress
The tracks of age upon her face.
Now careless grown of airs polite,
Her noonday nightcap meets the sight;   400
Her hair uncombed collects together,
With ornaments of many a feather;
Her stays for easiness thrown by,
Her rumpled handkerchief awry,
A careless figure half undressed,
(The reader's wits may guess the rest;)

All points of dress and neatness carried,
As though she'd been a twelvemonth married;
She spends her breath, as years prevail,
At this sad wicked world to rail,   410
To slander all her sex *impromptu*,
And wonder what the times will come to.

[The Marriage Bargain]

Tom Brainless, at the close of last year,
Had been six years a rev'rend Pastor,
And now resolved, to smooth his life,
To seek the blessing of a wife.
His brethren saw his amorous temper,
And recommended fair Miss Simper,
Who fond, they heard, of sacred truth,
Had left her levities of youth,   420
Grown fit for ministerial union,
And grave, as Christian's wife in Bunyan.
On this he rigged him in his best,
And got his old grey wig new dressed,
Fixed on his suit of sable stuffs,
And brushed the powder from his cuffs,
With black silk stockings, yet in being,
The same he took his first degree in;
Procured a horse of breed from Europe,
And learned to mount him by the stirrup,   430
And set forth fierce to court the maid;
His white-haired Deacon went for aid;
And on the right, in solemn mode,
The Reverend Mr. Brainless rode.
Thus grave, the courtly pair advance,
Like knight and squire in famed romance.
The priest then bowed in sober gesture,
And all in scripture terms addressed her;
He'd found, for reasons amply known,
It was not good to be alone,   440
And thought his duty led to trying
The great command of multiplying;
So with submission, by her leave,
He'd come to look him out an Eve,
And hoped, in pilgrimage of life,
To find an helpmate in a wife,

A wife discreet and fair withal,
To make amends for Adam's fall.
    In short, the bargain finished soon
A reverend Doctor made them one.   450
    And now the joyful people rouse all
To celebrate their priest's espousal;
And first, by kind agreement set,
In case their priest a wife could get,
The parish vote him five pounds clear,
T'increase his salary every year.
Then swift the tag-rag gentry come
To welcome Madam Brainless home;
Wish their good Parson joy; with pride
In order round salute the bride;   360
At home, at visits and at meetings,
To Madam all allow precedence;
Greet her at church with rev'rence due,
And next the pulpit fix her pew.

                                        1772–1773

FROM

M'Fingal

FROM CANTO III

The Liberty Pole

Now warm with ministerial ire,
Fierce sallied forth our loyal 'Squire,
And on his striding steps attends
His desperate clan of Tory friends.
When sudden met his wrathful eye
A pole ascending through the sky,
Which numerous throngs of Whiggish race
Were raising in the market place.
Not higher school-boy's kites aspire,
Or royal mast, or country spire;   10
Like spears at Brobdignagian tilting,
Or Satan's walking-staff in Milton.
And on its top, the flag unfurled
Waved triumph o'er the gazing world,
Inscribed with inconsistent types

Of *Liberty* and *thirteen stripes.**
Beneath, the crowd without delay
The dedication-rites essay,
And gladly pay, in ancient fashion,
The ceremonies of libation;   20
While briskly to each patriot lip
Walks eager round the inspiring flip:†

    .   .   .

  By this, M'Fingal with his train
Advanced upon th' adjacent plain,
And full with loyalty possessed,
Poured forth the zeal, that fired his breast.
  "What mad-brained rebel gave commission,
To raise this May-pole of sedition?
Like Babel, reared by bawling throngs,
With like confusion too of tongues,   30
To point at heaven and summon down
The thunders of the British crown?
Say, will this paltry pole secure
Your forfeit heads from Gage's power?
Attacked by heroes brave and crafty,
Is this to stand your ark of safety;
Or driven by Scottish laird and laddie,
Think ye to rest beneath its shadow?
When bombs, like fiery serpents, fly,
And balls rush hissing through the sky,   40
Will this vile pole, devote to freedom,
Save like the Jewish pole in Edom;
Or like the brazen snake of Moses,
Cure your cracked skulls and battered noses?
  "Ye dupes to every factious rogue
And tavern-prating demagogue,
Whose tongue but rings, with sound more full,
On th' empty drumhead of his skull;
Behold you not what noisy fools
Use you, worse simpletons, for tools?   50
For Liberty, in your own by-sense,
Is but for crimes a patent license,
To break of law th'Egyptian yoke,

---

  * The American flag. It would doubtless be wrong to imagine that the stripes bear any allusion to the slave trade. [All the notes are Trumbull's.]
  † Flip, a liquor composed of beer, rum and sugar; the common treat at that time in the country towns of New England.

And throw the world in common stock;
Reduce all grievances and ills
To Magna Charta of your wills;
Establish cheats and frauds and nonsense,
Framed to the model of your conscience;
Cry justice down, as out of fashion,
And fix its scale of depreciation;*   60
Defy all creditors to trouble ye,
And keep new years of Jewish jubilee;
Drive judges out,† like Aaron's calves,
By jurisdiction of white staves,
And make the bar and bench and steeple
Submit t' our Sovereign Lord, The People;
By plunder rise to power and glory,
And brand all property, as Tory;
Expose all wears to lawful seizures
By mobbers or monopolizers;   70
Break heads and windows and the peace,
For your own interest and increase;
Dispute and pray and fight and groan
For public good, and mean your own;
Prevent the law by fierce attacks
From quitting scores upon your backs;
Lay your old dread, the gallows, low,
And seize the stocks, your ancient foe,
And turn them to convenient engines
To wreak your patriotic vengeance;   80
While all, your rights who understand,
Confess them in their owner's hand;
And when by clamors and confusions,
Your freedom's grown a public nuisance,
Cry 'Liberty,' with powerful yearning,
As he does 'Fire!' whose house is burning;
Though he already has much more
Than he can find occasion for."

. . .

This said, our 'Squire yet undismayed,
Called forth the Constable to aid,   90

* Alluding to the depreciation of the Continental paper money. Congress finally ascertained the course of its declension at different periods,
by what was called, A Scale of Depreciation.
† On the commencement of the war, the courts of justice were everywhere shut up. In some instances, the judges were forced to retire, by the
people, who assembled in multitudes, armed with white staves.

And bade him read, in nearer station,
The Riot-act and Proclamation.
He swift, advancing to the ring,
Began, "Our Sovereign Lord, the King"—
When thousand clam'rous tongues he hears,
And clubs and stones assail his ears.
To fly was vain; to fight was idle;
By foes encompassed in the middle,
His hope, in stratagems, he found,
And fell right craftily to ground;   100
Then crept to seek an hiding place,
'Twas all he could, beneath a brace;
Where soon the conq'ring crew espied him,
And where he lurked, they caught and tied him.
 At once with resolution fatal,
Both Whigs and Tories rushed to battle.

· · ·

M'Fingal, rising at the word,
Drew forth his old militia-sword;
Thrice cried "King George," as erst in distress,
Knights of romance invoked a mistress: 110
And brandishing the blade in air,
Struck terror through th' opposing war.
The Whigs, unsafe within the wind
Of such commotion, shrunk behind.
With whirling steel around addressed,
Fierce through their thickest throng he pressed,
(Who rolled on either side in arch,
Like Red Sea waves in Israel's march)
And like a meteor rushing through,
Struck on their pole a vengeful blow.   120
Around, the Whigs, of clubs and stones
Discharged whole vollies, in platoons,
That o'er in whistling fury fly;
But not a foe dares venture nigh.
And now perhaps with glory crowned
Our 'Squire had felled the pole to ground,
Had not some Pow'r, a Whig at heart,
Descended down and took their part
(Whether 'twere Pallas, Mars or Iris,
'Tis scarce worth while to make inquiries);   130
Who at the nick of time alarming,

Assumed the solemn form of Chairman,
Addressed a Whig, in every scene
The stoutest wrestler on the green,
And pointed where the spade was found,
Late used to set their pole in ground,
And urged, with equal arms and might,
To dare our 'Squire to single fight.
The Whig thus armed, untaught to yield,
Advanced tremendous to the field: 140
Nor did M'Fingal shun the foe,
But stood to brave the desp'rate blow;
While all the party gazed, suspended
To see the deadly combat ended;
And Jove in equal balance weighed
The sword against the brandished spade;
He weighed; but lighter than a dream,
The sword flew up, and kicked the beam.
Our 'Squire on tiptoe rising fair
Lifts high a noble stroke in air,   150
Which hung not, but like dreadful engines,
Descended on his foe in vengeance.
But ah! in danger, with dishonor
The sword perfidious fails its owner;
That sword, which oft had stood its ground,
By huge trainbands encircled round;
And on the bench, with blade right loyal,
Had won the day at many a trial,
Of stones and clubs had braved th' alarms,
Shrunk from these new Vulcanian arms.   160
The spade so tempered from the sledge,
Nor keen nor solid harmed its edge,
Now met it, from his arm of might,
Descending with steep force to smite;
The blade snapped short—and from his hand,
With rust embrowned the glittering sand.
Swift turned M'Fingal at the view
And called to aid th' attendant crew,
In vain; the Tories all had run,
When scarce the fight was well begun;   170
Their setting wigs he saw decreased
Far in th' horizon tow'rd the west.
Amazed he viewed the shameful sight,
And saw no refuge, but in flight:

But age unwieldy checked his pace,
Though fear had winged his flying race;
For not a trifling prize at stake;
No less than great M'Fingal's back.
With legs and arms he worked his course,
Like rider that outgoes his horse,   180
And labor's hard to get away, as
Old Satan struggling on through chaos;
Till looking back, he spied in rear
The spade-armed chief advanced too near.

        .   .   .

The fatal spade discharged a blow
Tremendous on his rear below:
His bent knee failed, and void of strength
Stretched on the ground his manly length.
Like ancient oak o'erturned, he lay,
Or tower to tempests fall'n a prey,   190
Or mountain sunk with all his pines,
Or flow'r the plow to dust consigns,
And more things else—but all men know 'em,
If slightly versed in epic poem.
At once the crew, at this dread crisis,
Fall on, and bind him, ere he rises;
And with loud shouts and joyful soul,
Conduct him prisoner to the pole.
When now the mob in lucky hour
Had got their en'mies in their power,   200
They first proceed, by grave command,
To take the Constable in hand.
Then from the pole's sublimest top
The active crew let down the rope,
At once its other end in haste bind,
And make it fast upon his waistband;
Till like the earth, as stretched on tenter,
He hung self-balanced on his center.
Then upwards, all hands hoisting sail,
They swung him, like a keg of ale,   210
Till to the pinnacle in height
He vaulted, like balloon or kite.
As Socrates of old at first did
To aid philosophy get hoisted,
And found his thoughts flow strangely clear,

Swung in a basket in mid air:
Our culprit thus, in purer sky,
With like advantage raised his eye,
And looking forth in prospect wide,
His Tory errors clearly spied,   220
And from his elevated station,
With bawling voice began addressing.
    "Good Gentlemen and friends and kin,
For heaven's sake hear, if not for mine!
I here renounce the Pope, the Turks,
The King, the Devil and all their works;
And will, set me but once at ease,
Turn Whig, or Christian, what you please;
And always mind your laws so justly,
Should I live long as old Methus'lah,   230
I'll never join in British rage,
Nor help Lord North, nor Gen'ral Gage;
Nor lift my gun in future fights,
Nor take away your Charter-rights;
Nor overcome your new-raised levies,
Destroy your towns, nor burn your navies;
Nor cut your poles down while I've breath,
Though raised more thick than hatchel-teeth:
But leave King George and all his elves
To do their conq'ring work themselves."   240
    This said, they lowered him down in state,
Spread at all points, like falling cat;
But took a vote first on the question,
That they'd accept this full confession,
And to their fellowship and favor,
Restore him on his good behaviour.
    Not so our 'Squire submits to rule,
But stood, heroic as a mule.
"You'll find it all in vain," quoth he,
"To play your rebel tricks on me.   250
All punishments, the world can render,
Serve only to provoke th' offender;
The will gains strength from treatment horrid
As hides grow harder when they're curried.
No man e'er felt the halter draw,
With good opinion of the law;
Or held in method orthodox
His love of justice, in the stocks;

Or failed to lose by sheriff's shears
At once his loyalty and ears.   260

· · ·

I'll stand the worst; for recompense
I trust King George and Providence.
And when with conquest gained I come,
Arrayed in law and terror home,
Ye'll rue this inauspicious morn,
And curse the day, when ye were born,
In Job's high style of imprecations,
With all his plagues, without his patience."
   Meanwhile, beside the pole, the guard
A Bench of Justice had prepared.*   270
Where sitting round in awful sort
The grand Committee hold their Court;
While all the crew, in silent awe,
Wait from their lips the lore of law.
Few moments with deliberation
They hold the solemn consultation;
When soon in judgment all agree,
And Clerk proclaims the dread decree;
"That 'Squire M'Fingal having grown
The vilest Tory in the town,   280
And now in full examination
Convicted by his own confession,
Finding no tokens of repentance,
This Court proceeds to render sentence:
That first the Mob a slip-knot single
Tie round the neck of said M'Fingal,
And in due form do tar him next,
And feather, as the law directs;
Then through the town attendant ride him
In cart with Constable beside him,   290
And having held him up to shame,
Bring to the pole, from whence he came."
   Forthwith the crowd proceed to deck
With haltered noose M'Fingal's neck,
While he in peril of his soul
Stood tied half-hanging to the pole;

* An imitation of legal forms was universally practiced by the mobs
in New England, in the trial and condemnation of Tories. This marks
a curious trait of national character.

Then lifting high the ponderous jar,
Poured o'er his head the smoking tar.

．　．　．

And now the feather-bag displayed
Is waved in triumph o'er his head,　　　　300
And clouds him o'er with feathers missive,
And down, upon the tar, adhesive:
Not Maia's son, with wings for ears,
Such plumage round his visage wears;
Nor Milton's six-winged angel gathers
Such superfluity of feathers.
Now all complete appears our 'Squire,
Like Gorgon or Chimaera dire;
Nor more could boast on Plato's plan
To rank among the race of man,　　　　310
Or prove his claim to human nature,
As a two-legg'd unfeathered creature.

．　．　．

And now the Mob, dispersed and gone,
Left 'Squire and Constable alone.
The Constable with rueful face
Leaned sad and solemn o'er a brace;
And fast beside him, cheek by jowl,
Stuck 'Squire M'Fingal 'gainst the pole,
Glued by the tar t' his rear applied,
Like barnacle on vessel's side.　　　　320
But though his body lacked physician,
His spirit was in worse condition.
He found his fears of whips and ropes
By many a drachm outweighed his hopes.
As men in jail without mainprize
View every thing with other eyes.
And all goes wrong in church and state,
Seen through perspective of the grate:
So now M'Fingal's Second-sight
Beheld all things in gloomier light;　　　　330
His visual nerve, well purged with tar,
Saw all the coming scenes of war.
As his prophetic soul grew stronger,
He found he could hold in no longer.
First from the pole, as fierce he shook,

His wig from pitchy durance broke,
His mouth unglued, his feathers fluttered,
His tarred skirts cracked, and thus he uttered:
    "Ah, Mr. Constable, in vain
We strive 'gainst wind and tide and rain!   340
Behold my doom! this feathery omen
Portends what dismal times are coming.
Now future scenes, before my eyes,
And second-sighted forms arise.
I hear a voice, that calls away,
And cries, 'The Whigs will win the day.'
My beck'ning Genius gives command,
And bids me fly the fatal land;
Where changing name and constitution,
Rebellion turns to Revolution,   350
While Loyalty, oppressed, in tears,
Stands trembling for its neck and ears.["]

1782

TIMOTHY DWIGHT

Columbia, Columbia, to Glory Arise

Columbia, Columbia, to glory arise,
The queen of the world, and child of the skies!
Thy genius commands thee; with rapture behold,
While ages on ages thy splendors unfold.
Thy reign is the last, and the noblest of time,
Most fruitful thy soil, most inviting thy clime;
Let the crimes of the east ne'er encrimson thy name,
Be freedom, and science, and virtue, thy fame.

To conquest, and slaughter, let Europe aspire;
Whelm nations in blood, and wrap cities in fire;   10
Thy heroes the rights of mankind shall defend,
And triumph pursue them, and glory attend.
A world is thy realm: for a world be thy laws,
Enlarg'd as thine empire, and just as thy cause;
On Freedom's broad basis, that empire shall rise,
Extend with the main, and dissolve with the skies.

Fair Science her gates to thy sons shall unbar,
And the east see thy morn hide the beams of her star.
New bards, and new sages, unrival'd shall soar
To fame, unextinguish'd, when time is no more;   20
To thee, the last refuge of virtue design'd,
Shall fly from all nations the best of mankind;
Here, grateful to heaven, with transport shall bring
Their incense, more fragrant than odors of spring.

Nor less shall thy fair ones to glory ascend,
And Genius and Beauty in harmony blend;
The graces of form shall awake pure desire,
And the charms of the soul ever cherish the fire;
Their sweetness unmingled, their manners refin'd
And virtue's bright image, instamp'd on the mind,   30
With peace, and soft rapture, shall teach life to glow,
And light up a smile in the aspect of woe.

Thy fleets to all regions thy pow'r shall display,
The nations admire, and the ocean obey;
Each shore to thy glory its tribute unfold,
And the east and the south yield their spices and gold,
As the day-spring unbounded, thy splendor shall flow,
And earth's little kingdoms before thee shall bow,
While the ensigns of union, in triumph unfurl'd,
Hush the tumult of war, and give peace to the world.   40

Thus, as down a lone valley, with cedars o'erspread,
From war's dread confusion I pensively stray'd—
The gloom from the face of fair heav'n retir'd;
The winds ceas'd to murmur; the thunders expir'd;
Perfumes, as of Eden, flow'd sweetly along,
And a voice, as of angels, enchantingly sung:
"Columbia, Columbia, to glory arise,
The queen of the world, and the child of the skies."

w. c1778
p. 1793

FROM

Greenfield Hill

Ye Muses! dames of dignified renown,
Rever'd alike in country, and in town,
Your bard the mysteries of a visit show;
For sure your Ladyships those mysteries know:
What is it then, obliging Sisters! say,
The debt of social visiting to pay?

'Tis not to toil before the idol pier;
To shine the first in fashion's lunar sphere;
By sad engagements forc'd, abroad to roam,
And dread to find the expecting fair, at home!   10
To stop at thirty doors, in half a day,
Drop the gilt card, and proudly roll away;
To alight, and yield the hand, with nice parade;
Up stairs to rustle in the stiff brocade;
Swim thro' the drawing room, with studied air;
Catch the pink'd beau, and shade the rival fair;
To sit, to curb, to toss, with bridled mien,
Mince the scant speech, and lose a glance between;
Unfurl the fan, display the snowy arm,
And ope, with each new motion, some new charm: 20
Or sit, in silent solitude, to spy
Each little failing, with malignant eye;
Or chatter, with incessancy of tongue,
Careless, if kind, or cruel, right, or wrong;
To trill of us, and ours, of mine, and me,
Our house, our coach, our friends, our family,
While all th' excluded circle sit in pain,
And glance their cool contempt, or keen disdain:
T' inhale, from proud Nanking, a sip of tea,
And wave a curtsey trim, and flirt away;   30
Or waste, at cards, peace, temper, health and life,
Begin with sullenness, and end in strife,
Lose the rich feast, by friendly converse given,
And backward turn from happiness, and heaven.

It is, in decent habit, plain and neat,
To spend a few choice hours, in converse sweet;
Careless of forms, to act th' unstudied part,
To mix in friendship, and to blend the heart;
To choose those happy themes, which all must feel,
The moral duties, and the household weal,   40
The tale of sympathy, the kind design,
Where rich affections soften, and refine;
T' amuse, to be amus'd, to bless, be bless'd,
And tune to harmony the common breast;
To cheer, with mild good-humor's sprightly ray,
And smooth life's passage, o'er its thorny way;
To circle round the hospitable board,
And taste each good, our generous climes afford;
To court a quick return, with accents kind,
And leave, at parting, some regret behind.   50

Such, here, the social intercourse is found;
So slides the year, in smooth enjoyment, round.

Thrice bless'd the life, in this glad region spent,
In peace, in competence, and still content;
Where bright, and brighter, all things daily smile,
And rare and scanty, flow the streams of ill;
Where undecaying youth sits blooming round,
And Spring looks lovely on the happy ground;
Improvement glows, along life's cheerful way,
And with soft lustre makes the passage gay.   60
Thus oft, on yonder Sound, when evening gales
Breath'd o'er th' expanse, and gently fill'd the sails,
The world was still, the heavens were dress'd in smiles,
And the clear moon-beam tipp'd the distant isles,
On the blue plain a lucid image gave,
And capp'd, with silver light, each little wave;
The silent splendor, floating at our side,
Mov'd as we mov'd, and wanton'd on the tide;
While shadowy points, and havens, meet the eye,
And the faint-glimmering landmark told us home was
  nigh.   70

1794

JOEL BARLOW

FROM

Advice to the Privileged Orders

Introduction

The French Revolution is at last not only accomplished, but its accomplishment universally acknowledged, beyond contradiction abroad, or the power of retraction at home. It has finished its work, by organizing a government, on principles approved by reason; an object long contemplated by different writers, but never before exhibited, in this quarter of the globe. The experiment now in operation will solve a question of the first magnitude in human affairs: Whether theory and practice, which always agree together in things of slighter moment, are really to remain eternal enemies in the highest concerns of men?

The change of government in France is, properly speaking, a renovation of society; an object peculiarly fitted to hurry the mind into a field of thought, which can scarcely be limited by the concerns of a nation, or the improvements of an age. As there is a tendency in human nature to imitation; and as all the apparent causes exist in most of the governments of the world, to induce the people to wish for a similar change; it becomes interesting to the cause of humanity, to take a deliberate view of the real nature and extent of this change, and find what are the advantages and disadvantages to be expected from it.

There is not that necromancy in politics, which prevents our foreseeing, with tolerable certainty, what is to be the result of operations so universal, in which all the people concur. Many truths are as perceptible when first presented to the mind, as an age or a world of experience could make them; others require only an indirect and collateral experience; some demand an experience direct and positive.

It is happy for human nature, that in morals we have much to do with this first class of truths, less with the second, and very little with the third; while in physics we are perpetually driven to the slow process of patient and positive experience.

The Revolution in France certainly comes recommended to us under one aspect which renders it at first view extremely inviting: it is the work of argument and rational conviction, not of the sword. The *ultima ratio regum* had nothing to do with it. It was an operation designed for the benefit of the people; it originated in the people, and was conducted by the people. It had therefore a legitimate origin; and this circumstance entitles it to our serious contemplation, on two accounts: because there is something venerable in the idea, and because other nations, in similar circumstances, will certainly be disposed to imitate it.

I shall therefore examine the nature and consequences of a similar revolution in government, as it will affect the following principal objects, which make up the affairs of nations in the present state of Europe:

I. The Feudal System,
II. The Church,
III. The Military,
IV. The Administration of Justice,
V. Revenue and Public Expenditure.

It must be of vast importance to all the classes of society, as it now stands classed in Europe, to calculate beforehand what they are to gain or to lose by the approaching change; that, like prudent stock-jobbers, they may buy in or sell out, according as this great event shall affect them.

Philosophers and contemplative men, who may think themselves disinterested spectators of so great a political drama, will do well to consider how far the catastrophe is to be beneficial or detrimental to the human race; in order to determine whether in conscience they ought to promote or discourage, accelerate or retard it, by the publication of their opinions. It is true, the work was set on foot by this sort of men; but they have not all been of the same opinion relative to the best organization of the governing power, or how far the reform of abuses ought to extend. Montesquieu, Voltaire, and many other respectable authorities, have accredited the principle, that republicanism is not convenient for a great state. Others take no notice of the distinction between great and small states, in deciding, that this is the only government proper to ensure the happiness, and support the dignity of man. Of the former opinion was a great majority of the constituent national assembly of France. Probably not many years will pass, before a third opinion will be universally adopted, never to be laid aside: That the republican principle is not only proper and safe for the government of any people; but that its propriety and safety are in proportion to the magnitude of the society and extent of the territory.

Among sincere enquirers after truth, all general questions on this subject reduce themselves to this: Whether men are to perform their duties by an easy choice or an expensive cheat; or, whether our reason be given us to be improved or stifled, to render us greater or less than brutes, to increase our happiness or aggravate our misery.

Among those whose anxieties arise only from interest, the inquiry is, how their privileges or their professions are to be affected by the new order of things. These form a class of men respectable both for their numbers and sensibility; it is our duty to attend to their case. I sincerely hope to administer some consolation to them in the course of this essay. And though I have a better opinion of their philanthropy, than political opponents generally entertain of each other, yet I do not altogether rely upon their presumed sympathy with their fellow-citizens, and their supposed willingness to sacrifice to the public good; but I hope to convince them, that the establishment of general liberty will be less injurious to those who now live by abuses, than is commonly imagined; that protected industry will produce effects far more astonishing than have ever been calculated; that the increase of enjoyments will be such, as to ameliorate the condition of every human creature.

To persuade this class of mankind, that it is neither their duty nor their interest to endeavor to perpetuate the ancient forms of government, would be an high and holy office; it would be the greatest act of charity to them, as it might teach them to avoid a danger that is otherwise unavoidable; it would preclude the occasion of the people's indulging what is sometimes called a ferocious disposition, which is apt to grow upon the revenge of injuries, and render them less harmonious in their new station of citizens; it would prevent the civil wars, which might attend the insurrections of the people, where there should be a great want of unanimity,—for we are not to expect in every country that mildness and dignity which have uniformly characterized the French, even in their most tumultuous movements; it would remove every obstacle and every danger that may seem to attend that rational system of public felicity to which the nations of Europe are moving with rapid strides, and which in prospect is so consoling to the enlightened friends of humanity.

To induce the men who now govern the world to adopt these ideas, is the duty of those who now possess them. I confess the task, at first view, appears more than Herculean; it will be thought an object from which the eloquence of the closet must shrink in despair, and which prudence would leave in the more powerful arguments of events. But I believe at the same time that some success may be expected; that though the harvest be great, the laborers may not be few; that prejudice and interest cannot always be relied on to garrison the mind against the assaults of truth. This belief, ill-grounded as it may appear, is sufficient to animate me in the cause; and to the venerable host of republican writers, who have preceded me in the discussions occasioned by the French revolution, this belief is my only apology for offering to join the fraternity, and for thus practically declaring my opinion, that they have not exhausted the subject.

Two very powerful weapons, the force of reason and the force of numbers, are in the hands of the political reformers. While the use of the first brings into action the second, and ensures its cooperation, it remains a sacred duty, imposed on them by the God of reason, to wield with dexterity this mild and beneficent weapon, before recurring to the use of the other; which, though legitimate, may be less harmless; though infallible in operation, may be less glorious in victory.

1792

The Hasty Pudding

CANTO I

Ye Alps audacious, through the heavens that rise,
To cramp the day and hide me from the skies;

Ye Gallic flags, that o'er their heights unfurled,
Bear death to kings and freedom to the world,
I sing not you. A softer theme I choose,
A virgin theme, unconscious of the muse,
But fruitful, rich, well suited to inspire
The purest frenzy of poetic fire.
　　Despise it not, ye bards to terror steeled,
Who hurl your thunders round the epic field;　　　　10
Nor ye who strain your midnight throats to sing
Joys that the vineyard and the stillhouse bring;
Or on some distant fair your notes employ,
And speak of raptures that you ne'er enjoy.
I sing the sweets I know, the charms I feel,
My morning incense, and my evening meal,—
The sweets of Hasty Pudding. Come, dear bowl,
Glide o'er my palate, and inspire my soul.
The milk beside thee, smoking from the kine,
Its substance mingled, married in with thine,　　　　20
Shall cool and temper thy superior heat,
And save the pains of blowing while I eat.
　　Oh! could the smooth, the emblematic song
Flow like the genial juices o'er my tongue,
Could those mild morsels in my numbers chime,
And, as they roll in substance, roll in rime,
No more thy awkward, unpoetic name
Should shun the muse or prejudice thy fame;
But rising grateful to the accustomed ear,
All bards should catch it, and all realms revere!　　　　30
　　Assist me first with pious toil to trace
Through wrecks of time, thy lineage and thy race;
Declare what lovely squaw, in days of yore,
(Ere great Columbus sought thy native shore)
First gave thee to the world; her works of fame
Have lived indeed, but lived without a name.
Some tawny Ceres, goddess of her days,
First learned with stones to crack the well-dried maize,
Through the rough sieve to shake the golden shower,
In boiling water stir the yellow flour:　　　　40
The yellow flour, bestrewed and stirred with haste,
Swells in the flood and thickens to a paste,
Then puffs and wallops, rises to the brim,
Drinks the dry knobs that on the surface swim;
The knobs at last the busy ladle breaks,

And the whole mass its true consistence takes.
 Could but her sacred name, unknown so long,
Rise, like her labors, to the son of song,
To her, to them I'd consecrate my lays,
And blow her pudding with the breath of praise. 50
If 'twas Oella whom I sang before,
I here ascribe her one great virtue more.
Not through the rich Peruvian realms alone
The fame of Sol's sweet daughter should be known,
But o'er the world's wide climes should live secure,
Far as his rays extend, as long as they endure.
 Dear Hasty Pudding, what unpromised joy
Expands my heart, to meet thee in Savoy!
Doomed o'er the world through devious paths to roam,
Each clime my country, and each house my home, 60
My soul is soothed, my cares have found an end;
I greet my long-lost, unforgotten friend.
 For thee through Paris, that corrupted town,
How long in vain I wandered up and down,
Where shameless Bacchus, with his drenching hoard,
Cold from his cave usurps the morning board.
London is lost in smoke and steeped in tea;
No Yankee there can lisp the name of thee;
The uncouth word, a libel on the town,
Would call a proclamation from the crown. 70
For climes oblique, that fear the sun's full rays,
Chilled in their fogs, exclude the generous maize;
A grain whose rich, luxuriant growth requires
Short, gentle showers, and bright, ethereal fires.
 But here, though distant from our native shore,
With mutual glee, we meet and laugh once more.
The same! I know thee by that yellow face,
That strong complexion of true Indian race,
Which time can never change, nor soil impair,
Nor Alpine snows, nor Turkey's morbid air; 80
For endless years, through every mild domain,
Where grows the maize, there thou art sure to reign.
 But man, more fickle, the bold licence claims,
In different realms to give thee different names.
Thee the soft nations round the warm Levant
Polanta call; the French, of course, *Polante.*
E'en in thy native regions, how I blush
To hear the Pennsylvanians call thee *Mush!*

On Hudson's banks, while men of Belgic spawn
Insult and eat thee by the name *Suppawn*.   90
All spurious appellations, void of truth;
I've better known thee from my earliest youth:
Thy name is *Hasty Pudding!* thus my sire
Was wont to greet thee fuming from his fire;
And while he argued in thy just defense
With logic clear he thus explained the sense:
"In haste the boiling caldron, o'er the blaze,
Receives and cooks the ready powdered maize;
In haste 'tis served, and then in equal haste,
With cooling milk, we make the sweet repast.   100
No carving to be done, no knife to grate
The tender ear and wound the stony plate;
But the smooth spoon, just fitted to the lip,
And taught with art the yielding mass to dip,
By frequent journeys to the bowl well stored,
Performs the hasty honors of the board."
Such is thy name, significant and clear,
A name, a sound to every Yankee dear,
But most to me, whose heart and palate chaste
Preserve my pure, hereditary taste.   110

   There are who strive to stamp with disrepute
The luscious food, because it feeds the brute;
In tropes of high-strained wit, while gaudy prigs
Compare thy nursling, man, to pampered pigs;
With sovereign scorn I treat the vulgar jest,
Nor fear to share thy bounties with the beast.
What though the generous cow gives me to quaff
The milk nutritious: am I then a calf?
Or can the genius of the noisy swine,
Though nursed on pudding, thence lay claim to mine?   120
Sure the sweet song I fashion to thy praise,
Runs more melodious than the notes they raise.

   My song, resounding in its grateful glee,
No merit claims: I praise myself in thee.
My father loved thee through his length of days!
For thee his fields were shaded o'er with maize;
From thee what health, what vigor he possessed,
Ten sturdy freemen from his loins attest;
Thy constellation ruled my natal morn,
And all my bones were made of Indian corn.   130
Delicious grain, whatever form it take,

To roast or boil, to smother or to bake,
In every dish 'tis welcome still to me,
But most, my Hasty Pudding, most in thee.
   Let the green succotash with thee contend;
Let beans and corn their sweetest juices blend;
Let butter drench them in its yellow tide,
And a long slice of bacon grace their side;
Not all the plate, how famed soe'er it be,
Can please my palate like a bowl of thee.   140
Some talk of hoe-cake, fair Virginia's pride!
Rich johnny-cake this mouth has often tried;
Both please me well, their virtues much the same,
Alike their fabric, as allied their fame,
Except in dear New England, where the last
Receives a dash of pumpkin in the paste,
To give it sweetness and improve the taste.
But place them all before me, smoking hot,
The big, round dumpling, rolling from the pot;
The pudding of the bag, whose quivering breast,   150
With suet lined, leads on the Yankee feast;
The charlotte brown, within whose crusty sides
A belly soft the pulpy apple hides;
The yellow bread whose face like amber glows,
And all of Indian that the bakepan knows,—
You tempt me not; my favorite greets my eyes,
To that loved bowl my spoon by instinct flies.

CANTO II

   To mix the food by vicious rules of art,
To kill the stomach and to sink the heart,
To make mankind to social virtue sour,
Cram o'er each dish, and be what they devour;
For this the kitchen muse first framed her book,
Commanding sweats to stream from every cook;
Children no more their antic gambols tried,
And friends to physic wondered why they died.
   Not so the Yankee: his abundant feast,
With simples furnished and with plainness dressed,   10
A numerous offspring gathers round the board,
And cheers alike the servant and the lord;
Whose well-bought hunger prompts the joyous taste,
And health attends them from the short repast.

While the full pail rewards the milkmaid's toil,
The mother sees the morning caldron boil;
To stir the pudding next demands their care;
To spread the table and the bowls prepare;
To feed the household as their portions cool
And send them all to labor or to school.   20

Yet may the simplest dish some rules impart,
For nature scorns not all the aids of art.
E'en Hasty Pudding, purest of all food,
May still be bad, indifferent, or good,
As sage experience the short process guides,
Or want of skill, or want of care presides.
Whoe'er would form it on the surest plan,
To rear the child and long sustain the man;
To shield the morals while it mends the size,
And all the powers of every food supplies,—   30
Attend the lesson that the muse shall bring,
Suspend your spoons, and listen while I sing.

But since, O man! thy life and health demand
Not food alone, but labor from thy hand,
First, in the field, beneath the sun's strong rays,
Ask of thy mother earth the needful maize;
She loves the race that courts her yielding soil,
And gives her bounties to the sons of toil.

When now the ox, obedient to thy call,
Repays the loan that filled the winter stall,   40
Pursue his traces o'er the furrowed plain,
And plant in measured hills the golden grain.
But when the tender germ begins to shoot,
And the green spire declares the sprouting root,
Then guard your nursling from each greedy foe,
The insidious worm, the all-devouring crow.
A little ashes sprinkled round the spire,
Soon steeped in rain, will bid the worm retire;
The feathered robber with his hungry maw
Swift flies the field before your man of straw,   50
A frightful image, such as schoolboys bring
When met to burn the Pope or hang the King.

Thrice in the season, through each verdant row,
Wield the strong plowshare and the faithful hoe;
The faithful hoe, a double task that takes,
To till the summer corn and roast the winter cakes.

Slow springs the blade, while checked by chilling rains,

Ere yet the sun the seat of Cancer gains;
But when his fiercest fires emblaze the land,
Then start the juices, then the roots expand;   60
Then, like a column of Corinthian mold,
The stalk struts upward and the leaves unfold;
The bushy branches all the ridges fill,
Entwine their arms, and kiss from hill to hill.
Here cease to vex them; all your cares are done:
Leave the last labors to the parent sun;
Beneath his genial smiles, the well-dressed field,
When autumn calls, a plenteous crop shall yield.

  Now the strong foliage bears the standards high,
And shoots the tall top-gallants to the sky;   70
The suckling ears their silky fringes bend,
And pregnant grown, their swelling coats distend;
The loaded stalk, while still the burden grows,
O'erhangs the space that runs between the rows;
High as a hop-field waves the silent grove,
A safe retreat for little thefts of love,
When the pledged roasting-ears invite the maid
To meet her swain beneath the new-formed shade;
His generous hand unloads the cumbrous hill,
And the green spoils her ready basket fill;   80
Small compensation for the twofold bliss,
The promised wedding, and the present kiss.

  Slight depredations these; but now the moon
Calls from his hollow tree the sly raccoon;
And while by night he bears his prize away,
The bolder squirrel labors through the day.
Both thieves alike, but provident of time,
A virtue rare, that almost hides their crime.
Then let them steal the little stores they can,
And fill their granaries from the toils of man;   90
We've one advantage where they take no part—
With all their wiles, they ne'er have found the art
To boil the Hasty Pudding; here we shine
Superior far to tenants of the pine;
This envied boon to man shall still belong,
Unshared by them in substance or in song.

  At last the closing season browns the plain,
And ripe October gathers in the grain;
Deep-loaded carts the spacious corn-house fill;
The sack distended marches to the mill;   100

The laboring mill beneath the burden groans,
And showers the future pudding from the stones;
Till the glad housewife greets the powdered gold,
And the new crop exterminates the old.
Ah who can sing what every wight must feel,
The joy that enters with the bag of meal,
A general jubilee pervades the house,
Wakes every child and gladdens every mouse.

CANTO III

The days grow short; but though the falling sun
To the glad swain proclaims his day's work done,
Night's pleasing shades his various tasks prolong,
And yield new subjects to my various song.
For now, the corn-house filled, the harvest home,
The invited neighbors to the husking come:
A frolic scene, where work, and mirth, and play,
Unite their charms to chase the hours away.
Where the huge heap lies centered in the hall,
The lamp suspended from the cheerful wall,   10
Brown, corn-fed nymphs, and strong, hard-handed-beaux,
Alternate ranged, extend in circling rows,
Assume their seats, the solid mass attack;
The dry husks rustle, and the corncobs crack;
The song, the laugh, alternate notes resound,
And the sweet cider trips in silence round.
    The laws of husking every wight can tell;
And sure no laws he ever keeps so well:
For each red ear a general kiss he gains,
With each smut ear she smuts the luckless swains;   20
But when to some sweet maid a prize is cast,
Red as her lips and taper as her waist,
She walks the round and culls one favored beau,
Who leaps the luscious tribute to bestow.
Various the sport, as are the wits and brains
Of well-pleased lasses and contending swains;
Till the vast mound of corn is swept away,
And he that gets the last ear wins the day.
Meanwhile, the housewife urges all her care,
The well-earned feast to hasten and prepare.   30
The sifted meal already waits her hand,
The milk is strained, the bowls in order stand,

The fire flames high; and as a pool—that takes
The headlong stream that o'er the milldam breaks—
Foams, roars, and rages with incessant toils,
So the vexed caldron rages, roars, and boils.

First with clean salt she seasons well the food,
Then strews the flour, and thickens all the flood.
Long o'er the simmering fire she lets it stand;
To stir it well demands a stronger hand;   40
The husband takes his turn; and round and round
The ladle flies; at last the toil is crowned;
When to the board the thronging huskers pour,
And take their seats as at the corn before.

I leave them to their feast. There still belong
More useful matters to my faithful song.
For rules there are, though ne'er unfolded yet,
Nice rules and wise, how pudding should be ate.
Some with molasses line the luscious treat,
And mix, like bards, the useful with the sweet.   50
A wholesome dish, and well deserving praise,
A great resource in those bleak wintry days,
When the chilled earth lies buried deep in snow,
And raging Boreas dries the shivering cow.

Blest cow! thy praise shall still my notes employ,
Great source of health, the only source of joy;
Mother of Egypt's god,—but sure, for me,
Were I to leave my God, I'd worship thee.
How oft thy teats these pious hands have pressed!
How oft thy bounties proved my only feast!   60
How oft I've fed thee with my favorite grain!
And roared, like thee, to see thy children slain!

Ye swains who know her various worth to prize,
Ah! house her well from winter's angry skies.
Potatoes, pumpkins, should her sadness cheer,
Corn from your crib, and mashes from your beer;
When spring returns, she'll well acquit the loan,
And nurse at once your infants and her own.
Milk then with pudding I should always choose;
To this in future I confine my muse,   70
Till she in haste some further hints unfold,
Well for the young, nor useless to the old.
First in your bowl the milk abundant take,
Then drop with care along the silver lake
Your flakes of pudding; these at first will *hide*

Their little bulk beneath the swelling tide;
But when their growing mass no more can sink,
When the soft island looms above the brink,
Then check your hand; you've got the portion due;
So taught our sires, and what they taught is true.   80
    There is a choice in spoons. Though small appear
The nice distinction, yet to me 'tis clear.
The deep-bowled Gallic spoon, contrived to scoop
In ample draughts the thin, diluted soup,
Performs not well in those substantial things,
Whose mass adhesive to the metal clings;
Where the strong labial muscles must embrace
The gentle curve, and sweep the hollow space
With ease to enter and discharge the freight,
A bowl less concave, but still more dilate,   90
Becomes the pudding best. The shape, the size,
A secret rests, unknown to vulgar eyes.
Experienced feeders can alone impart
A rule so much above the lore of art.
These tuneful lips that thousand spoons have tried,
With just precision could the point decide,
Though not in song; the muse but poorly shines
In cones, and cubes, and geometric lines;
Yet the true form, as near as she can tell,
Is that small section of a goose-egg shell,   100
Which in two equal portions shall divide
The distance from the center to the side.
    Fear not to slaver; 'tis no deadly sin.
Like the free Frenchman, from your joyous chin
Suspend the ready napkin; or, like me,
Poise with one hand your bowl upon your knee;
Just in the zenith your wise head project,
Your full spoon, rising in a line direct,
Bold as a bucket, heeds no drops that fall;
The wide-mouthed bowl will surely catch them all!   110

w. 1792–1793
p. 1796

ROYALL TYLER

(1757–1826)

Much like the Connecticut Wits in his values, Tyler was another writer who copied the English while insisting that America should develop its own manners, life, and literature and refrain from imitating the customs of Europe. Born in Boston and a graduate of Harvard (1776), he took part in the military expedition that put down Shays' Rebellion. As a lawyer, in 1787 he visited New York on business pursuant to the Rebellion and saw the first play of his life—Sheridan's *School for Scandal*. He probably also saw Vanbrugh's *The Provoked Husband* and O'Keeffe's *The Poor Soldier*. Apocrypha has it that three weeks later he had written *The Contrast*. Although the play may seem silly (but delightfully so) to modern audiences, it is important in the development of our literature. *The Contrast* demanded a native image of our national character and presented two types that have never left us. One is the strong silent man, later especially associated with the idea of the West (Gary Cooper's "Yup" has been our most popular recent manifestation); the other is the Brother-Jonathan Yankee who, merged with the "real man," became the prototype of Uncle Sam. A sharp satirist, Tyler saw both the virtue and weakness of American newness and innocence, themes that underline some of our most important literature.

In 1791, Tyler moved to Vermont, was Chief Justice of the state's supreme court from 1807 to 1813, and taught part of that time at the state university.

His works include *The Contrast* (1787); *The Algerine Captive* (1797); and *The Yankey in London* (1809).

Editions and accounts of the man and his works are to be found in J. B. Wilbur and H. T. Brown, eds., *The Contrast* (1920); F. Tupper, "Royall Tyler: Man of Law and Man of Letters," *Vermont Historical Society Proceedings* (1928); A. H. Quinn, "Royall Tyler," *Dictionary of American Biography* (1936); A. H. Nethercot, "The Dramatic Background of Royall Tyler's *The Contrast,*" *American Literature,* XII (1941); A. W. Peach and G. F. Newbrough, eds., *Four Plays by Royall Tyler* (1941), Volume XV of *America's Lost Plays;* J. Lauber, "*The Contrast*: A Study in the Concept of Innocence," *English Language Notes,* I (1963); and R. B. Stein, "Royall Tyler and the Question of Our Speech," *New England Quarterly,* XXXVIII (1965).

The Contrast

Characters

COL. MANLY	JESSAMY	MARIA
DIMPLE	JONATHAN	LETITIA
VAN ROUGH	CHARLOTTE	JENNY
	SERVANTS	

SCENE: New York

PROLOGUE

Exult each patriot heart!—this night is shown
A piece, which we may fairly call our own;
Where the proud titles of "My Lord! Your Grace!"
To humble Mr. and plain Sir give place.
Our Author pictures not from foreign climes
The fashions, or the follies of the times;
But has confin'd the subject of his work
To the gay scenes—the circles of New-York.
On native themes his Muse displays her pow'rs;
If ours the faults, the virtues too are ours.
Why should our thoughts to distant countries roam,
When each refinement may be found at home?
Who travels now to ape the rich or great,
To deck an equipage and roll in state;
To court the graces, or to dance with ease,
Or by hypocrisy to strive to please?
Our free-born ancestors such arts despis'd;
Genuine sincerity alone they priz'd;

Their minds, with honest emulation fir'd,
To solid good—not ornament—aspir'd;
Or, if ambition rous'd a bolder flame,
Stern virtue throve, where indolence was shame.

But modern youths, with imitative sense,
Deem taste in dress the proof of excellence;
And spurn the meanness of your homespun arts,
Since homespun habits would obscure their parts;
Whilst all, which aims at splendor and parade,
Must come from Europe, and be ready made.
Strange! we should thus our native worth disclaim,
And check the progress of our rising fame.
Yet one, whilst imitation bears the sway,
Aspires to nobler heights, and points the way,
Be rous'd, my friends! his bold example view;
Let your own Bards be proud to copy you!
Should rigid critics reprobate our play,
At least the patriotic heart will say,
"Glorious our fall, since in a noble cause.
"The bold attempt alone demands applause."
Still may the wisdom of the Comic Muse
Exalt your merits, or your faults accuse.
But think not, 't is her aim to be severe;—
We all are mortals, and as mortals err.
If candor pleases, we are truly blest;
Vice trembles, when compell'd to stand confess'd.
Let not light Censure on your faults, offend,
Which aims not to expose them, but amend.
Thus does our Author to your candor trust;
Conscious, the free are generous, as just.

ACT FIRST

SCENE 1.

An Apartment at CHARLOTTE'S. CHARLOTTE *and* LETITIA *discovered.*

LETITIA. And so, Charlotte, you really think the pocket-hoop unbecoming.

CHARLOTTE. No, I don't say so: It may be very becoming to saunter round the house of a rainy day; to visit my grandmamma, or go to Quakers' meeting: but to swim in a minuet, with the eyes of fifty well-dressed beaux upon me, to trip it in the Mall, or walk on the battery, give me the luxurious, jaunty, flowing, bell-hoop. It would have delighted you to have seen me the last evening, my charming girl! I was dangling o'er the battery with Billy Dimple; a knot of young fellows were upon the platform; as I passed them I faltered with one of the most bewitching false steps you ever saw, and then recovered myself with such a pretty confusion, flirting my hoop to discover a jet black shoe and brilliant buckle. Gad! how my little heart thrilled to hear the confused raptures of, "Demme, Jack, what a delicate foot!" "Ha! General, what a well-turn'd—"

LETITIA. Fie! fie! Charlotte (*stopping her mouth*). I protest you are quite a libertine.

CHARLOTTE. Why, my dear little prude, are we not all such libertines? Do you think, when I sat tortured two hours under the hands of my friseur, and an hour more at my toilet, that I had any thoughts of my aunt Susan, or my cousin Betsey? though they are both allowed to be critical judges of dress.

LETITIA. Why, who should we dress to please, but those who are judges of its merit?

CHARLOTTE. Why a creature who does not know Buffon from Souflee—Man!—my Letitia—Man! for whom we dress, walk, dance, talk, lisp, languish, and smile. Does not the grave Spectator assure us, that even our much bepraised diffidence, modesty, and blushes, are all directed to make ourselves good wives and mothers as fast as we can. Why, I'll undertake with one flirt of this hoop to bring more beaux to my feet in one week, than the grave Maria, and her sentimental circle, can do, by sighing sentiment till their hairs are gray.

LETITIA. Well, I won't argue with you; you always out talk me; let us change the subject. I hear that Mr. Dimple and Maria are soon to be married.

CHARLOTTE. You hear true. I was consulted in the choice of the wedding clothes. She is to be married in a delicate white satin, and has a monstrous pretty brocaded lute-string for the second day. It would have done you good to have seen with what an affected indifference the dear sentimentalist turned over a thousand pretty things, just as if her heart did not palpitate with her approaching happiness, and at last made her choice, and arranged her dress with such apathy, as if she did not know that plain white satin, and a simple blond lace, would shew her clear skin, and dark hair, to the greatest advantage.

LETITIA. But they say her indifference to dress, and even to the gentleman himself, is not entirely affected.

CHARLOTTE. How?

LETITIA. It is whispered, that if Maria gives her hand to Mr. Dimple, it will be without her heart.

CHARLOTTE. Though the giving the heart is one of the last of all laughable considerations in the marriage of a girl of spirit, yet I should like to hear what antiquated notions the dear little piece of old fashioned prudery has got in her head.

LETITIA. Why you know that old Mr. John-Richard-Robert-Jacob-Isaac-Abraham-Cornelius Van Dumpling, Billy Dimple's father, (for he has thought fit to soften his name, as well as manners, during his English tour) was the most intimate friend of Maria's father. The old folks, about a year before Mr. Van Dumpling's death, proposed this match: the young folks were accordingly introduced, and told they must love one another. Billy was then a good natured, decent, dressing young fellow, with a little dash of the coxcomb, such as our young fellows of fortune usually have. At this time, I really believe she thought she loved him; and had they then been married, I doubt not, they might have jogged on, to the end of the chapter, a good kind of a sing-song lack-a-daysaical life, as other honest married folks do.

CHARLOTTE. Why did they not then marry?

LETITIA. Upon the death of his father, Billy went to England to see the world, and rub off a little of the patroon rust. During his absence, Maria like a good girl, to keep herself constant to her known true-love, avoided company, and betook herself, for her amusement, to her books, and her dear Billy's letters. But, alas! how many ways has the mischievous demon of inconstancy of stealing into a woman's heart! Her love was destroyed by the very means she took to support it.

CHARLOTTE. How?—Oh! I have it—some likely young beau found the way to her study.

LETITIA. Be patient, Charlotte—your head so runs upon beaux.—Why she read Sir Charles Grandison, Clarissa Harlow, Shenstone, and the Sentimental Journey; and between whiles, as I said, Billy's letters. But as her taste improved, her love declined. The contrast was so striking betwixt the good sense of her books, and the flimsiness of her love-letters, that she discovered she had unthinkingly engaged her hand without her heart; and then the whole transaction managed by the old folks, now appeared so unsentimental, and looked so like bargaining for a bale of goods, that she found she ought to have rejected, according to every rule of romance, even the man of her choice, if imposed upon her in that manner—Clary Harlow would have scorned such a match.

CHARLOTTE. Well, how was it on Mr. Dimple's return? Did he meet a more favorable reception than his letters?

LETITIA. Much the same. She spoke of him with respect abroad, and with contempt in her closet. She watched his conduct and conversation, and found that he had by travelling acquired the wickedness of Lovelace without his wit, and the politeness of Sir Charles Grandison without his generosity. The ruddy youth who washed his face at the cistern every morning, and swore and looked eternal love and constancy, was now metamorphosed into a flippant, pallid, polite beau, who devotes the morning to his toilet, reads a few pages of Chesterfield's letters, and then minces out, to put the infamous principles in practice upon every woman he meets.

CHARLOTTE. But, if she is so apt at conjuring up these sentimental bugbears, why does she not discard him at once?

LETITIA. Why, she thinks her word too sacred to be trifled with. Besides, her father, who has a great respect for the memory of his deceased friend, is ever telling her how he shall renew his years in their union, and repeating the dying injunctions of old Van Dumpling.

CHARLOTTE. A mighty pretty story! And so you would make me believe, that the sensible Maria would give up Dumpling manor, and the all-accomplished Dimple as a husband, for the absurd, ridiculous reason, forsooth, because she despises and abhors him. Just as if a lady could not be privileged to spend a man's fortune, ride in his carriage, be called after his name, and call him her known dear lovee when she wants money, without loving and respecting the great he-creature. Oh! my dear girl, you are a monstrous prude.

LETITIA. I don't say what I would do; I only intimate how I suppose she wishes to act.

CHARLOTTE. No, no, no! A fig for sentiment. If she breaks, or wishes to break, with Mr. Dimple, depend upon it, she has some other man in her eye. A woman rarely discards one lover, until she is sure of another.— Letitia little thinks what a clue I have to Dimple's conduct. The generous man submits to render himself disgusting to Maria, in order that she may leave him at liberty to address me. I must change the subject. (*Aside, and rings a bell. Enter* SERVANT.) Frank, order the horses to.— Talking of marriage—did you hear that Sally Bloomsbury is going to be married next week to Mr. Indigo, the rich Carolinian?

LETITIA. Sally Bloomsbury married!— Why, she is not yet in her teens.

CHARLOTTE. I do not know how that is, but, you may depend upon it, 't is a done affair. I have it from the best authority. There is my aunt Wyerley's Hannah (you know Hannah—though a black, she is a wench that was never caught in a lie in her life); now Hannah has a brother who courts Sarah, Mrs. Catgut the milliner's girl, and she told Hannah's brother, and Hannah, who, as I said before, is a girl of undoubted veracity, told it directly to me, that Mrs. Catgut was making a new cap for Miss Bloomsbury, which, as it was very dressy, it is very probable is designed for a wedding cap: now, as she is to be married, who can it be to, but to Mr. Indigo? Why, there is no other gentleman that visits at her papa's.

LETITIA. Say not a word more, Charlotte. Your intelligence is so direct and well grounded, it is almost a pity that it is not a piece of scandal.

CHARLOTTE. Oh! I am the pink of prudence. Though I cannot charge myself with ever having discredited a tea-party by my silence, yet I take care never to report any thing of my acquaintance, especially if it is to their credit, —*discredit*, I mean—until I have searched to the bottom of it. It is true, there is infinite pleasure in this charitable pursuit. Oh! how delicious to go and condole with the friends of some backsliding sister, or to retire with some old dowager or maiden aunt of the family, who love scandal so well, that they cannot forbear gratifying their appetite at the expence of the reputation of their nearest relations! And then to return full fraught with a rich collection of circumstances, to retail to the next circle of our acquaintance under the strongest injunctions of secrecy,—ha, ha, ha!—interlarding the melancholy tale with so many doleful shakes of the head, and more doleful, "Ah! who would have thought it! so amiable, so prudent a young lady, as we all thought her, what a monstrous pity! well, I have nothing to charge myself with; I acted the part of a friend, I warned her of the principles of that rake, I told her what would be the consequence; I told her so, I told her so."— Ha, ha, ha!

LETITIA. Ha, ha, ha! Well, but Charlotte, you don't tell me what you think of Miss Bloomsbury's match.

CHARLOTTE. Think! why I think it is probable she cried for a plaything, and they have given her a husband. Well, well, well, the puling chit shall not be deprived of her plaything: 't is only exchanging London dolls for American babies— Apropos, of babies, have you heard what Mrs. Affable's high-flying notions of delicacy have come to?

LETITIA. Who, she that was Miss Lovely?

CHARLOTTE. The same; she married Bob Affable of Schenectady. Don't you remember?

(*Enter* SERVANT.)

SERVANT. Madam, the carriage is ready.

LETITIA. Shall we go to the stores first, or visiting?

CHARLOTTE. I should think it rather too early to visit; especially Mrs. Prim: you know she is so particular.

LETITIA. Well, but what of Mrs. Affable?

CHARLOTTE. Oh, I'll tell you as we go; come, come, let us hasten. I hear Mrs. Catgut has some of the prettiest caps arrived, you ever saw. I shall die if I have not the first sight of them. (*Exeunt.*)

SCENE 2.

A Room in VAN ROUGH'S *House.* MARIA *sitting disconsolate at a Table, with Books, etc.*

Song

I

The sun sets in night, and the stars shun the day;
But glory remains when their lights fade away!
Begin, ye tormentors! your threats are in vain,
For the son of Alknomook shall never complain.

II

Remember the arrows he shot from his bow;
Remember your chiefs by his hatchet laid low:
Why so slow?—do you wait till I shrink from the pain?
No—the son of Alknomook will never complain.

III

Remember the wood where in ambush we lay;
And the scalps which we bore from your nation away:
Now the flame rises fast, you exult in my pain;
But the son of Alknomook can never complain.

IV

I go to the land where my father is gone;
His ghost shall rejoice in the fame of his son:
Death comes like a friend, he relieves me from pain;
And thy son, Oh Alknomook! has scorn'd to complain.

There is something in this song which ever calls forth
my affections. The manly virtue of courage, that fortitude
which steels the heart against the keenest misfortunes, which
interweaves the laurel of glory amidst the instruments of
torture and death, displays something so noble, so exalted,
that in despite of the prejudices of education, I cannot
but admire it, even in a savage. The prepossession which
our sex is supposed to entertain for the character of a
soldier, is, I know, a standing piece of raillery among the
wits. A cockade, a lapell'd coat, and a feather, they will
tell you, are irresistible by a female heart. Let it be so.—
Who is it that considers the helpless situation of our sex,
that does not see we each moment stand in need of a
protector, and that a brave one too. Formed of the more
delicate materials of nature, endowed only with the softer
passions, incapable, from our ignorance of the world, to

guard against the wiles of mankind, our security for happiness often depends upon their generosity and courage:—
Alas! how little of the former do we find. How inconsistent!
that man should be leagued to destroy that honor, upon
which, solely rests his respect and esteem. Ten thousand
temptations allure us, ten thousand passions betray us; yet
the smallest deviation from the path of rectitude is followed
by the contempt and insult of man, and the more remorse-
less pity of woman: years of penitence and tears cannot
wash away the stain, nor a life of virtue obliterate its
remembrance. Reputation is the life of woman; yet courage
to protect it, is masculine and disgusting; and the only safe
asylum a woman of delicacy can find, is in the arms of a
man of honor. How naturally then, should we love the
brave, and the generous; how gratefully should we bless
the arm raised for our protection, when nerv'd by virtue,
and directed by honor! Heaven grant that the man with
whom I may be connected—may be connected!— Whither
has my imagination transported me—whither does it now
lead me?— Am I not indissolubly engaged by every obligation of honor, which my own consent, and my father's
approbation can give, to a man who can never share my
affections, and whom a few days hence, it will be criminal
for me to disapprove—to disapprove! would to heaven that
were all—to despise. For, can the most frivolous manners,
actuated by the most depraved heart, meet, or merit, anything but contempt from every woman of delicacy and
sentiment? (VAN ROUGH, without. Mary!) Ha, my father's
voice— Sir!—

(*Enter* VAN ROUGH.)

VAN ROUGH. What, Mary, always singing doleful ditties,
and moping over these plaguy books.

MARIA. I hope, Sir, that it is not criminal to improve my
mind with books; or to divert my melancholy with singing
at my leisure hours.

VAN ROUGH. Why, I don't know that, child; I don't know
that. They us'd to say when I was a young man, that if a
woman knew how to make a pudding, and to keep herself
out of fire and water, she knew enough for a wife. Now,
what good have these books done you? have they not made
you melancholy? as you call it. Pray, what right has a girl
of your age to be in the dumps? haven't you every thing
your heart can wish; an't you going to be married to a

young man of great fortune; an't you going to have the quit-rent of twenty miles square?

MARIA. One hundredth part of the land, and a lease for life of the heart of a man I could love, would satisfy me.

VAN ROUGH. Pho, pho, pho! child; nonsense, downright nonsense, child. This comes of your reading your story-books; your Charles Grandisons, your Sentimental Journals, and your Robinson Crusoes, and such other trumpery. No, no, no! child, it is money makes the mare go; keep your eye upon the main chance, Mary.

MARIA. Marriage, Sir, is, indeed, a very serious affair.

VAN ROUGH. You are right, child; you are right. I am sure I found it so to my cost.

MARIA. I mean, Sir, that as marriage is a portion for life, and so intimately involves our happiness, we cannot be too considerate in the choice of our companion.

VAN ROUGH. Right, child; very right. A young woman should be very sober when she is making her choice, but when she has once made it, as you have done, I don't see why she should not be as merry as a grig; I am sure she has reason enough to be so— Solomon says, that "there is a time to laugh, and a time to weep"; now a time for a young woman to laugh is when she has made sure of a good rich husband. Now a time to cry, according to you, Mary, is when she is making choice of him: but, I should think, that a young woman's time to cry was, when she despaired of *getting* one.— Why, there was your mother now; to be sure when I popp'd the question to her, she did look a little silly; but when she had once looked down on her apron-strings, as all modest young women us'd to do, and drawled out ye-s, she was as brisk and as merry as a bee.

MARIA. My honored mother, Sir, had no motive to melancholy; she married the man of her choice.

VAN ROUGH. The man of her choice! And pray, Mary, an't you going to marry the man of your choice—what trumpery notion is this?— It is these vile books (*throwing them away*). I'd have you to know, Mary, if you won't make young Van Dumpling the man of *your* choice, you shall marry him as the man of *my* choice.

MARIA. You terrify me, Sir. Indeed, Sir, I am all sub-mission. My will is yours.

VAN ROUGH. Why, that is the way your mother us'd to talk. "My will is yours, my dear Mr. Van Rough, my will is yours": but she took special care to have her own way though for all that.

MARIA. Do not reflect upon my mother's memory, Sir—

VAN ROUGH. Why not, Mary, why not? She kept me from speaking my mind all her *life,* and do you think she shall henpeck me now she is *dead* too? Come, come; don't go to sniveling: be a good girl, and mind the main chance. I'll see you well settled in the world.

MARIA. I do not doubt your love, Sir; and it is my duty to obey you.— I will endeavor to make my duty and inclination go hand in hand.

VAN ROUGH. Well, well, Mary; do you be a good girl, mind the main chance, and never mind inclination.— Why, do you know that I have been down in the cellar this very morning to examine a pipe of Madeira which I purchased the week you were born, and mean to tap on your wedding day.— That pipe cost me fifty pounds sterling. It was well worth sixty pounds; but I overreached Ben Bulkhead, the supercargo: I'll tell you the whole story. You must know that—

(Enter SERVANT.*)*

SERVANT. Sir, Mr. Transfer, the broker, is below. *(Exit.)*

VAN ROUGH. Well, Mary, I must go.— Remember, and be a good girl, and mind the main chance. *(Exit.)*

MARIA. *(Alone)* How deplorable is my situation! How distressing for a daughter to find her heart militating with her filial duty! I know my father loves me tenderly, why then do I reluctantly obey him? Heaven knows! with what reluctance I should oppose the will of a parent, or set an example of filial disobedience; at a parent's command I could wed awkwardness and deformity. Were the heart of my husband good, I would so magnify his good qualities with the eye of conjugal affection, that the defects of his person and manners should be lost in the emanation of his virtues. At a father's command, I could embrace poverty. Were the poor man my husband, I would learn resignation to my lot; I would enliven our frugal meal with good humor, and chase away misfortune from our cottage with a smile. At a father's command, I could almost submit, to what every female heart knows to be the most mortifying, to marry a weak man, and blush at my husband's folly in every company I visited.— But to marry a depraved wretch, whose only virtue is a polished exterior; who is actuated by the unmanly ambition of conquering the defenseless; whose heart, insensible to the emotions of patriotism, dilates at the plaudits of every unthinking girl: whose laurels are the sighs and tears of the miserable victims of his specious behavior.— Can he, who has no regard for the peace and happiness of other families, ever have a due regard for the peace and happiness of his own? Would to heaven that my father were not so hasty in his temper! Surely, if I were to state my reasons for declining this match, he would not compel me to marry a man—whom, though my lips may solemnly promise to honor, I find my heart must ever despise. (*Exit.*)

END OF THE FIRST ACT

ACT SECOND

SCENE 1.

(*Enter* CHARLOTTE *and* LETITIA)

CHARLOTTE. (*At entering*) Betty, take those things out of the carriage and carry them to my chamber; see that you don't tumble them.— My dear, I protest, I think it was the homeliest of the whole. I declare I was almost tempted to return and change it.

LETITIA. Why would you take it?

CHARLOTTE. Didn't Mrs. Catgut say it was the most fashionable?

LETITIA. But, my dear, it will never sit becomingly on you.

CHARLOTTE. I know that; but did not you hear Mrs. Catgut say it was fashionable?

LETITIA. Did you see that sweet airy cap with the white sprig?

CHARLOTTE. Yes and I longed to take it; but, my dear, what could I do?— Did not Mrs. Catgut say it was the most fashionable; and if I had not taken it, was not that awkward gawky, Sally Slender, ready to purchase it immediately?

LETITIA. Did you observe how she tumbled over the things at the next shop, and then went off without purchasing any thing, nor even thanking the poor man for his trouble?— But of all the awkward creatures, did you see Miss Blouze, endeavoring to thrust her unmerciful arm into those small kid gloves?

CHARLOTTE. Ha, ha, ha, ha!

LETITIA. Then did you take notice, with what an affected warmth of friendship she and Miss Wasp met? when all their acquaintances know how much pleasure they take in abusing each other in every company?

CHARLOTTE. Lud! Letitia, is that so extraordinary? Why, my dear, I hope you are not going to turn sentimentalist.— Scandal, you know, is but amusing ourselves with the faults, foibles, follies and reputations of our friends;—indeed, I don't know why we should have friends, if we are not at liberty to make use of them. But no person is so ignorant of the world as to suppose, because I amuse myself with a lady's faults, that I am obliged to quarrel with her person, every time we meet; believe me, my dear, we should have very few acquaintances at that rate. (SERVANT *enters and delivers a letter to* CHARLOTTE, *and Exit.*) You'll excuse me, my dear. (*Opens and reads to herself.*)

LETITIA. Oh, quite excusable.

CHARLOTTE. As I hope to be married, my brother Henry is in the city.

LETITIA. What, your brother, Colonel Manly?

CHARLOTTE. Yes, my dear; the only brother I have in the world.

LETITIA. Was he never in this city?

CHARLOTTE. Never nearer than Harlem Heights, where he lay with his regiment.

LETITIA. What sort of a being is this brother of yours? If he is as chatty, as pretty, as sprightly as you, half the belles in the city will be pulling caps for him.

CHARLOTTE. My brother is the very counterpart and reverse of me: I am gay, he is grave; I am airy, he is solid; I am ever selecting the most pleasing objects for my laughter, he has a tear for every pitiful one. And thus, whilst he is plucking the briars and thorns from the path of the unfortunate, I am strewing my own path with roses.

LETITIA. My sweet friend, not quite so poetical, and little more particular.

CHARLOTTE. Hands off, Letitia. I feel the rage of simile upon me; I can't talk to you in any other way. My brother has a heart replete with the noblest sentiments, but then, it is like—it is like—Oh! you provoking girl, you have deranged all my ideas—it is like—Oh! I have it—his heart is like an old maiden lady's bandbox; it contains many costly things, arranged with the most scrupulous nicety, yet the misfortune is, that they are too delicate, costly, and antiquated, for common use.

LETITIA. By what I can pick out of your flowery description, your brother is no beau.

CHARLOTTE. No, indeed; he makes no pretension to the character. He'd ride, or rather fly, an hundred miles to relieve a distressed object, or to do a gallant act in the service of his country: but, should you drop your fan or bouquet in his presence, it is ten to one that some beau at the farther end of the room would have the honor of presenting it to you, before he had observed that it fell. I'll tell you one of his antiquated, anti-gallant notions.— He said once in my presence, in a room full of company —would you believe it—in a large circle of ladies, that the best evidence a gentleman could give a young lady of his respect and affection, was, to endeavor in a friendly manner to rectify her foibles. I protest I was crimson to the eyes, upon reflecting that I was known as his sister.

LETITIA. Insupportable creature! tell a lady of her faults! If he is so grave, I fear I have no chance of captivating him.

CHARLOTTE. His conversation is like a rich old fashioned brocade, it will stand alone; every sentence is a sentiment. Now you may judge what a time I had with him, in my twelve months' visit to my father. He read me such lectures, out of pure brotherly affection, against the extremes of fashion, dress, flirting, and coquetry, and all the other dear things which he knows I dote upon, that, I protest, his conversation made me as melancholy as if I had been at church; and heaven knows, though I never prayed to go there but on one occasion, yet I would have exchanged his conversation for a psalm and a sermon. Church is rather melancholy, to be sure; but then I can ogle the beaux, and be regaled with "here endeth the first lesson"; but his brotherly *here,* you would think had no end. You captivate him! Why, my dear, he would as soon fall in love with a box of Italian flowers. There is Maria now, if she were not engaged, she might do something.— Oh! how I should like to see that pair of penserosos together, looking as grave as two sailors' wives of a stormy night, with a flow of sentiment meandering through their conversation like purling streams in modern poetry.

LETITIA. Oh! my dear fanciful—

CHARLOTTE. Hush! I hear some person coming through the entry.

(*Enter* SERVANT.)

SERVANT. Madam, there's a gentleman below who calls himself Colonel Manly; do you choose to be at home?

CHARLOTTE. Show him in. (*Exit* SERVANT.) Now for a sober face.

(*Enter* COLONEL MANLY.)

MANLY. My dear Charlotte, I am happy that I once more enfold you within the arms of fraternal affection. I know you are going to ask (amiable impatience!) how our parents do,—the venerable pair transmit you their blessing by me—they totter on the verge of a well-spent life, and wish only to see their children settled in the world, to depart in peace.

CHARLOTTE. I am very happy to hear that they are well. (*Coolly*) Brother, will you give me leave to introduce you to our uncle's ward, one of my most intimate friends.

MANLY. (*Saluting* LETITIA) I ought to regard your friends as my own.

CHARLOTTE. Come, Letitia, do give us a little dash of your vivacity; my brother is so sentimental, and so grave, that I protest he'll give us the vapors.

MANLY. Though sentiment and gravity, I know, are banished the polite world, yet, I hoped, they might find some countenance in the meeting of such near connections as brother and sister.

CHARLOTTE. Positively, brother, if you go one step further in this strain, you will set me crying, and that, you know, would spoil my eyes; and then I should never get the husband which our good papa and mamma have so kindly wished me—never be established in the world.

MANLY. Forgive me, my sister—I am no enemy to mirth; I love your sprightliness; and I hope it will one day enliven the hours of some worthy man; but when I mention the respectable authors of my existence,—the cherishers and protectors of my helpless infancy, whose hearts glow with such fondness and attachment, that they would willingly lay down their lives for my welfare, you will excuse me, if

I am so unfashionable as to speak of them with some degree of respect and reverence.

CHARLOTTE. Well, well, brother; if you won't be gay, we'll not differ; I will be as grave as you wish. (*Affects gravity.*) And so, brother, you have come to the city to exchange some of your commutation notes for a little pleasure.

MANLY. Indeed, you are mistaken; my errand is not of amusement, but business; and as I neither drink nor game, my expences will be so trivial, I shall have no occasion to sell my notes.

CHARLOTTE. Then you won't have occasion to do a very good thing. Why, there was the Vermont General—he came down some time since, sold all his musty notes at one stroke, and then laid the cash out in trinkets for his dear Fanny. I want a dozen pretty things myself; have you got the notes with you?

MANLY. I shall be ever willing to contribute as far as it is in my power, to adorn, or in any way to please my sister; yet, I hope, I shall never be obliged for this, to sell my notes. I may be romantic, but I preserve them as a sacred deposit. Their full amount is justly due to me, but as embarrassments, the natural consequences of a long war, disable my country from supporting its credit, I shall wait with patience until it is rich enough to discharge them. If that is not in my day, they shall be transmitted as an honorable certificate to posterity, that I have humbly imitated our illustrious WASHINGTON, in having exposed my health and life in the service of my country, without reaping any other reward than the glory of conquering in so arduous a contest.

CHARLOTTE. Well said heroics. Why, my dear Henry, you have such a lofty way of saying things, that I protest I almost tremble at the thought of introducing you to the polite circles in the city. The belles would think you were a player run mad, with your head filled with old scraps of tragedy: and, as to the beaux, they might admire, because they would not understand you.— But, however, I must, I believe, venture to introduce you to two or three ladies of my acquaintance.

LETITIA. And that will make him acquainted with thirty or forty beaux.

CHARLOTTE. Oh! brother, you don't know what a fund of happiness you have in store.

MANLY. I fear, sister, I have not refinement sufficient to enjoy it.

CHARLOTTE. Oh! you cannot fail being pleased.

LETITIA. Our ladies are so delicate and dressy.

CHARLOTTE. And our beaux so dressy and delicate.

LETITIA. Our ladies chat and flirt so agreeably.

CHARLOTTE. And our beaux simper and bow so gracefully.

LETITIA. With their hair so trim and neat.

CHARLOTTE. And their faces so soft and sleek.

LETITIA. Their buckles so tonish and bright.

CHARLOTTE. And their hands so slender and white.

LETITIA. I vow, Charlotte, we are quite poetical.

CHARLOTTE. And then, brother, the faces of the beaux are of such a lily white hue! None of that horrid robustness of constitution, that vulgar corn-fed glow of health, which can only serve to alarm an unmarried lady with apprehensions, and prove a melancholy memento to a married one, that she can never hope for the happiness of being a widow. I will say this to the credit of our city beaux, that such is the delicacy of their complexion, dress, and address, that, even had I no reliance upon the honor of the dear Adonises, I would trust myself in any possible situation with them, without the least apprehensions of rudeness.

MANLY. Sister Charlotte!

CHARLOTTE. Now, now, now brother (*interrupting him*), now don't go to spoil my mirth with a dash of your gravity; I am so glad to see you, I am in tip-top spirits. Oh! that you could be with us at a little snug party. There is Billy Simper, Jack Chassé, and Colonel Van Titter, Miss Promonade, and the two Miss Tambours, sometimes make a party, with some other ladies, in a sidebox at the play. Everything is conducted with such decorum,—first we bow round to the company in general, then to each one in particular, then we have so many inquiries after each other's health, and we are so happy to meet each other, and it is so many ages since we last had that pleasure, and, if a married lady is in company, we have such a sweet dissertation upon her son Bobby's chin-cough, then the curtain rises, then our sensibility is all awake, and then by the mere force of apprehension, we torture some harmless expression into a double meaning, which the poor author never dreamt of, and then we have recourse to our fans, and then we blush, and then the gentlemen jog one another, peep under the fan, and make the prettiest remarks; and then we giggle and they simper, and they giggle and we simper, and then the curtain drops, and then for nuts and oranges, and then we bow, and it's pray Ma'am take it, and pray Sir keep it, and oh! not for the world, Sir: and then the curtain rises again, and then we blush, and giggle, and simper, and bow, all over again. Oh! the sentimental charms of a side-box conversation! (*All laugh.*)

MANLY. Well, sister, I join heartily with you in the laugh; for, in my opinion, it is as justifiable to laugh at folly, as it is reprehensible to ridicule misfortune.

CHARLOTTE. Well, but brother, positively, I can't introduce you in these clothes: why, your coat looks as if it were calculated for the vulgar purpose of keeping yourself comfortable.

MANLY. This coat was my regimental coat in the late war. The public tumults of our state have induced me to buckle on the sword in support of that government which I once fought to establish. I can only say, sister, that there was a time when this coat was respectable, and some people even thought that those men who had endured so many winter campaigns in the service of their country, without bread, clothing, or pay, at least deserved that the poverty of their appearance should not be ridiculed.

CHARLOTTE. We agree in opinion entirely, brother, though it would not have done for me to have said it: it is the coat makes the man respectable. In the time of the war, when we were almost frightened to death, why, your coat was respectable, that is, fashionable; now another kind of coat is fashionable, that is, respectable. And pray direct the tailor to make yours the height of the fashion.

MANLY. Though it is of little consequence to me of what shape my coat is, yet, as to the height of the fashion, there you will please to excuse me, sister. You know my sentiments on that subject. I have often lamented the advantage which the French have over us in that particular. In Paris, the fashions have their dawnings, their routine and declensions, and depend as much upon the caprice of the day as in other countries; but there every lady assumes a right to deviate from the general *ton,* as far as will be of advantage to her own appearance. In America, the cry is, what is the fashion? and we follow it, indiscriminately, because it is so.

CHARLOTTE. Therefore it is, that when large hoops are in fashion, we often see many a plump girl lost in the immensity of a hoop petticoat, whose want of height and *em-bon-point* would never have been remarked in any other dress. When the high head-dress is the mode, how then do we see a lofty cushion, with a profusion of gauze, feathers, and ribbon, supported by a face no bigger than an apple; whilst a broad full-faced lady, who really would have appeared tolerably handsome in a large headdress, looks with her smart chapeau as masculine as a soldier.

MANLY. But remember, my dear sister, and I wish all my fair country-women would recollect, that the only excuse a young lady can have for going extravagantly into a fashion, is, because it makes her look extravagantly handsome.— Ladies, I must wish you a good morning.

CHARLOTTE. But, brother, you are going to make home with us.

MANLY. Indeed, I cannot. I have seen my uncle, and explained that matter.

CHARLOTTE. Come and dine with us, then. We have a family dinner about half past four o'clock.

MANLY. I am engaged to dine with the Spanish ambassador. I was introduced to him by an old brother officer; and instead of freezing me with a cold card of compliment to dine with him ten days hence, he, with the true old Castilian frankness, in a friendly manner, asked me to dine with him to-day—an honor I could not refuse. Sister, adieu— Madam, your most obedient— (*Exit.*)

CHARLOTTE. I will wait upon you to the door, brother; I have something particular to say to you. (*Exit.*)

LETITIA. (*Alone*) What a pair!— She the pink of flirtation, he the essence of everything that is *outré* and gloomy. — I think I have completely deceived Charlotte by my manner of speaking of Mr. Dimple; she's too much the friend of Maria to be confided in. He is certainly rendering himself disagreeable to Maria, in order to break with her and proffer his hand to me. This is what the delicate fellow hinted in our last conversation. (*Exit.*)

SCENE 2.

The Mall.

(*Enter* JESSAMY.)

Positively this Mall is a very pretty place. I hope the city won't ruin it by repairs. To be sure, it won't do to speak of in the same day with Ranelagh or Vauxhall; however, it's a fine place for a young fellow to display his person to advantage. Indeed, nothing is lost here; the girls have taste, and I am very happy to find they have adopted the elegant London fashion of looking back, after a genteel fellow like me has passed them. Ah! who comes here? This, by his awkwardness, must be the Yankee colonel's servant. I'll accost him. (*Enter* JONATHAN.) Votre très— humble serviteur, Monsieur. I understand Colonel Manly, the Yankee officer, has the honor of your services.

JONATHAN. Sir!—

JESSAMY. I say, Sir, I understand that Colonel Manly has the honor of having you for a servant.

JONATHAN. Servant! Sir, do you take me for a neger,— I am Colonel Manly's waiter.

JESSAMY. A true Yankee distinction, egad, without a difference. Why, Sir, do you not perform all the offices of a servant? Do you not even blacken his boots?

JONATHAN. Yes; I do grease them a bit sometimes; but I am a true blue son of liberty, for all that. Father said I should come as Colonel Manly's waiter to see the world, and all that; but no man shall master me: my father has as good a farm as the colonel.

JESSAMY. Well, Sir, we will not quarrel about terms upon the eve of an acquaintance, from which I promise myself so much satisfaction,—therefore sans ceremonie—

JONATHAN. What?—

JESSAMY. I say, I am extremely happy to see Colonel Manly's waiter.

JONATHAN. Well, and I vow, too, I am pretty considerably glad to see you—but what the dogs need of all this outlandish lingo? Who may you be, Sir, if I may be so bold?

JESSAMY. I have the honor to be Mr. Dimple's servant,

or, if you please, waiter. We lodge under the same roof, and should be glad of the honor of your acquaintance.

JONATHAN. You a waiter! By the living jingo, you look so topping, I took you for one of the agents to Congress.

JESSAMY. The brute has discernment notwithstanding his appearance.— Give me leave to say I wonder then at your familiarity.

JONATHAN. Why, as to the matter of that, Mr.—pray, what's your name?

JESSAMY. Jessamy, at your service.

JONATHAN. Why, I swear we don't make any great matter of distinction in our state, between quality and other folks.

JESSAMY. This is, indeed, a leveling principle. I hope, Mr. Jonathan, you have not taken part with the insurgents.

JONATHAN. Why, since General Shays has sneaked off, and given us the bag to hold, I don't care to give my opinion; but you'll promise not to tell—put your ear this way—you won't tell?— I vow, I did think the sturgeons were right.

JESSAMY. I thought, Mr. Jonathan, you Massachusetts men always argued with a gun in your hand.— Why didn't you join them?

JONATHAN. Why, the colonel is one of those folks called the Shin—shin—dang it all, I can't speak them lignum vitæ words—you know who I mean—there is a company of them—they wear a China goose at their button-hole— a kind of gilt thing.— Now the colonel told father and brother,—you must know there are, let me see—there is Elnathan, Silas, and Barnabas, Tabitha—no, no, she's a she —tarnation, now I have it—there's Elnathan, Silas, Barnabas, Jonathan, that's I—seven of us, six went into the wars, and I stayed at home to take care of mother. Colonel said that it was a burning shame for the true blue Bunker-hill sons of liberty, who had fought Governor Hutchinson, Lord North, and the Devil, to have any hand in kicking up a cursed dust against a government, which we had every mother's son of us a hand in making.

JESSAMY. Bravo!— Well, have you been abroad in the city since your arrival? What have you seen that is curious and entertaining?

JONATHAN. Oh! I have seen a power of fine sights. I went to see two marble-stone men and a leaden horse, that stands out in doors in all weathers; and when I came where they was, one had got no head, and t' other wer'nt there. They said as how the leaden man was a damn'd tory, and that he took wit in his anger and rode off in the time of the troubles.

JESSAMY. But this was not the end of your excursion.

JONATHAN. Oh, no; I went to a place they call Holy Ground. Now I counted this was a place where folks go to meeting; so I put my hymn-book in my pocket, and walked softly and grave as a minister; and when I came there, the dogs a bit of a meeting-house could I see. At last I spied a young gentlewoman standing by one of the seats, which they have here at the doors—I took her to be the deacon's daughter, and she looked so kind, and so obliging, that I thought I would go and ask her the way to lecture, and would you think it—she called me dear, and sweeting, and honey, just as if we were married; by the living jingo, I had a month's mind to buss her.

JESSAMY. Well, but how did it end?

JONATHAN. Why, as I was standing talking with her, a parcel of sailor men and boys got round me, the snarl headed curs fell a-kicking and cursing of me at such a tarnal rate, that, I vow, I was glad to take to my heels and split home, right off, tail on end like a stream of chalk.

JESSAMY. Why, my dear friend, you are not acquainted with the city; that girl you saw was a— (*Whispers.*)

JONATHAN. Mercy on my soul! was that young woman a harlot!— Well, if this is New York Holy Ground, what must the Holy-day Ground be!

JESSAMY. Well, you should not judge of the city too rashly. We have a number of elegant fine girls here, that make a man's leisure hours pass very agreeably. I would esteem it an honor to anounce you to some of them.— Gad! that announce is a select word; I wonder where I picked it up.

JONATHAN. I don't want to know them.

JESSAMY. Come, come, my dear friend, I see that I must assume the honor of being the director of your amusements. Nature has give us passions, and youth and opportunity stimulate to gratify them. It is no shame, my dear Blueskin, for a man to amuse himself with a little gallantry.

JONATHAN. Girl huntry! I don't altogether understand. I never played at that game. I know how to play hunt the squirrel, but I can't play anything with the girls; I am as good as married.

JESSAMY. Vulgar, horrid brute! Married, and above a hundred miles from his wife, and think that an objection to his making love to every woman he meets! He never can have read, no, he never can have been in a room with a volume of the divine Chesterfield.— So you are married?

JONATHAN. No, I don't say so; I said I was as good as married, a kind of promise.

JESSAMY. As good as married!—

JONATHAN. Why, yes; there's Tabitha Wymen, the deacon's daughter, at home, she and I have been courting a great while, and folks say as how we are to be married; and so I broke a piece of money with her when we parted, and she promised not to spark it with Solomon Dyer while I am gone. You wouldn't have me false to my true love, would you?

JESSAMY. May be you have another reason for constancy; possibly the young lady has a fortune? Ha! Mr. Jonathan, the solid charms; the chains of love are never so binding as when the links are made of gold.

JONATHAN. Why, as to fortune, I must needs say her father is pretty dumb rich; he went representative for our town last year. He will give her—let me see—four times seven is—seven times four—nought and carry one;—he will give her twenty acres of land—somewhat rocky though —a bible, and a cow.

JESSAMY. Twenty acres of rock, a bible, and a cow! Why, my dear Mr. Jonathan, we have servant maids, or, as you would more elegantly express it, wait'resses, in this city, who collect more in one year from their mistresses' cast clothes.

JONATHAN. You don't say so!—

JESSAMY. Yes, and I'll introduce you to one of them. There is a little lump of flesh and delicacy that lives at next door, wait'ress to Miss Maria; we often see her on the stoop.

JONATHAN. But are you sure she would be courted by me?

JESSAMY. Never doubt it; remember a faint heart never —blisters on my tongue—I was going to be guilty of a vile proverb; flat against the authority of Chesterfield.— I say there can be no doubt, that the brilliancy of your merit will secure you a favorable reception.

JONATHAN. Well, but what must I say to her?

JESSAMY. Say to her! why, my dear friend, though I admire your profound knowledge on every other subject, yet, you will pardon my saying, that your want of opportunity has made the female heart escape the poignancy of your penetration. Say to her!— Why, when a man goes a-courting, and hopes for success, he must begin with doing, and not saying.

JONATHAN. Well, what must I do?

JESSAMY. Why, when you are introduced you must make five or six elegant bows.

JONATHAN. Six elegant bows! I understand that; six, you say? Well—

JESSAMY. Then you must press and kiss her hand; then press and kiss, and so on to her lips and cheeks; then talk as much as you can about hearts, darts, flames, nectar and ambrosia—the more incoherent the better.

JONATHAN. Well, but suppose she should be angry with I?

JESSAMY. Why, if she should pretend—please to observe, Mr. Jonathan—if she should pretend to be offended, you must— But I'll tell you how my master acted in such a case: He was seated by a young lady of eighteen upon a sofa, plucking with a wanton hand the blooming sweets of youth and beauty. When the lady thought it necessary to check his ardor, she called up a frown upon her lovely face, so irresistibly alluring, that it would have warmed the frozen bosom of age: remember, said she, putting her delicate arm upon his, remember your character and my honor. My master instantly dropped upon his knees, with eyes swimming with love, cheeks glowing with desire, and in the gentlest modulation of voice, he said— My dear Caroline, in a few months our hands will be indissolubly united at the altar; our hearts I feel are already so—the favors you now grant as evidence of your affection, are favors indeed; yet when the ceremony is once past, what will now be received with rapture, will then be attributed to duty.

JONATHAN. Well, and what was the consequence?

JESSAMY. The consequence!— Ah! forgive me, my dear

friend, but you New England gentlemen have such a laudable curiosity of seeing the bottom of every thing;— why, to be honest, I confess I saw the blooming cherub of a consequence smiling in its angelic mother's arms, about ten months afterwards.

JONATHAN. Well, if I follow all your plans, make them six bows, and all that; shall I have such little cherubim consequences?

JESSAMY. Undoubtedly.— What are you musing upon?

JONATHAN. You say you'll certainly make me acquainted?— Why, I was thinking then how I should contrive to pass this broken piece of silver—won't it buy a sugar-dram?

JESSAMY. What is that, the love-token from the deacon's daughter?— You come on bravely. But I must hasten to my master. Adieu, my dear friend.

JONATHAN. Stay, Mr. Jessamy—must I buss her when I am introduced to her?

JESSAMY. I told you, you must kiss her.

JONATHAN. Well, but must I buss her?

JESSAMY. Why, kiss and buss, and buss and kiss, is all one.

JONATHAN. Oh! my dear friend, though you have a profound knowledge of all, a pugnancy of tribulation, you don't know everything. (*Exit.*)

JESSAMY. (*Alone*) Well, certainly I improve; my master could not have insinuated himself with more address into the heart of a man he despised.— Now will this blundering dog sicken Jenny with his nauseous pawings, until she flies into my arms for very ease. How sweet will the contrast be, between the blundering Jonathan, and the courtly and accomplished Jessamy!

END OF THE SECOND ACT

ACT THIRD

SCENE 1.

DIMPLE's *Room.* DIMPLE *discovered at a Toilet, Reading.*

"Women have in general but one object, which is their beauty." Very true, my lord; positively very true. "Nature has hardly formed a woman ugly enough to be insensible to flattery upon her person." Extremely just, my lord; every day's delightful experience confirms this. "If her face is so shocking, that she must, in some degree, be conscious of it, her figure and air, she thinks, make ample amends for it." The sallow Miss Wan is a proof of this.— Upon my telling the distasteful wretch, the other day, that her countenance spoke the pensive language of sentiment, and that Lady Wortley Montague declared, that if the ladies were arrayed in the garb of innocence, the face would be the last part which would be admired as Monsieur Milton expresses it, she grin'd horribly a ghastly smile. "If her figure is deformed, she thinks her face counterbalances it." (*Enter* JESSAMY *with letters.*) Where got you these, Jessamy?

JESSAMY. Sir, the English packet is arrived.

DIMPLE. (*Opens and reads a letter enclosing notes.*) "Sir, I have drawn bills on you in favor of Messrs. Van Cash and Co. as per margin. I have taken up your note to Col. Piquet, and discharged your debts to my Lord Lurcher and Sir Harry Rook. I herewith enclose you copies of the bills, which I have no doubt will be immediately honored. On failure, I shall empower some lawyer in your country to recover the amounts. I am, Sir, Your most humble servant, John Hazard." Now, did not my lord expressly say, that it was unbecoming a well-bred man to be in a passion, I confess I should be ruffled. (*Reads.*) "There is no accident so unfortunate, which a wise man may not turn to his advantage; nor any accident so fortunate, which a fool will not turn to his disadvantage." True, my lord: but how advantage can be derived from this, I can't see. Chesterfield himself, who made, however, the worst practice of the most excellent precepts, was never in so embarrassing a situation. I love the person of Charlotte, and it is necessary I should command the fortune of Letitia. As to Maria!—I doubt not by my *sang-froid* behavior I shall compel her to decline the match; but the blame must not fall upon me. A prudent man, as my lord says, should take all the credit of a good action to himself, and throw the discredit of a bad one upon others. I must break with Maria, marry Letitia, and as for Charlotte—why, Charlotte must be a companion to my wife.—Here, Jessamy!

(*Enter* JESSAMY.)

DIMPLE. (*Folds and seals two letters.*) Here, Jessamy, take this letter to my love. (*Gives one.*)

JESSAMY. To which of your honor's loves?— Oh! (*Reading*) to Miss Letitia, your honor's rich love.

DIMPLE. And this (*delivers another*) to Miss Charlotte Manly. See that you deliver them privately.

JESSAMY. Yes, your honor. (*Going.*)

DIMPLE. Jessamy, who are these strange lodgers that came to the house last night?

JESSAMY. Why, the master is a Yankee colonel; I have not seen much of him; but the man is the most unpolished animal your honor ever disgraced your eyes by looking upon. I have had one of the most *outré* conversations with him!— He really has a most prodigious effect upon my risibility.

DIMPLE. I ought, according to every rule of Chesterfield, to wait on him and insinuate myself into his good graces.— Jessamy, wait on the colonel with my compliments, and if he is disengaged, I will do myself the honor of paying him my respects.— Some ignorant unpolished boor—

(JESSAMY *goes off and returns.*)

JESSAMY. Sir, the colonel is gone out, and Jonathan, his servant, says that he is gone to stretch his legs upon the Mall— Stretch his legs! what an indelicacy of diction!

DIMPLE. Very well. Reach me my hat and sword. I'll accost him there, in my way to Letitia's, as by accident; pretend to be struck with his person and address, and endeavor to steal into his confidence. Jessamy, I have no business for you at present. (*Exit.*)

JESSAMY. (*Taking up the book*) My master and I obtain our knowledge from the same source;—though, gad! I think myself much the prettier fellow of the two. (*Surveying himself in the glass*) That was a brilliant thought, to insinuate that I folded my master's letters for him; the folding is so neat, that it does honor to the operator. I once intended to have insinuated that I wrote his letters too; but that was before I saw them; it won't do now; no honor there, positively.— "Nothing looks more vulgar (*reading affectedly*), ordinary, and illiberal, than ugly, uneven, and ragged nails; the ends of which should be kept even and clean, not tipped with black, and cut in small segments of circles"— Segments of circles! surely my lord did not consider that he wrote for the beaux. Segments of circles! what a crabbed term! Now I dare answer, that my master, with all his learning, does not know that this means, according to the present mode, to let the nails grow long, and then cut them off even at top. (*Laughing without.*) Ha! that's Jenny's titter. I protest I despair of ever teaching that girl to laugh; she has something so execrably natural in her laugh, that I declare it absolutely discomposes my nerves. How came she into our house!— (*Calls.*) Jenny! (*Enter* JENNY.) Prithee, Jenny, don't spoil your fine face with laughing.

JENNY. Why, mustn't I laugh, Mr. Jessamy?

JESSAMY. You may smile; but, as my lord says, nothing can authorize a laugh.

JENNY. Well, but I can't help laughing— Have you seen him. Mr. Jessamy? Ha, ha, ha!

JESSAMY. Seen whom?—

JENNY. Why, Jonathan, the New-England colonel's servant. Do you know he was at the play last night, and the stupid creature don't know where he has been. He would not go to a play for the world; he thinks it was a show, as he calls it.

JESSAMY. As ignorant and unpolished as he is, do you know, Miss Jenny, that I propose to introduce him to the honor of your acquaintance.

JENNY. Introduce him to me! for what?

JESSAMY. Why, my lovely girl, that you may take him under your protection, as Madam Ramboulliet, did young Stanhope; that you may, by your plastic hand, mold this uncouth cub into a gentleman. He is to make love to you.

JENNY. Make love to me!—

JESSAMY. Yes, Mistress Jenny, make love to you; and, I doubt not, when he shall become domesticated in your kitchen, that this boor, under your auspices, will soon become *un aimable petit Jonathan.*

JENNY. I must say, Mr. Jessamy, if he copies after me, he will be vastly monstrously polite.

JESSAMY. Stay here one moment, and I will call him.— Jonathan!—Mr. Jonathan!— (*Calls.*)

JONATHAN. (*Within*) Holla! there.— (*Enters.*) You promise to stand by me—six bows you say. (*Bows.*)

JESSAMY. Mrs. Jenny, I have the honor of presenting

Mr. Jonathan, Colonel Manly's waiter, to you. I am extremely happy that I have it in my power to make two worthy people acquainted with each other's merit.

JENNY. So, Mr. Jonathan, I hear you were at the play last night.

JONATHAN. At the play! why, did you think I went to the devil's drawing-room!

JENNY. The devil's drawing-room!

JONATHAN. Yes; why an't cards and dice the devil's device; and the play-house the shop where the devil hangs out the vanities of the world, upon the tenterhooks of temptation. I believe you have not heard how they were acting the old boy one night, and the wicked one came among them sure enough; and went right off in a storm, and carried one quarter of the play-house with him. Oh! no, no, no! you won't catch me at a play-house, I warrant you.

JENNY. Well, Mr. Jonathan, though I don't scruple your veracity, I have some reasons for believing you were there; pray, where were you about six o'clock?

JONATHAN. Why, I went to see one Mr. Morrison, the *hocus pocus* man; they said as how he could eat a case knife.

JENNY. Well, and how did you find the place?

JONATHAN. As I was going about here and there, to and again, to find it, I saw a great crowd of folks going into a long entry, that had lanterns over the door; so I asked a man, whether that was not the place where they played *hocus pocus?* He was a very civil kind man, though he did speak like the Hessians; he lifted up his eyes and said— "they play *hocus pocus* tricks enough there, Got knows, mine friend."

JENNY. Well—

JONATHAN. So I went right in, and they showed me away clean up to the garret, just like a meeting-house gallery. And so I saw a power of topping folks, all sitting round in little cabins, just like father's corn-cribs;—and then there was such a squeaking with the fiddles, and such a tarnal blaze with the lights, my head was near turned. At last the people that sat near me set up such a hissing—hiss —like so many mad cats; and then they went thump, thump, thump, just like our Peleg threshing wheat, and stampt away, just like the nation; and called out for one Mr. Langolee,—I suppose he helps act the tricks.

JENNY. Well, and what did you do all this time?

JONATHAN. Gor, I—I liked the fun, and so I thumpt away, and hiss'd as lustily as the best of 'em. One sailor-looking man that sat by me, seeing me stamp, and knowing I was a cute fellow, because I could make a roaring noise, clapt me on the shoulder and said, you are a d——d hearty cock, smite my timbers! I told him so I was, but I thought he need not swear so, and make use of such naughty words.

JESSAMY. The savage!— Well, and did you see the man with his tricks?

JONATHAN. Why, I vow, as I was looking out for him, they lifted up a great green cloth, and let us look right into the next neighbor's house. Have you a good many houses in New York made so in that 'ere way?

JENNY. Not many: but did you see the family?

JONATHAN. Yes, swamp it; I see'd the family.

JENNY. Well, and how did you like them?

JONATHAN. Why, I vow they were pretty much like other families;—there was a poor, good natured, curse of a husband, and a sad rantipole of a wife.

JENNY. But did you see no other folks?

JONATHAN. Yes. There was one youngster, they called him Mr. Joseph; he talked as sober and as pious as a minister; but like some ministers that I know, he was a sly tike in his heart for all that: He was going to ask a young woman to spark it with him, and—the Lord have mercy on my soul!—she was another man's wife.

JESSAMY. The Wabash!

JENNY. And did you see any more folks?

JONATHAN. Why they came on as thick as mustard. For my part, I thought the house was haunted. There was a soldier fellow, who talked about his row de dow dow, and courted a young woman: but of all the cute folk I saw, I liked one little fellow—

JENNY. Aye! who was he?

JONATHAN. Why, he had red hair, and a little round plump face like mine, only not altogether so handsome. His name was Darby:—that was his baptizing name, his other name I forgot. Oh! it was, Wig—Wag—Wag-all, Darby Wag-all;—pray, do you know him?— I should like to take a sling with him, or a drap of cider with a pepper-pod in it, to make it warm and comfortable.

JENNY. I can't say I have that pleasure.

JONATHAN. I wish you did, he is a cute fellow. But there was one thing I didn't like in that Mr. Darby; and that was, he was afraid of some of them 'ere shooting irons, such as your troopers wear on training days. Now, I'm a true born Yankee American son of liberty, and I never was afraid of a gun yet in all my life.

JENNY. Well, Mr. Jonathan, you were certainly at the play-house.

JONATHAN. I at the play-house!— Why didn't I see the play then?

JENNY. Why, the people you saw were players.

JONATHAN. Mercy on my soul! did I see the wicked players?— Mayhap that 'ere Darby that I liked so, was the old serpent himself, and had his cloven foot in his pocket. Why, I vow, now I come to think on 't, the candles seemed to burn blue, and I am sure where I sat it smelt tarnally of brimstone.

JESSAMY. Well, Mr. Jonathan, from your account, which I confess is very accurate, you must have been at the play-house.

JONATHAN. Why, I vow I began to smell a rat. When I came away, I went to the man for my money again: you want your money, says he; yes, says I; for what, says he; why, says I, no man shall jocky me out of my money; I paid my money to see sights, and the dogs a bit of a sight have I seen, unless you call listening to people's private business a sight. Why, says he, it is the School for Scandalization.— The School for Scandalization!— Oh, ho! no wonder you New York folks are so cute at it, when you go to school to learn it: and so I jogged off.

JESSAMY. My dear Jenny, my master's business drags me from you; would to heaven I knew no other servitude than to your charms.

JONATHAN. Well, but don't go; you won't leave me so.—

JESSAMY. Excuse me.— Remember the cash. (*Aside to him, and—Exit.*)

JENNY. Mr. Jonathan, won't you please to sit down. Mr. Jessamy tells me you wanted to have some conversation with me.

(*Having brought forward two chairs, they sit.*)

JONATHAN. Ma'am!—

JENNY. Sir!—

JONATHAN. Ma'am!—

JENNY. Pray, how do you like the city, Sir?

JONATHAN. Ma'am!—

JENNY. I say, Sir, how do you like New York?

JONATHAN. Ma'am!—

JENNY. The stupid creature! but I must pass some little time with him, if it is only to endeavor to learn, whether it was his master that made such an abrupt entrance into our house, and my young mistress's heart, this morning. (*Aside.*) As you don't seem to like to talk, Mr. Jonathan —do you sing?

JONATHAN. Gor, I—I am glad she asked that, for I forgot what Mr. Jessamy bid me say, and I dare as well be hanged as act what he bid me do, I'm so ashamed. (*Aside.*) Yes, Ma'am, I can sing—I can sing Mear, Old Hundred, and Bangor.

JENNY. Oh! I don't mean psalm tunes. Have you no little song to please the ladies; such as Roslin Castle, or the Maid of the Mill?

JONATHAN. Why, all my tunes are go to meeting tunes, save one, and I count you won't altogether like that 'ere.

JENNY. What is it called?

JONATHAN. I am sure you have heard folks talk about it, it is called Yankee Doodle.

JENNY. Oh! it is the tune I am fond of; and, if I know anything of my mistress, she would be glad to dance to it. Pray, sing?

JONATHAN. (*Sings.*)

Father and I went up to camp,
  Along with Captain Goodwin;
And there we saw the men and boys,
  As thick as hasty pudding.
            Yankee Doodle do, etc.

And there we saw a swamping gun,
  Big as log of maple,
On a little deuced cart.
  A load for father's cattle.
            Yankee Doodle do, etc.

> And every time they fired it off,
> It took a horn of powder,
> It made a noise—like father's gun,
> Only a nation louder.
>> Yankee Doodle do, etc.

> There was a man in our town,
> His name——

No, no, that won't do. Now, if I was with Tabitha Wymen and Jemima Cawley, down at father Chase's, I shouldn't mind singing this all out before them—you would be affronted if I was to sing that, though that's a lucky thought; if you should be affronted, I have something dang'd cute, which Jessamy told me to say to you.

JENNY. Is that all! I assure you I like it of all things.

JONATHAN. No, no; I can sing more, some other time, when you and I are better acquainted, I'll sing the whole of it—no, no—that's a fib—I can't sing but a hundred and ninety verses: our Tabitha at home can sing it all.— (*Sings.*)

> Marblehead's a rocky place,
> And Cape-Cod is sandy;
> Charleston is burnt down,
> Boston is the dandy.
>> Yankee Doodle do, etc.

I vow, my own town song has put me into such topping spirits, that I believe I'll begin to do a little, as Jessamy says we must when we go a courting— (*Runs and kisses her.*) Burning rivers! cooling flames! red hot roses! pig-nuts! hasty-pudding and ambrosia!

JENNY. What means this freedom! you insulting wretch. (*Strikes him.*)

JONATHAN. Are you affronted?

JENNY. Affronted! with what looks shall I express my anger?

JONATHAN. Looks! why, as to the matter of looks, you look as cross as a witch.

JENNY. Have you no feeling for the delicacy of my sex?

JONATHAN. Feeling! Gor, I—I feel the delicacy of your sex pretty smartly (*rubbing his cheek*), though, I vow, I thought when you city ladies courted and married, and all that, you put feeling out of the question. But I want to know whether you are really affronted, or only pretend to be so? 'Cause, if you are certainly right down affronted, I am at the end of my tether;—Jessamy didn't tell me what to say to you.

JENNY. Pretend to be affronted!

JONATHAN. Aye, aye, if you only pretend, you shall hear how I'll go to work to make cherubim consequences. (*Runs up to her.*)

JENNY. Begone, you brute!

JONATHAN. That looks like mad; but I won't lose my speech. My dearest Jenny—your name is Jenny, I think? My dearest Jenny, though I have the highest esteem for the sweet favors you have just now granted me—Gor, that's a fib though, but Jessamy says it is not wicked to tell lies to the women. (*Aside.*) I say, though I have the highest esteem for the favors you have just now granted me, yet, you will consider, that as soon as the dissolvable knot is tied, they will no longer be favors, but only matters of duty, and matters of course.

JENNY. Marry you! you audacious monster! get out of my sight, or rather let me fly from you. (*Exit hastily.*)

JONATHAN. Gor! she's gone off in a swinging passion, before I had time to think of consequences. If this is the way with your city ladies, give me the twenty acres of rock, the bible, the cow, and Tabitha, and a little peaceable bundling.

SCENE 2.

The Mall.

(*Enter* MANLY.)

It must be so, Montague! and it is not all the tribe of Mandevilles shall convince me, that a nation, to become great, must first become dissipated. Luxury is surely the bane of a nation: Luxury! which enervates both soul and body, by opening a thousand new sources of enjoyment, opens, also, a thousand new sources of contention and want: Luxury! which renders a people weak at home, and accessible to bribery, corruption, and force from abroad. When the Grecian states knew no other tools than the ax and the saw, the Grecians were a great, a free, and a happy people. The kings of Greece devoted their lives to the service of their country, and her senators knew no other superiority over their fellow-citizens than a glorious pre-eminence in danger and virtue. They exhibited to the world a noble spectacle,—a number of independent states united by a similarity of language, sentiment, manners, common interest, and common consent, in one grand mutual league of protection.— And, thus united, long might they have continued the cherishers of arts and sciences, the protectors of the oppressed, the scourge of tyrants, and the safe asylum of liberty: But when foreign gold, and still more pernicious, foreign luxury, had crept among them, they sapped the vitals of their virtue. The virtues of their ancestors were only found in their writings. Envy and suspicion, the vices of little minds, possessed them. The various states engendered jealousies of each other; and, more unfortunately, growing jealous of their great federal council, the Amphictyons, they forgot that their common safety had existed, and would exist, in giving them an honorable extensive prerogative. The common good was lost in the pursuit of private interest; and that people, who, by uniting, might have stood against the world in arms, by dividing, crumbled into ruin;—their name is now only known in the page of the historian, and what they once were, is all we have left to admire. Oh! that America! Oh! that my country, would in this her day, learn the things which belong to her peace!

(*Enter* DIMPLE.)

DIMPLE. You are Colonel Manly, I presume?

MANLY. At your service, Sir.

DIMPLE. My name is Dimple, Sir. I have the honor to be a lodger in the same house with you, and hearing you were in the Mall, came hither to take the liberty of joining you.

MANLY. You are very obliging, Sir.

DIMPLE. As I understand you are a stranger here, Sir, I have taken the liberty to introduce myself to your acquaintance, as possibly I may have it in my power to point out some things in this city worthy your notice.

MANLY. An attention to strangers is worthy a liberal mind, and must ever be gratefully received. But to a soldier, who has no fixed abode, such attentions are particularly pleasing.

DIMPLE. Sir, there is no character so respectable as that of a soldier. And, indeed, when we reflect how much we owe to those brave men who have suffered so much in the service of their country, and secured to us those inestimable blessings that we now enjoy, our liberty and independence, they demand every attention which gratitude can pay. For my own part, I never meet an officer, but I embrace him as my friend, nor a private in distress, but I insensibly extend my charity to him.— I have hit the Bumkin off very tolerably. (*Aside.*)

MANLY. Give me your hand, Sir! I do not proffer this hand to everybody; but you steal into my heart. I hope I am as insensible to flattery as most men; but I declare (it may be my weak side), that I never hear the name of soldier mentioned with respect, but I experience a thrill of pleasure, which I never feel on any other occasion.

DIMPLE. Will you give me leave, my dear colonel, to confer an obligation on myself, by showing you some civilities during your stay here, and giving a similar opportunity to some of my friends?

MANLY. Sir, I thank you; but I believe my stay in this city will be very short.

DIMPLE. I can introduce you to some men of excellent sense, in whose company you will esteem yourself happy; and, by way of amusement, to some fine girls, who will listen to your soft things with pleasure.

MANLY. Sir, I should be proud of the honor of being acquainted with those gentlemen;—but, as for the ladies, I don't understand you.

DIMPLE. Why, Sir, I need not tell you, that when a young gentleman is alone with a young lady, he must say some soft things to her fair cheek—indeed the lady will expect it. To be sure, there is not much pleasure, when a man of the world and a finished coquette meet, who perfectly know each other; but how delicious is it to excite the emotions of joy, hope, expectation, and delight, in the bosom of a lovely girl, who believes every tittle of what you say to be serious.

MANLY. Serious, Sir! In my opinion, the man, who, under pretensions of marriage, can plant thorns in the bosom of an innocent, unsuspecting girl, is more detestable than a common robber, in the same proportion, as private violence is more despicable than open force, and money of less value than happiness.

DIMPLE. How he awes me by the superiority of his sentiments. (*Aside.*) As you say, Sir, a gentleman should be cautious how he mentions marriage.

MANLY. Cautious, Sir! No person more approves of an intercourse between the sexes than I do. Female conversation softens our manners, whilst our discourse, from the superiority of our literary advantages, improves their minds. But, in our young country, where there is no such thing as gallantry, when a gentleman speaks of love to a lady, whether he mentions marriage, or not, she ought to conclude, either that he meant to insult her, or, that his intentions are the most serious and honorable. How mean, how cruel, is it, by a thousand tender assiduities, to win the affections of an amiable girl, and though you leave her virtue unspotted, to betray her into the appearance of so many tender partialities, that every man of delicacy would suppress his inclination towards her, by supposing her heart engaged! Can any man, for the trivial gratification of his leisure hours, affect the happiness of a whole life! His not having spoken of marriage, may add to his perfidy, but can be no excuse for his conduct.

DIMPLE. Sir, I admire your sentiments;—they are mine. The light observations that fell from me, were only a principle of the tongue; they came not from the heart—my practice has ever disapproved these principles.

MANLY. I believe you, Sir. I should with reluctance suppose that those pernicious sentiments could find admittance into the heart of a gentleman.

DIMPLE. I am now, Sir, going to visit a family, where, if you please, I will have the honor of introducing you. Mr. Manly's ward, Miss Letitia, is a young lady of immense fortune; and his niece, Miss Charlotte Manly, is a young lady of great sprightliness and beauty.

MANLY. That gentleman, Sir, is my uncle, and Miss Manly my sister.

DIMPLE. The devil she is! (*Aside.*) Miss Manly your sister, Sir? I rejoice to hear it, and feel a double pleasure in being known to you.— Plague on him! I wish he was at Boston again with all my soul. (*Aside.*)

MANLY. Come, Sir, will you go?

DIMPLE. I will follow you in a moment, Sir. (*Exit

MANLY.) Plague on it! this is unlucky. A fighting brother is a cursed appendage to a fine girl. Egad! I just stopped in time; had he not discovered himself, in two minutes more I should have told him how well I was with his sister.— Indeed, I cannot see the satisfaction of an intrigue, if one can't have the pleasure of communicating it to our friends. (*Exit.*)

END OF THE THIRD ACT

ACT FOURTH

SCENE 1.

CHARLOTTE'S *Apartment.* CHARLOTTE *leading in* MARIA.

CHARLOTTE. This is so kind, my sweet friend, to come to see me at this moment, I declare, if I were going to be married in a few days, as you are, I should scarce have found time to visit my friends.

MARIA. Do you think then that there is an impropriety in it?— How should you dispose of your time?

CHARLOTTE. Why, I should be shut up in my chamber; and my head would so run upon—upon—upon the solemn ceremony that I was to pass through—I declare it would take me above two hours merely to learn that little mono-syllable—*Yes.* Ah! my dear, your sentimental imagination does not conceive what that little tiny word implies.

MARIA. Spare me your raillery, my sweet friend; I should love your agreeable vivacity at any other time.

CHARLOTTE. Why this is the very time to amuse you. You grieve me to see you look so unhappy.

MARIA. Have I not reason to look so?

CHARLOTTE. What new grief distresses you?

MARIA. Oh! how sweet it is, when the heart is borne down with misfortune, to recline and repose on the bosom of friendship! Heaven knows, that, although it is improper for a young lady to praise a gentleman, yet I have ever concealed Mr. Dimple's foibles, and spoke of him as of one whose reputation I expected would be linked with mine: but his late conduct towards me, has turned my coolness into contempt. He behaves as if he meant to insult and dis-gust me; whilst my father, in the last conversation on the subject of our marriage, spoke of it as a matter which laid near his heart, and in which he would not bear contradiction.

CHARLOTTE. This works well: oh! the generous Dimple. I'll endeavor to excite her to discharge him. (*Aside.*) But, my dear friend, your happiness depends on yourself:— Why don't you discard him? Though the match has been of long standing, I would not be forced to make myself miserable: no parent in the world should oblige me to marry the man I did not like.

MARIA. Oh! my dear, you never lived with your parents, and do not know what influence a father's frowns have upon a daughter's heart. Besides, what have I to allege against Mr. Dimple, to justify myself to the world? He carries himself so smoothly, that every one would impute the blame to me, and call me capricious.

CHARLOTTE. And call her capricious! Did ever such an objection start into the heart of woman? For my part, I wish I had fifty lovers to discard, for no other reason, than because I did not fancy them. My dear Maria, you will forgive me; I know your candor and confidence in me; but I have at times, I confess, been led to suppose, that some other gentleman was the cause of your aversion to Mr. Dimple.

MARIA. No, my sweet friend, you may be assured, that though I have seen many gentlemen I could prefer to Mr. Dimple, yet I never saw one that I thought I could give my hand to, until this morning.

CHARLOTTE. This morning!

MARIA. Yes;—one of the strangest accidents in the world. The odious Dimple, after disgusting me with his conversation, had just left me, when a gentleman, who, it seems, boards in the same house with him, saw him coming out of our door, and the houses looking very much alike, he came into our house instead of his lodgings; nor did he discover his mistake until he got into the parlor, where I was: he then bowed so gracefully; made such a genteel apology, and looked so manly and noble!—

CHARLOTTE. I see some folks, though it is so great an impropriety, can praise a gentleman, when he happens to be the man of their fancy. (*Aside.*)

MARIA. I don't know how it was,—I hope he did not think me indelicate—but I asked him, I believe, to sit down, or pointed to a chair. He sat down, and instead of having recourse to observations upon the weather, or hackneyed criticisms upon the theatre, he entered readily into a conversation worthy a man of sense to speak, and a lady of delicacy and sentiment to hear. He was not strictly handsome, but he spoke the language of sentiment, and his eyes looked tenderness and honor.

CHARLOTTE. Oh! (*eagerly*) you sentimental grave girls, when your hearts are once touched, beat us rattles a bar's length. And so, you are quite in love with this he-angel?

MARIA. In love with him! How can you rattle so, Charlotte? am I not going to be miserable? (*Sighs.*) In love with a gentleman I never saw but one hour in my life, and don't know his name!— No: I only wished that the man I shall marry, may look, and talk, and act, just like him. Besides, my dear, he is a married man.

CHARLOTTE. Why, that was good natured.— He told you so, I suppose, in mere charity, to prevent your falling in love with him?

MARIA. He didn't tell me so (*peevishly*); he looked as if he was married.

CHARLOTTE. How, my dear, did he look sheepish?

MARIA. I am sure he has a susceptible heart, and the ladies of his acquaintance must be very stupid not to—

CHARLOTTE. Hush! I hear some person coming
(*Enter* LETITIA.)

LETITIA. My dear Maria, I am happy to see you. Lud! what a pity it is that you have purchased your wedding clothes.

MARIA. I think so. (*Sighing.*)

LETITIA. Why, my dear, there is the sweetest parcel of silks come over you ever saw. Nancy Brilliant has a full suit come; she sent over her measure, and it fits her to a hair; it is immensely dressy, and made for a court-hoop. I thought they said the large hoops were going out of fashion.

CHARLOTTE. Did you see the hat?— Is it a fact, that the deep laces round the border is still the fashion?

DIMPLE. (*Within*) Upon my honor, Sir!

MARIA. Ha! Dimple's voice! My dear, I must take leave of you. There are some things necessary to be done at our house.—Can't I go through the other room?
(*Enter* DIMPLE *and* MANLY.)

DIMPLE. Ladies, your most obedient.

CHARLOTTE. Miss Van Rough, shall I present my brother Henry to you? Colonel Manly, Maria,—Miss Van Rough, brother.

MARIA. Her brother! (*Turns and sees* MANLY.) Oh! my heart! The very gentleman I have been praising.

MANLY. The same amiable girl I saw this morning!

CHARLOTTE. Why, you look as if you were acquainted.

MANLY. I unintentionally intruded into this lady's presence this morning, for which she was so good as to promise me her forgiveness.

CHARLOTTE. Oh! ho! is that the case! Have these two penserosos been together? Were they Henry's eyes that looked so tenderly? (*Aside.*) And so you promised to pardon him? and could you be so good natured?—have you really forgiven him? I beg you would do it for my sake. (*Whispering loud to* MARIA) But, my dear, as you are in such haste, it would be cruel to detain you: I can show you the way through the other room.

MARIA. Spare me, my sprightly friend.

MANLY. The lady does not, I hope, intend to deprive us of the pleasure of her company so soon.

CHARLOTTE. She has only a mantua-maker who waits for her at home. But, as I am to give my opinion of the dress, I think she cannot go yet. We were talking of the fashions when you came in; but I suppose the subject must be changed to something of more importance now.—Mr. Dimple, will you favor us with an account of the public entertainments?

DIMPLE. Why, really, Miss Manly, you could not have asked me a question more *mal-apropos*. For my part, I must confess, that to a man who has traveled, there is nothing that is worthy the name of amusement to be found in this city.

CHARLOTTE. Except visiting the ladies.

DIMPLE. Pardon me, Madam; that is the advocation of a man of taste. But, for amusement, I positively know of nothing that can be called so, unless you dignify with that title the hopping once a fortnight to the sound of two or three squeaking fiddles, and the clattering of the old tavern windows, or sitting to see the miserable mummers, whom you call actors, murder comedy, and make a farce of tragedy.

MANLY. Do you never attend the theatre, Sir?

DIMPLE. I was tortured there once.

CHARLOTTE. Pray, Mr. Dimple, was it a tragedy or a comedy?

DIMPLE. Faith, Madam, I cannot tell; for I sat with my back to the stage all the time, admiring a much better actress than any there;—a lady who played the fine woman to perfection;—though, by the laugh of the horrid creatures around me, I suppose it was comedy. Yet, on second thoughts, it might be some hero in a tragedy, dying so comically as to set the whole house in an uproar.— Colonel, I presume you have been in Europe?

MANLY. Indeed, Sir, I was never ten leagues from the continent.

DIMPLE. Believe me, Colonel, you have an immense pleasure to come; and when you shall have seen the brilliant exhibitions of Europe, you will learn to despise the amusements of this country as much as I do.

MANLY. Therefore I do not wish to see them; for I can never esteem that knowledge valuable, which tends to give me a distaste for my native country.

DIMPLE. Well, Colonel, though you have not traveled, you have read.

MANLY. I have, a little: and by it have discovered that there is a laudable partiality, which ignorant, untraveled men entertain for everything that belongs to their native country. I call it laudable;—it injures no one; adds to their own happiness; and, when extended, becomes the noble principle of patriotism. Traveled gentlemen rise superior, in their own opinion, to this: but, if the contempt which they contract for their country is the most valuable acquisition of their travels, I am far from thinking that their time and money are well spent.

MARIA. What noble sentiments!

CHARLOTTE. Let my brother set out from where he will in the fields of conversation, he is sure to end his tour in the temple of gravity.

MANLY. Forgive me, my sister. I love my country; it has its foibles undoubtedly;—some foreigners will with pleasure remark them—but such remarks fall very ungracefully from the lips of her citizens.

DIMPLE. You are perfectly in the right, Colonel—America has her faults.

MANLY. Yes, Sir; and we, her children, should blush for

them in private, and endeavor, as individuals, to reform them. But, if our country has its errors in common with other countries, I am proud to say America, I mean the United States, have displayed virtues and achievements which modern nations may admire, but of which they have seldom set us the example.

CHARLOTTE. But, brother, we must introduce you to some of our gay folks, and let you see the city, such as it is. Mr. Dimple is known to almost every family in town;—he will doubtless take a pleasure in introducing you.

DIMPLE. I shall esteem every service I can render your brother an honor.

MANLY. I fear the business I am upon will take up all my time, and my family will be anxious to hear from me.

MARIA. His family! But what is it to me that he is married! (*Aside.*) Pray, how did you leave your lady, Sir?

CHARLOTTE. My brother is not married (*Observing her anxiety*); it is only an odd way he has of expressing himself. — Pray, brother, is this business, which you make your continual excuse, a secret?

MANLY. No, sister: I came hither to solicit the honorable Congress that a number of my brave old soldiers may be put upon the pension-list, who were, at first, not judged to be so materially wounded as to need the public assistance. — My sister says true: (*To* MARIA) I call my late soldiers my family.—Those who were not in the field in the late glorious contest, and those who were, have their respective merits; but, I confess, my old brother-soldiers are dearer to me than the former description. Friendships made in adversity are lasting; our countrymen may forget us; but that is no reason why we should forget one another. But I must leave you; my time of engagement approaches.

CHARLOTTE. Well, but brother, if you will go, will you please to conduct my fair friend home? You live in the same street;—I was to have gone with her myself— (*Aside*) A lucky thought.

MARIA. I am obliged to your sister, Sir, and was just intending to go. (*Going.*)

MANLY. I shall attend her with pleasure. (*Exit with* MARIA, *followed by* DIMPLE *and* CHARLOTTE.)

MARIA. Now, pray don't betray me to your brother.

CHARLOTTE. (*Just as she sees him make a motion to take*

his leave.) One word with you, brother, if you please. (*Follows them out.*)

        (*Manent* DIMPLE *and* LETITIA.)

DIMPLE. You received the billet I sent you, I presume?

LETITIA. Hush!— Yes.

DIMPLE. When shall I pay my respects to you?

LETITIA. At eight I shall be unengaged.

        (*Re-enter* CHARLOTTE.)

DIMPLE. Did my lovely angel receive my billet? (*To* CHARLOTTE.)

CHARLOTTE. Yes.

DIMPLE. What hour shall I expect with impatience?

CHARLOTTE. At eight I shall be at home, unengaged.

DIMPLE. Unfortunate! I have a horrid engagement of business at that hour.— Can't you finish your visit earlier, and let six be the happy hour?

CHARLOTTE. You know your influence over me. (*Exeunt severally.*)

SCENE 2. VAN ROUGH's *House.*

        (VAN ROUGH, *alone.*)

It cannot possibly be true! The son of my old friend can't have acted so unadvisedly. Seventeen thousand pounds! in bills!—Mr. Transfer must have been mistaken. He always appeared so prudent, and talked so well upon money-matters, and even assured me that he intended to change his dress for a suit of clothes which would not cost so much, and look more substantial, as soon as he married. No, no, no! it can't be; it cannot be.— But, however, I must look out sharp. I did not care what his principles or his actions were, so long as he minded the main chance. Seventeen thousand pounds!— If he had lost it in trade, why the best men may have ill-luck; but to game it away, as Transfer says—why, at this rate, his whole estate may go in one night, and, what is ten times worse, mine into the bargain. No, no; Mary is right. Leave women to look out in these matters; for all they look as if they didn't know a journal from a ledger, when their interest is concerned, they know what's what; they mind the main chance as well as the best of us.— I wonder Mary did not tell me she knew of his spending his money so foolishly. Seventeen thousand pounds! Why, if my daughter was standing up

to be married, I would forbid the banns, if I found it
was to a man who did not mind the main chance.— Hush!
I hear somebody coming. 'T is Mary's voice: a man with
her too! I shouldn't be surprised if this should be the
other string to her bow.— Aye, aye, let them alone; women
understand the main chance.— Though, i' faith, I'll listen
a little. (*Retires into a closet.*)

(MANLY *leading in* MARIA.)

MANLY. I hope you will excuse my speaking upon so
important a subject, so abruptly; but the moment I entered
your room, you struck me as the lady whom I had long
loved in imagination, and never hoped to see.

MARIA. Indeed, Sir, I have been led to hear more upon
this subject than I ought.

MANLY. Do you then disapprove my suit, Madam, or
the abruptness of my introducing it? If the latter, my
peculiar situation, being obliged to leave the city in a
few days, will, I hope, be my excuse; if the former, I will
retire: for I am sure I would not give a moment's in-
quietude to her, whom I could devote my life to please. I
am not so indelicate as to seek your immediate approbation;
permit me only to be near you, and by a thousand tender
assiduities to endeavor to excite a grateful return.

MARIA. I have a father, whom I would die to make
happy—he will disapprove—

MANLY. Do you think me so ungenerous as to seek a
place in your esteem without his consent? You must—
you ever ought to consider that man as unworthy of you,
who seeks an interest in your heart, contrary to a father's
approbation. A young lady should reflect, that the loss of a
lover may be supplied, but nothing can compensate for the
loss of a parent's affection. Yet, why do you suppose your
father would disapprove? In our country, the affections are
not sacrificed to riches, or family aggrandizement:—should
you approve, my family is decent, and my rank honorable.

MARIA. You distress me, Sir.

MANLY. Then I will sincerely beg your excuse for ob-
truding so disagreeable a subject and retire. (*Going.*)

MARIA. Stay, Sir! your generosity and good opinion of
me deserve a return; but why must I declare what, for these
few hours, I have scarce suffered myself to think?—I am—

MANLY. What?—

MARIA. Engaged, Sir;—and, in a few days, to be married to the gentleman you saw at your sister's.

MANLY. Engaged to be married! And have I been basely invading the rights of another? Why have you permitted this?— Is this the return for the partiality I declared for you?

MARIA. You distress me, Sir. What would you have me say? You are too generous to wish the truth: ought I to say that I dared not suffer myself to think of my engagement, and that I am going to give my hand without my heart?— Would you have me confess a partiality for you? If so, your triumph is complete; and can be only more so, when days of misery, with the man I cannot love, will make me think of him whom I could prefer.

MANLY. (*After a pause*) We are both unhappy; but it is your duty to obey your parent,—mine to obey my honor. Let us, therefore, both follow the path of rectitude; and of this we may be assured, that if we are not happy, we shall, at least, deserve to be so. Adieu! I dare not trust myself longer with you. (*Exeunt severally.*)

END OF THE FOURTH ACT

ACT FIFTH

SCENE 1.

DIMPLE'S *Lodgings.* JESSAMY *meeting* JONATHAN.

JESSAMY. Well, Mr. Jonathan, what success with the fair?

JONATHAN. Why, such a tarnal cross tike you never saw!— You would have counted she had lived upon crab-apples and vinegar for a fortnight. But what the rattle makes you look so tarnation glum?

JESSAMY. I was thinking, Mr. Jonathan, what could be the reason of her carrying herself so coolly to you.

JONATHAN. Coolly, do you call it? Why, I vow, she was fire-hot angry: may be it was because I buss'd her.

JESSAMY. No, no, Mr. Jonathan; there must be some other cause: I never yet knew a lady angry at being kissed.

JONATHAN. Well, if it is not the young woman's bashfulness, I vow I can't conceive why she shouldn't like me.

JESSAMY. May be it is because you have not the graces, Mr. Jonathan.

JONATHAN. Grace! Why, does the young woman expect I must be converted before I court her?

JESSAMY. I mean graces of person; for instance, my lord tells us that we must cut off our nails even at top, in small segments of circles;—though you won't understand that— In the next place, you must regulate your laugh.

JONATHAN. Maple-log seize it! don't I laugh natural?

JESSAMY. That's the very fault, Mr. Jonathan. Besides, you absolutely misplace it. I was told by a friend of mine that you laughed outright at the play the other night, when you ought only to have tittered.

JONATHAN. Gor! I—what does one go to see fun for if they can't laugh?

JESSAMY. You may laugh;—but you must laugh by rule.

JONATHAN. Swamp it—laugh by rule! Well, I should like that tarnally.

JESSAMY. Why you know, Mr. Jonathan, that to dance, a lady to play with her fan, or a gentleman with his cane, and all other natural motions, are regulated by art. My master has composed an immensely pretty gamut, by which any lady, or gentleman, with a few years' close application, may learn to laugh as gracefully as if they were born and bred to it.

JONATHAN. Mercy on my soul! A gamut for laughing —just like fa, la, sol?

JESSAMY. Yes. It comprises every possible display of jocularity, from an *affettuoso* smile to a *piano* titter, or full chorus *fortissimo* ha, ha, ha! My master employs his leisure-hours in marking out the plays, like a cathedral chanting-book, that the ignorant may know where to laugh; and that pit, box, and gallery may keep time together, and not have a snigger in one part of the house, a broad grin in the other, and a d——d grum look in the third. How delightful to see the audience all smile together, then look on their books, then twist their mouths into an agreeable simper, then altogether shake the house with a general ha, ha, ha! Loud as a full chorus of Handel's, at an Abbey-commemoration.

JONATHAN. Ha, ha, ha! that's dang'd cute, I swear.

JESSAMY. The gentlemen, you see, will laugh the tenor; the ladies will play the counter-tenor; the beaux will squeak the treble; and our jolly friends in the gallery a thorough bass, ho, ho, ho!

JONATHAN. Well, can't you let me see that gamut?

JESSAMY. Oh! yes, Mr. Jonathan; here it is. (*Takes out a book.*) Oh! no, this is only a titter with its variations. Ah, here it is. (*Takes out another.*) Now you must know, Mr. Jonathan, this is a piece written by Ben Jonson, which I have set to my master's gamut. The places where you must smile, look grave, or laugh outright, are marked below the line. Now look over me.— "There was a certain man" —now you must smile.

JONATHAN. Well, read it again; I warrant I'll mind my eye.

JESSAMY. "There was a certain man, who had a sad scolding wife,"—now you must laugh.

JONATHAN. Tarnation! That's no laughing matter, though.

JESSAMY. "And she lay sick a-dying";—now you must titter.

JONATHAN. What, snigger when the good woman's a-dying! Gor, I—

JESSAMY. Yes; the notes say you must— "And she asked her husband leave to make a will,"—now you must begin to look grave;—"and her husband said"—

JONATHAN. Ay, what did her husband say?— Something dang'd cute, I reckon.

JESSAMY. "And her husband said, you have had your will all your life time, and would you have it after you are dead too?"

JONATHAN. Ho, ho, ho! There the old man was even with her; he was up to the notch—ha, ha, ha!

JESSAMY. But, Mr. Jonathan, you must not laugh so. Why, you ought to have tittered *piano,* and you have laughed *fortissimo.* Look here; you see these marks, A. B. C. and so on; these are the references to the other part of the book. Let us turn to it, and you will see the directions how to manage the muscles. This (*Turns over*) was note D you blundered at.— "You must purse the mouth into a smile, then titter, discovering the lower part of the three front upper teeth."

JONATHAN. How! read it again.

JESSAMY. "There was a certain man"—very well!—"who had a sad scolding wife,"—why don't you laugh?

JONATHAN. Now, that scolding wife sticks in my gizzard so pluckily, that I can't laugh for the blood and nowns of me. Let me look grave here, and I'll laugh your belly full where the old creature's a-dying.—

JESSAMY. "And she asked her husband"—(*Bell rings.*) My master's bell! he's returned, I fear— Here, Mr. Jonathan, take this gamut; and, I make no doubt but with a few years' close application you may be able to smile gracefully. (*Exeunt severally.*)

SCENE 2.

CHARLOTTE'S *Apartment*.

(*Enter* MANLY.)

MANLY. What, no one at home? How unfortunate to meet the only lady my heart was ever moved by, to find her engaged to another, and confessing her partiality for me! Yet engaged to a man, who, by her intimation, and his libertine conversation with me, I fear, does not merit her. Aye! there's the sting; for, were I assured that Maria was happy, my heart is not so selfish, but that it would dilate in knowing it, even though it were with another.— But to know she is unhappy!— I must drive these thoughts from me. Charlotte has some books; and this is what I believe she calls her little library. (*Enters a closet.*)

(*Enter* DIMPLE *leading* LETITIA.)

LETITIA. And will you pretend to say, now, Mr. Dimple, that you propose to break with Maria? Are not the banns published? Are not the clothes purchased? Are not the friends invited? In short, is it not a done affair?

DIMPLE. Believe me, my dear Letitia, I would not marry her.

LETITIA. Why have you not broke with her before this, as you all along deluded me by saying you would?

DIMPLE. Because I was in hopes she would ere this have broke with me.

LETITIA. You could not expect it.

DIMPLE. Nay, but be calm a moment; 't was from my regard to you that I did not discard her.

LETITIA. Regard to me!

DIMPLE. Yes; I have done everything in my power to break with her, but the foolish girl is so fond of me, that nothing can accomplish it. Besides, how can I offer her my hand, when my heart is indissolubly engaged to you?—

LETITIA. There may be reason in this; but why so attentive to Miss Manly?

DIMPLE. Attentive to Miss Manly! For heaven's sake, if you have no better opinion of my constancy, pay not so ill a compliment to my taste.

LETITIA. Did I not see you whisper her to-day?

DIMPLE. Possibly I might—but something of so very trifling a nature, that I have already forgot what it was.

LETITIA. I believe, she has not forgot it.

DIMPLE. My dear creature, how can you for a moment suppose I should have any serious thoughts of that trifling, gay, flighty coquette, that disagreeable—

(*Enter* CHARLOTTE.)

DIMPLE. My dear Miss Manly, I rejoice to see you; there is a charm in your conversation that always marks your entrance into company as fortunate.

LETITIA. Where have you been, my dear?

CHARLOTTE. Why, I have been about to twenty shops, turning over pretty things, and so have left twenty visits unpaid. I wish you would step into the carriage and whisk round, make my apology, and leave my cards where our friends are not at home; that you know will serve as a visit. Come, do go.

LETITIA. So anxious to get me out! but I'll watch you. (*Aside.*) Oh! yes, I'll go; I want a little exercise.— Positively (DIMPLE *offering to accompany her*), Mr. Dimple, you shall not go, why, half my visits are cake and caudle visits; it won't do, you know, for you to go.— (*Exit, but returns to the door in the back scene and listens.*)

DIMPLE. This attachment of your brother to Maria is fortunate.

CHARLOTTE. How did you come to the knowledge of it?

DIMPLE. I read it in their eyes.

CHARLOTTE. And I had it from her mouth. It would have amused you to have seen her! She that thought it so great an impropriety to praise a gentleman, that she could not bring out one word in your favor, found a redundancy to praise him.

DIMPLE. I have done everything in my power to assist

his passion there: your delicacy, my dearest girl, would be shocked at half the instances of neglect and misbehavior.

CHARLOTTE. I don't know how I should bear neglect; but Mr. Dimple must misbehave himself indeed, to forfeit my good opinion.

DIMPLE. Your good opinion, my angel, is the pride and pleasure of my heart; and if the most respectful tenderness for you and utter indifference for all your sex besides, can make me worthy of your esteem, I shall richly merit it.

CHARLOTTE. All my sex besides, Mr. Dimple—you forgot your tête-à-tête with Letitia.

DIMPLE. How can you, my lovely angel, cast a thought on that insipid, wry-mouthed, ugly creature!

CHARLOTTE. But her fortune may have charms?

DIMPLE. Not to a heart like mine. The man who has been blessed with the good opinion of my Charlotte, must despise the allurements of fortune.

CHARLOTTE. I am satisfied.

DIMPLE. Let us think no more on the odious subject, but devote the present hour to happiness.

CHARLOTTE. Can I be happy, when I see the man I prefer going to be married to another?

DIMPLE. Have I not already satisfied my charming angel that I can never think of marrying the puling Maria. But, even if it were so, could that be any bar to our happiness; for, as the poet sings—

"Love, free as air, at sight of human ties,
"Spreads his light wings, and in a moment flies."

Come then, my charming angel! why delay our bliss! The present moment is ours; the next is in the hand of fate. (*Kissing her.*)

CHARLOTTE. Begone, Sir! By your delusions you had almost lulled my honor asleep.

DIMPLE. Let me lull the demon to sleep again with kisses. (*He struggles with her; she screams.*)
(*Enter* MANLY.)

MANLY. Turn, villain! and defend yourself.—
(*Draws.* VAN ROUGH *enters and beats down their swords.*)

VAN ROUGH. Is the devil in you? are you going to murder one another? (*Holding* DIMPLE.)

DIMPLE. Hold him, hold him,—I can command my passion.

(*Enter* JONATHAN.)

JONATHAN. What the rattle ails you? Is the old one in you? Let the colonel alone, can't you? I feel chock full of fight,—do you want to kill the colonel?—

MANLY. Be still, Jonathan; the gentleman does not want to hurt me.

JONATHAN. Gor! I—I wish he did; I'd show him Yankee boys play, pretty quick— Don't you see you have frightened the young woman into *hystrikes?*

VAN ROUGH. Pray, some of you explain this; what has been the occasion of all this racket?

MANLY. That gentleman can explain it to you; it will be a very diverting story for an intended father-in-law to hear.

VAN ROUGH. How was this matter, Mr. Van Dumpling?

DIMPLE. Sir,—upon my honor—all I know is, that I was talking to this young lady, and this gentleman broke in on us, in a very extraordinary manner.

VAN ROUGH. Why, all this is nothing to the purpose: can you explain it, Miss? (*To* CHARLOTTE.)

(*Enter* LETITIA *through the back scene.*)

LETITIA. I can explain it to that gentleman's confusion. Though long betrothed to your daughter (*To* VAN ROUGH), yet allured by my fortune, it seems (with shame do I speak it), he has privately paid his addresses to me. I was drawn in to listen to him by his assuring me that the match was made by his father without his consent, and that he proposed to break with Maria, whether he married me or not. But whatever were his intentions respecting your daughter, Sir, even to me he was false; for he has repeated the same story, with some cruel reflections upon my person, to Miss Manly.

JONATHAN. What a tarnal curse!

LETITIA. Nor is this all, Miss Manly. When he was with me this very morning, he made the same ungenerous reflections upon the weakness of your mind as he has so recently done upon the defects of my person.

JONATHAN. What a tarnal curse and damn too!

DIMPLE. Ha! since I have lost Letitia, I believe I had as good make it up with Maria—Mr. Van Rough, at present

I cannot enter into particulars; but, I believe I can explain everything to your satisfaction in private.

VAN ROUGH. There is another matter, Mr. Van Dumpling, which I would have you explain:—pray, Sir, have Messrs. Van Cash and Co. presented you those bills for acceptance?

DIMPLE. The deuce! Has he heard of those bills! Nay, then, all's up with Maria, too; but an affair of this sort can never prejudice me among the ladies; they will rather long to know what the dear creature possesses to make him so agreeable. (*Aside.*) Sir, you'll hear from me. (*To* MANLY.)

MANLY. And you from me, Sir.—

DIMPLE. Sir, you wear a sword.—

MANLY. Yes, Sir:— This sword was presented to me by that brave Gallic hero, the Marquis De La Fayette. I have drawn it in the service of my country, and in private life, on the only occasion where a man is justified in drawing his sword, in defence of a lady's honor. I have fought too many battles in the service of my country to dread the imputation of cowardice.— Death from a man of honor would be a glory you do not merit; you shall live to bear the insult of man, and the contempt of that sex, whose general smiles afforded you all your happiness.

DIMPLE. You won't meet me, Sir?— Then I'll post you for a coward.

MANLY. I'll venture that, Sir.— The reputation of my life does not depend upon the breath of a Mr. Dimple. I would have you to know, however, Sir, that I have a cane to chastise the insolence of a scoundrel, and a sword and the good laws of my country, to protect me from the attempts of an assassin.—

DIMPLE. Mighty well! Very fine, indeed!—ladies and gentlemen, I take my leave, and you will please to observe, in the case of my deportment, the contrast between a gentleman, who has read Chesterfield and received the polish of Europe, and an unpolished, untraveled American. (*Exit.*)

(*Enter* MARIA.)

MARIA. Is he indeed gone?—

LETITIA. I hope never to return.

VAN ROUGH. I am glad I heard of those bills; though it's plaguy unlucky: I hoped to see Mary married before I died.

MANLY. Will you permit a gentleman, Sir, to offer himself as a suitor to your daughter? Though a stranger to you, he is not altogether so to her, or unknown in this city. You may find a son-in-law of more fortune, but you can never meet with one who is richer in love for her, or respect for you.

VAN ROUGH. Why, Mary, you have not let this gentleman make love to you without my leave?

MANLY. I did not say, Sir—

MARIA. Say, Sir!—I—the gentleman, to be sure, met me accidentally.

VAN ROUGH. Ha, ha, ha! Mark me, Mary; young folks think old folks to be fools; but old folks know young folks to be fools.— Why, I knew all about this affair:— This was only a cunning way I had to bring it about— Hark ye! I was in the closet when you and he were at our house. (*Turns to the company*.) I heard that little baggage say she loved her old father, and would die to make him happy! Oh! how I loved the little baggage!— And you talked very prudently, young man. I have inquired into your character, and find you to be a man of punctuality and mind the main chance. And so, as you love Mary, and Mary loves you, you shall have my consent immediately to be married. I'll settle my fortune on you, and go and live with you the remainder of my life.

MANLY. Sir, I hope—

VAN ROUGH. Come, come, no fine speeches; mind the main chance, young man, and you and I shall always agree.

LETITIA. I sincerely wish you joy (*Advancing to* MARIA); and hope your pardon for my conduct.

MARIA. I thank you for your congratulations, and hope we shall at once forget the wretch who has given us so much disquiet, and the trouble that he has occasioned.

CHARLOTTE. And I, my dear Maria,—how shall I look up to you for forgiveness? I, who, in the practice of the meanest arts, have violated the most sacred rights of friendship? I can never forgive myself, or hope charity from the world, but I confess I have much to hope from such a brother; and I am happy that I may soon say, such a sister.—

MARIA. My dear, you distress me; you have all my love.

MANLY. And mine.

CHARLOTTE. If repentance can entitle me to forgiveness, I have already much merit; for I despise the littleness of my past conduct. I now find, that the heart of any worthy man cannot be gained by invidious attacks upon the rights and characters of others;—by countenancing the addresses of a thousand;—or that the finest assemblage of features, the greatest taste in dress, the genteelest address, or the most brilliant wit, cannot eventually secure a coquette from contempt and ridicule.

MANLY. And I have learned that probity, virtue, honor, though they should not have received the polish of Europe, will secure to an honest American the good graces of his fair country-woman, and, I hope, the applause of THE PUBLIC.

THE END

1787

PHILIP FRENEAU

(1752–1832)

The son of a substantial New York family, Philip Morin Freneau moved to New Jersey when he was ten and entered Princeton to prepare for the ministry when he was sixteen. In college he became the friend of James Madison and of Hugh Henry Brackenridge (later the author of *Modern Chivalry*). With his two friends, Freneau became a supporter of the liberal Whig viewpoint, aligning himself with political attitudes that were to strengthen in him throughout the course of his experiences. He also came to love poetry and considered the possibility of a literary career. He and Brackenridge wrote the Commencement Poem for the Class of 1771, *The Rising Glory of America*. Diminishing funds following the death of his father forced Freneau to some immediately remunerative occupation. Disliking teaching, he went to the West Indies, where he was to write some of his best romantic poems; but the war turned his talents in other directions. After a brush with the British in 1778, he enlisted in the Revolutionary forces and became a blockade runner. As third mate of the ship *Aurora*, he was captured and spent six weeks in the brutal conditions of a British prison ship in New York Harbor. This experience left him with ineradicable scars of hatred for any vestige of aristocracy, Toryism, colonialism, or monarchism. He became an ardent propagandist, writing some of the most vehement pieces of anti-British poetry and prose to come out of the Revolution.

After the war, having edited the bitterly anti-Tory *Freeman's Journal* in Philadelphia from 1781 to 1784, he went back to sea as a captain in order to make a living. In 1790 he married

Eleanor Forman and settled in New York as a writer. He continued his career by editing the *Daily Advertiser*. As a journalist, his efforts were centered on the struggle between Jeffersonianism and Hamiltonianism; in 1791 he moved to Philadelphia to establish the *National Gazette*, the sharpest voice of attack upon the Hamiltonian *Gazette of the United States*. In the strong feelings generated by political issues, Freneau became deeply involved in the charges and countercharges exchanged by the two parties. He felt that the party of Hamilton was betraying the Revolution, the common man, democracy, and decency, and in his furious defense of Jeffersonian principles he once caused the conservative and belabored Washington to call him "that rascal Freneau." His undying partisan support of the French Revolution lost him subscribers and he moved back to New Jersey to publish *The Jersey Chronicle* (1795–1796), which also failed. He returned to New York to publish the *Time-Piece and Literary Companion* (1797–1798)—and again failed. For a while he had to go back to sea in order to support himself, and all the while, in whatever moments of calm he could find, he experimented with romantic poetry of nature, description, and imagination.

During his lifetime the reviews of his poems were largely bitter attacks on his political beliefs. Indeed, much of his poetry is topical satire, neoclassical in style. Some of it was praise of the Age of Reason. What remain his best works, however, are the imaginative poems that mark him as our most talented writer of the early transition between eighteenth- and nineteenth-century literature, and, with Edward Taylor, our second major poet of the seventeenth and eighteenth centuries. He died as he had lived—in a violent storm: aged eighty, he was killed by exposure to a blizzard.

Among the titles of his bibliography are *The American Village* (1772); *The British Prison-Ship* (1781); *The Poems of Philip Freneau* (1786); *A Journey from Philadelphia to New York* (1787); *The Miscellaneous Works of Mr. Philip Freneau* (1788); *Poems Written between the Years 1768 & 1794* (1795); *Letters on Various Interesting and Important Subjects* (1799); *Poems* (1809); and *A Collection of Poems* (1815).

Accounts of the man and his works are to be found in F. L. Pattee, ed., *The Poems of Philip Freneau*, 3 vols. (1902–1907); V. H. Paltsits, *A Bibliography of the Separate and Collected Works of Freneau* (1903); H. H. Clark, ed., *Poems of Freneau* (1929); L. Leary, *That Rascal Freneau* (1941); L. Leary, ed., *The Last Poems of Philip Freneau* (1946); N. F. Adkins, *Philip Freneau and the Cosmic Enigma* (1949); P.

Marsh, ed., *The Prose Writings of Philip Freneau* (1956); P. Marsh, "Philip Freneau's Fame," *Proceedings of the New Jersey Historical Society*, *LXXX* (1962); P. Marsh, ed., *A Freneau Sampler* (1963); and L. B. Holland, "Philip Freneau: Poet in the New Nation," *The Literary Heritage of New Jersey* (1965).

The Power of Fancy

Wakeful, vagrant, restless thing,
Ever wandering on the wing,
Who thy wondrous source can find,
Fancy, regent of the mind;
A spark from Jove's resplendent throne,
But thy nature all unknown.

This spark of bright, celestial flame,
From Jove's seraphic altar came,
And hence alone in man we trace,
Resemblance to the immortal race.   10

Ah! what is all this mighty whole,
These suns and stars that round us roll!
What are they all, where'er they shine,
But Fancies of the Power Divine!
What is this globe, these lands, and seas,
And heat, and cold, and flowers, and trees,
And life, and death, and beast, and man,
And time—that with the sun began—
But thoughts on reason's scale combined,
Ideas of the Almighty mind!   20

On the surface of the brain
Night after night she walks unseen,
Noble fabrics doth she raise
In the woods or on the seas,
On some high, steep, pointed rock,
Where the billows loudly knock
And the dreary tempests sweep
Clouds along the uncivil deep.

Lo! she walks upon the moon,
Listens to the chimy tune   30
Of the bright, harmonious spheres,
And the song of angels hears;
Sees this earth a distant star,
Pendant, floating in the air;
Leads me to some lonely dome,
Where Religion loves to come,

Where the bride of Jesus dwells,
And the deep-toned organ swells
In notes with lofty anthems joined,
Notes that half distract the mind.   40
   Now like lightning she descends
To the prison of the fiends,
Hears the rattling of their chains,
Feels their never-ceasing pains—
But, O never may she tell
Half the frightfulness of hell.
   Now she views Arcadian rocks,
Where the shepherds guard their flocks,
And, while yet her wings she spreads,
Sees crystal streams and coral beds,   50
Wanders to some desert deep,
Or some dark, enchanted steep,
By the full moonlight doth shew
Forests of a dusky blue,
Where, upon some mossy bed,
Innocence reclines her head.
   Swift, she stretches o'er the seas
To the far-off Hebrides,
Canvas on the lofty mast
Could not travel half so fast—   60
Swifter than the eagle's flight
Or instantaneous rays of light!
Lo! contemplative she stands
On Norwegia's rocky lands—
Fickle Goddess, set me down
Where the rugged winters frown
Upon Orca's howling steep,
Nodding o'er the northern deep,
Where the winds tumultuous roar,
Vext that Ossian sings no more.   70
Fancy, to that land repair;
Sweetest Ossian slumbers there;
Waft me far to southern isles
Where the softened winter smiles,
To Bermuda's orange shades,
Or Demarara's lovely glades;
Bear me o'er the sounding cape,
Painting death in every shape,
Where daring Anson spread the sail

Shatter'd by the stormy gale—   80
Lo! she leads me wide and far,
Sense can never follow her—
Shape thy course o'er land and sea,
Help me to keep pace with thee,
Lead me to yon' chalky cliff,
Over rock and over reef,
Into Britain's fertile land,
Stretching far her proud command.
Look back and view, thro' many a year,
Caesar, Julius Caesar, there.   90

    Now to Tempe's verdant wood,
Over the mid-ocean flood
Lo! the islands of the sea—
Sappho, Lesbos mourns for thee:
Greece, arouse thy humbled head,
Where are all thy mighty dead,
Who states to endless ruin hurled
And carried vengeance through the world?
Troy, thy vanished pomp resume,
Or, weeping at thy Hector's tomb,   100
Yet those faded scenes renew,
Whose memory is to Homer due.
Fancy, lead me wandering still
Up to Ida's cloud-topped hill;
Not a laurel there doth grow
But in vision thou shalt show,—
Every sprig on Virgil's tomb
Shall in livelier colors bloom,
And every triumph Rome has seen
Flourish on the years between.   110

    Now she bears me far away
In the east to meet the day,
Leads me over Ganges' streams,
Mother of the morning beams—
O'er the ocean hath she ran,
Places me on Tinian;
Farther, farther in the east,
Till it almost meets the west,
Let us wandering both be lost
On Taitis' sea-beat coast,   120
Bear me from that distant strand,
Over ocean, over land,

To California's golden shore—
Fancy, stop, and rove no more.
   Now, though late, returning home,
Lead me to Belinda's tomb;
Let me glide as well as you
Through the shroud and coffin too,
And behold, a moment, there,
All that once was good and fair—   **130**
Who doth here so soundly sleep?
Shall we break this prison deep?—
Thunders cannot wake the maid,
Lightnings cannot pierce the shade,
And though wintry tempests roar,
Tempests shall disturb no more.
   Yet must those eyes in darkness stay,
That once were rivals to the day?—
Like heaven's bright lamp beneath the main
They are but set to rise again.   **140**
   Fancy, thou the Muses' pride,
In thy painted realms reside
Endless images of things,
Fluttering each on golden wings,
Ideal objects, such a store,
The universe could hold no more:
Fancy, to thy power I owe
Half my happiness below;
By thee Elysian groves were made,
Thine were the notes that Orpheus played;   **150**
By thee was Pluto charmed so well
While rapture seiz'd the sons of hell—
Come, O come—perceived by none,
You and I will walk alone.

                                 1770

The Deserted Farm-House

This antique dome the insatiate tooth of time
   Now level with the dust has almost laid;—
Yet ere 'tis gone, I seize my humble theme
   From these low ruins, that his years have made.

Behold the unsocial hearth! where once the fires
    Blazed high, and soothed the storm-stay'd traveler's
      woes;
See! the weak roof, that abler props requires,
    Admits the winds, and swift descending snows.

Here, to forget the labors of the day,
    No more the swains at evening hours repair,   10
But wandering flocks assume the well known way
    To shun the rigors of the midnight air.

In yonder chamber, half to ruin gone,
    Once stood the ancient housewife's curtained bed—
Timely the prudent matron has withdrawn,
    And each domestic comfort with her fled.

The trees, the flowers that her own hands had reared,
    The plants, the vines, that were so verdant seen,—
The trees, the flowers, the vines have disappear'd,
    And every plant has vanish'd from the green.   20

So sits in tears on wide Campania's plain
    ROME, once the mistress of a world enslaved;
That triumph'd o'er the land, subdued the main,
    And Time himself, in her wild transports, braved.

So sits in tears on Palestina's shore
    The Hebrew town, of splendor once divine—
Her kings, her lords, her triumphs are no more;
    Slain are her priests, and ruin'd every shrine.

Once, in the bounds of this deserted room,
    Perhaps some swain nocturnal courtship made,   30
Perhaps some *Sherlock* mused amidst the gloom;
    Since Love and Death forever seek the shade.

Perhaps some miser, doom'd to discontent,
    Here counted o'er the heaps acquired with pain;
He to the dust—his gold, on traffic sent,
    Shall ne'er disgrace these moldering walls again.

Nor shall the glow-worm fopling, sunshine bred,
   Seek, at the evening hour this wonted dome—
Time has reduced the fabric to a shed,
   Scarce fit to be the wandering beggar's home.   40

And none but I its dismal case lament—
   None, none but I o'er its cold relics mourn,
Sent by the muse—(the time perhaps misspent)—
   To write dull stanzas on this dome forlorn.

           1775

FROM

The House of Night

A Vision

Trembling I write my dream, and recollect
A fearful vision at the midnight hour;
So late, Death o'er me spread his sable wings,
Painted with fancies of malignant power!

      . . .

Dark was the sky, and not one friendly star
Shone from the zenith or horizon, clear,
Mist sat upon the woods, and darkness rode
In her black chariot, with a wild career.

And from the woods the late resounding note
Issued of the loquacious Whip-poor-will,   10
Hoarse, howling dogs, and nightly roving wolves
Clamor'd from far off cliffs invisible.

Rude, from the wide extended Chesapeke
I heard the winds the dashing waves assail,
And saw from far, by pictures fancy form'd,
The black ship traveling through the noisy gale.

At last, by chance and guardian fancy led,
I reach'd a noble dome, rais'd fair and high,
And saw the light from upper windows flame,
Presage of mirth and hospitality.   20

And by that light around the dome appear'd
A mournful garden of autumnal hue,
Its lately pleasing flowers all drooping stood
Amidst high weeds that in rank plenty grew.

. . .

No pleasant fruit or blossom gaily smil'd.
Nought but unhappy plants and trees were seen,
The yew, the myrtle, and the church-yard elm,
The cypress, with its melancholy green.

. . .

And here and there with laurel shrubs between
A tombstone lay, inscrib'd with strains of woe,   30
And stanzas sad, throughout the dismal green,
Lamented for the dead that slept below.

. . .

Then up three winding stairs my feet were brought
To a high chamber, hung with mourning sad,
The unsnuff'd candles glar'd with visage dim,
'Midst grief, in ecstasy of woe run mad.

A wide-leaf'd table stood on either side,
Well fraught with phials, half their liquid spent,
And from a couch, behind the curtain's veil,
I heard a hollow voice of loud lament.   40

Turning to view the object whence it came,
My frighted eyes a horrid form surveyed;
Fancy, I own thy power— Death on the couch,
With fleshless limbs, at rueful length, was laid.

And o'er his head flew jealousies and cares,
Ghosts, imps, and half the black Tartarian crew,
Arch-angels damn'd, nor was their Prince remote,
Borne on the vaporous wings of Stygian dew.

Around his bed, by the dull flambeaux' glare,
I saw pale phantoms— Rage to madness vext,   50
Wan, wasting grief, and ever musing care,
Distressful pain, and poverty perplext.

Sad was his countenance, if we can call
That *countenance,* where only bones were seen
And eyes sunk in their sockets, dark and low,
And teeth, that only showed themselves to grin.

Reft was his skull of hair, and no fresh fair bloom
Of cheerful mirth sat on his visage hoar:
Sometimes he rais'd his head, while deep-drawn groans
Were mixt with words that did his fate deplore.   60

. . .

But now this man of hell toward me turn'd,
And strait in hideous tone, began to speak;
Long held the sage discourse, but I forbore
To answer him, much less his news to seek.

He talk'd of tomb-stones and of monuments,
Of equinoctial climes and India shores,
He talk'd of stars that shed their influence,
Fevers and plagues, and all their noxious stores.

. . .

"Death in this tomb his weary bones hath laid,
"Sick of dominion o'er the human kind—   70
"Behold what devastations he hath made,
"Survey the millions by his arm confin'd.

"Six thousand years has sovereign sway been mine,
"None, but myself, can real glory claim;
"Great Regent of the world I reign'd alone,
"And princes trembled when my mandate came.

"Vast and unmatch'd throughout the world, my fame
"Takes place of gods, and asks no mortal date—
"No; by myself, and by the heavens, I swear,
"Not Alexander's name is half so great.   80

"Nor swords nor darts my prowess could withstand,
"All quit their arms, and bow'd to my decree,
"Even mighty Julius died beneath my hand,
"For slaves and Caesar's were the same to me!

"Traveler, wouldst thou his noblest trophies seek,
"Search in no narrow spot obscure for those:
"The sea profound, the surface of all land
"Is molded with the myriads of his foes."

. . .

Scarce had he spoke, when on the lofty dome
Rush'd from the clouds a hoarse resounding blast—   90
Round the four eaves so loud and sad it play'd
As though all music were to breathe its last.

Warm was the gale, and such as travelers say
Sport with the winds on Zaara's barren waste;
Black was the sky, a mourning carpet spread,
Its azure blotted, and its stars o'er-cast!

Lights in the air like burning stars were hurl'd,
Dogs howl'd, heaven mutter'd, and the tempest blew,
The red half-moon peep'd from behind a cloud
As if in dread the amazing scene to view.   100

The mournful trees that in the garden stood
Bent to the tempest as it rush'd along,
The elm, the myrtle, and the cypress sad
More melancholy tun'd its bellowing song.

No more that elm its noble branches spread,
The yew, the cypress, or the myrtle tree,
Rent from the roots the tempest tore them down,
And all the grove in wild confusion lay.

Yet, mindful of his dread command, I part
Glad from the magic dome—nor found relief;   110
Damps from the dead hung heavier round my heart,
While sad remembrance rous'd her stores of grief.

O'er a dark field I held my dubious way
Where Jack-a-lanthorn walk'd his lonely round,
Beneath my feet substantial darkness lay,
And screams were heard from the distemper'd ground.

Nor look'd I back, till to a far off wood
Trembling with fear, my weary feet had sped—
Dark was the night, but at the inchanted dome
I saw the infernal windows flaming red.   120

. . .

What is this Death, ye deep read sophists, say?—
Death is no more than one unceasing change;
New forms arise, while other forms decay,
Yet all is Life throughout creation's range.

The towering Alps, the haughty Apennine,
The Andes, wrapt in everlasting snow,
The Apalachian and the Ararat
Sooner or later must to ruin go.

Hills sink to plains, and man returns to dust,
That dust supports a reptile or a flower;   130
Each changeful atom by some other nurs'd
Takes some new form, to perish in an hour.

Too nearly join'd to sickness, toils, and pains,
(Perhaps for former crimes imprison'd here)
True to itself the immortal soul remains,
And seeks new mansions in the starry sphere.

When Nature bids thee from the world retire,
With joy thy lodging leave, a fated guest;
In Paradise, the land of thy desire,
Existing always, always to be blest.   140

1779

The Vanity of Existence

To Thyrsis

In youth, gay scenes attract our eyes,
    And not suspecting their decay
Life's flowery fields before us rise,
    Regardless of its winter day.

But vain pursuits, and joys as vain,
   Convince us life is but a dream.
Death is to wake, to rise again
   To that true life you best esteem.

So nightly on some shallow tide,
   Oft have I seen a splendid show;   **10**
Reflected stars on either side,
   And glittering moons were seen below.

But when the tide had ebbed away,
   The scene fantastic with it fled,
A bank of mud around me lay,
   And sea-weed on the river's bed.

                            1781

To the Memory of the Brave Americans

*Under General Greene, in South Carolina, who Fell in
the Action of September 8, 1781.*

At Eutaw Springs the valiant died;
   Their limbs with dust are covered o'er—
Weep on, ye springs, your tearful tide;
   How many heroes are no more!

If in this wreck of ruin, they
   Can yet be thought to claim a tear,
O smite your gentle breast, and say
   The friends of freedom slumber here!

Thou, who shalt trace this bloody plain,
   If goodness rules thy generous breast,   **10**
Sigh for the wasted rural reign;
   Sigh for the shepherds, sunk to rest!

Stranger, their humble graves adorn;
   You too may fall, and ask a tear;
'Tis not the beauty of the morn
   That proves the evening shall be clear.—

They saw their injured country's woe;
   The flaming town, the wasted field;
Then rushed to meet the insulting foe;
   They took the spear—but left the shield.   20

Led by thy conquering genius, Greene,
   The Britons they compelled to fly;
None distant viewed the fatal plain,
   None grieved, in such a cause to die—

But, like the Parthian, famed of old,
   Who, flying, still their arrows threw,
These routed Britons, full as bold,
   Retreated, and retreating slew.

Now rest in peace, our patriot band;
   Though far from nature's limits thrown,   30
We trust they find a happier land,
   A brighter sunshine of their own.

1781

To Sir Toby

A Sugar Planter in the Interior Parts of Jamaica

If there exists a hell—the case is clear—
Sir Toby's slaves enjoy that portion here:
Here are no blazing brimstone lakes, 'tis true;
But kindled Rum too often burns as blue,
In which some fiend, whom nature must detest,
Steeps Toby's brand and marks poor Cudjoe's breast.
   Here whips on whips excite perpetual fears,
And mingled howlings vibrate on my ears;
Here nature's plagues abound, to fret and tease,
Snakes, scorpions, despots, lizards, centipedes.   10
No art, no care escapes the busy lash;
All have their dues—and all are paid in cash.
   The eternal driver keeps a steady eye
On a black herd, who would his vengeance fly,
But chained, imprisoned, on a burning soil,
For the mean avarice of a tyrant, toil!

The lengthy cart-whip guards this monster's reign—
And cracks, like pistols, from the fields of cane.

    Ye powers who formed these wretched tribes, relate,
What had they done, to merit such a fate!   20
Why were they brought from Eboe's sultry waste,
To see that plenty which they must not taste—
Food, which they cannot buy, and dare not steal,
Yams and potatoes—many a scanty meal!—

    One, with a gibbet wakes his negro's fears,
One to the windmill nails him by the ears;
One keeps his slave in darkened dens, unfed,
One puts the wretch in pickle ere he's dead:
This, from a tree suspends him by the thumbs,
That, from his table grudges even the crumbs!   30

    O'er yond' rough hills a tribe of females go,
Each with her gourd, her infant, and her hoe;
Scorched by a sun that has no mercy here,
Driven by a devil, whom men call overseer—
In chains, twelve wretches to their labors haste,
Twice twelve I saw, with iron collars graced!—

    Are such the fruits that spring from vast domains?
Is wealth, thus got, Sir Toby, worth your pains!—
Who would your wealth on terms like these possess,
Where all we see is pregnant with distress—   40
Angola's natives scourged by ruffian hands,
And toil's hard product shipp'd to foreign lands.

    Talk not of blossoms and your endless spring;
What joy, what smile, can scenes of misery bring?—
Though Nature here has every blessing spread,
Poor is the laborer—and how meanly fed!—

    Here Stygian paintings light and shade renew,
Pictures of hell, that Virgil's pencil drew:
Here, surly Charons make their annual trip,
And ghosts arrive in every Guinea ship,   50
To find what beasts these western isles afford,
Plutonian scourges, and despotic lords:—

    Here, they, of stuff determined to be free,
Must climb the rude cliffs of the Liguanee;
Beyond the clouds, in skulking haste repair,
And hardly safe from brother traitors there.

1784

The Hurricane

Happy the man who, safe on shore,
Now trims, at home, his evening fire;
Unmoved, he hears the tempests roar,
That on the tufted groves expire:
Alas! on us they doubly fall,
Our feeble bark must bear them all.

Now to their haunts the birds retreat,
The squirrel seeks his hollow tree,
Wolves in their shaded caverns meet,
All, all are blest but wretched we—   10
Foredoomed a stranger to repose,
No rest the unsettled ocean knows.

While o'er the dark abyss we roam,
Perhaps, with last departing gleam,
We saw the sun descend in gloom,
No more to see his morning beam;
But buried low, by far too deep,
On coral beds, unpitied, sleep!

But what a strange, uncoasted strand
Is that, where fate permits no day—   20
No charts have we to mark that land,
No compass to direct that way—
What Pilot shall explore that realm,
What new Columbus take the helm!

While death and darkness both surround,
And tempests rage with lawless power,
Of friendship's voice I hear no sound,
No comfort in this dreadful hour—
What friendship can in tempests be,
What comforts on this raging sea?   30

The bark, accustomed to obey,
No more the trembling pilots guide:
Alone she gropes her trackless way,
While mountains burst on either side—

Thus, skill and science both must fall;
And ruin is the lot of all.

1785

The Wild Honey Suckle

Fair flower, that dost so comely grow,
Hid in this silent, dull retreat,
Untouched thy honied blossoms blow,
Unseen thy little branches greet:
   No roving foot shall crush thee here,
   No busy hand provoke a tear.

By Nature's self in white arrayed,
She bade thee shun the vulgar eye,
And planted here the guardian shade,
And sent soft waters murmuring by;   10
   Thus quietly thy summer goes,
   Thy days declining to repose.

Smit with those charms, that must decay,
I grieve to see your future doom;
They died—nor were those flowers more gay,
The flowers that did in Eden bloom;
   Unpitying frosts, and Autumn's power
   Shall leave no vestige of this flower.

From morning suns and evening dews
At first thy little being came: 20
If nothing once, you nothing lose,
For when you die you are the same;
   The space between, is but an hour,
   The frail duration of a flower.

1786

The Indian Burying Ground

In spite of all the learn'd have said,
   I still my old opinion keep;
The posture that we give the dead,
   Points out the soul's eternal sleep.

Not so the ancients of these lands—
    The Indian, when from life released,
Again is seated with his friends,
    And shares again the joyous feast.

His imaged birds, and painted bowl,
    And venison, for a journey dressed,   10
Bespeak the nature of the soul,
    Activity, that knows no rest.

His bow, for action ready bent,
    And arrows, with a head of stone,
Can only mean that life is spent,
    And not the old ideas gone.

Thou, stranger, that shalt come this way,
    No fraud upon the dead commit—
Observe the swelling turf, and say
    They do not lie, but here they sit.   20

Here still a lofty rock remains,
    On which the curious eye may trace
(Now wasted, half, by wearing rains)
    The fancies of a ruder race.

Here still an aged elm aspires,
    Beneath whose far-projecting shade
(And which the shepherd still admires)
    The children of the forest played!

Here oft a restless Indian queen
    (Pale Shebah, with her braided hair)   30
And many a barbarous form is seen
    To chide the man that lingers there.

By midnight moons, o'er moistening dews,
    In habit for the chase arrayed,
The hunter still the deer pursues,
    The hunter and the deer, a shade!

And long shall timorous fancy see
    The painted chief, and pointed spear,

And Reason's self shall bow the knee
  To shadows and delusions here.
40
1788

The Indian Student

Or, Force of Nature

From Susquehanna's farthest springs
Where savage tribes pursue their game,
(His blanket tied with yellow strings.)
A shepherd of the forest came.

Not long before, a wandering priest
Expressed his wish, with visage sad—
"Ah, why (he cried) in Satan's waste,
Ah, why detain so fine a lad?

"In white-man's land there stands a town
Where learning may be purchased low—   10
Exchange his blanket for a gown,
And let the lad to college go."—

From long debate the council rose,
And viewing Shalum's tricks with joy
To Cambridge Hall, o'er wastes of snows,
They sent the copper-colored boy.

One generous chief a bow supplied,
This gave a shaft, and that a skin;
The feathers, in vermilion dyed,
Himself did from a turkey win: 20

Thus dressed so gay, he took his way
O'er barren hills, alone, alone!
His guide a star, he wandered far,
His pillow every night a stone.

At last he came, with foot so lame
Where learned men talk heathen Greek,
And Hebrew lore is gabbled o'er,
To please the Muses,—twice a week.

Awhile he writ, awhile he read,
Awhile he conned their grammar rules—   30
(An Indian savage so well bred
Great credit promised to the schools.)

Some thought he would in law excel,
Some said in physic he would shine;
And one that knew him, passing well,
Beheld, in philip, a sound Divine.

But those of more discerning eye
Even then could other prospects show,
And saw him lay his *Virgil* by
To wander with his dearer bow.   40

The tedious hours of study spent,
The heavy-molded lecture done,
He to the woods a-hunting went,
Through lonely wastes he walked, he run.

No mystic wonders fired his mind;
He sought to gain no learned degree,
But only sense enough to find
The squirrel in the hollow tree.

The shady bank, the purling stream,
The woody wild his heart possessed,   50
The dewy lawn, his morning dream
In fancy's gayest colors dressed.

"And why (he cried) did I forsake
My native wood for gloomy walls;
The silver stream, the limpid lake
For musty books and college halls.

"A little could my wants supply—
Can wealth and honor give me more;
Or, will the sylvan god deny
The humble treat he gave before?   60

"Let seraphs gain the bright abode,
And heaven's sublimest mansions see—

I only bow to Nature's God—
The land of shades will do for me.

"These dreadful secrets of the sky
Alarm my soul with chilling fear—
Do planets in their orbits fly?
And is the earth, indeed, a sphere?

"Let planets still their course pursue,
And comets to the Center run—
In Him my faithful friend I view,
The image of my God—the Sun.

"Where Nature's ancient forests grow,
And mingled laurel never fades,
My heart is fixed;—and I must go
To die among my native shades."

He spoke and to the western springs,
(His gown discharged, his money spent,
His blanket tied with yellow strings,)
The shepherd of the forest went.

1790

Ode

God save the Rights of Man!
Give us a heart to scan
Blessings so dear:
Let them be spread around
Wherever man is found,
And with the welcome sound
Ravish his ear.

Let us with France agree,
And bid the world be free,
While tyrants fall!
Let the rude savage host
Of their vast numbers boast—
Freedom's almighty trust
Laughs at them all!

Though hosts of slaves conspire
To quench fair Gallia's fire,
Still shall they fail:
Though traitors round her rise,
Leagu'd with her enemies,
To war each patriot flies,   20
And will prevail.

No more is valor's flame
Devoted to a name,
Taught to adore—
Soldiers of Liberty
Disdain to bow the knee,
But teach Equality
To every shore.

The world at last will join
To aid thy grand design,   30
Dear Liberty!
To Russia's frozen lands
The generous flame expands:
On Afric's burning sands
Shall man be free!

In this our western world
Be Freedom's flag unfurl'd
Through all its shores!
May no destructive blast
Our heaven of joy o'ercast,   40
May Freedom's fabric last
While time endures.

If e'er her cause require!—
Should tyrants e'er aspire
To aim their stroke,
May no proud despot daunt—
Should he his standard plant,
Freedom will never want
Her hearts of oak!

1795

On Mr. Paine's Rights of Man

Thus briefly sketched the sacred RIGHTS OF MAN,
How inconsistent with the ROYAL PLAN!
Which for itself exclusive honor craves,
Where some are masters born, and millions slaves.
With what contempt must every eye look down
On that base, childish bauble called a crown,
The gilded bait, that lures the crowd, to come,
Bow down their necks, and meet a slavish doom;
The source of half the miseries men endure,
The quack that kills them, while it seems to cure.   10

    Roused by the REASON of his manly page,
Once more shall PAINE a listening world engage:
From Reason's source, a bold reform he brings,
In raising mankind, he pulls down kings,
Who, source of discord, patrons of all wrong,
On blood and murder have been fed too long:
Hid from the world, and tutored to be base,
The curse, the scourge, the ruin of our race,
Their's was the task, a dull designing few,
To shackle beings that they scarcely knew,   20
Who made this globe the residence of slaves,
And built their thrones on systems formed by knaves
—Advance, bright years, to work their final fall,
And haste the period that shall crush them all.

    Who, that has read and scanned the historic page
But glows, at every line, with kindling rage,
To see by them the rights of men aspersed
Freedom restrained, and Nature's law reversed,
Men, ranked with beasts, by monarchs willed away,
And bound young fools, or madmen to obey: 30
Now driven to wars, and now oppressed at home,
Compelled in crowds o'er distant seas to roam,
From India's climes the plundered prize to bring
To glad the strumpet, or to glut the king.

    COLUMBIA, hail! immortal be thy reign:
Without a king, we till the smiling plain;
Without a king, we trace the unbounded sea,
And traffic round the globe, through each degree;
Each foreign clime our honored flag reveres,

Which asks no monarch, to support the STARS: 40
Without a king, the laws maintain their sway,
While honor bids each generous heart obey.
Be ours the task the ambitious to restrain,
And this great lesson teach—that kings are vain;
That warring realms to certain ruin haste,
That kings subsist by war, and wars are waste:
So shall our nation, formed on Virtue's plan,
Remain the guardian of the Rights of Man,
A vast Republic, famed through every clime,
Without a king, to see the end of time.   50

1795

Stanzas to an Alien

Remote, beneath a sultry star
Where Mississippi flows afar
I see you rambling, God knows where.

Sometimes, beneath a cypress bough
When met in dreams, with spirits low,
I long to tell you what I know.

How matters go, in this our day,
When monarchy renews her sway,
And royalty begins her play.

I thought you wrong to come so far   10
Till you had seen our western star
Above the mists ascended clear.

I thought you right, to speed your sails
If you were fond of loathsome jails,
And justice with uneven scales.

And so you came and spoke too free
And soon they made you bend the knee,
And lodged you under lock and key.

Discharged at last, you made your peace
With all you had, and left the place   20
With empty purse and meager face.—

You sped your way to other climes
And left me here to tease with rhymes
The worst of men in worst of times.

Where you are gone the soil is free
And freedom sings from every tree,
"Come quit the crowd and live with me!"

Where I must stay, no joys are found;
Excisemen haunt the hateful ground,
And chains are forged for all around.   30

The scheming men, with brazen throat,
Would set a murdering tribe afloat
To hang you for the lines you wrote.

If you are safe beyond their rage
Thank heaven, and not our ruling sage,
Who shuts us up in jail and cage.

Perdition seize that odious race
Who, aiming at distinguish'd place,
Would life and liberty efface;

With iron rod would rule the ball   40
And, at their shrine, debase us all,
Bid devils rise and angels fall.

Oh wish them ill, and wish them long
To be as usual in the wrong
In scheming for a chain too strong.

So will the happy time arrive
When coming home, if then alive,
You'll see them to the devil drive.

                                        1798

On a Honey Bee

Drinking from a Glass of Wine and Drowned Therein

Thou, born to sip the lake or spring,
   Or quaff the waters of the stream,

Why hither come, on vagrant wing?—
   Does Bacchus tempting seem—
      Did he for you this glass prepare?—
      Will I admit you to a share?

Did storms harass or foes perplex,
   Did wasps or king-birds bring dismay—
Did wars distress, or labors vex,
   Or did you miss your way?—   10
      A better seat you could not take
      Than on the margin of this lake.

Welcome!—I hail you to my glass:
   All welcome, here, you find;
Here, let the cloud of trouble pass,
   Here, be all care resigned.—
      This fluid never fails to please,
      And drown the griefs of men or bees.

What forced you here we cannot know,
   And you will scarcely tell—   20
But cheery we would have you go
   And bid a glad farewell:
      On lighter wings we bid you fly,
      Your dart will now all foes defy.

Yet take not, oh! too deep a drink,
   And in this ocean die;
Here bigger bees than you might sink,
   Even bees full six feet high.
      Like Pharaoh, then, you would be said
      To perish in a sea of red.   30

Do as you please, your will is mine;
   Enjoy it without fear—
And your grave will be this glass of wine,
   Your epitaph—a tear;
      Go, take your seat on Charon's boat,
      We'll tell the hive, you died afloat.

                           1809

To a Caty-Did

In a branch of willow hid
Sings the evening Caty-did:
From the lofty locust bough
Feeding on a drop of dew,
In her suit of green array'd
Hear her singing in the shade
   Caty-did, Caty-did, Caty-did!
   While upon a leaf you tread,
Or repose your little head,
On your sheet of shadows laid,   10
All the day you nothing said:
Half the night your cheery tongue
Revell'd out its little song,
   Nothing else but Caty-did.

From your lodgings on the leaf
Did you utter joy or grief?—
Did you only mean to say,
I have had my summer's day,
And am passing, soon, away
To the grave of Caty-did:—   20
   Poor, unhappy Caty-did!

But you would have utter'd more
Had you known of nature's power—
From the world when you retreat,
And a leaf's your winding sheet,
Long before your spirit fled,
Who can tell but nature said,
Live again, my Caty-did!
   Live and chatter, Caty-did.

Tell me, what did Caty do?   30
Did she mean to trouble you?—
Why was Caty not forbid
To trouble little Caty-did?—
Wrong, indeed at you to fling,
Hurting no one while you sing
   Caty-did! Caty-did! Caty-did!

Why continue to complain?
Caty tells me, she again
Will not give you plague or pain:—
Caty says you may be hid,   40
Caty will not go to bed
While you sing us Caty-did.
    Caty-did! Caty-did! Caty-did!

But, while singing, you forgot
To tell us what did Caty not:
Caty-did not think of cold,
Flocks retiring to the fold,
Winter, with his wrinkles old,
Winter, that yourself foretold
    When you gave us Caty-did.   50

Stay securely in your nest;
Caty now, will do her best,
All she can, to make you blest;
But, you want no human aid—
Nature, when she form'd you, said,
"Independent you are made,
My dear little Caty-did:
Soon yourself must disappear
With the verdure of the year,"—
And to go, we know not where,   60
    With your song of Caty-did.

                                                    1815

On the Uniformity and Perfection of Nature

On one fix'd point all nature moves,
Nor deviates from the track she loves;
Her system, drawn from reason's source,
She scorns to change her wonted course.

Could she descend from that great plan
To work unusual things for man,
To suit the insect of an hour—
This would betray a want of power,

Unsettled in its first design
And erring, when it did combine   10

The parts that form the vast machine,
The figures sketch'd on nature's scene.

Perfections of the great first cause
Submit to no contracted laws,
But all-sufficient, all-supreme,
Include no trivial views in them.

Who looks through nature with an eye
That would the scheme of heaven descry,
Observes her constant, still the same,
In all her laws, through all her frame.   20

No imperfection can be found
In all that is, above, around,—
All, nature made, in reason's sight
Is order all and all is right.

                                                    1815

On the Religion of Nature

The power that gives with liberal hand
    The blessings man enjoys, while here,
And scatters through a smiling land
    The abundant products of the year;
        That power of nature, ever bless'd,
        Bestow'd religion with the rest.

Born with ourselves, her early sway
    Inclines the tender mind to take
The path of right, fair virtue's way
    Its own felicity to make.   10
        This universally extends
        And leads to no mysterious ends.

Religion, such as nature taught,
    With all divine perfection suits;
Had all mankind this system sought
    Sophists would cease their vain disputes,
        And from this source would nations know
        All that can make their heaven below.

This deals not curses on mankind,
  Or dooms them to perpetual grief,   20
If from its aid no joys they find,
  It damns them not for unbelief;
     Upon a more exalted plan
     Creatress nature dealt with man—

Joy to the day, when all agree
  On such grand systems to proceed,
From fraud, design, and error free,
  And which to truth and goodness lead:
     Then persecution will retreat
     And man's religion be complete.   30

                          1815

On the Universality and Other Attributes of the God of Nature

All that we see, about, abroad,
What is it all, but nature's God?
In meaner works discovered here
No less than in the starry sphere.

In seas, on earth, this God is seen;
All that exist, upon him lean;
He lives in all, and never strayed
A moment from the works he made:

His system fixed on general laws
Bespeaks a wise creating cause;   10
Impartially he rules mankind
And all that on this globe we find.

Unchanged in all that seems to change,
Unbounded space is his great range;
To one vast purpose always true,
No time, with him, is old or new.

In all the attributes divine
Unlimited perfectings shine;
In these enwrapt, in these complete,
All virtues in that centre meet.   20

This power doth all powers transcend,
To all intelligence a friend,
Exists, the greatest and the best
Throughout all the worlds, to make them blest.

All that he did he first approved,
He all things into being loved;
O'er all he made he still presides,
For them in life, or death provides.

1815

INDEX OF AUTHORS, TITLES, AND
FIRST LINES OF POEMS